I0772342

BB EASTON

THE
COMPLETE
RAIN
TRILOGY

BB EASTON

PRAYING FoR RAIN

THE RAIN TRILOGY BOOK 1

Rain

I'M SITTING IN *A booth at Burger Palace. I don't remember how I got here, or when, but the empty seat across from me tells me that I came alone.*

The place smells like classic greasy burgers and fries. My stomach snarls in response.

God, I'm starving.

I glance across the bustling fast-food restaurant at the giant digital menu on the wall and notice four banners hanging on either side of the checkout counter. They're huge, hanging from the ceiling all the way down to the floor. Only, instead of showing pretty models eating airbrushed cheeseburgers, these things look like propaganda for the Antichrist. Each one is bright red with the silhouette of a hooded figure on horseback in the middle. One is holding a massive sword over his head. Another one has a scythe, like the Grim Reaper. One is swinging a mace, and the fourth one is charging forward with a flaming torch. Even though I can't see their faces, I almost feel like their demonic eyes are staring right at me.

This is a fucked up marketing campaign, *I think, searching the terrifying banners for more information.*

The only text I see on them anywhere is a simple date in bold white font at the top of each one.

April 23.

What the hell?

I look around the restaurant for more clues, but all I find are happy little families sucking soda out of red cups with hooded horsemen on them. A little boy carries a Big Kid

Box to his seat with an image of the Grim Reaper guy on it. A little girl licks blood-red ice cream out of a cracked black cone. And, on every wrapper, every poster, every napkin, straw, and ketchup packet, there's the same date.

April 23? *I rack my brain.* April 23. What the hell is going to happen on April twen—

Before I can finish my thought, the lights flicker off and the doors burst open. Wind whips through the small restaurant like a tornado, sending drinks crashing and people scrambling, as four hooded figures on giant smoke-breathing horses charge in.

Suddenly, the banners, the ad campaign—it all makes sense.

Today is April 23.

And we're all gonna die.

Smoke and screams and chaos fill the air as I scurry to the floor beneath my table, backing all the way up to the wall and hugging my knees to my chest.

I can't breathe. I can't blink. I can't think. All I can do it cover my ears and try to block out the screams of mothers and children as I peer into the darkness.

Flames climb up the black-and-red banners, illuminating a wasteland before me. Furniture overturned. Bodies strewed about the wreckage. Severed heads, missing limbs, torsos impaled on table legs. My hands move from my ears to my mouth as I muffle a scream.

Don't let them hear you.

Thick black smoke begins to curl and creep into my hiding spot, making my eyes water and my throat burn. I can hardly see past the table now, and suppressing the cough and the panic building in my throat is getting harder and harder to do.

I know I need to run—I have to—but my legs won't cooperate. I'm stuck in the fetal position, rocking like a child, as I pull my T-shirt over my mouth and nose.

I scream at myself inside my head, but it's my mother's voice that finally gets my ass in gear. "Are you going to stay home all day and wallow, like your father, or are you gonna get out there and try to help somebody?" *Her scolding from this morning rings in my ears louder than the cries of the burning, impaled women and children all around me.*

I want to help. Even if, right now, the only person I can help is myself.

Placing my palms on the filthy floor, I slowly bring my knees down so that I'm on all fours.

I can do this.

Taking one last breath, I straighten my back and prepare to crawl to safety. I can't see the exits through all the smoke, but I can see the two blood-spattered hooves that come to a stop directly in front of me when I take my first step.

I wake up at the tail end of a scream, just like I do every morning. Just like we all do, ever since the nightmares began.

Grabbing my cell phone off the charger, I hold my breath and read the date.

April 20.

I sigh and toss it back onto the nightstand.

I used to feel so relieved when I woke up from the nightmare. Back when I still had hope that some scientist somewhere was gonna figure it out. But everybody on the planet has been dreaming about the four horsemen of the apocalypse coming on April 23 for almost a year now, and we still don't have answers.

After a few months, most of the world's top researchers either resigned in defeat, died from heart attacks, or went crazy from the stress of trying to figure it out. Every day, the news got worse, the crime rate skyrocketed, and eventually, the newscasters just stopped reporting. Without answers or hope or, hell, even fake news to calm us down, most people have just accepted that the world is going to end on April 23.

Myself included.

I still feel relieved when I wake up from the nightmare, but now, it's only because I can't wait for it to be over.

Three more days. I only have to do this shit for three more days.

I drag myself out of bed and groan at my reflection in the bathroom mirror. Choppy, chin-length black hair frames my pale face, the same way that yesterday's smudged eyeliner frames my sunken blue eyes.

Where the fuck did my hair go?

My eyes scan the filthy countertop for a brush and land on my long black braid, still bound with an elastic band, lying in a heap next to an empty bottle of codeine cough syrup.

Way to go, Rain. Get high and cut all your hair off. Real original.

I try to remember what happened last night, but it's not even a blur. It's just gone. Like the hair that I pick up and toss onto my overflowing trash can on my way to turn on the shower.

We've been advised to use our bathtubs for water storage in case our town's supply gets cut off, but the way I see it, if we're all going to die anyway, why not enjoy a hot shower first?

And by *enjoy*, I mean cry under the stream until the water turns cold.

I towel-dry my hack job of a hairdo, throw on a tank top and a pair of plaid flannel pajama pants, and shove my feet into an old pair of cowboy boots. I used to want to look cute when I left the house. Now, I just want to look homeless. Bronzer, beachy waves, cleavage, cutoff jeans—all those things attract attention. The bad kind. The kind that gets you robbed or raped. At least, around here.

As much as I'd like to spend the next three days in bed with my head under the covers, I'm fucking starving, and all we have here is dried spaghetti noodles, a can of lima beans, and a bottle of expired pancake syrup. Our supplies have been running low ever since the gangs took over the neighborhood grocery stores. They'll let you *shop*, but you have to be willing to pay in their *preferred currency*, which, when you're a nineteen-year-old girl…

Let's just say I haven't gotten that desperate yet.

Luckily, Burger Palace is still serving. And *they* take cash. I just have to get in and out without drawing too much attention to myself.

I pick the Twenty One Pilots hoodie up off my floor and resist the urge to bury my nose in the soft cotton like I used to. I know Carter's scent is long gone, just like him—and thank God for that. The last thing I need is another reminder that my stupid boyfriend chose to spend his last few weeks on earth in Tennessee with his family instead of here with me.

Asshole.

I yank the sweatshirt on over my head, completing my frumpiest look yet, and stomp down the stairs. The scene in the living room is pretty much the same as it is every morning. My father is passed out in his recliner, facing the front door, with a fifth of whiskey tucked in the crook of his elbow and a shotgun across his lap. I'd probably take more pity on him if he hadn't always been a mean-ass drunk.

But he has.

He's just a *paranoid* mean-ass drunk now.

I can't even bear to look at him. I cover my mouth with the sleeve of my sweatshirt to keep from gagging on the smell of piss as I snatch his prescription bottle of hydrocodone off the table.

I think you've had enough, old man.

Popping one of the little white pills into my mouth, I pocket the rest and cross the living room.

I grab my dad's keys off the hook by the front door and lock the doorknob on my way out. Even though I know how to drive, I don't bother taking my dad's truck. The roads are so clogged with wrecked and abandoned vehicles that they're basically impassable now.

Traffic laws were one of the first things to go after the nightmares began. Everybody started driving a little faster, having a few extra drinks, ignoring those pesky red lights and stop signs, and forgetting that turn signals had ever existed. There were so many accidents that the tow trucks and traffic cops and ambulance drivers couldn't keep up, so eventually, they just quit trying. The wrecks piled up and caused more wrecks, and then, when the gas stations closed, people started leaving their vehicles wherever they ran out of gas.

Franklin Springs, Georgia, has never exactly been a classy place, but now, it looks like one big demolition derby arena. I would know. I live right off the main two-lane highway that cuts through town. In fact, the *Welcome to Franklin Springs* sign hangs right across the street from my house. Of course, somebody recently spray-painted a giant UC over the RAN in Franklin, so the sign reads *Welcome to Fucklin Springs* now.

Can't imagine who would do such a thing.

The quickest way into town would be to walk along the highway about a mile or so, but it also feels like the quickest way to get raped or robbed, frumpy outfit or not, so I stick to the woods.

As soon as my feet hit the pine needle–covered trail behind my house, I feel like I can finally relax. I inhale the humid spring air. I listen to the birds chattering away up in the trees. I try on a smile; it doesn't feel right. And I pretend, for just a moment, that everything's okay again, like it used to be.

But, when I step out of the woods and feel the heat of a nearby car fire on my face, I remember.

Life sucks, and we're all gonna die.

I flip my hood over my head and tiptoe around the corner of the library, watching out for the three Rs: rioters, rapists, and rabid dogs. The dogs don't really have rabies, but so many people have died in the weeks leading up to April 23 that their pets are starting to band together and hunt as a team.

So. Many. People.

Images of those I've lost flicker behind my eyes, dim and grainy, fighting to get a feeling past the hydrocodone. But the painkiller does its job, and within moments, I'm fuzzy and numb again.

When the coast is clear, I shove my hands in the front pocket of my hoodie to keep all my shit from falling out and scurry across the street. Cars and trucks are lurched on the curbs, overturned in the ditches, and abandoned with doors wide open in the middle of the lanes. I try not to think about how many of those cars might still have people in them as I reach out and pull open the Burger Palace door.

When I walk in, I half-expect to see flaming banners and demons slaying people on horseback, but it's just the entire miserable town of Franklin, crammed inside and yelling at each other.

God, it's loud. People who've lived here their whole lives are shoving fingers in each other's faces, arguing about who was next in line. Babies are crying. Mothers are crying. Toddlers are screaming and running around like wild animals. And everybody smells like liquor.

I sigh and begin to make my way to the back of the line when I notice that my third-grade teacher, Mrs. Frazier, is standing at a cash register. It's her turn to order, but she's too busy cursing out Pastor Blankenship, who's behind her in line, to get on with it. I'm sure Mrs. Frazier wouldn't mind if I—

I slip in front of her at the cash register, hoping she keeps screaming long enough for me to order.

"Hi, and welcome to Burger Palace!" A girl wearing a Burger Palace cap and polo shirt beams at me from across the counter. "May I take your order?"

I glance down the line and notice three more employees, all sporting the same exaggerated grin.

What the hell are they giving these people? Molly? Crystal meth?

"Uh … yeah." I keep my voice low. "I'll have a soda and a large fry."

"Would you like to Apocasize that?"

I blink. Twice. "I'm sorry, what?"

"Apocasize it!" She gestures up at one of the digital screens behind her, where an animated thirty-two-ounce drink and bucket of fries are holding hands and skipping around a fire. "It's not like we have to worry about carbs anymore, am I right?"

My eyebrows pull together. "Uh … no, I guess not." I hear Mrs. Frazier call Pastor Blankenship a cunt behind me and know I'd better wrap it up. "Sure, whatever. How much does that cost?"

Perky Polly on Molly taps her monitor a few times. "That'll be forty-seven fifty."

"For a soda and fries?" I blurt.

She shrugs, never letting her smile slip.

"Jesus," I mutter under my breath as I dig in my hoodie pocket for some cash.

Price-gouging pieces of—

I set the contents of my pocket on the counter to sort through them, and with that one simple, absentminded gesture, all holy hell breaks loose. Perky Polly leaps across the counter, clawing at my little orange prescription bottle, at the exact same moment that Pastor Blankenship swipes one long arm out to grab it. Their fists collide, knocking the plastic bottle to the floor, which I manage to get a foot on before it can roll away. But, as I kneel down to pick it up, Mrs. Frazier launches herself at my back and sends us both crashing into the counter.

The entire crowd surges forward, pinning us to the stainless steel surface as they push and pull and claw at the salvation in my fist with greedy, desperate hands. I scream as one of them rips out a chunk of my hair. I hiss as another rakes her nails across my cheek. I bite and elbow as many others as I can. Howls and grunts and frustrated curses pour out of me as I struggle against the mob. The weight of them is crushing, pushing me down. I curl into a ball on the floor, clutching the bottle to my chest with both fists as I wince and take their beating.

Then, just as suddenly as it began, it stops. The ringing in my ears registers a moment later. Someone fired a gun. Or a freaking cannon from the sound of it.

The room goes quiet, and the crowd freezes, but I don't look up.

It could be a trick. It could be somebody just trying to distract me so that somebody else can snatch my pills. It could be—

I wince as the hot metal muzzle of a gun sears my temple.

"I'll be taking this." I hear the stranger's voice just before a firm hand wraps around my upper arm and yanks me to my feet.

I stand in a daze and face my attackers. They don't even have the decency to look ashamed. In fact, they don't look at me at all. Their eyes, a few pistols, and at least one rifle are all trained on the person holding a gun to my head. They're not mad that he's about to kidnap me. They're mad that he's kidnapping my pills.

"Who the hell are you?" Mr. Lathan, our former postman, growls from the back of the crowd. One of his eyes is squeezed shut as he stares down the length of his rifle, ready to fire.

My abductor shrugs as he walks me backward toward the door. "Doesn't really matter, does it?"

I watch the glow of anger in everyone's eyes cloud over with despair as they take in the meaning of his words.

Today is April twentieth. Nothing matters anymore.

I don't struggle. I don't even turn around and look at him. I let him drag me behind the building and pray that, whatever he does, he does it quick.

So much for not drawing attention.

I realize along the way that I'm limping, but I can't seem to pin down the location of my injury. And my mouth tastes like blood, but it doesn't hurt. And my body feels all floaty and light even though I just got jumped by half the town.

Damn, this hydrocodone is some powerful shit.

I giggle at the absurdity of my situation as the gunman behind me guides me toward a parked dirt bike with the heel of his palm on my shoulder.

"What's so funny?" His voice is soft, just like his touch as we come to a stop.

I turn to answer him and almost choke on my own spit. The words dry up in my mouth as I stare into the mossy-green eyes of a guy not much older than me. A tall, gorgeous guy who should be on a poster in my bedroom, not kidnapping me from Burger Palace.

I expected my captor to be some middle-aged, beer-gutted, gray-bearded, bald guy, not … *this*. *This* guy is perfect. It's like his parents were so rich that they went to the doctor and selected his DNA from a menu before he was conceived—high cheekbones, straight nose, soft eyes, strong eyebrows, and full lips that he's chewing on absentmindedly.

But the rest of him doesn't look rich at all. He's wearing a white ribbed tank top under a blue floral Hawaiian shirt, his jeans have holes in them, and the disheveled brown hair tucked behind his ear looks like it hasn't seen a pair of scissors in years.

Mine, on the other hand …

I run my fingers through my hacked-off locks, suddenly feeling super self-conscious about my frumpalicious appearance.

My captor raises his dark eyebrows a little higher, indicating that he's still waiting for me to tell him what's so funny.

I think about the painkillers that made me giggle, which causes me to remember all the other stuff I pulled out of my pocket along with that little orange bottle. "Shit!" I gasp, frantically patting my lower belly, feeling for the contents of my hoodie pocket. "I left all my money on the counter in there! And my keys!" I grimace and pinch the bridge of my nose. "God, I'm such an idiot."

"You still got those pills?" The boy pulls back one side of his unbuttoned Hawaiian shirt and shoves his handgun into a brown leather holster.

"Uh … yeah …" I wrap my fist a little tighter around the plastic bottle.

"Good." He flicks his chin toward the dirt bike behind me. "Get on."

"Where are we going?"

He lets his shirt fall back into place and pins me with a look that I can't quite read. It's been so long since I've seen somebody display anything other than the swollen red eyes of despair, the gnashing teeth of mob rage, the panicked twitchiness of fear, or the distant stare of sweet, drug-induced numbness that his calm, focused demeanor confuses the hell out of me.

"Shopping."

I pull my eyebrows together as he strides past me.

"Shopping?"

The stranger stops next to the dirt bike and shoves a black helmet onto his head, ignoring my question.

"A helmet. Really?" I snort. "We only have three days to live, and you're worried about safety regulations. You're not one of those *lifers*, are you?"

Lifer is a term the media coined months ago to describe those disgustingly optimistic members of our society who simply refused to believe that the end was near. You used to be able to tell them apart by their stupid, smiling faces and cheerful greetings. But, now, they look just like the rest of us—mad, sad, scared, or numb.

"I'm not a lifer. I just have shit to do, and it's not gonna get done if my head is splattered all over the asphalt." The boy straddles the black-and-orange machine and turns his masked face toward me. "Get on."

I consider my options. I can't exactly run back into the restaurant and ask for help. I'm in no condition to fight. I might be able to toss the painkillers in one direction and run as fast as my beat-up legs will go in the other, which could work if all he wants is the pills. But then what? Limp home and survive on pancake-syrup soup until the four horsemen of the apocalypse come to get me?

Yeah, I think I'd rather be kidnapped.

CHAPTER 2

Rain

I CLIMB ON BEHIND my captor and wrap my arms around his waist like girls do in the movies. I've never ridden a motorcycle before or a dirt bike or whatever this thing is, but I like that it gives me an excuse to hug this boy. I sigh and rest my cheek on a yellow hibiscus on the back of his Hawaiian shirt. I know it's not a real hug, but it still feels pretty damn good. I guess I haven't hugged anybody since …

A memory gnaws at the edges of my consciousness. It must be a sad one—I can tell by the way it gets harder to breathe—so I push it back down with all the others.

If I can just keep them locked up until April 23, I won't ever have to feel them again.

The lifer stomps down on some kind of lever, and we take off like a rocket. I squeal as we round the building, holding on to him tighter with my right hand so that I can use my left to give Burger Palace the middle finger.

I smile with my cheek still pressed against his back and wonder what he smells like. All I can smell is spilled gasoline from the wrecked and abandoned cars we're weaving through at top speed. That, and the occasional overflowing dumpster.

Left, right, left, left, right.

The fluid movement and throaty roar of the engine are exhilarating and soothing, all at the same time. I want it to last forever, but a few moments later, my chauffeur slows down and turns right, pulling into the Huckabee Foods parking lot.

Somebody spray painted an F over the H on the sign so that it says *Fuckabee Foods* now, but I'm too busy freaking out to admire my handiwork.

The grocery store? No, no, no, no, no. Is this *why he took me? To whore me out for food? Shit!*

The parking lot is almost empty, except for a handful of motorcycles and a few delivery trucks that either got stranded or hijacked. We pull up next to a bread truck, and I feel the blood begin to pulse through my body.

I'm gonna do it. Now or never. Here we—

The second we're parked, I throw my leg over the side of the dirt bike and take off running toward the highway. At least, I thought I was going to take off running. As soon as I try, I remember that I just got the shit kicked out of me and can't manage much more than a hobble.

I get maybe ten feet away when a pair of large hands clamps down on my waist and a head of shiny brown hair appears under my arm. With one motion, the lifer stands up straight, scooping me off the ground with his shoulder in my lower back.

I scream and cling to his head with both hands as my world is turned upside down.

"No!" I shriek. "Put me down!" I thrash. "Fuck you!" I kick and pull at his hair with both hands.

The lifer suddenly bends his knees, causing his shoulder to jam into my kidney. "Fucking. Stop." He punctuates each word with a heavy breath as he struggles to keep a grasp on my flailing body.

"I'm not going in there," I pant. "You can't make me. I'd rather starve than—ugh! Ahh! Oof!"

The bastard is walking back toward the dirt bike now, and every step sends his shoulder a little deeper into my back.

He sets me on my feet between his bike and the bread truck, and then he turns me around to face him. His viselike grip has moved from my waist to my shoulders, his hair is in his face, and his eyes are narrowed in frustration.

"I need food," he spits through his clenched teeth. "They have it. And you're gonna help me get it. Now, if you will just *shut the fuck up* and listen to me, I'll make sure you get out of there with your precious little virtue intact."

I roll my eyes. "Virtue? Pssh. That shit's been gone since eighth grade."

Captain Serious completely ignores my perfectly timed joke and stares at the yellow Twenty One Pilots logo on my black hoodie. "Do you have a shirt on under that?"

"Uh … yeah."

"Tuck it in."

I sneer at him, but the witty comeback turns to dust in my mouth as the boy strips off his Hawaiian shirt. Where I expect to see the birdcage chest and spindly arms of a teenager, I find the rippled, muscular torso of a man. A grown-ass man with actual biceps … and tattoos on those biceps … and abs that I can count even through his ribbed tank top.

I feel myself physically pull away from him. Guys are fun. Guys are my friends. Guys I can handle. But men …

Men scare the shit out of me.

Especially the ones in this town.

I watch as he takes off his brown leather shoulder holster next. The gun inside must be heavy, judging by the way the veins on his arm pop out as he wraps the straps around the weapon and tucks it into the wheel well of the bread truck. Unarmed, the *man* shrugs his blue floral shirt back on, and I quickly go back to the business of shirt-tucking.

"You ready?" His eyes fall to the drawstring waistband of my plaid pajama pants, which I'm tying in a tight knot to keep my shirt in.

"No," I sass, peeking up at him through my lashes.

He rolls his eyes before tucking his disheveled brown hair behind his ears. The motion is so sweet that I almost forget about all the tattoos and muscles. He becomes a guy again.

And a guy is much easier to trust than a man.

"Just keep your mouth shut and follow my lead, okay? We're gonna be in and out."

I bite my tongue and nod, letting him guide me toward the entrance of Fuckabee Foods with a hand on the small of my back. A neckless meathead with facial tattoos is sitting in a folding lawn chair out front. He's holding an Uzi and staring at a glowing device on his lap. He's so engrossed that he doesn't look up until we're almost standing right in front of him.

"You got service?" my abductor asks, glancing at the episode of *American Chopper* playing on the guy's tablet.

"Fuck no," he snaps, furrowing his unibrow. "But I downloaded some shit before the cell towers went down." He taps the side of his head with a thick index finger. "You gotta be smart, man." The redneck who looks like he just escaped death row cuts his eyes to me and sneers, "Looks like you payin' with a *dime* today, huh?"

I have to fight back a wave of panic as his gaze slides down the length of my body.

"This?" He chuckles, giving me the side-eye. "*This*, unfortunately, is my sister. I wouldn't wish her on my worst enemy, man." He leans forward and whispers loud enough for me to hear him, "She's a biter."

I cross my arms and cock my head to one side, trying to play the part of the bratty younger sister as the ogre eyes me suspiciously.

"If you ain't sharin' the pussy, you better come correct, boy. My men ain't gonna be real happy about not gettin' a taste of that"—he licks his lips as I try not to dry-heave under his stare—"unless you got somethin' even better for 'em."

"Your men like the taste of *Hydro?*"

I don't know what the hell he's talking about until that asshole reaches into his pocket and produces an orange canister full of little white pills.

My hands fly to my stomach, squeezing and patting my now-empty hoodie pocket. "No!" I shriek, reaching out to snatch my pills back, but Human Shrek grabs them first.

With a victorious grin, he pops the cap off and shakes a handful into his mouth. "These better be real," he mumbles, crunching them to paste between his yellowed teeth. "If I ain't feeling somethin' by the time y'all leave, y'all motherfuckers is dead."

Um, you just crushed, like, five extended-release hydrocodone. I think you might be the one who's dead, dumbass.

Standing, he pats us down with the hand not holding the semiautomatic weapon and then hands us two plastic grocery bags from the stash hanging off the back of his chair. "Fill 'em up and get the fuck out. Twenty minutes."

As soon as the sliding glass doors close behind us, I turn and punch my captor in the stomach. "What the hell?" I hiss. "Those were mine—"

Before my temper tantrum has a chance to get started, I'm up against a wall with a hand clamped over my mouth.

"Let's get one thing straight." *Hawaii Five-O's* pupils bore into mine like lasers, but his voice is nothing more than a whisper. "I don't *care* what *you* need. I'm here to get what *I* need. And what *I* need is food, supplies, and for you to shut the fuck up." He glances out the front door where our new friend is sitting with his back to us. "Unless, of course, you *want* homeboy's buddies to hear you. I'm sure they'd love to see the hot piece of ass he just let in here."

My eyes go wide as his palm disappears from my face. I should be upset, enraged even, but as I stare up at the grumpiest asshole I've ever met—other than my dad, of course—my stupid mouth pulls into a sideways smile.

Did he just call me hot?

My captor doesn't smile back. He simply shakes his head in a way that says, *This bitch is crazy,* and then taps an invisible watch on his exposed wrist. "Nineteen minutes. Let's go."

My smile disappears.

I hustle to keep up with him as he heads toward the center aisles. The deeper into the store we go, the louder the voices of the new occupants become and the stronger the stench of rotting food. Of course, the center aisles house all the nonperishables, which is exactly what he appears to be stocking up on. Protein bars, squeezie pouches filled with pureed fruits and vegetables, beef jerky, trail mix …

"What's your name?" I whisper as he bends over and reaches one long arm all the way to the back of a shelf to grab the last can of beef stew. The place has been ransacked.

He looks up at me with that same flat expression. Then, he stands and drops the can into one of the bags, ignoring my question.

"You're not gonna tell me?" I whisper-pout.

Mr. Grumpy raises one eyebrow in response, then turns away from me and continues browsing the looted aisles.

"I have to call you *something*," I whisper-whine as he reads the nutrition label on a packet of ramen noodles. He puts them back. "If I guess it, will you at least nod?"

His jaw clenches, and his eyes cut to mine. "If I tell you, will you shut the fuck up?" His voice is a barely audible hiss.

I grin and nod, pretending to lock my lips shut with an invisible key.

"It's Wes."

I open my mouth to reply, then snap it shut again when his eyebrows shoot up in a silent warning.

Sorry, I mouth, holding my hands up. *I'll be quiet.*

I follow him to the cereal aisle where cornflakes and colorful, dried marshmallows crunch beneath our feet like autumn leaves, no matter how lightly we tread. As we near the end, a chorus of deep laughter bursts into the building and bounces off the rafters. *Wes* pushes me behind him and peers around the corner. Turning back to me, he places a finger to his lips, then points it in the direction of the next aisle over. The voices, too loud and rowdy to belong to sober men, travel away from us, down a path of what sounds like broken glass and sticky soda.

With tender feet, we turn left and tiptoe down aisle twelve. Hardware.

Wes stops in front of a wall of hanging tools, and I watch him with my mind occupied by two very different thoughts. Part of me can't stop thinking about his name—*Wes. I wonder what it's short for. Wesley probably. Or Wesson, like that big-ass gun he was carrying. Or maybe it's something fancy, like Westchester*—while the other part of me wonders how in the hell he's going to fit anything else into those bags. Sharp corners bulge in every direction, threatening to slice the thin plastic to shreds, yet he keeps pulling items off the wall—a flashlight, a pocketknife, a pack of lighters, and a can opener.

Then, he turns his gaze on me.

Suddenly, I know what it feels like to be a flashlight or a pocketknife or a pack of lighters or a can opener. It feels good, being looked at like that. Being chosen by this *man*. But also scary. And exhilarating. Especially when he begins walking toward me.

I hold his stare as he approaches and hold my breath when he stops right in front of me … and spreads his arms.

I don't question the invitation. I don't hesitate for a second. I step forward, wrap my arms around his waist, and rest my cheek on the hard plane of muscle above his heart. Mine thunders in my chest as I wait for his embrace, but my captor doesn't hug me back. Instead, he reaches around me, pulls the neck of my baggy sweatshirt out, and drops the packaged supplies down the back of my tucked-in tank top.

My cheeks blaze with mortification as the items slide down my bare skin, one by one.

Plunk, plunk, plunk, plunk.

God, I feel stupid.

The second the last one drops, I'm gone. I don't care about the cereal crunching under my boots or the laughing, slurring men nearby or the ogre with the Uzi waiting for us outside. All I care about is getting the fuck away from that asshole before he sees my stupid red face.

I'm almost to the exit when a trio of guys who look like they just crawled out from under a meth lab step between me and the sliding glass doors. The red bandanas showing off their redneck gang affiliation are the only colorful thing about their otherwise drab, unwashed appearances. There's a gross, predatory look in their bloodshot eyes that would send me running … if it wasn't for the handguns sticking out of their waistbands.

"What's the rush, pretty girl? You just got here."

I recognize one of them from school. He was in the grade above me, I think. At least, he was until he stopped going.

"Well, goddamn." His pale face splits into a grin, revealing a set of blackened teeth. "If it isn't little Rainbow Williams." He clicks his tongue and violates me with his cloudy eyes. "Look at you … all grown up."

I want to act cool and pal around with him like we're old friends, but I can't even remember his damn name.

I can't remember anything anymore.

I start to panic, flying through every possible name I can think of in my mind, but all I can get out is, "Hey … man."

"Looks like you and your boyfriend here"—all three guys lift their eyes to a spot over my shoulder—"were trying to leave without paying your taxes."

Taxes.

My stomach drops.

I manage to twist my face into a fake smile. "Oh! No … see, we worked it out with …" I gesture toward the doorman on the other side of the glass behind them, hoping he'll verify our payment situation, but when I glance over at him, he's not in his chair at all.

He's lying facedown on the sidewalk, being sniffed and nibbled on by a pack of wild dogs.

My guts churn as the reality of our situation comes crashing down around me. We are unarmed and outnumbered, and the only person who might have been able to help us just freaking overdosed.

I glance over my shoulder at Wes. His jaw flexes as he chews on the inside of his bottom lip. He's staring straight ahead, refusing to look at me, and I know why.

Because the lifer has something to live for.

"Can I go?" he asks in a bored voice, meeting the stares of all three gangsters as if they were obnoxious children making him late for work.

I almost want to laugh. A complete stranger took me at gunpoint and delivered me to my worst nightmare, and I let him do it because I liked the way he looked at me.

The nightmare! That's it! Any minute now, the four horsemen are going to burst through that door and kill us all! It's just the nightmare! It has to be! Wake up, Rain! Wake up!

I swing my head left and right, desperately searching for a telltale black-and-red banner, a stitch of April 23 propaganda, some flames, smoke, *something,* but the only things hanging on the walls are TV monitors showing videos of happy white people eating three-dollar bags of Doritos.

It's not a dream. It's just me, three rapists, and the guy trying to sell me to them.

Gulp.

The thugs glance at each other and then back at the man behind me.

The one on the left glares at him and spits on the ground. "Yo pussy-ass ain't even worth the bullet."

"Go on, pretty boy," the one on the right says through his gold grill, flicking his head toward the door. "Get the fuck out."

The one I recognize stares right at me, licking his thin, chapped lips. "You never said shit to me when we was in school, but now, I'm gon' have you screamin' my name."

Dread slithers through my veins as all three rotten grins close in on me, and tears sting my eyes as I watch the lifer walk right on past, leaving me to pay for his precious groceries. The sliding glass doors behind the hillbilly mafia open as my only hope strolls toward them. He stops in the doorway and gives me one last look over his shoulder. But his face isn't cold and callous, like I expected. It's not even remorseful. What I find there is sharp and direct. Wes's pupils narrow and cut to the display shelf beside him and back. Like a command.

Or a warning.

I don't have time to figure out what it means before Wes brings two fingers to his mouth and lets out the loudest whistle I've ever heard.

The dogs outside lift their heads, and before the rednecks in red even have a chance to turn all the way around, Wes grabs a bag of chips off the shelf next to him and rips the damn thing wide open. Salty orange triangles rain down on the threesome as a pack of starving dogs rushes through the open sliding doors. My brain screams at me to run, but all I can do is stand there with my mouth hanging open as the dogs overtake my attackers, snarling and yelping and gnashing and clawing at anything and everything between them and the promise of food.

As I stare at the scene before me, a hand clamps down around my wrist and drags me out the door. I don't look at the ogre on the sidewalk as we pass. I don't stop to take his machine gun or hunt for my pill bottle—two things I know I'll kick myself for later. I don't even limp. All I can think about as Wes and I run across the parking lot is getting away from that hellhole as quickly as possible.

Once we're behind the bread truck, Wes shoves the grocery bags into my arms and grabs his gun holster from the wheel well. "You okay?" he asks, shrugging the brown leather harness on over his shirt.

"Yeah," I huff, shoving my arms elbow deep into the straps of the plastic bags so that they won't fall off during the ride.

"Good." He pulls his black helmet down over his face.

Good.

My cheeks tingle as I climb onto the bike behind him. The second my ass hits the seat, I plaster myself to Wes's back, and we peel out of the parking lot and onto the highway. Shots ring out from somewhere behind us, but I don't look back.

Of course, I don't look forward either.

When you're three days away from the apocalypse, there's not much to look forward to.

Rain

RIGHT, LEFT, RIGHT, RIGHT, *left.*

We weave back through the wreckage on the highway, and I'm lulled into a trance. The adrenaline from our escape begins to wear off—taking the last of my hydrocodone high along with it—and my mind begins to wander into dangerous places. No memories come. Just feelings. Bad ones. And the occasional unwanted picture in my head. I don't know which ones are from real life and which ones are from the nightmares.

I don't want to know.

I squeeze my eyes shut and try singing to myself, but every song that comes to mind is sad. Or violent. Or sad and violent. "Semi-Automatic" by Twenty One Pilots makes me think of "10 A.M. Automatic" by The Black Keys, which makes me think of "Black Wave" by K. Flay, which makes me think of "Blood in the Cut" by K. Flay, which makes me think of "Cut Yr Teeth" by Kississippi, which makes me think of "Cut My Lip" by Twenty One Pilots.

I begin searching for a happy Twenty One Pilots song—there has to be one—when Wes makes a sharp right, pulling into Hartwell Park. I hold on to him tighter through the turn, food bags cutting off the blood supply to my lower arms, and try to figure out what the hell we're doing there.

The place has seen better days. Burger Palace wrappers, crushed beer cans, and cigarette butts have been strewn around like confetti after a party, and in addition to all the other graffiti, *somebody* went and spray-painted a giant letter S on the sign so that it reads *Shartwell Park* now.

Okay, that one's my personal favorite.

Wes drives right up onto the grass and parks next to the playground. I let go of him, reluctantly, and climb off the dirt bike. Setting the plastic bags on the ground, I massage the divots out of my arms to try to get the blood flowing into my hands again.

As soon as his helmet is off, Wes grabs the bags and heads up a yellow ladder to the top of the playground equipment. I tilt my head back and squint up at him as he disappears over the ledge. "Why did you stop *here*? You just really like slides or something?"

"Dogs can't climb ladders," he calls back over the sound of plastic rustling and cardboard ripping.

Oh shit.

Looking around to make sure there's no sign of the three Rs, I climb up the ladder and find Wes sitting with his back against the railing, already popping the last bite of a protein bar into his mouth.

"Damn. You *were* hungry."

He wads up the wrapper and tosses it into the sea of garbage below us before offering the opened box to me. The gesture is kind, but his eyes are hard as he crunches on a cheekful of chemically engineered nutrients.

"Uh, thanks." I slide a protein bar out of the box and peel back the wrapper. The moment my teeth sink into that brick of salty sweetness, an involuntary moan rumbles in the back of my throat. It's the first thing I've eaten that hasn't come out of a deep fryer at Burger Palace in days. Maybe longer.

"That was really fucking stupid back there."

I swallow and risk a glance at my angry companion. Even though he's sitting and I'm standing, the look on his face still scares the hell out of me.

"Oh … yeah. Sorry about that."

"I told you I'd get you out of there *if* you kept your mouth shut and followed my lead. You didn't follow shit."

I wince and manage an awkward half-smile. "I followed you, like, *almost* the whole time." My half-smile turns into a grimace.

"Yeah, and you ran your fucking mouth almost the whole time, too." Wes drops his dagger-like stare and begins rummaging through the bags again.

"I said I was sorry, okay? Maybe, next time, you should kidnap somebody a little less impulsive."

Wes rips the top off another box, ignoring me.

I cross my arms over my chest and try to pout, but it's kind of hard when he's twisting the cap off a pouch of squeezie applesauce like a five-year-old.

"Man"—I giggle—"you do *not* know how to apocalypse. We're gonna die in three days, and you're over here, worried about the five food groups."

Wes stills with the pouch poised an inch from his parted lips. "Who's *we?*"

"Um, you, me"—I spread my arms and look out over the empty landfill of a park—"everybody."

"I'm not gonna die," Wes says before wrapping his lips around the opening of the pouch.

Something about the way he's looking up at me makes my cheeks tingle.

I laugh it off and snap my fingers at him. "I knew you were a lifer! I knew it!" I sit down across from him and lean forward. "So, tell me, lifer, if we're not gonna die, what do *you* think the nightmares mean? You think the four horsemen of the apocalypse are just gonna show up on April 23 to braid our hair and play patty-cake?" At the mention of braids, I reach up and touch the place where mine used to be.

Yep. Still gone.

Wes leans forward and jams a finger in my direction. "I told you, I'm not a fucking lifer. I didn't say, *we're* not gonna die. I said, *I'm* not gonna die. I don't know what the dream means, and I don't give a shit. All I know is that whatever it is … I'm gonna survive it."

I almost choke on my protein bar. Burying my lower face in my elbow, I cough up bits of powdered peanut butter and stare at the delusional man sitting across from me. "You're gonna *survive* it?"

Wes lifts his shoulders in a half-assed shrug as the pouch between his lips flattens to nothing.

"How are you gonna survive something if you don't even know what it is?"

Another shrug. Another wrapper hits the ground.

"Been doin' it my whole life." Wes's voice is soft again, and this time, his eyes don't meet mine when he speaks.

Something inside of me twists at his admission, and I lower my voice to match his. "So, you're like, some kind of survivalist then?"

"Sure." The word comes out harsh and flat, like he doesn't want to talk about it.

That's fine with me. I'm an expert at not talking about shit. Or dealing with it at all if I don't have to.

I lean back against the railing and yelp as the items he shoved down my shirt earlier clang against the yellow metal poles. The corner of one package stabs me in the spine while the corner of another pokes me in the ass through my pajama bottoms. "Ow! God! Damn!"

With a huff, I turn around so that my back is toward him and untuck my tank top, letting all of his precious supplies fall into his lap. Wes chuckles softly, and I look at him over my shoulder.

Big mistake.

The man in the Hawaiian shirt is smiling down at the tools I just dumped on him like it's Christmas morning. His lashes are long and dark against his high cheekbones, a lock of soft brown hair has fallen out from behind his ear, and all I want to do is crawl into his lap so that maybe he'll look at me the same way.

But he won't because, unlike that flashlight, pocketknife, pack of lighters, and can opener, I'm a tool that's already served its purpose. Wes got his food, and any minute, he's going to toss me aside like all those wrappers on the ground below us.

Through the railing behind Wes, my eyes catch movement on the other side of the playground. An older couple just arrived, and they're each pushing a small child on a swing. The kids are giggling and kicking their feet, completely oblivious to the garbage and sadness all around them, but their parents' vacant, numb, washed-out stares say it all.

They're going to watch each other die in three days, and the only thing they can do about it is stay high and try not to cry in front of the kids.

I tear my eyes away from their pain, as all of mine begins to rise to the surface. Every punch and kick I took this morning makes itself known. The rejection I know is coming—when Wes announces that he doesn't need me anymore—burns like fire beneath my skin. Every loss I've suffered and the ones I know are coming pound against my skull, demanding to be acknowledged. I feel it all and all at once.

I grab my hoodie pocket, desperate for relief, but it's empty. Of course.

Because Wes stole my pills to buy these fucking groceries.

Turning back around, I shove my hands into my windblown hair and try to catch my breath, but I can't. I can't breathe. I can't get my fingers through the tangled strands. And I can't believe I was stupid enough to let this guy take the only thing I had that would make this pain go away. I yank harder. Breathe harder. I rock back and forth, trying to soothe myself, but nothing's working.

"Hey … you okay?"

"No!" I shout, but I only hear it in my mind. My lungs are expanding and contracting—I can feel it—but the air's not getting in.

The air's not getting in!

"Rainbow …"

"Rain!" I snap, clutching the sides of my head.

"*Rainbow,*" a sweet voice calls in my head. "*Rainbow, baby, time to come inside …*"

The image of a beautiful, smiling woman with dark blonde hair flashes behind my eyes before my flailing consciousness bats it away.

No!

"Rain …" Wes's voice is measured and calm.

He's talking to me like I'm a caged animal, so I behave like one.

I fucking run.

CHAPTER 4

Wes

"RAIN!" I SHOUT AFTER her, but she's already halfway across the parking lot.

Her limp is worse than before, but she's managing. I lean back against the railing and watch her disappear into the woods.

What the fuck was that?

I glance over my shoulder at the family she was staring at just a second ago and wonder if she knew them or something.

Whatever. It's not my problem.

My stomach growls, reminding me exactly what my problem is. Or was, before I scored a week's worth of food, thanks to that little black-haired psycho. I'm actually glad she ran off. That one had *desperate clinger with daddy issues* written all over her, and the last thing I need is another mouth to feed.

I dig through the plastic bags until I find the can of beef stew. I'm sure it'll taste like fucking dog food, but it has enough calories and protein to get me through the rest of the day.

I pick up the packaged can opener in my lap, and I swear, it fucking smells like her. Lifting the cardboard to my nose, I close my eyes and inhale, remembering the way she wrapped her little arms around me in the grocery store. Her hair smelled just like this—vanilla or cupcakes or some girlie shit. Made my dick hard.

Yeah, and then she stormed off and almost got herself gang-raped.

My heart beats like an iron fist against my ribs as I picture her standing there, watching me leave, big blue eyes full of fear, big black hoodie almost down to her knees.

Stop it. You don't need her anymore. Supplies, shelter, self-defense. That's it.

My blood pumps harder as I remember the way she tried to fight me off in the parking lot. Bitch actually pulled my hair. Nobody's ever pulled my fucking hair before.

Supplies, shelter, self-defense.

I picture the little crease in her forehead and the swelling claw marks on her cheek after I yanked her ass out of Burger Palace, standing there, debating whether or not to get on the bike with me. As if she had a choice.

Supplies, shelter, self-defense.

Then, I see her the way I found her—balled up on the floor, so tiny, taking the beating of a lifetime because she refused to hand over her precious painkillers.

Damn it!

I chuck the can back into the bag and grab my shit. My stomach protests as I leap down to the trash-covered woodchips below and begin tying the grocery bags to my handlebars with violent knots. I have to get Rain back, and it has nothing to do with the fact that she smells like sugar cookies or looks like a broken china doll dressed by a blind person or because of the way her tits and thighs felt pressed against me on the back of my bike. I have to get Rain back because I know something she doesn't.

Rainbow Williams is a fucking survivor.

And I'm not done using her yet.

I follow the trail she took through the woods on my bike, but it only leads as far as a strip shopping center down the road from the park. The place is deserted, hollowed out from a fire. If I had to guess, I'd say the looters probably took whatever drugs they could find in the dentist's office and left the rest to burn.

That's the only thing of any real value anymore. Pills. Pussy. The thrill of pyromania. Cash is worthless—unless you want to Apocasize your French fries at Burger Palace. And our government is so full of shit that nobody even listens to those lying assholes anymore. According to them, the US dollar is "stronger than ever," and we should all just "remain calm" until "the source of the nightmares is identified."

Of course, that message has been playing on a prerecorded loop for the last few weeks because not even the newscasters are showing up for work anymore. They're all at home with their families or out getting fucked up and lighting shit on fire like the rest of us.

I drive around the building and pick up the trail again, heading back the way I came. Even though I haven't been back to Franklin Springs since I was nine, I still know these woods like the back of my hand. I think I spent more time in them, avoiding my cunt of a mother and her parade of drunken boyfriends, than I ever did under her roof.

Or anyone's roof, for that matter. After I was placed in foster care, I bounced from shitty home to shittier home until I finally aged out of the whole shitty system. Now, I bounce from roommate to roommate instead.

The trail runs parallel to the main highway, stopping and restarting at almost every business along the way. A few forks jut off of it here and there, cutting through the woods to nearby neighborhoods. I'm starting to think I might have waited too long. Rain could be anywhere by now. She's probably inside some perfect little house somewhere, eating a perfect little meal, telling her perfect little family about the asshole who kidnapped her from Burger Palace.

I pop the clutch and shift into second. Then, third. I don't know if it's because I think I can still find her or if it's because I'm so fucking mad at myself for letting her go, but I tear down the trail so fast that I don't even realize where I am until the woods clear, and I find myself barreling across a huge parking lot, headed toward one very familiar-looking bread truck.

Fuck!

I hit the brakes and skid to a stop beside the truck. I listen for shots, yelling, barking, anything, but my bike is loud as fuck, so I kill the engine and wait. My gun has been a fucking paperweight ever since I used my last bullet saving Rain's ass at Burger Palace this morning, but I draw it anyway and walk my bike forward until I have a clean view of the main entrance through the driver's window.

Huckabee Foods looks exactly the way we left it—bloated corpse facedown on the sidewalk, overturned lawn chair, probably a few mauled gangbangers on the other side of the sliding glass doors. But, most importantly, no imminent threats. I breathe out a sigh of relief and holster my gun, wondering how the fuck I could be stupid enough to end up back here. I was being reckless. I don't *do* reckless.

But I know somebody who does.

Before I can crank the throttle and get the fuck out of there, something tells me to give the entrance a second look. I do, and that's when I notice that the dead guy is no longer lying on his stomach. He's rolled over onto his side. And there, squatting next to him, is the little black-haired bitch who did the rolling.

Rain's hoodie-covered body is kneeling in front of the corpse, holding one side of him up with her shoulder while she digs through the pockets of his baggy jeans. The guy's face is fucking horrifying—eyelids half-open, mouth slack, dried puke covering one side of it—but Rain is going through his shit like she's hunting through a clearance bin at Walmart.

A little fucking survivor. I knew it.

When she finds what she's looking for, Rain lets the guy's body fall back down with an unceremonious *plop*. She focuses all of her attention on something small and orange in her hands. I want to stand up and give her a slow clap for having bigger balls than I do, but I'm pretty damn sure that whatever gang produced Thug-Life Shrek and the meth-head trio, it has plenty more soldiers to spare inside.

Rain shakes a pill into her mouth. Then she caps the bottle and shoves it down the neck of her sweatshirt, tucking it into her bra. I smirk, remembering how that same bottle practically fell out of her hoodie pocket and into my hand when I threw her over my shoulder earlier.

She's learning.

Shaking my head, I stomp down on the kick-start.

Rain got what she came for. Now, it's my turn.

I pull out from behind the bread truck, expecting Rain to spin around with a smile on her face at the sound of my approaching engine.

Instead, she spins around, holding homeboy's Uzi.

It's still strapped to his massive body, but she keeps the barrel trained on me as she struggles to free it. By the time I pull up to the curb next to her, her cheeks are pink from exertion. I sit and wait with a smug smile under my helmet, knowing good and goddamn well that this girl isn't going to shoot m—

Br-r-r-r-r-ap!

The crescendo of a machine gun sounds at the exact same time that a white-hot pain slashes through my shoulder. I look to Rain in disbelief that the bitch actually pulled the trigger, but she isn't facing me anymore. She's facing the main entrance where two more of society's red bandana rejects are lying on the ground, bleeding all over a bed of broken glass.

Rain's startled eyes dart over to me before she drops the Uzi and leaps to her feet. She hesitates, then makes a mad dash for my bike, stopping to pick up one of the fallen gangbanger's pistols along the way.

Supplies, shelter, and self-defense, I recite in my head as Rain wraps her soft little body around mine.

Two down, one to go.

Rain

I JUST KILLED A guy.

Two guys. I think I just killed two guys.

As I bounce up and down on the back of Wes's speeding dirt bike, I replay what just happened in my head. I don't *relive* it. I simply watch it, like a bad TV show, while I wait for the hydrocodone to kick in and make it all go away.

I see the reflection of the sliding glass doors opening in Wes's shiny black helmet. I see red bandanas coming out of that door. I see guns pointed at Wes. Then, I see the men holding those guns fall down as the sliding glass doors explode behind them. It looks like sparkly crystal confetti in the air. Everything is so loud. I can't believe Wes actually shot those guys. I turn back around and look at him.

But he isn't holding a gun.

I close my eyes and smoosh my cheek against Wes's shoulder blade a little harder. Then, I throw that instant replay clip into the fortress of Shit I'm Not Going to Think About Ever Again Because None of This Matters and We're All Going to Die.

Wes's body begins to twist and flex in my arms like he's trying to do something while he drives, so I sit up and peek over his shoulder. He has one hand on the handlebars while the other is messing around with his holster. I wonder if he needs my help, but before I can offer, Wes draws his gun and tosses it into the woods.

I turn my head, following the revolver with my eyes as it disappears into the underbrush. Then, I gasp as the pistol I forgot I was even holding is pulled free from my hand. Wes holsters his new gun—*my* gun—and I feel his body shake with laughter.

Asshole.

I smack him on the shoulder and hear him yelp, even over the roar of the engine.

When I look down, there's blood on my hand.

Oh my God.

Wes pulls to a stop on the side of the trail and yanks his helmet off. "What the fuck?"

"I'm sorry! I didn't know!" I slide off the leather seat and reach for the sleeve of Wes's shirt. The pink flower printed there is now bright red. "Let me look at it."

Wes glares at me and nods. Once.

He mercilessly chews on the inside of his bottom lip as I carefully pinch the edge of his sleeve. Lifting the fabric, I see a deep gash across his upper arm. It's nasty—about two inches long and half an inch wide—but not bleeding too badly. It's as if the heat from the bullet cauterized the wound.

"Well, I've got good news and bad news."

Wes raises an annoyed eyebrow at me.

"The good news is that it's just a flesh wound. The bad news is that you ruined your pretty shirt."

Wes pulls his shoulder away from me and yanks his sleeve back down. "*I* ruined it?"

"Don't look at me! The only reason those guys came outside and shot at you was because they heard *your* loud-ass bike!"

"Well, *my* loud-ass bike wouldn't have been there if *you* hadn't run away."

"Well, *you* didn't have to come get me, did you?"

Wes purses his lips and looks at me the way he would a shelf of canned goods or a rack of tools. Like he's considering my value. "Yes, I did."

He props his bike on the kickstand, and my heart begins to pound as he stands up and faces me. The vehicle is in between us, like a line in the sand.

"As much as I hate to admit it"—his face softens, just a little—"you're pretty useful when you're not trying to get us both killed."

I swallow and straighten my spine, forcing myself to look him in the eye. It's hard to act tough when you're looking at something that *pretty*. Hell, it's hard to remember what I was about to say.

Wait. What was I about to say? Oh, right.

"What makes you think I wanna help *you*?"

"What makes you think I give a shit what you want?" Poof. Softness gone.

"Gah, Wes! You don't have to be such a dick. You could just ask nicely, you know?"

Wes pulls *my* gun out of his holster and points it at my head with a smirk. "I don't have to ask nicely. I'm the one with the gun."

I roll my eyes and cross my arms over my chest.

"You know what I like about Glocks?" Wes's smirk widens into a sneer. "The safety is right here." He taps his index finger against the trigger. *Tap, tap, tap.* "You don't even have to cock the hammer back before you shoot. You just ... squeeze."

"Ugh! Fine! I'll help you!" I throw my arms in the air. "You don't have to be so dramatic about it."

Wes chuckles as he shoves the gun back into his holster. It reminds me of how he looked at the playground. Dark eyelashes fanned across his cheeks. Perfect smile. Rusty laugh. Only this time, it doesn't hurt to look at him.

Because this time, he wants me to stay.

"I need gas," Wes announces, giving his gunshot wound another quick glance. It must hurt like a bitch.

"Gas stations around here are all dry. Only way to get gas now is to siphon it."

"Cool." Wes climbs back onto the bike and looks over at me. "Know where we can find a hose?"

"And a bandage?" I glance down at the ruined sleeve of his Hawaiian shirt.

"Yeah."

"Yeah"—I swallow, trying to push the tightness out of my throat—"I do."

Wes

RAIN LEADS ME DOWN the trail, back through the park, and all the way to a library across from good ole Burger Palace.

"I can't believe that car is still on fire," she shouts over the growl of the engine as we pass a smoking sedan in the parking lot. "It's been burnin' all day!"

She directs me to go around to the back of the library and points to the spot in the trees where the trail continues. I head toward it but notice movement out of the corner of my eye. I turn my head and reach for my gun but relax when I see that it's just a dude … giving another dude a blow job.

"Sorry!" Rain shouts to the startled men with a giggle as we dive back into the pines.

This part of the trail isn't as well traveled, so I slow down, and for the first time all day, I don't feel like I'm running to or from anything. I suck in a deep breath, wishing I could smell the pines through my helmet, and feel Rain's warm body shuddering against mine as she continues to laugh.

Then a sapling branch whips across my mangled shoulder, and I debate burning the entire fucking forest to the ground.

"There!" Rain's finger shoots out in the direction of a clearing up ahead. "That's my house!"

Her house? This should be interesting. I'm sure her parents are gonna be real excited about their precious Rainbow bringing a gun-toting homeless guy with a weeping flesh wound home for dinner.

The trail ends in the backyard of a small wooden two-story that looks like it hasn't been painted since the South lost the Civil War. At one point, it might have been blue. Now, it's just a weathered gray, spotted with mildew and peppered with woodpecker holes.

I pull around to the front of the house and park in the driveway next to a rust-colored '90s-era Chevy pickup truck.

Any minute, I'm expecting a middle-aged guy with a beer gut and a shotgun to come bursting out the front door, chewing on tobacco and yelling at me to, *Go on now! Git!*

Maybe I should keep my helmet on a little longer ...

Rain hops off the back of my bike and runs over to a spigot on the side of the house. She cranks the handle and lifts the end of a green garden hose to her mouth. Her eyes close in ecstasy as she drinks, making me realize how thirsty I am. I don't know if I've had anything to drink all day.

I stride over and wait my turn, noticing that one side of her hair is getting wet. I want to reach out and tuck it behind her ear, but I don't. That's a boyfriend move, and the last thing I need is for this chick to get the wrong idea about us.

I don't do *us*. All *us* does is get you hurt or killed, so I throw an E on the end of that bitch, and I *use*.

My foster parents used me to get money from the state. I used them to get food, water, and shelter. The girls at school used me to fill their needy little attention buckets and make each other jealous. I used them as a nice warm place to put my dick. The guys used me to score them drugs or guns or cool points or the answers to next week's history exam. I charged them a shitload to do it. This is the way the world works, and watching Rain clutching that hose in her fist—sucking from the stream with her little pink tongue at the edge of her slightly open mouth—makes me think of a few new ways I could use her, too.

As if she could hear my inappropriate thoughts, Rain lifts her big blue eyes to mine.

I smirk down at her. "There something wrong with your sinks?"

Rain jerks the hose away from her mouth and coughs.

"You okay?"

"Yeah, I just ..." She hacks some more, wiping her mouth on the back of her sleeve. "I lost my keys, remember? I can't get in."

"Whose truck is that? Can't they let you in?" I jerk my thumb in the direction of the rust bucket on wheels.

"That's my dad's, but …" Her face goes white as her eyes dart left and right, looking for a lie. "He's deaf. *And* he hangs out in his man cave upstairs all day, so he won't hear me knocking."

"Or see you knocking," I add.

"Right." Rain shrugs dramatically.

"Where's your mom?" I take the hose from her and drink while I wait for her to make up another bullshit story.

"She's at work."

I take a breath between gulps. "Nobody's at work."

"No, for real!" The pitch of her voice shoots up along with her eyebrows. "She's an ER nurse. The hospital is still open."

I give her a doubtful glare. "How does she get there?"

"Motorcycle."

"What kind of motorcycle?"

Rain's face reddens. "I don't know! A black one!"

I laugh and shut off the water. There are a dozen smart-ass responses on the tip of my tongue, but I decide to keep my mouth shut. If this girl doesn't want me to know that she lives alone—which is pretty fucking obvious from her bullshit responses—then that's what I'm gonna let her think.

Besides, I can't say that I blame her. I'm sure *Invite a strange man into your house after he pulls a gun on you* is in the top ten list of shit single girls are taught not to do.

Invite a strange man into your house after he pulls a gun on you twice is probably in the top five.

Rain turns her flustered head toward the Chevy. "You can siphon the gas out of my dad's truck since the roads are too trashed to drive it anyway. I guess just use the"—her eyes dart back to me as I flick open my new pocketknife and slice off about five feet of hose—"hose."

"Thanks." I smirk. Walking over to the rust bucket, I cut the length of hose in my hand into two pieces—a long one and a short one. Then, I pop open the gas cap and stick both inside the opening. "Hold these, okay?"

Rain hops over like her ass is on fire. I find it interesting that she's completely incapable of following directions unless I'm asking her for help.

She probably would have been a nurse, like her mom, I think. *If her mom even is a nurse.*

I pull off my holster, making sure not to graze my shoulder wound with it, and set it on the ground. I see the way Rain is eyeing it, so I push it further away with my foot. "Uh-uh-uh."

"That's *my* gun." Rain pretends to pout as I take off my Hawaiian shirt and stuff it into the openings around the hoses.

I move her hands so that she's holding the shirt and the hoses in place.

"Can't you just, like, stick a tube in there and suck on it?" Rain asks as I walk my bike closer to the truck.

"Sure, if I wanted to get a mouthful of gasoline."

Rain rolls her eyes, and the expression makes her seem so young. That giant Twenty One Pilots hoodie doesn't help.

"How old are you?" I ask, tilting my bike sideways so that the gas tank will be lower than the truck's.

"Nineteen."

Bullshit.

"How old are you?" she asks as I stick the end of the long hose into my gas tank.

"Twenty-two."

Keeping my bike tilted at just the right angle, I lean over to where Rain is holding everything in place and blow into the short tube. She gasps a moment later when we hear the sound of liquid splashing against the bottom of my gas tank.

"Where did you learn how to do that?" Rain's eyes are wide, her voice is breathy, and her mouth has fallen open in a little O.

I begin to think of a few other ways I could put that look on her face when I remember that she asked me a question. "YouTube."

"Oh, right." She laughs. "The internet's been down for a week, and I already forgot about YouTube."

An awkward silence stretches between us as we're forced to stand there, each holding our own end of the hose.

Rain breaks it and manages to make things even more awkward. "I can't believe we only have three days left."

"Speak for yourself," I snap.

"Oh, right." Rain furrows her brow, considering my statement. "Hey, can I ask you a question?"

I shrug. "You're going to anyway."

"If whatever's coming is as bad as everyone thinks it is, then why are you trying so hard to survive it? I mean, what if you end up being the last person on Earth?"

"Then, I'd be king of the fucking world," I deadpan. The tank is almost full, so I stand the bike upright to stop the flow.

Rain lets out a sad laugh as I pull out the hose and screw the gas cap back on. "Yeah, you'd be king of the whole busted, ruined planet."

I shrug and push the kickstand back out. I never talk about my shit, but there's something about the way this girl is hanging on my every word that makes them just start falling out of my mouth. "The way I see it, if I can survive the fucking apocalypse, then it makes everything I've been through mean something, you know? Like, instead of breaking me … they made me unbreakable."

Rain's big, sad eyes begin to glisten, making me wish I'd kept my fucking mouth shut. I don't want her pity. I want her compliance. I want her resources. And, if I'm being honest, I wouldn't mind bending her over the hood of this truck right now either.

"Who is *they?*" she asks as I pull her death grip off the hoses and toss them into the overgrown grass.

"Doesn't matter." I pick my holster up off the ground and carefully pull it back on over my wifebeater. "All that matters is that, if I'm still here and they're not, then I won."

"Well, whoever they are"—Rain gives me a small smile as I fan my shirt in the air to smooth out the wrinkles—"I hope they die last."

A laugh bursts out of me as I look at Rain's angelic face. She starts laughing too, then snatches my lucky shirt out of my hands.

"Oh my God, were you seriously about to put this back on?" She cackles. I grab my shirt and try to pull it out of her hands, but she clings to it with dear life. "How are you gonna survive the apocalypse wearing a shirt soaked in gasoline?"

"I don't exactly see any laundromats around here, do you?" I fake left and grab the shirt when she veers right, but she still doesn't let go.

"I can wash it."

"What? When your mom gets home from work and lets you in?"

Rain's face pales, and she releases my shirt.

Fuck. I didn't mean to call her out.

"Yeah," she says, her eyes losing focus and dropping to my chest, "when my mom gets home."

Shit. Now, she looks all sad and freaked out. Her hand is in her hair again. That's never good. This bitch does stupid shit when she's freaking out.

"Hey," I say, trying to snap her out of it. "You wanna eat?" I drape my shirt over my good shoulder and begin untying the grocery bags hanging from my handlebars. "I saw a tree house in your backyard. We should eat up there—"

"In case the dogs smell the food," Rain finishes my sentence with a faraway look on her face.

"No." I grin, holding the bags with my good arm and guiding her into the almost-knee-high grass with my other. "Because it's probably full of Justin Bieber posters. He's so fucking dreamy."

Rain snorts through her nose like a pig. "Oh my God." She cackles. "Did you just make a joke?"

I raise an eyebrow at her and keep walking. "I would never joke about the Biebs."

As Rain falls into step beside me, snickering at my stupid fucking joke, I realize that I might have been wrong earlier.

I already feel like the king of the world.

Rain

I SHOVE ALL THE thoughts of my mother back into the Shit I'm Never Going to Think About Again Because None of This Matters and We're All Going to Die fortress, pull up the drawbridge, and light that bitch on fire.

Three more days.

As I climb the ladder to my rickety old tree house, I realize that it's already starting to get dark outside.

Make that two and a half more days.

All I have to do is not think about her for two and a half more days, and then I won't have to think about her ever again.

I pop another pill while I wait for Wes to climb the ladder, just to make extra sure that shit stays locked up tight.

I take the bags from him as he climbs over the top of the ladder.

The tree house isn't much. It's basically just a rotting plywood box with a couple of dirty-ass beanbag chairs and an old boom box inside, but when I was a kid, it was Cinderella's castle, Jack Sparrow's pirate ship, and Wonder Woman's invisible plane, all rolled into one.

The ceiling is so low that Wes doesn't even bother trying to stand up. He simply crawls over to a beanbag chair and makes himself at home. He stretches his long legs out in front of him and crosses them at the ankles as he rummages through the grocery bags. His feet almost stick out the door. It reminds me of Alice in Wonderland when she grew too fast and got stuck in the White Rabbit's house.

"So," I say, plopping into the beanbag next to him as he concentrates on working that damn can opener that stabbed me in the back earlier, "you got anything in there that *doesn't* look like dog food?"

Wes hands me one of the bags without looking up.

I pull out a stick of beef jerky and gesture toward the clunky radio with it. "Hey, do you want to listen to some music? I think I have my mom's old Tupac CD in here. It's not *Justin Bieber*, but ..."

Wes smirks at my joke and pops a chunk of potato into his mouth. "Save your batteries. We won't have power much longer."

His statement wipes the smile right off my face.

Oh, right. Apocalypse. Yay.

I take in Wes's dirty clothes as he starts pulling chunks of beef, carrots, and potatoes out of the can with his fingers like a starved raccoon. His messy hair. His total lack of personal belongings.

"So ..." I pretend to look for a way to open the jerky package. "Where did you come from?"

"Here," Wes says between bites.

I laugh. "You are *so* not from here. I've lived here my whole life, and I've never seen you before."

Wes gives me a look that says he does not appreciate being called a liar, then deadpans, "I lived here until I was nine. Then, I ... moved around a lot."

"Really? Do you still have family here?"

Wes shrugs and returns to his canned dinner.

"You don't know? Who are you staying with?" I still haven't touched my jerky.

Why am I so nervous to talk to this guy? He's just a guy. Of manly age and stature. Okay, he's a fucking *man* and I don't know him and he has a gun and he's currently my only source of food that isn't a condiment.

"You."

Wait. What?

"Ohhh no. You can't stay with me. Are you fucking kidding? My parents would—"

"Not in there." Wes gestures toward my house with a cube of beef pinched between his thumb and index finger. Then, he tosses it into his mouth and points toward the floor. "Out here."

"Oh." I relax a teensy, tiny bit. "I guess that's okay."

"I wasn't asking," Wes mumbles as he chews, plucking a carrot out of his can next.

"Where are your parents?" I ask, still trying to put all the pieces together.

Wes tosses back the wet orange vegetable. "I never met my dad, and my mom's locked up."

"Oh, damn. I'm sorry."

"Don't be. She deserves worse." Wes's voice is emotionless as he selects a potato.

"Uh … brothers or sisters?"

His annoyed eyes cut to mine but only for a second before he returns to his meal. "No."

"Then, why—"

Wes's head snaps up. "I came back because I found a bomb shelter here when I was a kid. Okay? Out in the woods." He takes a deep breath through his nose and releases it. When he continues, his voice is a little less defensive. "My plan was to find it this afternoon, after I got supplies … but I burned all my daylight looking for your ass instead."

Wes and I both look out the door at the same time. A dark blue has fallen over the sky, covering our sunset and tucking it in for the night. That's what Wes's comment feels like. I know he meant it to be a jab, but it landed on me like a blanket.

Wes chose finding *me* over finding shelter for the night.

I stare at his profile as his gaze returns to the can he's holding. I want to reach out and run my finger down the bridge of his perfect nose. I want to trace the edge of his strong jaw and feel the sandpaper scratchiness of his evening stubble against my fingertip. I want to press that finger between his full pink lips and let him bite it off if he wants to.

Because if Wes thinks he needs me, I'm determined to prove him right.

A chill racks my body as the last of the sun's warmth disappears along with the color from the sky. "I'll be right back," I say, chucking the beef jerky and trail mix back into one of the bags and scrambling over to the ladder.

Wes doesn't question where I'm going, but his gaze is a silent warning. If I try to run again, he'll find me.

I try not to smile about that until I'm halfway down the ladder.

Wes

GREAT JOB, ASSHOLE. YOU *made her fucking run again.*

Look, there she goes.

I sit up and watch Rain's hoodie-shrouded silhouette sprint across the backyard and disappear around the side of the house like she can't get away from me fast enough.

Maybe she just needs to pee.

Well, if she's not back in sixty fucking seconds, I'm going after her.

About thirty-five seconds later, I hear a loud crash, like the sound of a window breaking. I lurch forward, ready to jump out of that fucking tree house and see what the hell is going on, but before I make it to the ladder, I see a light come on inside the house. Followed by another one, and another one. I shake my head and flop back down in my seat.

That bitch just broke into her own damn house.

I toss a handful of trail mix into my mouth and watch as lights go on and off in various rooms.

What the hell is she doing in there?

It's pitch-black outside now, so I dig the flashlight out of one of the grocery bags and turn it on, setting it down so that it shines at the opposite wall. It illuminates a pack of cigarettes sticking out of a crack between the floorboard and wall.

Fuck yeah.

I dig them out—Marlboro Reds—and flip open the lid. When I turn the box over to shake one out, nothing but tobacco dust pours into my hand.

Goddamn it.

I throw the box into the corner and hear the sound of a door slamming in the distance. Seconds later, Rain is full-on sprinting across the lawn with her arms full of God knows what. The house is dark again.

Rain grunts as she climbs the ladder with her arms full, but instead of her head emerging first, a bundle of blankets and pillows comes flying over the threshold before her. Then, a tiny hand setting a bottle of whiskey down on the plywood floor with a thud, followed by the face and body of the girl it belongs to.

Rain is wearing a backpack that's almost as big as she is. She shrugs it off her shoulders and sits cross-legged next to it in the middle of the floor. Tearing it open, Rain begins talking a mile a minute.

"So, I got you some blankets and a towel and a pillow, and I filled up a couple of water bottles in case you get thirsty. Oh, and I got you some toilet paper and an extra toothbrush and all these little travel-sized toiletries from the one time my parents took me to the beach. We stayed at a real hotel that time, not just a friend of my dad's that he told me to call *Uncle This* or *Uncle That*, like all our other 'vacations.'" She put finger quotes around the word *vacations* and continues unpacking. "I remember I tried to order fried chicken from the hotel restaurant, and a lady in the back started screaming, 'Fried chicken? Fried chicken!' And then she stormed out the front door and threw her apron on the floor next to my booth on her way out. When our waiter came back, he said, 'Welp, the cook just quit. How 'bout some grilled cheese?'"

Rain cackles at the memory. The sound is manic. Pressured.

"I would have gotten you some warmer clothes too, but mine won't fit you and my dad's are in his room and"—she goes back to digging in the backpack even though it's empty now, her left knee bouncing so hard and so fast that it begins to shake the tree house—"I don't wanna go in there."

Abandoning the backpack, Rain grabs the bottle of Jack Daniel's and takes a swig, wincing and hissing in agony as it goes down. Then, another. And another.

"Hey"—I reach over and pull the bottle from her hand, and she releases it without a fight—"you okay?"

"I'm fine!" She cuts her eyes away and shoves her hands into her hair.

I know she's a pill head, but Hydro doesn't do *this*. Whatever *this* is, it happened inside that house.

Now she's rocking back and forth again.

Awesome.

"Rain."

Her eyes lift to mine, partially illuminated from my flashlight, and there's a wild desperation in them that makes me realize I read this entire situation wrong.

Rain doesn't live alone.

Rain lives with a fucking monster.

"You're scared of him, aren't you?"

"Who? I'm not scared." Rain glances over at the house as if he can hear her, knee bouncing, breaths shallow.

"Yes, you are. Look at you."

She swallows and looks down at her knee. As she stills her leg, Rain's chin buckles and begins to wobble instead.

My teeth clench so hard I feel like they might shatter. Jerking my chin toward the house, I manage to grind out, "That motherfucker hurt you?"

She claps her hands, completely covered by her hoodie sleeves, over her mouth and nose. Then, she closes her eyes and shakes her head. I can't tell if she's answering my question or trying to rid herself of some unwanted memory, but I don't care.

"Stay out here tonight."

Rain opens her eyes but doesn't take her hands away from her face.

"Let me rephrase that." I sit up and jam my finger into the plywood floor. "You're staying out here tonight."

When Rain doesn't argue, I lean back and take a long pull from the bottle in my hand.

Damn, that's good.

I toss the bag of trail mix into her lap. "Eat. I got shit to do tomorrow, and you're gonna be worthless if you're starving."

"You want me to come?" Rain mumbles into her hands.

Even with her face partially covered and the only light in the tree house coming from a pocket flashlight aimed at the wall, I can see the hope in her big blue eyes.

Fuck. Why did I say that? I don't need her anymore.

Because she's useful, I tell myself. *She's a resource—that's all—and she's the best one you've got.*

I tip the neck of my bottle at her. "You can come—as long as you promise not to eat all the fucking M&M's outta there."

Rain lowers her hands, revealing a smile that she's trying to hide by biting her lip, and uses them to dig through the bag of trail mix in her lap. Pulling her hand out, she holds up one perfectly round piece of red candy between her fingers. Then, she fucking flicks it at me. It's so dark on my side of the tree house that I can't see where it went, but I hear it bounce off the plywood wall somewhere to my right.

"Bitch." I chuckle, taking another swig of whiskey.

That little comment earns me two more M&M's to the head.

"Oh, it's on now!" I grab the stick of beef jerky and lunge forward, swatting her with it until she's nothing but a giggling, hoodie-covered heap on the plywood floor. Then, I sit back, smug in my victory, and survey my spoils for the day.

Supplies? Check.

Shelter? Check.

Self-defense? Check.

Slightly psychotic teenager with a pill habit, daddy issues, and impulse control problems?

I smirk at the hiccupping heap of girl in the fetal position across from me.

Jackpot.

Wes

I TAKE A DEEP *breath and exhale as I shift into second gear. I don't even care that I probably just sucked up two lungfuls of pollen. The woods here have been calling me home ever since I left thirteen years ago. Everything is just the way I remember, except greener. Taller. And, now that I'm exploring them on a Yamaha instead of some busted, old thrift-store sneakers … faster.*

We managed to shove all the food and supplies into Rain's backpack, but since there was no way she could wear that big-ass thing and not fall off the back of my bike, I decided to wear it and let her sit in front of me.

Worst. Decision. Ever.

Rain's ass rubbing against my dick is making it fucking impossible to keep my raging hard-on down. I've tried thinking about politics. About baseball. About Will Ferrell's naked, hairy ball sack. But nothing's working. My mind keeps going back to how easy it would be to just pull those little pajama bottoms down and let Rain bounce on my dick for real.

We drive over a patch of tree roots in the path, and I swear to God, that bitch arches her back and presses against me even harder through the bumps.

I can't fucking take it anymore.

"Throttle," I growl into her ear as I release the right handlebar.

We slow down for just a second before Rain grabs the handle. She twists the shit out of it, and we shoot forward. I laugh as she dials it back and can feel how hard she's breathing where her back meets my chest. I have to keep the clutch engaged with my left hand, but now, my right hand is free to do something about the evil little tease sitting in my lap.

Wrapping my arm around her waist, I tuck my nose into the neck of her hoodie and inhale the warm, sugary scent coming off of her heated skin. Rain's heavy breaths all but stop. Then, she angles her head to the side, just a little.

It's all the invitation I need. She keeps her eyes on the path and steers us with jerky movements as my tongue forges a trail of its own up her neck.

Fuck. She even tastes like vanilla.

I slide my hand up her body until it's filled with the weight of her perfect, round tit. Then, I smile because I can tell how hard her nipple is, even through her sweatshirt. I circle it with my thumb and feel her moan vibrate against my chest.

She can't even hide how badly she wants this, and thank fuck for that because, with my cock pressed against her ass, neither can I.

I trace the outline of her ear with my tongue as I work her other nipple, squeezing and kneading and wishing like hell that I could flip her around, yank that hoodie up, and suck it between my teeth.

I glance up just to make sure Rain isn't about to drive us off a cliff. Then, I slide my hand lower and push my fingers beneath the loose drawstring waistband of her soft flannel pajama pants. They skate over a silky pair of panties. I cup her pussy and bite her earlobe, waiting for her to tell me to stop, to swat my hand away.

But she doesn't. Instead, Rain reaches behind her back with her free hand and grabs my dick through my jeans.

Fuck.

Yes.

I'm determined to drive her just as crazy as she's been driving me this entire ride, so I rub two fingers from her clit to her hole in slow, gentle strokes, over her panties. But Rain's impulsive ass manages to unbutton my fly and get my zipper down in seconds. The moment her smooth fingers wrap around my cock, my plan to tease her mercilessly goes right out the window. It feels so fucking good that I yank her panties aside and slide two fingers into her slick, hot pussy.

Rain's head falls back to my shoulder, so I look up and try to concentrate on the trail while she whimpers and fucks my hand.

But we aren't on the trail anymore. At least, not any trail I've ever been on.

This one cuts through a forest of dead trees that are in the process of being consumed by sharp, thorny vines. The taller branches, brittle and gray and bent toward the white sky, have red banners hanging from them. We're going so fast that I can't read what any of them say, but I can tell that each one is branded with the silhouette of a hooded figure on horseback.

The vines reach up from the forest floor like octopus tentacles, winding around the ancient trees and squeezing them until the wood splinters and breaks and crumbles into the ocean of hungry thorns.

"Faster!" I yell to Rain, but she doesn't crank the throttle.

She begins pumping my dick even harder instead.

Fuck, it feels good.

I shove my fingers into her deeper and rub her clit with my thumb and thrust into her hand even though I know that if I don't kick it into third gear right fucking now, we're both going to die.

I can hear myself yelling inside my own head.

What the fuck are you doing?

I can see myself, a slave to my stupid desire for this crazy girl.

She's going to get you killed, dipshit! Ditch the bitch and get the fuck out of here!

But I'm powerless. Rain is in control now, and she's driving us straight toward certain death.

A tree snaps up ahead, and the sound echoes through the woods like a gunshot. As it crashes to the ground, one of its branches falls across the trail. I can clearly see the banner attached to it now, waving like a flag on the way down.

Just above the image of a faceless horseman wielding a flaming club is the date April 23.

I don't have time to contemplate what that means because, a split second later, I'm flying over the handlebars and somersaulting down the rocky, root-covered trail. When I finally stop rolling, I smack my head on something hard. My cranium explodes in pain. I sit up, clutching my dented skull, and begin frantically looking around for Rain. Blood trickles down my arm as I swivel toward the sound of cavalry in the distance.

Four monstrous black horses are barreling toward me through the forest—heads down, smoke pouring from their flared nostrils—ripping through the brambles and branches like party streamers. They leave nothing but flames and scorched earth in their wake as their faceless, cloaked riders point their weapons—a sword, a scythe, a mace, and a flaming club—toward the colorless sky.

"Wes!" Rain's voice calls out.

I swing my dented head left and right, but I don't find her until I turn all the way around. She landed in a thicket of thorn bushes, and all I can see is her face and halo of black hair before the vines constrict around her body and pull her under.

"Wesssss!"

"No!" I run toward her, but the vines grab my legs, their thorns digging into my clothes and skin like fish hooks, and pull me down, too.

Trees pop and hiss and collapse all around me as the heat from the approaching fire intensifies. I struggle to free myself, slicing my hands open as I rip the sharp vines from my body. With every push and pull and grunt and shove, I get closer to the place where Rain disappeared.

My vision is blurry and red. My head feels like it's about to implode. My hands are shredded and almost worthless, but with one last thrash, I make it out. I stumble toward the spot where I last saw Rain, calling her name with every labored step, but when I get there, she's gone.

Leaving nothing behind but a puddle of water.

I peer into it—exhausted, confused, desperate—but all I find is my own frantic, bloodied reflection staring back at me.

Then the image splashes away, stomped out by one giant black hoof.

April 21
Rain

"WES. WES, WAKE UP. It's just the nightmare. You're okay. You're here."

Wes is sleeping sitting up. His good shoulder and the side of his head are leaning against the wall of the tree house, and he has my old comforter pulled up to his chin. He yelled my name so loud in his sleep that it woke me up. Luckily, I hadn't been asleep long, so my horsemen hadn't shown up yet, but from the looks of things, Wes's are on the other side of his eyelids right now. His entire face is tensed up, as if he's in pain, and he's breathing hard through his nose.

"Wes!" I want to shake him, but I'm afraid to touch his shoulder. I bandaged it up before we went to sleep last night, and it was pretty gross. I decide to squeeze his thighs and shake his legs instead. "Wes! Wake up!"

His eyelids flash open. They're alert and alarmed, and they land on me like a laser scope.

I hold my hands up. "Hey! You're okay. It was just the nightmare. You're safe."

Wes blinks. His eyes dart all over the tree house, out the door behind me, and then land back on mine. He's still breathing heavy, but his jaw relaxes a little.

"You're okay," I repeat.

Wes takes a deep breath and scrubs a hand down his face. "Fuck. What time is it?"

"I don't know. I stopped carrying my phone when the cell towers went down." I look out the door and notice a faint orange haze where the treetops meet the sky. "Maybe six thirty? The sun's coming up."

Wes nods and sits up, rubbing the side of his head where it was pressed against the wall all night.

"That was a bad one, huh?" I ask, taking in his battle-worn appearance.

He stretches as much as he can in the confined space and gives me a sleepy-eyed stare. "Not all of it."

Something in his tone of voice or maybe the look in his eye makes my cheeks flush. "Oh. Uh, that's good." I turn and begin rummaging through the backpack, trying to hide my blush.

"Did you fix your hair?" I don't look up, but I can feel his eyes on me. "It's all shiny."

"Oh." I laugh. "Yeah. I woke up when I heard my mom get home last night, so I went inside to say hey. I figured, while I was in there, I might as well take a shower, brush my teeth, change my clothes …" My voice trails off when I realize that I'm rambling. I look down at the skinny jeans and hiking boots sticking out from under my hoodie as a prickly heat begins to crawl up my neck. I wanted something that was cute but woodsy. You know, *bomb-shelter chic*. Now, I'm wishing I'd just put a bag over my head.

Wes leans forward and peeks around my hair, which I straightened with a flat iron and evened out with a pair of scissors after the jagged braid-ectomy I gave myself the other night.

"Are you wearing *makeup*?"

"Yeah! So?"

Oh my God, I'm yelling.

"You just look … different."

"Whatever." I grab the travel-sized toiletry kit and the towel out of the backpack and shove them into his chest. "*You* can go take a shower with the hose."

"Damn." Wes chuckles. "That's cold."

"Literally." I grin. "Go on. I wouldn't want you to lose your precious *daylight*." I throw his words from last night back in his face as he crawls past me toward the door.

"You're not coming?"

"To watch you wash yourself? No, thanks." I roll my eyes and do my best to pretend like his perfectly chiseled abs disgust me.

"That's good 'cause there's gonna be some serious shrinkage."

I laugh as Wes climbs down the ladder. Then, I remember something. As soon as he gets to the bottom, I lean out the doorway and drop his Hawaiian shirt onto his face.

Wes pulls the royal-blue fabric off his head and holds it to his nose. "Holy shit. You washed it?"

"Yeah. It smells better now, but that blood is never coming out."

The smile that beams back up at me makes my body tingle all over.

"Thanks." Wes drapes the shirt over one shoulder and gives me a wicked side-eye. "You sure you don't wanna come wash my back?"

"Ha! And see your *shrinkage*? I'll pass."

Wes shrugs with a sideways smile and walks across the yard toward the side of the house. The second he's out of sight, I let out the breath I was holding and shove my hand up inside my hoodie. Grabbing the bottle of hydrocodone I stashed in my bra, I pull it out and shake a little white pill into my hand. I toss it back with a sip from one of the water bottles and realize that the liquid inside is sloshing like crazy, thanks to my trembling hand.

Better make that two.

Wes

I DON'T CARE HOW heavy that backpack is; after the dream I had this morning, Rain's ass is wearing it, *and* she's sitting on the back.

I shove my helmet on over my towel-dried hair but pause before kick-starting the bike. I'm afraid the sound of the engine will cause Rain's shithead of a father to come running out, guns blazing, but maybe she was telling the truth about him being deaf after all.

Maybe she was telling the truth about her mom, too.

I look around for her mom's fabled motorcycle—the "black one"—but there's no sight of it. I guess she could have parked in the garage, but from the looks of this place, that door probably doesn't even work anymore.

I pull my helmet off and turn to Rain, who is struggling to climb on behind me with that big-ass pack on. "What did your mom say about the dirt bike in the driveway?"

"Huh?" she asks, swinging her leg over the seat with a grunt.

"Your mom? Did she ask about my bike? She would have had to drive around it to get into the garage."

"Oh. Right." Rain wraps her arms around my ribs as tight as she can to keep from falling backward. "I told her I was letting a friend stay in the tree house."

I can't tell if she's lying or not. She sounds convincing, but her eyes look a little extra crazy. Maybe it's just all that mascara. I fucking hate it. I don't need Rain to get hotter. I need her to get uglier so that I can fucking focus on surviving the next two days.

"Don't you need to go inside and tell her bye?"

"No. She's sleeping."

"And your dad?"

"Passed out in his chair."

"Well, shouldn't you, like, leave a note telling her where you're going or something?"

Rain cocks her head to the side and raises her eyebrows. "Wes, I'm nineteen years old."

I shrug. "I don't know how this family shit works, okay?"

She sighs and drops the attitude. It only lasts a second, but in that moment, I see the real Rain. Underneath all those fake smiles and that sassy attitude is a black ocean of sadness crashing against a crumbling lighthouse of hope.

"Neither do I," she admits. Then, she presses her cheek to my shoulder. *Fuck me.*

I stomp down on the kick-start and head through the backyard, realizing that my dream this morning wasn't just a nightmare; it was a premonition.

The way Rain's body feels wrapped around mine, the way she looks, all dolled up like we're going on a fucking date, the way she wants to help me even though nobody's fucking helping her, I'm distracted by it. All of it. This bitch is going to get into my head, make me veer off course, and get us both killed. I know it like I know my own name, yet here we go anyway, into the woods.

CHAPTER 12

Rain

WE'VE BEEN OUT HERE for hours. The morning chill is long gone. Now, it's just hot and humid and hazy as hell, thanks to the pollen bomb that seems to have gone off somewhere nearby. Maybe that's why these people built a bomb shelter. It wasn't to protect them from nuclear fallout. It was to protect them from breathing all this crap in the air.

Wes is so serious about finding this place. *So* serious. Last night and this morning, he actually joked around with me a little bit, but ever since we left the house, he's been all business. I feel like I can't get a good read on him. Sometimes, he's relaxed and funny and … I don't know … kind of flirty? Then, other times, he looks at me like he hates me. Like I'm his annoying little sister, and he's sick of me tagging along.

Maybe it's because I'm not being very helpful right now. He's nicer when I'm helping him.

All I'm doing is walking around, poking the ground with a big stick.

Wes said the bomb shelter was underground, and the only entrance was a metal door, like a big, square manhole on the ground. It must have been built in the '60s, back when family fallout shelters were all the rage, but by the time Wes found it, the only thing left of the house it belonged to was a crumbling stone chimney.

We've been looking for that damn chimney all morning. I don't have the heart to tell Wes that I've spent my whole life in these woods and have *never* seen an old stone chimney, but I guess it's possible that it fell over after he left. A lot can happen in thirteen years.

Hell, here lately, a lot can happen in thirteen minutes.

"Are you *sure* it was behind Burger Palace?" I ask in a teensy, tiny voice.

We've poked every square foot of earth back here, and that door is either buried so deep in pine needles that a stick isn't gonna do the trick or we're in the wrong place.

"Yes, I'm fucking sure. I lived right down there," Wes growls, shoving his finger in the opposite direction of the highway. "I used to walk by that goddamn chimney every day on my way to …" His voice trails off and he shakes his head, trying to get rid of the memory. "Ugh!" Wes drops the backpack on the ground and sits next to it on a fallen tree trunk, pressing his fingertips into his forehead. His freshly washed hair falls over his face, curling at the ends where it was tucked behind his ear.

I take a seat a few feet down from him on the log and unzip the pack, pretending to look for a bottle of water or something. "Sorry we haven't found it yet. I'm sure we're close. Some stupid kid probably knocked the chimney down or something."

Wes doesn't even look at me.

You're making it worse. Just shut up.

I see the bag of trail mix, so I pull it out and extend it toward Wes. "M&M?" I smile, giving the bag a little shake.

Wes turns his head toward me—one eye hidden behind that curtain of hair—and gives me an almost smile. It's just a twitch at the corner of his mouth really, and I can't tell if it's a *thanks, but no thanks* kind of twitch or the *I'm glad you're here* kind or the dreaded *you're annoying the shit out of me, and I'm just tolerating you until I can figure out how to get rid of you* kind. Before I realize what I'm doing, I reach out with my free hand and tuck that hair back behind Wes's ear so I can get a better look at his confusing expression.

Which makes his almost smile disappear completely.

Shit.

Wes is now giving me the same look he gave me behind Burger Palace yesterday. The one that freezes the air in my lungs. The one that is focused and emotionless and intimidating as hell. I wonder what he's thinking about when he looks at me like that. What he's hiding.

I realize that I'm staring at him with my hand poised awkwardly in midair behind his ear, so I drop my eyes and yank my arm back. "We're gonna find it," I blurt out, unable to think of anything else to say.

"Yeah? And what if we don't?"

I peek back up at him from under my mascara-coated lashes. "We die?"

Wes nods real slow and chews on the corner of his mouth as he studies me. "Why do I get the feeling that you're not too upset about that?"

Because I'm not.

Because I'm looking forward to it.

Because I'm too chickenshit to do it myself.

I shrug and settle on, "Because it means I get a do-over."

"No, it doesn't," Wes snaps, sitting up straighter. "It means you *are* over. Don't you get that? It means you lost, and they won."

I want to tell him that I'm okay with that, whoever "they" are, but I know it'll only lead to more questions. Questions I don't want to answer. Questions that will rattle the locks on Fort Shit I'm Not Going to Think About Ever Again Because None of This Matters and We're All Going to Die. So, I keep my mouth—and the drawbridge—shut tight.

Besides, if Wes knows I'm just using him as a distraction, that I don't actually *want* to survive whatever the hell is coming for us, he might not let me tag along anymore. And tagging along with this asshole is kinda my only reason for living at the moment.

I sigh and look around the woods, praying for a burst of inspiration that will help me convince him that we're in this together.

Blowing out a breath, I lean forward and place my elbows on my knees. "If only we had a metal detector or something."

"That's it!" Wes snaps his fingers and points at me in the same motion.

I glance over at him and give myself an internal high five when I see his beautiful, megawatt smile beaming back at me.

"That's fucking it! Rain, you're a goddamn genius!" Wes stands up and ruffles my hair before lifting the backpack off the ground and holding the straps open for me to slip into. "Where's the closest hardware store?"

I push my messed up hair out of my face and point toward the highway. "Let's go!"

"Okay, okay," I grumble, standing up and turning around so that he can drop that fifty-pound behemoth on my shoulders. "But, if there's a redneck with a machine gun at the door, we're coming up with a plan B."

Wes laughs and spins me around to face him, gripping me by the shoulders so the pack doesn't take me down. The way he's looking at me right now, the way his strong hands feel on my body, the way his hopeful smile causes an entire swarm of butterflies to take flight in my belly, I'd probably face down five tattooed rednecks with machine guns if that was what it took to keep him happy. But I don't tell him that.

A girl has to play a *little* hard to get.

Wes

I HAVE TO CUT through the Burger Palace parking lot on my way to the highway. The line of people waiting to get in wraps around the building at least twice, but it's hard to tell through all the fistfights. His royal highness, King Burger, is smiling down at the yelling, kicking, screaming, chest-shoving, hair-pulling mob from his throne up on the digital Burger Palace sign. I've always hated that motherfucker, even as a kid. I remember the way his glowing face would laugh at me as I dug through his dumpsters.

Rich prick.

I swerve to avoid hitting a naked toddler in the middle of the parking lot.

As I slow down to turn onto the highway, I notice that one of the floor-to-ceiling windows on the front of the library across the street has been broken out. A techno beat so loud I can hear it over my engine is pouring out of the place, and inside, colored lights are swirling around like it's a rave. I imagine a bunch of teenage kids inside, guzzling cough syrup and passing out STDs like party favors, but as I pull onto the highway, a topless grandma comes stumbling out, holding what I swear to God looks like a—

"Dildo!" Rain screams, pointing directly at the old lady as we pass by.

I laugh and shake my head. "Guess the Franklin Springs orgy is BYOD."

I don't think I said it loud enough for Rain to hear me through my helmet, but she cackles and smacks me on my good shoulder.

"BYOD!" she squeals. "Oh my God, that thing was, like, a foot long!"

I twist the throttle and take off, causing her arms to snap back around my body and her fingertips to dig into my sides. It's fucking stupid, but I don't like Rain paying attention to somebody else's cock. Even if that cock is made of rubber and belongs to Abraham Lincoln's widow.

It's getting harder and harder to navigate the highway, not just because of the abandoned and wrecked vehicles every ten feet, but because—thanks to the overflowing dumpsters and trash cans all over town—the road is now covered in garbage, too. I really have to slow down and concentrate to avoid hitting something, but that doesn't stop me from glancing up when we pass Rain's house.

It looks exactly the way it did last night, except now there's a baseball-sized hole in the middle of the glass window on the front door.

Crazy bitch. I smirk.

As we drive past, I wonder what the hell went on in there last night. Rain seemed so upset when she came back from getting all those supplies, but while I was sleeping, she turned around and went right back in. Maybe she waited until her dad passed out. Or maybe her mom really did come home. Or maybe she just—

Bam!

A bump under the tires pulls my attention back to the road, and suddenly, it feels like I'm trying to drive through quicksand. The bike is dragging ass, and I have to grip the handlebars harder to keep the damn thing tracking straight.

"Shit!"

I pull off to the side of the road and want to punch myself in the face. This is exactly what I knew would happen. I let myself get distracted for one fucking second, and now, I have a flat tire. I don't even know what I ran over; that's how checked out I was.

I prop the bike up on the kickstand, yank my helmet off, and turn around, prepared to tell Rain to go the fuck home. I want to scream it at her actually. I want to jam my finger into her perfect little face and make her cry off all that fucking makeup. Maybe then she'll stop following me around like a lost puppy, and I'll finally be able to focus again.

But when I stand up, Rain loses her grip on my torso. Her eyes go wide, and her arms flail in huge circles as she falls off the back of the bike, landing on her giant backpack like an upside-down turtle.

"What the fuck, Wes?" she cries, rolling from side to side in a pathetic attempt to get up.

A laugh from the bowels of my tarnished black soul bursts out of me as I watch her struggling on the ground. She cuts me an *eat shit* look that only lasts a second before she starts laughing, too. When she accidentally snorts like a pig, her hoodie-covered hands fly to her mouth in mortification.

"Just take the pack off!" I cry through my laughter, watching her alternate between struggling to get up and succumbing to her own giggle fit.

Rain pulls her arms out of the straps as I reach down and lift her shuddering body off the ground. The moment she's upright, she falls into my chest, snorting and hiccupping and burying her beet-red face in my freshly washed shirt.

And, just like in the nightmare, her touch is all it takes for me to lose complete control—of the situation, of my willpower, of my own body. Instead of giving her a swat on the ass and sending her home like I know I should, I watch like a prisoner in my own mind as my arms wrap around her tiny shoulders and pull her in closer.

No! What the fuck are you doing, pussy? Cut her loose!

I scream at myself, call myself every name in the book, but the voice in my head is drowned out by the euphoric rush I get from holding this girl. She coils my shirt in both fists. Burrows her face into my neck. Her breath comes in short, hot bursts as she giggles against my skin. Her nose is cold. And all I can do is watch in humiliation as the meat puppet I live inside of tips its face down and smells her fucking hair.

Oh my God, you're pathetic.

Sugar cookies. She laughs like a farm animal. She looks like a discarded porcelain doll that raided a teenage boy's closet. And she smells like fucking sugar cookies.

Let her go, dipshit! Supplies! Shelter! Self-defense! That's *what you need!*

But the warning falls on deaf ears because now my stupid fucking cock has gone rogue, too. Why not? Nothing else is listening to me. It springs to life and rams itself into my zipper, seeking Rain's attention as well. I take a small step back, just enough to keep from shoving my hard-on into her belly like a full-fledged creep, but she responds to my step back with one of her own.

And that's it.

The moment is over.

The laughter is gone.

We drop our arms, and we begin walking.

I carry the backpack and push my bike—the front tire almost completely flat—as Rain falls in step beside me. I'm still hard, and I probably will be forever, thanks to the way she's blushing and twirling her hair in her fingers. I decide to concentrate on watching the road for debris—what I should have been doing in the first place.

"So … how much farther until we get to the hardware store?" I ask, staring at the pavement in front of me.

"Uh …" Rain looks off in the distance like she can see it.

This part of the highway is nothing but old farmhouses, like hers, with a few untended fields and a shit-ton of trees in between them. No one is growing anything. No one even has horses on their land. Just a bunch of junk cars and a few rusty old sheds.

"Maybe, like, fifteen, twenty minutes? It's on the other side of this hill, down past the skating rink."

I chuckle and shake my head.

"What?"

"You just sounded so country."

Rain scoffs. "If you think *I* sound country, then you haven't heard—"

"No, it's not your accent," I cut her off. "It's just the way everybody down here tells you the distance in minutes instead of miles and uses landmarks instead of street names."

"Oh my God." Rain's mouth falls open. "We *do* do that!"

I smile even though my bullet wound is starting to scream from pushing my bike up this never-ending hill.

She tilts her head to one side, watching me. "You said *everybody down here*. Where were you before you came back? Somewhere up north?"

"You could say that." I smirk, giving her a half-second of eye contact before resuming my death glare at the littered pavement. "I lived in South Carolina for a while, but before that, I was in Rome."

"Oh, I think I've been to Rome. That's close to Alabama, right?"

I snort. "Not Rome, Georgia. Rome, Italy."

"No way!"

Rain reaches over and smacks me on the arm, narrowly missing my bullet wound. I wince and suck in a breath, but she doesn't even notice.

"Oh my God, that's amazing, Wes! What were you doing in Italy?"

"Being a colossal piece of Eurotrash mostly."

Rain leans forward, devouring my words one by one like kernels of popcorn. So, I just keep spewing them.

"After I left Franklin Springs, I never stayed anywhere longer than a year—a few months usually—and then I'd get bounced to the next piece-of-shit house in the next piece-of-shit town. As soon as I aged out of the system, I knew I wanted to get as far away from here as fucking possible. I was sick of small towns. Sick of school. Sick of having no fucking control over where I went or how long I stayed. So, on my eighteenth birthday, I checked all the airline sales, found a last-minute deal to Rome, and the next morning, I woke up in Europe."

"The system?" Rain's dark eyebrows bunch together. "Like foster care?"

"Uh, yeah. Anyway"—I kick myself for letting that slip. It's not that I'm embarrassed about it. I just don't particularly want to talk about the worst nine years of my life right now. *Or ever*—"Rome is fucking incredible. It's ancient and modern, busy and lazy, beautiful and tragic, all at the same time. I had no idea what I was gonna do once I got there, but as soon as I stepped off the plane, I knew I was gonna be all right."

"How?" Rain is so engrossed in my story that she steps on a muffler lying in the street and almost busts her ass.

I try not to laugh. "Almost everybody was speaking English. There were signs in English, menus in English, the street musicians were even playing pop songs in English. So … I cashed in my dollars for euros, bought a spare guitar off one of the street performers, and spent the next few years strumming classic rock songs in front of the Pantheon for tips."

I glance over, and Rain is staring at me like *I'm* the fucking Pantheon. Eyes huge, lips parted. I have to reach out and pull her toward the bike so that she doesn't hit her head on the tire of the flipped Honda minivan we're walking next to.

"Did you have to sleep on the street?" she asks, unblinking.

"Nah, I always found somebody to crash with."

That makes her blink. "Somebody, huh? You mean, some *girl*." When I don't correct her, she rolls her eyes so hard, I half-expect them to fall out of their sockets. "Did you point guns at their heads and make them pay for your groceries, too?"

I raise an eyebrow at her and smirk. "Only the ones who talked back."

Rain scrunches up her nose like she wants to stick her tongue out at me. "So, why'd you leave if you had it so good with your classic rock and your Italian women?" she sasses.

My smile fades. "It was after the nightmares started. Hey, watch out."

I point to a shard of glass sticking up at a weird angle in Rain's path. She glances at it just long enough to avoid it and then returns her rapt attention to me.

"Tourism totally dried up. I couldn't make shit playing on the street anymore, and I couldn't get a real job without a visa. I didn't really have a choice, as usual. My roommate was an American whose parents offered to pay for our plane tickets back to the States, so … that's how I ended up in South Carolina."

"Did you love her?"

Rain's question catches me completely by surprise.

"Who?"

"Your 'roommate.'" Her big eyes narrow to slits as she makes sarcastic finger quotes around the word *roommate*.

I hate how much I like it.

"No," I say honestly. "Did you love *him*?"

"Who?"

I drop my eyes to the yellow letters emblazoned across her perky tits. "The guy you stole that hoodie from."

Rain's eyes drop to her sweatshirt, and she stops dead in her tracks.

I guess that's a yes.

Crossing her arms over the band logo, Rain lifts her head and stares at something off in the distance behind me. It reminds me of the way she looked when she was watching that family at the park yesterday.

Right before she flipped the fuck out.

Shit.

"Hey … look. I'm sorry. I didn't mean to …"

"That's his house."

Huh?

I follow the direction of her gaze until I'm turned around, staring at a yellow farmhouse with white trim, set back about a hundred feet from the road. It's nicer than her parents' place, bigger, too, but the yard is just as overgrown.

"The boy next door, huh?" I try to keep the malice out of my voice, but knowing that the piece of shit who upset Rain is somewhere inside that house makes me see red.

When Rain doesn't answer, I turn around and find her standing with her back to me. I stomp my kickstand down, prepared to chase her ass if she decides to bolt again, but the rattle of pills against plastic tells me that Rain isn't going anywhere.

She's found a different form of escape.

Rain pops a painkiller into her mouth and shoves the bottle back inside her bra. The whole time, I can practically hear the blood rushing to my extremities.

Whoever this kid is, he's gonna die.

"Rain, I need you to give me one good reason why I shouldn't storm up those steps, drag this punk out by the throat, and force him to eat his own fingers after I cut them off with my pocketknife."

Rain lets out a sad laugh and turns to face me again. "Because he's gone."

I blow out a breath. *Thank fuck.*

"He left with his family a few weeks ago. They wanted to spend *April 23* in Tennessee, where his parents are from," Rain scoffs and rolls her eyes.

April 23. That's what people call it when they don't want to say *the apocalypse.* Like it's a fucking holiday or something.

Rain looks back at me with a mixture of heartbreak and hate in her narrowed eyes, and fuck, do I know that feeling. The hate makes the heartbreak easier to take. Or, at least, it did for me.

Now, I don't feel it at all.

Reaching across my bike, I wrap an arm around her shoulders and pull her toward me. Rain leans across the pleather seat to hug me back, and both my heart and cock swell in response. All I want to do is kiss the shit out of her until she forgets that this idiot farm boy ever existed, but I don't. Not because she's too vulnerable. But because I don't trust myself to stop.

"Hey. Look at me," I say, trying my hardest not to smell her fucking hair again.

Two big blue irises peek up at me from under two black-smudged eyelids, and the need I see in them makes my soul ache.

"Take it from somebody who's a professional at getting left …" I force a grin. "All you gotta do is say *fuck 'em* and move on."

"I don't know how." Rain's eyes are pleading, begging for something to take the pain away.

I recognize the look, but I don't even remember what it feels like anymore.

Because I'm the one who does the leaving now.

Pain doesn't even know my forwarding address.

"It's easy." I smirk. "First, you say, *fuck*. Then, you say, *'em.*"

Rain smiles, and my eyes drop to her lips. They're dry and swollen from almost crying, and when they whisper the words, "Fuck 'em," I swear, I almost come in my pants.

"Good girl," I whisper back, unable to look away from her mouth. "Now, let's go light his house on fire."

"Wes!" Rain squeals, smacking me on the chest with a tiny smile. "We're not lighting his house on fire."

She turns and starts walking toward the hardware store again, and I let her lead the way. Not because I don't want to torch that little shit's house. I do.

But because there is a dead woman staring at me from behind the wheel of that overturned minivan.

Rain

BY THE TIME WE get to Buck's Hardware, I feel amazing. The sun is shining, my pills have kicked in, Wes is being nice to me again, and I cannot *wait* to climb that sign and paint a much-needed F over that B.

God, I can't believe I told him about Carter.

What did you expect? You took him right past the guy's house.

I'm such an idiot.

Note to self: take the trail from now on.

I nod to myself as I follow Wes across the parking lot. He's all serious again, slowing down and reaching for his gun as we approach the busted front door. God, it must be exhausting, trying to survive the apocalypse.

I'm just trying to stay high enough to keep from crying all the time, and that's hard enough.

Wes props his bike on the kickstand next to the front door and shoots a warning glance at me over his shoulder. The way he looks reminds me of the way he described Rome. Soft and hard. Old and young. Pale green eyes shadowed by thick, dark brows. Soft brown hair grazing a hard, stubbled jaw. A floral Hawaiian shirt covering jagged black tattoos. I'm attracted to the boy in him and scared of the man in him, and I'm pretty sure I'd take a bullet for both of them even though I don't even know their last name.

But, honestly, I'd probably take a bullet for anybody right about now. This *waiting around to die* thing is killing me.

The glass in the front door has been smashed out, and Wes doesn't seem too happy about it. He pauses against the wall next to the door with his gun drawn and jerks his head, indicating that I'm supposed to join him *next to* the entrance instead of standing right in front of it like a dumbass.

Oh, right.

I hop over to the wall beside Wes, and that's when I hear faint, deep voices inside the building.

Wes turns toward me so that our faces are inches apart, and I hold my breath. I know he's not going to kiss me—that wouldn't even make sense—but my body doesn't seem to know that. It tenses all over and buzzes and hums as Wes's lips graze the edge of my ear.

"I'm gonna give you the backpack so that I can move around more easily in there. You stay out here and watch the bike."

I shake my head violently. "No. I'm coming too."

"No, you're not," Wes hisses between his clenched teeth.

He drops his eyes, and I feel his hand wrap around mine. I look down with my heart in my throat as Wes wraps my fingers around the handle of his gun.

"I won't be able to focus with you in there, and trust me, those guys won't be able to either." Wes's eyes slide up my body to my face, and they take what little power I have along with them. "Stay out here. Please."

I swallow and nod, feeling the weight of his trust fall on my shoulders along with the backpack. Then, he turns and opens the door.

I don't know how he does it, but the glass beneath his feet doesn't even crunch as he tiptoes in and silently closes the door behind him. I watch through the broken glass as he disappears from view.

This is bad.

My painkillers are in full effect, and I can't tell if he's been gone five seconds or five minutes. One of my arms feels heavier than the other.

That's weird. I bend my right elbow and notice a small black handgun in my fist. I blink at it. *How did that get there?*

Thunder booms in the distance even though the sun is shining. Nothing makes sense anymore. I should be in college right now. I should be working part-time at some shitty diner and getting an apartment with Carter and adopting a cat and naming it Blurryface. But, instead, I'm standing outside of Buck's Hardware, holding a gun and guarding a stranger's dirt bike while he sneaks inside to steal a metal detector so that we can find a hidden bomb shelter to live in because the four horsemen of the apocalypse are coming in two days, according to an unexplained dream we've all been having.

I hear the thunder again, only this time, it's coming from inside the building.

Crash!

My heart lurches into my throat as the sounds of struggle—muffled grunts, skin hitting skin, skin hitting the floor, merchandise hitting the floor—come pouring out through the hole in the door. I don't think; I just react. I yank on the handle with my free hand and charge inside, my giant backpack jostling with every step. This place hasn't been ransacked like Huckabee Foods, but on the left side of the store an endcap shelf of fertilizer has been knocked over, and there are plastic containers and little round granules everywhere.

I run in that direction. I don't see anyone yet, but I hear Wes's voice coming from the back of the store.

"Rain, get the fuck out!"

"Rain?" another masculine voice says.

I recognize it immediately.

"Quint?" I almost slip in the spilled fertilizer as I turn the corner and find Quinton Jones, my buddy since kindergarten, standing at the end of the aisle with his daddy's hunting rifle trained on Wes.

Wes has his back to me and appears to be holding Lamar Jones, Quint's little brother, like a human shield. I can't tell from here, but the way his arm is poised, my guess is that he has a certain pocketknife pressed to Lamar's throat as well.

"Quint!" I squeal. "I didn't know you guys were still in town!"

My classmate keeps his gun trained on Wes, but his dark features pull up into a big grin when he sees me. "Rainbow Williams! Got-damn! Where you been, fam?"

I make a beeline for my buddy, but the second I get within arm's reach of Wes, he grabs me, shoving Lamar toward his brother and using me as a human shield instead. I don't even realize he's taken the gun back until I see it stretched out in front of us, aimed at Quint.

Wes's breath is warm against my cheek when he says, "You can tell him hi from here."

I laugh in surprise and wave at the kid I used to play Power Rangers with on the playground. "Hi, Quint." I giggle. "This is my new friend, Wes. Wes, this is Quint and Lamar. Quint was in my grade at school." I turn my head toward Wes and whisper loud enough for everyone to hear, "He's a lifer."

Quint rolls his black-brown eyes at me and elbows his brother. "Here we go with this shit again."

Lamar works his jaw back and forth, which I can now see looks a little swollen, and glares at Wes. He's grown his hair out since the last time I saw it. The top is in short dreadlocks now. I like it.

Wes holsters his gun but keeps his left arm wrapped tightly around my shoulders. I like that, too.

"So, you don't believe in the nightmares?" he asks Quint. His tone is lighter, friendlier.

I know what he's doing. And it seems to be working.

Quint lowers the rifle, stabbing it into the ground like a cane, and launches into one of his numerous conspiracy theories. "All you have to do is look at who's dyin' and who's gettin' rich to know that there's some fucked up shit goin' on. If you ask me, I think this whole thing, the nightmares and all of it, was planned by the government to get all the poor folks and the brown folks to kill each other off. Let the trash take itself out, you know?"

"Yeah, and the Burger Palace CEO is in on it," Lamar chimes in.

His voice sounds deeper than I remember. I don't know if it's because of puberty or because he's trying to sound tough in front of Wes. Either way, it's kinda funny.

Wes snorts in agreement. "That motherfucker is making a killing."

I laugh. "For real! They tried to charge me, like, eighty-seven dollars to *Apocasize* my meal yesterday!"

"See?" Lamar raises his hand in my direction. "That's what I'm talkin' about!"

Quint pushes Lamar's arm back down. "So, what brings y'all to Buck's Hardware on this fine day?" he asks, eyeing us a little more suspiciously.

Wes tilts his head in the direction of the front door. "My bike got a flat."

"And we need a metal detector," I blurt out, earning me a glare and a shoulder squeeze from Wes.

Oops.

"A metal detector?" Quint repeats, raising an eyebrow.

"Y'all lookin' for buried treasure?" Lamar chuckles and cups his swelling jaw with a wince.

"Yeah. I'm pretty sure my dad's got all kinds of stuff buried in the backyard. Y'all know him."

Quint and Lamar smirk and give each other a knowing look. Everybody in this town thinks Phil Williams is a crazy, old, drunken hermit who doesn't leave the house. They're not exactly wrong.

"What about you?" I ask, trying to steer the conversation away from the subject of my dad as quickly as possible.

"Just came in to grab some motor oil." Quint gives Lamar the same look that Wes just gave me, but Lamar ignores him. "We're gettin' outta here."

"Really? How?" I ask. "The roads are so bad; we couldn't even get from Burger Palace to here without a flat."

Lamar grins. "Oh, we ain't worried 'bout flats."

Quint glares at his brother, who isn't getting the hint, and then turns his attention toward me. "Well, we best be goin'." His dark eyes flick from me to Wes and back again. "You good?"

There's something in his tone that tells me he wouldn't hesitate to put a bullet in this white boy if I asked him to. I love him for that.

I glance over my shoulder at Wes and smile. "Yeah, I'm good."

Wes doesn't let me go until the door shuts behind Quint and Lamar. Then, he spins me around and grips my shoulders so hard I feel like he's going to crush them in his bare hands. I wince and brace myself for the lecture that I know is coming about *blah, blah, blah, you never listen, blah, blah, blah, I told you whatever*, but instead, I hear Wes suck a deep breath in through his nose and exhale it just as hard. I open one eye and peek at him. His jaw is clenched, his eyes are narrowed, but he's not yelling. Not yet anyway.

I lift my other eyelid and give him a tiny cringe of a smile. "Don't be mad. I know you said—"

But before I can finish my apology, Wes pulls my body flush against his and smashes his lips even harder against mine. My body goes rigid for a second, completely caught off guard, but when he grabs the back of my head and slides his warm tongue into my gasping mouth, an atom bomb of desperation goes off inside of me. I press up onto my tiptoes and kiss him back, sparklers and bottle rockets going off behind my eyes. Wes tears the backpack off my shoulders and tosses it to the ground before slamming me up against the shelves of weed killer behind me. I can feel him everywhere. His hands are clutching the back of my neck, cupping my face, gripping my waist, grabbing my ass. His chest is pressed against my chest. His thigh is shoved between my legs, and when he rocks his hips forward, I feel another part of him—full and hard—against the side of my belly.

"Wes." My plea is barely audible as it disappears into his relentless mouth.

Wes responds by gripping my hips and grinding against me harder. I feel my core coil and tighten as the entire world, both inside my mind and outside this store, disappears.

"You never … fucking … listen," he growls between kisses.

"I know," I pant, hooking my knee over his hip and shifting so that his hardness is now between my legs. "I'm sorry."

Wes's pace becomes even more punishing. I cling to his shoulders and suck on his swirling tongue and hold my breath as tiny earthquakes begin to rock my body. My legs tremble as the pressure builds.

"Wes …"

I tilt my hips forward, taking the full brunt of his force. Feeling him there—*right there*—separated by only a few layers of fabric and knowing he's just as desperate for me as I am for him, does me in. I whimper against his lips and pulsate around nothing as the earth shifts beneath me, and I'm suddenly falling.

But I don't hit the ground.

The shelf does.

Along with about two hundred plastic jugs of weed killer.

I open my eyes at the sound of the crash to find Wes smirking down at me, lips swollen and eyes hooded. He has a death grip on one of my arms, which he releases slowly as I turn and look behind us at the damage.

My cheeks burn white-hot when I realize what just happened. How pathetic I am. Wes is a sex god, and I just came in my panties and knocked over a shelf of weed killer from a kiss. I can't even face him.

Thunder booms outside—for real this time—and I feel his stubble graze my cheek.

"As much as I'd love to pick up where we left off, I think it's about to rain. We'd better go." He smacks me on the ass and walks off, giving me and my bright red face a much-needed moment to compose ourselves.

So … that happened, I think, staring down at the damage we did.

I wait for my next thought to come—for me to overanalyze every aspect of that interaction; for me to admire the way the shelves were spaced just far enough apart so that, if one fell, it wouldn't cause a domino reaction; for me to freak out and find a way to make the whole awkward situation worse— but there's nothing inside my head except for a warm, soft, fuzzy kind of glow. I wait and wait, blinking at our mess, smiling to myself, but still nothing comes.

I don't know how long I stand there, admiring the emptiness in my mind, but it's the closest thing to relief I've felt in weeks.

Wes managed to do what all the alcohol and painkillers in the world haven't. With nothing more than his body and his attention, he made it all just go away. All the memories. All the loss. All the worthlessness and loneliness and hopelessness and fear. For a few minutes, I was free of it all.

God, I hope he does it again.

As I wander the aisles of Buck's Hardware, I let my mind actually contemplate the possibility of survival. Maybe living a little longer wouldn't be so bad … if I were with Wes. Maybe we could make each other happy in our bomb shelter built for two. Maybe, once we find it, we can do what we just did again but without clothes on.

Blurry, grainy images of Carter's boyish face begin to tiptoe around the edges of my chemically induced bliss. He's only been gone about a month, but I can hardly remember what he looked like anymore. What his voice sounded like. What it felt like when we'd sneak out and make love on a blanket under the stars, hidden by the waist-high grass in Old Man Crocker's untended field.

It hadn't felt like whatever Wes just did; I know that much.

Or had it? I can't remember.

I walk two or three laps around the store in a daze before I spot Wes kneeling next to his dirt bike just outside the front door. He tucks his hair behind his ear as he fiddles with the tire, and I can't help but admire his gorgeous profile. It's crazy to think that somebody that beautiful came out of Franklin Springs. I'm glad he got out when he did. He doesn't belong here. The people here are … simple. Or, at least, they *were* before the nightmares began. Now, most of them have left town, killed themselves, or gotten themselves killed.

Not that I'm one to judge. I was thinking about doing one of those three things myself—until Wes showed up.

I take another lap, actually paying attention to the merchandise this time, and discover that Buck's Hardware does not carry metal detectors. My hope deflates like the tire on Wes's bike. How am I supposed to tell him that we came all the way out here and got a flat for nothing? I can't. I won't. I just need to think. I close my eyes and try to concentrate, but nothing comes. It's ironic. This whole time, all I've wanted to do was erase everything in my brain, and now that Wes and the painkillers have finally done it, I need the damn thing back.

I wander the store some more, and just when I'm about to admit defeat, I notice a few giant magnets, grouped together on a shelf near the door. They look like round metal weights with a hole in the middle, and the sign below them says they can lift up to ninety-five pounds.

"Thank you, Jesus," I whisper, raising my palms to the drop-tile ceiling.

I find some yellow nylon rope on a different aisle and use a pair of gardening shears to cut off two six-foot-long lengths of it. I thread one through the hole in each magnet and tie it off, figuring that Wes and I can just drag the magnets behind us as we walk through the woods. If they can lift almost a hundred pounds, surely we'll feel a tug if we pass over a big metal door beneath the pine needles. Right? It might work.

It has to work.

I run outside with the backpack and my makeshift magnets-on-a-rope, eager to show Wes my new invention. He looks up at me from where he's reflating his newly patched tire with a hand pump, and all my excitement leaves me in a single breath. Just beyond the store's covered entrance, the sky has gone from bright blue to slate gray. Sizzling yellow lightning bolts shoot out of the clouds in the distance, and big, fat raindrops are hitting the asphalt parking lot so hard it looks like it's boiling.

"You were right about the rain," I mumble, staring at what's become of our beautiful spring afternoon.

A clap of thunder booms so loud and so close it rumbles a piece of glass loose from the broken door. I jump at the sound of it shattering on the concrete behind me.

Wes glances at me over his shoulder.

"Can we … can you drive that thing in the rain?"

He raises his eyebrows like that was the stupidest question ever asked. "It's a *dirt* bike. A little mud ain't gonna hurt it."

I smile, hearing the country in his voice for the first time.

Guess he's from Georgia after all.

"You afraid of a little rain? 'Cause I can take you home if—"

"No!" I blurt out before reclaiming my chill. "No, it's fine. I don't mind."

Wes gives me the side-eye, then returns to pumping the tire. "The sooner we find that shelter, the better. I have a feeling the locals are about to burn this whole shitty town to the ground."

"What makes you think that?"

"Because I drove through at least twenty other shitty little towns just like this one on my way here from Charleston, and they were all burning. *Including* Charleston. That's why I left."

"Oh."

I'm such a fucking idiot. Wes arrived in Franklin Springs without so much as a toothbrush, and I never even wondered why.

Thanks, hydrocodone.

"You had to leave because of the fires?"

"Yep," Wes replies in a clipped tone, squeezing the tire to test its fullness. "I was living on Folly Island and waiting tables at this little tiki bar." He's not looking at me, but at least he's talking. "The owners were good people. They let me play guitar on the weekends so I could earn extra tips."

Wes talked about playing guitar in Rome, too. I don't know why, but I have such a hard time picturing him as a musician. I mean, sure, he looks like he just walked offstage with that grunge rock hair and effortlessly cool outfit—not to mention, his stupefyingly gorgeous face—but all the artists and musicians I know are sweet and sensitive. Wes isn't even in the same zip code as sweet and sensitive.

"After everything started shutting down," he continued, giving the tire a few more pumps of air, "they said they'd keep serving 'til they ran out of food. I didn't have shit else to do, so I volunteered to help 'em out."

I smile to myself, picturing Wes grouchily waiting tables by the beach in jeans, combat boots, and a Hawaiian shirt—his half-assed attempt at beachwear.

"On Friday night, some locals came barging in, screaming about fires. The phone lines were already down, so by the time word got to us, half the island had already burned … including the house I'd been living in." Wes screws the cap back on the tire nozzle as the wind changes direction and begins spraying us with sideways rain.

I shield my face with my forearm. "Oh my God, Wes. I'm so sorry. Did anybody get hurt?"

He stands and wipes his dirty hands on his jeans. "My roommate got out with minor burns, but I didn't wait around to find out about anyone else. I traded my wallet and everything in it with my buddy down the street in exchange for his dirt bike, stole a gun and holster out of his closet before I left, and got the fuck out of town." Right on cue, the wind blows Wes's lightweight shirt like a beautiful floral curtain, exposing the deadly weapon he keeps tucked away underneath.

"But I met you Saturday morning."

Finally, Wes looks at me—or *squints* at me, thanks to the spitting, sideways rain. "Drove all night. I figured, if the world's gonna burn, I'd better get my ass underground."

"And here you are."

Wes looks around and raises one dark, unimpressed eyebrow. "Yeah. Here I am."

"You know, I'm kinda glad your house burned down." I smile, clutching the weights even tighter.

The corner of his grumpy mouth curls upward as those liquid green eyes drop to my chest. "Whatcha got there?"

I look down. "Oh! I made metal detectors!" I hold up the large gray discs to show him my ingenious invention. I can't quite feel my face, thanks to all the painkillers, but if I could, I'm sure it would be sore as hell from this stupid grin.

A deep laugh rumbles in Wes's chest. I feel it vibrate through my body, causing every hair to stand at attention. The air is charged—and not just from the thunder and lightning.

Tell me I did good.

Tell me you're proud of me.

Tell me you'll keep me forever and ever.

Wes opens his mouth, but none of those things come out. Instead, he takes two steps toward me, reaches out, plucks the magnets from my hands like they weigh nothing, and says, "I'm kind of glad my house burned down, too."

My smile widens into a maniacal grin. I rear back to tackle-hug him when an explosion so loud it sounds like an atom bomb causes us both to duck and cover. The lightning strike rattles what's left of the glass out of the front doors and reverberates through the metal awning above us like a tuning fork. My ears are ringing so badly; I barely register that Wes is shouting at me. I blink at him and try to shake off my daze.

"That was the fucking roof! Come on!"

Wes spins me around and shoves the magnets into our already-overstuffed backpack. Then, he throws on his helmet and straddles the bike. The second my arms wrap around his middle, he stomps on the kick-start and plunges us face-first into the storm. I point toward a gap in the woods across the street where the trail starts. Then—clinging to Wes with my free hand—I struggle to yank the hood of my sweatshirt out from under the backpack and onto my head as we fly through what feels like a never-ending waterfall. The rain is pounding on us so hard I wonder if it's hailing.

Once we get into the woods, the rain doesn't hurt as much, but it's just as heavy, flooding the trail with thick brown mud.

"Wipe my visor!" Wes shouts back to me, unable to let go of the throttle or the clutch.

I use my left hand like a windshield wiper, but the second I stop, Wes shouts at me to keep doing it.

"Just take it off!" I shout back, but Wes shakes his head in response.

Another bolt of lightning explodes about a hundred yards in front of us. I shriek as sparks fly from the pine tree it struck, followed by cracks and snaps as it crashes to earth.

Skidding sideways, Wes suddenly stops and pulls the helmet off his head. "I can't see shit!"

"Me either," I yell, holding on to him with both hands and pressing my forehead against his back. My hoodie is soaked through, but at least it's keeping the rain out of my eyes.

More crashes pop and echo all around us as dead branches fall from great heights.

Wes mutters something I can't quite hear before taking off again. I hold on tight, keeping my head down as he accelerates. The force of the rain intensifies, telling me that we're not in the woods anymore, so I look up.

And immediately want to vomit.

Wes is barreling across an open field toward the last place I want to be right now.

The one place he knows is empty.

A yellow farmhouse with white trim.

Wes

I DRIVE RIGHT UP onto that little shit's patio and use my helmet to break out the glass in his back door. I hope Rain wasn't lying about his family being out of town. The only thing country folk love more than God is their goddamn guns. This could get ugly.

I reach inside and unlock the deadbolt, grateful that it's the old-school kind that doesn't require a key. Turning around, I find Rain standing on the porch with her hood over her head, staring at the house like it's gonna eat her alive. I grab her by the elbow and yank her inside as another bolt of lightning drops into the woods like a bomb.

Once the door's shut—or what's left of it—I push the wet hair out of my face and stomp across the kitchen. I can't fucking believe this shit. There's a concrete fallout shelter less than a mile away, but I'm standing in a wooden tinderbox in the middle of a lightning storm.

I flip the light switch, and two fluorescent bulbs overhead flicker to life with a dull hum.

At least the power hasn't gone out yet.

I don't even bother checking the water. There's enough of it dumping out of the sky right now to keep us alive forever.

The kitchen is just as countrified as I expected—beige wallpaper with roosters all over it, rooster-shaped cookie jars, little rooster salt and pepper shakers.

"Your boyfriend sure loves cocks," I tease, but when I turn around, Rain is right where I left her, standing by the back door, staring at the puddle spreading under her feet. "You okay?"

Her shoulders are hunched, and her face is completely hidden underneath that dripping wet hood. "I … I don't wanna be here," she mumbles without looking up.

"Well, that makes two of us." I open the cabinet closest to me. Dishes. *Next.* More dishes. *Next.* Mugs with motherfucking roosters on them. "You think your boyfriend left anything to eat?"

If I thought I had a chance of fucking this girl, I'd stop reminding her of the fact that she has a boyfriend who is still possibly alive, but A) I can't remember the little shit's name, so I have to call him "your boyfriend," and B) based on the fact that we're standing in his *goddamn kitchen* right now, I'm pretty sure sex is off the menu.

A ceramic rooster stares directly into my soul just before I slam the fourth cabinet.

Cockblocked. Literally.

I probably could have driven a little farther and taken us to Rain's house instead, but after the way she acted last night, I know for a fact that she doesn't want to be there either.

"I'm gonna go change," she mutters. Her hiking boots squeak against the linoleum floor as she passes through the kitchen and into the living room.

Her mood is example number four thousand eighty-five of why it's always better to do the leaving than to be left.

After searching the cabinets, drawers, and pantry and finding nothing but roach killer and rooster-themed bullshit, I take a chance on the fridge. I realize it's a long shot, and I'm right. The fucker is cleaned out. The only things inside are a few ketchup packets from Burger Palace and half a stick of butter. But the freezer, I think I heard angels singing when I opened that thing. Ice cream, corn dogs, frozen waffles, sausage biscuits, steamer bags of vegetables, and the cherry on top … a frosty half-full bottle of Grey Goose vodka.

This fucker's mom just became my new hero, rooster collection and all.

I unscrew the cap and help myself as a little rag doll appears in the doorway. Her face looks absolutely dejected as she stands there, wearing a Franklin Springs High basketball jersey and shorts and holding a sopping wet bundle of clothes out in front of her.

"What the fuck are you wearing?" I cough, wiping my mouth with the back of my hand.

"It's all I could find," she snaps, a blush staining her cheeks as she glances down at the uniform hanging off her curves. Her voice is quiet and remorseful, but I don't give a shit.

Rain is mine. I stole her. I'm using her. I made her come less than an hour ago, and I don't appreciate her parading around in front of me with some other asshole's jersey on.

"His fucking name is on your back."

"It's all I could find!" she shouts, surprising me with her sudden anger. "He took everything!"

I have a feeling we're not talking about clothes anymore, so I pull open the freezer door, hoping to change the subject before things get heavy again. "Not *everything*."

Rain's eyes go wide, and her little mouth falls open. "Corn dogs?" she whispers, her gaze shifting from me to the bounty in the freezer and back.

"And ice cream … if you eat your veggies." I pull out a steamer bag of frozen broccoli and pop it into the microwave across from the fridge. My stomach growls louder than the thunder outside at the prospect of eating a hot meal. I don't know if it's closer to lunch or dinnertime, but I'm pretty sure the protein bar I shoved into my face this morning was the only thing I've eaten all day.

"Oh my God, a real dinner." The awe in her voice makes me want to puff up my chest with pride even though all I'm doing is pressing buttons on a microwave.

"I'm, uh … gonna do some laundry. You want me to wash that?" Rain's gaze slides down my body, reminding me that my clothes are dripping wet and splattered with mud.

"Sure." I bite the inside of my cheek, trying not to smirk. If this bitch wants my clothes, she can have them.

Unlacing my boots, I step out of each one and leave them in a muddy heap in the middle of the kitchen. Then, I pull my shirt off, nice and slow, and try not to wince when my sopping wet bandage comes off with it. Rain doesn't notice though. In fact, she's not looking at my face or my shoulder at all. She's staring directly at my abs. My white tank top is glued to my chest like I'm in a wet T-shirt contest, so I flex shamelessly as I take off my holster and set it on the counter, followed by everything in my pockets.

I'm not stupid. I know I look like every girl's wet dream, and I use it to my advantage whenever possible. My looks and my resourcefulness are the only tools I've been given in this life. Everything else I've had to beg for, borrow, or fucking steal. Including the little black-haired tool drooling in front of me.

Unbuttoning my jeans, I hear Rain giggle. Not exactly the reaction I was hoping for. I look up to find her beaming—eye makeup ruined from the rain, hair towel-dried and shaggy. She's a mess and a mindfuck, but when she smiles, it steals the air from my lungs.

"More flowers?" She chuckles, her eyes glued to my crotch.

Glancing back down, I realize that I'm wearing my floral-print boxer shorts, the ones my asshole roommate gave me as a joke for Christmas.

"They came with the uniform." I smirk, pushing my jeans the rest of the way down. That shuts her up.

Rain's eyes go wider as she drinks in the outline of my semi-hard cock, plastered down by the clinging fabric of my wet boxers.

His name might be emblazoned across her back, but her nipples are straining against the fabric because of *me*.

I step out of my jeans and hook my thumbs into the waistband of my boxers. Just as I'm about to slide them down, Rain squeezes her eyes shut and squeals. Dropping the bundle in her hands to the floor, she suddenly grabs the sides of her basketball shorts and yanks them down. The jersey is long enough to cover her ass, but I still get a clean shot of those full, perfect tits when she bends over to step out of the shorts.

"Here!" she chirps, holding the shiny blue fabric out toward me with her eyes still closed. "Put these on!"

I chuckle as I toss my wet clothes onto the pile at her feet. As I stalk toward Rain, wearing nothing but a self-satisfied grin, I'm one hundred percent confident that she's forgotten all about What's-his-face. At least, for now. Hell, the way she's blushing and biting that plump bottom lip as I approach, she might have forgotten her *own* name.

I take the shorts from her hand and step into them, taking my sweet-ass time. Once they're on, I clear my throat, prompting Rain to open her eyes. I'm crowding her space, so close she has to crane her neck back to look up at me. The microwave dings, but neither of us pays it any attention.

"Thanks."

Her eyes drop to my chest. I know without looking what she's staring at. I can see her counting.

"Thirteen?"

It was the first tattoo I ever got. Thirteen jagged tally marks, right above my heart. Usually, when girls ask about it, I just make some shit up. *Thirteen is my lucky number.* Or, *My mom's birthday was August thirteenth.* Or, *It's the number of touchdown passes I threw to win the state championship back in high school.*

But Rain isn't going to fuck me, no matter what I say—at least, not in this house—so I tell her the truth.

"It's the number of foster homes I was in."

She doesn't bat an eye at my admission. She just lets them roam over my flesh. "What about this one?"

She's staring at the rose and dagger on my right shoulder, just above my bullet wound. I laugh. "Have you ever heard that song 'Eurotrash Girl'?"

Rain nods and looks up at me.

"Well, there's a part where he talks about getting a tattoo of a rose and a dagger in Berlin, so one weekend, when some friends and I took the train to Berlin for Oktoberfest, we all got rose and dagger tattoos."

"Uh, I'm pretty sure he talks about getting crabs in Berlin, too." Rain wrinkles her nose and gives me the side-eye. "Or was that Amsterdam?"

"No, I think Amsterdam's where he sold his plasma."

"Right." She grins. "And spent all the money on a guy in drag."

"It happens to the best of us." I shrug, eliciting another giggle from Rain.

"What's the story behind this one?" Her eyes drift down to my elbow.

I roll my arm over, showing the whole thing.

I snort a laugh through my nose. "I had a buddy who wouldn't let his tattoo artist go near his elbow because he heard it was the most painful place to get inked, so while he was getting some work done on his bicep, I got another artist at the shop to do a bull's-eye right on my elbow, just to be a dick."

Rain laughs, the smile finally reaching her eyes. "Did it hurt?"

"Like a bitch."

Water from the clothes on the floor trickles over to my bare feet as Rain's eyes devour the stories etched in my skin. I wanted to use my body to taunt her, punish her, but instead, she's reading it like an open book. When her gaze slides over to the wilted lily tattoo on my ribs, I've never felt more exposed.

"Did that one hurt?" She touches it with a cold fingertip, tracing the stem down my side.

"Yeah." I swallow. "Every fucking day of my life."

Her eyebrows pull together as she searches my skin for signs of injury. Gentle fingers skate over the drooping pink petals—one for every month of her short life.

"Lily was my sister." I don't even know why I'm telling her. Maybe so that she'll stop fucking touching me like that.

Rain lifts her head but not her fingers. Those she splays over my ribs, covering the ink like a bandage.

"I'm sorry." The sincerity in her big blue eyes is so genuine, the hurt in her voice so raw, I get the sense that Rain isn't sympathizing with me. She's commiserating.

The microwave dings a reminder, and I couldn't be more thankful for the interruption.

"Show's over," I call over my shoulder as I walk toward the beeping machine.

A cloud of steam hits me in the face when I open the door. Setting the bag of cooked broccoli on the counter, I spin around to grab the rest of our dinner out of the freezer.

"You wanted a corn dog, right?"

I grab a box of corn dogs and a few individually wrapped sausage, egg, and cheese biscuits. Then, I turn toward Rain. Her mouth is open in a way that makes me want to put something inside of it. Food will do. My tongue would do better. My dick would be a fucking miracle.

"I'll take that as a yes." I smirk.

Rain blinks the emotion off her face and scoops the bundle of clothes off the floor, inadvertently flashing me again in the process. I snicker as I watch her scamper into the laundry room on the far side of the kitchen.

I return my attention to the glowing microwave and try not to think about the tingling sensation left on my skin where Rain's cold hand just was. A hollow, metallic clang and repetitive swishing sounds from the washing machine signal her return. Rain says nothing as she stands beside me, our stomachs growling in unison as we watch our processed meat products twirl under the halogen lights.

Then, one wall-rattling clap of thunder brings it all to a standstill. With a flash and a rumble, the house goes dark. The dance stops. And those once-blinking numbers on the microwave disappear for good.

"Shit." I open the door and pull out our food. It's still cold to the touch, but it seems thawed at least.

A gust of wind whips through the broken back door, causing Rain to shiver and cross her arms over her chest.

"Does …" I'm about to say *your boyfriend* but stop myself at the last minute. "Does *this house* have a fireplace?"

Rain nods, staring at her corn dog like it's a beloved family member on life support.

"It's gonna pull through," I tease, squeezing her shoulder. Which earns me a smack on the arm.

Fuck, that hurt. I make a mental note to ask Rain to patch me up again tonight. My bullet wound is starting to throb like a motherfucker.

I grab my lighter, the broccoli, and the bottle of vodka and follow Rain out of the kitchen, focusing on her round ass instead of the name above it. The living room has a vaulted ceiling and has been decorated with plaid furniture and the heads of decapitated animals. Not exactly my taste, but the fireplace is nice. It's big and stone and filled with actual logs. Not those fake-ass gas-burning things.

I place everything on the hearth and grab a *Field & Stream* magazine off the coffee table. Ripping out a few pages, I twist them into a stick and light the end on fire. Rain sits cross-legged on the carpet beside me, careful to keep the jersey tucked between her legs. She's holding the corn dog in one hand and the biscuits in the other.

"Just so you know …" I say, holding the makeshift torch against the smallest piece of wood until it catches. "Mine's bigger."

Rain furrows her thin eyebrows at me and then bursts out laughing when my eyes shift from her face to the breaded wiener in her hand.

Fuck, I love that sound.

"Why are you in such a good mood?" She smiles as I take the food from her and lay it on the hearth to warm up.

"Because I'm about to eat the shit out of these biscuits."

And because nobody's trying to kill me at the moment.

And because I might get to sleep in an actual bed tonight.

And because I got to see your tits … twice.

"This whole time, I thought you were a jerk, and it turns out, you were just hangry?"

"Oh, I'm still a jerk." I grab the bottle of vodka off the hearth and press the ice-cold glass against her outer thigh just to make my point.

"Ahh! Okay, okay! You're still a jerk!" she screams, swatting it away.

I chuckle and twist off the cap, giving her a salute with the neck of the bottle before tipping it back. The vodka goes down smooth, dulling away the hard edges of the day.

I extend the bottle toward Rain but pull it back at the last second. "Just a sip, okay? You're on that Hydro shit, and the last thing I need is for you to puke or die."

Rain smiles as she accepts my offering, and something warm spreads inside my chest that has nothing to do with the fire or the alcohol. As I watch her eyelids flutter shut and her pretty pink lips wrap around the frosty glass bottle, I wish like hell that it were me. Any part of me. Every part of me.

"That's enough," I bark, snatching it out of her hand.

She laughs and coughs against the back of her wrist. "God, I hate vodka."

"What else do you hate?" I ask, surprisingly interested in learning more about my newly acquired resource.

I tear open the bag of broccoli and set it on the carpet in front of us. Rain's hand plunges inside, pulling out a fistful of little green trees.

"I'm fucking starving," she mumbles, popping one into her mouth.

"You didn't answer my question."

She shrugs. "I don't know … everything?" I watch the joy drain from her face as she stares into the fire. "All of this. This town, the nightmares, what they make people do, just waiting around to die. I hate all of it."

"You wanna know what I hate?" I ask, nudging her with my elbow. "Actually, it's more of a who."

"Who?" she croaks, clearing the emotion from her throat.

"Tom Hanks."

"Tom Hanks!" Rain squeals and shoves my leg. "Nobody hates Tom Hanks! He's the nicest guy in America!"

"I call bullshit," I say, leaning forward to rustle the logs with a fire poker. "It's all just an act. I'm not falling for it."

Rain snorts like a pig—*again*—which makes her laugh even harder, and I realize this is the most fun I've had in a long time. I poke one of the biscuits on the hearth and decide that our dinner is warm enough.

Thunder booms off in the distance as I hand the dick-on-a-stick to Rain. She grins and bites the tip off.

"Savage." I cringe.

We both go quiet as we inhale our meals. As the minutes stretch on, I can almost see our thoughts accumulating on the carpet between us, heavy and dark.

The dirty ones are mine.

I wonder how many little pricks from high school stuck their dick in that perfect mouth. How many of them were invited and how many just took advantage of a pretty little throwaway. I wonder what she would be doing right now if I hadn't pulled her out of Burger Palace. What she would be doing if the nightmares had never started. I wonder if she's going to go home again in the middle of the night or if she'll spend the whole thing here with me.

Rain's cheeks, full of food, flush pink when she catches me staring. "What?" Her voice is defensive as she brushes invisible crumbs away from her mouth.

"I'm just trying to figure you out."

"Good luck. I've been tryin' for years." Rain slides the last bite of corn dog off the stick with her fingers and pops it into her mouth.

"What were you like in high school?"

"I dunno." She shrugs. "Blonde."

"Blonde?" I snort.

"That was the only thing I was ever good at. Being blonde. Being pretty. Being a perfect little trophy. I wasn't real outgoing, so most people just thought I was a stuck-up bitch, but I got good grades. I made my mama proud. I dated the basketball star and went to church every Sunday. You know, small-town shit."

As she talks, I begin to see glimmers of that girl in the one I'm looking at. The mascara smudged under her eyes. The half-inch of blonde roots I never noticed before. The killer fucking curves she was hiding under all that baggy clothing. Rainbow the bombshell became Rain the badass.

But both of them are just disguises.

I snap my fingers as it hits me. "You're a chameleon."

Rain gives me an offended glare. "What, like I'm fake?"

"No. You're *adaptive*. You change how you look to suit your environment, to survive, like a chameleon."

Rain rolls her eyes at me. "And what are *you*?"

"Me?" I point to myself with the bottle of vodka in my hand. "I'm good at figuring people out." I give her a wink and take another swig. Wincing from the burn, I twist the cap back on. "Guess it's a by-product of changing homes every six to twelve months."

I set the bottle down on the carpet next to me, but when I glance back over at Rain, she's not looking at me anymore. She's staring at the corn-dog stick in her hands.

"Wes?" she asks, twirling the wood between her fingers.

"Yeah ..."

Rain tosses the stick into the fire. It flickers blue as it catches, probably from all the fucking chemicals and preservatives.

"What happened to your sister?"

Fuck.

I swallow and decide to just rip the Band-Aid off.

"She starved to death."

There. I said it. Let's move on.

Rain's eyes shoot open as she turns to face me. "What?" She shakes her head, confusion rippling her forehead. "How?"

"Neglect." I shrug. "She was only eight months old. My mom was an addict and could hardly take care of herself, and our dads were both out of the picture. I managed to get myself to school and scavenge for food in the dumpster behind Burger Palace, but I never once thought about feeding my sister. She was just a baby, you know? I didn't even think she ate food."

"Oh my God, Wes."

Rain's mouth falls open like she's going to say more, but I cut her off, "She used to cry all the time. *All* the fucking time. I would play in the woods or at my friends' houses every chance I got so that I wouldn't have to hear it. Then, one day, the crying just ... stopped."

I remember the relief I felt, followed by the horror of finding her lifeless body, faceup in her crib.

"The cops came when I called 911, and that was the last time I saw my mom. My case worker said I could go see her in jail, but ..."

I shake my head and glance at Rain, waiting for the typical condolences to come pouring out of her parted lips. *I'm so sorry. That's just awful. Blah, fucking blah.* But she's not even looking at me. She's staring into the fire again, a million miles away.

"My mom got pregnant when I was about eight or nine, too."

My stomach drops. Rain never mentioned having a younger sibling, so I'm pretty sure this story doesn't have a happy ending.

"I was so excited. I loved playing with baby dolls, and I was about to have a real one that I could play with every day."

"Did she have a miscarriage?" I ask, hoping the answer is yes.

Rain shakes her head. "My daddy gets real mean when he's been drinking. He never puts his hands on me, but sometimes, when he gets like that, my mama—"

Rain suddenly goes so still. It's as if somebody turned her off. She stops talking. She stops breathing. She even stops blinking. She just stares into that damn fire as all the color drains from her face.

"Rain …"

She clamps her hands over her mouth and nose, and I know any minute the rocking and hair-pulling are going to begin.

Oh shit.

"Hey." I put a hand on her bare shoulder, but she recoils from my touch. "Rain, tell me what's going on."

She shakes her head, a little too hard. "Nothing," she lies, forcing herself to meet my stare. "I'm just … I'm really sorry about your sister." The sadness in her voice is sincere, but when she yawns, it's fake as hell. "I'm so tired. I think I'm gonna go to bed, okay?" Rain doesn't even wait for my response before she's practically running out of the room.

What.

The fuck?

I hear a door slam down the hall but no crying. At least, not yet. I'm sure she's too busy digging a little white pill out of a little orange bottle.

Whatever. I am not going after her crazy ass. I'm gonna sit right here, enjoy this fire, drink this entire bottle of vodka, and pass the fuck out.

I take a nice long pull from the ice-cold bottle and hear what sounds like music coming from down the hall.

So what? Maybe she falls asleep listening to music.

Then, I recognize the song—"Stressed Out" by Twenty One Pilots.

Twenty One fucking Pilots.

She's in *his* room, listening to *his* music, wearing *his* clothes, like she still belongs to *him*. But she doesn't, and it's high fucking time that she got that through her head.

Fueled by three or four or six shots of vodka and Rain's erratic behavior, which is obviously contagious, I stand up and stomp down the dark hallway she disappeared into, mad that my bare feet don't make any sound on the worn-out carpet. I want her to hear me coming. I want my footsteps to rattle off the walls.

This bullshit ends now.

My eyes take a second to adjust to the dark. I see three doors in the hallway before it turns left, but only one is shut. I walk right over to it and give it a hard shove. The music gets louder as it swings open, and there, sitting cross-legged in the center of a bare mattress, is Rain, rocking and staring at a glowing MP3 player in her hands.

"Get up," I shout.

Rain jumps. Her head swivels toward me, but she doesn't move.

"I said, get the fuck up!" My voice booms in What's-his-face's tiny bedroom, but I don't even try to rein it in. I don't even think I can right now.

I'm furious that I see a nine-year-old version of myself in her lost eyes, and I want to slap it out of her. I'm furious that something is hurting her, and she won't let me murder it. But mostly I'm furious that I didn't find her soon enough to stop whatever it is from happening in the first place.

Rain hops up, standing next to the bed with the glowing device in her hands, and stares at me. She's not crying. She's not running. And, for the first time since I laid eyes on her, she's awaiting her next command like a good little soldier.

"I need you to get something through that pretty little head of yours right now." I take two steps into the room and point my finger directly at her face. "Everybody ... fucking ... leaves. I don't know what's going on with your family, and honestly, it doesn't matter. Because people are temporary. Everyone you love, everyone who's hurting you—they will all fucking leave, one way or another. They might die, they might get locked up, or they might just throw you away once they find out how fucked up you are, but they ... will ... leave ... you." I drop my hand and take a breath through my nose, trying to calm myself down.

Shaking my head, I close the distance between us with a final step and continue in a slightly less homicidal tone. "*Our* job ... is to say *fuck 'em* and survive anyway. That's it, Rain. That's our only job. That took me twenty-two years to figure out, and I wish you had twenty-two years to figure it out, too, but you don't. You have two fucking days. So, I need you to man the fuck up because I can't do *my* job without *you*." Emotion—one I don't remember feeling since I was a kid—strangles me, cutting off my voice before the last syllable of my confession.

Rain shakes her head as a new song begins to play. "That's not true." Her voice is quiet but strong. "Because I'm not gonna leave *you*."

The singer begs her to save his heavy, dirty soul, but she drops him onto the bed and buries her face in *my* heavy, dirty soul instead.

Her embrace on my bare chest makes me feel like I've been skinned alive. I'm nothing but raw pink meat in her arms. My scales, my fur, my leathery hide ... it's all been ripped away. Rain's touch penetrates through every layer of defense I thought I had, reaching places that have never seen the light of day. I hate this feeling. Every muscle in my body tenses in response to the pain, but I hold her to me anyway.

Wrapping my arms around her warm, curvy body, I slide a hand up her back and thread my fingers into her short, damp hair. "Oh, I *know* you're gonna leave me," I growl, pulling her head back so that she's looking up at me in the dark. "So, until then, I'm gonna use ... you ... up."

Rain presses up onto her toes at the same moment that I dive for her parted lips, and our mouths collide like the train wreck that we are. I tilt my head sideways and plunge my tongue into her mouth, unable to get my fill. I'm gripping her hair too tight, but I'm powerless to release her. Instead, I slip my free hand under that sad excuse for clothing and grip her full, round ass. My heart jackhammers in my chest as I swallow her responsive moan.

Her hands slide up my back and around to my front, skirting over my pecs and locking behind my neck. I feel her nipples against me, hard as pebbles beneath that unworthy dipshit's jersey, so I pull it off over her head and toss it to the floor. I can barely see her in the darkness, but I don't need to. My hands read the curves of her body as they skim every square inch of her goose bump–covered flesh. She shivers as I knead her perfect tits, and when I break our kiss to pull one perky, needy nipple into my mouth, her hand reaches for me.

She grips me through the silky fabric of the athletic shorts, which were already tented and struggling to contain what she's done to me. My cock is at full attention, swollen and throbbing in her hand, as she gently holds my head to her breast. Her touch is so tender; it causes another surge of emotion to tighten around my throat. It hurts, the way she touches me. It's fucking killing me.

And I'm going to let it.

Rain slides her hand up and down over my shaft through the slippery material as I suck and tongue and worship her other nipple. My every breath on her flesh elicits a reaction, and when I kiss my way back up to her mouth, when I slide both hands over her full ass and tease her slick folds from behind, that reaction is a purr so sweet it vibrates every nerve in my body like a guitar string.

Rain dips her fingers into the waistband of my shorts and guides them down, carefully releasing me. Then, her lips take the same amount of care as they travel from my mouth to my jaw, forging a trail of lingering kisses down my neck and sternum. She takes a step back and bends at the waist as she continues her descent. All I can do is stand here and let her cut me open. That's what her trail of kisses feels like—the slice of a fucking scalpel. She's peeling back my layers, exposing all of my unlovable insides, and she's pretending that she likes what she sees.

But she doesn't. No one ever has, and no one ever will.

The second she sinks to her knees, just before she puts that lying mouth on my cock, I grab her by the hair and pull her head back to face me. "You don't have to do this," I rasp. And, for once, I'm shocked to realize that I mean it.

I want to be inside of her but not like this. This is how the bar flies try to please me. The tourists and college girls and drunken divorcées. They get down on their knees and look up at me like porn stars while they suck me off, practically begging me to fall in love with them.

Daddy issues, all of them.

This bitch has daddy issues, too, and here she is, looking up at me with big, desperate eyes, about to put my cock in her mouth to win my approval … just like the rest of them.

"You don't want …" Rain's voice trails off as I drop to my knees, too.

Grabbing the backs of her thighs, I pull her forward until she's straddling my lap. Her tits are flush against my chest, her lips are once again grazing mine, and I've got her plump, round ass in both hands.

"Perfect," I whisper.

Rain smiles against my mouth as she begins to slide her wet pussy along the length of my shaft. I devour that smile. I chew it up and swallow it. And I feel it burn like fire inside of me, illuminating things I thought were gone forever.

Things I hoped would stay that way.

I don't want to press her to have sex. Hell, I don't even know if she's done it before. But, when Rain threads her fingers into my hair and cradles my head in her hands and sinks down onto me with a gasp, I'm suddenly the one feeling inexperienced. This isn't sex. This is so far outside the realm of sex that I don't even know where I am.

All I know is that it hurts. There's pressure everywhere. My chest feels like it's about to explode. My head is pounding. My eyes burn like I've been pepper-sprayed. And my balls are already tightening in response to Rain's warm welcome.

I wrap my arms around her waist and try to accept everything she's giving me even though it cuts me to the bone. I try to give it back, but I feel clunky and uncoordinated. I don't know how to do what she's doing. I don't even know if there's anything left of me to give.

She's not afraid as she pulls me in fully, grinds against me, and sears me with her napalm kisses. It's like she's done this a hundred times before. And that's when I realize … she has.

In this very room.

With someone else.

Rain's not making love to *me*. She's making love to *him*.

The pressure I was feeling suddenly disappears. I can breathe again. I'm not in danger. There is no threat. This is simply a transaction—sex in exchange for a little boyfriend role-play.

Well, that's too fucking bad. If Rain wants to fuck somebody, she's gonna have to settle for *me*.

Grabbing her ass with both hands, I rear up onto my knees and chuckle as she squeals and wraps her arms and legs around me. I stand and drop her onto the mattress, crawling over her like a predator as the MP3 player tumbles to the floor. The singer is whining about some girl who left a tear in his heart. I feel bad for the guy. He really shouldn't let himself get that attached.

I form a plank over Rain's body, careful not to touch her as I line myself up with her tight little slit. That's all she's getting from me. *I* do the using in this relationship, and tonight, I'm using her for sex. Boyfriend role-play not included.

The moment I plunge inside of her, Rain wraps her thick thighs around my waist and laces her fingers together behind my neck. "Come here," she whispers, tugging me toward her, and the huskiness in her voice has me dropping to my elbows to kiss her.

Rain's lips are brutally soft. Her touch, too. I thrust into her harder, hoping she'll take the hint and drop the act, but she's determined to make this fantasy happen. I'm just about to flip her over and take her from behind when a single syllable stops me in my tracks.

"Wes …"

Wes.

Not What's-his-face.

Wes.

"Yeah?" I rasp, that fucking noose tightening around my throat again.

Rain's hands slide to my cheeks. "What's your name? Your whole name?"

I wish I could see her face. I wish I could see the sincere curiosity I hear in her voice shining out of those big blue doll eyes.

"Wesson Patrick Parker." I swallow, but the noose only tightens.

"I thought you might be a Wesson." Rain presses her little feet against my ass and tilts her hips up, drawing me back into her molten heaven.

"What's yours?" I manage to choke out, burying myself in it to the hilt.

"Rainbow Song Williams."

I retreat slowly, missing her with every inch, and thrust back in again. "What does it mean?"

Rain moans softly and wraps her arms around my back. I slide my hands under her shoulders and lie flush on top of her, wondering if she can feel my heart pounding the way I can.

"It's the title of a song by that band, America, from the '70s." Rain nuzzles her face into the side of my neck and plants a kiss there. "It's kinda sad actually. It's about a girl who fell asleep on a rainbow while she was hiding from blowing leaves and broken dreams."

I brace myself on my forearms and look into the reflective pools of her eyes. "It sounds like you." I watch them crinkle at the corners as she smiles, and before she can say another word, I surprise myself by sitting back on my haunches and pulling her up with me. Rain sinks down onto my dick again, and we're just like we were before—her ass in my hands, her parted lips on mine, and her fingers running through my hair.

Fucking perfect.

Her movements are less tender now. More desperate. Mine feel less awkward, more confident. Rain nips at my tongue with her teeth as she slides up and down on my cock. I slap her ass and grin as she tugs on my hair in response. This isn't what she did in the dark with What's-his-face. This is what she does in the dark with *me*. And, when she moans my name again, I fucking know it.

"Wes," she chants, her voice a breathy plea as her ass slaps against my thighs, and her tight little slit squeezes me even harder. "Wes …"

The feeling of Rain coming all over my cock with my name on her lips and my head in her hands is unlike anything I've ever experienced before. It shatters me. A tear rips through my heart as I clutch her panting, writhing body—just like that Twenty One Pilots motherfucker said it would—because I want this. I want her. But how can I keep her when everybody fucking leaves?

My hips jerk and my balls tighten as I thrust up into her. I know I should pull out. I always pull out. But, as my dick swells and stiffens inside her pulsating body, I just … can't. Not this time. Nothing has ever felt more right in my whole fucked up life, so I decide to let myself have it. I'm a selfish bastard, and I want this.

I want Rain.

With a final surge, I coil my arms tighter around her waist and pour everything I fucking have into a girl I just met yesterday. As my cock jerks and spurts hot cum inside her still-trembling body, the pressure in my chest and the noose around my throat fade away, replaced with something warm and fuzzy and completely foreign.

Hope.

April 22
Rain

"THAT ONE LOOKS LIKE *a cupcake.*" *I smile, squinting up into the afternoon sky.*

Wes and I are lying on a red-and-white-plaid blanket in the middle of Old Man Crocker's overgrown field, watching a parade of clouds float by. He pulls me into his side and kisses the top of my head. I feel it sizzle all the way down to my toes, like a bolt of lightning.

"You're adorable ... because that's clearly the dog shit emoji."

"Oh my God." I giggle. "You're right!"

"I know." Wes shrugs, my head on his shoulder rising and falling along with the movement. "I'm always right."

"What do you think that one is?" I ask, pointing to a human-shaped blob traveling by.

Wes picks a blade of grass and begins twirling it between his fingers. "The one that looks like a guy holding an ax over a teddy bear? Must be Tom Hanks. Fuckin' asshole."

I snort and cover my mouth with my hand.

"You know you sound like a pig when you do that?" Wes teases.

"You know you look *like a pig when you eat?" I tease back.*

"Guess we're made for each other." Wes lifts my left hand from his chest and slides the blade of grass he was playing with, looped and knotted to look like a ring, onto my fourth finger.

My breath catches as I wiggle my finger in the air, half-expecting it to glint in the sun like a diamond.

I prop myself up on my elbow and smile down at his beautiful face, trying to figure out how somebody who looks like he belongs on a poster in a teenage girl's bedroom could possibly think he was made for me.

Wes props himself up, too, mirroring me, and places a sweet kiss on my grinning mouth. "I can't wait until all of this shit is over, and it's just you and me."

He kisses me again, slower and deeper, sending a jolt of electricity straight between my legs that time. I don't know if I pull him on top of me or if he guides me down, but somehow, I end up on my back again, this time with Wes hovering over me. His hair falls like a curtain over the side of his face, shielding us from the sun.

"I can't wait either," I reply with swollen lips and flushed cheeks. "When it's all over, we should go find a mansion ... up on a hill ... and paint terrible portraits of each other all over the walls."

Wes drops his lips to my neck, just below my ear, and whispers, "What else should we do?"

He kisses me there. Then, a little lower. Then, a little lower. The pillowy softness of his lips combined with the abrasive drag of his stubble causes my toes to curl into the blanket.

"Uh ..." I try to think, but it's difficult with Wes's tongue sliding along my collarbone. "We should find a convertible ... and clear the highway ... and drive it as fast as we can."

Wes makes his way over to my shoulder, sliding the spaghetti strap of my sundress down along his path. "What else?" he murmurs against my heated flesh.

Wes's fingertips graze my skin as he slides the straps of my dress down to my elbows. The thin yellow fabric rolls off my chest, and Wes follows it with a trail of kisses.

"I ..." I don't even know what I'm saying anymore. My thoughts are scrambled, and my attention is focused completely on the scratchy-soft feel of this beautiful man. I reach up to stroke his silky hair and say the first thing that comes to mind, "I want you to learn how to fly a plane"—I gasp as his curious tongue swirls around my exposed nipple—"and take me somewhere I've never been."

"Like where?" he asks, continuing his descent, taking my dress and inhibitions with him as he kisses his way down my stomach.

"Somewhere with ... windmills ... and flower gardens ... and-and little thatched-roof cottages." I arch my back involuntarily as I feel the tip of Wes's finger trace the seam of my body over my lace panties.

This is heaven, I think, feeling the sun's warmth on my skin and Wes's tender touch all the way down to my soul. That's the only explanation. I died, and this is my reward for letting my mom drag me to church all those years.

"What do you want to do when it's just the two of us?" I ask, glancing down the length of my body.

Wes lifts his mossy-green eyes, narrowed in wicked playfulness and hooded by bold, dark eyebrows. "This," he says before disappearing under my skirt.

"Rainboooow!" A voice as familiar as the name it's calling floats past us on the wind.

Mom?

I sit up and peek over the top of the tall grass. My mother is standing on our front porch across the street with her hands cupped around her mouth.

"Rainboooow! It's time to come hoooome!"

"Mom!" I struggle to pull my dress up, eager to run to her.

I've missed her so much. But, as I go to stand, the ground begins to rumble. I grab Wes for stability as the knee-high grass shoots up all around us. In seconds, it grows as tall as Wes, caging us in. A ripping sound pulls my attention to our blanket, which is splitting down the middle as more blades of grass burst out of the earth, separating us like the bars of a jail cell.

"No!" I scream, grabbing Wes with both hands. I pull him to my side of the blanket just before the last grassy rod explodes from the ground.

Panting, I glance at his face, expecting to see anger or confusion or that look of focused determination he pulls on when he's trying to hide his feelings from me, but there's just … nothing.

His features are as expressionless as a wax figure, and his eyes look right through me when he opens his mouth and says, "Time to go home, Rain."

He slowly raises one arm and points to something behind me. I turn and see that a trail has opened up in the side of our grassy, six-foot-high cell.

I exhale in relief and tug on Wes's still-outstretched hand, but his feet are rooted to the ground.

"Come on!" I shout, tugging again. "I'm not leaving you here!"

"Everybody leaves." His voice is monotone as he recites his personal mantra.

I feel like I'm in Oz, and he's the Scarecrow—familiar but confused as he mindlessly points me away from him.

"Rainboooow!" My mom's voice sounds farther away.

We have to go.

"Come on!" I tug on Wes's outstretched hand again, this time yanking hard enough to get his feet moving.

We enter the narrow path, and I have to pull him every single step of the way.

Until it forks.

Shit!

I glance down both trails, noticing that each one appears to end in another fork.

"Give me a boost," I say, walking behind Wes and putting my hands on his shoulders.

He mechanically does as I asked, giving me his hand as a foothold so that I can climb up onto his back. When I peer over the top of the grass, my stomach sinks. Old Man Crocker's field has morphed into a giant, intricate maze. I can still see my mother standing on the porch across the street, but it feels like she's twice as far away now, shielding her eyes from the sun as she looks for me in the field.

"Mom!" I call out, waving my hands above my head. "Mom! Over here!"

Something catches her attention, but it's not me. The earth rumbles again as I turn to follow the line of her gaze. I watch in amazement as a green stem grows up out of the middle of the field, as thick and tall as a telephone pole. Once it's reached its full height, it blooms.

I expect to be dazzled by velvety flower petals or palm leaves the size of water slides, but instead, the stem opens and releases a single black-and-red banner that unfurls all the way to the ground.

My heart plummets along with it, landing in the acid bath of my stomach without so much as a splash.

Three more stems spring from the quaking earth. Three more ominous banners bloom, each depicting a different hooded figure on horseback.

And a date, written at the top in bold.

"Wes, what day is it?" I cry, already knowing the answer but praying for a miracle.

His body is as rigid as his voice is emotionless when he replies, "Why, it's April 23, of course."

"Go!" I shout, gripping his shoulder and pointing toward my house. "Run, Wes! Run!" I watch as my mother recoils from the evil banners, walking backward into the house and shaking her head in disbelief. "She's gonna leave, Wes!"

"Everybody leaves," he recites again, his feet rooted to the spot.

"Shut! Up!" I scream, hitting him as hard as I can. My blow lands on the side of his head. It feels like I punched a pillow, but when I look down, Wes's head is lying on his shoulder, and straw is sticking out of a huge tear in the side of his neck.

"Oh, Wes," I sob, trying to stuff the straw back in. "I'm sorry. I'm so sorry." I lift his head back into place and hold it steady with my hands. I realize that his once-shiny brown hair has turned to brittle hay, his skin beige burlap.

The ground rumbles again.

I'm afraid to look, but my head swivels around anyway. There, at the edge of the field, stand four black horses—eight feet tall at the shoulder, smoke billowing from their flared nostrils—and their faceless, cloaked riders. They don't appear to be pursuing us though, and for a moment, I allow myself to hope that perhaps the field is somehow off-limits to them. I exhale a sigh of relief, but it leaves my throat as a scream when the horseman on the far right lowers his flaming torch to the top of the grass.

"Run!" The word tears out of me as I urge Wes to move, nudging and pushing and kicking his straw-filled body, but he just stands there like the empty scarecrow he is, staring at a wall of grass.

I climb off of him and tug on his lifeless arm. Smoke and flames climb toward the sky behind him as the sound of my mother's motorcycle roars behind me.

"She's leaving! You're gonna burn! Please, Wes! Please come with me!"

Tears blur my vision and burn my cheeks as I stare into the dead button eyes of a soulless man.

"Everybody leaves," he repeats mindlessly. His straw-filled brain unable to listen to reason.

Fire consumes the wall of grass behind him, blacking out the sky with smoke as I tug his arm completely off. Straw flies from the severed sleeve as I toss it into the blaze and wrap myself around his burning, hot waist.

"You're wrong," I sob into his tattered plaid shirt just before it goes up in flames. "I'm not leaving you."

The heat sears the flesh from my arms, but I don't let go.

Not until I wake up.

I open my eyes slowly, waiting for the intense heat to disappear, but it doesn't. The body that I'm wrapped around is just as hot as the one from my nightmare.

"Wes?" I sit up and take in the scene before me.

Carter's bedroom in the light of day is even more depressing than it was last night. His open closet is full of athletic equipment and basketball trophies and a tangle of wire coat hangers. His empty dresser drawers are pulled open at random lengths like a sideways city skyline. And the man I slept with on Carter's bare mattress is curled up beside me in the fetal position, shivering and sweating and running from his own horsemen.

My eyes roam over Wes's naked body. His furrowed forehead is covered in tiny beads of moisture, his strong body is shivering despite the heat waves radiating off of it, and his bullet wound is on full display in all its gory, oozy glory.

Shit!

I was supposed to keep it clean and bandaged, but just like everything else, I forgot.

Yesterday just disappeared so quickly, I try to explain to myself. *Everything was crazy with the flat tire and the storm and being in this house and …*

I feel my cheeks heat and the corners of my mouth curl upward as I remember what else we did yesterday. The way Wes kissed me like I was his last meal. The way he held me and called it *perfect.* The way he poured himself into me, filling the emptiness that I'd once thought was bottomless. Wes showed me depths I hadn't known he possessed last night, and I drowned in them, happily.

Wesson.

My smile widens at the thought of his name. I don't want to feel happy about what I did. What *we* did. I want to feel guilty and terrible and disgusting. I just cheated on the only boy I'd ever loved … or thought I loved … in his own bed, for God's sake, but … in the words of Wesson Patrick Parker …

Fuck 'em.

Carter left me here to die.

Wes is the only thing that makes me not want to.

I slide off the bed and sit cross-legged on the floor next to my backpack. I quietly dig past the food and water until I find the first aid kit I packed. There's plenty of ointment and bandages in there, but Wes needs antibiotics and probably some painkillers. That gory mess looks like it probably hurts a hell of a lot worse than he's been letting on.

I pull the orange prescription bottle out of the front pocket of my backpack where I stashed it while I was changing out of my wet clothes. Holding it up to the light, I'm surprised to see how many pills I have left. Thinking back, I realize that I haven't taken a single one since yesterday afternoon. I haven't needed to. Wes's kisses are my new memory-erasing drug, and if I'm really lucky—which I'm not—those won't run out.

I set the hydrocodone next to the first aid kit and tiptoe down the hall. I don't know why I feel the need to be so quiet. Maybe it's because I don't want to wake Wes up. Or maybe it's because I've spent the last few years trying to *avoid* being caught naked in Carter Renshaw's house.

I glance at the fireplace on my way through the kitchen, suddenly remembering that we left it burning before bed. But the blaze is long gone, the glass doors shut tight. I smile and shake my head. *Wes the survivalist.* I should have known he would come back out here in the middle of the night to take care of it.

Evidently, Boy Scout duty wasn't the only thing Wes was up to last night. I head toward the kitchen on my way to the laundry room but do a double take when I realize that our clothes have been laid out all over the couches and tables and floor in front of the fireplace. I remember the power outage and giggle, picturing a very naked Wes pulling our wet clothes out of the washing machine and cursing up a storm when he figured out that the dryer wouldn't work.

I pull on the plaid flannel shirt and ripped black jeans I packed for today, pleasantly surprised at how dry they are, and fold the rest of our clothes into a nice little stack—with Wes's Hawaiian shirt on top, of course.

Hugging the stiff, wrinkled cotton to my chest, I scurry through the house, opening the blinds for light and checking the bathrooms for leftover antibiotics, which I find in practically every drawer and medicine cabinet I check.

"If April 23 doesn't kill us all, antibiotic resistance will. Now, take those."

I chuckle as my mom's smart-ass comment from months ago surfaces in the recesses of my mind. I was recovering from a sinus infection, and she made sure I took every last damn antibiotic I'd been prescribed. She even watched me swallow them like a prison nurse.

Sudden awareness slaps the amused smirk right off my face.

A memory. Shit.

Pushing it away, I toss a fourth unfinished prescription bottle onto my stack of clothes and step into the master bathtub to open the blinds. The sliver of sky I see above the pines is still angry and gray, but it's stopped raining. I focus on that tiny miracle. On the glimmer of hope that we might find the shelter today.

We have to find it today.

All we have left is today.

When I turn to go check on Wes, a scream bursts out of me. Pill bottles tumble into the bathtub, rattling like handfuls of gravel against the porcelain.

"Fuck," I gasp, clutching the folded bundle to my chest. "You scared the shit outta me!"

The tall, muscular, tattooed man blocking my exit leans his uninjured shoulder against the doorframe. "You scared me first."

He's completely unashamed of his nudity, but I'm too concerned about his pale, clammy face and bluish, heavy eyelids to appreciate the view.

"One of the horsemen took you from me. Pulled you right out of my arms, and …" His voice trails off and he shakes his head, ridding himself of whatever torturous fate I just suffered in his mind. "When I woke up, you were gone."

"I'm sorry." I frown, setting the pile of clothes on the edge of the tub.

I walk over and wrap my arms around the sweet, sleepy, naked man. Wes pulls me in and kisses the top of my head, and I'm reminded how warm he is. Too warm.

"I went to find you some antibiotics," I mutter into his bare chest.

His skin is damp and smells like sweat.

"I let your bullet wound get infected." I feel the weight of guilt settle over me, pressing me into the floor as I say the words out loud. "I'm so sorry, Wes. I'll take better care of it, I promise. Look"—I let go of him and head toward the bathtub, eager to get away from the disappointed look that I'm sure he's giving me right now—"I found you some medicine."

"Is that why I feel like shit? I thought it was just the vodka." Wes's joke lands on me like a slap of shame.

"Yeah, that's why you feel like shit."

My guts twist as I gather the bottles in my hands and scan their labels. There are two prescriptions of Keflex that, together, might make close to a whole round. I walk over to the counter and busy myself with combining the pills into one container, reading the dosing instructions—anything to keep from looking at Wes.

Instead, I find myself looking into the open, lifeless eyes of the two guys who shot at him. An image of them lying on the ground flashes before me, as clear and gruesome as a crime scene photo. Their slack facial muscles, the red mess, the glass everywhere. I killed them. I killed two people less than forty-eight hours ago, and I haven't even thought about them since. I wince and squeeze my eyes shut, gripping the edge of the counter until the vault finally does its job and swallows the memory back down.

I should be relieved, but I'm not. My heart begins to sputter, and my palms begin to sweat. That was two memories in less than ten minutes.

What if more come? What if—

I need to take another pill. I need to take two. I can't do this …

I vaguely register the sight of Wes's naked form coming to stand next to me as I stare through the mirror over the sink.

"You okay?"

Righting myself, I pull on a fake grin and glance up at the reflection of his pale face. "Yeah." I shake a white tablet into my hand and offer it to him. "Just take one of these every six hours until they're"—Wes pops the medicine into his mouth and swallows before I've even finished my sentence—"gone. I, uh, have some antibiotic ointment, too, and bandages, but we need to clean your wound first."

I feel Wes staring at me as my eyes dart around the bathroom, looking for a diversion. I feel the heat radiating off his body, trying to fight the infection I caused. And I feel the question on his lips before he speaks it.

My armpits start to sweat.

Great. Now, we're both sweating.

A shower. We need to shower.

I run over to the shower and turn on the faucet.

"I'll just clean your wound in here," I call over my shoulder. "It'll be easier this way and we might as well take advantage of the hot water before the gas gets cut off and the bomb shelter probably doesn't have running water at all …" I'm rambling. I can hear myself talking a mile a minute, but there's nothing I can do about it. I can't even look at him.

He'll know. He'll see all my secrets, and he'll just *know*. I can't let that happen. He said it himself; people leave when they figure out how fucked up you are, and I need him to stay. I need him to distract me. I need him to get better …

I undo the top two buttons on my flannel before my hands start to shake, and I just yank the whole thing off over my head. My bra puts up even more of a fight. I can feel Wes watching me as I struggle with the clasp.

"Hey," he says, his voice as soft and cautious as his footsteps as he crosses the bathroom to help.

Once he reaches me, I drop my hands in defeat and let him unfasten it, concentrating on the way his fingertips feel against my skin.

"Breathe, okay?" he whispers, guiding my opened bra down my arms and onto the floor at my feet. "Just breathe."

I do as he said, inhaling the steamy air through my nose until my lungs can't hold anymore. My whole body sags as I exhale.

Wes's hands grip the muscles on either side of my neck and squeeze, almost to the point of pain, before releasing and moving a few inches down to my shoulders. He squeezes and releases again, moving down to my biceps.

By the time his hands are at my wrists, I'm a limp noodle, leaning backward against his hot, clammy chest.

"You're thinking about what happened at the grocery store, aren't you?"

I nod even though that's just the tip of the iceberg. Just a pebble tossed on top of the mountain of shit I'm trying to keep submerged.

"Well, don't. You saved my life by taking those guys out, and now, you're doing it all over again with this." Wes sweeps his hand over to the cluster of orange bottles on the counter behind us.

Dropping his chapped lips to my bare shoulder, he reaches in front of me to unbutton my jeans. Wes slides my pants and panties down my legs as I splay my trembling hands on the steamy shower door and step out of them.

Standing back up, Wes wraps his arms around me from behind. His erection nuzzles into the crease of my ass, but his embrace doesn't feel sexual. It feels like he's trying to hold me together.

"Why are you doing all this for me?"

My stomach churns out a fresh batch of acid as my heart begins to pound through my back against Wes's chest.

How do I answer that without sounding even crazier than he already suspects that I am?

Because I think I might be in love with you.

Because, before I met you, I hadn't smiled in a month.

Because I don't want to lose you.

Because you're my only reason for living.

"Look at me."

I hold my breath as Wes turns my body around to face him. Then, with a swallow, I lift my head and accept my fate. I let him see me in all my naked, bruised, fucked up glory. Even sick, Wes's beauty takes my breath away. His pale green eyes are rimmed in red—tired and determined, hopeless and hopeful. His dark eyebrows pull together as he chews on the inside of his bottom lip. He's looking at me like I'm a precious puzzle, and everything else fades away. More than the pills or the memories or the fear of what tomorrow will bring, I realize that I am a slave to that *look*. I would do anything, give *anything*, to spend what's left of my short life watching Wes watching me.

He asks his question again, "Why are you doing this, Rain? Why are you taking care of me?"

"Because ... I like taking care of people?" It's not a lie. "I was gonna start nursing school last fall, but then, you know, everything went to shit. But, seeing as how I can't even keep my first patient from getting an infection, it's probably for the best."

I attempt a smile, but Wes doesn't return it. His intense, bloodshot eyes dart back and forth between mine while he makes up his mind about me. Then, he nods.

"What?" My cheeks suddenly feel as if I'm the one with the fever.

"Nothing. Come on. Shower's hot."

I blink, and Wes is gone, replaced with a plume of steam from the opening and closing of the shower door.

I follow him in and freeze at the sight of his head thrown back under the spray. Rivulets of warm water crisscross over his chest and slide into the valleys between his abs. Wes is no more than a foot away from me, but I feel as though I couldn't touch him even if I wanted to. He's shut me out, and I don't even know why.

I feel like, if things were normal right now, this is the part where Wes would tell me he'd call me on his way out the door, never to be heard from again.

I don't know what I did, but I messed up. I gave the wrong answer, and now, I'm being shunned for it.

"Wes." My wavering, raspy voice is almost completely drowned out by the roar of the shower. I clear my throat and continue, a little louder, "Wes."

He turns to look at me but flinches and curses under his breath as the hard spray lands directly on his gaping wound.

Without thinking, I reach out and cup my hands above the gash, shielding it from the onslaught. "Just stand here for a minute," I say, angling him so that the water hits his back and runs down his arm, cleaning out the injury without all the blunt force trauma.

Wes jerks his shoulder, pulling his arm out of my hand. "I can take it from here. You're off the clock, *Nurse Williams*." He says it like an insult. I feel it land in my gut like a sucker punch.

"Are you mad at me?"

"Nope."

I glance up and notice immediately that the hopefulness I saw just a few minutes ago has been replaced with a cement wall, painted green and lined with spiky black lashes like razor wire.

"I just don't wanna be your little *patient*, okay? I can take care of myself. I've been doing it my whole life."

And there it is.

"I've been doing it my whole life."

Nobody has ever taken care of Wes before. Not because they genuinely wanted to. Not because they cared.

"I care." My eyes go wide as my own words hit my ears. I glance up at Wes in a panic, wondering if he heard me, too. Praying to God that he didn't.

Wes stills, his bottom lip curled inward slightly as if he's just about to start chewing on it. Blood pounds in my ears louder than the water drumming on his skin as I wait for him to react, but he doesn't so much as blink.

Fuck.

A subtle hardness makes its way into the edges and angles of Wes's face. His eyes narrow, just a bit. His jaw flexes. His nostrils flare. I can't tell what he's fighting back, but whatever it is, it scares me.

"Listen to me," he grinds out from between his clenched teeth. "I'm not your fucking boyfriend, okay? I'm the guy who put a gun to your head two days ago. Remember? You don't know me, you don't fucking love me, and you never will. So, stop …" Wes shakes his head and glances around the inside of the shower, hunting for the words he needs in the swirling mist. "Stop … *this*. Stop pretending like you give a shit."

His accusation makes me livid.

"Stop pretending like I don't!" I shout, balling my hands into fists at my sides as the emotion I've been trying to hide from him bubbles up and boils to the surface. "Stop pretending like you're this unlovable monster when you're the boldest, bravest, most … most beautiful person I've ever met!" My fingernails dig into my palms as fury surges through my body. "And stop pretending like I'm only here because you kidnapped me. You didn't kidnap me, and you know it. You saved me, Wes. And every time you look at me, you do it all over again!"

It happens at once, but the first thing I register is Wes's lips on my lips. His kiss is needy and desperate and tastes like my tears. I feel his hands clutching the back of my head next. Then, I begin to process the cold, hard tiles against my back. He's kissing me like he did at the hardware store when he realized that we weren't going to get shot—up against the shelves, angry and relieved and unable to express it any other way.

But, this time, there are no clothes between us, no hang-ups or reservations, and no storm brewing outside. This time, when I hitch my thigh over the V of his hip, he's able to slide against me without a barrier. This time, when I angle myself so that he's lined up perfectly, he fills me until my back drags up the wall, and my toes barely touch the ground. This time, I feel him everywhere. His feverish skin warms me from the outside in. His palms glide over my wet curves like he's molding them from clay. And his heart— I feel that too—is pounding away just as hard as mine.

This connection is more intense than anything I've ever experienced. It's as if he becomes someone else when we touch. No, it's as if he becomes *himself*. The real Wesson. The one who is loving and passionate and aching for affection. I cling to that version as he takes me higher, pressing me into the wall and wrapping my other thigh around his waist. His strength is the only thing keeping me from falling, in more ways than one, and when I feel him swell inside of me, so does my heart.

I tighten my legs around his waist and pull him even closer, wanting as much of him as I can get. And he gives it to me, driving forward until his body rocks against my sensitive flesh, triggering an explosion of convulsions between my legs and fireworks behind my eyes. Wes follows me over the edge, groaning against my lips as his pulsing, jerking surge of heat fills me deep and makes me glow.

I don't remember how long it's been since my last birth control shot, and honestly, I don't care. The only thing that matters right now is that, if I die tomorrow—and I very well might—it will be with a smile on my face and Wesson Patrick Parker by my side.

Wes

I SUCK A BREATH in through my nose and exhale through my gritted teeth as I sit on the edge of Fuckface's bed and let Rain play doctor with my bullet wound.

She wrinkles her forehead and gives me an apologetic look. "Sorry, I know it hurts. I'm almost done."

It's not the gaping hole in my arm that hurts; it's the one in my fucking soul that has me looking around for something to bite down on. The one that wants to shove Rain across the room and scream at her to stop touching me like that. It's the part of me that's never had somebody kiss my stupid fucking boo-boos that wants to rip the bandage out of her hand and slap it on myself. This shit is unbearable.

"There you go." She smiles, sealing the edges of the bandage down with gentle fingers.

I catch her leaning in with her fat pink lips pursed, but I jump to my feet before she can actually kiss it. She might as well stab me in the fucking heart. Every kind thing Rain does for me is just one more reminder of everything I've been missing my whole fucking life. And, honestly, I'd rather not know.

I was so much happier when people used me for a paycheck from the government or a fuck boy, and I used them for a roof over my head or a place to stick my dick. I knew where I stood. Things were simple, relationships were temporary, and I knew all the rules. Hell, I'd invented them.

But this shit with Rain is fucking with my head. I don't know what's real anymore. I don't know if she actually cares about me or if she's just using me as a stand-in for her missing boyfriend. I don't know if I'm keeping her around because she's useful or if I've gone and done the one thing I swore I would never do to another person as long as I lived.

Gotten attached.

I feel Rain watching me as I pace the floor of her *real* boyfriend's bedroom like a caged animal. "We've gotta go." I don't have to tell her why. Tomorrow's date is hanging over our heads like the blade of a guillotine.

Rain nods once. She looks younger today without all that makeup on. Her wet hair hangs limp around her face and stops bluntly at her chin. The sleeves of her plaid flannel shirt are too long and bunched in her fists. And her wide blue eyes blink up at me with the trusting innocence of a child.

This isn't just about me anymore, and that fact makes finding the bomb shelter even more imperative.

I pull my holster on over my wifebeater and cover it with my Hawaiian shirt. I couldn't sleep last night until I got my gun from the kitchen. I can't ever sleep unless I know there's a weapon within arm's reach. Even as a kid, I used to stash a kitchen knife under my pillow at night.

I wish I could say I'd never had to use it.

Rain slides off the bed and kneels beside the backpack while I pull on my jeans and boots. She shoves her extra clothes, the first aid kit, and my meds inside, but not the hydrocodone. That she uncaps and shakes into her palm without making a sound. I watch out of the corner of my eye as she covertly pushes a little white pill into her mouth and tucks the orange bottle into her bra through the neck of her shirt.

At first, I thought she didn't want me to see her dosing because she was afraid I'd take her pills again, but the more I watch her, the more I realize she's not afraid; she's ashamed. She's ashamed of her dependence.

I know the fucking feeling.

Crash!

The sound of glass breaking down the hall shatters our silence. Rain and I freeze, our eyes locking as a chorus of giggles and curse words echo through the house.

"See? I told you they left." A girl's voice.

"Damn. I was really hoping I'd get to fuck Carter Renshaw before I died." Another girl.

"We all were, honey." A guy.

Their laughter fills the house as the color drains from Rain's face.

"You know them?" I whisper.

Rain simply nods and covers her mouth with her sleeves.

"I don't know why the hell he wasted all his time with *Rainbow Williams*." The way this bitch says her name makes me wish she were a guy so that I could go out there and bash her face in.

"Uh … 'cause she's gorgeous," the guy replies, lisping a little on the last S.

I want to bash his face in, too.

"I guess, if you're into that whole goody-goody, Little Miss Perfect thing. But Carter was captain of the basketball team. He should have been dating a cheerleader."

Rain's eyes drop to the floor, and I see red.

"Oh, like you?" the other girl sasses back.

"Yeah. Duh."

I hear cabinet doors opening and shutting as the trio continues their shit-talking in the kitchen. With the bedroom door wide open and no other sound in the house, we can still hear them clearly. *Too* clearly.

"Well, *I* made out with him senior year, so maybe he just had a thing for blondes."

Rain's eyes flick to mine, wide with shock.

"Oh my God, you little slut!" the cheerleader cackles. "I can't believe you never told me!"

"Are you serious? You would have told the whole school by Monday, and Rainbow probably would have killed herself by Tuesday."

"Ugh, you're so right."

I watch Rain shrink, disappearing into her flannel shirt until only her flushed pink face is visible.

"For real. After we kissed, Carter actually told me he wanted to break up with her, but he was afraid it would, like, send her over the edge. She always seemed so depressed, you know?"

"Oh, I know. And then she dyed her hair black and started wearing that awful hoodie. I wanted to be like, *Girl, I know the world's ending and all, but you are dating Carter Renshaw. Get some highlights and cheer the fuck up.*"

My irritation flares with the mention of that fucker's hoodie but cools as soon as I realize that Rain's not wearing it today. In fact, she hasn't put any of his clothes back on since last night.

"I don't know," the guy chimes in. "I think Carter should have been on the DL with a certain fluffy queen from drama club instead. Wouldn't that have just been scandalous?"

I reach over and give Rain's thigh a squeeze. "You want me to kill 'em?" I whisper, only partly joking.

The corner of Rain's mouth lifts in a half-assed smile, but the look on her face is one hundred percent kicked puppy.

Crouching down, I look her dead in the fucking eyes and whisper, "Hey, what's our job?"

The other corner of her mouth quirks up to match the first. "To say *fuck 'em* and survive anyway?"

I smirk at my star student, feeling a swell of possessive pride fill my chest. "Very good, Miss Williams," I whisper. "Very—"

"Oh my God, you guys! Corn dogs!"

"That's it. These fuckers are gonna die."

The impulse to shoot them where they stand sends a thrill down my spine as I pull the 9-millimeter out of my holster. I let the magazine drop into my open palm and count the number of bullets left—or I should say, *bullet*.

"Fuck," I hiss, slamming the clip back into the handle.

Rain shushes me and places a finger to her lips.

I sigh and whisper the bad news, "I only have one bullet left. You're gonna have to pick the one you hate the most."

Rain giggles into her sleeves, and the sight makes my heart pound like a fucking gorilla's fist against my chest. She's nothing like the girl those bitches described. She's strong and resilient and sweet and—lucky for one of them—forgiving.

"I don't want you to kill them," she admits, looking up at me from under her naturally black lashes, a sheepish smile tugging at the corners of her mouth.

"Why not?"

"Because they just made me feel *so* much better."

Either that pill kicked in way faster than I expected or she's finally snapped.

"You feel *better*? After hearing *that*?" I gesture toward the empty hallway with my gun.

Rain nods, swallowing me whole with her expanding pupils. "If Carter cheated, then that means I don't have to feel bad anymore. About"—her eyes drop to the floor as she shrugs, but when they find mine again, they're glimmering with courage—"*us*."

Us. Fuck me.

I don't do us! I want to fire back, but the words die in my mouth as I realize that they're no longer true. When I look into that beautiful, hopeful, frightened face, the only thing I see is everything I've ever wanted.

Us.

From the kitchen, we hear the microwave door slam shut and a plate land with a thud on the counter. "Damn it! I forgot the power's out!"

A snort bursts out of Rain before I clap my hand over her mouth, choking on my own laughter. We tumble to the carpet, and I reach out, pushing the door almost completely shut with my hand, hoping it will muffle some of the sounds we're making.

"Guess those assholes aren't gonna get to eat your corn dogs after all," I whisper, my lips grazing her ear.

"Shh-h-h-h-h." Rain giggles even though she's the one making all the damn noise. Her body shakes underneath me with suppressed laughter as I drop my lips to her shushing mouth.

I vaguely process the sounds of shouting and squealing and banging around in the kitchen, but my senses are too busy feasting on a rainbow to pay them much attention anymore.

Rain smells different today, like fruity shampoo instead of sugar cookies, but the feel of her hasn't changed a bit. Her soft, round edges are obedient—molding to fit the shape of my cupped hands, smoothing flat against my hard planes—but her tongue is a defiant little cocktease. It coaxes me deeper just to disappear with a wet *smack* as her lips slide down the length of my tongue. The tiny, breathy noises she makes as her hips rise up to meet mine are the sexiest sounds I've ever fucking heard, and the sight of her beneath me—eyes shut, back arched, lips parted—could only be better if she were naked.

"Wes …"

That one whispered word has me ready to tear the buttons off her fucking shirt. I push up onto my forearms to do just that when her eyes pop open, wide and worried.

"Wes, do you smell smoke?"

I sit up and inhale, coughing immediately as my lungs reject the hazy gray air tumbling in from the hallway. "Fuck!"

I grab Rain by the arms and yank her to her feet, but we both start coughing as soon as we're upright. The air is so much thicker up here. So much hotter. It burns my eyes and sears my nostrils as I fight to suck the oxygen from it.

"Get down!" I command, pulling Rain to the ground as I drop to my knees. Crawling over to the door, I look down the hallway and listen for signs of life, but all I hear are the sounds of destruction coming from the kitchen.

Rain is right behind me as we make our way toward the living room, which looks like it's been inhabited by a swirling black thundercloud. A crash so loud it sounds like a stack of dishes falling off the back of a pickup truck cuts through the thickened air. I ignore it as we emerge from the hallway, my sights set on the closest exit. I turn left and head toward the front door, careful to avoid the broken glass those little shits left everywhere on their way in. When I reach the handle and throw that fucker open, I gulp two lungfuls of humid air before turning to help Rain navigate the glass.

"Rain?"

Another crash, even louder than the first, rattles the walls as I peer into the blackness, looking for my girl.

"Rain!"

"I'll be right"—*cough*—"back!" Rain's voice sounds strangled as it filters through the smog.

"What the fuck are you doing?" I scream. When I don't get a response, I barrel headfirst into the house. "Rain!"

Knowing her, she probably went to go check on those dumb fucks in the kitchen, so I charge into the living room, heading toward the source of the smoke at the back of the house. After a few feet, the air gets so thick and hot and hard to breathe that I have to drop to my elbows and army crawl the rest of the way.

"Rain!" I call one last time before making it to the entryway of the kitchen, which now resembles the fiery fucking gates of hell.

The entire back wall of cabinets is engulfed in flames. They're burning so bright and so hot it's as if they were varnished with bacon grease. The stove appears to be the source of the inferno—or I should say, the mangled, melting tower of Tupperware piled on top of the gas burners, which have been turned on full blast. The bottom has already burned out of the cabinets to the left and right of the stove, hence the crashing dishes we heard, and it looks like the roof is gonna be the next thing to give.

There's no sign of Rain or the motherfuckers who set the fire, so I turn around and crawl back the way I came.

At least, I *think* it's the way I came. The air is so black I can't see my own hand in front of my face. I stop as my coughing gets the better of me, but the sound of the ceiling buckling above propels me forward. My heart races faster with every foot of ground that I cover. I should have reached the front door by now. I should have at least hit a wall. Regret coils around my throat, stealing the air from my lungs.

"Rain!" I snarl between lungfuls of poison, her name leaving an even worse taste in my mouth than the noxious fumes I'm breathing for her.

I knew from that very first day that she was going to be the death of me. I knew it, and I let it happen anyway.

"*Us*," I hear her soft voice coo in my head.

The sound makes me want to puke.

This is what us *gets you. It gets you fucking killed.*

I hear her voice again and assume I must be hallucinating until I realize that she's not saying *us*.

She's saying, "Wes! Wes! Oh my God!"

I feel her tiny hands reach out to me in the dark, gripping my arms, touching my face. The relief I feel that she's alive is overshadowed by the rage burning inside me hotter than a Tupperware fire.

"Just a few more feet. Watch out for the glass."

I feel something sharp cut into my forearm as the light of day becomes a gauzy reality up ahead. Rain shuffles backward out the door as I follow, tumbling onto the porch where I alternate between coughing and dry-heaving until the world finally stops spinning. All the while, I can feel her concerned hands all over me.

"Fucking stop!" I yell, swatting her away as I crawl over to the edge of the porch. I hack up something black and spit it into the bushes below. My head is pounding, and my heart is too as I try to figure out what the fuck to say to her.

"I'm so sorry." Her voice is a trembling whisper as she sits on the porch next to where my head is hanging over the ledge. "I just ran back to the bedroom real quick to get the backpack. All your medicine was in there. I couldn't just leave it. But, when I got back, you were gone. I ran around the whole house looking for you before I realized you'd gone back inside."

Her story soothes my anger a little bit but not the festering truth gnawing away at the pit of my stomach—the truth that love and survival are mutually exclusive in my world. I allowed myself to think, for just a few hours, that maybe this time would be different. Maybe I would finally get to have both. Maybe God doesn't fucking hate me.

"Wes, say something. Please."

"We should get off the porch."

Rain jumps to her feet and reaches out to help me up, but I wave her off and use the railing to pull myself up. Stumbling down the stairs, I look for the sun, trying to figure out what time it is. I can't even find it through the plume of black smoke billowing into the sky above the house, but based on the way the trees' shadows are clinging to the right side of their trunks, I'd say it's already after noon.

Fuck.

Once again, I find myself tempted to tell her to go home. To scream it at her, but when I turn to deliver the blow, I just can't. Rain's forehead is wrinkled in concern. Her blue eyes are rounded in remorse. And when she blinks, twin tears sparkle in the sunlight as they slide down her cheeks.

"Come here," I demand, feeling my chest swell and crack and splinter as she leaps forward and buries herself in it.

"I was so scared," she wails, fisting the back of my shirt as sobs rack her body. "I thought … I thought I'd lost you!"

I run my hand over her hair as her words pierce my heart like daggers, the pain more intense than my bullet wound or my soot-stained lungs.

I've finally found what I've been missing my whole life, and if I keep it, it will kill me.

No wonder Rain was wearing a black hoodie when I met her.

She's the fifth fucking horseman of the apocalypse.

CHAPTER 18

Rain

HEAT SCORCHES MY BACK as the house goes up in flames behind me, but I can't let go of Wes. Not yet.

Two nights ago, I had a nightmare about Burger Palace, and the next morning I got attacked inside of one. Last night, I had a dream that we burned in a fire, and it almost happened a few hours later. What if these aren't just coincidences? What if the nightmares are coming true?

I remember what Wes said about dreaming that I was taken away from him last night, and my fists curl into his shirt.

The sound of a bomb going off behind me pulls a scream from my lungs. I bury my face in Wes's shirt and feel his hand cover the back of my head. I try to relax, but his grip is too hard. His posture too rigid.

"What was that?" I ask without looking up, hoping it was just the stove exploding or the roof caving in.

When Wes doesn't answer right away, I glance up at his jaw, tight and grinding. His eyes cut to mine, and his chest puffs up beneath my cheek.

Exhaling through his flared nostrils, Wes finally replies, "My bike."

We walk around the side of Carter's burning house, and sure enough, Wes was right. He'd parked his bike right against the house, next to the back door, and when the fire finally chewed through the kitchen wall, Wes's gas tank got so hot that it exploded.

As we walk past the debris on our way toward the trail—a handlebar here, a fender there—the only thing I can think of to say is, "I'm sorry."

"It's fine," he says without looking at me. "I don't need it anymore anyway." His curt response gives me chills. It's detached and automatic, like he's said it a million times to rationalize a million different losses.

"I don't need it anymore anyway."

Will he feel that way when the horsemen take me from him, too?

This morning, he wouldn't have. This morning, he said the nightmare scared him, that waking up without me *scared* him. But now, I don't know. It's like the real Wes died in that fire, and all I got back is the outer shell.

We're silent as we enter the woods and begin our walk down the trail, concentrating on avoiding the mud puddles and fallen branches in our path.

"I guess it's a good thing we're not on the bike," I say, stepping over the trunk of a fallen pine tree. "This trail is a mess."

"Yeah," Wes deadpans, clearing the obstacle without even looking down.

His eyes are fixed on something up ahead. I follow his gaze and feel my already-heavy heart sink even more. Wes is staring at the side of my tree house.

"Did you go see your mom last night?"

"Uh … no," I stammer, stepping over another fallen tree. "I … went early this morning, before you woke up."

Wes nods slowly, pressing his lips together in a hard line as his eyes drop to my hiking boots. The hiking boots he probably saw on Carter's bedroom floor when he woke up.

Right where I'd left them the night before.

My sinking heart goes into a full-on free fall at the realization that Wes knows I'm lying, but that's the only sensation the drugs allow me to feel. I don't look at my house at all as we pass. It's not there. It doesn't exist. Nothing exists, except for my feet on this trail. No past. No future. No feelings. No fear. Just the *squish, squish, splash* of mud beneath my boots and the sound of birds busily rebuilding their nests after the storm.

I breathe the cool, humid air and sigh. With the gray clouds overhead and the woodsy smell of burning leaves on the breeze, it feels more like fall than spring.

But people don't burn leaves in the spring.

Looking around, I notice a plume of smoke rising above the trees up ahead. I wonder if we got turned around somehow and are actually headed back toward Carter's house. This doesn't smell like Carter's fire though—all that melting plastic and wood varnish. This fire smells cozy and delicious.

Wes doesn't seem to appreciate the scent as much as I do. As we get closer, his cough gets worse. I guess his poisoned lungs have had enough smoke inhalation for one day. Pulling his shirt over his nose, Wes lets a yellow hibiscus filter his oxygen as we press on, emerging from the woods behind the raging inferno that was once the Franklin Springs public library.

"I guess the orgy got a little out of hand," Wes muses between coughs as we round the side of the building.

When I realize that the homey smell I was enjoying is actually the scent of burning books, something like sadness begins to settle around me, but the hydrocodone tosses it off like an unwanted blanket.

Wes coughs into his shirt as we cross the street, hacking something up and spitting it onto the littered asphalt. He's so pale. His lips are almost bluish, and the sweaty sheen from this morning is back.

"You okay?" I ask as soon as we step into the Burger Palace parking lot, but Wes doesn't seem to hear me.

His eyes are trained on the thirty-foot-tall digital billboard overhead. "How the fuck is that sign on if the power's out?" he mutters.

"They probably have a generator for it." I roll my eyes. "God forbid we have to go a day without seeing stupid King Burger on his stupid fucking horse."

Horse.

I eye the flashing multicolored image of King Burger on his trusty steed, Mister Nugget, as we pass below. He's holding his French fry staff in the air like a sword—or a mace or a scythe or a flaming club—and a nagging sense of déjà vu tugs at the edges of my fuzzy consciousness.

The sound of gunfire inside the restaurant chases it away.

Wes grabs my hand and takes off running toward the woods as people come pouring out of every exit, screaming and shrieking and calling out the names of their loved ones.

Some of whom I've known my whole life.

"*Fuck 'em,*" Wes's voice says inside my head as the *splish, splish, splash* of mud beneath my feet returns.

Fuck 'em, I repeat, this time in my own voice.

I don't look back, and I don't let go. I run hand in hand with this beautiful stranger, over roots and beneath branches, feeling more alive than I ever have.

Wes, on the other hand ...

When we finally make it back to the place we were searching yesterday, he doubles over and places his hands on his knees, coughing and hacking until his face goes from ashen to purple.

I struggle to yank the backpack off his stubborn, hunched-over shoulders and push him to sit on the fallen log we rested on yesterday. I pull a bottle of water out of the bag and hand it to him. Wes chugs almost the whole thing before taking a breath.

Reaching into the neck of my shirt, I pull the little orange bottle out of my bra and unscrew the cap. "Here," I sigh, shaking one of my few remaining painkillers into my palm. "This'll make you feel better."

"I don't want to fucking feel better," Wes snaps, shoving my hand away.

I gasp as the tiny, precious tablet goes flying, disappearing a few feet away in a fat bed of wet pine needles.

"I want to find that goddamn bomb shelter!"

Ignoring my shocked expression, Wes shoves his arm elbow deep into the backpack next to me, rooting around until he finds the giant magnets in the bottom. "The *only* thing that's gonna make me feel better is being in a cement bunker underground before midnight." Wes shoves one of the homemade metal detectors in my direction. "Come on."

I accept the magnet with a frown. "Will you at least eat something first?"

"I'll eat when I find the fucking shelter!" he yells, pushing to his feet. "I'll rest when I find the fucking shelter. I'll take your pills—"

"When you find the fucking shelter. Okay, I get it." I nod, blinking back startled tears.

"Do you?" he snaps, tossing the magnet on the ground in front of his muddy boots and pulling the rope taut. "Because I feel like all you've done since we met is sidetrack me and try to get me killed."

"I know," I mumble, my eyes drifting over to the place where my pill disappeared. I could really use it right about now. Standing, I wander over to the mound of pine needles, hoping to find a glimmer of white in all that brown. I stare down at the crisscrossing lines on the ground, a chaotic pattern as pointless as my short, stupid life.

I'm sorry, I want to say. *I was just trying to help*, I think to myself. *You're better off without me.*

But the words don't come out of my mouth.

I'm too distracted by the shape of the mound in front of me. Bending over, I shove my hands into the wet pine straw, but they don't disappear into the mulchy mess like they should. Instead, my fingertips jam into something large and hard just below the surface. When I brush the needles away, my mouth falls open at the sight of a large stone block ... attached to another stone block with crumbling white mortar.

"Wes!" I shout, frantically uncovering the chain of stones. "Wes, I found it! I found the chimney!"

A split second later, Wes is at my side, kissing my temple and apologizing profusely as we work together to unearth the fallen chimney. Once we locate the base, he knows exactly where to look for the hatch. He turns and takes about ten steps away, like a pirate measuring paces on a treasure map, and then he drops the magnet. This time, there's no bounce when it lands on the soft forest floor. Hopeful green eyes lock on to mine as Wes tugs on the rope. The metal disc doesn't budge.

I stand, rooted to the spot, as he falls to his knees and begins clawing at the carpet of leaves and needles beside the magnet. As the surface of a rusted metal door begins to take shape under his determined hands, I feel as if he's lifting a weight off of me as well.

We're going to be okay.

I was helpful.

Wes will be happy with me again.

"Shit," he hisses, uncovering a rusty old padlock secured to the side of the door. Giving it a tug, Wes drops it with a clang against the door. Bracing his hands on his thighs, he furrows his brow at the new challenge, as if he were trying to unlock it with the sheer force of his mind. After a moment, he nods. Then, he reaches into the side of his open shirt and pulls the 9-millimeter out of his holster. "Go stand behind that tree. I'm gonna shoot the lock off, and I don't want you to get hit by the ricochet."

With a nod, I scurry behind the nearest oak tree and feel my heart pound as I wait for the shot to ring out. I should be excited, but this sensation fighting through the drugs feels closer to dread. This is our last bullet.

What if he misses? What if he gets hit by the ricochet? What if—

The sudden blast rattles my eardrums as it crashes and echoes off the trees. When I open my eyes and lower my hands from my ears, I wait for confirmation that it's safe to come out, but all I hear is the exaggerated *squeeeeeeak* of a metal door being opened.

Then, nothing.

With a deep breath, I peek around the trunk of the tree. Wes is on his knees, soft brown hair hiding his face, white knuckles curled around the edge of the open doorway. He did it. He fucking did it. And with hours to spare. Wes should be running around, shouting in triumph, but instead, he looks like he's kneeling before the executioner. I can't figure out why until I look into the void.

And see his tortured face staring back.

Wes

Water.

The entire … fucking … bomb shelter …

Is filled with water.

When I threw open that door, I didn't see salvation. I saw the happiness drain from my own eyes. I saw the smile rot off my own fucking face. In my reflection, I saw myself for what I'd always been—helpless, hopeless, powerless.

Nothing.

I have nothing. I've accomplished nothing. I've survived a lifetime of hell for nothing. And tomorrow, I'm going to return to nothing, just like everybody else. I'm not special. I'm not a survivor. I'm a fucking sham.

"Go home, Rain," I say, closing my eyes. It's bad enough that I have to hear the words coming out of my mouth. I don't want to have to see them, too.

"Wes." Her tiny voice is almost a whisper as the straw rustles beneath her approaching feet.

I hold my hand out, as if that will keep her from coming any closer. "Just … go home. Go be with your parents."

"I don't want to," she whines. "I want to stay here. With you."

I lift my head as anger surges through my bloodstream. "You only have a few hours left to live, and you're gonna waste them on somebody you don't even know? What the fuck is wrong with you? I have nothing to offer you. No supplies, no shelter, no fucking means of self-defense!" I throw the gun in my hand as hard as I can past Rain and into the forest. "I can't save you. I can't even save myself. Go the fuck home and be with your family while you still have one."

Rain doesn't even turn her head as the weapon sails by. Her pleading, glistening eyes are trained on me and me alone. "I don't care about any of that, Wes. I … I care about *you*."

"Well, you shouldn't," I snarl, gritting my teeth as I prepare to break what's left of my own sputtering heart. "I was just using you to help me get what I wanted, and here it is, in all its flooded glory." I sweep a hand over the cesspool in front of me and let out a disgusted laugh. "So go the fuck home, Rain. I don't need you anymore."

The lie tastes like arsenic on my tongue and hits Rain with a force almost as deadly. Her mouth drops open, and her eyes blink rapidly as she struggles to process the poison I just spat at her. I expect her to argue with me. To come back with more teenage girl whining about whatever it is she *thinks* she feels for me. But she doesn't.

She swallows.

She nods.

She tucks her head to hide her quivering chin.

And then she says the words that cut deeper than any goodbye I've ever suffered through.

"I just wanted to help."

CHAPTER 20

Rain

MY FEET FEEL LIKE cinder blocks as I stumble back down the trail toward the highway, struggling to open the childproof bottle in my shaking hands.

Don't fucking cry.

Don't you dare fucking cry.

My eyes, my throat, my lungs—they burn worse than when I was crawling through Carter's smoke-filled house. But I have to hold back the tears. I have to. If I cry for *him*, then I'll have to cry for all of them. And I can't do that. I won't.

"Go home, Rain."

I look behind me, but Wes isn't following. The only thing I have left of him is his cruel, dismissive voice. I walk faster, trying to get away from it.

"Go be with your parents."

He told me he would use me up. That I would leave him. I didn't believe it at the time, but all it took was five simple words for him to prove himself right.

"I don't need you anymore."

With a desperate grunt, I rip the cap off and throw it as hard as I can against a tree. I don't look to see where it lands. It doesn't matter anymore. Nothing does.

Wes was my only hope. My only shot at life after April 23. Without him, my hours are numbered.

Without him, I don't want the ones I have left.

CHAPTER 21

Wes

AS I LISTEN TO RAIN'S footsteps getting farther away, I feel a pure, unbridled hatred begin to fester in my soul. I don't hate the nightmares or the flooded shelter or even Rain for doing exactly what I told her to. I hate the man staring back at me. I want to wrap my fucking hands around his neck and squeeze until I have the pleasure of watching all the life drain from his eyes. Because he's the one who made her leave.

He's the one who makes everyone leave.

His fucking face is nothing more than a lie. He uses it to trick people into thinking he's trustworthy. Attractive. Confident. Strong. But he's an ugly, lying piece of shit that people can't wait to get away from as soon as they see past the facade.

I spit in his worthless fucking face, watching it distort into ripples just before I slam the metal door with a primal scream.

The clang vibrates through my arms and into my chest and rattles a cough from my smoke-stained lungs. When the silence falls back around me, it comes with a strange sense of calm.

The man is gone.

I don't know who I am without him, but I feel lighter. Younger. Freer. I no longer have anything to fear because every bad thing that could possibly happen to me has already happened. Because of him.

And, now, he's locked away for good.

I pick up Rain's backpack, noting how heavy it is. As my feet begin to move, my strides feel too long. My point of view unusually high. I'm a kid again, in a grown-up's body, walking home with a backpack full of food scored from the dumpster behind Burger Palace like I did every afternoon.

The trail is wider than I remember. Muddier, too. But the birds are singing the same songs they always have, and the trees smell just as piney. I almost expect Mama and Lily to be waiting for me when I get home. Mama will probably be passed out on the couch with that thing in her arm or arguing with her "friend" in the bedroom. Lily will probably be screaming in her crib. Her little face will light up when I walk in the room, but she'll start crying again after a minute or two. Mama said babies do that. They just "cry all the damn time."

When I cut through the Garrisons' backyard, I notice that their swing set is gone. I used to spend hours playing on that thing with their son, Benji. The Patels' house, next door, looks like it hasn't been lived in for years. The grass comes past my knees, and a few windows are broken out. Junk cars line the road, which is littered with broken television sets, glass vases, dishes— anything that the big kids might like to smash. I let my feet carry me across the destruction, but with every crunch of my boots, it becomes more and more apparent that the squat beige house at the end of the street isn't my home anymore.

And it hasn't been for a long, long time.

"Four-five-seven Prior Street," I told the woman on the phone when I called 911 like *they'd taught me at school.*

"What's your emergency?"

"My baby sister stopped crying."

"Son, is this a prank phone call?"

"No, ma'am. She … she won't wake up. She's all blue, and she won't wake up."

"Where is your mommy?"

"She won't wake up either."

The mailbox still says *457*, but the house looks nothing like I remember. For starters, it's been painted—light gray with bright white trim—and the shutters, well, it has some. The rotten front steps that used to wobble when I ran down them, always on the verge of missing the bus, have been replaced, and hanging from the side of the porch, where the giant wasp's nest used to be, is a blue-and-red plastic baby swing.

My chest constricts as I instinctively listen for the sound of crying.

But there's only silence.

I run to the porch, clearing all four steps in a single leap, and press my face to one of the windows on either side of the freshly painted front door.

"Hello?" I bang on the door with my fist before trying to get a better view in through one of the other windows. "Hello!" I pound on the glass with my open palm.

Even though the framed photos hanging on the wall above the couch show a family of smiling strangers, I can't help but picture my mom and my sister the way I found them that day. One passed out and dead to the world, the other …

Before I know it, I'm grasping the sides of the doorframe and kicking the motherfucker in. Wood splinters around the deadbolt as the door swings open violently. I burst into the living room and realize immediately that the place doesn't smell like cigarette smoke and sour, spilled milk anymore. The walls inside have been painted a light gray as well, and the furniture is simple and clean.

"Hello?" I move more cautiously into the hallway, my heart chugging like a freight train.

When I peek into the first room, my old room, I don't find a mattress on the floor, surrounded by a collection of flashlights in case the power went out. I find a computer desk and two matching bookcases filled with books.

Lily's crib was in my mom's room because the extra bedroom had a padlock on it. She never told me what was in there, but now, the door is wide open.

Adrenaline pushes me forward as my eyes land on a white crib, positioned against the far wall with rays of late afternoon sunlight hitting it sideways from the window. The zoo animals hanging from the mobile watch me approach, holding their breath along with me as I relive that day with every step.

I remember the relief I felt that she'd stopped crying, followed by the realization that her skin wasn't the right color. That her open eyes were fixed on nothing. That her once-chubby cheeks were sunken, her knuckles raw from incessant chewing.

But when I look into *this* crib, it's as if I'm experiencing that day in reverse. First comes the dread and then the relief.

There is no Lily. No death. No failure. Only a fitted sheet covered in pink giraffes and gray elephants and a tiny pillow embroidered with three simple words.

You are loved.

I pick it up and read it again, blinking away the sudden, stinging tears blurring my vision.

You are loved.

I grit my teeth and try to breathe through the pain.

You are loved.

I want to throw the pillow to the ground and stomp on it, but instead, I find myself clutching it to my chest, pressing it as hard as I can against the place that aches the most. I hear the words again, repeated in my mind, and realize that the voice doing the whispering isn't my own.

It belongs to a different neglected girl. One with sad blue eyes too big for her delicate face. One who found a way to care for me, even when she wasn't being cared for herself.

One that I just threw back to the wolves.

I might not have been able to save Lily, but I'm not that same scared little boy anymore.

I'm a man now.

A man who lies.

A man who steals.

But a man who will do whatever it takes to protect his girl.

Wes

THE ENERGY IN TOWN has escalated into a fever pitch of desperation. The parking lot fistfights and burning buildings and rioters smashing car windows and stray dogs snarling over Burger Palace wrappers blur together as I power through the anarchy with my head down. Glancing up only to note how quickly the sun is sinking behind the trees, I walk faster.

I know April 23 won't technically be here until midnight, but from the looks of this place, I think hell is going to show up ahead of schedule.

As I hustle across the highway, I pass a group of shitfaced good ole boys hanging out on the tailgate of a stranded F-250. They have the doors open, blasting some obnoxious country song from the truck's CD player. They don't seem to notice me, but as soon as I get within arm's reach, one of the fuckers reaches out and grabs my backpack. It all happens so fast. One minute, I have my sights set on the smoking shell of a library across the street, and the next, I have a forty-year-old man on the pavement with my pocketknife pressed against his throat.

His stunned, glassy eyes lift to something over my head as his buddy in the truck yells, "Mikey! Git my rifle!"

Shit.

Backpack in hand, I take off running, disappearing behind a Chevy Suburban just before three bullets pierce the hood and fender. Their laughter fades behind me as I tear past the library. The exterior walls are still intact, but the fire inside has eaten through the roof and is now shooting fifteen feet into the air. A few extremely stoned-looking Franklin Springs citizens have gathered around to watch it burn.

I hope Rain made it through here okay, I think as my feet hit the trail.

If she even went home. Fuck. What if she didn't go home?

I rack my brain for other places I should search, but nothing comes to mind. Carter's house is gone. Her friends have all left town, if she even had any. The businesses around here are either boarded up, burned down, or occupied by thugs. She has to be there. She has to.

What the hell do I say to her dad?

"Hi. I'm the guy your daughter was with while you were worried sick about her for the last two and a half days. Sorry about that."

Maybe he really is deaf. If that's the case, I won't have to say anything.

As I jog, I wonder if Rain knows sign language.

I wonder if her mom will be home.

I wonder if she even has a mom anymore.

I don't slow down, the closer I get. In fact, I pick up the pace as soon as the tree house comes into view, hurdling over the fallen oak where Rain told me she went home this morning.

Why would she lie about that? What is she hiding?

Whatever it is, I have a feeling it's inside that house.

And I just shoved her back toward it with both hands.

Fucking asshole.

An idea, a wild hope, ignites in my mind as I take the wooden ladder rungs two at a time. But, when I lift my head above the threshold of the tree house, all I find are two beanbag chairs, some protein bar wrappers, and an empty bottle of whiskey. No Rain. Just remnants from our first night together.

I look over my shoulder at her house and see it the way I saw it then. The faded gray siding. The darkened windows. It looks just as empty as it did that night, but it's not. It can't be.

I hop down and feel the impact deep in my shoulder wound. It's still throbbing, but I think my fever has gone down. I slide the backpack onto my good shoulder and dig the bottle of Keflex out of the front pocket—just another reminder of all the ways Rain tried to help me.

Popping one into my mouth, I cross the overgrown backyard with a renewed determination to find her and return the favor.

I round the corner, passing her old man's pickup truck in the driveway, and march up the weather-beaten steps to her front door. With my heart in my throat, I raise my fist to knock, but the sound coming through the broken window in the door makes my blood run cold.

It's a song.

It's a Twenty One fucking Pilots song.

"Rain?" I call through the hole in the door, hoping she'll just walk over and let me in. Like anything in my life has ever been that easy.

"Rain!" I yell louder, the artery in my neck pulsing with every second that ticks by unanswered.

The only response I get back is that singer's whiny-ass voice telling me that he can't sleep because everyone has guns for hands.

Unable to stand here any fucking longer, I reach out and turn the knob. It rotates in my hand freely.

Moving so that my body is against the wall and out of view, I yell, "I'm coming in," and nudge the door open with my foot. When the action isn't met with a spray of bullets, I take a deep breath and look around the doorframe.

Then, I immediately retreat.

Gasping for air with my back against the wooden siding, I try to process the scene inside.

A dark living room. Blinds drawn shut.

A coffee table. A couch. An old-school TV.

And a man.

Sitting in a recliner, facing the door.

With a shotgun across his lap.

And his brains splattered all over the wall behind him.

With every breath I draw, the smell becomes more and more unbearable.

The smell of death. The smell of dried blood and exposed gray matter.

The song starts over.

I pull the small flashlight from my pocket and breathe into my shirt as I tiptoe into the house. Broken glass crunches under my boots.

"Rain?" I call again, swallowing down the bile rising in my throat.

I tell myself not to look as I walk past Mr. Williams to check the kitchen, but morbid fucking curiosity gets the best of me. Swinging the flashlight in his direction, I have to clamp my teeth together so hard they almost crack to keep from puking. The entire back of his head is mushy pulp, mingling with the fluffy insides of the recliner. The streaks on the once-country-blue wall behind him have long dried to a deep rust, indicating where the bigger chunks were before they slid off and calcified on the crusty, bloodstained carpet.

I don't see an entrance wound on his bloated old face, but the blood spilling over his lower lip and into his gray beard tell me that somebody put that shotgun into his mouth before pulling the trigger.

Probably him.

The color of the blood and the stench in the fucking air also tell me that this shit did not just happen. I'd say this guy's been sitting here for …

My guts twist, and this time, no amount of teeth-clenching will keep me from hurling all over the carpet as the last two and a half days scream by in reverse.

The drugs. The secrecy. The mood swings.

The way she refused to let me come inside the house.

The way she said he wouldn't hear her knocking, wouldn't see her at the door.

The way she came running out of here that night like she'd seen a …

I brace myself on my knees and puke again.

Oh God.

Fuck.

He's been here this whole fucking time.

The song starts over.

And now she's in here with him.

Wiping my mouth on the back of my hand, I walk over to the stairs by the open front door. As much as I hate to trap in the smell, I kick it shut. The last thing we need is wild dogs sniffing out the body.

The beam from my flashlight leads the way as I trudge up the stairs, listening for movement, crying, *anything.* But there's nothing. Nothing but that goddamn song and the sound of my own rushing pulse as I finally reach the upstairs hallway.

Five doors.

Three closed.

Here we go.

"Rain?" I call again, but I know she won't answer. I try not to consider why as I shine my flashlight into the first open door on the right.

The sight of a black braid makes my breath catch, but I exhale in relief when I realize that it's sitting on top of an overflowing trash can. Next to a toilet. Beside a sink.

There's no one inside. It's just an empty bathroom.

A thought occurs to me as I throw open the next door and find nothing but towels and sheets.

Maybe Rain *killed the bastard. I saw her mow down two motherfuckers at Huckabee Foods like it was nothing. She could have killed him too, if it were self-defense.*

I want to believe it. I want to picture Rain as the victor in this fucked up situation. I want to find her rocking in a corner somewhere because she's batshit crazy.

Not because she's broken.

The song starts over as I approach the last door on the right.

"Rain?" I knock lightly before turning the knob, not wanting to startle whoever might be inside. "It's Wes. Can I come in?" I crack the door and brace for impact, but the only thing that hits me in the face is that same putrid smell from downstairs.

Fuck.

I pull my shirt over my nose and pray to every fucking god I can think of as I approach the lump on the bed.

Please don't let it be her. Please don't let it be her. Please, God. I know you fucking hate me, but just … fuck. Don't let it be her.

I watch helplessly as the yellow beam from my flashlight slides up the side of a four-poster bed and across the surface of a patchwork quilt covered in flowers. The bedspread has been pulled up over the person's face—or over the place where it used to be, judging by the size and location of the maroon stain on the fabric—but I don't pull it down.

I don't need to. The blonde hair fanned out over the shredded pillow—soaked in blood as thick as tar and sprinkled with fluffy down feathers—tells me everything I need to know.

There's no saving Mrs. Williams.

I just hope I'm not too late to save her daughter.

My legs are moving and my guts are churning and my hands are gripping the flashlight like a lifeline.

Not because I'm scared.

But because now, I know exactly where she is.

The music is louder at this end of the hall, so the last room on the left has to be the one. I stomp across the carpeted corridor and twist the knob. I don't knock first. I don't wait in the hallway and push the door open from a safe distance. All of my survival instincts go out the fucking window as I burst through the last obstacle standing between me and my girl.

The first thing that registers is the smell. It isn't putrid or coppery, like the rest of the house. It's as warm and sugary as vanilla cake. I close the door behind me and breathe in like a drowning swimmer breaking the surface of the water. The familiar scent fills my lungs and lifts my spirits. Looking around the room, I find the source of the smell everywhere. Lit candles illuminate every nook and cranny in Rain's small bedroom. I turn my flashlight off and stick it back in my pocket as I take in the cozy space. Clothes and notebooks cover the floor. Bookcases filled with messily arranged paperbacks and trinkets line the left wall. A daybed and side table take up most of the right. And there, on that bed, is my very own Sleeping Beauty.

Rain is lying on her stomach on top of the covers, a vision of perfection in a house of fucking horrors.

I cross the room in two steps. The first thing I do is grab Rain's glowing cell phone off the nightstand and jam my finger against the pause symbol on the screen. I set it back down and exhale in relief as that fucking song stops, and silence settles around us.

Rain is facing the wall, so I sit on the edge of her bed and run my hand over her shiny black hair. It feels smooth beneath my palm. Smooth and real.

Nothing matters outside of these four walls. The chaos, the danger, the festering death. It doesn't exist. It's just me, my sleeping angel, and a glowing, silent sense of peace.

"Rain," I whisper, leaning over to kiss her temple. But, when my lips meet her flesh, my illusion of happiness comes crashing down.

Her skin is cold. Too cold.

"Rain." I shake her shoulder and watch as her limp body jostles lifelessly.

"Fuck! Rain!" I leap to my feet and roll her toward me so that I can see her face.

And it's like looking into Lily's all over again.

Purple lips.

Purple eyelids.

Ashen skin.

I'm too late.

I'm too fucking late.

"Wake up, Rain! Come on, baby! Wake up!"

My eyes and hands search every inch of her body for a bullet wound, a slit wrist, something that would explain why she's not *fucking waking up*. But there's nothing. No blood. No injuries. It's not until I rip open her flannel shirt that I find my answer.

Or rather don't find it.

Rain's precious bottle of hydrocodone is gone.

"Goddamn it, Rain!" My voice breaks on her name like a tidal wave against a seawall as I jam my fingers against her jugular, searching for a pulse I know I won't find.

"Goddamn it," I whisper, pulling her lifeless body into my arms.

I drape her long arms over my shoulders and hug her to my chest.

"I'm so sorry." The words come out as voiceless sobs.

I grip her body tighter and bury my face in her neck. Her toes barely touch the carpet as I rock her back and forth. She used to like that. It made her feel better.

"I'm so fucking sorry."

I coil my arms around her ribs, hugging her like I hugged that lying fucking pillow.

You are loved, it said.

I cough out a bitter, sorrowed laugh, tasting my own tears on her cold, clammy skin.

I *was* loved.

And here's the fucking proof.

Rain survived the murder-suicide of her parents, the loss of her friends and boyfriend, and the disintegration of her whole fucking town, but it was *my* neglect that finally broke her.

Just like Lily.

For the first time in my life, I think about killing myself. I could just lie down beside Rain, hold her in my arms, and with Mr. Williams's shotgun, add one more corpse to this fucked up house of death.

But I can't. That's my fucking curse. I'm a survivor.

And when I feel Rain's pulse, weak and fleeting against my cheek, I know I was right about her all along.

She's a survivor too.

April 23
Rain

"LOOK." WES GRABS MY arm as we cross the highway, pointing at the digital billboard above Burger Palace. "The sign is still on. What the fuck?"

I snort and roll my eyes. "They probably have a special generator for it. God forbid we have to go a day without seeing stupid King Burger on his stupid fucking horse."

I give the animated asshole the side-eye as we approach, which he seems to return.

His cartoon eyes land on me as his deep voice booms from the loudspeakers. "What did you say, young lady?"

I look at Wes, who shrugs in response, and then back at the digital sign.

"I'm talking to yoooou!" The ground shakes beneath my feet as King Burger points his French fry staff in my direction. It becomes three-dimensional and a thousand times longer, extending out of the screen and stopping inches away from my face.

"I ... I'm sorry," I say, glancing up the length of the French fry at the raging monarch above.

"I will not tolerate profanity in my kingdom!"

I open my mouth to apologize again, but when I do, King Burger shoves his French fry staff right down my throat.

"Get those foul words out of your mouth," he bellows as I gag and cough and gasp for air.

It's not until I'm puking all over the sidewalk that he finally lets up.

"There you go." His voice is kinder now. Softer. "Get it all out."

I puke again, but this time, when I open my eyes, I'm hovering over a toilet bowl in a dark room. Someone is rubbing my back.

He's saying things like, "I'm so sorry," and, "That's my girl."

It sounds like Wes, but before I can turn to look at him, he shoves two fingers down my throat and makes me hurl again.

I swat at him, but my hands hit nothing. Wes evaporates like smoke, leaving me alone and on my knees. I'm no longer hugging a toilet. I'm in the woods, kneeling in wet pine straw and staring down into the watery entrance of the flooded bomb shelter. As my stomach gives one last heave, I reach into my mouth and pull something long and silky from the depths of my stomach. It just keeps coming, yard after yard. Once it's finally out, I spread it over the ground to see it better.

But I already know what it is.

A black-and-red banner.

With a demonic silhouetted horseman in the center.

And a date at the top.

Today's date.

I swing my head left and right, listening for hooves, looking for Wes. But I don't find him in the forest. I find him when I look back down at my reflection.

Is that what I look like? *I wonder, reaching up to touch my stubbly jaw, but my reflection doesn't copy me.*

Instead, it beats on the surface of the murky water with a closed fist, eyes wide and full of panic.

"Wes!" I reach out to touch his face in the water, but the surface is as smooth and hard as glass. I pound on it with both hands, but they bounce right off.

Wes's eyes are pleading. Huge bubbles leave his mouth and break against the barrier between us as he tries to tell me something.

"Wes! Hang on!" I wrap the banner around my fist and punch as hard as I can, but my blows land like pillows against the unbreakable water.

As I stop to catch my breath, I realize that Wes isn't fighting anymore. His face is calm now, and his eyes are full of remorse and acceptance.

"No!" I scream at him, pounding the surface again. "No, Wes! Fight!"

But he doesn't. He presses a hand to the glass as his face sinks away from me. His eyes lift to something over my shoulder just before they disappear into the black.

I don't have to turn around to know what he was looking at. I can feel the horse's hot, hellish breath on the back of my neck. I bow my head, ready to accept my fate, and feel the wind from a swinging mace ruffle my hair. I squeeze my eyes shut and brace for impact, but the spiked ball doesn't connect with my skull.

It shatters the glass beneath my hands.

Without thinking, I plunge into the cold, murky water, looking, reaching, grasping for Wes. But I can't find him. I swim deeper but never hit bottom. I swim to the left and right but never find a wall. I don't come up for air until my lungs begin to burn. I kick furiously to get back to the surface, clenching my teeth and holding my nose to keep from inhaling water in my desperation to breathe, but just as I prepare to crest the top of the water, I hit my head on it instead.

No!

Looking up, I pound on the glassy surface, sucking in lungfuls of water as the mace-wielding horseman watches me drown. From this angle, I can see that he does have a face under that hood after all.

A beautiful one with soft green eyes and full, smirking lips.

I bolt upright, clutching my chest and gasping for air. Every breath makes my raw throat sting. When I open my eyes, I find myself staring at a toilet. My toilet. There's a pillow on the floor by the door, which is letting a little bit of daylight in around the edges. A few candles on the counter provide the rest of the light. I recognize them from my room.

I rub my pounding temples as I try to figure out how I ended up on the bathroom floor.

The smell of vomit lingering under the vanilla is my first clue.

The man watching me from the bathtub is my second.

Wes is lying down in the tub, fully clothed. His muddy boots are propped up on the ledge, and his head is on the opposite corner. His eyelids are heavy, like I just woke him up, but his blown-out pupils are alert and trained on me.

He doesn't say anything at first, and neither do I. We just stare at each other, both waiting for the hammer to drop, and when we finally speak, it's at the exact same time.

"You slept almost all day," Wes says.

"You're really here," I blurt out.

Wes nods, and the look on his face isn't happy.

It's sad and sympathetic.

Reality wraps around my empty stomach and crushes it like an aluminum can as the meaning behind that look takes hold.

"You saw," I whisper.

Wes nods again, pressing his lips into a hard line. "I'm so sorry, Rain. About everything, but … fuck. I just … I had no idea."

"I'm so sorry." His words hit me like an ice-cold bucket of reality.

My chin buckles as my gaze drifts over to one of the candles. I stare at the flame until I convince myself that that's why my eyes are burning.

I'm so sorry makes it real. The way he's looking at me right now makes it real. The fact that he saw it too makes it real.

I reach into the neck of my flannel, desperate for something to shut down the pain, but my shirt has been ripped wide open, and my pills are long gone.

Because I took them all.

And *he* made me throw them up.

Grief and shame and irrational rage blur my vision and turn my hands into fists. I was going to die without ever having to feel this. Without ever having to miss them. I was going to stay numb and distracted until April 23 and then the horsemen would take me to wherever they had gone and we'd be together again like it never happened. I had a plan, but then Wes showed up and ruined everything. Now he's here and he's saying he's sorry and he's looking at me like my parents are dead and my painkillers are gone and it all hurts so fucking much and—

"I hate you!" I shout. The words echo off the walls, and tears blur my vision, so I squeeze my eyes shut and scream it again, "I hate you!"

I grab a hairbrush off the counter and throw it as hard as I can at him. Wes catches it just before it hits him in the face.

"You ruined everything! I hate you! I hate you! I hate you!"

"I know," he says, deflecting a toothbrush holder and a bottle of soap. "I'm so sorry, Rain."

"Stop saying that!"

I lunge toward the bathtub, hoping to claw his stupid green eyes out. The same ones that watched me drown in my nightmare. The same ones that are watching me drown now. But Wes grabs my wrists as I come across the edge of the bathtub and pulls me in with him.

I land on his chest, and his solid arms lock around me, pinning me in place.

"Let me go!" I howl, writhing in his grasp and kicking the tub with my bare feet. "Don't touch me! Let me go!"

But Wes just holds me tighter, shushing me like a child. I struggle and fight and kick and flail, but when I feel his lips press against the top of my head, when I feel his arms rock me from side to side, all the anger leaves my body.

In the form of a sob.

"Shh ..." Wes runs a hand over my hair, and it reminds me of the way my mom used to do it before she left for work.

I picture her exactly the way she looked the morning before it happened. Stressed. Frazzled. Her dirty-blonde hair gathered in a lopsided ponytail. Her blue hospital scrubs stained with coffee.

"Mom, we have less than a week left. Why are you still going to work? Will you please just stay home? Please? I hate being here with Dad. He just drinks and takes those painkillers for his back and messes with his guns all day. He doesn't even talk to me anymore. I think he's, like, snapped or something."

"Rainbow, we've talked about this. Not everything is about you. Other people need me, too. Now more than ever."

"I know, but—"

"No buts. There are two types of people in this world, honey—wallowers and workers. When the going gets tough, I deal with it by working, by trying to help. Which type of person are you going to be? Are you going to stay home all day and wallow, like your father, or are you gonna get out there and try to help somebody?"

"I want to help," I said, dropping my eyes to her scuffed white sneakers.

"Good. Because, when this thing blows over—and I'm sure it will—a lot of people are going to need your help."

Even though it hurts to remember her, it's also surprisingly comforting. It's almost like she's right here with me. I can still hear her voice, still smell the hazelnut-flavored coffee on her breath as she kissed my cheek. The worst part isn't seeing her again; the worst part is knowing that she's been here the whole time, but I've kept her locked away.

She deserves to be remembered.

Even if it's only for a few more hours.

When my cries die down and I finally catch my breath, Wes runs a soothing hand down my back.

"Better?" he asks, his voice barely above a whisper.

I nod, surprised to find that I actually mean it. My parents might be gone, and tomorrow might not exist, but here, in this bathtub, with the one person who came back for me, I do feel a little bit better.

"You wanna tell me what happened?"

With my cheek on his chest and my eyes lost in the flickering candlelight, I nod again. I want to get it out of me. I want to finally be free.

"I … I couldn't sleep that night, so I snuck outside to smoke one of my dad's cigarettes. I had a few stashed in my dresser, and I thought it might help calm my nerves. He'd gotten so paranoid about the rioters and the dog attacks that I knew he'd flip out if he saw me going outside that late, so I was super quiet. I even smoked out in the tree house because I was afraid he'd see me on the porch."

I take a deep breath and focus on the rhythm of Wes's heartbeat beneath my cheek. "Just as I was finishing my cigarette, I heard a gunshot. It was so loud; it sounded like it came from inside the house, but I thought that was crazy. Then, I heard another one."

"Your room," Wes says, stroking my hair. "I saw the hole blasted in your bed when I carried you in here last night."

I nod, staring at nothing. "He thought I was asleep under the covers, like her."

I lift a shaking hand to my mouth and then still when I realize I'm not holding a cigarette. I can almost feel the grass slashing at my bare legs as I flew across the backyard and around to the front of the house, grabbing the handle on the front door as the third blast went off.

"I saw it happen." I squeeze my eyes shut, trying to stop the flow of fresh tears. "I saw my dad—"

Wes wraps his arms around me tighter and begins rocking me from side to side again.

"And, when I called my mom's name, she didn't answer …" I catch my sobs in my flannel-covered hand, remembering the way she looked before I pulled the quilt over her head. I kissed her goodnight over the covers and told myself that she was just sleeping. That they were both just sleeping.

Then, I shut the door, polished off a bottle of cough syrup, and I went to sleep, too.

"I'm so sorry," Wes whispers into my hair.

There are those words again. *"I'm so sorry."*

But, for some reason, when Wes says them this time, they don't hurt.

They help.

Wes

I LEAD RAIN DOWN the stairs and out the back door with my hand over her eyes and my stomach in knots.

"Can I look now?"

"Not yet," I say, guiding her off the patio and into the knee-high grass.

We walk about thirty feet until we're standing in the shade of a giant oak tree on the right side of the property.

Last night, once I was sure that Rain didn't have anything left to throw up, I didn't know what the fuck to do with myself. I couldn't sleep in that house. I couldn't stand to be in there a second longer than I had to with those fucking corpses just a few rooms away. And knowing that Rain was going to have to face all that as soon as she woke up … completely sober, I knew I had to do something before I lost my shit.

I just hope it was the right thing.

With a deep breath, I uncover her eyes. "Okay. You can look now."

Even though I spent all night and most of the day on it, the job isn't pretty. The graves are shallow and the mounds are muddy and the crosses are made from sticks fastened together with grass, but at least I got those fuckers out of her house and into the dirt where they belong.

I chew on my bottom lip as I watch Rain open her eyes. After everything she's been through, the last thing I want to do is hurt her more, but when she covers her mouth and nose with her hands and looks up at me, it's not tears of pain I see in her big blue eyes. It's tears of gratitude.

I pull her against me, feeling every bit the same way. She's here, and she's okay. Even though I might only have her for a few more hours, or even minutes, every single second feels like an answered prayer.

The first one in my entire fucking life.

Prayer. That reminds me …

"Do you want to say anything?" I ask, kissing the top of her head.

She nods against my chest and lifts her glassy eyes to mine. "Thank you," she says, and the sincerity in her voice cuts me to the fucking core. "I don't … I can't believe you did all this. For *me*."

I smile and brush a tear away from her cheek with my thumb. "I'm beginning to realize there's not much I *wouldn't* do for you."

That makes Rain smile, too. "Like what?"

"What wouldn't I do for you?"

She nods, a glimmer of mischief returning to her sad red eyes.

"I don't know … piss on Tom Hanks if he were on fire?"

Rain snorts out a snotty laugh and covers her nose with the crook of her elbow as she giggles. It's the most adorable thing I've ever seen. As I watch her, I try to commit every sound, every freckle, every eyelash to memory. I know it's stupid. I know I can't take these memories with me any more than I can take her, but I hang on anyway.

If the horsemen want her, they're going to have to pry her out of my cold, dead hands.

When her laughter dies down, I gesture toward the graves with a flick of my chin. "I meant, is there anything you want to say to *them*?"

"Oh." Rain's face falls as she turns to look at the twin mounds of dirt again. "No," she says with a heartbroken yet somehow hopeful look on her face. "I'll tell them in person when I see them again."

I nod, hoping that time comes later rather than sooner.

"So, what do we do now?" Rain sniffles, looking around. "What's the new plan?"

"My only plan is to sit in that tree house"—I point in the direction of the wooden box a few yards away—"watch the sun set with this super-hot girl I kidnapped a few days ago, and then maybe make her dinner. I saw that this place has spaghetti and pancake syrup."

Rain pulls her thin, dark eyebrows together. "You mean, you're just … giving up?"

"No," I say, taking her by the hand and leading her toward our home away from fucked up home. "I've just had a change of priorities; that's all."

"What could you possibly prioritize over surviving?" Rain asks, becoming eye-level with me as she steps onto the first rung of the tree-house ladder.

"Living." I smile.
Then, I lean forward and kiss my girl while I still can.

143

Rain

LIVING.

The moment Wes's lips touch mine, I understand exactly what he means. All the death—both past and future—falls away, and there's only him. My *living*, breathing present.

I'm overwhelmed with love for him. I love him for coming back for me. I love him for saving my life even though I only have a few hours of it left. I love him for doing for my parents what I was too weak to do myself.

"I love you," I whisper against his lips, needing to say it out loud. Needing him to hear it.

Wes doesn't respond at first. He simply closes his eyes and presses his forehead to mine. Whatever he's about to say feels important, so I hold my breath as he takes one big enough for the both of us.

"The moment I saw you, I knew I was fucked." His voice is raspy and low. "I knew it when I used my last bullet to pull you out of Burger Palace instead of saving it. I knew it when I pulled that stupid fucking stunt with the dogs instead of leaving you at Huckabee Foods. I knew it when I got shot for you, when I got a flat tire because of you, and when I went back into a burning building to find your ass. The whole time, I thought you were distracting me from my mission, but it wasn't until you left that I realized you *were* my mission." Wes opens his eyes, and his pupils drink me in. "I think I came here to find *you*, Rain. I'm just sorry it took me so long to figure that out."

"Don't be sorry," I whisper around the lump in my throat. "I'm sorry. It sounds like I've been a real pain in the ass."

Wes laughs, and the vision is so beautiful that I feel like I'm looking into the sun. I take a picture of him with my mind, the way he looks right now—backlit by an orange sky, white teeth glowing in his crescent smile, and a lock of brown hair grazing his perfect cheekbone. I want to remember this moment forever.

Even if forever is only for tonight.

"I fucking love you," he says with that perfect smile just before it crashes against mine.

I let go of the ladder and wrap my arms around Wes's neck, knowing without a shred of doubt that he won't let me fall. What I don't expect is for him to grab the backs of my thighs and wrap them around his waist in the process. It's fitting that I'm no longer attached to the earth because that's how I feel whenever I kiss Wes—supported, secure, suspended above my problems.

His tongue and teeth aren't gentle as they take what they want, and neither is his body as it presses mine against the ladder. Desperation fuels us as we bite and suck and push and pull. We have so much lost time to make up for and so little of it left to spare. April 23 is almost over, and every heartbeat that pumps through my veins is another second I've wasted not making love to this man.

I lock my ankles behind Wes's back as he reaches over my head to grab the ladder. Squeezing my eyes shut, I hold on tight as he begins to climb, never once breaking our kiss. As soon as Wes reaches the top, we become a blur of hands and zippers and shirts and skin.

I lift my ass off the plywood floor as Wes shimmies my pants and panties off. Then, I part my knees for him as he frees himself from his jeans. As he climbs over me, I reach for him, desperate for him to fill me—to make me whole again—but Wes stills and gazes down at me instead.

"What is it?" I ask, reaching up to cup his stubbled cheek.

Two deep lines have formed between his dark eyebrows. I feel mine do the same.

"Nothing. I just … wanted to look at you …"

One last time, his sad smile says.

I don't want to see that look, so I kiss it away as I lift my hips to let him in.

But something happens as soon as Wes and I are joined. All that time that felt like it was slipping away? It doesn't just slow down. It stops. We inhale. We exhale. We kiss. We connect. And when we finally start moving again, it's with the lazy grace of melting ice cream.

Because that's all we are.
Something to be savored before it disappears.

Wes

"THIS IS SO NICE." *Rain sighs as she rests her head on my shoulder.*

The Franklin Springs Cinema wasn't exactly hard to break into. Now, figuring out how to work the projector, that took a minute.

"I would have taken you to dinner too, but I can't exactly afford to pay sixty-eight bucks for an Apocasized King Meal right now."

Rain giggles and pats the cardboard bucket in her lap. "I'd rather eat stale popcorn for the rest of my life than step foot in that place again."

"That's good because it might come down to that." I smile and kiss the top of her head.

It feels so fucking weird, being on a date with this girl. I mean, I've dated lots of girls, but it was always an exchange. An understood transaction. With Rain, I just ... want to make her happy.

"Aquaman?" she asks as the opening credits begin to roll.

"What? It was that or Dumbo."

A flirty grin tugs at the corners of her mouth. "I'm not complaining."

"Oh, really? You gotta thing for Jason Momoa, huh?"

"No." She drops her eyes, and I can see the blush rising to her cheeks, even in the darkened auditorium. "But I might have a thing for another guy with tattoos."

"I fucking hope so," I say, pulling her into my lap as her squeals compete with the booming speakers.

When I glance back at the screen, Jason Momoa is carrying a rescued fisherman into a bar. The camera pans from a table full of fishermen to the counter where he's ordering a shot of whiskey. The movement is so fluid, so fast, that I almost miss it, but I swear, on the wall of the bar, I saw a red banner with a black horseman on it.

"Did you see that?" I ask without taking my eyes off the screen.

"See what?"

"That banner."

Rain looks around the room. "Where?"

"Not here." I point to the screen. "In the movie."

"Really?"

I set her on her feet and stand up. "We should go."

"Why? We just got here."

"Because …" I gesture toward the screen as Jason Momoa snatches the bottle from the bartender and begins to chug. Then, I do a double take. The label on the bottle reads April 23. "Rain! Look!"

But, by the time she swings her head toward the screen, Jason has already smashed the bottle on the ground.

"Wes, I don't see anything."

"I think that's the point."

I grab her hand and sprint out of the auditorium and toward the main exit. The second we enter the lobby, four black-and-red banners unfurl from the ceiling, separating us from our escape. We're running too fast to stop, so I sweep my arm out to push one aside … and watch the image of the horseman dissolve into tiny pixels of light around my hand. I turn around, but from behind, it looks just as real as the others.

"Wes, come on!"

Rain is tugging on my arm, but I barely feel it as I stare at the back of the floor-to-ceiling strip of fabric. Reaching out, I run my fingers along the surface again. I feel absolutely nothing as they pass through, leaving a digital trail of multicolored pixels in their wake.

"Look." I do it again, this time sticking my whole arm through. "It's not real."

"Is that real?" The terror in her voice grabs my attention.

I swing my head around as the double doors burst open, and a smoke-spewing horse from hell charges through. The faceless, hooded motherfucker on his back swings his steel sword over his head in a flourish of swoops. I manage to push Rain out of the way before he strikes, closing my eyes and bracing for impalement, but when his blade slices through me, it feels like nothing more than a whoosh of air.

By the time I open my eyes, the horseman, the banners, all of it is gone.

It's just me and Rain and a profound revelation.

None of this is real.

When I open my eyes, it takes me a minute to remember where I am. It's dark outside, and I'm sore as fuck—both from digging graves all day and from sleeping on a plywood floor.

And probably from a few of the positions I twisted Rain into before I passed out.

I sit up and find her sitting with her back against the wall of the tree house and her legs straight out in front of her. She's staring out the entrance, lost in thought. That is, until I stretch and five different joints all crack at once.

She jumps and turns toward me, her shoulders sagging in relief a moment later. "I was wondering when you were gonna wake up."

"I didn't even realize I'd fallen asleep," I grumble, rubbing the back of my neck. "How long was I out?"

"I don't know. An hour, maybe two?"

"And still no horsemen, huh?"

Rain shakes her head. "I've been hearing gunshots in the distance but no hooves. This shit is killing me, Wes. It wasn't so bad when you were awake and …" She drops her eyes, and I can almost see her blush in the dark. "But, the whole time you were asleep, I've just been sitting here, waiting for the world to end. Why hasn't it happened yet? What the fuck are they waiting for?" Her voice cracks at the end, and I know it won't be long before she cracks, too.

I crawl over to her and kiss her worried brow. "I had a dream just now; it was like the nightmare, but … I think it was trying to tell me something. Come on." I kiss her again before climbing down the ladder.

"No, Wes! Where are you going?" she shrieks, peering down at me. The whites of her wide eyes almost glow in the dark as they jerk left and right, looking for any sign of danger.

"I'm going to prove to you that there's nothing to be afraid of. Come on."

Rain climbs down the ladder on trusting, trembling legs and holds my hand like a vise as we walk across the yard. The sounds of faraway gunshots and howling dogs and shattering glass tell me that I might have spoken too soon. Just because the horsemen aren't real doesn't change the fact that the whole world has lost its goddamn mind.

We still have plenty to be afraid of.

I pull the flashlight from my pocket and light our way as we enter through the back door, careful not to shine it anywhere near the mangled recliner. I lead Rain upstairs and feel her sweaty palm begin to shake in my grasp.

God, I hope I'm right.

We head into her room where she immediately shuts and locks the door behind us. Her hands are covering the lower half of her face, and it looks like she's on the verge of hysterics.

"Wes, just tell me what the hell is going on! Please!"

I grab her phone off the nightstand and swipe it open as quickly as possible. "I have to show you."

"The cell towers are down, remember? There's no service."

"You were listening to music earlier," I say, hunting for the app.

"Just what I have saved on my phone."

There.

I press the blue music note icon and find what I'm looking for. Turning the screen toward Rain, I point to the little black dot I noticed last night when I paused that incessant fucking song.

She crosses the room and stares at it in confusion.

"That's just a blown-out pixel." The screen illuminates the disappointment on her face.

"Maybe."

I turn the phone back around and take a screenshot of the music app. Using the camera tool, I zoom in on the image as much as I can. Then, I save it and zoom in on the second version even more. Sure enough, once it's large enough, the blip takes on the unmistakable silhouette that's been haunting our dreams for almost a year.

Rain's mouth falls open as she sees the image take shape. "What does it mean?"

"It means someone's fucking with us." I begin opening and closing every app on her phone, searching for more abnormalities. It doesn't take long to find another one. "Shit."

"What?"

I turn the phone toward her. "Open Instagram and pay attention to what you see before the feed comes up." I watch her face as a red light splashes across it. "Did you see it?"

Her eyes are two perfect circles as they lift back to mine. "Was that the banner?"

"It flashed too fast to be sure, but I know it was red and black."

Rain sits on the bed next to me and stares at the floor, taking it all in. "So, you're saying somebody's been *planting* these images in our heads?"

I nod, feeling sick to my stomach. "Subliminal messaging. And this is just what we can find on your phone. I'm sure we were being exposed to way more through TVs and tablets and—"

"Billboards."

Rain and I lock eyes as we try to make sense of our new reality.

"Who would do this?" she asks.

"I don't know. Could be anyone from a couple of hackers on a power trip to some third-world dictator trying to destroy modernized society."

"So, does this mean the apocalypse isn't coming? It was all just a sick joke to make us go crazy?"

I illuminate the screen on her phone again, turning it toward her so that she can see the clock for herself. "Considering that it's after midnight, I think it's safe to say that the apocalypse isn't coming."

"April twenty-*fourth*." Her voice is barely a whisper as I watch her face go through the entire range of human emotion, illuminated by the digital glow. Relief. Elation. Grief. Regret. Then, as the sound of approaching destruction begins to rise in the distance, pure, unfiltered dread.

The sound is like a never-ending car accident—metal scraping metal, crunching glass, and squealing steel.

And it's getting closer.

"Pack your shit and get ready to run," I snap, thrusting the phone into her hand. "Does your dad have any more guns?"

She nods blankly. "In the master closet."

I run across the hall with my flashlight, holding my breath to cope with the lingering stench of death in the room. Throwing open the closet door, I shine my light in all directions, not knowing where to look. There are scrubs and shoes and suits and dresses and—

Bingo.

The light lands on a black briefcase sitting on the floor next to the door— the kind that takes a code to open. Luckily, I have the code—in the form of a pocketknife. Jamming my blade underneath the brass plate, I pop the case open in three seconds flat, and the sight inside takes my breath away.

A Smith & Wesson .44 Magnum. Six-inch barrel. Black with a wooden grip.

Rain's dad must have been a *Dirty Harry* fan.

I lift the beast out of the molded foam cutout it's nestled into and check the cylinder.

And it's fully fucking loaded.

I shake my head in disbelief and kiss the barrel before tucking it into my holster.

For some reason, God likes me today. I hope I don't fuck it up.

When I get back to Rain's room, she's kneeling in front of her open window, gripping the ledge as she waits for whatever the fuck is coming. Her backpack is on her shoulders, almost bursting, and I can see that she's wearing a hoodie underneath it.

I cross the room and lean against the wall next to the window. "That sweatshirt had better not have a Twenty One Pilots logo on it." I smirk.

Rain looks up at me with fear carved into her beautiful face. "*That's* what you're thinking about right now?"

From here, I can see that the sweatshirt says *Franklin Springs High.*
Thank fuck.

I bend over and kiss her worried, wrinkled little forehead. "Try to relax, okay? The horsemen aren't real. Whatever is coming, it's human. And, if it's human"—I pull the left side of my Hawaiian shirt open to show her my newest acquisition—"we can kill it."

Rain's shoulders sag as she gives me a brave nod. "Sit."

She pats the carpet, and I notice a fresh bandage, antibiotic ointment, a pill, and a glass of water laid out on a paper towel beside her.

The sight makes me feel like I've been punched in the heart.

"Wes?"

I bite my lip and try to focus on the grinding, crashing, squealing noises approaching outside and not the stinging sensation behind my eyes.

"Baby, are you okay?"

Baby.

I've never been anybody's fucking baby, not even when I *was* a baby. But, for some fucked up reason that I don't understand, I'm hers. Maybe, one day, being treated like I matter won't hurt so goddamn much, but I hope not. I hope it guts me every time, forever, as a reminder that this girl is a fucking miracle.

"Yeah," I whisper, clearing my throat as I drop to my knees beside her.

Rain gives me a shy smile as she goes to work on my arm, jumping a little from the grinding, gnashing, crashing sounds getting closer outside. I pop the Keflex into my mouth and swallow it without taking my eyes off her.

"Why are you staring at me like that?" she asks, looking up at me through her long, dark lashes.

"Because I fucking love you."

The smile on her face lights up the dark room. It's the prettiest thing I've ever seen, and I suddenly can't wait for whatever is coming to get here so that I can kill it and turn its teeth into jewelry for her to wear.

Especially when another crash makes her gasp and cover that beautiful smile with both hands.

We look back outside as lights illuminate the highway. The overturned Corolla to the right of the driveway begins to lurch and move, scraping across the asphalt as Rain's eyes lift to mine.

"Listen to me." I cup her face in my hands, stealing her attention. Commanding it. "The horsemen aren't real. Do you hear me? Whatever that is, people are behind it. People who are gonna fucking die if they try to hurt a hair on your head."

Rain nods as the lurching sedan at the end of her driveway rolls sideways and takes out her mailbox. We both turn at the same time, watching as the force behind the shove comes into view.

"Is that a—"

"Bulldozer!" Rain takes off like a shot.

I grab my flashlight and take off after her, but by the time I make it downstairs, the front door is already wide open.

"Fuck! Rain, stop!"

I don't catch up to her until she's almost at the end of her driveway, jumping up and down and waving her arms. The bulldozer slows down as I dart in front of her, shoving her behind my back and grabbing the revolver under my arm.

"Well, got-damn!" a voice shouts from the cabin of the idling machine.

I shine my flashlight toward it and find Quinton and Lamar—the brothers from the hardware store—shielding their eyes from the beam.

I lower the light but keep my hand on my gun.

"You got it working!" Rain yells, jumping up and down behind me.

"I told y'all we weren't gonna get no damn flat!" Lamar shouts over the snarling engine.

"Finally got the damn thing up and runnin'," Quinton adds, "and none too soon. Rednecks in town done lost their damn minds."

"We're getting the fuck outta here," Lamar adds. "Y'all comin'?"

"Yes!" Rain shouts, peeking out from around my arm.

Quinton gives her a little salute, and I don't know if I want to blow his head off for looking at her like that or pat him on the back for making her so damn happy. Personally, I don't give a shit if we stay or go. As long as Rain is with me, we could live in a hollowed-out tree for all I fucking care. Supplies, shelter, self-defense—those are just icing on the vanilla-flavored cake now.

"We'll be right behind ya." I holster my gun and give the guys a nod.

I don't trust them—I don't trust anybody with a dick around my girl—but the survivor in me recognizes a good resource when it sees one.

I follow Rain as she tears back into the house, flying through the kitchen and into the garage. I shine the light ahead of me as I step into the musty, humid space and find a very excited Rain standing next to a very badass Kawasaki Ninja.

"Do you know how to drive it?" she asks, the contents of her backpack jostling with every bounce. "My mom never taught me."

"Fuck yeah, I do." I grin.

Rain runs over to the wall and grabs the keys off a hook while I shine the light above us, finding the emergency release latch for the garage door. I pull the red handle and then walk over and shove the heavy-ass door all the way up. The scraping and crashing of Quinton and Lamar's bulldozer clearing the highway fills the garage, but it doesn't sound like hell anymore.

To Rain, it sounds like heaven.

When I turn around, she's watching me, holding a black helmet and grinning with that wild, impulsive look in her eye. That look usually ends with me almost getting killed trying to save her ass, but I don't mind anymore. In fact, I have a feeling that's why I'm here.

Rain holds the helmet out to me, so I take it.

And shove it onto her head.

And kiss the visor with a smile.

Rain climbs on behind me and holds on tight as I fire up the Ninja. It purrs like a fucking kitten and has almost a full tank of gas.

Looking skyward, I say a silent, *Thank you,* as I twist the throttle, launching us out of the garage and onto the midnight highway beyond.

Rain squeals in delight, giving the house of horrors her middle finger as we pass.

I might not know where we're going or what we'll find when we get there, but I do know that, whatever it is, it's gonna have to go through me to get to her.

Me and my new pal, God.

PLAYLIST

THIS PLAYLIST IS A collection of songs that I either mentioned in *Praying for Rain* or that I felt illustrated a feeling or a scene from the book. I am grateful to each and every one of the brilliant artists listed below. Their creativity fuels mine.

You can stream the playlist for free on Spotify: https://spoti.fi/37b4BcH.

"400 Lux" by Lorde

"Alone Together" by Fall Out Boy

"Baby" by Bishop Briggs

"Black Wave" by K. Flay

"Cut Yr Teeth" by Kississippi

"Dark Blue" by Jack's Mannequin

"Eurotrash Girl" by Cracker

"Guns for Hands" by Twenty One Pilots

"Hard Times (Acoustic)" by Guster

"Hold On" by Flor

"Heavydirtysoul" by Twenty One Pilots

"I Know Places" by Taylor Swift

"I'm With You" by Vance Joy

"Little Heaven" by Toad the Wet Sprocket

"Love Story" by G-Eazy & Halsey

"My Blood" by Twenty One Pilots

"On Your Porch" by The Format

"Stolen" by Dashboard Confessional

"Twinkle" by Whipping Boy

"Wrestle Yü to Hüsker Dü" by The Dirty Nil

"You Can't Look Back" by Taking Back Sunday

BB EASTON

FIGHTING FOR RAIN

THE RAIN TRILOGY BOOK 2

*This book is dedicated to anyone who was ever afraid
but did the damn thing anyway.
Especially you, Staci.*

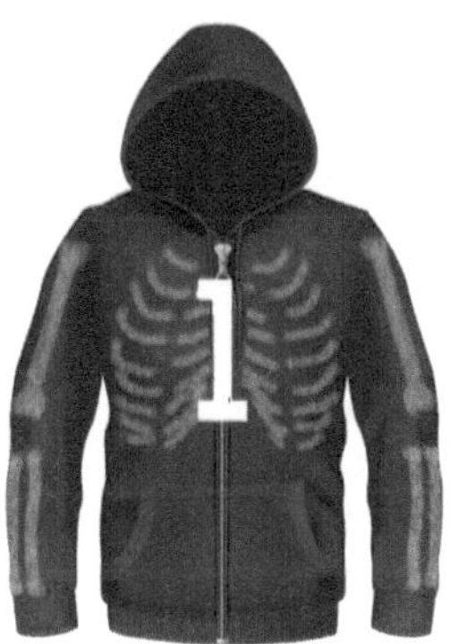

April 24, 1:35 a.m.
Rain

WITH MY ARMS AROUND Wes's waist and the roar of a motorcycle engine drowning out my thoughts, I turn and watch my house disappear behind us. My home. The only one I've ever known. The trees and darkness swallow it whole as we speed away, but they don't take my memories of what happened there. I wish they would. I wish I could pull this ache out of my chest and throw it into that house like a hand grenade.

I also wish I weren't wearing this damn motorcycle helmet. Wes should be wearing it. He's the survivalist. I don't really care if my head gets cracked open. All I want to do is lay my cheek on his back and let the wind dry my tears. Besides, the inside of it smells like hazelnut coffee and cold-cream moisturizer. Just like my mama.

Who's now buried in a shallow grave behind that house.

Right beside the man who killed her.

I might have survived April 23, but not all of me made it out alive. Rainbow Williams—the perfectly preppy, straight A–earning, churchgoing, trophy girlfriend of Franklin Springs High School basketball star Carter Renshaw—is buried back there too, right next to the parents she was trying so hard to please.

All that's left of me now is Rain.

Whoever the hell that is.

I curl my fingers into Wes's blue Hawaiian shirt and look over his shoulder at the black highway laid out before us. My friends, Quint and Lamar, are up ahead in their daddy's bulldozer, clearing a path through all the wrecked and abandoned vehicles that piled up during the chaos before April 23, but it's so dark that I can barely see them. All I can see is the road directly in front of our headlight and a few sparks in the distance where the bulldozer's blade is grinding against the asphalt. All I can smell are my memories. All I can feel is Wes's warm body in my arms and a sense of freedom in my soul, growing with every mile we put between us and Franklin Springs.

And, right now, that's all I need.

The rumble of the road and the emotional exhaustion of the past few days have me fighting to keep my eyes open. I nod off, I don't even know how many times, as we crawl along behind the bulldozer, jerking awake the moment I feel that first twitch of sleep.

Wes slows to a stop so that he can turn to face me. A lock of hair falls over one cheek, but the rest is pushed straight back and tangled from the wind. His pale green eyes are almost the only feature I can make out in the dark. And they don't look too happy.

"You're scaring the shit out of me. You've got to try to stay awake, okay?" Wes shouts over the sound of metal scraping asphalt up ahead.

I glance past him and see the headlights of the bulldozer shining on the roof of an overturned eighteen-wheeler. It's blocking the entire highway, but Quint and Lamar are hard at work, trying to push it out of our path.

I pull Mama's helmet off my head and feel her disappear along with her scent. It's replaced with the smell of spring pollen, pine trees, and gasoline.

"I know," I shout back with a guilty nod. "I'm trying."

A burst of sparks flies behind Wes as the bulldozer gives the tractor-trailer another good shove.

Wes puts the kickstand down and gets off the bike. "This is gonna take them a while. Maybe you should stand up and walk around a little. Might help you wake up."

He's just a silhouette, backlit by the haze from the headlight, but he's still the most beautiful thing I've ever seen—tall and strong and smart and *here*, even after everything he just witnessed. As I place my palm in his, the tiny orange sparkles of light glittering in the background match the ones dancing across my skin, giving me goose bumps, even under my hoodie.

I can't see his expression, but I feel Wes smiling down at me. Then, suddenly, his energy shifts. As I slide off the bike, he grips my hand tighter, lifting his head and inhaling so deeply that I can hear it, even over the grinding, crunching sounds coming from the bulldozer.

"Shit." The profile of his perfect face comes into view as he turns his head to look over his shoulder. "I think I smell—"

Before the word can even leave Wes's lips, the eighteen-wheeler explodes in a ball of fire. White-hot light fills my eyes and scorches my face as Wes tackles me to the ground.

I don't feel the impact. I don't hear the debris landing all around us. I don't even hear my own voice as I shout my friends' names. All I can hear are the thoughts in my head, telling me to get up. To run. To help.

Wes is looking down at me now. His lips are moving, but I can't tell what he's saying. Another explosion goes off, and I cover my face. When I lower my hands, he's gone.

I sit up and see Wes's silhouette running toward the bulldozer.

Which is now engulfed in flames.

"Quint!" I scream, taking off in a sprint toward the passenger side as Wes heads toward the driver's side. "Lamar!"

I climb up onto the track, thanking God that the fire hasn't made it through the blown-out windshield yet, and pull the door open. Inside, Quint and Lamar are slumped over in their seats, covered in broken glass. Wes is unbuckling Quint's seat belt. His head snaps up when I open the door, and his dark eyebrows pull together.

"I told you to stay the fuck there!"

"I couldn't hear you!" I lean into the cab, struggling to move Lamar's body so that I can unbuckle his seat belt.

"Rain, stop!" Wes snaps at me as he lifts Quint's lifeless body into his arms.

"I can help!" I get the belt off and give Lamar's shoulder a hard shake. His eyes flutter open as something begins to hiss and pop under the flaming hood. "Come on, buddy. We gotta go."

Lamar twists in his seat to try to climb out, but he winces and pulls his eyes shut again.

"Lamar," I shout, tugging on his shoulders. "I need you to walk. Right now."

His head rolls toward me, and the light from the flames illuminates a deep gash across his forehead. The dark red blood glistens against his dark brown skin. I pull on his arms harder, but he's so heavy.

"Lamar! Wake up! Please!"

Two hands clamp around my waist and pull me out of the cab just before a blur of Hawaiian print swoops in to take my place.

"Go!" Wes shouts as he pulls Lamar from the bulldozer. "Now!"

I jump off the track to get out of his way and run toward the motorcycle. As I get closer, I notice Quint's body lying on the ground next to it.

It isn't moving.

As I rush to him, my mind goes back to the day we met. We were in the same preschool class, and I found Quint off by himself on the first day of school, quietly eating Play-Doh behind Ms. Gibson's desk. He begged me not to tell on him. I didn't, of course. Instead, I sat and ate some with him just to see what all the fuss was about.

I found out years later that his daddy used to beat him whenever he got in trouble, so he got real good at not getting caught. His little brother, Lamar, didn't seem to learn the same lesson. He got caught all the time, but Quint always took the blame.

I kneel next to my very first friend and reach for his throat, hoping to find a pulse, but I don't get that far. I find a shard of glass sticking out of his neck instead.

"Oh my God." The words fall from my mouth as I grab his wrist, pushing and prodding and praying for a heartbeat.

Wes sets Lamar down next to me as another explosion rattles the ground below us. I scream and cover my head as the hood of the bulldozer lands with a clang about thirty feet away and skids to a stop.

Wes leans over and puts his hands on his knees to catch his breath. "He okay?" he asks, gesturing to Quint with a flick of his head.

"He's alive, but …" I drop my eyes to the glass sticking out of his neck and shake my head. "I don't know what to do."

God, I wish Mama were here. She would know. She was an ER nurse.

Was.

Now, she's dead.

Just like we're going to be if we don't get the hell out of here before that gas tank explodes.

I look around and realize that, with the light from the flames, I can actually tell where we are now. The sides of the highway are cluttered with all the cars and trucks that Quint and Lamar pushed out of our way, but the faded green exit sign on the side of the road says it all.

PRITCHARD PARK MALL

NEXT RIGHT

My eyes meet Wes's, and without saying a word, we get to work. He stashes the motorcycle in the woods, I drag the hood of the bulldozer over to make a stretcher for Quint, and Lamar shakes off his daze enough to stand and help carry his brother past the wreckage.

When we get to the exit ramp, Pritchard Park Mall sits at the bottom, shining in the moonlight like a worthless mountain of crumbling concrete. It's been rotting away ever since the last store closed up shop about ten years ago, but the land isn't valuable enough for anyone to even bother tearing it down.

"Fuck. Look at that place," Wes groans. He's holding one side of the makeshift stretcher while Lamar and I struggle with the other. "You sure about this?"

"I don't know where else to go," I huff, shifting my grip on the corner of the yellow hood. "We can't put Quint on the bike to take him home, we can't leave him here, and we can't sleep in the woods because the dogs will sniff out the food in our pack."

A howl rises over the sound of burning metal, pushing us to move faster.

"You okay, man?" Wes asks Lamar, changing the subject. He doesn't want to talk about what we might find inside this place any more than I do.

Lamar just nods, staring straight ahead. Quint's smart-ass little brother hasn't said a word since he came to, but at least he can walk. And follow directions. That's actually an improvement for him.

When we get to the bottom of the ramp, we find a chain-link fence circling the perimeter of the mall property. The sounds of gunshots, terrified screams, and revving engines fill the air—probably Pritchard Park rioters celebrating the fact that they survived April 23, but they obviously don't care about looting the mall.

They're smart enough to know there's nothing left to loot.

We walk along the fence until we find a spot that's been flattened. Then, we cross the parking lot and head toward what used to be the main entrance.

We pass a few cars with For Sale signs in their broken windows, kick a couple of hypodermic needles along the way, and eventually make it to a row of metal and glass doors. At least half of the windows have been broken out already, which makes the hair on the back of my neck stand up.

We're not the first ones here.

The bulldozer hood won't fit through the door, so we set it down on the sidewalk as carefully as we can.

"I'll go in first," Wes says, pulling the gun from his holster.

"I'm coming with you," I announce before glancing over at Lamar. "You stay with him."

But Lamar's not listening. He's staring at his big brother like he hung the moon.

And then fell from it.

"Don't you dare touch that glass," I add, pointing to Quint's neck. "He'll bleed out. Do you hear me?"

Lamar nods once but still doesn't look up.

When I turn back toward Wes, I expect him to argue with me about coming with him, but he doesn't. He simply offers his elbow for me to take and gives me a sad, exhausted, exquisite smile.

"No fight?" I ask, wrapping my hand around his tattooed bicep.

Wes kisses the top of my head. "No fight," he whispers. "I'm not letting you out of my sight."

Something in his words makes my cheeks flush. I should be afraid of walking into an abandoned mall with no electricity at night in the aftermath of The Apocalypse That Never Happened, but as Wes tucks me behind his back and pulls the broken door open, the only thing I feel is an overwhelming sense of belonging. I would follow this man to the ends of the earth, which, from the looks of it, might be right here at Pritchard Park Mall.

Wes guides us through the open door and eases it closed with the tiniest click. We tiptoe over the broken glass like professionals, and Wes leads the way with his gun stretched out in front of us.

The smell of a decade's worth of dust and mildew is overpowering. I have to clench my teeth and cover my nose with the sleeve of my hoodie to keep from coughing. The only source of light inside is the moon shining in through a few dirty skylights, but I came here so many times as a kid that I know the layout by heart.

At the end of this hall, there should be a fountain in the middle of a two-story atrium. I remember there being escalators behind it and elevators on the left—cool glass ones that I used to beg Mama to ride over and over and over. Branching out from the atrium, there are four hallways—this one leading to the main entrance, the north hallway that leads to the old food court, and two more on the left and right that lead to the big department stores that Mama always said we couldn't afford to shop at.

Even though I remember coming here as a kid, there's no sense of nostalgia. No warm familiarity. It's so dark and so vacant that I feel as though I'm walking on the moon and being told that it used to be Earth.

As the crumbling edges of the stone fountain come into view, the sound of voices in the distance has me pulling Wes to a stop.

I push up onto my tiptoes until my lips graze the shell of his ear. "Do you hear that?" I whisper. "It sounds like—"

"Freeze!" a voice shouts as the silhouette of a man holding a rifle appears from behind the fountain.

Instinctively, I hold my hands up and step in front of Wes. "Don't shoot!" I shout back. "Please! Our friends outside are hurt. We just need a place to spend the night."

"Rainbow?" His voice softens, and I recognize it instantly.

It's one I've heard say my name a thousand different times in a thousand different ways. It's one I never thought I'd hear again, and after I met Wes, never wanted to. It's the voice of the boy who left me behind.

"Carter?"

I thought April 24 was going to be a new beginning.

Turns out, it's just the beginning of the end.

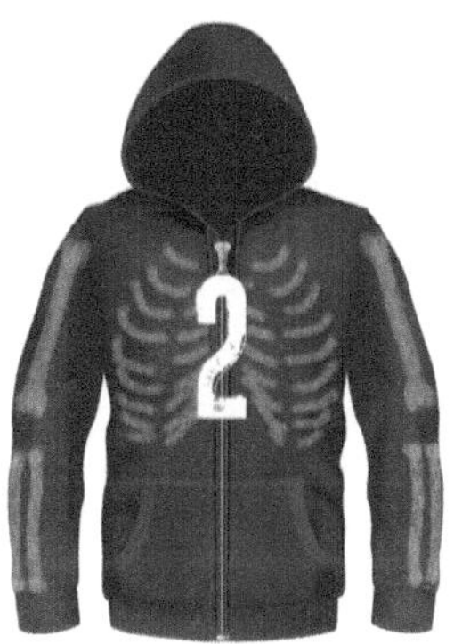

Wes

CARTER.

His name on her lips hits my ears like a blaring, screaming alarm clock, waking me from the best dream of my life.

It all seemed so real. I can still feel the heat of her thighs around my waist and see the tears glistening in her big blue eyes when she told me she loved me. When she promised she'd never leave. And I believed her.

Like a fucking dumbass.

The impending apocalypse made people do crazy shit. Some burned entire cities to the ground. Some, like Rain's psychopathic dad, committed murder-suicides just to get it all over with. And me? I let myself believe the desperate ramblings of a lost, lovesick teenager.

But the four horsemen never came for us.

Reality did.

And from the looks of him, he's about six foot three.

Even though I feel like the world is tilting on its axis and there's an invisible knife twisting in my pancreas, I keep my cool as Reality jogs toward my girl.

No, not my girl. *His* girl.

I've done this so many times; it's almost second nature now. Standing in the Department of Child and Family Services while yet another foster parent gave me back. Standing against the lockers in my fuckteenth high school, acting like I didn't give a shit whether anyone talked to me or not. Standing behind the bar at work, watching whatever chick I was fucking at the time kiss her boyfriend goodbye in the parking lot.

Fold your arms across your chest. Keep your posture loose. Look bored. You are bored. People are so fucking boring. Yawn. Light a cigarette. Damn, no cigarettes.

Rain doesn't move as he approaches. She doesn't lift her arms for a hug, but that doesn't stop LeBron James from wrapping his four-foot-long arms around her and lifting her off the ground.

My teeth clench together, and my blood fucking boils as he goes to kiss her, but on the outside, I'm the picture of indifference.

Do what you want. I don't care.

You don't care.

Nobody fucking cares.

Rain turns her head before his lips can make contact and grunts, "Ugh! Carter, what are you doing? Put me down!"

He's just a shadow, but the whites of his eyes almost glow in the dark as they go wide and glance over at me.

I smirk and raise an eyebrow, but it's just for show. Kind of like Rain's performance right now. I'm not stupid enough to think this means she isn't going to go back to him. I know she is. I've seen this episode before.

"What am I doing?" His voice wavers as he sets her back on her feet. "I fucking missed you! I never thought I'd see you again. And you're *here*. You're … *alive*."

Rain shoves him with both hands, and he takes a step backward, more out of shock that she pushed him than her actual strength.

"No thanks to you!" she screams. *Screams.* It knocks the dust off the rafters and scares a bird into flight.

I grip the handle of my gun and listen for footsteps. That pigeon can't be the only thing she just woke up.

"What was I supposed to do?" Carter reaches for her, and she shoves him again. "I had to go with my family!"

Yep. This is the part where she guilt-trips him for leaving …

"One town over? I thought you were in Tennessee!"

"We were in a bad car accident and got stranded here." The giant huffs and drags a hand through his hair. "I'll tell you about it in the morning, okay? Come here."

"Stranded?" Rain swats his giant hands away. "You could *walk* back to Franklin Springs from here! It's twenty miles, max!"

"You know it's not safe to be on the roads! Especially with all the supplies we'd be carrying."

"You wanna talk to me about not being safe? You have no *idea* what I went through while you were gone!"

Aaaaand this is the part where she uses me to make him jealous …

"I almost died! Wes, how many times did I almost die?" She keeps her back to me as Carter's head swivels in my direction.

Even though my throat is so tight that I can hardly breathe and I have to put my hands in my pockets to keep him from seeing that they're balled into fists, I manage to keep my voice unaffected when I say, "I dunno. Ten? Twelve? I lost count."

"Who the hell is *he*?" Carter thrusts a massive hand in my direction, and Rain looks at me over her shoulder.

I lock eyes with her, my feelings safely hidden behind a well-worn costume of confident apathy, and silently ask the same question.

Yeah, Rain. Who am I? Your substitute boyfriend? Your April 23 distraction? Your meal ticket? Chauffeur? Gravedigger and personal bodyguard? Just say it so that I can get the fuck out of here and go find something to break.

Rain takes a deep breath and smiles at me in a way that almost makes me think she means it. Her porcelain face lights up, illuminating the dust-thickened air around her, and her shiny blue doll eyes look wild and alive. I know that look. That's the look she gets before she does something stupid and impulsive.

"He's my fiancé." She beams.

Motherfucker.

My shoulders slump, and any doubt I had about her motives leaves me in a bitter, sharp sigh.

"Fiancé?" Carter jerks his head back as if he's been punched, but Rain isn't even facing him anymore.

She's walking toward me with a sway to her hips and a smirk on her beautiful fucking face.

"I just left a month ago! And besides, why the fuck would you get engaged if you thought we were gonna die yesterday?"

"I knew we weren't gonna die," Rain says, standing beside me and wrapping a delicate hand around my bicep. "Wes is a survivalist."

Carter throws his free hand in the air in exasperation as I look down at my girl. *His* girl.

Fine. I can play this game—the one where she pretends to care, and I pretend to believe her. I've been playing it my whole life. At least now, I know where I stand.

I thought April 24 was going to be a new beginning.

Turns out, it's just the same old shit but with no Wi-Fi.

"Hey, guys? We got trouble!" Lamar's voice coming from the mall entrance breaks up our happy little reunion.

We turn and run toward him as the sound of motorcycles revving and guns firing and people shouting builds outside.

"Shit," Carter hisses. "Bonys."

"What are Bonys?" Rain asks, but as Carter pushes the door open with one long arm, we're able to see for ourselves.

Dozens of motorcycle riders have blazed over the downed section of fence around the mall and are doing doughnuts and firing semiautomatic weapons into the air in the parking lot. Bullets leave their guns in orange bursts as they howl at the moon, matching the Day-Glo orange stripes painted on their clothes to look like skeleton bones.

"Oh my God! Is that Quint?" Carter slides his rifle around so that it's hanging down his back and leans over to get a better look at the guy we left outside.

In this light, I can see that Carter is no Franklin Springs redneck. The guy has brown skin and a mop of curly, dark hair, and he's wearing a fucking Twenty One Pilots T-shirt.

I think about the oversize Twenty One Pilots hoodie Rain was wearing when I first met her, and I have to resist the urge to kick his teeth in.

"We can't fit the hood through the door, so we're gonna have to lift him." Rain is in doctor mode, which is pretty much the only time she takes the lead on anything. "Wes, help me hold Quint's head and neck still, so the glass doesn't move. Lamar and Carter, you guys each take a leg. Come on! Now!"

Luckily, the doorway is shadowed by an awning, so the Bonys haven't noticed us yet. We do as Rain said and move Quint's lifeless body inside. The first empty store on the left has its metal gate down and locked, but the third shop is wide open. We shuffle inside and set Quint on the floor behind the checkout counter.

A faded sign on the wall announces that this place used to be called Savvi Formalwear.

Formalwear. In Pritchard Park. No fucking wonder this place went out of business.

Lamar kneels next to his brother and holds his hand while he feels for a pulse, and the sight of them knocks the air out of my lungs. I know that fucking feeling. I know what it's like to lose your only sibling. To find her quiet and cold in her crib. The moment I see Lily's blank, bluish face in my mind, I feel like I'm being choked. Strangled. I can't get out of there fast enough. I mumble something about guarding the door as I stumble backward out of the store.

Rain calls after me, asking for her first aid kit, so I tear her backpack off my shoulders and toss it onto the floor as I bolt.

I don't stop until I get to the entrance, bracing my forearms on the metal door handle and sucking in lungfuls of humid air through the broken glass.

Fuck, I hate it here.

The Bonys—or whatever they're called—are still tearing it up outside. I watch them in a jealous rage. Carter seemed afraid of them, but they look like they're having a good fucking time if you ask me. Not a care in the—

Suddenly, the entire mob takes off toward the road in front of the mall. It's so dark that I can't make out what triggered them to leave until their headlights close in on a dude riding a bicycle with a backpack on. Even from across the parking lot, I can see the terror on his face as they descend upon him like piranhas. His screams are loud enough to rise over the roar of their engines, and when they finally race off, there's nothing but some twisted metal and a fleshy lump in the road where a living, breathing man just was.

"Oh, good. They're gone." Rain's breathy voice sounds like heaven compared to the noises I just heard.

I tear my eyes away from the cadaver in the street and turn toward her, relieved to see that she's alone. I open my arms and hug her—I don't know why. I guess I just need to hold her before the next thing comes to try to take her away.

Rain hugs me back, and for a minute, we just stand there and take it all in.

"How's Quint?"

Rain sighs. "He's alive, but I don't know how long I can keep him that way. If I take the glass out, he'll lose too much blood, so I just cleaned him up and left it in. I'm hoping his body will push it out on its own. I heard that's a thing."

I force a reassuring smile and kiss the top of her head. "Yeah, that's a thing."

"Lamar's gonna stay with him tonight."

"Good."

"And Carter went back to his post by the fountain. He said he's on guard duty tonight."

"So, he's watching us right now."

Rain nods against my chest. "Probably."

I let her go and take a step back, searching her face for signs of sincerity. "And that whole thing about us being engaged …"

Rain blushes and drops her eyes. "I had a dream a few nights ago that we were lying in Old Man Crocker's field, and you made me a little engagement ring out of a blade of grass." Rain lifts her left hand and stares down at her empty finger. "It seemed so real, you know? Until you turned into a scarecrow and the four horsemen of the apocalypse came and set you on fire."

"You sure you weren't just trying to make your boyfriend jealous?"

Rain drops her hand and looks at me as if I just spat on her shoes. "Are you serious right now?"

"As a fucking heart attack."

"I said it because that's how I feel, Wes. I don't want to call you my *boyfriend.* I've had one of those, and it didn't feel like this." Rain casts a glance over her shoulder at the dark hallway stretching out behind her and the man-child sitting in the shadows beyond. "But considering that you didn't even fight for me back there, I'm guessing that you don't feel the same way."

I grab Rain by the jaw and pull her into the shadows of the storefront doorway right next to us. I hate the way her eyes go wide in fear, but it's taking all of my self-control not to scream in her face right now.

"Listen to me," I hiss through gritted teeth. "When I found you last night, I thought you were fucking dead." I spit the words out, remembering how heavy her lifeless body felt in my arms. How her hands dangled at her sides and her head fell back as I clutched her to my chest and cried against her cold, slack cheek. "For the first time in my life, I thought about killing myself. If I hadn't finally found your pulse, I was prepared to lie down right next to you and blow my own fucking brains out, so don't tell me how the fuck I feel."

Rain's mouth falls open in my palm as her eyebrows pull together in pain. "Wes …"

"I'll fight to keep you alive. I'll fight to keep you safe. But I will *never* fight to keep you, or anyone, from leaving me."

A tear slips from the corner of Rain's glassy eye and rolls down the edge of my index finger to her parted lips. Reaching out, she places one tiny hand over my heart, over the place where thirteen jagged tally marks tell the world how many foster homes I was kicked out of, how many times I wasn't good enough, how many times I fought to stay and was left behind anyway.

Then, she says the words that make me want to put my fist through the glass shop window beside her head, "You'll never have to."

I tilt her face up and kiss her salty, wet mouth until her breath becomes ragged and her hands begin to claw at my belt buckle. Carter can't see us—I made sure of that when I pulled her over here—so I know this isn't just for show. Rain actually believes the four little words she just whispered.

If only they were true.

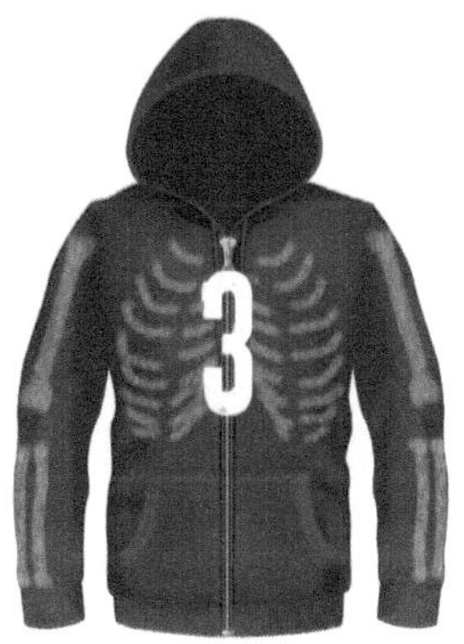

Rain

"PLEEEEEASE!" I CRY, TUGGING on Mama's hand and leaning with my whole body toward the Hello Kitty store. "I promise I won't beg for nuthin'! I just wanna look. Real quick! Pleeeeease?"

"Rainbow, stop it," Mama snaps, looking around at all the other shoppers. "You're making a scene."

"But Tammy-Lynn got a Hello Kitty binder for her birthday!"

Mama's eyes get softer, and I know I got her. She never lets me get nuthin' at the mall unless it's my birthday, and it just so happens that I'm gonna be eight in exactly three days.

"One thing, okay? And you can't have it until your birthday."

"Yes, ma'am!"

This time, when I yank Mama's hand, she lets me pull her into the store, and it's like a Hello Kitty wonderland in there. Purses and T-shirts and lamps and stuffed animals and bath mats and bedsheets and, "Oh my God, slap bracelets! Look, Mama! Look!"

"One thing, Rainbow. And hurry up. We still have to get you some new shoes for school."

Shoes!

I run to the shoe wall and drool as rows and rows of Sanrio characters stare back at me from the sides of sneakers and sandals and even fuzzy little bedroom slippers. But one pair calls out to me. I grab the black low-top Converse with Badtz-Maru's cute little face right on top.

"I want these, Mama! Please?"

My mother scrunches her face up as she takes the shoebox out of my hands. "The grumpy penguin? Out of everything in this store, you want the black grumpy-penguin shoes?"

I bite my lip and nod all my nods.

Mama turns the box sideways in her hands and reads the description of my favorite Hello Kitty character out loud. "Bad Badtz-Maru is a mischievous little penguin who has dreams of becoming the king of everything one day. Although he's bossy and he has a bit of an attitude problem, Badtz is a loyal friend to Pandaba and Hana-Maru. When he's not getting into trouble, Badtz-Maru can be found collecting pictures of movie stars who play his favorite bad guys?" *Mama's voice goes up at the end like she's asking a question. "Rainbow!"*

"What, Mama? He's my favorite! Look how cute he is!"

"Cute? He's scowling."

I stick my finger out and stroke his frowny little canvas beak. "He just needs somebody to love him. That's all."

Mama sighs and slaps the lid on the box. "Fine, but only because it's your birthday."

We check out, and I don't even let the cash register lady put my shoes in a bag. I just hug the whole box to my chest and wait for the receipt to print. It prints and prints and gets longer and longer until it touches the floor.

I look up at the lady, but she's gone. Everybody's gone. The store is empty, and it smells bad, like the attic. Everywhere I look, the lights are off, and the shelves are empty. Even the shoe rack. The counter that was just shiny and white a second ago is now covered in dust so thick that I could write my name in it with my finger.

The receipt is still printing, so I follow it out the door and into the hallway. The benches are rusty now. The floor tiles are all cracked, and some even have grass growing in between them. And the sale banners that used to hang from the ceiling don't say Sale no more. They're all red with demon people riding black, smoke-breathing horses on them.

I don't like it here. I wanna go home.

I turn in circles, trying to find Mama, but she's gone too.

It's just me and Bad Badtz-Maru. Even though he's just on a pair of shoes, I know he'll protect me. He's going to be the king of everything one day.

I follow the receipt out the door and into the parking lot. It's empty now. More scary banners hang from the light posts, but I ain't afraid of them. I'm mad *at them. They made everything go away. They made Mama go away. So I stomp over to a junky old car and climb up on top of it, all the way to the roof. Then, I reach up and pull one of those banners right down.*

"There!" I yell, throwing it on the dirty ground. "See? You're not so—"

But I don't get to let all my words out before these real, real loud motorcycles drive up super-fast from all around me. The people driving them are dressed like skeletons, and some of their helmets have spikes on them.

I wonder for a minute if they're friends with the demon horse riders. I hug my shoebox tighter, hoping they won't be mad about me ripping down their friends' banner, but then they do something even worse than ripping the banners down. They start lighting them on fire!

I cheer and put my fist in the air like people do in the movies.

They hate the horsemen too! Maybe they'll help me. Maybe they know where everybody went. Maybe they can take me to my mama.

A few of the skeleton people see me and start driving their motorcycles in a circle around the car I'm on.

I smile. "See, Badtz," I whisper to my shoebox. "It's gonna be okay. We found some new friends."

There's a guy on the back of one of the motorcycles, and he's pouring something all over the car out of a big red jug. Some of it even splashes up onto my shoes.

"Hey!" I shout, taking a step back.

I wonder if maybe the guy driving will tell his friend that he's spilling his water, but he doesn't. Instead, he pulls to a stop right in front of me, flips open a fancy lighter—the silver kind that Daddy uses to light his cigarettes—and tosses it onto the hood of the car.

I wake up with a gasp, my eyes darting left and right, looking for signs of danger faster than my foggy brain can process what they're seeing.

I'm sitting on the ground inside the mall. My back is against Wes's chest. His arms are around my shoulders. In front of me, I can see the broken-out windows of the main entrance. It must have rained while we were asleep. There's a puddle creeping toward us from the door.

And one of my hiking boots is already soaked.

We're tucked inside of the same store entrance we hid in last night. The metal gate is down and locked, but I know without even peeking through the slats which shop it used to be. I can practically smell the Hello Kitty bath bombs and body sprays clustered around the checkout stand.

Wes tightens his grip around my body and grinds his teeth in his sleep. I want to let him hold me a little longer, but I can tell that whatever he's dreaming about is about as fun as being set on fire by Bonys.

"Wes." I tap his thigh, which is about all I can do with the death grip he has on me. "Wake up, babe. It's morning."

Wes swallows and yawns and rubs my upper arms with his hands as he comes to. "Hmm?"

"It's morning. We made it."

Wes shifts his weight and sits up straighter behind me. Then, he lets his forehead drop to my shoulder with a groan. "You woke me up for that?"

I laugh. "I thought you were having a nightmare. Did you see the horsemen?"

He grumbles something into my hoodie that sounds like a no.

"Really? Me either! I saw the banners, but the horsemen never came." I frown, thinking about how the Bonys were about to light me on fire, but at least it was something new. After spending a year dreaming about the four horsemen of the apocalypse killing everyone on April 23, getting burned alive by a deranged motorcycle gang feels like an improvement.

"Yeah, I saw the banners too." Wes yawns and lifts his head. "But then everybody turned into zombies and tried to eat us. I got to hack your boyfriend up with a machete though, so it wasn't all bad."

"Wes!" I turn sideways in his lap, ready to snap at him for using the B-word again, but the sight of him hits me like a ton of bricks.

His soft green eyes are rimmed with red. His jaw is peppered with stubble. His face is covered in dirt and ash, and the collar of his blue Hawaiian shirt has Quint's blood on it. The reality of what we've been through comes crashing down around me as I gaze into Wes's beautiful, battle-worn face.

It happened. All of it. The eighteen-wheeler explosion. The overdose. The house fire. The shoot-out at Fuckabee Foods. My parents …

Wes gets blurry as my eyes fill with tears. I squeeze them shut, trying to block out the images of my daddy in his armchair and my mama in her bed. Their faces … oh my God.

They're really gone, and the apocalypse never came to make it all go away.

I cover my mouth with the sleeves of my hoodie and look up at Wes. "What are we gonna do now?" My voice breaks along with the dam holding back my tears.

Wes pulls me against his chest and wraps his arms around me as an ocean of grief drags me under. "Don't you remember what I told you?" he asks, rocking my jerking, trembling body from side to side.

I burrow my face into the side of his neck and shake my head, gasping between sobs.

How can I remember what to do? I've never lost my entire family in one day before.

But Wes has.

"We say *fuck 'em* and survive anyway."

"Right." I nod, remembering his pep talk from two days ago.

"So, what do we need to survive today?"

I sniffle and lift my head. "You're asking *me*?"

"Yep. In order to say *fuck 'em* and survive anyway, the first thing you have to do is say *fuck 'em*, and the second thing you have to do is figure out what you need to survive. So, figure it out. What do we need?"

"Uh …" I wipe the snot and tears from my face with my hoodie sleeve and sit up. "Food?"

"Good." Wes's tone is surprisingly not sarcastic. "Do we have any?"

"Um …" I look around until I spot my backpack in the opposite corner of the entryway. "Yes. And water but not much."

"What else do we need?"

I look at the puddle inching closer to us. "A better place to sleep."

"Okay. What else?"

My eyes drop to the torn, bloodstained spot on Wes's sleeve. "You need to take your medicine. You need a new bandage too, but my hands aren't clean enough to do it."

"So, we'll add *find soap* to the list."

I nod again, surprised at how relieved I feel. Empowered almost.

"So we need supplies and shelter …" he summarizes. "What else?"

"Hmm …" I pull my eyebrows together and look around, hoping to find some clue in the dank, dusty, cobweb-covered hallway.

Wes clears his throat and taps the handle of the gun sticking out of his holster.

"My daddy's gun?"

"Self-defense." He smirks. "Supplies. Shelter. Self-defense. Every day, when you wake up, I want you to ask yourself what you need to survive that day, and then your job is to go find it."

"That's it?"

"That's it."

"Okay." I nod once, like a soldier accepting a mission. "So today, we need soap and water and a better place to sleep."

I like this—having a goal again. Taking direction. It feels like it did back when we were searching for the bomb shelter. When it was just me and Wes against the world. It was almost fun.

Wes smiles, but his tired green eyes don't even crease at the corners. There's a sadness in them that feels new. He usually looks so determined, so focused. Now he just looks … resigned.

"See?" he says, letting his fake grin fall as two miserable mossy eyes bore through me. "You got this."

"*We* got this," I correct.

"Yeah." Wes swats me on the side of my butt and waits for me to climb off his lap. "Well, *we* have to take a piss, so … time to get up."

We both stand, and I watch as he stretches and cracks his neck from side to side. He's gone—I can feel it. The fiery, passionate Wes that I was just beginning to get to know has become the Ice King again. Cold. Hard. Good at slipping through my fingers.

The air temperature seems to drop ten degrees as he breezes past me and over to the main entrance. When he doesn't hear anything outside, he pushes it open with his gun drawn and disappears into the foggy morning.

Wes said my job was to figure out what I need to survive and go get it.

But I already let it walk out the front door.

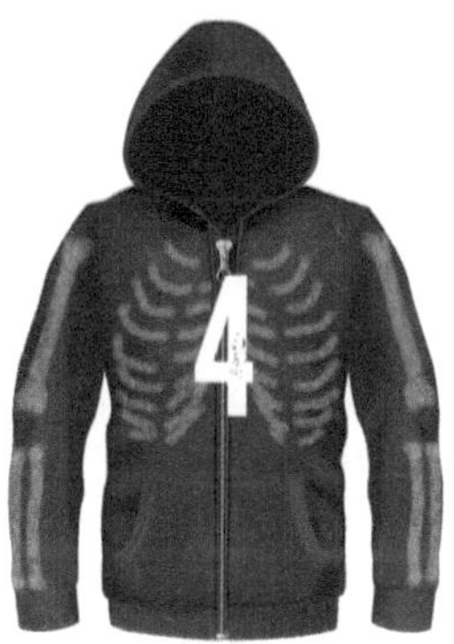

Wes

I'VE GOT MY DICK in one hand and my gun in the other as I piss on a dead bush outside of Pritchard Park Mall. No sign of the Bonys yet. I have a feeling they're not exactly morning people.

Fuck knows I'm not.

I zip my shit up, wishing like hell that I had a cigarette.

Rain's dad probably had a whole stash in their house somewhere.

I look past the parking lot, through the chain-link fence, and up the ramp to the overpass. The eighteen-wheeler wreckage is maybe a hundred feet before the exit, hidden from view by the woods—just like Rain's mom's perfectly good motorcycle. I feel the weight of the key in my pocket, calling to me.

Leave before you get left, it says.

I chew on my bottom lip. Then, I reach into my pocket and pull out the key.

Leave before you get left.

I look down at the keychain in my palm for the first time since grabbing it last night. Attached to the metal ring is a frayed strip of leather, knotted on both ends and strung with a dozen mismatched plastic beads. The ones in the middle spell out *I ♥ MOM.*

Leave, dumbass—

"Wes? Are you still out here?"

"Yeah." I spin around as Rain peeks her head out of one of the broken entrance doors.

Her big, round, puffy eyes lock on to me, and a giant smile spreads across her tear-streaked face. "One down, two to go."

I pull my eyebrows together, but before I can ask what she's talking about, Rain pushes the door open with her boot and holds her sparkling clean hands up so that I can see them.

"I found soap!"

I pocket the keychain and follow Rain back to the tux rental place where Quint and Lamar spent the night. Quint is still behind the counter, unconscious. His neck is bandaged, but the shard of glass is still there, poking out through the gauze. Lamar is sitting on the floor next to him with his back to the wall, and gauging by the bags under his eyes, I think he stayed up all night watching his brother breathe.

"The employee bathroom still has soap in the dispenser!" Rain chirps, pointing toward a hallway on the right side of the shop. "No running water though. I had to use some of the bottled stuff. Sit." She gestures toward the checkout counter.

I lean against it and toss a glance at Lamar. "You okay, man?"

He nods, but his eyes never leave his brother's face.

I wish I had something encouraging to say, like, *I'm sure he'll be okay*, or, *Rain will fix him up*, but the motherfucker hasn't moved a muscle since I pulled him out of that bulldozer last night. For all we know, he could be brain-dead.

Rain sets her backpack on the counter next to me and starts rummaging through it. She pulls out what's left of the antibiotics, a bottle of water, a first aid kit, and a handful of protein bars. I twist the cap off the orange pill bottle and shake a white tablet into my mouth as she peels back my bandage and takes a peek.

She exhales in relief and pulls it the rest of the way off. "It looks so much better, Wes."

I glance down at the mangled gash on my shoulder, laid open by that fucker's bullet, and hear Lamar suck his teeth behind us.

"Better than *what*? Got*damn*, that shit is *nasty*."

I cough out a bitter laugh. "You shoulda seen the other guy."

I picture those two gangbangers dropping to the ground in a spray of bullets and blood and broken glass. Then, I remember the horror I saw on Rain's face the moment she realized that she was the one who'd pulled the trigger.

It's the same look that's on her face now.

Shit.

I reach over and give her arm a squeeze. I forgot that she's not exactly happy about being a murderer.

Rain pretends not to notice as she places a new bandage on my upper arm, pressing the edges down with delicate fingers. Her touch makes all the other broken, hollowed-out places in me scream and beg for her attention too.

Goddamn, it hurts.

"Where's your daddy, Lamar?" Rain asks, changing the subject away from the shooting.

"Home." He punctuates his one-word sentence by spitting a wad of phlegm on the ground.

"He still alive?" Rain asks, trying to sound nonchalant, but I can hear her swallow that lump in her throat from here.

"I fuckin' hope not," Lamar grumbles.

She tucks her chin to her chest and begins shoving everything back into her backpack, probably to hide the fact that her hands are shaking.

Lamar opens his mouth like he's about to ask her about her own piece-of-shit dad, but then he shoots to his feet and sucks a deep breath in through his nose. "Y'all smell that?"

"Smell wha—" I inhale and can practically taste scrambled eggs on my tongue. "Holy shit."

"Breakfast time, bitches!" Lamar slaps the filthy counter and heads out the door.

I guess the only thing that can pull him away from his big brother is the promise of food that doesn't come out of a can. Typical teenage boy.

"What about Quint?" Rain asks, her eyes shifting from the open doorway over to me.

"He's not going anywhere." I sigh, tossing the protein bars back into Rain's backpack. "Come on. Let's go see what your boyfriend made you for breakfast."

Rain

Neither of us speaks as we walk through the atrium, following the smell of food.

I try to be tough, like Wes. I stand tall, take long steps to match his, but everything I look at reminds me of her. The escalators I used to beg Mama to let me ride over and over are just metal stairs now. The glass elevator with the big, glowing buttons I loved to press is stuck on the bottom floor—its only passengers a few Burger Palace wrappers and a plastic chair. The three-tier fountain that Mama and I used to throw pennies into is now full of weeds and baby pine trees. And, instead of Christmas music, all I hear is broken tiles clattering under our boots and the sound of voices coming from the direction of the food court.

Everything hurts. My eyes burn. My chest aches. My family is gone. The world I knew is gone. And all I want to do is curl up in that plastic chair in that broken elevator and cry myself to death.

But I know Wes won't let me, so I keep going. I keep trying to breathe. I keep trying to remember what was on my survival to-do list. But mostly, I keep trying to figure out what I can do to get Wes back. *My* Wes. Not this detached tough-guy version.

As we pass through the atrium and approach the food court, I wish the walk had been longer. I'm not ready for this.

There are people everywhere. I was expecting Carter and his family and maybe a few other stragglers who had made their way here after getting stopped by the wreck, but this is at least twenty people, talking and laughing and sitting at tables that have been clustered into small groups. The left and right sides of the food court are lined with fast-food counters. The back wall has an exit that's been barricaded shut with tables. The merry-go-round in the corner is still there, but it's tilted to one side and blanketed in cobwebs. And in the center, Carter's dad is standing next to a flaming barrel with a metal grate on top, cooking something in a cast iron skillet.

"Mr. Renshaw!" I cry, bounding over to the human teddy bear.

Carter's dad looks like a lumberjack Santa Claus—all beard and belly—and he always gives the best hugs.

His face lights up when he sees me, which is half a second before I tackle him and burst into tears.

"Come on now …" He chuckles, his deep voice vibrating against my cheek. "I ain't that ugly, am I?"

"Rainbow? Oh my goodness, child." Mrs. Renshaw's voice is husky and warm as she walks up and smooths her hand over my shorter hair.

She's tall and heavyset, like Carter's dad, but that's where their similarities end. Mrs. Renshaw is a no-nonsense black woman who was an assistant principal at our school before the world fell apart. She used to have a sleek, shoulder-length bob, like a TV reporter, but now her hair is cropped in a super-short Afro, probably due to the lack of hair salons in the Pritchard Park Mall.

"Shh …" she coos. "We should be celebratin', not cryin'. It's April 24. Come on now. Let's get you somethin' to eat. You must be starved."

When Carter's mom goes to fix me a plate of scrambled eggs from the skillet, I notice Wes standing a few feet away. The way he's watching us, with those intense eyes and that bored expression, makes me cry even harder. Because as much as I love Carter's parents, it's Wes's arms I want to be wrapped in right now. It's his punishing kisses and powerful hands that could make this pain go away. It's his love that could replace what I've lost.

But he's gone too.

Just like in my dream, Wes is nothing more than a scarecrow now, waiting to be burned.

Once I catch my breath, Mrs. Renshaw sits us down at a table nearby. The fake wooden surface is cleaner than anything I've seen in the mall so far, just like the metal chairs surrounding it. They obviously get some use. Carter and Lamar are at the table next to us along with Sophie, Carter's ten-year-old sister. She rushes over and hugs me from behind. Her dark corkscrew curls are wild, same as the other boy who's watching me right now.

Carter's eyes are a warm brown, but his stare is cold and questioning as it flicks from me to Wes.

"We haven't been properly introduced," Mrs. Renshaw says, extending her hand across the table to Wes.

"Oh, sorry." I pull my gaze from Carter to his mother. "Mrs. Renshaw, this is Wes. Wes, this is Carter's mom and dad." I reach up and tug on one of the curls smooshed against the side of my face. "And this little brat is Sophie."

"Hi!" Sophie giggles and squeezes me one more time before taking her seat by her brother.

"Wes and Rainbow here are *engaged*," Carter announces to the group, his voice oozing sarcasm.

Everyone's eyes fall on me as I squirm in my seat and stare at my untouched plate of food.

"Engaged?" Carter's mom echoes, dropping her fork.

I can't even speak. My cheeks burn with embarrassment and rage and shame as people who thought I would one day be their daughter-in-law stare at me like I have two heads.

"Yep," Carter sneers, looking at me like a cat that just found a rubber mouse. "Why don't you tell us how he popped the big question, Rainbow? Or did *you* ask *him*?"

"Carter!" his mother hisses in warning. "Stop it."

I go to push my chair out, ready to run away and hide until my face goes back to its regular color, but Wes's arm clamps around my shoulders before I can take off. He still feels cool and distant, but his icy aura is soothing now, like a balm.

"Can I tell the story, sweetheart?" Wes's voice is steady and strong, like his fingers as they stroke my upper arm.

I nod and slump against his side, wishing I could disappear altogether.

"So, after *you* left Rain in Franklin Springs with her deranged father … he took a shotgun to her mom's face while she was asleep, blasted a hole in Rain's bed—which he didn't know was empty at the time—and then redecorated the living room with his own brains."

I wince and cover my face with my hoodie sleeves as everyone in the food court gasps and goes silent.

"I met her … I don't know … was it the next day, baby?"

I nod against his chest, too stunned to cry and too mortified to look up.

"When I found her, she was high as a kite, getting her ass kicked in the middle of Burger Palace over a bottle of painkillers."

"Oh, Rainbow. I'm so—"

"She goes by Rain now, and I'm not finished," Wes snaps, cutting off Carter's mother. "Since you guys left, she lost her parents, got shot at, got trapped in a house fire, tried to overdose, and … what else, honey? Oh yeah, she almost got blown up in an eighteen-wheeler explosion last night. So, if you're asking how we got *engaged* instead of why she's crying and looks like she's been through a war zone, you never fucking cared about her in the first place."

I wait for Carter's mom to slap him across the face, but all I hear is a single slow clap coming from the group of tables at the back of the food court. I open one eye and see a girl about my age, maybe younger, walking toward us with the swagger of a gangster. She looks like she might have had green hair at one point, but it's faded to the color of decaying leaves and is twisted into messy dreadlocks. Her rounded nose has a hoop through it, and her baggy black T-shirt and pants look like they came from the men's big and tall section at Walmart.

Everyone in the food court cowers as she passes.

"That's the most fun we've had around here since the internet went down." She twists her full lips into a smirk, still clapping at a painfully slow rate.

Wes's grip around my shoulders loosens, and his energy goes cool again.

"What's your name, *Hawaii Five-0*?" Her hazel eyes are the same color as her yellowish-greenish-brownish hair. They cut over to me once and darken before darting back over to the man next to me.

"Wes," he says flatly.

"Well, *Wes*, welcome to my kingdom." She spreads her arms and glances around the food court. "I'm Q. That stands for queen, 'cause I'm the muhfuckin' monarch up in here. Me and my crew been runnin' this place goin' on three years now. You and y'all other stray cats"—she flicks her fingernails at the rest of us sitting around the table—"are guests in my castle. That means y'all gon' have to pull y'all's weight, or you gon' get put out." Her angular eyebrows shoot up in warning as she points toward the barricaded exit.

"Ya boy Carter here"—she points a lazy finger at my ex—"is on patrol duty. *Duck Dynasty* over here hunts birds and deer and shit from up on the roof. And mama bear"—she points to Mrs. Renshaw—"cooks it all up real nice. But y'all …" Q taps her fingertips to her lips as her eyes roam from Wes to me to Lamar. Then, she snaps her fingers. "Y'all gon' be my scouts."

"Scouts?" Wes's body language is relaxed, but his tone is challenging.

"That's right. We're runnin' low on shit now that all y'all strays are up in here. *Somebody* got to do some shoppin'."

"I can't leave," I blurt out. "Please. Let me do something else. We have a hurt friend, and somebody has to stay here to take care of him."

Q eyes me suspiciously. "You good at shit like that?"

"Like what?"

"Like nurse-type shit."

I sit up and nod. "My mom is … *was* … an ER nurse. She taught me a lot."

Q snaps again and points one long fingernail right between my eyes. "Good. You gon' be my medic. And you can start with that one." She swings her finger from my face to Mr. Renshaw's.

I glance at Mr. Renshaw and watch the color drain out of his rosy cheeks. "Don't let me down now." Q cackles as she sashays back to her table, full of other rough-looking, gun-toting, unwashed teens. "I'd hate to have to feed y'all to the Bonys."

They're runaways, I realize.

We're all just strays and runaways.

Turning to Carter's dad, who hasn't spoken a word since we sat down, I ask, "Why do you need a medic, Mr. Renshaw?"

He gives me a sad smile. "That ain't important right now. What's important is that you know how sorry we are about your folks, Rainbo—I mean, Rain." Carter's grizzly bear of a dad looks at Wes, remembering what he said about my name, and gives him a solemn nod.

Mrs. Renshaw reaches across the table and squeezes my hand. "I am so sorry, baby girl." Her dark brown eyes glisten as they bore into mine. "I knew we shoulda taken you with us—you and your mama. I won't ever forgive myself for that, but at least we're all together now."

Lamar and Sophie both get up to hug me and give their condolences, but my attention is focused solely on Carter. The boy I grew up with. The boy I gave all my firsts to. The *man* who should be consoling me right now. But instead, he's just staring at me like he doesn't know what to say.

"Rainbow …" he finally mutters.

"Rain," I snap back.

His honey-colored eyes fill with remorse, and for a second, I regret being so mean. That face … I was in love with that face for as long as I can remember. I know every angle. Every expression and smile and dimple. It kills me to see him hurting. I want to curl up in his lap and let him wrap his long arms around me like he used to …

But then I remember overhearing Kimmy Middleton say she made out with him senior year, and suddenly, I don't feel so bad anymore.

"Hey, Carter, remember Kimmy?" I watch the guilt crawl across his handsome face, and it's all the validation I need. "She burned your house down."

"What?" Mrs. Renshaw screeches. "Our house?"

Carter's eyes go wide and dart from me to his parents.

Sophie starts to cry.

Mr. Renshaw stands up, slams his chair in, and stomps away with a definite limp.

"What happened to him?" I ask, desperately wanting to change the subject after the bomb I just dropped on them. "Why does he need a medic?"

Mrs. Renshaw shakes her head and looks over her shoulder as her husband hobbles toward the atrium. "We got in a bad accident on our way out of town. As soon as we left for Tennessee, it was obvious that everybody on the highway was under the influence of something. People were speedin' and weavin' all over the road. We had only made it to Pritchard Park when a car up ahead of us pulled in front of a tractor-trailer and made it jackknife right in the middle of the road. It ended up rolling about three times and blocking the entire highway. There was a huge pileup, and we were caught right in the middle of it."

"Oh my God." I cover my mouth with the sleeve of my hoodie. "That pileup is why we're here too. We couldn't get around it, and when we tried …" My voice trails off as I glance over at Lamar.

He's staring blankly in the direction of the tuxedo shop, like he can see his brother from here.

Mrs. Renshaw is looking at her children the same way. "Sophie and Carter were okay—thank God. But Jimbo …" She shakes her head. "His leg was crushed in the accident, and he won't let anybody look at it. I'm afraid it's bad."

"So that's why you guys didn't come home?" I ask. "Because he couldn't walk that far?"

Mrs. Renshaw nods.

"Plus, the dogs and Bonys," Carter adds, staring at the table like a kid in the principal's office. "We never would have made it."

"So we decided to stay here. We had enough food and supplies in the car to last us this long, and Q has been gracious about sharing the drinking water from their rain barrels with us."

Q.

I glance over at the runaways' table and catch her watching us.

No. Not *us*.

Wes.

"When we woke up this morning and the apocalypse hadn't happened, I thought …" Mrs. Renshaw's chin buckles. "I thought maybe things would go back to normal. Maybe we could go back home."

Carter's mom tries to hold it together, but as soon as she looks over at Sophie, her face crumples like a paper towel. I've never seen Mrs. Renshaw cry before, and knowing that my words made her do it makes me want to throw up. I was so cruel. My mama had taught me better than that. I was trying to hurt Carter on purpose, and this is what I get.

Carter, Sophie, and I all jump up at the same time to comfort her. Sophie kneels at her side and clasps her hand while Carter and I end up standing on either side of her, squeezing her shoulders and rubbing her back.

"I'm so sorry," I mutter, speaking to Mrs. Renshaw but finding my eyes drifting up to Carter's.

"Me too." His deep voice vibrates around me, taking me to a million different places at once.

I know what his voice sounds like when he's sleepy, when he's sick, when he's lying, when he wants me to take my clothes off, when he's angry, when he's frustrated, and when he's playing the part of Mr. Popular. I know what it sounded like when he was six years old and lost his two front teeth at the same time. And now, I know what it sounds like when he's just plain lost.

"You can have my house, Mrs. Renshaw," I say, tearing my eyes away from her son. "I'm never going back there again."

Wes

"WES, WAIT!" RAIN CALLS out, but I just keep walking.

I'd rather give myself a root canal than sit around for another second of this precious little family reunion.

"Rainbow!" Carter yells after her.

I turn around at the sound of his voice, only because I want to watch her choose him. *Them*. I need to see it. I need to feel the twist of the knife because I know that's the only fucking way I'll be able to let her go.

"Sorry. I meant, *Rain* …" Carter has this bullshit, pitiful puppy-dog look on his pretty-boy face, and I want to put my fucking fist through it. "Can we go somewhere and talk? Please?" He pulls his eyebrows up so high that they disappear behind his mop of curly black hair. Then, he bites his bottom lip.

Motherfucker. I know that look. I invented that fucking look.

"Not right now, Carter," Rain says, picking up her untouched plate of eggs. "I have to go check on Quint."

Not right now? How about not fucking ever?

I feel my muscles tense and my teeth grind together as I glare at the piece of shit in the Twenty One Pilots T-shirt, but by the time his eyes land back on me, I'm loose as a motherfucking goose. I roll my neck and stick my hands in my pockets like I'm waiting in line at the DMV, not thinking of all the ways I could crack his skull open.

Rain turns and walks toward me, her face flushing when she realizes I stopped to watch their little exchange, but I keep my face slack and my posture relaxed.

You're not mad. You're bored. Bored, bored, bored.

Everybody knows how this show is gonna end. Rain becomes a Renshaw. She gets her happy little family back. They have two-point-five kids who can dunk from the foul line and don't even need therapy. The. Fucking. End.

I wait for her to catch up. Only a jealous, bitter asshole would turn his back and keep walking right now, and I'm not jealous.

Nope. I'm just so fucking bored.

Rain's face looks tortured as she approaches, and I feel the fire inside me die down. Her right cheek still has three pink claw marks on it from when she got attacked at Burger Palace. Her lips are chapped. Her hair is matted. And her big, round eyes look like two empty swimming pools now.

Drained.

Dull.

Desperate.

I hate how badly I want to be the one to fill them back up.

A moment before Rain closes the distance between us, gasps and shrieks and, "Oh my God!"s fill the food court. I look past her and see that every digital monitor behind every fast-food counter is on and glowing red.

"Wes?" Rain's voice is barely a whisper as she comes to stand beside me. "What's going on?"

I watch as the black silhouette of a hooded horseman holding a scythe flashes on-screen for less than a second.

"Did you see that?"

I nod.

Another one flashes—this time, the horseman with the sword. Then, another and another. Faster and faster, their images appear and disappear until the screens are just pulsating black-and-red pools.

People scream.

Sophie dives for her mother's arms.

And Rain grips my bicep so hard that her nails break the skin.

"Maybe this is just the nightmare," I say in a half-assed attempt to make her feel better.

"It's not, Wes. It's real."

"None of this is real, remember? It's all just a hoax."

"Citizens," a female voice with a French accent booms through the speakers, drawing my attention back to the screens.

The face of a middle-aged woman with mousy-brown hair, sharp features, and dark red lipstick fills the left side of the screen while the word *citizens* is written in at least twelve different languages on the right side.

"My name is Dr. Marguerite Chapelle. I am the director of the World Health Alliance. If you are seeing this broadcast, congratulations. You are now part of a stronger, healthier, more self-sufficient human race."

Rain and I look at each other as dread slithers across her face and into my veins.

The camera zooms out, and Dr. Chapelle is sitting at a sleek white table with an older man on either side of her. Behind them, on risers, are at least eighty other assholes, all wearing suits that probably cost more than the mortgage payments on their Malibu summer homes.

The smug bastard front and center is our fucking president.

"For the past year, the World Health Alliance has been working in conjunction with the United Nations"—she gestures to the world leaders standing behind her—"to implement a solution to the global population crisis. A *correction*, if you will. We call this correction Operation April 23."

"Wes, what is she talking about?" Rain whispers, gripping my arm tighter.

"Approximately three years ago, our top researchers discovered that, at the rate that our population was growing, Earth's natural and economic resources would be depleted in less than a decade. To put it bluntly, human beings were facing extinction, and the cause was simple—our species had abandoned the law of natural selection."

The camera pans to the man on her left, a skinny guy with a haircut like Hitler's. The caption below his face says, *Dr. Henri Weiss, World Health Alliance Researcher.* "Every s-species on the planet is s-subject to the law of natural selection," he says, tugging at his collar and taking a sip from his glass of water. His accent sounds German, and he looks like he's about to shit himself. "It is the very f-foundation of evolution. Since the dawn of living organisms, the weaker, more infirm members of the s-s-species die off, and the strongest, most intelligent, most well-adapted members live the longest and procreate the most. This p-process promotes the survival of the species by ensuring that each g-g-generation inherits only the most adaptive genetic traits and by p-p-preventing resources from being depleted by nonproductive s-s-s-subgroups."

The camera slides back to the French bitch. "Over the past century, human beings have become the first species to ever circumvent the law of natural selection. Through advances in technology and lavish government programs, we have been actively prolonging the lives of our weakest, most disabled, and most dependent members of society to the great detriment of our entire species."

She gestures to President Dickhead standing behind her.

"The American government, for example, spends over one trillion dollars each year housing, feeding, and caring for its disabled, incarcerated, and unemployed citizens—citizens who contribute nothing in return. As a result, the World Health Alliance calculated last January that the number of disabled and nonproductive members of our species outnumbered able-bodied, productive members for the first time in the history of any species. Immediate action had to be taken."

The camera cuts to the man on her right who looks a little like Mr. Miyagi from *The Karate Kid*. The caption below his name reads, *Dr. Hiro Matsuda, World Health Alliance Researcher.* "We needed a way to thin the herd, so to speak, while ensuring that the strongest, healthiest, most intelligent members of our species would survive. Engineering a super virus or inciting a world war would have been … counterproductive … due to the loss of healthy, able-bodied citizens that would have resulted. Therefore, my team and I came up with a plan to introduce a global stressor so intense that it would trigger our least resilient citizens to behave in self-destructive ways while simultaneously encouraging our most resilient citizens to become even stronger and more self-reliant."

The images of the horsemen appear again, eliciting gasps from the audience, but this time, they're presented as icons at the bottom of the screen.

"The Four Horsemen of the Apocalypse, the Grim Reaper, Death— these archetypes have appeared in almost every society throughout history. By planting these iconic images in every digital media source worldwide— paired with a single date: April 23—we were able to tap directly into the collective human subconscious and plant the idea of an impending doomsday."

"Oh my God, Wes," Rain whispers, looking up at me like a child who just found out that the Easter Bunny wasn't real. "Those images you found in my phone—you were right."

"Worldwide subliminal messaging." I shake my head.

Only it wasn't at the hands of some evil corporation or a band of sniveling computer hackers on a power trip, like I thought. It was worse.

It was our own fucking government.

"We all owe Dr. Matsuda, his team, and our world leaders a debt of gratitude." The French bitch grins. "Operation April 23 was a brilliant success. Our researchers estimate that our global population has been decreased by as much as twenty-seven percent with most of the relief coming from our nonproductive subgroups."

"What does that even mean?" Rain whispers.

"It means that most of the people who died because of the April 23 hoax were either crazy, sick, poor, or old."

I watch Rain's face go pale, and I wish I could take it back.

Shit.

I pull her against my chest and press my lips to the top of her head. I don't even know what to say. All I can do is stand here and hold her while the government tells her they're happy that her parents are dead.

"In an effort to protect the law of natural selection going forward and to ensure that our population never again faces extinction due to our irresponsible allocation of resources to the weakest, most dependent members of society, all social services and subsidies are to be discontinued.

Life support measures are to be discontinued. Government-provided emergency services are to be discontinued, and all incarcerated members of society will be released."

The entire food court erupts in outraged shouts and hushed murmurs as people try to process what the fuck this lady just said.

"You are encouraged to resume your daily lives. Power, water, and cell service have been restored, and the images you just saw have been removed from all digital media. Go back to work. Provide for your families. Protect yourself and your community. Your government will no longer do these things for you. And should you see evidence of a person or group of persons defying the laws of natural selection, you are required to dial 55555 on any cellular device to report the misconduct. Agents from your area will be dispatched immediately to detain the suspect. The future of our species depends on your cooperation. Good luck, and may the fittest survive."

The monitors go black as the reality of our situation slowly begins to take hold.

It was all just a fucking hoax.

They invaded our dreams.

They terrorized us from the inside out.

They drove us insane and watched while we self-destructed.

Then they smiled and said it was for our own good.

I wish I could say I was surprised, but after everything I've been through, this just feels like a regular Tuesday. Get shit on. Get beat down. Get told it's your fault. Then, get kicked to the curb with everything you own in a trash bag over your shoulder.

Yep, that sounds about right.

The only family in the room is clinging to one another for support. Offering comfort. Rationalizing that everything is going to be okay. Encouraging each other to trust in our leaders and do as they say.

Meanwhile, the homeless kids in the back of the room are jumping up and down, cheering and waving their guns in the air, while Q stands on a table shouting, "It's the wild, wild west, muhfuckas! Pew, pew, pew!"

The way Rain is wrapped around me, it's obvious which group she belongs in.

It's also obvious that I don't belong here at all.

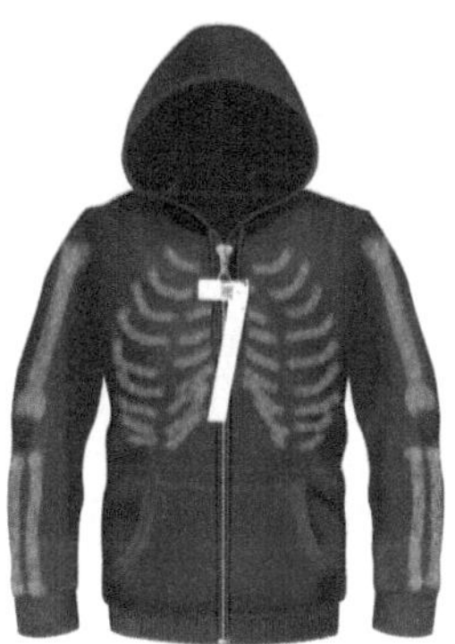

Rain

"DUDE, THIS PLACE HASN'T had power in, like, forever, right? How in the hell did they make the TVs come on?" Lamar asks from his perch on the counter, his heels banging into the cabinets below with every swing of his restless legs.

Wes shrugs. "I dunno, man. Maybe they flipped the entire power grid on just for the broadcast?"

I'm only half-listening to their conversation. The rest of me is busy staring at the unconscious boy behind the counter. The one with the glass shard sticking out of a bloody bandage on the side of his neck. The one I'm supposed to fix somehow.

The one I'm *going* to fix somehow.

"Rain?" Wes asks.

"Huh?" I reply without taking my eyes off of Quint.

"You okay? You haven't said a word since the announcement."

"*The announcement*," I mutter, turning to face Wes. "Is that what we're gonna call it from now on? Like the way everybody called the apocalypse *April 23* 'cause it sounded nicer?"

Wes chews on his bottom lip like he does when he's trying to figure something out.

When he's trying to figure *me* out.

"I know that was a lot to process, okay? *I know.* But I need you to stay focused. Don't freak out on me."

"I'm not freaking out."

Wes tosses a doubtful glance at Lamar.

"I'm not. Maybe I just don't feel like talking about the fact that the government just publicly patted themselves on the back for makin' my dad try to kill his whole family."

Wes exhales hard through his nose and nods. "Yeah, I get that."

"I know he was *nonproductive*. He was depressed … unemployed, paranoid, mean as a snake, addicted to everything he could get his hands on … but what about *her*?" The prickly heat of anger in my flushed face fades as my throat tightens with emotion. "She was so good, Wes." I picture my mama's beautiful, frazzled, selfless face, and I want to cry. She was the most productive member of society I'd ever met. There are so many things I want to say, so many feelings I haven't expressed yet, but they're all too damn painful, so I cover my mouth with the sleeves of my sweatshirt and hold them all in.

I stare at Wes's lips, hoping the words coming out of his mouth will help take my mind off the ones lodged in my throat.

"I know. But we can't change what happened. All we can do is say *fuck 'em* and survive anyway, right? So, how are we gonna survive today? Do you remember your list?"

I swallow down all the things left unsaid and force myself to answer him.

"I … I was supposed to find soap, water, and shelter." I take a deep breath and straighten my back. "I already found soap, and Mrs. Renshaw said that Q has water barrels, so that only leaves shelter."

The lips I'm staring at widen and part, revealing Wes's dazzling smile. I don't get to see it often, but when I do, it warms my skin like the sun, seeping into my pores and filling me with pride.

I feel my own lips curve upward, mirroring his. I did something right.

"That's my girl," Wes says with that grinning mouth, but the moment the words pass over his upturned lips, his smile deflates like a popped balloon. He didn't like the way they tasted. This new, detached Wes didn't like calling me *his* girl.

So my lips fall flat too.

We stand there for a minute—me staring at his serious mouth and him staring at mine—until Wes finally takes a step back and gestures with his hand toward the door. "Let's go find you some shelter."

You.

"Let's go find you *some shelter."*

I want to take his arm as I make the short trip across the store, but I'm afraid I'll prick my finger on the barbed-wire fence he's building between us.

I don't know what's going on with Wes, but he's eerily quiet as we walk down the hallway. I yank on the metal gates and locked doors of every storefront we pass, but he just follows four feet behind me with his arms folded across his chest.

The distance between us feels like it's doubling with every step I take.

I turn right at the fountain and head down the hallway, angry tears stinging my eyes.

Hope momentarily chases them away when I spot an old shoe store up ahead with the gate raised. I poke my head inside and peek over the empty chest-high shelves. The vinyl benches that were once used to try on shoes have been clustered together in the center of the store and arranged like living room furniture. Carter's dad is sitting on one with his head bowed as Carter's mom and sister stand with their backs to me, probably telling him all about *the announcement.*

"Never mind," I whisper, slinking backward out of the store. "This one's taken."

When I turn to continue my walk, I find Wes waiting for me with his back against the graffiti-covered wall outside the shoe store. His Hawaiian shirt is open, revealing his bloodstained white tank top and the hint of a gun holster underneath. His head is tilted back, staring up at one of the skylights as if it were clear enough to actually see through, and his profile is the picture of perfection. The sight of him takes my breath away, replacing it with a hollow, empty ache in my chest.

He looks exactly like the man I fell in love with a few days ago. The one who rescued me from an angry mob, got shot for me, ran back into a burning building to find me, and buried my parents' bodies just to help take away my pain. He looks like the man who refused to let me go when everybody else had left me behind.

But he did let me go. He must have.

Because this guy sure as hell ain't him.

"You're not even helping me look," I snap, stomping past his cool exterior without stopping.

"You're right." Wes's voice is infuriatingly calm as he pushes off the wall.

"Is this some kind of test?" I hiss, rattling the next gate a little harder. "I have to do everything on my own from now on, is that it?"

"Nope," Wes says from somewhere behind me. "I'm not helping 'cause I'm not staying here."

"What?" I turn to face him, blood thumping in my ears. "Why not?"

That damn eyebrow goes up again. "Hmm. Maybe 'cause there's no running water. No electricity. Maybe I don't feel like being the errand boy for a group of crazy-ass, gun-toting homeless kids. Or, I don't know, maybe I don't wanna live down the hall from your fucking ex and his little Norman Rockwell family."

"What do you want me to do, Wes?" I turn my back on him and stomp toward the next storefront.

"Leave. With me. Right now. We can find a new place. One with water and power and doors that lock and walls that don't have black fucking mold growing on them."

I sigh, letting my hand linger on the rusty metal. "I can't leave Quint here. You know that."

"So, we'll take him with us. We could drive the Ninja back to town, gas up your dad's truck, and then come back and get him."

"What about Lamar?" My voice takes on a shrill tone as a strange sense of panic washes over me.

"He could ride in the back with Quint."

I turn and walk past the next entrance without stopping. The gate is up, but it's obvious somebody's been living in there for a while now. Maybe a few somebodies. Clothes and mattresses and beer cans and random, mismatched patio chairs are strewed around like confetti.

"What about Mr. Renshaw?" I ask, quickening my pace. "He's hurt too."

"You can make all the excuses you want. I know the real reason you don't want to leave."

"Oh, yeah? What's that?"

Because I'm too scared. Because I'm too sad. Because no one is trying to rape or rob me in here. Because nothing in here reminds me of home.

When Wes doesn't say anything, I turn to find him watching me with that emotionless expression on his filthy, beautiful face.

"You think I want to stay because of *him*?" I snap.

Wes raises one eyebrow as he nonchalantly chews on the inside corner of his mouth.

"Oh my God. I have friends here, Wes. I have a—"

"*Family*?" His tone is smooth as ice, but his eyes are hard and accusing.

"No … a *purpose*. I can help people here. I feel safe in here. Out there …" I shake my head, thinking about what's waiting beyond those doors. "Out there, it's nothing but Bonys and bad memories."

Wes opens his mouth to reply as I yank on the next metal gate. I brace myself for the impact of his words, but instead, my ears are assaulted by the sound of squealing gears when the gate jerks to life in my hands.

The rusty metal squeaks and shimmies as it rolls up to the ceiling, revealing the hollowed-out interior of an old Barnes & Noble bookstore.

My mouth falls open as I step inside. "Oh my God. This used to be my favorite place in the whole mall."

It's dark inside, but there's enough light from the skylights in the hallway to see my way around. The checkout stands are to the left of the entrance, right where I remember. The coffee shop, or what's left of it, is to the right. There are rows and rows of empty shelves in the center of the store and dust-covered tables lining the main aisle.

"I remember Mama bringing me here for story time when I was a kid," I continue, talking more to myself than to Wes. "They had a train set right back there, and these little stools that looked like tree trunks, and"—I gasp as my eyes climb up a wooden ladder in the far-left corner of the store, leading up the trunk of a cutout, cloud-shaped oak tree—"a tree house!"

I sprint down the main aisle, looking for signs of life between every row of shelves. When I don't find anything except for trash, standing water, and the occasional forgotten book, I head over to the children's area.

Please don't let anyone be up there. Please, God. Please let me have this one thing …

I reach out with a hopeful hand to grasp the ladder, but Wes beats me to it. Taking the rungs two at a time, he climbs to the top and shines his pocket flashlight into the wooden shelter. Then, without a word, he clicks it off and hops back down, landing before me with a graceful thud.

"Well?"

"Well, what?" His face is unreadable, but the air around him is charged.

"Any runaways living up there?"

"Nope." Wes props his elbow on the ladder and leans over me, causing me to tilt my head back to make eye contact. "It's all yours."

"You mean, ours," I whisper, frozen to the spot by his icy stare.

Wes shakes his head. Slowly.

Panic shoots through my veins as I realize what he's saying.

"Don't go." I shake my own head, much faster, as sudden, uncontrollable tears blur my vision. "Please. Please stay here with me. I can't do this without you, Wes."

"Yes, you can."

"I don't want to!"

I step up onto the bottom rung of the ladder and place my hands on Wes's shoulders, so that we're eye-to-eye. "Remember yesterday? We were just like this. I was on the ladder of my tree house, and you were on the ground, and the sun was setting over there"—I point one hand in the direction of the hazy, sunlit entrance—"and I told you I loved you, and you said you loved me too."

"You thought the world was about to end." Wes's tone is condescending and doubtful, but his hands on my waist are begging me to make him believe.

"So did you."

"I meant what I said."

"So did I, Wes. I still do."

Seconds go by as I let that sink in. Wes doesn't say a word. He doesn't move a muscle, but his heart is beating so hard that I can feel the air vibrating off his chest in sonic waves. His hands tighten around my middle, and his nostrils flare as he sucks in silent breaths.

I can almost hear the sound of cracking ice.

I force a smile even though I'm terrified and bring one hand up to stroke his rough cheek. "Hey … if I'm not allowed to freak out, then you're not allowed to either."

Wes nods his head maybe a fraction of an inch. It's so subtle that I almost miss it, but in that whisper of movement, he lets me see the real him. The one who is panicking just as badly as I am.

"Look around, baby. It's still just you and me … and a tree house." I smile and gesture above my head. "Carter being here doesn't change anything. I don't want to stay because of him. I know that's what you think, but you're wrong. I want *you*. I love *you*. Don't you see that?"

Wes swallows the distance between us in a single step and crashes his lips against mine. When he presses my back against the ladder and invades my mouth with his tongue, I taste his relief. When he lifts my thigh over his hip and rocks against me, I feel his desperation. And when his hand slides up the back of my head and fists my hair, I feel his need.

This isn't a goodbye kiss.

It can't be.

I raise my arms and gasp for air as Wes pulls my hoodie and tank top off over my head in one motion. Then, I dive for his mouth again. The only time I feel truly alive is when I'm kissing this man. He's like a live wire—calm and quiet on the outside but a raging electrical storm within. One touch, and I'm rooted to the spot, lit up and blazing hot as his power surges through me. It scrambles my thoughts, blasts through all my fears, and leaves me humming and vibrating and yearning for more.

Wes strips himself of his shirt, holster, and tank top. Then, as soon as his hands are free, they reach for me. Rough palms caress my exposed skin and tear at the clothes preventing them from touching more. Wes yanks my lacy bra down around my waist and feasts on the curve of my neck as he kneads my aching breasts. I arch my back and cling to the ladder rung above my head as his soft, warm mouth trails wet kisses down my chest. All I can do is hold on, paralyzed by the current of pleasure flowing through me, as Wes swirls and sucks and drags his tongue over each of my tight, tender nipples.

He places one of my feet on his thigh and makes quick work of my bootlaces. In a few seconds, both of my hiking boots join the growing pile of clothes on the ground, and Wes's hands move straight to my zipper. I go to reach for him, but he places my hand back on the wooden slat above me.

"Don't move," he growls, yanking my jeans and panties down my thighs. "I want you just like this."

Once I'm completely naked, Wes takes a step back and admires me. Stretched out on the ladder. Arms up. Back arched. Breasts wet from his mouth and heaving with my every breath.

Even in the dark of the bookstore and behind that curtain of brown hair, I see the moment his eyes darken. A shiver cascades down my spine as Wes licks his full bottom lip and unfastens his jeans. I swallow as his thumbs hook into his waistband, shoving his pants and boxers down just enough to free himself, and I feel my heart sink as his hand wraps around his hard cock.

I wanted to make love to Wes.

But it looks like the Ice King just took his place.

Wes's eyes don't meet mine as he stalks toward me. They linger on my body as he strokes his length. Even though my heart is breaking, slick heat trickles between my thighs as my back arches toward his ghost. I'll take this man any way I can get him even if the version I'm getting isn't him at all.

"Fuck," Wes hisses, snaking his hands down my sides, over my hips, and around to squeeze my full ass.

Wes spreads me apart as he pulls my body toward him, guiding his thickness into the slippery mess between my thighs. He groans, pushing my hips away from him and pulling them right back. I hold on to the ladder with both hands as he drags his smooth flesh between my folds. His head is bowed as he watches himself disappear between my thighs.

He won't look at me.

He won't even look at me.

"Wes," I cry, my voice breaking with need.

His eyes snap up, softened by surprise, and I catch a glimmer of the man inside. Reaching out with one hand, I cup his hard jaw, holding it in place so that he can't look away.

"Stay with me," I beg, my eyes darting back and forth between his. I hope he hears me. I hope he feels all the ways that I mean those words.

Hooking my thigh over his hip, Wes presses the tip of himself against the core of me. He blinks, but he doesn't look away as he fills me slowly. His pale green eyes are a tortured mix of agony and ecstasy as they bore into mine, but they're honest, and they're open, and for once, they do as I say.

They stay.

Wes's jaw muscles flex beneath my fingertips as we click into place, and for a moment, we're as close as two people can be. The intensity of that stare is paralyzing. The feeling of his bare skin against mine, intoxicating. The heat of his breath and the thump of his heart and the pulsing need where we're joined are overwhelming.

Then, he closes his eyes.

He withdraws.

And when he thrusts forward again, it's not sweet and slow.

It's hard and cold.

Wes's fingertips bite into my thigh, holding me in place as his hips surge forward in deep, punctuated, violent motions. He's fucking me like he's stabbing me. Like he's trying to rid himself of his pain by burying it in my flesh.

So, I cling to the wooden rung above my head and take it. All of it.

Because Wes's pain still feels better than mine.

His eyebrows crease, and his lips part. And all I want to do is make whatever he's feeling go away. So, I lean forward and do the only thing there is left to do. I press a kiss to his perfect lips.

Wes stills for a moment. Then, he wraps his arms around my body so tight that I can hardly breathe. He devours my mouth, taking everything I have to give as he fills me to my limit.

Wrapping my arms around his neck, I coil my right leg around his waist for support as he grinds against my over-sensitized flesh. I was wrong before. *This* is as close as two people can get.

Wes isn't showing me his brave face or his guarded face. He isn't showing me his face at all.

He's showing me his fear.

The moment I feel him swell and jerk inside of me, my body detonates, contracting around him suddenly and violently. I whimper into his mouth with every surge of pleasure and swallow his quiet moans of pain.

He doesn't pull out, doesn't break our connection. He holds me and kisses me until he's making love to me again, and I'm hit with a sickening sense of déjà vu.

This is exactly how he made love to me yesterday up in my tree house—passionately, endlessly—as if it were our last night on earth.

I didn't think this was a goodbye kiss, but maybe I was wrong.

Because the last time Wes tried to tell me goodbye, it felt exactly like this.

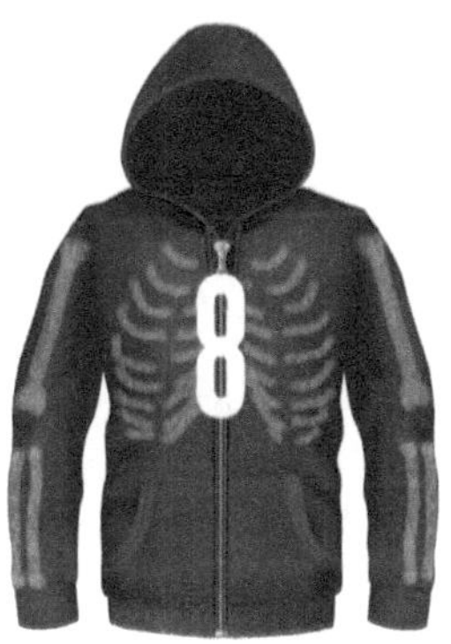

Wes

IT'S DARK AS NIGHT up in the tree house, but I don't need light to see Rain. She fucking glows. The blunt edge of her black hair, the straight line of her nose, the curves of her body, and the overlap of her arms across her chest. I can see every swoop and bend of her in perfect detail.

I'm fucking obsessed.

Which is why I need to go right the fuck now.

I drape Rain's clothes over her naked, napping body, tuck her hoodie under her head, and place my pocketknife in her tiny fist. She grips it and pulls it close as I kiss her on the forehead one last time. I let my lips linger, inhaling the fading scent of vanilla on her skin just to torture myself. Then, I climb out of the tree house with a noose of emotion wrapped around my neck.

Leave before you get left has never fucking hurt like this.

I have to get out of here before I do something stupid, like change my mind. I won't be able to breathe again until this place is a blip in my rearview—along with the girl who almost got me. Fool me once, shame on you. Do that shit thirteen more times, and guess what. I'm motherfucking foolproof.

I throw my clothes back on, check to make sure I still have the key to the Ninja in my pocket, and look around for the backpack.

Goddamn it.

I stomp out of the bookstore and try to focus on how disgusting this place is instead of the growing black hole in my chest. The floor is covered in trash and dust and cracked tiles with weeds growing in between them. The walls are covered with graffiti and shittily drawn dicks. And I can hear fucking frogs croaking somewhere in the atrium.

Frogs.

I turn left at the petri dish of a fountain and head straight to the tuxedo shop.

Rain's backpack is sitting on the counter, right where she left it, so I unzip it and dig around for what I need. I'm only going to take my antibiotics, a few bandages, maybe a protein bar or two, and a bottle of water. I can find the rest when I get back to town. I pocket the pills and shove a beige brick of food into my mouth, not even bothering to taste it as I hunt for the water bottles. When I find them, they're both empty.

Whatever. I'll just find a house with a garden hose on my—

The sound of moaning and coughing behind the counter scatters my thoughts.

Don't look. He's not your problem. This is the same guy who pulled a rifle on you in the hardware store, remember? Fuck him.

I look anyway.

Fuck me.

Quint's dark eyes are wide open, and his chest is heaving like he just ran a marathon. He tries to sit up, winces, and falls back to the ground as his hand flies up to touch his neck.

"No!" I leap over the counter and grab his wrist before he does any damage.

His brother is sitting next to him, passed out cold with his head against the checkout stand cabinets.

Quint's wild eyes lock on to mine.

"You're okay, man," I say, placing his hand on his chest, but from this close, I can see that he is definitely not fucking okay.

His skin is hot to the touch and covered in beads of sweat. His lips are chapped and pale. His shirt is soaked. And a trickle of blood is seeping from the bandage with every panicked pulse of his jugular.

Quint opens his mouth to try to ask me something but winces again as the glass shifts from the motion.

I glance at Lamar and debate whether or not to wake him up, but the kid has been on twenty-four-hour watch since we got here and could use the fucking shut-eye.

"Don't try to talk, okay? You were in an accident. We couldn't get you back to Franklin Springs, so we brought you to Pritchard Park Mall. You're in the old Savvi Formalwear right now. That's pretty boss, right?"

Quint tries to smile but cringes and bites his bottom lip from the pain.

Shit.

"You took some glass to the neck, man, but Rain's got you patched up. She'll be by to check on you in a few, okay?"

Quint grabs my wrist and looks at me with eyes the color of my cold, dead heart.

"Am I …" he whispers, pausing to suck in a breath and grimace from the pain.

"Hell no," I lie. "Don't even say it. You're gonna be fine."

Quint squeezes his eyes shut and grits his teeth as his face crumples. A high-pitched keening sound comes from somewhere deep inside his body, and I can't fucking take it anymore.

"You're gonna be okay," I say more forcefully, but I don't know who I'm trying to convince—myself or Quint. "You want some water? I'm gonna get you some water."

I stand up and grab the empty bottles on my way out the door.

Fuck.

This.

Place.

I have to concentrate on not crushing the plastic bottles in my fists as I stomp toward the food court.

Fuck.

These.

People.

A fat-ass toad jumps from the edge of the fountain into the murky, mucous-like water inside as I pass.

Supplies.

Shelter.

Self-defense.

I kick a broken tile.

I'm getting this motherfucker some water.

Then, I'm getting the fuck out of here.

The second I walk into the food court, I set my sights on the bitch at the back table. Q. She and the rest of her minions are still celebrating the end of civilization. A few tattooed misfits with random parts of their heads shaved are playing cards and taking shots from a bottle of bottom-shelf tequila. A beanpole in a jean jacket with the sleeves cut off is playing a goddamn accordion while a burly, bearded guy in a pair of unwashed overalls strums along on the banjo. A few crusty teens are gathered around a cell phone, elbowing each other like they're watching porn, and Q is kicked back in a plastic chair, smoking a joint, with a busted pair of black motorcycle boots propped up on the table and her black men's pants cut off at the knees.

Fucking gutter punks.

"Well, well, well." Q coughs, holding the smoke in her lungs. "If it ain't our new roomie, *Hawaii Five-0.* Everybody say, 'Hi, *Hawaii Five-0.*'"

"Hi, *Hawaii Five-0*," the clan drawls without looking up.

"Where's the luau?" Q exhales and passes the joint to her right.

I want to bark at her that I don't have time for her bullshit, but I smirk through my rage and hold up the empty water bottles. "Know where I can fill these?"

Q gets an evil glimmer in her gangrene-colored eyes and sits forward. She drops her feet to the floor and sits with her legs spread wide apart, like a dude.

"Water's for employees only, Surfer Boy." Q eyes me up and down. Her eyebrows and eyelashes are thick and dark. Her brownish-greenish-yellowish dreadlocks are flipped over the top of her head, spilling over one shoulder and ending somewhere below the full tits she's hiding underneath that baggy T-shirt. And the gold hoop in her nose glints in the light as she grins, deciding she likes what she sees.

I don't need this shit.

"You know what? I'll find it somewhere else. Thanks."

I turn to leave, but the sound of Q's plastic chair scraping the ground stops me in my tracks.

"Hold up."

I look at her over my shoulder with my *not interested in your bullshit* face firmly in place.

"Let's take a little field trip. I wanna show you somethin'."

"I don't have time for—"

"Listen, muhfucka. I let you stay in my castle last night. I gave you my protection from the Bonys. I fuckin' fed yo' ass. You can give me five minutes."

She's right. I might not like this bitch, but right now, she's the best resource I've got.

"Fine. Five."

"I'm sorry. I think what you meant to say is, *Thank you, Yo Majesty.*" Q stands and brushes her dreads over her shoulder with a dramatic sweep of her hand.

"Thanks," I mutter as Q turns and walks away from the table, gesturing for me to follow her with a flick of her long-ass fingernails.

"We gon' have to work on that last part." She cackles over her shoulder.

I feel the eyes of everyone in the food court on my back as we walk across the room and through a swinging half-door next to one of the fast-food counters.

"You ever see *Charlie and the Chocolate Factory*, Surfer Boy?"

"Uh, yeah. Why?" I mutter as we turn down a series of skinny, unlit hallways behind the restaurant kitchens.

Q pulls the latch on a heavy metal door and yanks it open, revealing a set of metal stairs. "Because I'm about to show you the April 23 version." Q grins and gestures for me to go up the stairs first.

Fuck it. Here we go, down the rabbit hole.

I can't see shit in the stairwell, but after what I found at the top of the last dark staircase I climbed, I'm pretty sure whatever I'm about to see couldn't possibly be worse. When I get to the landing at the top, I reach my hands out in front of me and feel the smooth surface of a metal door.

"Open it," Q says behind me, so I find the handle and give it a shove.

When the door swings open, the sun slaps me in the face so hard that it damn near blinds me. I lift my forearm to shield my eyes, and Q chuckles behind me.

"Go on."

I step out onto the roof, and the first thing I notice is the sound of birds clucking ... just before something huge goes flapping past my face.

"The fuck?" I drop my hand and squint in the direction that it traveled, finding a flying fucking hen landing on the roof of a plastic playhouse surrounded by chicken wire.

At least six more fat-ass chickens are inside the makeshift coop, staring at me with shifty orange eyes.

"That one's Asshole." Q nods toward the ball of feathers that almost took my head off. "We let her out during the day because ... well, she's a fuckin' asshole if we don't."

I look around in disbelief. Q was right. This place is insane. They have rows and rows of blue plastic rain barrels, dozens of containers—everything from old washing machines to tires—spilling over with fruits and vegetables, some of the biggest pot plants I've ever seen, and beyond the junk yard of a garden is a giant inflatable pool surrounded by mismatched patio furniture.

"You did all this?" I ask, trying to ignore the chicken staring at me in my peripheral vision.

"Hell nah." Q snorts, wrinkling up her nose. "I told you, I'm the queen up in here. I don't do shit. My people did all this." Q sweeps her hand out over her dominion as she turns and walks down the path separating the water collection area from the garden.

"Where did you guys get all this stuff?" I ask, following a few feet behind her.

Q shrugs. "Walmart."

I snort out a laugh as she comes to a stop next to a propane camping stove by the water barrels.

"Lysol used to sneak over there with a pair of bolt cutters every few days to steal shit outta the lawn and garden section. Opie used to swipe chickens and tools and shit from a farm somewhere around here. And Pizza Face yanked that pool right outta some kid's backyard."

"Those your *scouts?*"

"Were. Until the Bonys showed up." Something flashes across Q's face before she flicks her fingers at the teakettle sitting on top of the single-burner stove. "You gotta boil that shit before you drink it …"

"I thought you said water was for employees."

"That's why I brought you up here, Surfer Boy." Q points off into the distance. "You see that pharmacy, 'bout two blocks down? Now, Bonys already done broke into it, but I know there's gotta be some good shit left. You scope it out for me; I'll give you all the water you can drink. Bring me back some tampons and toilet paper …" Q's catlike eyes drift south as the corner of one angled eyebrow crawls north. "I'll be ya best muhfuckin' friend."

I open my mouth to tell her I'm not staying, but something she said makes me bite my tongue.

There's a pharmacy.

Right across the fucking street.

I sigh and scrub a hand down my face. "Fine. But I'm gonna need that water up front."

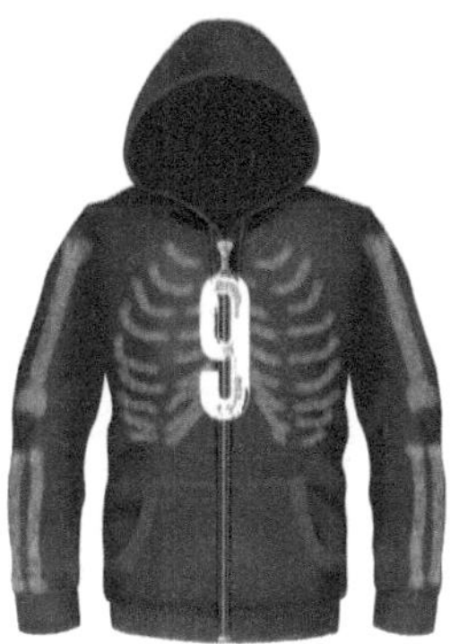

Wes

TWO BLOCKS.

I sling Rain's empty backpack over my good shoulder and push open the exit door. I might be an asshole, but even I can't let a guy die on the floor of an abandoned mall without at least checking the pharmacy down the street for meds first.

God, you better be watching. I deserve some serious extra credit for this shit.

The sun is already beginning to slide behind the pines next to the exit ramp, so I pick up the pace as I walk across the parking lot. I listen for the sound of motorcycles, gunshots, dogs barking, *anything*, but it's eerily quiet. The road in front of the mall has a few vehicles on it, but they're still and silent. Instead of engines and car horns, all I hear are birds and broken glass under my feet.

It looks like an urban wasteland out here. It sounds like a goddamn nature preserve. And, for a moment, it feels like I really am the last asshole on earth.

This is exactly how I pictured April 24. No people. No rent. No debate about whether to stay or leave anybody or anyplace. Just me and the shit of the earth.

Only in my head, it felt a hell of a lot better than this.

I step over a section of flattened chain-link fence and look down the street in both directions. The pharmacy is so close that I could be there in about two minutes if I stuck to the road, but considering that the last bastard

I saw walk down this highway is still lying on it about fifty yards away, I decide to cross the street and walk behind a strip shopping center instead.

I draw my gun as I slide along the side of the brick building, taking care not to let the gravel crunch too loudly under my boots. The farther away I get from the street, the worse the smell. I dismiss it as just another overflowing dumpster—until I recognize it.

It's the same way Rain's house smelled when I found her parents.

My stomach twists and my heart pounds as I take a breath and glance around the corner of the building.

Yep.

There's a dead body back there all right.

A dead body being chewed on by a pack of fucking dogs.

I stifle a gag, but the noise in the back of my throat doesn't go unnoticed. One head pops up from the pack. Then, another. And another. By the time the first bark sounds, I'm in a full sprint and already halfway to the dumpster behind the building. I grab the top edge and swing myself up as a dozen mangy dogs descend upon me. Thank fuck the lid was closed. The dogs bark and snarl and rake their claws down the sides of the metal box I'm standing on while I catch my breath and try not to look at the carcass on the ground a few feet away.

Think, motherfucker.

I glance to the right. The pharmacy is next to the shopping center, separated by a parking lot, but it's too damn far to make a run for it. I have no food—I emptied the backpack before I left so that I could fit more supplies inside of it—and I am *not* shooting a bunch of golden retrievers and Labradoodles.

One of the dogs yelps and bucks a smaller dog off its back.

Fuck, they're trying to climb each other now.

Climb …

I hold my breath as I look down the length of the building. Then, I exhale when I spot what I'm looking for.

A fire escape.

The ladder is about forty feet away though.

More yelps and growls break out below as I try to figure out how to distract these guys long enough to make it across the pavement. Half of them still have their collars on, so I know they haven't been wild for long. I bet if I had a tennis ball, most of them would still chase it.

They're not predators; they're just fucking starving.

A breeze blows through the alley behind the shopping center, causing the stench of death and whatever's decomposing in the dumpster to intensify. I pull my shirt over my nose and mouth, trying like hell to keep from puking, when my eyes land on a sign next to one of the metal back doors.

Parkside Bakery.

Bakery.

Food!

Before I even finish formulating my plan, I drop to my knees, reach down into the dog soup below me, grab the handle on the sliding side door of the dumpster, and yank that motherfucker open.

The bastards go insane, clawing and jumping and climbing over one another to try to get inside. I pull my hand back just as a Jack Russell terrier with gnashing teeth makes it to the top of the dogpile. He chomps down on a paper bag just inside the open door and rips it open with a violent shake of his head. I don't wait to see what comes falling out. Whatever it is, it's enough to keep them distracted as I leap to the ground and take off for the ladder.

I grit my teeth and try not to look at the battered body on the ground as I sprint past it, but the sight of purple dreadlocks in my peripheral vision tells me more than I wanted to know.

I'm not the first scout Q has sent on this mission.

Bile climbs up my throat, but I push it down and run harder. When I make it to the ladder without being chased, I decide to keep running. I don't stop to look both ways before I cross the parking lot between the shopping center and the pharmacy, and I don't fucking slow down. I'm done being cautious. I'm done with this whole goddamn day. I just want to get in, get out, and get the fuck out of Pritchard Park forever.

I draw my gun and duck through the shattered sliding glass door. Usually, I would tiptoe around in case someone was inside, but honestly, I *hope* someone's inside. There's a rage building inside of me that I wouldn't mind unleashing on a Day-Glo skeleton right about now.

Fuck Quint for getting hurt.

Fuck Carter for having a pulse.

Fuck the World Health Assholes for doing this to us.

Fuck Q for sending me on this goddamn death march.

Fuck Rain for making me want to believe in shit that history has proven will never fucking exist for me.

"If anybody's in here, come the fuck out!" I snarl, sweeping my head from left to right. The place is silent. "You have three seconds to show yourself, or I will shoot your ass on sight!"

When I don't hear anything, except for the blood rushing in my ears from the run and my untapped wrath, I do a quick survey of what's left in the store. The checkout station has been ransacked. There's not a single pack of cigarettes, candy bar, or bag of chips left on the shelves, but the rest of the store looks pretty much the same.

I guess makeup and greeting cards aren't exactly a top priority when you think the world's about to end.

The pharmacy is in the back corner, past all the convenience store bullshit, so I unzip the backpack and make my way down the aisles, chucking shit in along the way. Tampons, toothpaste, shampoo, hand sanitizer, protein bars, peanut butter … I can't believe all this stuff is still here. In Franklin Springs, this place would have been taken over by thugs weeks ago.

Oh shit.

The realization stops me in my tracks and then sends me sprinting past everything else in the store and diving over the pharmacy counter.

The Bonys probably *did* have guys posted in here twenty-four/seven … up until yesterday. They thought the world was gonna end just like everybody else, so they were out, getting fucked up and killing pedestrians for fun. I saw them. But when they finally shake off their hangovers and figure out that the world didn't end and it was all just a hoax …

The rumble of motorcycle engines in the distance fuels me as I scour the labels on row after row of identical white bottles with incomprehensible Latin words printed on them.

Goddamn it!

I don't know what any of this means. Nobody ever took me to the doctor as a kid. The only drugs I know are the ones with street value, and of course, those are long gone.

Rain would know what to look for.

Rain.

I unzip the front pouch on her backpack and read the label on the pills she swiped from Carter's house for my bullet wound.

KEFLEX (cephalexin) Capsules, 250 mg

I kiss the label and drop the almost-empty bottle back into the bag. The roaring of engines grows louder as I scan the shelves for anything starting with a K.

Forget about the drugs! Run, dumbass!

Epinephrine … flurazepam …

Go! Now!

Glucophage … hydralazine …

What are you doing? Do you think that Quint kid would be up in here, finding meds for you right now? Fucking run!

Keppra—no. Shit. Too far … Keflex!

The moment my fingers graze the five-hundred-count bottle of antibiotics, the crunch of broken glass under boot heels roots me to the spot.

"Argh!" a deep voice growls just before the sound of something being smashed echoes off the high ceiling. "They took all the goddamn smokes!"

I crouch down on the floor between two pharmacy shelves as a second pair of feet comes crunching into the store.

"Ah, man," a younger voice says, so quietly I can barely hear him. "They took all the Mr. Goodbars."

"Fuck Mr. Goodbar!" the older asshole yells, followed by the sound of hollow cardboard containers tumbling to the ground. "If you don't find me a cigarette, a cuppa coffee, and something for this gotdamn migraine in the next five minutes, I'ma beat yer ass, boy."

"I—"

"Four minutes!"

"Okay, fine."

I unzip the backpack, tooth by plastic tooth, and slide the Keflex bottle in as quietly as possible.

"I'ma check the break room for a coffeepot," the older asshole grumbles. "Anybody tries to come in that door … shoot 'em."

Shit.

I look around, frantically trying to find a better place to hide. The shelves of drugs run perpendicular to the pharmacy counter, so even though I'm crouched down, anyone walking by would be able to see me. The only safe place would be under the counter, but with all the shit in this backpack, there's no way I could get over there without making noise.

So, I do the only thing I can; I wrap both hands around the smooth wooden handle of Rain's dad's .44 Magnum, and I say a silent prayer to my new pal, God.

"Hey, Vipe, I found a carton of Virginia Slims!"

"I ain't smokin' no *Vagina Slimes!*" The asshole's voice is much louder than before.

Closer.

Every muscle in my body tenses, including my trigger finger, as the old bastard walks into view. His thinning gray hair is pulled back in a low ponytail. His leathery skin is pockmarked and sunburned. His beer gut sticks a solid foot out in front of him, and his black biker jacket has been spray-painted with neon-orange stripes resembling skeleton bones.

He stops right in front of the counter, and my finger tightens around the trigger. But he doesn't see me. Instead, he turns his back and pulls a bottle of Excedrin off the shelf across from the pharmacy counter.

"Maybe I should grab some Vagisil for that pussy of yours while I'm back here." He cough-laughs into his fist while I stare down the barrel of my gun, aiming directly for his bald spot.

My heart is pounding so hard I can feel every vein pulse and swell as they force the blood into my muscles. I know this feeling. This is exactly how I used to feel every single night, lying in an unfamiliar bed, clutching whatever weapon I'd stashed under my pillow, waiting for some other balding, beer-gutted piece of shit to come find me.

The bloated Bony pops the cap on the Excedrin bottle and tosses a few into his mouth before turning his head toward something out of my view.

"What you doin', boy?"

"I'm just gonna grab some allergy meds. This pollen is killin' me."

"The *pollen* is killin' you?"

The hungover old fuck shakes his head, and I know what's coming next before it even happens. He's gonna call that kid a little bitch and throw that bottle of Excedrin at him.

He turns his head sideways, so I aim for his temple.

"The pollen's killin' you?" He raises his voice, cocks his arm back, and lets the painkillers fly. I hear them bounce off of something before hitting the ground with a rattle. "How the fuck did I end up with a pussy wipe for a son? I shoulda put a pillow over your face the day your mama shit you out!"

My fingers tighten around the gun in my hands; I wish it were that motherfucker's neck.

"Sorry, sir," the kid mumbles.

"Get the fuck outta my sight!" the dickhead yells, throwing his hand in the direction of the pharmacy.

Shit.

Even though there are about three aisles of drugs between the pharmacy door and me, they're open shelving units. I can see everything. I see the door handle slowly rotate down. I see the door swing open with a creak. I see the ripped jeans, black-and-orange skeleton hoodie, and shaggy hair of a kid who can't be older than fourteen.

His posture is hunched over, as if he wants to curl in on himself until he disappears, and he's too busy staring at the floor to notice the man hiding in plain sight ten feet away.

Something on the shelf in front of him catches his attention, and he leans over even further to pick a small purple box off the shelf.

Zyrtec. Thank fuck.

Take it and go. Take it … and …

The kid's eyes lift suddenly, as if I'd spoken out loud, and lock directly on to mine.

Well, one of them does.

The other one is swollen shut and black as hell.

His good eye goes wide as it lands on my gun, so I quickly lower it and raise a finger to my lips.

Please don't make me shoot you, kid. For fuck's sake …

The boy bristles but not because of me. Because of the sound of footsteps in the hallway behind him.

"Hey, you little cocksucker …" Daddy Dearest appears in the doorway, and I can smell last night's liquor on him from here. "You find a coffeepot back h—"

His beady, bloodshot eyes drift from his cowering son to whatever—or whoever—the kid is staring at, and the second they land on me, I'm on my feet. Backpack in one hand, gun in the other, I sprint for the counter, hoping to clear it before the bastard can get a clean shot on me, but the sound of skin hitting skin stops me in my tracks.

The man shouts a few choice expletives at the kid, but I can't hear them. All I can hear is that backhand. It reverberates through my jaw, just like it did the first time *I* got hit in the mouth. The sting of pain, followed by the burn of humiliation.

Words like, "Shoot him, stupid," and, "Give me that fuckin' gun. *I'll* do it," slide off my back and land on the floor in a meaningless pile of syllables as I turn and face every motherfucker who ever put his hands on me, all rolled into one.

The rage that has been building inside of me all day now feels like a tiny match … that just got dropped into a can of gasoline.

I surrender all control of my body—give it over willingly—and watch like a spectator as I charge straight toward that piece of shit. His rodent-like eyes widen in shock just before my shoulder careens into his bloated fucking belly, sending him stumbling backward into the wall.

The noises make it to my brain first—something plastic clattering to the ground, boots shuffling over dirty floors, the dull smack of knuckles hitting teeth, the melodic ping of those teeth hitting the tiles—and then the physical sensations begin to come through. The rush of adrenaline through my bloodstream, the crunching pain in my right hand every time it connects with his face, the delicious strain of muscles in my left arm as I fight to keep him upright against the wall. Vaguely, I register his flailing arms, his dirty fingers trying to punch and poke whatever parts of me he can reach, but he can't hurt me.

Nobody can.

Not anymore.

A new sound rises over the pounding of blood in my ears, and it pulls me back to reality like a bucket of cold water.

It's a small, cracking voice demanding in an unconvincing tone that I, "Stand back."

Fuck. The kid.

I release his old man and step back with my hands in the air as the bastard's limp body slides down the wall.

"Back up," he says again, pointing a .32 at me with shaking hands.

I do as he said, my knuckles screaming in pain and my chest expanding violently with every breath I suck in.

"'Bout fuckin' time, you piece of shit," the old man spits through the fleshy pulp that used to be his lips. His eyes are swollen to mush. A river of blood runs from his broken nose down his mouth and chin. And when he rolls his head toward the kid, he garbles, "Shoot him, stupi—" but he doesn't get a chance to finish his command.

A bullet above his right eye shuts him up forever.

I flinch as the blast echoes around me. I turn with my hands still raised and face the corpse's maker. His posture is taller, his good eye narrowed in resolve.

He's not looking at me when he lowers his gun, and he's not speaking to me when he says—no, declares—"I'm. Not. Stupid."

The heat of the moment changes from charged and frenetic to stifling and heavy.

This is the world we live in now.

No social workers were coming to help this kid.

No Department of Child and Family Services.

No cops or judges or family attorneys were gonna fight for him.

And there won't be any coming to investigate this crime scene either.

This is the new justice system.

And right now, I'm scared to ask myself which one is better.

The kid finally looks at me, shock giving way to shame as he awaits my judgment, but I have none to give him.

Instead, I grab my backpack—pain shooting through almost every muscle, knuckle, and rib in my body—and head toward him on my way out the door.

I pause right before I pass, placing a hesitant hand on the kid's trembling shoulder. "Fuck 'em," I spit out, my eyes fixed on the empty hallway beyond the door and the empty life waiting for me beyond that. "Say *fuck 'em* and survive anyway."

1 0

April 25
Rain

I WAKE FROM A dreamless sleep, only to find myself lying in a pitch-black nightmare.

When I sit up and blink into the darkness of the tree house, my shirt tumbles off my bare chest and lands in my lap. My right hip is sore as hell from lying on the plywood floor. I rub it absentmindedly as I wait for my eyes to adjust to the darkness. I must have slept all the way through the afternoon and into the night. There isn't a speck of daylight filtering in from the hallway anymore.

But I don't need light to know that Wes is gone.

I can feel it.

His heat, his scent, his quiet, simmering intensity—all of it. Gone. The only evidence that he was even here are the clothes draped over my naked body and the pocketknife tucked into my fist.

He might as well have stabbed it into my heart.

I squeeze the textured handle as hard as I can. I squeeze it until my fingernails cut into my palm and my biceps begin to shake. I squeeze it even harder than I squeeze my eyes shut as I fight to keep the tears at bay.

Supplies. Shelter. Self-defense.

Wes left me with the last thing he thought I needed to survive.

Without him.

Stop it. Maybe he just had to pee. Maybe he went to find water.

I pull my shirt on over my head and feel around for my jeans.

Oh God. Maybe he's in trouble.

Worry swallows my despair and sends me scrambling down the tree house ladder. I trip over my boots at the bottom, pausing just long enough to shove my feet into them.

My vision adjusts to the dark, allowing me to avoid the edges and corners of the bookshelves as I trudge past. My footsteps sound flat and heavy, as if the grief I'm carrying has actual weight.

Please let him be okay. Please, God. I'll do anything.

The hallway is silent, except for the occasional cricket or frog, but I shatter that silence with every puddle I accidentally splash through and every broken tile I send skidding across the filthy floor.

My brain lies to me, my eyes seeing Hawaiian prints and haunting eyes in every reflection and shadow I pass. When they finally land on the fountain, I gasp as the silhouette of a man rises beside it. Hope fills my heart and then gushes out through a fresh tear when the figure lifts a rifle to his shoulder.

"Don't shoot." I hold my hands up. "It's Rain."

"Holy shit, Rain! You're still here?" Carter's voice echoes through the atrium as he lowers his weapon and jogs toward me.

When his long arms pull me to his chest, another wave of déjà vu from last night crashes over me. Carter hugged me like this before he knew that Wes and I were together. When he still thought I was his.

The only reason he would hug me like that now is if—

"He's gone, isn't he?"

Carter's body goes stiff. Then, he nods against the top of my head.

"Nobody's seen him since yesterday afternoon. Or you." Carter drops his arms and takes a step back so that he can look down at me. "But here you are."

I can't see his face, but I know he's smiling from the tone of his voice.

Wes is missing, and Carter's smiling.

I take a step back, too. "Does anyone know where he went? We have to find him, Carter. What if he's hurt?"

"He's not fucking hurt," Carter huffs, turning to walk toward the fountain. He leans over and lifts something off the ground. It's about the size and shape of a small boulder.

"I found this tonight while I was patrolling." He points a finger at the south hall. "Just inside the main entrance."

Carter hands me the large bundle. It's heavy in my arms and rough against my skin, but it's not the feel that tells me I'm holding my own backpack; it's the smell. The subtle scent of Daddy's cigarettes and Mama's hazelnut coffee that used to linger on everything it touched in the house. It hits me like a sucker punch, stealing my breath and making my eyes burn.

"It's full of supplies." Carter's tone is smug and accusing. "I knew it was yours because of the keychain hanging from the zipper. At first, I thought you must have dropped it off for Quint before you left, but since you're still here—"

"He left it for me."

Carter has the decency to shut his mouth as I hug the overstuffed bag to my chest.

It's fitting that it's so full. It's as if everything I've lost is crammed inside.

My parents. My home. My old life.

My Wes.

I smell them on the canvas, feel the weight of them in my arms.

But they're not here.

They're gone, and they're never coming back.

I make it to the edge of the fountain before my knees buckle. Curling my body around the backpack, I slide to the floor, holding on to it for dear life as I rock back and forth.

My eyes are fixed on nothing, and that's exactly what I feel.

Nothingness.

It is deep and wide and dark and damp.

It smells like stale cigarettes and morning coffee.

It swirls, like cemetery fog, around me. Clouding my vision. Numbing my pain.

None of this matters, it whispers. It always knows just what to say.

But then I feel something else wrap around me. Something warm and solid and wonderful.

He is heavy, like the backpack, but grounding.

He smells like home too, in his own way.

He is real, and he is here, and when I look up at the tender concern in his eyes, the fog lifts.

And the pain comes. It rips through me like a rusty machete as I bury my face in Carter's T-shirt, as my emotions decide they've found a safe place to go and flee my body in torrents.

I cry and mourn and twist my fists in the soft cotton while Carter shushes me and pulls me closer.

Which only makes me cry harder.

Not because of everything I've lost.

But because of the one thing I actually got back.

My best friend.

"Carter?" a shaky voice calls from the end of the hall leading toward the main entrance.

"Yeah?" he replies into the darkness, clearing his throat.

"I don't know what to do, man. He's ... he's gettin' worse."

"Lamar?" I wipe my eyes and sit up.

"Rainbow?" The elation in Lamar's voice surprises me. "Rainbow! You're still here!"

The sound of sneakers pounding the tiles echoes down the hall, reaching me seconds before he does.

"You gotta come. Right now. He's ... I can't ... I don't ... you gotta help him, Rainbow. Please!" Lamar's voice cracks, reminding me just how young he is.

Fourteen? Fifteen maybe?

I've been so caught up in my own shit that I never stopped to think how hard all this must be for him. Underneath all that attitude, he's still just a kid.

I hold out my hands and let him pull me to my feet, missing the warmth of Carter's arm around my shoulders the moment it falls away. I know without turning around that he'll bring my backpack.

He always used to carry it for me at school.

As Lamar tugs me toward the tuxedo shop, I notice the first traces of morning light peeking in through the broken windows in the main entrance doors. They illuminate the doorway of the Hello Kitty store where Wes told me he'd never fight to keep me from leaving.

If only I had fought harder to make him stay.

Or maybe I should have agreed to leave with him, like he wanted me to, I think as I follow Lamar into the tuxedo shop, but when I come around the end of the counter and see Quint's body convulsing on the floor, I know that's not true.

This is exactly where I'm supposed to be.

In fact, this is the only place I *want* to be.

No smells. No triggers. No angry mobs. No dead bodies.

In here, I have a purpose. In here, I have friends. Out there ...

In my mind, I reopen the fortress of Shit I'm Not Going to Think About Ever Again Because None of This Matters and We're All Going to Die, take everything outside those doors—my old house, the bodies buried in fresh dirt behind it, the beautiful boy in the Hawaiian shirt who saved my life and broke my heart, motorcycles and loose dogs and tree houses and burning buildings—and shove it all inside.

Then, I unzip the backpack Carter set on the counter, and I get to work.

May 1 (One Week Later)
Rain

"YOU ATE YOUR BREAKFAST!" Carter's cheerful voice shatters the silence in the tuxedo shop as his six-foot-three frame fills the doorway.

"Yeah ..." Quint clears his throat. "Kep' it down this time, too."

Carter's bright face darkens as his eyes flick from mine to the boy sitting next to me behind the counter.

"That's great, man," he replies with a smile that only I know is fake.

I know all his smiles.

"Has your *nurse* eaten anything today?" Carter's gaze slides over to me.

Quint shrugs as I drop my eyes and pull the sleeves of my hooded sweatshirt over my hands.

Carter presses his full lips into a thin line and nods slightly.

Thanks to the antibiotics, hand sanitizer, and gauze I found in my backpack, I was able to kill Quint's infection, remove the glass from his neck, and by some miracle, keep him from bleeding out while I bandaged him up, but knowing that Wes was the one who had delivered those supplies only made the festering stab wound in my own heart grow deeper.

"Rain ... can I talk to you outside?"

I lock my hoodie sleeves in my fists and shake my head.

"Not *outside*, outside, just ... in the hallway."

Quint gives me a nudge with his elbow. "Go on, girl. You ain't left this room in days. I'll be a'ight."

With a huff, I pull myself to stand. Every muscle in my body rejoices over finally being used as I follow Carter out the door. Once I'm in the hallway, I lean against the wall outside the tuxedo shop and stare straight ahead.

"You're not even gonna look at me?"

"I will … if you stand over here." I gesture toward the wall across from me with a hoodie-covered fist and then press my knuckles to my lips. The black cotton doesn't smell like home anymore.

Thank God.

"Uh … okay?" Carter pads into view with his hands in his pockets and his eyebrows raised in uncertainty. "This better?"

I nod.

"I guess that answers my question."

"What question?" I mumble into my hoodie sleeve.

"I have an errand to run. I thought it might be fun if you came with, but seeing as how you won't even *look* at the exit, I'm guessing that's a no."

"Yeah, that's a no. Are we done?" I close my eyes as I turn to go back into the tuxedo shop, not wanting to accidentally catch a glimpse of what's outside those doors. In my mind, it's all gone. And that's exactly how I want it to stay.

"Rain …"

Carter's long fingers wrap around my bicep, and I go limp, letting him pull me against his chest without an ounce of protest. I hate how badly I need his hugs. Anyone's hugs.

"You haven't eaten anything in days. You haven't left the mall since you got here. Hell, you've barely even left the tuxedo shop. All you do is obsess over Quint and Lamar. I get that you want to help and all, but you need to take a break and get some fresh air before you lose your shit."

"This air is good enough."

"Maybe we could take a walk around here and then … go say hi to my folks? They've been asking about you."

"Well, you can tell 'em I'm right here." I straighten my spine and take a step backward out of his embrace.

Carter runs a hand through his loose curls in exasperation. Then, his eyes widen and lips curve with the makings of what is probably a bad idea. "You know what? I'm gonna do that. Be right back."

I watch him walk away with long, determined strides before I shuffle back to the safety of Savvi Formalwear.

Inside, Quint gives me a smirk. I wrapped his neck in so much gauze that it looks like he's wearing a diaper as a necklace. His eyes are sunken, and his lips are dry. But the fact that he's vertical and smiling feels like a handful of glitter sprinkled on top of the stagnant black cesspool that is my life.

Especially when he sweeps a hand in front of his gauze choker and rasps, "I see you eyein' my pearls."

I snort. "You got me."

"Hater." Quint winces and stifles a laugh as I join him behind the counter. "So ... you gonna tell me what that was all about?"

I roll my eyes and plop down on the three-by-eight-foot patch of tile that I now call home. "Nope."

The sound of a throat being cleared causes both of our heads to snap toward the doorway. I push up onto my knees just enough to see Carter entering the store, followed by a very unhappy-looking grizzly bear of a man with a very pronounced limp.

"Since you won't leave your post, I figured I'd bring you a new patient to work on." Carter beams.

"Is that why you brought me down here? Dammit, boy!" Mr. Renshaw turns to leave but wobbles on his feet and has to grab Carter's arm for stability.

"Mr. Renshaw! Stay right there!" I run to the back.

I grab a rolling desk chair from what used to be the office and push it out to the center of the store where Carter's dad is breathing heavily and wiping his brow with the back of his hand. He gives me a pained smile from somewhere behind his bushy, overgrown gray beard and then flops onto the mildewed vinyl seat with a grunt.

"Jeepers. I done told y'all, I'm fine," Mr. Renshaw gasps.

"Ah, come on, old man. Rain needs a new patient. The one she's got is boring." Carter jerks his chin in Quint's direction. Then, he leans down and whispers in his dad's ear, loud enough for everybody to hear, "And he's startin' to smell."

Carter ducks suddenly as a roll of medical tape goes whizzing past his head.

"I heard that, asshole," Quint coughs out from behind the counter.

They all burst out laughing as Carter stands and gives Quinton another smile that I know all too well. It's the same one he used to give Sophie after he teased her to the point of her smacking him.

Brotherly love.

"Glad you're feeling better, man," Carter says more seriously, walking over to the counter and reaching behind it to give Quint some kind of dude handshake/fist bump thing.

The three of us were in the same grade back in Franklin Springs, and even though Carter and Quint didn't hang out that much, they've known each other since they were kids.

"Me too." Quint's words are strangled with pain, but his voice is getting a little stronger every day.

"Would you get out of here?" I huff. "You're upsetting my patients."

Carter chuckles as he strolls toward the door. I close my eyes as he passes, catching his subtle, masculine scent.

"Hey, Carter?" I blurt out just before he leaves.

Turning back around, my best friend flashes me a Hollywood smile and points a finger gun at me. "I knew it. I knew you'd rather hang out with me than stay here with a cripple and an angry, old man."

I crack a smile—my first one in days. I don't know how he does it, but Carter has always been able to make me laugh, no matter how badly I don't want to.

"Uh, *no*." I roll my eyes. "I was just wondering where you're going."

"Relax, Rainbow Brite." Carter beams.

And my heart sinks like the *Titanic*. I know that smile too. It's one that I saw more and more of toward the end of our relationship.

Carter has a secret.

"You won't even miss me … *much*." With a wink, he disappears into the hallway, and I turn to glare at my new patient.

"He gets it from you, you know."

Mr. Renshaw chuckles and wipes the last few beads of sweat from his brow. The walk over must have really taken it out of him. As soon as his laughter fades, I can almost feel his defenses go up.

"Don't worry," I say, taking a seat on the edge of the counter a few feet away. "I'm not gonna make you show me."

Mr. Renshaw relaxes into his chair. "You ain't?"

"I already know it's broken."

His nostrils flare. "How do you s'pose that?"

"By your limp. That car accident was over a month ago. If you're still limping this badly, it means something's broken, and it's not gonna heal unless you get it set and stop hobbling around on it like you've been doing."

Mr. Renshaw's rosy cheeks go pale, confirming my suspicions.

Crap. It really is broken.

"I … I didn't think it mattered, what with the end of the world comin' and all," Mr. Renshaw grumbles through his wiry gray beard. His once-bright eyes are dull, pinched at the corners in pain and red from countless sleepless nights.

"Is that why you wouldn't let anybody see it?"

He shrugs and shifts uncomfortably in his seat. "Didn't wanna worry 'em any more than they already was."

Quint and I share a quick, sympathetic glance before I hop off the counter and cross the room.

Placing a hand on Mr. Renshaw's shoulder, I say, "Welp, the world's not ending after all, so what do you say we get you fixed up?"

He shakes his head, pulling his hurt leg a little further under the chair. "No?"

"I 'preciate you tryin' to take care of me, Rainbow; I do. But I think it's best to just let it be."

"Why don't you let me be the judge of that?"

Not that I have any idea what I'm doing.

I glance down at his leg—I don't even touch it—and the jumpy old bastard swivels away from me in his seat with a loud, "No!" He drops his eyes with an embarrassed chuckle. "I mean ... I'm fine. Thanks anyway, young lady."

I huff loud enough for him to hear me. Mama used to say that the burliest men were always the biggest babies when it came to boo-boos.

Mama.

The second her beautiful, tired, stressed-out face comes to mind, I frantically grasp at the nothingness, pulling it on like a hazmat suit right before the sadness slams into me.

Once I'm safe in my feelingless fog again, I look back down at Mr. Renshaw. His face is just as guarded as mine.

"I guess we're done here then, huh?"

His bushy eyebrows lift in surprise. "You ain't gonna argue with me?"

I shake my head and swivel his chair toward the door. Using it like a wheelchair, I roll him out into the hallway. "I know better than to argue with a Renshaw. Y'all are almost as stubborn as you are cocky."

"Hey," Mr. Renshaw snaps. "If God didn't want me to brag, he shouldn't've made me so damn pretty."

I shake my head as I roll the old man back home.

When we get to the shoe store, I'm greeted by an enthusiastic tackle hug from Sophie and a sad-eyed, *sorry about your parents* hug from Mrs. Renshaw. Both of them make me want to cry.

And also remind me why leaving the tuxedo shop is such a bad idea.

It takes almost all the energy I have to crank my mouth up into a smile. I can't remember the last time I ate ... or even stood up for this long. Spots begin to dance along the edges of my vision.

"He's all yours," I say, walking backward out of the store as the room begins to tilt. "I, uh ... I gotta get back to Quint. See ya later ..."

Once I'm in the hallway, I tear my eyes away from their disappointed faces and head back to Savvi so fast that I'm practically jogging. I keep my gaze glued to the floor and count my steps along the way to keep my eyes and mind from wandering to dangerous places.

Ninety-one, ninety-two, ninety—

As soon as I cross the threshold into my new home, I finally look up.

And find Q staring back at me.

She's leaning against the counter with her arms folded across her chest and a look on her face that says she didn't come to say hi.

"What's up, Doc?" she deadpans.

"Hey, Q. How're you?" I cringe at the fake cheerfulness in my voice.

It's like I'm in high school all over again, cranking up my Southern accent and trying to play nice with the mean girls who are just waiting around to steal my boyfriend or snip off pieces of my ponytail when I'm not looking. Well, too bad for Q; the boy and the hair are already gone.

Like everything else.

"Just came to check on my future scout." Q tosses her dreads over one shoulder as she casts a backward glance over the counter at Quint. "Looks like you been earnin' your keep, nurse lady." Her toxic, waste-colored eyes flick back to me. "'Specially since you ain't even been takin' your share."

The accusation in her tone tells me that I did something wrong, but hell if I know what.

"I'm sorry, my share of what?" I ask as sweetly as possible.

"Don't give me that Southern belle bullshit. I'm talkin' 'bout food. You know, that shit you need to stay alive? You got a stockpile around here that you ain't tellin' me about?"

When I don't answer, her slimy gaze slides over the rest of the store. Searching. "You wanna live in *my* kingdom, Snow White, you gotta share yo' spoils, undastand?"

I nod, swallowing hard, as Q walks past the mannequin stand where my overstuffed backpack is hidden underneath. Just before she breezes past me, she stops, so close I can smell the weed smoke trapped in her hair, and runs a long fingernail down my jaw.

"By the way"—her lip curls as she digs her razor-sharp talon into the underside of my chin—"you look like shit."

I clamp my jaw shut and hold her stare. I'm not about to give this bitch the satisfaction of seeing me wince, but I'm not dumb enough to slap her away either.

I need this place too much.

Q finally drops her hand with a cackle and waltzes past me toward the door. "Bet that's why ya man left."

Rain

THE MALL IS QUIET. *Quint is resting after the best day he's had since we got here, and Lamar is sound asleep with his head on my shoulder. I should be happy. Or at least content. But I feel nothing.*

I hope it lasts.

Footsteps in the hallway approach, but I'm not afraid. I'm safe here—inside this building, behind this counter. Nothing has tried to attack, shoot at, or rape me since I arrived.

Which is exactly why I'm never, ever leaving.

When the clomp, clomp, clomp *of heavy feet enter the tuxedo shop, I expect to see Carter's mop of dark curls appear above the counter—he likes to pop in while he's doing his nightly rounds—but the face I see when I look up grabs the knife handle sticking out of my heart and twists it with invisible hands. Pain, sharp and suffocating, slices through my numbness, but I don't show it. If I flinch, if I blink, he might disappear again forever.*

Wes stares at me with that infuriatingly blank expression. The one he wears when he's thinking.

He's always thinking.

I can see him perfectly, even in the dark. Shiny brown hair, flipped up at the bottom from being tucked behind his ear. Soft green eyes hooded by strong, dark eyebrows. He shaved while he was gone. And washed his clothes. I know because the hibiscus on the shoulder of his blue Hawaiian shirt isn't blood red anymore. As my eyes slide across his broad chest, I realize that all of the flowers are different now. In fact, they're not flowers at all.

They're hooded figures on horseback.

Yellow and orange and deep, dark pink.

I sigh, and for the first time since he arrived, I allow myself to close my eyes.

"You're not really here, are you?"

He doesn't reply, and I know that when I open my eyes, he'll already be gone. Vanished like a ghost into the night. With a sigh, I look up and find Wesson Patrick Parker kneeling right in front of me.

God, he's so beautiful.

I hold my breath, afraid that he might scatter like a dandelion if I'm not careful, but ... I'm not careful. I reach out with impulsive fingers and tuck his hair behind his ear. When he doesn't disappear, I exhale, letting my hand linger on his cheek.

"Why did you leave?"

Wes leans into my touch and closes his eyes. "Self-defense."

Of course. Wes's recipe for survival. Supplies, shelter, and self-defense.

"What are you defending yourself from, Wes? Nothing will hurt you here."

His eyes flick open, and I feel his jaw clench in my palm.

"The only *thing that will hurt me is here," he grinds out, eyes as hard as polished jade.*

"If you're talking about Carter—"

"I'm talking about you."

"Me"—I shake my head and huff out a frustrated laugh—"hurt you? Are you serious right now? You left me, Wes. You broke my heart. You wanna talk about survival? I can't survive without my heart."

"Bullshit," Wes snaps. "I've been doing it since the second I walked out those doors."

I hold his stare and my breath until my eyes water and my lungs burn.

Then, as if we both run out of patience and oxygen at the same time, we lunge for one another. His fingers dive into my hair. My hands grip the back of his neck. We erase the distance with a violent desperation, and just before our lips collide, Wes whispers my name.

"Rain ... wake up."

My eyes flutter open to find a very different man blinking at me in concern. This one has eyes like warm Tennessee whiskey, not cool, mossy stones. They're friendly, not fiercely guarded, and they don't stare through me; they simply stare at me.

"Hey, sleepyhead," Carter whispers with a smile, his perfect teeth almost glowing in the dark.

"Hey," I croak, rubbing my eyes.

"You remember the plan?"

"Mmhmm." I go to stretch but stop short when I feel Lamar's head resting on my shoulder. "Can you ..." I gesture toward the bag of bones slumped on top of me and roll my neck in relief when Carter gently shifts Lamar so that he's lying with his head on Quint's thigh.

"Carter?" I whisper as he helps me to my feet. "Do you still dream about the horsemen?"

He pauses, looking up and to the left as he tries to remember. "Damn. You know what? I don't think I do. Why? Are you still having the nightmares?"

I shake my head as we walk out into the hallway. "No. I still see the horsemen, but they're not scary anymore … I think they're fading away."

"That's good. Now, you can start dreaming about me again."

Carter wags his eyebrows at me, and I elbow him in the ribs.

"God, you're just as bad as your dad."

"Speaking of the old man, you sure you know what you're doing?"

I swallow. "No, but the way his foot looks like it's sticking out in the wrong direction a little bit—and the fact that he can walk on it at all—makes me think it might just be a greenstick fracture."

"And you can fix that?"

I cringe and look up at Carter. "Maybe? I saw the vet do it to our dog, Sadie, when she got hit by a car that one time."

"That was in eighth grade!"

"You got any better ideas?" I snap.

Carter shrugs. "You sure it won't just, like, heal on its own?"

I glare up at him. "It's been a month, Carter. Does it seem like it's healing on its own?"

He holds up his hands in surrender. "Okay. Damn."

"Sorry," I mumble, pulling my hoodie sleeves into my fists. "I'm just nervous."

Carter wraps a long arm around my shoulders and jerks me against his side. "You got this," he says, planting a quick kiss on the top of my head. "If you think you can fix it, you can."

I relax a little, soaking up his warmth and support like a dry sponge, but all too soon, we're at the shoe store. Carter goes in first, leading me through the web of old shoe racks by the hand.

"The girls are sleeping here," he whispers, pointing over a shelf at the clearing in the center of the store.

I look in their direction, but it's pointless. It's too dark to see anything more than a foot in front of my face.

"We put the old man in the back tonight. He snores like a damn freight train when he's been drinkin'."

"Drinking?"

Bright white teeth flash at me in the dark. Carter slows his pace and leans down to whisper in my ear, "I mighta scored a bottle of some *very* bottom-shelf tequila today. Thought it might help with the pain."

His breath is warm on my neck, his fingers are laced through mine, and even though I don't want him this close … I need *somebody* this close. Anybody.

Carter pushes open a swinging metal door, and if I didn't know better, I'd swear a construction crew was behind it, taking a jackhammer to the concrete floor.

"Jesus Christ. How much did he drink?"

"Let's just say, this is the first time he's slept through the night since we got here."

Carter pulls a small flashlight out of his pocket to light our way. We pass a few floor-to-ceiling metal shelving units before finding Mr. Renshaw passed out diagonally across a surprisingly comfy-looking sleeping bag.

"What the hell? Y'all have sleeping bags?" I smack Carter on the arm.

He chuckles. "A couple. We packed them for our trip to Tennessee. With all of our relatives heading to my Grandma's house, we thought there was a pretty good chance that we'd end up sleeping on the floor until ... you know."

"April 23?" I roll my eyes.

"Yeah."

The air between us grows heavy as I start to think about the day he left. The gates on Fort Shit I'm Not Going to Think About Ever Again Because None of This Matters and We're All Going to Die rattle, but they hold fast. That's an outside-the-mall memory. We don't allow those out anymore.

"Come on," I whisper in the silence between snores. "Let's get this over with."

Carter and I follow the beam of his flashlight to a very unconscious James "Jimbo" Renshaw. Kneeling by his sock-covered feet—nobody goes barefoot around here—I take a deep breath and push the hem of his left pant leg up to his knee.

"Holy shit," Carter blurts. The beam of light darts across the floor and up the wall as he jerks back in response to his daddy's mangled shin.

"No, no. It's okay. Look." I gesture for Carter to shine the light back down. "See how his leg is bent right here?"

"Yeah, I fucking see it. I'll never *unsee* it."

"I think his bone just kinda cracked, like this." I hold up one straight finger and then bend it a little in the middle. "It didn't break the skin, there's not a lot of bruising, and he's still able to put a little weight on it, so ..." I swallow, my mouth suddenly going dry. "So, I think he just needs that fracture reset."

"What, like, we can just pop it back into place?"

"Well, it's been a few weeks, so it probably already has a good bit of tissue growth on it ..."

"Oh my God." Carter sits down next to me and rests his elbows on his knees. The beam of light lands on a cinder-block wall about fifteen feet away. "Are you trying to tell me that we're gonna have to re-break his fucking leg?"

I give him a tiny smile that feels more like a wince. "Just a little."

I count Mr. Renshaw's snores until Carter finally responds.

Five … six … sev—

"Fuck it." He throws his hands up. "It's not gonna get better if we do nothing, right?"

I nod, trying my best to seem confident when, really, the thought of what I'm about to do makes me want to puke.

"We need to make a splint to keep his leg straight while it heals."

Carter swings the flashlight across the empty warehouse. "There's nothing in here but shelves and …" The beam lands on a haphazard stack of wooden slatted things piled up in the far corner of the room. "Pallets!"

He jumps up and disappears into the darkness. I watch the circle of light bounce across the warehouse until it reaches the pile of wooden trash. A second later, Carter's foot crashes into it like a grenade, sending splintered shards flying.

My gaze darts to Mr. Renshaw, but he doesn't even flinch from the ruckus.

I do though when I reach into my pocket and pull out a certain black pocketknife.

Not now, dammit. We are not gonna think about him now … or ever.

I slice open the toe of Mr. Renshaw's sock and slide it up to cover his calf just as Carter returns with an armful of wooden planks.

He sets the boards down and takes a step back with his hands in the air. "I can't do it. I can't fucking do it, Rain. You gotta do it."

"By myself? I don't know if I'm strong enough. There might be a lot of new bone growth to get through."

"Oh my God." Carter squeezes his eyes shut.

"Stop it!" I whisper-shout.

"It's my dad, Rain. What if it were *your* dad?" He clamps a hand over his mouth the second the words tumble out. "Fuck. I'm sorry. I'm so sorry. I didn't mean to … shit."

But I'm not looking at Carter anymore. I'm staring at the drunken, bearded, snoring, middle-aged man passed out on the floor before me, and suddenly, those outside-the-mall memories are having a real hard time staying locked up.

What if it *were* my dad?

What if it were the same unemployed, self-indulgent, depressed, angry bastard who treated my mama like a punching bag until the day he killed her?

What if?

Without another thought, I grab one of the wooden pallet slats, place it on the bent side of Mr. Renshaw's broken shin bone, and hold it in place with both hands. Then, with my teeth gritted and liquid fire in my veins, I press my foot against the bumped-out part on the opposite side and give it a good, hard shove.

"AHHHHHHH!"

I hang on to the board for dear life as Mr. Renshaw sits up and tries to jerk his leg away from me. Carter grabs his thigh and presses down to hold it in place as his dad slurs at the top of his lungs.

"BEAR DONE GOT ME, AGNES! GIT MY GUN!"

Then, his eyes roll back up in his head, and just as quickly as he came to, he passes out again, free-falling toward the concrete floor.

"Fuck!" Carter lets go of his thigh and dives with his hands out like the all-star athlete he was born to be, catching the back of his dad's head just before it splatters on the ground.

The two of us share a wide-eyed stare—him holding a head, me holding a leg—until the snoring resumes. Then, after a few deep breaths, we get to work on Mr. Renshaw's improvised splint.

Carter braces the straightened bone with four broken boards—over the sock so that he doesn't get splinters—and I carefully slide Mr. Renshaw's belt off to lash them around the middle. I take off his other sock and tie it around the top and use the drawstring from his sleeping bag to secure the bottom.

"Think it'll stay?" he whispers between snores.

"If he doesn't mess with it." I take a deep breath and blow it out, bracing my hands on the tops of my thighs. "Hey, Carter?"

"Yeah, Doc?"

"You got any more of that tequila?"

"Easy, tiger." Carter plucks the bottle from my hand as I swallow my third mouthful of what might as well be gasoline.

I wipe my mouth with the back of my hand, trying to hide my grimace as the tequila scorches its way down my throat to my empty stomach.

"God, these frogs are almost as loud as your dad."

Carter coughs out a laugh, trying not to choke as he lowers the bottle from his own lips. "For real!" He turns and glares into the fountain we're sitting on and lifts a finger to his lips, shushing the wildlife.

I giggle through my nose.

"Hey, Rain?"

"What?"

Carter sets the bottle on the floor and turns to face me, his features serious in the silvery glow from the skylights. Then, suddenly, he grabs my biceps and whisper-shouts, "BEAR DONE GOT ME, AGNES! GIT MY GUN!"

I burst out laughing, doubling over and clamping my hands over my mouth as I try not to be so damn loud. Of course, that only makes it worse. "Too soon!" I hiccup, waving one hand in surrender. "Too soon!"

"Sorry!" Carter has the best belly laugh. It's so boyish and sweet, like his face, betraying his manly, six-foot-three-inch packaging.

"For real though"—he claps a hand over my shoulder—"that was fucking badass back there. Thank you."

My laughter dies down. "Don't thank me yet. I could have made it worse, for all I know."

Carter slowly shakes his head from side to side. His hooded eyes have a hard time keeping up. "Unh-uh. You make everything better, Rainbow Brite."

"Pssh. You're drunk."

"I got somethin' for you today."

"Oh, yeah? Where'd you go anyway? You never told me."

"Every few days, Q has me take everybody's phones and shit out to my parents' car to charge 'em."

"I thought your car was busted."

"It is. Dented all to hell, right in the middle of the pileup, but it's got gas, and the engine still starts up, so ..." Carter reaches into the pocket of his basketball shorts and pulls out a shiny black device. "I charged your phone."

"Oh my God." I gasp and reach for it, turning it over in my hands like some kind of artifact from a past civilization. "Where did you find this?"

"It was in your backpack the night I found it."

My mood sours at the mention of that night, but Carter quickly changes the subject. "Check it out!" He taps his finger on the glass, lighting it up. The wallpaper used to be a picture of us, but after he left, I couldn't stand looking at him anymore, so I changed it back to the default screen. Now, it's just stupid blue digital swirls. "Your service even got turned back on."

I stare at the phone in my hand, racking my brain for the name of somebody I could call, but ... everyone I might want to talk to either left town before April 23 or ...

The screen goes black.

"Hey ... you okay?" Carter gives my shoulder a little squeeze.

I nod, staring at the blank screen, but it's a lie, and Carter knows it.

So, I sigh and shake my head. "I don't have anybody to call."

"What are you, forty? You don't use a phone for calling people, silly."

Carter snatches the phone out of my hand, and I watch his face light up blue as he *tap, tap, taps* on the screen. Seconds later, the soft strumming of a ukulele drifts over the croaking of the fountain frogs as Tyler Joseph sings about a house made of gold.

"You're supposed to use it to listen to your favorite band. Duh."

I smile politely at his proud, illuminated face beaming in triumph. Carter is trying so hard to cheer me up. Now's probably not the time to tell him that Twenty One Pilots was never my favorite band.

It was *his*.

"Thanks, Carter." I take the phone from him and set it on the fountain next to me, letting it play. "That was really sweet."

He nods, and his smile slowly fades. The two of us look around as we listen to the music. He nudges a loose tile back into place with his sneaker. I pick at my hoodie sleeves. He shifts a few inches closer to me. I hold my breath until I can feel my heartbeat in my neck.

"Your hair is shorter." Carter's voice rumbles in my ear as he reaches up and slides two fingers down the front strands of my black hack job.

I flinch and pull back slightly, tucking that side behind my ear. "Yep. And yours is longer."

"Car Radio" begins to play, the electronic beat mimicking my erratic pulse as Tyler raps about being unable to distract himself from his dark thoughts.

Maybe Twenty One Pilots is my favorite band after all.

"I can't believe you're here," Carter whispers, crowding my space.

I can smell the tequila on his warm breath, and the inside of my hoodie suddenly feels like a sauna.

"I thought about you every single day, Rainbow," he slurs, leaning down to press his forehead to the side of mine. "Every single second."

I place my hand on the fountain ledge beside me to help support his weight.

"I wanted to come home to see you so bad, but I couldn't stand the thought of having to say goodbye all over again. It'd almost killed me the first time."

Carter slides a hand up the outside of my thigh, and all I can hear is the sound of blood rushing in my ears.

"I missed you so much, ba—"

The second I feel his lips graze the corner of my mouth, I grab my phone and jump up. "I'd, uh … better go check on Quint," I mumble, walking away backward. "Night, Carter!"

I turn and sprint toward the tuxedo shop as the voice coming from my fist sings about not being the person their partner used to know.

I shut the device off and shove it into my pocket.

You and me both, Tyler. You and me both.

May 2
Rain

"KNOCK, KNOCK." I PEEK my head over the empty shelves and breathe a sigh of relief when I don't see Carter. "Anybody home?"

"Rainbow!" Sophie squeals, using her whole arm to wave at me from her seat on one of the black vinyl shoe store benches.

Mrs. Renshaw's face lights up too, but her husband—who is lying flat on his back on his own bench with his splinted leg propped up on an empty shelf—won't even look at me. He throws his elbow over his eyes and grumbles something unintelligible through his wiry gray beard.

"There's my hero!" Mrs. Renshaw stands and spreads her arms, ready to pull me in for a hug as soon as I make my way through the maze of aisles.

I walk directly into her embrace but find myself gritting my teeth to get through it and pulling away sooner than usual. My reaction surprises me. I love Mrs. Renshaw.

But she's not my mother.

I don't have one of those anymore, and hugging her only reminds me of that fact.

I quickly add *Mrs. Renshaw* to my mental list of triggers to avoid at all costs.

"I can't thank you enough for taking care of my big, stubborn baby over here," Mrs. Renshaw says, casting a sideways glance over at her groaning husband. "We are so, so blessed that the Lord brought you back into our lives."

"Uh … you're welcome?" I feel my cheeks heat as I follow her gaze over to my latest victim. "But I'm not so sure *he'd* agree with you about that."

"I can hear y'all, ya know," Mr. Renshaw growls.

I smile and walk over to him. "How's my favorite patient doin'?"

"Don't come near me, devil woman."

"I brought Advil."

Mr. Renshaw props himself up on his elbows. "'Bout damn time."

I glance down at his splinted leg while I dig the bottle of painkillers out of my hoodie pocket and smile when I see that it's not too swollen.

"You probably need these more for your pounding head than your leg," I tease, dropping two little brown pills in his palm.

"That damn Mexican tequila gets me every time. Now I know why they call it Montezuma's Revenge."

I laugh, nervously glancing around as Mr. Renshaw swallows his meds. "So, did you, like, send Carter to his room as punishment or something?"

Mrs. Renshaw snorts. "Oh, he's around here somewhere."

"He went looking for yooooou," Sophie adds in a singsong voice, batting her eyelashes.

Ugh. Great.

"So …" I change the subject back to the bearded elephant in the room. "Mr. Renshaw—"

"Oh, just call me Jimbo, dammit. This ain't no time for formalities."

Somebody's grouchy. Jeez.

"Okay, *Jimbo.* I think I straightened your shin bone out, so as long as you keep it in the splint and don't put any weight on it for a few weeks, it should heal correctly."

Or at least, better than before.

Maybe.

I hope.

"A few weeks!" Mr. Renshaw plops back down on his back and throws a meaty arm over his face.

"Oh, stop bein' so darn dramatic. As bad as that wreck was, you're lucky to still be alive," Mrs. Renshaw snaps.

"Yeah, Dad," Sophie chimes in.

"I mean it, Mr.—er, Jimbo. No walking or standing on it. For at least … eight weeks."

I don't know if that's even right. I just figured, if I told him eight, he might make it at least four or five.

"I can't find her anywhere, Mom. I don't know where else to—"

All of our heads swivel toward the entrance as Carter comes stomping into the store. His frustrated gaze lands on me, and I see a glimmer of embarrassment surface in his eyes before it's quickly masked by a bright, overconfident smile.

"He still breathing?" Carter chides, glancing down at his old man.

"Yeah, but I don't think he wants to be." I smirk back, appreciating that he's keeping things light and friendly.

"Boy, yer lucky I can't walk, or I'd be kickin' yer ass right about now."

Carter snorts out a laugh, all long, dark eyelashes and floppy black curls, but as I'm watching him, I get the feeling that someone else is watching me. I turn and glance over my shoulder, thinking I'm just being paranoid, but the smitten stare of Mrs. Renshaw is definitely glued to the side of my face. She flicks her eyes from me to her son, and I swear, if her irises weren't such a dark brown, I'd be able to see big red hearts floating in them.

Ohhhh, no. No, no, no.

"Well, I'll let y'all get back to your day. Just … let me know if you need anything," I say with a smile, speed-walking back through the haphazard rows of shelves between me and the door.

My eyes meet Carter's as I pass, and just when I think he's going to let me walk away without making it awkward, he spins on his heel and follows me out the door.

"Rain, wait!"

I don't wanna talk about it. I don't wanna talk about it. I don't wanna—

I turn around and force a smile. "What's up?"

"So, about last night …"

Damn.

"Carter, you don't have to—"

"Do you remember what I did with my flashlight? I can't find it anywhere, and everything is kind of a blur after you went *Karate Kid* on my dad's leg." He winces and rubs his forehead. "I'm pretty sure that tequila was just rat poison with a worm floating in it."

Carter gives me a small, sheepish smile as he stuffs his hands in the pockets of his athletic shorts, and of course, I know that smile just like all the others.

Carter's giving me an out.

Gratefully, I return the favor. Cocking my head to one side, I give him a scowl. "You mean, you don't remember running down the halls, shining it in everybody's rooms last night? You were shouting something like"—I put my fist to my mouth and lower my voice—"'FBI! Hand over all your marijuana, and nobody gets hurt!'"

Carter laughs and wraps an arm around my shoulders, steering me in the opposite direction of the atrium. "Man, I turn into a damn genius when I'm drunk."

You turn into something all right.

"Where are we going?"

"To have some fun."

My feet freeze, and for the second time in as many days, I feel the urge to run away from Carter Renshaw.

I don't know what's wrong with me. People don't run away from Carter; they run toward him. Literally. They can't even help it. He's just that magnetic. His smile, those eyes, that tall and chiseled body, his cocky swagger. I was just as much of a fangirl as every other female—and some of the males—at Franklin Springs High School. The only advantage I had was that I'd found him first.

I fell in love with the boy next door *before* he became the big man on campus, but once he became the big man on campus, I got the distinct feeling that he'd outgrown the girl next door. I saw his wandering eye, the way he let the cheerleaders feel him up in the hallway. I knew he wasn't always truthful about where he was or how often he had practice. And overhearing Kimmy say that they'd made out senior year only confirmed what I'd suspected all along.

That must be what this *no feeling* is about. This is about Carter breaking my trust and leaving me behind. It's definitely *not* about a certain Hawaiian shirt–wearing, gun-toting, green-eyed loner who's out there somewhere with my heart in his pocket.

Nope. It can't be. I deleted him.

"What? You don't like fun?" Carter asks, giving me a lazy grin.

"What *kind* of fun?"

"You'll see." He starts walking again with his arm still around my shoulders, obviously expecting my feet to just magically do what he wants, like everything else.

When they don't, Carter looks down at me in shock. Nobody tells him no. Especially not his sweet, eager-to-please little girlfriend, Rainbow Williams.

But that girl, *Rainbow*, she was lying to him just as much as he was lying to her. About the music she liked, her favorite movies, how much she loved to watch sports and suck his dick. Rainbow tried to be everything he ever wanted, and he still left her behind.

So, now, all he gets is Rain.

And *No* is that bitch's middle name.

"Tell me now, or I'm not going."

Carter's dark eyebrows pull together. "Seriously?"

I respond with a glare.

"Listen, I don't know what's up with your whole … *attitude*, but … it's kinda sexy." He grins.

"Ugh!" I huff and shrug off his arm, turning and stomping off the way we came.

I make it all of two steps before his hand clamps down around my bicep, and his boyish laugh bounces off the walls.

"Simmer down, Rainbow Brite."

"Don't call me that," I snap, trying to wriggle out of his grip, but his hand is so big his fingers practically wrap around my arm twice. "Let me go!"

"If I do, will you listen to me?"

I grunt and give up the fight, crossing my arms over my chest the second he lets go. I still have my back to him, so Carter walks around and stands in front of me. He's looking at me the way he looks at Sophie when she's being a brat.

"The guys and I are gonna play hockey in the old Pottery Barn, okay?" He points over my shoulder, but I don't look. "I thought you might want to come along. You always loved coming to my games back in the day. You can be my cheerleader."

He smirks, and I want to slap it off his face.

Be his cheerleader. Puh-leez.

"I'll come but only if I get to play."

The second the words are out of my mouth, I regret them very, very much. I don't know the first thing about hockey. I'm probably gonna make a total fool out of myself, twist an ankle, and …

Oh, whatever. None of this matters, and we're all gonna die. Right?

"*You* wanna play hockey?" he scoffs.

"You heard me." I crane my neck back to look him in the eye.

As Carter studies me, I decide that putting that puzzled look on his pretty face is worth whatever sprained ligament I'm about to suffer.

Finally, he shrugs. "Okay, but they're not gonna go easy on you."

God, if you're listening, please make them go easy on me.

We walk inside what used to be Pottery Barn, and I realize it's the first time I've ever been in one. I used to stare at the gorgeous window displays when I was a kid. Everything looked so shiny and expensive and stylish. Of course, Mama would never take me inside because she knew I'd probably break a four-hundred-dollar lamp within five seconds, but that only made my longing stronger. I told myself that the day I became a real grown-up would be the day I came here and bought the first thing that caught my eye without even looking at the price tag.

Well, here I am, and even though I'm ten years too late to do any shopping, I can still feel the spirit of every glittery picture frame and smell the essence of every scented candle that used to line these shelves. Even though they're covered in dust and water stains now, the wall-to-wall hardwood floors and white custom shelves lining the open space still feel just as luxurious as they did when I was a kid. And lucky for me, everything in the store is totally free now … as long as you're in the market for a mildewed cardboard box, a crate of broken dishes, or a random, cracked toilet seat.

A group of runaways is gathered in the center of the store, chatting. I recognize all four guys from Q's table—the accordion player in the patched-up jean jacket, the lanky teenagers with matching bullet belts and ripped skinny jeans, and the heavyset, bearded banjo player who's wearing suspenders to keep his threadbare corduroy pants from falling off.

"Well, if it ain't The Lumineers," Carter teases as we approach the group.

All eight eyeballs land on me, and instead of widening in predatory lust—like I was used to back in Franklin Springs—they narrow in disgust. These guys look at me the way their queen looks at me—like I'm a threat, a liar, an *outsider* who needs to be disposed of as soon as she's no longer useful. On the one hand, it's kinda refreshing to have a man look at me like something other than his next victim. But, on the other hand, I also kinda need to keep living here, so it might be time for me to dust off my Student Council smile and make some new friends.

Uggggggh.

With a deep breath and dead soul, I reach way down inside and find a tiny glimmer of the girl I once was. The one who could turn into whatever she needed to be, whenever she needed to be it. Usually, what I needed to be was Carter's agreeable little trophy at school, or Mama's picture-perfect daughter at church, or Daddy's gentle voice of reason at home. But right here, right now, all I need to be is *one of them.*

I scan their clothes, shoes, and visible tattoos for *anything* we might have in common, but I can't find a damn thing. I don't have dreadlocks. I don't recognize any of the band logos on their T-shirts or jacket patches. I can't even read their terrible tattoos. And they're all just wearing busted, old black Converse and combat boots.

I glance down at my jeggings, brown hiking boots, and Franklin Springs High sweatshirt and sigh.

"What's up, man?" the banjo player asks Carter without taking his eyes off me. "I hate to break it to you, but bringing your own personal cheerleader ain't gonna help you win."

More cheerleader jokes. Awesome.

"Oh, she ain't my cheerleader." Carter glances down at me with a smirk. "She's the nurse. I brought her, so she can patch you up as soon as I get done beatin' yo' ass."

The guys all laugh and walk toward each other, meeting in the center of the deserted store to high five and slap each other on the back.

Okay, I don't get it. Carter's dressed like a quintessential jock in his basketball shorts, three-hundred-dollar limited-edition sneakers, and Nike swoosh T-shirt while these guys look like something that crawled out of a punk rock band's tour bus after it rolled down the side of a mountain. And yet, here they are, laughing and talking shit like old friends.

Oh, right. Sports. They have sports in common. And penises.

I roll my eyes and sigh even harder. I should just go. I'm way out of my element, and I obviously can't muster the appropriate amount of enthusiasm or personality needed to make new friends right now.

Or ever again probably.

"Guys, this is Rain." Carter extends his hand backward and gives me a wink over his shoulder. "She's totally in love with me."

His grin is friendly, but his words land on me like a piano. I *was* in love with him—for my whole entire life actually—but now, those feelings are just a punch line for another one of his stupid, cocky jokes.

I glare at him, feeling hurt. Feeling embarrassed. Feeling like I want to spin around and retreat to my nice, safe cave and never come back out. But then I scan the expectant faces of the four strangers staring at me, and I realize something. He made fun of them too, and they didn't storm off like little bitches. They dished it right back out. Maybe that's what friends do here. Maybe Carter is just trying to be *friends* with me.

Maybe I can play this game after all …

"Carter," I deadpan, "the only person in love with you here is *you*." I tilt my head in the direction of the banjo player. "And maybe that guy."

The bullet-belt twins look at each other and then howl in unison, slapping their knobby knees through the holes in their skintight jeans. The accordion player snickers under his breath, and the banjo player's face pales for a second before splitting into a massive grin.

Cocking his head to one side, he raises a furry eyebrow and glances at Carter. "Sweetheart," he whispers, placing a delicate hand on Carter's forearm, "I thought we agreed we weren't gonna tell nobody."

I snort through my nose as I try to keep a straight face, and the entire group bursts into laughter.

Carter shakes off the banjo player's meaty hand and introduces me to the world's finest homeless hockey team. "Rain, this is Loudmouth …"

The denim-vest-wearing accordion player drops his eyes and tips the brim of his paperboy hat at me.

"Brangelina …"

The bullet-belt twins throw me a wink and an air kiss.

"And my secret lover, Tiny Tim."

The banjo player extends his proud belly and slides his thumbs behind his suspenders.

"So …" I shift my attention to the skinny gutter punks in the middle of the lineup. "Which one of you gets to be Angelina?"

"Ooh! Me!" they both shout in unison, raising their hands.

"Dude, your name is literally Brad," the one on the left snaps at the one on the right.

"That's just semantics. I make a way better Angelina. Just look at the cleft in this chin." He tilts his face toward the light streaming in from the hallway.

"What cleft?" The guy on the right squints and leans in closer. "Oh, that little thing? Here, let me make it bigger for you."

In the blink of an eye, Not Brad cocks his fist back and lets it fly, landing a blow right in the middle of Brad's chin. Brad's head snaps back, but he recovers quickly, putting Not Brad in a headlock and giving him an uppercut to the spleen.

"It's a touchy subject," Carter whispers in my ear as the two guys wrestle to the ground.

I look up to find him inches away, a smirk on his lips and pride shining out of his honey-colored eyes. That's another smile I know by heart.

The one that means I did good.

Once upon a time, that look was everything the future Mrs. Rainbow Renshaw ever wanted. I was willing to do whatever it took to earn Carter's approval. And when I did, that look was my reward. I would commit whatever I did to memory so that I could keep doing it just to get more of that look.

Now, the only look I want to see on Carter's face is his mouth hanging open when I beat his ass in hockey.

I clap my hands together, drawing the attention of the group. "As team captain, I choose Brangelina."

It turns out that hockey is just soccer with sticks, and I played church-league soccer until middle school—when I realized that church-league soccer wasn't cool. Of course, when I played, we used an actual ball and goals with nets, not a jagged piece of broken plate and sticks fashioned from wooden pallets, but otherwise, it's not really that different. Plus, Brangelina and I kinda make a perfect team. I hang back and play goalie while they run around Carter like tornadoes with ADHD. Poor guy is pretty much on his own out there. Tiny Tim's approach to goalkeeping consists of talking shit while moving as little as possible, and Loudmouth's main priority is strictly defense. As in, defending *himself* against having to interact with the puck by all means necessary.

Carter pulls his signature basketball spin move to evade Not Brad, but I block his breakaway shot with the side of my foot. I have to use the side of my foot because the stick I'm using is just two splintery pieces of pallet nailed together, and it wouldn't stop a marble. When nobody calls me on it, I raise my worthless stick in the air triumphantly.

"Boom!" I shout at Carter, but my gloating is cut short when the top half of my homemade stick swings down and practically chops my fingers off.

"Ahh!" I drop my stick and grab my hand, holding it as I bounce in place and hiss through my teeth.

"High-sticking!" Tiny Tim shouts, pointing at me like a suspect in a police lineup. "High-sticking!"

"What the hell is high-sticking?"

"High-sticking is when a player is struck by a stick that has been raised above waist-level," Loudmouth quietly recites to himself while staring at the ground.

"But I hurt *myself!*"

Carter smirks. "Sorry, babe. Rules are rules. You gotta go to the penalty box."

"Penalty box?" I swing my head from side to side. "What penalty box?"

Tiny Tim points to the mildewed cardboard box I noticed when we first walked in and grins through his grimy beard.

"You have *got* to be kidding me."

"Go on, princess." He chuckles, waving me off. "Two minutes for high-sticking. Do your time like a man."

I stick my tongue out at him as I stomp over to the soggy cube of cardboard. Loudmouth follows me with his head down, and once I'm sitting inside with my knees pulled to my chest, he adds the final touch.

He picks up the toilet seat lying on the ground next to the box, and just before the quiet little accordion player slips it over my head like a statement necklace, I notice that someone has scrawled the word *PENULTEE* on it in black permanent marker.

I glare at him, but it's pointless. His eyes are on the floor, and he's already halfway back to his safe little corner of the store.

The guys howl with laughter, and my pout lasts all of five seconds before I'm laughing right along with them.

"What's so funny?" a feline voice purrs from the entryway.

My head swivels to the left where Q is leaning against the wall, looking cool as hell with her lion's mane of dreads and her kicked-back posture, but she doesn't fool me. The intensity in her eyes and tightness in her muscles tell me that she's ready to pounce on the next gazelle that crosses her path.

In fact, she can't wait.

"The doc got a penalty for high-sticking against *herself!*" Tiny chuckles, wiping a tear from his eye.

Q raises a brow as she takes in the sight of me sitting in a cardboard box with a toilet seat around my neck before her gaze cuts back to the group. "Looks like y'all could use a third then."

"But … they're supposed to be down a player for two minutes," Tiny whines.

"Two minutes is up," Q snaps back, gliding across the room to pick up my stick.

She doesn't look at me again, but I get the message loud and clear.

I'm out when she says I'm out.

And not just in the game.

I watch from the box of shame as Brad and Carter face off in the center of the store. Q's presence seems to have shaken everybody up. They all seem so quiet and distracted. After tapping sticks with Brad, Carter easily gets the jump on him, sending the ceramic shard skidding across the hardwood, straight toward our goal. But right before it goes in, Q slams her stick—*my stick*—down on the ground sideways, blocking the entire goal with a triumphant smirk. The chunk of fine china ricochets off of it, and Carter's shoulders bunch up around his ears.

I know, if she had been anyone else, he would have laid into her for cheating, but with her being his only source of food, water, and shelter at the moment, he bites his tongue and glares at me instead.

I know, big guy. I know.

Loudmouth hustles after the broken piece of plate and sets it back in the center of the store.

"I got this," Q announces, leaving her post as goalie to take Not Brad's spot across from Carter.

Not Brad shrinks away from her the moment she gets close, but Carter holds his ground.

Placing the mangled end of his makeshift hockey stick on the ground next to the broken plate, Carter looks at Q expectantly. He's not just going to let her have this. He's still a competitor through and through, and as stupid as that might seem right now, I get it.

In this post–April 23 world, the only things you get to keep are the things you refuse to let someone else take away from you.

Carter taps his stick on the ground and lifts it a few inches in the air, waiting for Q to smack it with the end of hers—the signal that it's go time—but as usual, Q plays by her own rules. As soon as he lifts his stick off the hardwood, she whacks the ceramic puck as hard as she can, sending the shard careening directly into Tiny's portly gut. The room goes from silent to deafening as Tiny clutches his stomach with a guttural wail, and the puck falls to the floor with a heart-stopping shatter.

Q makes a show of dragging an inch-long fingernail down her tongue and using it to write the number one in the air. Then, she turns toward me, victory shining brightly in her vomit-colored eyes as she tosses her almost waist-length dreads over her shoulder.

"Take care of that," she barks, flicking her ring-adorned fingers in the direction of her latest victim. "And yo, when I said you looked like shit the other day …"

The corners of her full mouth twist into something truly evil as she stalks toward me. I try to keep my face neutral as she approaches, but when she reaches out to drag one of those talons along the edge of the toilet seat around my neck, I flinch.

"I was wrong," she coos, gripping the rim between her thumb and forefinger. A glimmer of malice flashes across her face just before she leans forward, placing her lips against my ear, and whispers the word, "Flush." Before I have time to react, she jerks her hand to the left, sending the toilet seat spinning around my neck like a horseshoe. Q throws her head back and cackles as sharp, stinging heat sears my cheeks and burns my eyes. "*Now*, you look like shit!"

She turns and sashays toward the entrance, still chuckling to herself, and Brangelina parts for her like the Red Sea. I quietly lift the toilet seat over my head and clutch it to my chest like a teddy bear. Carter squeezes Tiny Tim's shoulder while keeping his furious eyes locked on me. Loudmouth is practically rocking in the corner.

And, in that silence, we hear it.

The pounding.

Q stops for a second, listening like the rest of us, but when she spins around, it's like there's a completely different person in her place. Her face lights up, her mouth splits into a manic grin, and her wide eyes dart from person to person, scanning our expressions for signs that we hear it too.

Completely ignoring the fact that we're all glaring at her like she just stabbed our dog, Q snaps her fingers and yells, "Ohhhh shit! Y'all know what time it is?"

Tiny Tim shrugs off his anger and nods.

Loudmouth appears to be blushing.

Brangelina grins at each other and does a dramatic jump high five.

And Carter's lingering gaze heats my skin.

"It's bath time, muhfuckas!"

Rain

Q's HUSKY VOICE GROWS more and more distant as she takes off down the hallway, yelling, "Bath time, bitches!" at the top of her lungs.

Brangelina and Loudmouth follow, no questions asked, and even Tiny Tim, with a wince and a moan, saunters off behind them.

"Hey, Tiny?" I call as I step out of the cardboard box.

He stops in the store entrance and turns toward me. Sad brown eyes, tucked inside a frame of shoulder-length dreadlocks and bushy brown facial hair, stare back.

"Come see me in the tuxedo shop later, and I'll take care of that for you." I give him a sympathetic smile and glance down at the puncture wound he's covering with his thick hand.

Tiny salutes me with two fingers before trudging off in the same direction as his friends.

Suddenly, it's just Carter and me and the sound of the rain beating down on the roof. His eyes burn like liquid gold, molten hot with unexpressed rage, and are locked on me like I'm the void he wants to pour it all into.

"You okay?" he asks, stalking across the room toward me.

"I'm fine," I snap, dusting the dirt off my ass. "Is she always that much of a bi—"

Before I can finish my insult, Carter stops a foot in front of me and claps a huge hand over my mouth.

He scans the room with wide eyes and then whispers, "In case you haven't noticed, you're the only other girl here her age. Q doesn't like competition, so I suggest you keep your mouth shut and your head down if you want to stick around."

"Ugh!" I jerk away from him and cross my arms over my chest. "So I just have to take her shit?"

Carter's jaw clenches, and his nostrils flare. "Look, I don't like it either, okay? You think it's easy for me to sit back and watch somebody disrespect my friends like that? Fuck no. But we have nowhere else to go, do we? Not unless—"

"No," I cut him off before he can say another word about places that no longer exist.

Carter closes his mouth and nods. I didn't realize there was a glimmer of hope in his eyes until it was extinguished. "Okay then. Home sweet mall it is. Come on."

He extends his hand to me, but I just stare at it.

"Where are we going?"

"To take a shower."

"Shower?"

Carter rolls his eyes. "When it rains, everybody runs up to the roof to shower off. Q has a stash of soap and shampoo and shit up there. It's"—he lifts a shoulder in a nonchalant half-shrug—"*fun.*"

"Q," I spit her name out like it's a bloody, cracked tooth before something occurs to me. "Wait. So, everybody up there is … naked?"

Carter chuckles and takes my hand even though I didn't give it to him. "Told you it was fun."

"But … what about your parents? What about Sophie?"

He starts walking backward toward the door, tugging on my hand with a playful, overconfident grin on his face. "It's not really their scene. They duck out the back door of the shoe store and shower off behind the bushes." He gives my hand a tug. "Come on, Rainbow Brite … if you're lucky, I might let you wash my back."

Suddenly, my hand is free, and my feet are moving, and my face is hot, and I can hear Carter's smug voice behind me insisting that he was, "Just kidding."

But I don't stop. I don't care about his stupid joke. I have a much, much bigger problem right now.

I run straight back to the tuxedo shop and practically scream at Lamar to take Quint up to the roof to shower off. They look at me like I have two heads, but I can't rein in my panic. The walls are closing in, and I need them to get the hell out before I have a full-blown meltdown.

"Go!" I shout, shoving a finger in the direction of the door.

Quint is finally healthy enough to maybe handle a flight of stairs.

Maybe.

I hope.

"Just don't touch his bandage!"

"Okay, *Mom.* Jesus." Lamar holds his hands up before helping his big brother off the floor.

I want so badly to rush over to them, to help Lamar get him cleaned up, but … I just … I just *can't.*

As soon as they're out the door, I lift the white cube in the center of the store that was once a pedestal for a prom-ready mannequin and pull my backpack out from underneath. I sink to the floor and dig through the contents, feeling my chest tighten more and more with every passing second. A clap of thunder shakes the walls, pushing me to move faster.

I find the travel-sized toiletries that I packed from home and have to squeeze my eyes shut and count backward from twenty to keep from picturing the beachfront motel where those little bottles came from.

… three … two … deep breath … one.

Squeezing the shampoo and conditioner bottles in my fists, I focus solely on my surroundings and begin to walk backward out of the tuxedo shop entrance. Another clap of thunder makes me jump as I turn and continue to move in reverse toward the doors at the end of the hallway.

I can do this.

Step.

I don't have to look at anything.

Step.

Not that there's anything out there.

Step.

Nope.

Step.

Nothing at all.

I feel the rain spitting on the side of my face through the broken windows just before my back hits the smooth metal handle of one of the main entrance doors.

Every beat of my heart feels like a lightning strike, reverberating through my body and making me tremble. The entire hallway stretched out before me is empty, and although it's still early afternoon, the storm has darkened the mall to the point that I can't even see the fountain from here.

Good.

The darkness helps calm my nerves. It helps me lose myself and pretend.

I'm just gonna step out this door into another … wetter … part of the mall. That's all. I'm not going outside. There is no outside. This is the … the … mall shower room. Yeah.

I set the bottles on the ground and pull off my clothes as quickly as possible, throwing them in front of me far enough that they won't land in one of the puddles forming by the door. Then, I press my naked back to the door again, cherishing the feeling of cool metal against my heated skin.

I'm in the mall. And when I push through this door, I'll still be in the mall. No big deal.

I memorize which bottle is in which hand—*shampoo right, conditioner left*—and then, with a deep breath and my eyes screwed shut, I push against the door with my body. A gust of wind blows my hair into my face, but the feeling of rain pouring down on me doesn't come. Only a slightly stronger mist, still spitting at me sideways.

The awning! Dammit!

My heart lurches into high gear as I realize that I have farther to go. Instead of walking straight back into the open parking lot to get out from under the cover, I decide that I need to stay close to the building. I need something to keep me grounded. With my knuckles against the brick and the plastic bottles in my fists, I move sideways in the direction of the mist. The droplets grow larger with every blind step I take, and when they finally begin to soak my hair and chill my skin, I stop. I can't remember which bottle is the shampoo and which is the conditioner, and I'm too terrified to open my eyes and check. So, I choose one blindly, squeeze the contents into my hand, and begin to scrub my entire body furiously.

I hear a sizzle in the air before the next clap of thunder. It's so close that it shakes the ground under my feet and elicits excited screams and nervous laughter from the people on the roof.

People on the roof.

"No!" I yell, possibly out loud, as I push the fear down and try to tell myself that I'm not outside.

The world I left and all its hurts don't exist anymore. There is no trigger out here that could possibly hurt me. But I am, and it does, and when I take one more step out from under the cover of the awning—when I feel my feet sink into something earthy and soft and as familiar as barefoot Easter egg hunts and summer games of tag—I find it.

Thunder claps, and pain seizes me like a lightning bolt striking from the ground up. The grass under my feet hurts worse than anything I thought I might encounter out here, but I've missed it so much that I can't bring myself to move.

I miss it all so fucking much.

The shampoo running down my face smells like summer vacation, and I can't stop the tears or the memories from coming now. I remember my dad taking me out into the ocean so deep that I could barely touch and showing me how to find starfish with my toes. The heartbroken look on his face when Mama said we had to throw them all back. The one he smuggled home in his suitcase that caused the entire car to smell like dead fish for months.

The memories come faster and faster, slamming into me from all sides. Now, the overgrown grass is smashed beneath my knees, my shins. Cool mud squishes between my fingers as I dig them into the soft earth, desperate for something to hold on to as the pain slices through me.

Fireworks on the Fourth of July.

S'mores around the burn barrel after raking all the fall leaves.

Christmas movies. Curling up with Mama on the couch. Slightly crooked stockings. Very burnt cookies for Santa. Catching my dad at three in the morning, wrapping presents with a cigarette hanging out of his mouth.

And then I see Wes … beautiful, guarded, wounded Wes … asleep in my bathtub after burying them both.

I test my legs. I have to crawl away from this nightmare. I have to get back inside. I have to get away from the smells and the textures and the sounds of this deleted world. On wobbly limbs, I claw my way back to the door and don't stop until it's firmly closed behind me.

Pressing my back to the cool metal again, I suck in as many deep, mildew-scented breaths as it takes for my heart rate to finally begin to return to normal. When I open my eyes, I expect to feel relieved. I'm back in my safe new world now. I never have to open that door again.

But the second my gaze lands on the entrance of the Hello Kitty store, that's exactly what I do.

I turn and push that sucker wide open.

So that my puke will land on the sidewalk.

May 3
Rain

A KNOCK ON THE door makes me jump, causing the brittle pages of the ancient tuxedo catalog I'm sitting on to crinkle loudly.

"Come in," I call out, but my voice doesn't want to work, possibly due to the hours I've spent sobbing in this very spot since yesterday.

I clear my throat to try again but decide not to. I don't care who's there. I don't want them to come in.

The Savvi Formalwear office door opens anyway, letting in a slice of light from the hallway. It tears across the floor, missing me by inches.

"Yo, boss lady …" Lamar steps into the doorway. His silhouetted short, messy dreads bounce as his head swivels from left to right, scanning the dark room for signs of life. Then, he snorts out a laugh. "What the hell you doin' down there?"

I peer back at him as if I were viewing him from the grave. As if the activities of the living were beyond my grasp. Speaking. Feeling. Giving a damn. I remember doing those things. I just don't remember how I did them.

"You sittin' under the desk 'cause Mr. Renshaw took the rolly chair?" Lamar laughs. "Or was there a tornado warnin' I don't know about?"

I stare back, waiting for the words to come, but they don't.

I'm sorry. Rain's not here anymore. I cried her out. This is just her fleshy wrapper, left under a desk like a wad of chewing gum.

Lamar's smile fades as his eyes adjust to the darkness of the windowless office. When he finally gets a good look at me, he says, "Hey … you all right?"

Flipping my hood up over my head, I turn and face the wall.

"So, uh … Quint's feelin' a little better since gettin' cleaned up yesterday. I think I'ma try to take him to get breakfast. You wanna come?" There's a note of hope at the end of his question. "I hear they're makin' eeeeggggggs …"

I don't respond.

I hear the air leave his lungs, taking the wind out of his sails along with it.

"C'mon, Rainy Lady," he whines. "I had to help him shower *and* feed him by myself last night."

If there were a shred of feeling left in this husk of a body, the fact that Lamar is more concerned about getting help with his brother than finding out why I spent the entire night curled up in a ball under a desk in a dark room might hurt. But it doesn't. Nothing can hurt me anymore.

I'm not even here.

"Fine. I'll do it myself. Again!"

The door slam echoes in my ears for several minutes after he leaves. Or could it be hours? I don't know anymore. I feel like I'm floating in primordial ooze. Disconnected from reality. Disconnected from my thoughts and feelings. Disconnected from time.

The only thing I can feel is my body, and the longer I sit here, the more it makes itself known. My throbbing bladder, my growling stomach, my aching legs and back—they join together in a chorus of pain until I have no choice but to move.

With everyone still at breakfast, the store is quiet. I make my way down the hall on rubbery legs. I watch them as they lift and step, but my brain doesn't register the impact. It's as if I'm wearing virtual reality goggles.

Maybe I'm going crazy.

I open the door to the employee restroom and prop it open so that I can see what I'm doing as I shimmy my jeans down and sit on the edge of the sink to pee.

When I'm done, I continue to sit there, staring at a lacy spiderweb draped over a useless air-conditioning vent, admiring the dark gray nothingness swirling inside of me. Now that my bladder's not full anymore, I am empty.

Truly and completely.

I zip and button my jeans with numb, clumsy fingers and make my way back to my cave. This time, I walk with my entire shoulder hugging the wall. I keep my gaze fixed on the entrance to the store—it's too disorienting to look at my feet—but before I make it back to the office, a demon with slime-colored eyes and a mane made of snakes fills the doorway. Her jerky gaze lands on me—or what's left of me—and a sneer splits her face from ear to ear.

I know I should be afraid of her, but that feeling is gone too. All I can do is stare back and wait for her to attack.

"There you are, *Flush*."

She stalks toward me with the posture of a gangster even though she's wearing baggy black men's pants cut off at the knee, motorcycle boots, and a black T-shirt that's at least three sizes too big. She doesn't stop until she's standing right in front of me. Then, she yanks the hood off my head. Grabbing a handful of my hair, Q jerks me forward. I don't feel the pain. I only hear her take a long, deep breath as she lifts a fistful of my hair to her nose.

"Fresh as a fuckin' daisy." Q shoves my head backward, and her eyes blaze. "Riddle me this, bitch. How is it that you show up wit' nothin' but the clothes on yo' back, you ain't been eatin' my food, you ain't been usin' my muhfuckin' shampoo, yet here you is, alive and smellin' like a gotdamn rose bush?"

I stare at her from the safety of the nothingness and blink.

"Where's ... yo' ... shit?" She jams two fingers into my chest with each word, her face mere inches from mine.

"I'm sorry," I say, the sound of my own voice taking me by surprise. "Rain isn't home right now."

Q's face darkens, and her hand coils into my hair again, yanking my head down sideways.

"Rain don't have a home, bitch. This *my* home, and I'm here to collect my muhfuckin' rent." Her grip on my hair tightens to the point that I finally register the pain, and I'm almost relieved to feel it. "You got two seconds to tell me where the fuck yo' stash is before I put you *and* ya little boyfriends out."

Lifting my eyes, I glance over her shoulder at the white plaster mannequin in the center of the store. Q turns her head to follow my gaze. Then she shoves me to the ground and stomps off in that direction.

I watch from my sideways spot on the hall floor as the mannequin falls to the ground like a cut tree. The thud of it is quickly followed by the sound of a zipper and wild cackling laughter, but all I can focus on is the blank stare of the plaster man, lying in the same position as me. Expressionless. Empty. Unfazed.

Is this what I've become?

Q drags me by my hair down the hall to the food court, rambling on about Christmas coming early, but still, I feel nothing. Not when we get there and a hush falls over the crowd. Not when Carter slams his plate down and stands up with eyes full of fury. Not when Mr. Renshaw tries to do the same, only to wince and tumble back into his rolly chair with a frustrated grunt. I feel nothing when Mrs. Renshaw covers Sophie's eyes or when Lamar and Quint look on helplessly. And when Tiny, Loudmouth, and Brangelina chuckle as Q shoves me toward their table, my only thought is about Tiny's wound and how he never came by to let me take a look at it last night.

"From now on, we gon' call dis bitch muhfuckin' Santa Claus!" Q announces as she unzips my backpack and dumps the contents out in the middle of their table.

The runaways gasp and cheer and lunge for the pile, but Q slaps their hands away as she presents each item.

"Granola bars!" She holds the box up to an enthusiastic rabble from the table. "Slim Jims!"

"Yay!" The crowd cheers.

"What the fuck is dis? *GoGo squeeZ applesauce*?" She reads the label.

"Fuck yeah!"

"Band-Aids, aspirin, antihista-whatever-the-fuck." She blindly tosses each item over her shoulder, pelting me with medical supplies, before she goes completely still. "Oh, helllll nah."

Q glares at me with murderous eyes before holding up a variety box of Kotex. "Bitch, you had muhfuckin' tampons this *whole time*!"

I see a flash of movement and close my eyes just before the back of Q's hand meets my face, all four of her chunky silver rings slicing across my cheekbone.

Time stands still as pain explodes across the side of my face.

I feel like I'm on a sitcom where one of the characters is freaking out, so another character slaps them and yells, *Snap out of it!*

Well, Q's slap snaps me the fuck out of it. Only there's no laugh track. No commercial break. No lovable neighbor at the ready with a zinger of a punch line. It's just pain. And humiliation. And tears. And loss. All the feelings I've been so graciously disconnected from burst through my defenses like a tidal wave in the wake of that slap.

Once time begins to move again, I realize that the entire cafeteria has erupted into hysterics. Everyone is on their feet. Everyone is yelling. Carter has one of the runaways by his ripped T-shirt and is screaming in his face. Brad and Not Brad are hauling me to my feet, high-fiving my limp palms for taking "one helluva hit." Q is standing on the table, tossing peanut butter sandwich crackers into the crowd like dollar bills. And Lamar is scurrying around the madness, picking up the medical supplies that Q pelted me with.

Then, just as suddenly as the outburst began, it stops.

And everyone turns to face the glowing TV monitors behind the fast-food counters.

Meanwhile ...
Wes

THUMP ... THUMP ... THUMP ... SCRRRRAPE.

Fuck.

My heart begins to pound as I listen to my foster mom's boyfriend stumbling up the stairs.

Thump ... thump-thump ... WHAM.

The thin walls rattle as he careens into them, ricocheting up the stairs and down the hall like a three-hundred-pound racquetball.

"Fuck you," he mutters to no one, and I reach under my pillow to grab my knife.

Ms. Campbell went to bed hours ago, which means Limp Dick here didn't get to fight with her tonight. She's been doing that—going to bed earlier and earlier, taking enough sleeping pills to tranquilize a horse, just so that by the time he gets fuck-shit-up drunk, she'll already be passed out.

And it's been working—for her.

Slam! My door swings open so hard that the knob punches a hole in the Sheetrock wall.

I try not to flinch, but I can't help it.

I hope he didn't notice.

"Wake up, you worthlessss sack of shit."

I grip the handle of my pocketknife tighter and crack one eye open to glance at the motherfucker unfastening his belt as he lumbers toward my mattress. The hall light is on, *and I notice that the peeling wallpaper just outside my open door isn't faded yellow with light-blue cornflowers on it anymore.*

It's blood red with black hooded horsemen all over it. Each one is carrying a different weapon over his head as he charges—a sword, a scythe, a torch, a mace. But they don't scare me anymore.

And neither does this asshole.

Because now I know this is just a dream.

"Get up, boy!" the disgusting, sweaty, pig of a man staggering toward me yells as he slides his belt off and pulls it taut, making a snapping sound with the leather.

I close my eyes.

It's just a dream.

I'm in control.

He can't hurt me anymore.

I hold my breath and lift my pointer finger off the handle of my knife, smiling as a smooth, metal trigger magically appears beneath it.

"Ahhh!" I sit up and swing my gun out in front of me, ready to shoot the face off that sweaty, worthless piece of shit.

But no one's there.

I'm not in Ms. Campbell's foster home anymore. I'm alone, on a couch, being assaulted by the sunlight that's streaming in through a pair of dingy plastic blinds.

"Fuck," I groan, flopping back down onto the sofa and throwing my forearm over my eyes.

Even though I woke up before that motherfucker had a chance to beat the shit out of me, it feels like *somebody* did. My head throbs like it's been slammed repeatedly in a car door. My equilibrium thinks I'm on a dinghy in the middle of a hurricane. And I'm pretty sure everything inside my body has gone sour.

Hell, everything in my entire fucking *life*.

When I open my eyes again, I'm not sure what day it is or how long I've been here, but I know exactly where the fuck I am by the fading scent of death in the air.

I groan and rub my swollen lids.

From my sideways viewpoint on the couch, my eyes focus on an empty bottle of Grey Goose lying sideways on the coffee table, mirroring my miserable position.

I squeeze my eyes shut and pinch the bridge of my nose as I vaguely remember stomping through the rubble of Carter's burned-up house and pulling everything salvageable out of the still-intact freezer.

Including a handle of vodka.

My plan had been to find a new place to crash—maybe a nice, abandoned bachelor pad with a fully stocked beer fridge and a pool—but the highway was only clear maybe another block or two past Rain's house. With the riots in Franklin Springs still going strong, there was no point in risking a flat tire just to get another gun pulled on me in town by some jacked-up meth head who hadn't slept in three days.

So, I came to the one place I knew would be empty.

It had nothing to do with the fact that a certain rag doll–looking, mindfuck of a girl used to live here.

I just needed supplies and shelter.

And a shitload of vodka.

The sound of a car engine has me bolting upright again. I haven't heard a car on this road since I got here. I lean to the left so that I can see the road through the gap between the blinds and the window frame. The highway is only clear from here to the Pritchard Park exit, so whoever this is, they might be coming from the mall.

Staring into the sunlight only makes my head pound harder, but I hold my breath and squint through the pain. When the vehicle finally comes into view, I release that breath in the form of a snort. Slowing to a crawl in front of Rain's house is the motherfucking mailman. Dude doesn't even pull to a complete stop. He just throws a handful of envelopes at the mailbox lying on its side in the driveway and keeps on going.

Unbelievable.

So this is what, "You are encouraged to resume your daily lives," looks like. Bury your dead. Barricade your front doors. Scavenge for food. But hey, we got the utilities up and running again! Your bill is in the mail!

I scrub a hand down my face, feeling at least a week's worth of stubble beneath my palm, and decide to take advantage of those utilities before the county realizes the owners of this house are buried under two feet of red dirt in the backyard and cuts them off again.

I stand and wait a second for the room to stop spinning before I head for the stairs.

I spent the worst night of my life on the second floor of this house. The door on the right is where I found Mrs. Williams—or what was left of her after her husband blasted her face off. The door on the left is where I found Rain's lifeless body after she took a fistful of painkillers, lying on a mattress with a shotgun blast through it, too. And this bathroom—

I flip the light switch and wince as the fluorescent light illuminates what feels like a scene from another life.

Rain's pillow still sits on the floor by the toilet where I spent most of the night with my fingers down her throat. Her long, thick black braid is still lying on top of the trash can in the corner of the room. And vanilla-scented candles still cover every flat surface. I'd pulled them out of Rain's bedroom that night to block out the stench of death from the rest of the house, but now, I'd take blood and brains over sweet vanilla.

Because it reminds me of her.

When we first met, Rain smelled like sugar cookies, birthday cake, vanilla frosting with rainbow sprinkles—things I wished my mom had baked for me as a child, things I smelled and tasted at other kids' houses. Kids whose parents remembered their birthdays. Kids whose parents loved them.

That's what Rain smelled like to me—the kind of love I always wanted but never had.

But after a few days, she didn't smell like vanilla anymore.

She smelled like *me*.

I took every good, pure, sweet thing about Rain, chewed it up, and swallowed it.

I'm the reason she took all those pills that night.

I'm the reason she almost joined her parents in the dirt out back.

And I'm the reason she's probably lying naked in Carter's arms right now.

There's a reason none of my houses ever smelled like vanilla.

It's because love doesn't exist in my world.

I step over the pillow and turn the handle on the shower faucet as far as it will go. The pipes groan and rattle in protest, but a second later, water sprays from the faucet. I sigh and set my gun down on the counter, pushing some of the candles aside to make room. I pull off my Hawaiian shirt and lay it on the closed toilet lid. Then, I turn sideways to look at my bullet wound in the mirror. It's damn near healed.

I close my eyes and remember the way it felt when Rain put that first bandage on. Her touch was so gentle, but the pain it caused was excruciating. I'd wanted a woman to touch me like that my whole life, and once I felt it, I knew walking away would hurt worse than any fucking gunshot ever could.

I hate being right.

I blow out a shaky breath and go to strip off the rest of my clothes when the sound of voices has me reaching for my revolver.

Standing in the space between the sink and the open bathroom door, I press my back against the wall and listen. I can't make out what's being said over the sound of the shower, but I definitely hear someone downstairs.

A million different scenarios run through my mind, but the only one that makes sense is that it's pillagers snooping around for supplies. They're not gonna find much downstairs unless they check the freezer or swipe the keys to the motorcycle or truck, but the fact that they're talking at full volume despite hearing a running shower upstairs tells me that they're ballsy as fuck—and probably well-armed.

I tiptoe down the hall with my gun drawn. With each step closer to the living room I get, the clearer the voices become. The one talking right now is definitely male, which is good. I have no problem shooting the fuck out of a man. And, with another few steps, I can tell he's definitely a good ole boy. This isn't one of the Glock-toting gangbangers from the grocery store. This is one of the rifle-slinging, pickup truck–driving rednecks who tried to jump me in town.

I take the stairs as quietly as possible with my back against the wall. By the third stair, I begin to make out a few words here and there—words like *violation* and *willful disobedience*. By the fifth, I find their source—a glowing TV screen reflected in the framed poster above the couch.

I exhale and take the stairs a little less quietly the rest of the way to the living room but keep my gun drawn just in case.

"Governor Steele," a female reporter on the TV says. She's wearing so much makeup I suspect she's trying to hide the fact that she's just as hungover as I am. "Are you saying that what we're about to witness is a public trial of sorts?"

"No, ma'am," the bloated, old bastard answers, snatching the microphone out of her hand.

Turning to face the camera, Governor Steele puffs up his chest as a slow, evil smile curls up into his jowly, pockmarked cheeks. "What y'all are about to see heah … is a public execution."

I drop to the couch and set my gun on the coffee table.

"Excuse me," the reporter says, leaning into the microphone that Governor Fuckface stole from her. "Did you say … execution?"

"That's right, young lady. The events of April 23 have given the human race a new lease on life, and we must protect it at all costs. We were facing global extinction due to our bleeding hearts, and the only way to enshuh that never happens again is to protect the laws of natural selection *tooth and nail.*" The motherfucker pounds his doughy palm with the butt of the microphone. "In the words of the late, great Dr. Martin Luther King Junyuh, 'Desperate times call for desperate meashuhs.'"

"Governor, *sir,* I believe it was Hippocrates who said—"

He yanks the microphone even farther away from the leaning reporter. "We are no longuh countries divided! We are one race—the human race— and our sworn enemy is anyone who dares to defy the laws of natural selection again! The future of our very species depends on swift … just … *permanent* consequences." His jowls bounce as he shakes his fist in the air.

"But, Mr. Governor—"

The balding piece of shit actually shoves the reporter back with his forearm and takes a step toward the camera. "Today, y'all will see the lengths to which your government is willing to go to protect you from evah havin' to face the possibility of extinction again. We take this responsibility very seriously, which is why anyone reported to us for engaging in activities that save or sustain the life of someone with a terminal disability, injury, or illness will be tried within forty-eight hours and, if convicted, sentenced to death."

The camera pans to the right, past the shell-shocked reporter and the gold-domed Georgia State Capitol building behind them, and swivels around to face a grassy clearing surrounded by people.

"From now on," the governor continues, walking into view, "Plaza Park will be the final resting place for those who choose to defy the laws of natural selection in the great state of Georgia!"

The crowd cheers.

They actually fucking cheer.

"Because these criminals chose to violate the laws of naychuh, their bodies will be returned to naychuh as the ultimate atonement."

At the governor's gesture, the camera tilts down, revealing a four-by-four-foot hole dug out of the earth and a sapling with roots wrapped in burlap next to it.

"A Southern live oak, the majestic state tree of Georgia, will stand where these traitors fall as a reminduh that Mother Naychuh is the true lawmakuh now, and if we disobey her again, she will feed on us all."

He pauses for dramatic effect and then barks, "Bailiff, bring out the accused."

A tall, thin man in a cop uniform parts the crowd, dragging an older, white-haired guy behind him. He's wearing a prison uniform that looks like it's made out of the same burlap material the tree roots are wrapped in. His hands are bound behind his back. His eyes are blindfolded, and his mouth is gagged. He stumbles a few times as they trudge over the uneven grass, but he appears to be coming willingly.

My already-sour stomach turns putrid as I watch the bailiff stand him directly in front of the hole, facing the governor.

No. No, no, no, no, no …

"Doctuh Macavoy, you were arrested on April 29 at Grady Memorial Hospital for allegedly continuing the use of life-support procedyuhs after being ordered by your superiors to cease all Intensive Care Unit functions. During your trial on April 30, you were found guilty of this crime, and as such, you have been sentenced to death. If you have any last words, you may speak them now or forevuh hold your peace."

The bailiff removes the burlap gag from Dr. Macavoy's mouth.

He swallows, and with trembling lips and a quivering voice, he says, "Elizabeth Ann, I … I will love you forever and always. Take care of the girls for me. Tell them not to be sad. Tell them …" He sniffles. "Tell them whenever the wind blows, that's me giving them a hug."

By the time the gunshot rings out, I'm already halfway up the stairs.

Rain

I SQUEEZE MY EYES shut and cover my ears just in time, but I can still hear the gunshot blast and *slump* of a body falling into a hole even through my hands. The image of the gentleman in the burlap jumpsuit still blazes behind my eyelids, only now he is two men, both wearing red bandanas and pointing their pistols at Wes outside of Huckabee Foods. I watch their bodies jerk from the impact of my bullets. I hear their grunts and gurgles and gasps for air all over again as they fall onto a bed of broken glass at our feet. I feel the weight of the gun in my hand and the guilt on my conscience, and suddenly, I don't know who to feel sorrier for—the executed or the executioner.

When I finally open my eyes and lower my hands, the hole is gone. In its place stands a baby oak tree—even taller than the man who stood there before it—and Governor Steele, who's posing next to it with a golden shovel that has obviously never touched a speck of dirt. With every camera flash, his grin widens, and his pose becomes more and more heroic. But when the camera pans over to the reporter for final remarks, she has none to give. She simply stares into the lens, the blank look on her face mirroring my own until the screen goes black.

I stand, slack-jawed and silent, as the gravity of what I just witnessed settles around me. But I seem to be the only one. Within seconds, the uproar in the food court picks up right where it left off. They treat the broadcast like it was just another bad reality TV show, shocking at the time but forgotten as soon as it's over.

Q goes back to pelting the crowd with supplies from my backpack, working them into a frenzy as she mimics Governor Steele. "Return to naychuh, you filthy criminals! Pow! You a tree! Pow, pow! Now you a tree too! Hey! Stop movin', muhfucka! I said, you a tree!"

I stumble backward through the mosh pit of manic runaways until I bump into the burn barrel. Then, I spin around and head straight for the hallway. I pass Carter's family, clinging to one another at their table, but I don't stop when they call my name. I don't ever want to stop. For the first time since he left, I finally understand how Wes must have felt on his way out the door.

Because for the first time since I got here, I want to leave too.

But when I try to muster the courage to lift my head, to look out those broken windows I've been avoiding instead of down at my own two feet, I watch them turn and tread into the tuxedo shop instead.

Because, as much as I want to be, I'm nothing like Wes Parker.

I'm not brave.

I'm not strong.

I'm weak and scared and possibly going crazy.

That's probably why he left. Because Wes wears his past like armor while I wear mine like chains.

I lift the mannequin back onto the white cube in the center of the store. Then, I close the cabinet doors and checkout stand drawers that Q didn't slam shut while she was hunting for my supplies. I straighten the entire store, even adjusting the mannequin stands along the sides of the room so that they're perfectly spaced and symmetrical, until I feel my blood pressure go back to normal. Until the urge to scream and pull my hair out passes. Until I feel like I have a thimbleful of control in this fucked up new world.

When the boys come back, the place looks good as new, and so does Quint … almost.

I hop up onto the counter while Lamar dumps an armload of bandages, pills, and ointments on the dust-free surface next to me.

"Look at you, up and walkin' around. Did you get somethin' to eat?"

"Did I get somethin' to eat?" Quint winces in pain and lifts his fingertips to the bandage around his neck.

"You just got your ass handed to you by Queen Cuntface," Lamar finishes for him. "And you wanna know if he ate?"

I slam my hands over Lamar's mouth and shush him with wide, warning eyes.

Quint looks from him to the far corners of the room, as if he's searching for surveillance equipment.

"Are y'all for real?" Lamar mumbles before shoving my hands away. "I can't even call her a—"

"Shh!" Quint and I hiss in unison, waving our hands in his face.

But it's too late. Lamar's insult must have had the power to conjure Satan herself because Q waltzes in not one second later.

I slide off the counter, and Quint and I stand on either side of Lamar, as if we could actually protect him.

Her serpentine eyes slide across the three of us before settling on the boy in the middle. "Saw you and your bro here helpin' yaselves to a little breakfast this mornin'. Now, I been reeeeal patient wit' y'all, but now that I know ya girl here's been holdin' out on me, well ..." She spreads her arms wide and then slams her hands together with a loud clap. "Look at dat. My patience done run the fuck out."

"No!" I blurt out, bile and panic beginning to rise in my throat. "Please don't kick us out. Please. I ... I can't go back there. I ... we ..." My eyes swing from Quint's to Lamar's. "We don't have anywhere else to go!"

"Aww ... ain't that about a bitch? Maybe y'all shoulda thought about that before you fucked wit' ya landlord." Q's expression goes from sarcastic to murderous. "Get the fuck out."

"Please!" I cry, taking a step forward to reach for her arm.

Q yanks her arm out of my grasp before grabbing my shocked face with splayed fingers. Her thumbnail jams into my jawbone as the talons of her first two fingers stab into the swollen bags beneath my eyes, pulling my bottom lids down. She assesses me like a cat, trying to figure out if she wants to eat me now or play with me first.

"Touch me again, and I'ma take ya eyeballs and wear 'em as earrings, bitch."

I try to squeeze my eyelids shut and whisper, "I'm sorry," against her palm.

Q groans and releases my face with a shove. "I'll let y'all stay—on one condition." She turns her attention on the boys to my right and sneers, "These two lazy-ass muhfuckas start scoutin' ... *now*."

"No," I blurt and shake my head. "Please. They can't go out there. Quint still has an open wound, and Lamar ..." I turn and look at the smart-ass standing next to me. "He's just a kid."

"Boo-fuckin'-hoo, bitch." Q pretends to wipe a tear from her eye and flick it at me. "Scout or get the fuck out."

My frantic mind races through every possible choice. Even though the very thought of going outside makes me feel like the room is spinning and the walls are closing in, I can't risk getting kicked out or losing the only friends I have left.

With a heaving chest and sweating palms, I open my mouth to volunteer, but the voice that I hear isn't my own. It's deep and cool but with an edge that electrifies every cell in my body.

"I'll do it."

All four of our heads swivel toward the door, which is now filled with a presence I never thought I'd see again. His chestnut-brown hair is dark and wet. His pale green eyes are sad. Severe. His clothes are clean, his boots are muddy, and even from ten feet away, I can feel him. Hollow yet overflowing. Calm yet pulsing. Strong-willed and stubborn, yet … he's here.

He came back.

Wes's green gaze swallows me whole before he speaks again, "You still want to stay here?" His words are quiet, meant only for me.

I nod. It's a lie though. I don't want to stay here another second, but nodding is easier than admitting that something is so wrong with me that I can't even look outside without having a panic attack.

His soft gaze hardens as it settles on Q. "Then, I'll do it."

She claps her ring-adorned hands together and sashays toward Wes. Her full hips sway as if she were swinging an invisible tail. "I knew you'd be back, Surfer Boy," she coos, reaching up to pat him on the cheek.

Wes jerks his chiseled chin out of her reach, and she bursts out laughing.

"Oh, I forgot. You wanna keep us on the down-low." She casts an evil smirk at me over her shoulder before walking out the door.

Just before she disappears, Q turns to face Wes again. "You got until tomorrow to bring me some dish soap, lighter fluid, toothbrushes, deodorant, D batteries, and some gotdamn chocolate chip cookies, Surfer Boy. I ain't playin'."

Wes lifts an eyebrow at her but says nothing as she spins back around and prances away. When his gaze falls back on me, as cold and guarded as the day we met, I hold my breath.

"You're hurt." The words come out raspy and clipped after clawing their way through his clenched jaw.

I don't even know what to say to that.

Of course I'm fucking hurt. You left me. I needed you, and you left me.

But when Wes reaches out and runs a thumb over my bruised cheek, I wince and realize what he meant.

"Ugh." I turn my head away and hiss, "What do you care?"

"So, uh …" Lamar mumbles as he and Quint tiptoe around us. "If y'all need us, we're gonna be … avoiding the hell outta this conversation. Deuces."

He throws a peace sign up on their way out the door, and suddenly, it's just me.

And Wes.

Who is still staring at my freshly slapped cheek.

"Who did this to you?"

"It doesn't matter."

"Fucking tell me, Rain."

"Fine! You did this to me, *okay?* You. If you had been here, none of this would have happened!"

Wes drops his eyes, the lids stained purple from exhaustion.

Just like mine.

"I'm sorry." His voice is soft and sincere and makes me want to do stupid things like kiss his violet eyelids, so I turn and walk to the counter to put some space between us instead.

I sit on the dark gray surface next to the medical supplies. It's better over here. I feel like I can almost think now. Almost.

"I've never felt sorry for anything I've done before … but I'm sorry for this." Wes's eyes lift, and the remorse I see in them is all the apology I need.

I want to run to him and kiss the pain off his face, but I can't. I'm paralyzed by his presence. All I can do is hold my breath and stare as he crosses the room like a ghost.

"I don't expect you to understand what it's like to fear something that doesn't make any sense"—Wes takes a step toward me. Then, another—"but this"—he gestures between us with the flick of a finger—"this scares the shit out of me."

Step.

"I was trying to protect myself."

Step.

"But when I saw that broadcast today …" Wes shakes his head as the color drains from his face. "It made me realize that there's something I want to protect even more than myself."

Wes erases the gap between us with one final stride. His body comes to a stop between my dangling legs, and his palms find a home on my trembling thighs.

"I know you think you're safe here, but you're not. You taking care of Quint … all these witnesses …"

Wes cups my face just below my busted cheek. I close my eyes and lean into his touch even though it makes everything hurt that much worse.

"Piss off the wrong person, and they can make you disappear with one phone call, Rain."

I pull my eyes shut tighter and shake my head against his palm.

No one here would do that. Would they?

"Listen, I don't care if you hate me. I don't care how bad it hurts to see you with someone else. I don't care if you ever fucking speak to me again. I will suffer through all of that and more to make sure they don't fucking take you."

Wes slowly dips his head forward, but his lips don't land on my mouth. They fall like a feather onto the raised welt on my right cheekbone. The gesture is so gentle, so sweet, that it breaks my heart in two. I remember how Wes used to flinch and grit his teeth when I cared for his bullet wound. That's how I feel right now. His tenderness hurts, but only because it's making me realize how badly I needed it.

My eyes flutter open as a strange sense of déjà vu slithers into my veins. Panic replaces pain as I frantically search the flowers on Wes's shirt for telltale horseman silhouettes.

"Are you real?" I whisper, touching my fingertips to the orange hibiscus over his heart.

Wes drops his forehead to mine and slides a hand into the hair at the back of my head. "Are you?"

I reach for his breathtaking face with both hands, needing to kiss him, to touch him, to convince myself that this isn't just another cruel dream, but the sound of a clearing throat shatters the moment like a gunshot.

Wes's head whips around to face the entrance. Then, his hand forms a fist in my hair when he sees who our unexpected guest is.

Carter's jaw flexes and nostrils flare as he stands in the doorway, holding a green beer bottle with dandelions and wildflowers sticking out in all directions.

"I came to check on you, but"—he eyes Wes up and down with disgust before turning his disappointment back on me—"looks like you got *company*."

Something changes in his demeanor, and suddenly, he's Cocky Carter from high school, smirking as he crosses the room like he just sank a three-pointer to win the game.

Wes loosens his grip and leans against the counter, lazily rubbing the back of my neck.

Carter stops right in front of me and glances down at my split cheek. From here, I can see that he must have taken a pretty good hit during the food court scuffle too, because one side of his jaw is definitely swollen. His eyes flare behind his well-placed mask, but us getting smacked around by the runaways isn't what he came here to talk about.

"I just wanted to be the first one to tell you, happy birthday." He grins triumphantly, first at me and then at Wes, as he hands me the bouquet.

I accept it mechanically and stare at it in disbelief.

"It's May?" I ask quietly and to no one in particular.

"Yep. May 3." Carter puffs out his chest.

"I ..." The flowers blur as my eyes look past them and focus on the floor. "I didn't think I was gonna have another birthday."

I blink and look up to find Carter watching Wes with smug satisfaction on his face and Wes watching me with thinly veiled concern written all over his.

"Thank you, Carter," I whisper, giving him a one-armed hug while my free hand grips Wes's bicep. "I'll see you later, okay?"

I'm sure Carter and Wes are glaring at each other over my shoulder, but Wes won't give him the satisfaction of acting like he gives a shit.

"A'ight, Rainbow Brite," he says, shooting me with a finger gun and a wink as he walks backward toward the door. "Come by later. My folks wanna tell you happy birthday too."

I don't respond, and the second Carter's six-foot-three-inch frame is out of sight, I feel Wes's whole body tense up beside me.

I set the flowers down and turn to face him.

"Please don't freak out. Carter and I are just fr—"

"It's your birthday?" Wes's eyebrows lift and pull together.

"Oh. Uh … yeah. I guess it is." I smile, still trying to process the fact that I lived to see twenty after all.

"Fuck." He tucks his damp hair behind one ear and stares out into the empty hallway. "I didn't know."

I laugh. "If it makes you feel any better, I didn't know either."

"It doesn't," Wes deadpans.

Then, without warning, he leans over and seals his lips to mine. My thoughts scatter. My heart pounds. The lights behind my closed eyelids glow brighter. And the switch in my brain that once produced joy creaks and groans until it finally breaks loose from all the rust and cobwebs and begins dumping glitter into my bloodstream again.

I touch his shoulders, his face, his hair—anything I can get my hands on that will help me believe that he's really here.

He's really here.

Wes angles his head as he deepens our kiss, attacking me with a passion I haven't felt since …

No. No, no, no.

The glitter switch turns back off.

The lights dim.

My heart sinks like a cinder block, pulling my thoughts down with it.

Breaking the seal of our mouths by no more than a quarter of an inch, Wes tells me what I already know is coming.

"I gotta go."

"But … you just got here," I whisper, feeling the long fingers of despair beginning to wrap around my throat.

"I'll be right back. I promise." Wes gives me a determined stare and one last peck on the lips, but I'm too stunned to return it. "If I'm gonna get Q's shit while it's still light out, I gotta go now."

And, before I finish nodding, the best birthday present I ever got walks right back out the door.

Wes

"OF COURSE IT'S HER fucking birthday. Why would the day I show up empty-handed after disappearing on a weeklong bender *not* be her fucking birthday? God, I'm such a fucking asshole."

I stomp across the empty parking lot, talking to myself out loud and gesturing with my gun, not giving two shits who might see me. The only people who travel these streets anymore are Bonys and people too stupid or desperate to be afraid of them.

Looks like I just joined the second category.

The ground is wet from the storm last night, and the sky is still cloudy and gray. The wind blows my unbuttoned shirt around like a cape as I approach the intersection in front of the mall, and I like it. I like the electrical charge in the air. It feels like any-fucking-thing could happen. It feels like I could march right the fuck down this street into that pharmacy and take down anyone or anything that stands in my way.

It feels like I just kissed the shit out of Rainbow Williams.

I turn and take the sidewalk instead of going back behind the shopping center because, right now, I'm fucking invincible. Rain is still here. Nobody's called the cops on her yet for saving Quint. And she's not fucking Carter. I could tell the second that little bitch cleared his throat. If the two of them had hooked up, he would have come at me with his pop's rifle, not some smartass comment and a side-eye.

The next thing I know, I'm standing directly in front of the shattered CVS door. No wild dogs. No bloated, dreadlocked corpses. No homicidal maniacs on motorcycles.

I look to the swirling sky and give a little salute.

I guess God likes me when I'm trying not to be a piece of shit.

I knock on the metal frame of the door with the barrel of my gun. I know there's a chance some strung-out Bony is gonna blow my head off as soon as I peek inside, but I also know it's possible that the place is open for business again. The mail is running—sort of. The power's back on. Hell, Burger Palace never even fucking closed.

"Y'all open?" I call out, standing with my back against the bricks.

"Depends on how you're payin'," an apathetic adolescent voice replies.

I pull the door open and spot the Bony kid who saved my ass the last time I was here sitting behind the checkout stand, reading *Gearhead Magazine*. He's wearing a black hoodie with neon-orange skeleton stripes spray-painted on it, but it doesn't swallow him the way it did a week ago. He seems to fill it out a little better somehow, and the purple bruise around his eye has faded to a subtle greenish-yellow. I stop in the doorway when I notice that the .32 he used to blast his old man is sitting on the counter, aimed directly at me.

He lifts his eyes and does a double take as recognition wipes the apathy off his face.

"'Sup, kid?" I lift my chin.

"'Sup." His tone and expression are guarded, but he hasn't shot me yet, so that's good.

"They got you mannin' the place by yourself now?"

The kid lifts one shoulder in a half-assed shrug.

He's alone. Good.

"Listen …" I take a few steps farther into the store. "I need a few things. I'm hoping, maybe we can work something out."

The kid raises his non-bruised eyebrow. "You got weed?"

Fuck. Of course a fourteen-year-old kid is gonna want weed.

"No, but I think I know where I can get you some ammo for that .32."

I'm pretty sure Rain's dad had a small arsenal tucked away in the corners of that house. I just gotta dig a little more.

His eyebrow falls back into place, and he looks down at his magazine. "Nah. Got a full clip … except for one."

He glances back at me with hatred in his eyes, and I know exactly where that one bullet went.

"I got something else you might be interested in." I take another step closer. "I wouldn't normally offer this to a kid, but you seem like a smart guy."

I pull a bottle of hydrocodone out of my pocket and rattle the contents. I found it when I emptied Rain's dad's pockets before I buried him. I figured that bastard would have something with some street value on him.

The kid's eyes light up at the sight of that little orange bottle, and I know I got him.

"This shit's better than cash. You can get anything you want out there with this—as long as you *don't fucking eat it.*"

The little punk rolls his eyes and hands me a plastic bag from under the counter. "Three pills to fill up a shopping bag. Five, and I'll throw in a case of water."

I laugh and shake my head. "Dude, I think you and I are gonna be damn good friends."

Rain

I CAN'T BELIEVE I'M twenty.
 I can't believe Wes came back!
 I can't believe he's gone again.
 I hope he's okay out there.
 He'll be fine. I'm the one who got beat up, and I stayed in here.
 Q. What a bitch.
 At least she's letting us stay.
 She's gonna make my life a living hell though.
 Not that it wasn't already.
 But now Wes is back!
 But what's gonna happen when he remembers how much he hates this place?
 He's gonna leave again, and then what?
 I'll die. I'll fucking die.
 Or I could go with him.
 No, I can't do that. I can't even look out the window!
 Shit. He is gonna leave again, and if I'm not better by then, I'm gonna be stuck in here with Q forever.

My thoughts ping-pong back and forth in my mind as my body ping-pongs back and forth across the cracked-tile tuxedo shop floor. I've been pacing for what feels like hours. The light in the hall is starting to turn that yellowy-orange color that tells me night is coming. I can't be in here by myself in the dark. I'll go crazy ... er.

Keeping my same frantic pace, I turn my feet so that they lead me out into the hall instead of back across the room for the fifteen thousandth time.

Maybe I'll go see if there's any dinner left in the food court. That'll make Q happy. She always gets pissed when I don't eat her precious food.

As I approach the atrium, I hear her booming laughter coming at me from the opposite end of the hallway. Peeking around the fountain, I see Q leaving the food court, cackling and bumping shoulders with a few of the other runaways. I'm not ready to face her again. Not by myself and especially not if she has an audience.

She's worse when she has an audience.

Instead, I turn and haul ass down the hallway on the right. I don't care where I'm going as long as I get there before Q spots me.

I notice the shoe store up ahead and remember what Carter said about his family wanting to see me. The sound of Queen Bitch and her army of dreadlocked gutter punks echoes off the atrium walls behind me, so I turn and duck into the second to last place I want to be right now.

"Knock, knock …" I say, faking a smile as I make my way to the center of the shoe store as quickly as possible.

Sophie hops up and runs over to me, pulling me into their makeshift living room by the hand. "Rain! You came! C'mere! C'mere! We got surprises for you!"

Her mother must have braided her hair after the rain shower. It looks perfect and probably took hours. It's interesting that Mrs. Renshaw chopped all of her own hair off but still takes the time to fix her daughter's. Sadness tugs my spirits down, but I smile anyway and let the giggly ten-year-old pull me inside.

"Oh, Rainbow!" Mrs. Renshaw gasps, immediately jumping up and launching into a gospel-worthy version of "Happy Birthday."

Carter and his dad place their playing cards facedown on the bench in between them and join in, albeit with a lot less flare, and Sophie belts out the words louder than anyone.

My cheeks feel prickly and hot as everyone in the room stands and sings to me.

When the song is over, Carter walks over to me with a smug look on his face and his arms behind his back. "Ta-da!" he says, pulling one hand out to present me with a Twinkie, still in the wrapper.

A laugh bursts out of me as I reach for the spongy, golden brick of goodness. "Oh my God, where did you find this?"

"We packed some from home when we left for Tennessee. Damn things last forever." Pulling his other hand out from behind his back, Carter holds a small pocket flashlight right above the Twinkie and aims it at the ceiling. "Make a wish." He beams.

So, I do. I close my eyes and picture a beautiful, unreadable face. Eyes as soft and green as mint ice cream with features so hard they could have been chiseled from a glacier. Then, I blow.

I hear a tiny *click*, followed by cheering, and when I open my eyes, the beam of flashlight is off, as if I'd blown it out.

"Well, aren't you clever?" I tease, unwrapping the Twinkie as an excuse to look away from Carter's cocky-ass expression.

"That's what they call me—Clever Carter."

"Uh-huh." I smirk. Taking my first bite, I moan in appreciation as dry cake and creamy frosting fill my mouth. "Oh my God, why is dis so good?" I mumble around the delicious processed treat.

"I have something for you too!" Sophie chirps, bouncing over to me with a piece of cardboard in her hands. Swiping the flashlight from her big brother, Sophie clicks it on and shines it down on the inside of a shoebox lid. Inside, there's a drawing of a unicorn Pegasus surrounded by big, fluffy clouds and floating flowers.

"Is he shitting out a rainbow?" Carter asks, nudging Sophie with his elbow.

"Uh, no! That's her tail, stupid! The rainbow is over there!"

"Guys! Stop it!" Mrs. Renshaw snaps.

"I love it." I smile, taking the shoebox and hugging it to my chest. "Thank you, Sophie."

Sophie grins and sticks her tongue out at her brother.

"I got you something too, sweetheart." Mrs. Renshaw takes a softer tone as she reaches into the pocket of her dress. Gesturing for me to hold out my hand, she drops the item into my palm, and Sophie immediately shines the flashlight on it.

My mouth falls open. "Mrs. Renshaw—"

"Now, now. Don't you try to tell me no, child. I want you to have it."

The gold necklace in my hand glitters in the light, casting yellow flecks onto my fingertips like a tiny disco ball.

"I inherited that a few years back from my aunt Rosalyn. It's supposed to be a horseshoe, for good luck, but it always looked more like a rainbow to me." Mrs. Renshaw smiles at me with pride in her full cheeks, but I have no idea what I did to deserve it.

"Thank you so much. Really. But I can't accept this."

"Oh, pssh. You can, and you will. I don't need that old thing. I got everything I need right here."

Mrs. Renshaw glances from me to her children and then over at her husband, who is still standing. He's leaning on a display shelf with most of his weight on his good leg, but still.

"Jimbo," I yell, snapping my fingers at Carter's dad. "You'd better get off that leg right now."

Mr. Renshaw chuckles and reluctantly takes a seat. "Why are y'all givin' her all these presents when she's so damn mean to me?"

"We're givin' her all these presents *because* she's mean to you, Jimbo. Heck, a few more weeks with her around, and you might even start cleanin' up after yourself." Mrs. Renshaw wags her finger at her husband.

Carter reaches over and takes the necklace out of my hand, and I hold my breath as he unclasps it with fingers almost too large for the task.

"Woman, I do plenty around here—"

The Renshaws launch into one of their spirited fake fights as Sophie giggles in delight. No one is watching as Carter reaches out and slides the ends of his great-aunt's necklace around my neck. No one sees my discomfort as his fingers skate along my skin and disappear under my dark hair.

And when Mrs. Renshaw takes the flashlight out of her daughter's hand and shines it in her husband's face, no one notices the way I cringe and step back when Carter leans forward and whispers, "Happy birthday, Rainbow Brite. We love you. *I*—"

"What the hell are you doin', woman?"

"I just thought you might want a spotlight to go with that speech you rehearsed!"

Carter is looking at me expectantly, his hands resting on either side of my neck, as something almost imperceptible pulls my attention toward the hallway.

I turn my head slightly, staring off into the darkness of the back of the store as I listen for the sound of footsteps or voices behind me. Instead, I hear something that strikes a chord deep in my soul. A familiar tone, low and constant. Then another, in a slightly higher pitch. Then, one that bends from low to high, like a cresting wave.

"I … I gotta go," I say, stumbling toward the sounds and out of Carter's grasp. "Thank you for the birthday party."

Carter calls after me, but I'm laser-focused on finding the source of those notes. Into the darkened hall I sprint, looking left and right until I determine that the sound is definitely coming from the atrium.

More notes float through the air. I can barely hear them from here, but they fill me with hope and dread at the same time.

Bow, bow, bow, bummmmmmmm.

As I get closer to the atrium, I notice that the fountain seems to be glowing. There's a haze of amber light all around it and a scent in the air that I know by heart.

Because I picked it out myself.

Bath and Body Works Warm Vanilla Sugar candles.

Rain

THE AROMAS AND SOUNDS of home assault my senses as I fight with myself to stay in control.

Don't do this. Not now. Not here.

My chest tightens. I take deeper breaths, but the air's not getting in.

Don't panic. It's just a smell. A smell can't hurt you.

But it does. It hurts because I miss it so goddamn much.

I force myself to round the side of the fountain and come face-to-face with the only thing I want to see ... surrounded by everything that I fear.

Wes is sitting on the edge of the fountain, tuning a guitar that looks exactly like the one my dad used to play when I was a kid. My pink duffel bag—the one that Mama bought me before my first sleepaway camp—is wide open on the floor next to him, and everywhere I look, there are lit vanilla candles dotting the floor and fountain.

"Wes?" My voice comes out so screechy you would have thought I'd found him handling live cobras, not lazily tuning a guitar by candlelight.

Wesson Patrick Parker lifts his head, and for a moment, I'm suspended in the space between fear and reason. That brief moment of clarity where you're not being lied to by your emotions or manipulated by your logical mind. That tiny gap where everything moves in slow motion and you're able to see things as they really are.

And what I see is Wes looking at me with one bright, twinkling eye. His shiny brown hair has fallen in front of the other one, curling slightly at the bottom where it fits behind his ear, and his lips are parted in an easy smile.

The guitar he's holding, it's just a guitar. It can't hurt me. The candles he lit, the fragrance I smell—they can't hurt me either. This beautiful person brought these thoughtful things from my house, and for a moment, I am honored and humbled and crushed by the weight of my gratitude for him.

But then Wes points to a small beige throw blanket spread out on the floor a few feet away, the one Mama and I used to snuggle under when we would watch movies on her days off from the hospital, and at the sight of it, the scent of cigarettes and hazelnut coffee smashes into me like a wrecking ball.

Clarity, gone. Gratitude, demolished.

I am fear and feelings and anguish and, and …

"I can't," I mutter, shaking my head as the breaths come faster and faster. My feet scream at me to run, but I manage to keep them rooted to the floor— my need to stay close to Wes somehow overpowering my need to escape this situation.

"You can't what? Rain, are you okay? Why don't you sit down?" He gestures to the blanket again.

"I can't!" I force the words through my gritted teeth as my hands plunge into my hair. I tug hard, trying to distract myself from one type of pain with another.

"You can't sit?" His voice is low and soothing but laced with concern.

I shake my head, still tugging, still fighting with some unknown demon for control of my body.

"Okay …"

I hear the hollow thrum of the guitar being set aside and feel Wes's strong hands wrap around my waist. Guiding me toward him, he pulls down, gently, and my body follows his silent command. I land on his lap sideways and immediately bury my face in his warm neck.

"Can you sit *here*?" he asks, wrapping his arms around my hyperventilating body.

I nod. The weight of him soothes me like a heavy blanket. The scent of him reminds me of the present, not the past. And the utter *gravity* of him is enough to pull the panic out of my body through my pores.

I take a deep breath and am shocked when my lungs actually inflate. Then, I exhale so hard I feel dizzy.

Wes exhales too, but it doesn't sound relieved. It sounds defeated.

Letting go of me with one arm, he runs a hand through his hair. "I just keep fucking this up."

I shake my head, wanting to argue with him, but my words haven't come back yet.

"I wanted to get you something for your birthday while I was out, but then I realized that you wouldn't want anything. You don't care about *stuff*. In fact, the happiest I ever saw you was when you were climbing on the back of that motorcycle, ready to leave everything you owned behind. You didn't even know where we were going."

Wes wraps his arm back around me, and I realize that I'm not hyperventilating anymore. I'm not in my body at all. I'm lost in his words, wrapped in the rough timbre of his deep, soothing voice.

"So, I asked myself what I would have done for your birthday if April 23 had never happened. If things were normal, you know? And I don't think I would have gotten you anything. I think I would have put you on a plane and taken you to Coachella."

"Coachella?" The word tumbles from my lips as they curl into a curious smile.

"Mmhmm. It's a huge music festival in California. They have it every year in the spring. Or … *had* it." Wes's voice trails off.

"I've heard of it. Is it fun?"

He shrugs. "Never got a chance to go. It looked fun. Everybody would get fucked up and dance around with flowers in their hair." Wes reaches for something next to him. It's a little yellow daisy he probably stole out of Carter's bouquet.

The image of him doing it makes me smile.

"I want to see you like that," he says, tucking the flower behind my ear.

"What? Dressed up like a hippie?" I tease, my cheeks tingling as his fingertips slide through my hair.

"No … happy."

Happy.

I think about that word … about the fact that this man wants me to feel that word. I think about the fact that this man is here at all. And then something occurs to me.

"I am."

Wes gives me the side-eye.

"Now that you're here."

"So, what was all that about?" He gestures to the place where I was standing a few minutes ago.

"I can't …" I shake my head and try again. "I can't … see things … or … smell things …" I feel my chin begin to wobble, and the tears begin to pool, but I push through. I don't want to admit it out loud. It sounds so stupid and shameful and ridiculous, but there's a freedom building behind these words, pushing on them, begging to be let out. "I can't even touch things that remind me of home … without …"

"Having a meltdown?"

I drop my eyes and nod.

"And I just showed up with a duffel bag full of shit from your house." Wes pinches the bridge of his nose and shakes his head. "I'm so sorry, babe. I'll get rid of it. All of it."

"No," I snap. "Leave it. I need to …" I take a deep breath.

I need to get used to this.

I need to get over this.

I need to get better so that the next time you leave, I can leave with you.

"You sure?"

I nod, keeping my eyes screwed shut.

"Well, I can't pretend like we're at Coachella if you're sitting in my lap." Wes smirks. "Here." He moves a few candles and guides me to sit next to him on the ledge of the fountain.

Picking my dad's guitar back up, he asks if I have any requests.

"I don't know what you can play."

"I played on street corners in Rome all day, every day for two years. If I don't know it, I'll bullshit my way through it." He begins to strum absentmindedly. "What's your favorite song?"

"Uh …" I search my brain for something original. Something that feels like me. But all I come back with are Carter's favorite songs.

"Twenty One Pilots?" Wes asks.

"No," I blurt, opening my eyes to glare at Wes.

"Okay." He chuckles and holds up one hand, his other firmly wrapped around the neck of the guitar in his lap. "So, you don't know what your favorite song is?"

I shake my head.

"Challenge accepted." Wes grins, and without even looking, he shreds out a heavy metal riff that catches me off guard and makes me crack up.

"Okay, so not death metal. How about …" He plays another tune, something slower. His expert fingers bend the strings until they whine.

I tilt my head, trying to figure out where I've heard it before.

"If you don't recognize Garth, then you are definitely not a country fan. Okay, what about …"

Duh-nuh-nuh, chicka-chicka, duh nuh-nuh …

The opening notes of "Smells Like Teen Spirit" by Nirvana have me smiling and bobbing my head immediately.

"Actually, that doesn't help at all. Everybody loves Nirvana." Wes grins.

"What did people request the most?" I ask, wanting a little glimpse into Wes's life before the world fell apart.

I want to pretend like I'm a beautiful college student studying abroad, and he's a beautiful street musician sitting on a fountain in front of the Pantheon.

"I dunno. Whatever was popular. I can't even tell you how many times I had to play 'Call Me Maybe.'" Wes smiles. "But it was classic rock that got everybody singing—and more importantly, tipping. It didn't matter if they were young, old, rich, poor, or if they even spoke English. If I played The

Beatles, The Stones, Journey, The Eagles … I made fuckin' bank, and everybody walked away from my fountain happy."

Happy. There's that word again.

"Will you play me one?"

Wes eyes me up and down while the jukebox catalog in his head flips to the perfect song. Then, with a smirk, he says, "I got it."

Chicka duh nuh-nuh nuh-nuh, duh nuh-nuh …

My eyes light up, and my heart overflows as he plays a simple song about an American girl raised on promises, trying to find someplace in this great, big world where she can hide from her pain.

"I love it." I smile, swallowing back the lump in my throat.

"Tom Petty." He shakes his head. "Goddamn genius."

Lifting his eyes, Wes tips his chin at something over my shoulder. "Sup?"

My heart stops, but when I turn around, it's not Q and her crew; it's Quint and Lamar, tiptoeing toward us from the food court.

"Guess it's safe to go back into the tux shop now," Lamar jokes.

"You can hang out, if you want." Wes gestures toward the blanket on the floor that I refuse to look at. "We're just trying to figure out Rain's favorite song."

Lamar and Quint share some kind of silent brotherly communication.

Then, Lamar speaks up, "Ahh … fuck it. Ain't nothin' to do in the shop 'cept stare at this ugly motherfucker all night. We'll chill with y'all."

Quint shrugs, and Lamar helps him over to the blanket. Holding him from behind, Lamar helps Quint ease down into the sitting position without having to move his head. It makes my heart swell so much to see Lamar stepping up to help his brother that I don't even realize I'm looking at the blanket until both of them are sitting on it.

My eyes go wide as I jerk my gaze back to Wes's smug expression.

Oh, you think you're soooo smart.

Wes gives my thigh a little squeeze. Then, he turns his attention back on the Jones brothers.

"Do you guys know what Rain likes to listen to?"

"'Free Birrrrrrd'!" somebody shouts from up above us. Actually, two somebodies.

My head snaps up to find Brangelina standing at the top of the broken escalator with their fists in the air. They stomp down the metal stairs and take a seat halfway down.

"No, no, no!" Not Brad shouts. "I wanna hear …" He switches to his hip-hop voice. "I did it all for the nookie!"

"What?" Brad chimes in.

"The Nookie!"

"What?"

They sing the chorus back and forth as Wes leans over and whispers in my ear, "I am not fucking playing Limp Bizkit."

I giggle as Tiny Tim comes shuffling out of a dark second-story shop, holding his banjo over his head. "Did somebody say nookie?"

"Wes is trying to figure out my favorite song," I call over to them.

"She looks like a Taylor Swift girl to me," Tiny teases, taking a seat a few rows above Brangelina.

Wes looks back at me and raises an eyebrow. "You a Swiftie?"

I shrug, but before I can give him an answer, I notice a curvy silhouette stalking into the atrium from the hallway to the left—the one I never go down—shrouded in a cloud of smoke.

"Go ahead, Surfer Boy," Q calls out, her voice slurry and slow as she snaps her fingers in our direction. "Play me some T. Swift."

Wes glances down at me with hard eyes. The sharp line of his jaw flexes in the glow of the candles.

"You want me to play nice?" he whispers. The implication is clear.

You want to keep living here, or can I be a dick?

"No," I say, his question giving me an evil idea. "I want you to play 'Mean.'"

Wes smirks. "The song?"

I nod.

"You sure?"

I nod.

"All right, but you gotta sing it."

"What? No. Wes—"

"Yes." He lifts his thumb and slides it beneath the gash on my cheek, letting me know that he knows *exactly* who put it there. "You sing it."

"But … what if I don't know the words?"

"Everybody knows the words."

Before I can argue anymore, Wes's fingers land on the strings like he's played the song a hundred times, and the "Mean" train leaves the station. I feel my chest constrict as I glance over at Q, who is now sitting on the bottom stair of the escalator, glaring at me.

When it comes time for me to sing the first line, I choke, but Wes just plays the melody again, this time murmuring the lyrics under his breath. I almost go for it, but it's not until the third try that the words actually come out of my mouth.

They're quiet at first as I tell Q that she's a bully who enjoys picking on people weaker than her.

A little louder when I tell her that she has a voice like nails on a chalkboard.

And by the time we get to the chorus, I'm declaring—not to her, but to myself—that one day, I'm gonna leave this place, and all she's ever gonna be is mean.

"Yeeeeee-haw!" Tiny calls out as he joins in on his banjo, walking down the escalator stairs and right past Q, who takes a puff from her bowl and tries to act oblivious.

Brangelina stands up, arm in arm, and sways back and forth as they help me sing the second verse about how I walk with my head down because she's always pointing out my flaws.

But it's not until Loudmouth shows up out of nowhere, jamming out on his accordion like it's a cherry-red electric guitar with flames painted on it, that I finally feel confident enough to use my full voice. It's not pretty. It's not perfect. It sure as hell wasn't good enough for the Franklin Springs First Baptist Church choir. But when I look Q in the eyes and tell her she's a pathetic liar who's gonna die alone, it sounds pretty damn good to me.

Sophie comes running up beside me and starts dancing and singing at the top of her lungs, and by the last chorus, even Wes and too-cool-for-school Lamar are singing along.

When the song is over, Tiny Tim keeps it going about two minutes too long with the world's worst and most enthusiastic banjo solo. We all burst out laughing as he holds the instrument over his head like he just played Lollapalooza.

But the sound of gunfire shuts us up real quick.

As the blast echoes through the two-story atrium, making my heart stop and my hands reach for Wes, the body of the banjo explodes, showering Tiny in splintered wood.

Q stands up, unsteady on her feet, and replaces all of our laughter with a deep, stoned chuckle of her own. "Y'all muhfuckas a buncha … *comedians,* huh?" She swings a small black handgun around in her limp wrist, gesturing to all of us with the barrel. "Y'all a buncha rock stars now?"

She stumbles as she takes a few steps forward, a self-satisfied grin on her sleepy-eyed face. "Well, you know what rock stars eat?" A slow, evil laugh vibrates through her smiling lips. "They don't eat shit."

Her heavily lidded eyes land on Tiny, who's holding what's left of his decimated banjo and looking like he wants to cry. Walking over to him, she pokes his portly belly with the barrel of her gun and sneers, "So tomorrow, *y'all* ain't gon' eat shit."

Everyone holds their breath as Q sashays toward the hallway she came from, that slow, closed-mouth chuckle punctuating the silence as she drifts away.

Taking our joy along with her.

Wes

AS SOON AS Q walks off, I realize how badly we just fucked up.

Not only are we on that cunt's shit list now, but we got the runaways in trouble too.

One phone call. That's all it would take for Rain to get a bullet between the eyes on live TV, and we just made a whole lotta new enemies.

Everyone scatters back to their own corners of the mall, grumbling and giving us shitty looks, while Rain sits with her hoodie-covered hands over her mouth, staring at the dark hallway that Q just disappeared into.

"Soph! What the fuck was that? Get back in here!" a deep voice echoes from down the hallway behind us. I know without looking that it belongs to that smug little shit Carter.

"Coming!" Sophie calls out. Then, she turns to Rain with big, sad eyes. "I gotta go. Carter didn't want me to come out here. Happy birthday though."

"Thanks, big girl." Rain fakes a smile and spreads her arms for a hug. "You go tell your brother he's not the boss of you." She sounds so different when she talks to kids. Stronger. More confident. She sounds like a mom.

But a good one, not the piece-of-shit version I was cursed with.

As soon as the girl is gone, Rain's posture wilts like the dying daisy I tucked behind her ear.

"Q just fired a gun like, twenty feet away from her." She shakes her head. "She's fine."

"She's gonna go hungry tomorrow. Because of me."

"No, she's not." I cup Rain's jaw and turn her miserable, beautiful face toward mine. "Everybody here has food stashed somewhere. Nobody's gonna starve, okay?"

Rain's eyes land on the floor. "This isn't the end, Wes. Q is gonna do something else. She's gonna try to get me back for this."

"Not if you leave."

Shit.

Rain's chest rises and falls as her breathing speeds up, and I know I brought it up too soon.

"I …" She looks around—at the blanket, at the candles, at the guitar in my hands—and I prepare to hear another, *I can't.*

But instead, Rain mumbles, "I'm not ready."

"I'm not ready."

I can work with that.

I smile and tuck my knuckle under her chin, encouraging her to lift her head. I don't know how, but I feel more fucking connection in that half-inch of contact than I've ever experienced with another person in my whole waste of a life. I feel her struggle as if it were my own, and I guess, in a way, it is. The only difference between us is that she hides from her pain.

While I run away from mine.

Rain lifts her eyelids, heavy with fat black lashes, and looks at me with a silent plea.

"You will be," I answer with more confidence than I feel.

That earns me a tiny smile.

"Plus, we can't leave right now. I haven't found your favorite song."

That earns me a bigger smile.

"You really suck at this." She grins.

"Damn, woman. Give me a chance."

Rain giggles as I stand and pull her to her feet. I grab the duffel bag and guitar but leave the candles.

Maybe I'll get lucky, and we'll burn the place down.

I turn to start walking, but Rain doesn't follow. Her eyes are locked on that goddamn blanket, and before I can stop her, she's moving toward it.

Fuck me. Here we go.

I hold my breath as she lifts it off the ground. Draping it over her arms, Rain hugs the fuzzy woven fabric to her chest like a teddy bear, and I prep for the waterworks to start. I sling the guitar over my back and get ready to drop the duffel bag, so I can catch her when her knees buckle and the hair-pulling begins.

Her face crumples as she buries her nose in the cable-knit nightmare. A tear spills over her busted cheek.

But my girl stays strong.

With a deep, steadying breath, Rain lifts her head, looks at me in utter fucking sorrow, and says, "We need something to sleep on."

There's my little survivor.

Supplies over goodbyes.

I don't make a big deal about it, but inside, I'm fist-pumping like one of those *Jersey Shore* douche bags. I'm gonna get this girl outta here by the end of the week. I know it.

I sling the guitar back around to the front as we head toward the bookstore—*our* bookstore—to break the silence. "Okay, pop quiz …"

I play the guitar line from "Hey Ya!" by OutKast and laugh when she tucks the blanket under one arm and does the *clap, clap, clap* part.

"Nice. Didn't expect you to be a hip-hop fan."

"What?" She shrugs. "Everybody knows OutKast. They're from Georgia."

"True. How 'bout this one?"

I play the intro to "Call Me Maybe" and sigh in sheer fucking delight when her nose wrinkles and her head tilts to one side.

"No? What about this one?"

I pluck the first few notes of "Sugar, We're Goin' Down" as we walk into the almost-pitch-black bookstore, and Rain calls it before I even get to the chorus.

"Oh! Fall Out Boy! I love them."

I'm glad she can't see my face right now because my smile is smug as fuck.

"Did I pass?" Rain asks as I stop at the bottom of the tree house ladder to give her a hand up.

"I think I'm the one who passed." I give her a swat on the ass as she heads up and chuckle when she yelps in surprise. "I know your song."

"Oh, really?"

When I climb in behind her, Rain is sitting, facing me with her arms folded over her chest.

For a guy who has nothing to prove, I fucking love proving myself to this girl.

I sit with my back against the wall and strum lightly as I build my case.

"Yep. You like alternative music …" I switch to a gritty rock-'n'-roll riff and pause for a second when I realize that it's one that I wrote years ago after finding an old Gibson acoustic in Foster Mom Number Nine's basement. I've never played that song for anyone before.

I shake off the significance and keep talking, "But you also like girl-power anthems …" My notes morph into the *whoa, oh, oh, oh, oh-oh* part from "Single Ladies" by Beyoncé.

Rain laughs and does the little hand movement from the video, which only fuels my ego as I settle on a new tune. It's softer and slower and definitely sadder. I'm afraid it might be too much, considering how far she's come today, but fuck it. It's the truth, and right now, the truth—and this guitar—is all I got.

"I think you might be a Paramore girl."

I tell God he'd better fucking back me up on this one as my strumming gets louder. The simple, soulful melody is synchronized with every beat of my own bleeding heart as I open my mouth and sing the first line.

About a girl watching her daddy cry.

Rain clutches the blanket to her chest and listens as I tell her the story of a woman who's afraid to get hurt after watching her parents break each other's hearts. She tries to protect herself. She tries to avoid the pain of being left. But when she finally falls in love, she realizes that it's worth the risk.

I hope she's fucking right.

I can't really see Rain's expression in the dark, but as I let the final note fade out, I know I'm going to find tears before I even reach for her face.

"How did you do that?" She sniffles, and when she leans into my touch, I know I got her.

I shrug. "When you're in the system, you get good at figuring people out. Fast."

And when you're stuck with the same bunch of assholes your whole life, like Rain, I guess you get good at hiding.

She inhales deeply and sighs. "So, what's the name of my new favorite song?"

I place the guitar in the corner and crawl over to her. Laying her down, I take the wadded-up blanket out of her arms and set it behind her head like a pillow. "'The Only Exception.'"

Gazing down at her, I know now that that's *exactly* what she is for me. The only exception to all of my rules.

No getting attached.

Leave before you get left.

Supplies. Shelter. Self-defense.

Survival above all else.

Now, they've all been crossed out with a giant X, and next to them, in murderous block letters, are the words *Protect Rainbow Williams*. That's all I fucking care about now. Keeping her safe. Keeping her—period.

I was afraid she would hurt me, but while I was gone, I realized that she's the only fucking thing in my life that *doesn't* hurt.

"Wes?" she asks, her voice small and shaky as she slides her fingers into my hair and pushes it away from my face. "Will you still be here when I wake up?"

Guilt seizes my heart and squeezes it in its fucking fist. Bracing myself on my forearms, I lower myself onto her soft, warm body and press my lips to hers. Blood explodes through my veins on contact, but I don't move. I hold that kiss until I feel her relax beneath me. Until I know she'll believe me when I finally promise, "Forever."

Satisfied, Rain pulls my face back down to hers and kisses me like forever might actually exist. Slowly. Sweetly. Without the ticking clock of April 23 looming over our heads or the hooded horsemen from hell breathing down our necks. Without blood on our hands or ash in our hair. Without wonder or worry about how it will end. Because we started at the fucking end.

Now, we get to begin.

Tilting my head, I deepen our kiss and try not to smile when I feel Rain's hips rock against me in response. We might have forever, but I have a week's worth of pleasure to make up to this woman, and I think she's waited long enough.

Gripping her hip with my right hand, I press myself against her and feel a moan vibrate through her chest.

"I missed you," she whispers, weaving her fingers deeper into my hair.

"I …" I squeeze my eyes shut, forcing myself to speak around the knot of remorse in my throat, "I didn't think you would. No one ever has, so … I'm sorry. I'm so fucking sorry, Rain. If you want me, I'm yours."

"Forever," she repeats.

My promise sounds more like a prayer coming from her lips, so I dip my head lower and seal it with a kiss. Our bodies move instinctively as I pour my heart out through my mouth—kissing her deep and slow, like a love song.

And somehow, Rain knows all the words.

Her body rolls and writhes beneath me as our tongues swirl and our breathing becomes heavy. I grind against her faster, wanting to make her come just like this—with nothing more than a kiss and promise.

"Wes," she rasps, tilting her head back.

"Mmhmm …" I hum, sucking on her fat bottom lip.

"Wes …" Rain's voice sounds more frantic, but her hips keep working in tempo with mine. "These are my only panties!"

I chuckle against her panting mouth. "Not anymore. I grabbed you some extra clothes while I was at your house."

With that, Rain grabs my head and crushes her mouth to mine. The arch of her body underneath me, the needy moan in the back of her throat as she comes undone, the way she forgave me with open arms and is holding my face right now like I'm fucking precious—it overwhelms me, and suddenly, Rain isn't the only one who's going to come from a single kiss.

I push myself off of her, kneeling between her legs to try to calm down, but the sight of Rain basking in post-orgasmic bliss before me does nothing for my throbbing cock.

Opening her eyes, Rain takes one look at my face and then lets her gaze slide down my fully clothed body to the massive bulge right in front of her. With a swollen-lipped smirk, she reaches up and unfastens my belt.

I grab her wrist in warning. "Let me make you feel good a few more times first. I have a lot of making up to do."

"It's my birthday," she says with a devilish grin. "I can do whatever I want."

Can't argue with that logic.

I let go of her wrist and watch as Rain slowly unbuttons my jeans and spreads the fly open. Her fingers slide up the shaft of my swollen cock through my boxers, and it jerks against the waistband.

Fuuuuck, this girl is killing me.

Without sitting up, Rain shimmies my pants and boxers down over my ass and licks her lips as my cock falls free.

"Come down here," she says, her voice laced with need.

I don't understand what she means until Rain grabs my hips and tugs forward gently.

Oh shit.

"You want me to fuck your mouth?"

Even in the dark, I can see Rain's skin flush at my words. She drops her eyes and nods with a tight-lipped smile.

My balls tighten, and I do as she said, straddling her waist and leaning forward onto my hands. I drop my head and watch as her kiss-swollen lips part, and her little pink tongue slides across the head of my cock.

"Fuck," I hiss, trying to hold still as she wraps her warm mouth around me and sucks her way to the end.

"Rain, you don't have to—" I start, but I can't finish my sentence because if she doesn't keep doing what she's doing right now, I'll fucking die.

I hold my breath, afraid that if I move a single muscle, I'll hurt her, but once Rain sets a rhythm with her mouth and her hands, I'm powerless. My hips buck as she takes me deeper, works me faster, sucks me harder. Sweat rolls down my neck as I struggle to maintain control, but when she moans, throaty and raw, when I hear how fucking turned on she is, I lose control.

My entire body goes rigid as I pour myself into Rain's soft, warm mouth. Waves of pleasure roll down my spine as her tongue works me over, sucking and swallowing every last drop until I'm spent and empty and full at the same time.

Rain looks up at me with a smirk on her plump lips and pride in her pretty blue eyes.

"You're fucking up my apology." I smirk back.

Rain's mouth spreads into a full-on grin. "Sorry."

"Liar." I move backward down the length of her body until I'm straddling her thighs. "Now I gotta start all over."

Rain giggles as I pull her hoodie and tank top off over her head, and the sound is music to my fucking ears. She arches her back so that I can unfasten her bra, and the smooth curves of her body are a siren's song that I can't ignore. My fingers slide over her full tits, squeezing and rolling her perky pink nipples until her hips lift off the ground in need.

Fuck.

Even in the dark, Rainbow Williams is sexier than anything I've ever seen in the light.

She reaches for my open shirt, attempting to push it over my shoulders, so I shrug it off for her along with my holster. As I pull my tank top off over my head, I feel her gentle hand slide down and around my already-hard cock.

"Uh-uh," I tease, grabbing her hand and pinning it next to her head. "Not yet."

The side of Rain's mouth curls up, and my dick jerks in response, remembering how fucking good it felt to be in there.

"You can grab this." I place her hand on her boob and give it a little squeeze, earning me a giggle. "You can grab this." I lift her hand to the top of my head, where she gives my hair a tug. "Or you can grab this." I lace my fingers between hers and feel a sudden bolt of electricity binding us together the moment our palms meet. "Got it?"

Rain nods, but the humor is gone from her face. Tender, doe-eyed sweetness replaces it as she brings our joined hands to her lips and plants a kiss on one of my scarred, busted knuckles.

Something clicks inside my heart. I feel it, like a fresh battery being snapped into place, and I realize that the aching, echoing hole in my chest—the one I've lived with my whole fucking life—wasn't there because I was empty.

It was there so that Rain could reach in and fix me.

I press our joined hands to the plywood above her head and kiss her again, this time with all my working parts. This woman found me broken and made me whole, and I'm suddenly determined to do the same for her. I will get her the fuck out of here. I will give her a happy life, even in this shithole, lawless, dumpster fire of a world, and starting right now, I will love her the same way she loves me.

As if forever really exists.

Trailing wet kisses across her jaw and down her neck, I take my time, savoring the salt on her skin and the swell of her blood pumping beneath it. When I get to her nipple, I work it slowly, with my tongue, my lips, my teeth. I time my movements with the rise and fall of her perfect, heaving tits. But when I go to pull my hand away so that I can unfasten her jeans, Rain refuses to let go. I smile against her heated skin and pull our entwined fingers down together. Clumsily, I get her pants unbuttoned and fumble to untie her bootlaces with my one free hand.

But I don't mind. If Rain wants to hold my hand for the rest of her life, I'll fucking cut it off and give it to her.

Once I slide her jeans and ruined panties off over her bare feet, Rain parts her legs for me, and it feels like I'm being welcomed home.

With our hands still joined, I kiss my way from the inside of her ankle, up to her knee—which must be ticklish because it jerks and smacks me in the fucking mouth, causing Rain to giggle—and down to the soft, needy, glistening place that I plan on worshipping for the next few hours.

When I slide my tongue up her seam and around her clit, I do it only because I want to make her feel good. There's no pretense. No impatient foreplay so that I can get off and go to bed. I don't go straight for the spots I know will make her thighs tremble and her back arch just to speed things up. I settle in, and I let her body tell me what it wants. Long licks elicit hushed moans and slow body rolls. Swirling circles earn me short whimpers. A teasing finger causes her to buck her hips against my face, but two fingers, knuckles deep, have her head thrown back and her fist in my hair. Up and around, up and around, my tongue and my fingers ride the wave of her body, rising and falling with her quickening breaths. But still, I wait. I keep her in heaven as long as I can until her fist tightens in my hair and her thighs clamp around my ears and the first flutters of an orgasm tickle my fingers.

Then, I suck.

Rain's entire body contracts around me as she writhes and pants and growls the sexiest fucking sounds I've ever heard. I slide my fingers out and replace them with my tongue, wanting to drink every drop of her the way she did me.

"Fuck, Wes," Rain rasps, pulling my face up toward her with her free hand.

Her other one is still clutching mine, and the sight of our fingers entwined has my newly repaired heart acting like it's on the fucking fritz already. It skips a few beats entirely as I climb up her boneless, spent body and press a kiss to her love-drunk lips.

"I'm not done yet," I promise, sliding my aching cock over her slippery, swollen flesh.

Rain shoves her toes into the waistband of my jeans and pushes them as far down my legs as they will go.

"I'm gonna make you come once for every night that I was gone."

Rain's head falls back onto the plywood with a dramatic *thunk*, but her hips rise to meet mine, thrust for thrust.

I would chuckle at her mixed signals, but this feels too fucking good. I drop my forehead to hers as we move with and against each other, seeking friction in the slippery mess we've made. Our mouths collide in a torrent of tongues and teeth as the pace quickens until I can't fucking take it anymore. I need to be inside Rainbow Williams more than I need my next fucking breath.

Pulling her knee up to my ribs, I surge forward, filling her completely in one delicious fucking motion.

And Rain comes on contact.

Her nails dig into my back, and her moans echo down my throat as she pulses and arches and glows in my arms.

And I follow her into the light.

The darkness behind my eyelids goes white as I hold her shuttering body to mine. As I fill her with everything that I have. Everything that I am. Everything that I want to be for her. I could stay here like this forever, basking in the afterglow of my girl on fire.

But I can't.

Because I promised this woman six more orgasms.

And from now on, I'm a man of my word.

May 4
Rain

WHEN I WAKE UP, I feel as though I've been turned inside out. The pain I used to carry around in my mind and in my soul is now only in my back from sleeping on a plywood floor. My muscles, which used to feel restless from lying around all day, are now deliciously sore. And my heart—which, just yesterday, felt like a rotting, blackened organ oozing poison into my bloodstream—now feels ripe and red where it pitter-pats against Wes's side.

It feels happy. *I* feel happy.

I bury my smile in his bare chest and tighten my arm around his ribs. His presence feels like a miracle. Like a gift from God. Some people get new shoes or fancy cars or the latest iPhone for their birthdays. I got a whole person. *My* person.

And also, like, a dozen orgasms.

Wes stretches and turns in my arms, pressing his morning *situation* against my hip as he pulls me closer.

"No horsemen last night," he grumbles sleepily, kissing my forehead.

"None at all?"

"Hmm-mm." He shakes his head as much as he can with his lips still on my face. "You?"

I try to remember what I dreamed about and smile when it finally comes to me. "Me either. I dreamed that I was in outer space. I was stranded on this tiny planet, or maybe it was just an asteroid. I don't know how I got there, but I couldn't get home. I could see Earth, but every time I jumped off the rock and tried to swim to it, I would only get so far before the little planet's gravity would pull me back down. I was so frustrated. I started to panic."

Wes pulls me closer and rests his chin on the top of my head.

"Then, all of a sudden, this rocket came whizzing through the air. It looked like the Looping Starship ride at Six Flags. There was no roof, and everybody was screaming and laughing with their arms in the air. I waved for help, but they shouted at me that the ride was full. They were just gonna leave me there, but right before the ride passed me by, you leaned out as far as you could and pulled me in. You let me sit in your lap because all the seats were taken, and you wrapped your arms around me so that I wouldn't fall out."

I kiss Wes's warm chest and feel my skin prickle with a million tingling goose bumps.

"It was the best dream I've had in a long, long time."

Wes swells even more against my hip, but he ignores it and smooths a hand over my hair. "I would go to outer fucking space to get you."

I smile.

"But I would *never* let those motherfuckers ride on my spaceship. They can all burn in hell."

I laugh with my whole body … until it makes me realize how badly I need to pee.

"Wes, I gotta go," I huff, pushing on his chest.

"Nuh-uh," he groans, pulling me closer.

"No, Wes. I gotta *go*."

Catching my meaning, he releases me with a chuckle and sits up. "I'll come outside with you."

"No, it's fine. I'll be right back," I mutter, trying to pull my hoodie and jeans on as quickly as possible.

Wes slips his holster on, throws his Hawaiian shirt on over it—leaving it unbuttoned so that his chest is on full display—and slides his boxers on over his still-hard cock. "Nah, I'm ready. Let's go."

"Like that?" I giggle, glancing down.

"What?" Wes follows my gaze to see the head of his dick staring back up at him. "It'll calm down when the cold air hits it." He shrugs.

"Wes," I hesitate. "I don't go out there … anymore."

"Oh, you found a new spot?" he mumbles, buttoning his shirt to cover the issue. "Smart. That front entrance is pretty exposed."

"No …" I sigh, already hearing the shakiness return to my voice.

Wes's head snaps up, and suddenly, he's the Ice King again. Cold. Guarded. Quietly raging and highly alert.

"What happened?" he snaps.

"Nothing. I just—"

"Bullshit. What happened?"

"Ugh! I can't think when you get like this!"

"You don't need to think. You need to tell me what the fuck happened."

"I had a panic attack, okay?" I shout. "I touched the grass, and I just … I freaked out. I can't see the trees because they remind me of home. I can't look at the highway because it reminds me of home. I can't leave this damn building because everything out there triggers a memory, and memories trigger the pain, and the pain triggers the panic because if I can't shut it down immediately, it's so big and so awful that I think it might kill me, *okay*?"

I take a huge breath and blow it out through my lips as Wes studies me with unaffected eyes.

"No," he finally says, his mouth set in a hard line.

"No?"

Wes shakes his head. "No. It's not fucking *okay*. Get your shoes on. We're going outside."

"Watch your step."

I grip Wes's bicep harder as I step down off the curb and into the street.

At least, I assume it's the street.

"How're you doing?" he asks.

"I … uh …" I check in with myself and realize that I'm actually kind of okay.

With Wes's tank top tied around my head, I can't see anything. All I can hear is his voice. And with my boots on, the only thing I can feel is the pavement beneath my feet and his body touching mine.

I hate it when he's right.

"I'm … *fine*, I guess."

Wes chuckles. "It's a good thing nobody's out here because you don't look fine. You look like you're being fucking kidnapped."

"Wouldn't be the first time you kidnapped me," I joke. "Besides, you're too pretty to be a kidnapper. It defeats the purpose if girls go with you willingly."

"Hold up," Wes says, stopping to bend over and pick something up.

I hear a familiar metal rattle but can't figure out what it is.

"So, you think I'm pretty, huh?" Wes asks as we start walking again. I can hear the smirk in his voice.

"Boy, you know you're pretty. Don't go fishin' for compliments."

"Nah." Wes snorts. "I'm ugly wrapped in a pretty package. But *you* …" The deep rasp in his voice vibrates all the way down my spine as Wes leans in and presses his lips to my temple. "You're the most beautiful fucking thing

I've ever seen." I feel his fingertip slide down the bridge of my nose and over my mouth and chin as if he's admiring my profile. Then, it continues lower, stopping right between my breasts. "Even in here."

I blush, grateful for the blindfold so that I don't have to drop my eyes in embarrassment.

"Step up."

I do as he said and feel the asphalt turn to soft earth beneath my feet. A few feet later, he pulls me to a stop and turns me so that I'm facing something that blocks out the sun.

"We're here. You can take your blindfold off but only look straight ahead, okay?"

"Wes, I … I'm scared."

"I'm right here. You wanna sleep in a bed again someday? You wanna take a hot shower and eat food that wasn't cooked over a metal barrel?"

I nod, feeling my heart rate skyrocket.

"Well, this is the first step, baby. Take off your blindfold."

I take a deep breath, drawing as much strength from him as I can. I lost my mama and daddy. Wes lost his mom and sister. I was left behind by my boyfriend. Wes was rejected by thirteen different foster families. I dealt with mean girls at school. Wes was the new kid at half a dozen high schools. If he can stand out here and be ready for whatever happens next, then maybe I can too.

Sliding the ribbed tank top off my head, I bring it to my nose and inhale. The scent of Wes overpowers all my other senses, making me feel happy.

Making me feel brave.

I crack open my eyelids, letting in a tiny sliver of my surroundings, before I open them the rest of the way in surprise. We're standing two feet in front of the faded green PRITCHARD PARK MALL exit sign next to the highway.

Wes wraps a firm hand around my jaw, holding it straight. "Don't look anywhere but here, okay?"

"Okay," I reply, too curious to be afraid.

I hear the metallic rattle again and smile when it gets louder and faster.

"I noticed this can of spray paint on the ground the other day, and it made me think of you." Wes chuckles, shaking the can in his hand.

"Why me?" I smile.

"Oh, I dunno. Maybe because of the *Welcome to Fucklin Springs* sign in front of your house?"

I grin. "Shartwell Park is my personal favorite."

"So, you admit that you're a vandal?"

"I prefer the term *wordsmith*." I smirk, accepting the can of neon-orange spray paint in Wes's outstretched hand.

"See, take this sign." I pop the cap off with an experienced thumb. "A vandal would just draw a coupla dicks on it and move on." I cross out the *P* in Pritchard and easily turn the *R* into a letter *B*.

I can feel Wes grinning, but I'm too nervous to look over at him. Instead, I focus all my attention on the green-and-white—and now, neon-orange—sign in front of me.

"But not me." I give the can a few more shakes and cover the *RD* with two big, bold *S*s.

"*Bitchass Park Mall*," Wes reads aloud with pride. "I didn't even think to add the double *S*s at the end. Nice."

I turn and give him a little curtsy, but when I open my eyes, I not only see Wes; I see the entire mangled pileup behind him.

Quint and Lamar's daddy's bulldozer is a charred hunk of metal. The pavement around it, scorched and black. The tractor trailer on its side looks like a T-Rex took a bite out of it, and all around, pushed to the sides of the road, are the totaled and abandoned vehicles Quint cleared trying to get us through the pileup. I picture him lying on the pavement with that shard of glass sticking out of his neck. I picture Lamar, dazed and in shock with blood trickling into his eye from his lacerated eyebrow. I remember the sound of the explosion and the way twisted metal and broken glass rained down around us like confetti.

And then, I remember the way the inside of my mama's helmet smelled when I put it on.

Like hazelnut coffee.

Like *her*.

The scene in front of me goes blurry as the memories line up along the edges of my mind, ready to march in one by one to destroy me. The first one charges, and it's a doozy.

Christmas morning.

The last Christmas before April 23, I came downstairs to find Daddy passed out next to a puddle of his own vomit on the floor in front of the Christmas tree. Mama and I left him there while we opened presents. She brewed her coffee extra strong that morning. Made me some too. I don't know what else she put in that cup, but it made me feel warm and silly. We curled up under her blanket on the couch and watched *Christmas Vacation* on repeat until Daddy came to. It wasn't so fun after that.

"Hey," Wes says, blocking the sides of my face with his hands like blinders. "Stay with me."

I blink, pulling myself out of my head as his beautiful face comes into view.

"You did it." He beams, and the pride in his eyes is enough to make tears form in mine. "You're outside, fucking shit up like a little punk."

Wes jerks his thumb in the direction of the sign, and two warm streams slide down my cheeks as I turn to look at it. Not because I'm afraid to be out here.

But because I'm so incredibly thankful to be.

"I love you," I whisper, shifting my gaze back to the man who, just yesterday, I thought I'd never see again. "I love you so—"

Before I can finish my declaration, Wes silences me with his mouth. He blocks out the world with his hands over my ears, clutching my face as he kisses me hard. He chases the memories away with his tongue and lips and hips and smell. And I am plunged back into my favorite place.

The one where Wes and I are alone together.

A car horn breaks into my consciousness, causing me to go rigid in Wes's arms. I don't look, afraid of what I might find, but Wes does, and what he sees makes him grin against my lips. He lets go of me to salute something over my shoulder, so I give in to my curiosity and take a peek.

A small white mail truck comes puttering up next to us, and Eddie—the same mail carrier we've had since I was a kid—gives us a little wave before flipping a U-turn and heading back down the highway toward Franklin Springs.

"The mail is running?" I ask in shock.

"Sort of." Wes chuckles, lifting his tank top to re-cover my eyes. "C'mon. Let's head back. I'm starving."

"But Q isn't feeding us today," I remind him as he ties the white cotton in a knot behind my head, grateful that he's not going to push me to walk all the way back, unblindfolded.

"I told you, I have plenty of food." Wes presses a kiss to my unsuspecting lips, which part in a silent gasp as his hand slides between my legs. "That's not what I'm hungry for."

I feel so much better on the way back. Bolder. Braver. I lace my fingers between Wes's and swing our hands back and forth as we head down the exit ramp. The bright May sun warms the top of my head, and I suddenly want to feel it everywhere—on my cheeks, on my shoulders. I crave it like oxygen.

Once we're at the bottom of the ramp, I pull Wes to a stop next to the chain-link fence encircling the mall and yank my hoodie off over my head. His makeshift blindfold comes off in the process, and I freeze, both from the delicious warmth on my skin and from the war being waged inside my head.

"Rain?"

I think I can do it. I think I can open my eyes and be okay. With Wes beside me and the sun on my face, I feel like I could fly if I really wanted to.

I listen for anything that might sound … I don't know … triggering, but all I hear is the faint rumble of an engine in the distance.

Make that several engines.

"Shit," Wes spits, tightening his grip on my hand.

"Wes?"

"Bonys."

My eyes snap open and jerk in the direction of the break in the fence and then back up the ramp the way we came.

"We gotta run for it," Wes growls.

"It's too far!"

"Now, Rain!"

"No! Just … just … just put this on!" I take the can of spray paint in his hand and swap it out with my oversize Franklin Springs High sweatshirt.

Wes glances over my shoulder toward the sound of the rumble, but he doesn't argue. He yanks the hoodie on over his head in the time it takes to suck in one more steadying breath. It fits him perfectly, hugging his broad chest and shoulders, and I get to work, spraying neon-orange ribs across the front and back. Wes flips the hood over his head and pulls it down low to cover his eyes.

Tossing the empty can over the barbed wire, I stand with my back against the fence and pull Wes in front of me so that I'm mostly hidden from view.

"Kiss me!" I beg as five shiny street bikes crest the hill at the end of the street. "Like I don't want it!"

Wes doesn't hesitate, grabbing me by the throat and shoving his thigh between my legs. He angles his back toward the oncoming threat as he plunges his tongue into my mouth, and as much as I want to sag against the fence and let him, I have to pretend to fight him off.

I don't bother screaming—they won't hear me over the roar of those engines—but I make a show of shoving his immoveable chest and trying to push off the fence with my boot as he holds me in place. Wes rips my tank top halfway down the front and grabs my breast as the first motorcycle passes.

And, against my better judgment, I look.

The crew of madmen seems to move in slow motion as they take in the show. Their once-chromed-out choppers and slick black street bikes have been spray-painted with neon skulls and bones and bloody, flaming body parts just like the leather jackets and hoodies they wear. Each man has on a helmet or mask more terrifying than the one before it. Mohawked, blood-spattered, Day-Glo skulls eye us up and down as they drive by—machetes, nail-filled baseball bats, and sawed-off shotguns at the ready.

They sneer at me as I scream—for real this time—shoving Wes off of me just enough to break out into a full-on sprint.

Satisfied with our performance, the Bonys take off down the road as Wes chases after me, catching me by the wrist and spinning me around in his arms. He kisses me as furiously as he did the day I pulled him out of the Renshaws' burning farmhouse.

I might know all of Carter's smiles, but I'm quickly learning all of Wes's kisses.

This is his post-near-death-experience kiss.

I hate this kiss.

I hate the Bonys.

I hate this new world.

But mostly, I hate how good the sun feels on my skin right now because, once we go back inside, I'm pretty sure I'm never going to feel it again.

May 5
Wes

"Bailiff, bring out the accused!"

Governor Fuckface is turning into more and more of a glorified game show host with every broadcast. He sweeps his ham hock of an arm out to gesture toward the five convicts being ushered out of the capitol building—each one bound, gagged, and wrapped in a matching burlap jumpsuit—as if he were Vanna White, revealing today's grand prize on *Wheel of Fortune.*

I shovel a forkful of eggs into my mouth and wash it down with boiled rainwater as I watch them parade the guilty past the bloodsucking saplings that have already been planted. There must have been another execution while we were out yesterday because now there are three baby oak trees growing in Plaza Park.

In a few minutes, it will be eight.

Rain pushes the food around on her plate next to me as they read out the crimes of the accused. A few more hospital workers who refused to remove life support, a woman who continued tube-feeding her disabled husband, and a mother who saved her child's life with an EpiPen after he had an allergic reaction to a bee sting.

These are considered high crimes now, but murder and rape are totally legal.

Go fucking figure.

Just before the first of the accused gets to say her last words, I turn and cup my hands over Rain's ears. She's not watching the broadcast—her gaze has been glued to her untouched breakfast ever since it came on—but I know she's listening.

Her big blue eyes lift, and for a moment, it feels like we're the only two people in the room.

Bam!

I force a small smile as the sound of a body landing at the bottom of a dirt hole reverberates through my fucking soul.

Bam!

I smooth my thumbs over her cheekbones, being extra careful with the right side, which is now sporting a gnarly green-and-purple bruise.

Bam!

The third convict takes a bullet between the eyes as Rain drinks me in with hers. The corners of her full pink lips twitch as if she wanted to smile back, but she pulls them down and drops her gaze instead.

Bam!

I can't say that I blame her. I'm probably the only motherfucker who can smile while people are being executed on live TV.

Bam!

Because I'm the only motherfucker who gets to look at her while it happens.

Across from us, Quint pushes his plate away and cups a hand over his mouth in disgust while Lamar stares blankly at the screen as if he were just watching another bad horror flick.

I pull Rain's head against my chest, thankful that she's not freaking out, thankful that she's here with me instead of lying in the bottom of a dirt hole in Plaza Park, and I begin to get the feeling that the executions aren't the only thing people are watching in the food court.

I glance up and find Carter's parents staring at us from a few tables away. His sister is wearing headphones and playing on someone's cell phone—no doubt to protect her from the mass murders happening on live TV—but her folks are none too happy. Mrs. Renshaw has the Southern decency to look away, but Carter's dad holds my stare for what feels like hours. There's no challenge in his puffy, bloodshot eyes—the old bastard can hardly walk—just a deep sadness.

I know that feeling. I've lost her before too.

Carter didn't come to breakfast with them, and honestly, I don't fucking blame him. Just the *idea* of seeing Rain with someone else was enough to make me pack my shit and go. I want to feel bad for the guy, and I would, if he deserved my sympathy. But I know assholes like him. Popular. Good-looking. Entitled as fuck. Guys like that don't take rejection well. They throw tantrums like fucking toddlers when shit doesn't go their way. And wherever

Carter is right now, my guess is that he's plotting his next move, not licking his wounds.

I look around the room, taking a mental headcount, and a sinking feeling slithers into my gut.

The runaways are all accounted for at Q's table—watching their phones and smoking weed and aiming guns at each other's heads like they're Governor Fuckface on TV. Quint—who is now down to a large Band-Aid and a couple of aspirin a day—and Lamar are in a heated debate about whether they should steal a Jeep and find a place in the mountains or steal a convertible and try to find a beach house to squat in. And the Renshaws are huddled together as usual, all except for Carter.

He's the only one unaccounted for.

Until that motherfucker marches into the food court, carrying my duffel bag.

Carter shoots me an *eat shit* look as he heads straight toward Q's table, and I laugh—I actually fucking laugh—and shake my head.

So predictable.

Rain doesn't think it's funny though. She stiffens in my arms the second she sees him.

I want to reassure her that it's going to be fine. That no matter what happens, I won't let these dramatic little bitches hurt her. But I can't.

This is post-April 23.

All bets are off.

Carter stops directly in front of Q, commanding the attention of everyone in the food court, as he unzips my duffel bag and dumps it out on her table. Extra clothes for Rain, water bottles, trail mix, canned stew, dried fruit, beef jerky—all the shit I brought from Rain's house, plus all the nonperishables I've been hoarding from my trips to CVS—tumble out like bombs. The cans hit the table and roll to the floor in a series of loud clangs and bangs, and everybody holds their breath and waits for Q to drop a bomb of her own.

Her mouth curls up on one side as she admires both the spoils and the show. "Well, well, well … what do we have here, mall cop? You tryin' to buy a spot at the big-boy table?"

"This is Wes's bag!" Carter declares in his best Captain America voice. The authority in his tone has me rolling my eyes.

Fucker would have made a great mall cop.

"He's been hiding food, supplies, even bullets!" Carter turns and aims an accusing finger directly at me. "Kick. Him. Out."

It's an Oscar-worthy performance. I'll give him that.

Q cackles. It starts low and deep, only in her throat. Then, it builds into something loud and psychotic. Suddenly, food and clothes go flying as she comes across the table, grabbing Carter by the face and kissing the shit out of him. He pushes her off and stumbles backward as she stands in the middle of the table, towering over him.

"You wanna act like a little bitch? I'ma treat you like a little bitch."

"What the fuck?" Carter yells.

His mom gasps and covers Sophie's ears even though she's too engrossed in whatever she's watching to know what's going on.

"You think just 'cause I ride ya dick whenever I want that you can tell me what the fuck to do in *my* muhfuckin' castle?" Q drops to her feet directly in front of Carter and shoves a sharp fingernail into his chest. "You ain't shit, mall cop. If I should kick anybody out, it's yo' ass. *That* muhfucka's the best scout I eva had …" Q looks directly at me as her lip curls into a sneer, and her hips gyrate back and forth. "And he looks like he could eat the hell outta some pussy, too."

The word *pussy* is the match that detonates the powder keg. Loud metal scrapes echo all around us as a dozen chairs are pushed out at once. Carter's parents stand in disgust. The runaways leap to their feet to cheer on the madness. And I shove away from the table because Carter is stalking toward me with his hands balled into fists. I want to tell Rain to get the fuck out of here, but I don't have a chance. I'm too busy preparing for Carter to take a swing.

Which leaves her wide open for him to grab instead.

Carter wraps his long fingers around her biceps and crouches down so that they're eye-to-eye. "Rainbow, please. Just let me explain. It meant nothing, I swear!"

Rain grunts and tries to jerk away from him, but Carter doesn't let her go. He shakes her. He fucking shakes her, and her wide eyes asking me for help are the last thing I see before the darkness takes over.

The sound of Rain screaming is what filters in through my consciousness first. I blink—one, two, three times—and find myself kneeling on the ground. A mound of bloody flesh is gasping beneath me, spitting blood and teeth like a human volcano. I leap off of him and try to open my hands to reach for Rain, wherever she is, but my fists feel like they've been run through a meat grinder. There is more screaming as Mrs. Renshaw and Sophie drop to their knees beside the mangled man on the ground.

I watch their tears fall in slow motion, wondering if my bloody fists are the reason they're crying, just before I hear Rain cry out, "Noooo!"

My head snaps in the direction of her voice a split second before her tiny body collides with mine, sending us both tumbling to the floor. The wall-rattling blast of a hunting rifle being fired indoors has me back on my feet and running, dragging Rain by the hand along with me. I don't have to look behind us to know who fired the gun.

If somebody beat the shit out of my kid, I'd try to kill him too.

We pass the fountain without any other shots being fired and are in the home stretch toward the main entrance when Rain digs in her heels like we're about to run off the edge of a cliff.

"Wes, what are you doing?" Her voice is shrill and terrified, and I know that I'm not done fighting yet.

I turn and level her with a commanding stare, my eyes shifting between her and the fountain every other second. "We have to leave. Now."

"We can't!"

"Goddamn it, Rain! Either you can run or I can fucking carry you, but we have to leave right the fuck now!"

Both of our heads jerk up as we hear the *stomp, slide, stomp, slide* of Mr. Renshaw's limp coming down the hallway.

"So help me God, boy, if I catch you round here again, I'ma hang yer head on the wall like a twelve-point buck."

The metallic clank of a rifle being cocked sends us both into motion again. I shove open the heavy exit door and pull my girl into the blinding spring sunlight. Instead of hauling ass straight across the parking lot, I head for the closest parked car, using it as a barricade until I'm sure the coast is clear. Rain is breathing heavily beside me, and I can't tell if it's from exertion or panic, but I don't stop to find out.

I do what I do best.

I fucking run.

Rain

CARTER'S FACE. I CAN'T get the image of Carter's pulverized face out of my mind. The last time I saw a face that bloody …

I gasp and choke on a sob as the image of my mother lying in bed, never to wake up again, slams into my consciousness like a linebacker. It doesn't flicker, and it doesn't flash. It blocks out my vision like a gruesome bumper sticker over my eyes as Wes drags me up the exit ramp and into the woods. I count backward in my mind. I shake my head from side to side. I use my free hand to yank on my hair, but nothing's working.

We stop running. Wes is talking to me, but I can't hear him. I'm too busy trying to think of something else. Anything else. I open my eyes as wide as I can, looking all around us for a distraction, but everything reminds me of her. The woods, her motorcycle, the air in my lungs. It all reminds me that I'm alive and she's not. Wes straddles the bike, his mouth moving like he's giving me instructions, but I just blink at him. At his perfect face. Carter had a perfect face too, but Wes broke it. He broke it, just like my dad broke my mama's face. Made it ugly and bloody and gone.

Wes guides me to sit on the motorcycle. I let him manipulate my body like a rag doll.

Is this what the Paramore girl sang about? Watching your parents destroy each other just to fall in love and make the same mistake? Will Wes do the same thing to me one day?

I watch him as he picks up Mama's helmet. He shoves his wild hair behind one ear, black lashes fanning out across high cheekbones, and I know she's right. I *am* destined to make the same mistake. Because just like my mama, I've fallen madly in love with a man who is capable of doing terrible things with the best of intentions.

Wes's pale green eyes lift to mine, swimming with remorse and sharpened by fear, and I'm so lost in them that I don't realize what's happening until I'm being plunged into a dark, hazelnut-scented prison.

Wes starts the bike, and I hold on for dear life as grief wraps its powerful tentacles around me and drags me under. I can't hide from it anymore. I can't fight it off. I have no distractions. Nowhere to go. It's just me and this smell and this loss and this pain and this road taking me right back to my own personal hell.

I squeeze my eyes shut and press my forehead to Wes's back as a strangled cry fills my helmet. It is long and loud and primal and overdue.

I don't want to go back there. I don't want to go back there. I don't want to go back there. Please, God. Please don't let him take me back there.

I rock in my seat and repeat the mantra, finding some relief in the mindless repetition, but when the bike eventually begins to slow, a fresh wave of fear washes over me.

No, no, no, no, no, no, no.

I'm afraid to look up. Afraid to let go. Afraid to face the place that holds all of my best and worst memories. I'm not ready. It's too soon.

When the bike pulls to a stop, Wes turns and lifts the helmet off my head. I suck in a breath that doesn't smell like hazelnut coffee and exhale with my whole body.

"Fuck, Rain …" Wes whispers, brushing the matted black strands away from my swollen, wet cheeks.

I keep my eyes shut tight, content to sit here and let him touch me as long as we don't have to go inside. "I'm not ready," I mumble. It's the only explanation I can give him before my face crumples again.

"I know. I wanted to give you more time, but … time's never really been our fuckin' friend, has it?"

I shake my head, my eyes still glued shut.

"Do you think you could sit on the porch?"

I nod, not because I believe that I can, but because I *want* to believe that I can.

Wes guides me off the bike and walks me down the driveway and over to the front steps. My pulse speeds up with every step we take closer to my own living nightmare, but I push myself to keep walking.

It's just the porch. It's fine. It's just the porch.

Wes helps me sit on the top stair and then plops down behind me so that my entire shaking body is enveloped by his.

"You know how I brought all that stuff from your house when I came back?"

I nod and listen, eager for him to keep talking. Wes's voice is my favorite sound—deep and rough yet calm and quiet—and the way his chest rumbles against my back when he speaks helps me feel calmer, too.

"I stayed here while I was gone. That whole fucking time. I don't know if I told you that. Mostly, I just got drunk and felt sorry for myself, but when I wasn't passed out, I fixed the place up a little."

"Wait. You did what?" Without thinking, I turn in his arms and open my eyes.

Wes's lips pull into a sweet, boyish smile, and he shrugs. "I knew you'd come home eventually, and I didn't want you to have to see ... *all that* ... again. I found some paint in the garage. Got rid of the, um ... *damaged* furniture. Pulled up the carpet. Did you know you got hardwoods under there?"

I shake my head and laugh as my face wars with itself over whether to grin like a lunatic or cry like one.

So, I give up and do both. I laugh and cry and look into the eyes of a man who destroys beautiful things ... but who also makes destroyed things beautiful again. For me.

Then, I notice something over his shoulder.

"Wes ... is that a new front door?"

His smile spreads into a grin as he turns and looks at the country-blue slab of wood behind him with the big brass door knocker. "Look familiar?"

"Yeah, it does actually. But I don't—oh my God."

Wes chuckles and turns to face me. "The front half of Carter's house only got smoke damage, so I was able to salvage a few things. It doesn't exactly match the rest of the house, but at least it doesn't have a broken-out window in the middle of it."

Wes shifts his weight and pulls something out of his pocket. Taking my hand, he drops a single key into my palm. "Found this under Carter's doormat. Welcome home, Rain."

I stare at the tarnished metal, which suddenly feels as though it weighs as much as a house.

No, as much as a *home*.

"Listen, you don't ever have to go back in there if you don't want to. We can live in the fucking tree hou—"

My heart explodes as I dive for his mouth, planting a kiss on his perfect, parted lips. I don't care if I'm ready. I don't care if he's fucked up. I don't care if we're destined to break each other's hearts. No one has ever loved me like this, and Paramore was right.

That's worth the risk.

I pull away, clutching the key—still warm from Wes's pocket—like a single rose. "I wanna see."

Wes's eyes widen as his pupils dart back and forth between mine. "You sure?"

I nod, not sure at all, but wanting to be … for him. And for me.

"Come on," I say, using his broad shoulders to help me stand. "Show me what you've done with the place."

"Rain, you don't have to do this."

I shake my head and try to put on a brave face. "I want to."

With a single dip of his chin, Wes takes a step back, clearing my path to the front door.

But it doesn't feel like a door. It feels like I'm standing in front of a massive wooden drawbridge, and inside, banging against the surface and rattling the heavy chains, is everything I've been trying to keep locked away in my mind. Every trauma. Every fear. Every bittersweet, fading memory. I was afraid if I let them out, they would trample me, but as I slide the key into the lock with shaking fingers, the rattling goes quiet. When I turn the knob and give it a push, the door opens without so much as a squeak. And when Wes reaches in beside me and flicks the light switch by the door, all those gruesome beasts I expected to find have been replaced with glittering, golden butterflies.

The living room is wide open and full of light. Instead of stained, matted carpet, shiny hardwood the color of Coca-Cola is spread out before us. The only furniture in the room is a couch and a love seat, a coffee table, and the TV stand. The walls are light beige again instead of tobacco yellow. And when I inhale, I smell fresh paint instead of cigarettes and coffee.

"Wes … I …"

"Oh shit. Hang on …" Wes darts inside and grabs an empty liquor bottle off the coffee table. Holding it behind his back, he turns to face me, an innocent mixture of pride and shame on his handsome face.

"You did all this in a week?"

"Yeah …" Wes looks around for a place to stash the bottle. He sets it down next to the TV stand, where I can't see it. "It turns out that ripping up carpet feels a hell of a lot better than putting your fist through a wall."

Wes starts walking back toward me, but I don't let him get more than a few feet before I run and leap into his arms, peppering his face with kisses.

Wes laughs as I grip his stubbled cheeks, kissing his tired eyelids, his strong brows, his straight nose, and smooth forehead, and it's a sound I never thought this house would hear again.

"I love you," I declare between kisses.

"Love you more," Wes says before intercepting my lips with his own.

The moment the seam of our mouths meet, I feel as if I've been struck by lightning. I'm rooted to the earth through his strong body, captured and suspended in his glowing, buzzing stream of electricity. I grip his face harder as the current courses through us—blinding and devastating and healing and hot—and Wes angles his head to take me deeper, using my mouth as a vessel for everything left unsaid.

He kisses me feverishly, impatiently. As if he has more love to give me than time.

And that's when it hits me.

I know this kiss.

I know this kiss all too well.

Wes

I KNEW FROM THE moment I first laid eyes on Rainbow Williams that I would end up dying for her. I didn't want to believe it, I didn't know how or why, but when Rain needed help, God gave me a gun with a single bullet, a dirt bike, and a clear highway all the way to Franklin Springs. Out of all the sad sacks of shit he could have chosen for the job, he picked me, and for that, I'll be eternally grateful.

I just wish that fucker would have let me have more time with her. But, he's never given a shit about what I wanted before. Why start now?

When I first hear the rumble in the distance, I slow our kiss, pulling her soft body to me even tighter. I memorize every curve, every sigh, and I smile.

"I found a stash of cash in a tackle box in your parents' closet," I murmur against her lips. "It should be enough to keep the lights and water on until you can find a job."

"Wes?"

"And there's extra ammo in your dad's sock drawer." Holding her up with one arm, I snake a hand between us and pull the revolver out of my holster. "Keep this on you at all times. Sleep with it under your pillow, okay?"

I tuck the muzzle into the back of her jeans and pull her tank top down over it.

"Wes, you're scaring me."

The bump and crunch of tires over gravel signal that our time is up. Two car doors slam, followed by a third.

Rain's bright blue eyes go wide, and I hate the panic I see in them.

"Hey." I grab her face like I did during the execution today, forcing her to look at me. "It's okay. You're gonna be okay."

"What's gonna be okay? What's happening, Wes?" Rain's shrill voice is drowned out by an authoritative *bang, bang, bang* on the door.

"Georgia State PD. Open up!"

Rain shrieks and covers her mouth with her hands.

"We have the premises surrounded! Open up!"

"Oh my God, Wes! I have to hide!" she whispers under the sound of more pounding, her eyes darting all over the room.

"No, baby," I shush her, grabbing her face again. "They're not here for you. You did nothing wrong. Just promise me you won't go back to Bitchass Park, okay?" I give her a phony smile. "Stay here. You're safe here."

"What's happening, Wes?"

The banging intensifies to the point that I'm afraid they're going to break Rain's new goddamn door down.

"It's open!" I yell, holding her stare as long as I can.

The door flies open behind her, and in walks a brick shithouse of a cop, followed by the bitch who called them.

"That's him," she declares, pointing a righteous finger in my direction. "That's the man who procured the antibiotics."

Rain spins around at the sound of her voice, shock and betrayal twisting her beautiful features. "Mrs. Renshaw! What are you doing?"

Rain turns to the officer and spreads her arms wide, as if she can single-handedly protect me from the law. "It was me!" she shrieks. "Take me! I gave him the antibiotics! Not Wes!"

The cop flashes Carter's mother a questioning look as I walk around Rain's outstretched arms and kneel before her. Her teary eyes drop to mine, and her fingers thread into my hair as she shakes her head from side to side.

"No …"

"It was me. I saved Quinton Jones's life." My words are directed at the cop, but my eyes are holding Rain's heartbroken stare. "And even if it wasn't, you can't execute her …"

I press a kiss to Rain's belly and smile, knowing that a part of me will live on with her forever.

"She's pregnant."

PLAYLIST

THIS PLAYLIST IS A collection of songs that I either mentioned in *Fighting for Rain* or that I felt illustrated a feeling or a scene from the book. I am grateful to each and every one of the brilliant artists listed below. Their creativity fuels mine.

You can stream the playlist for free on Spotify: https://spoti.fi/2IG7oku

"A Little Death" by The Neighbourhood

"Alligator" by Of Monsters and Men

"Alive with the Glory of Love" by Say Anything

"Alone Together" by Fall Out Boy

"Baby Girl, I'm a Blur" by Say Anything

"Back to Your Love" by Night Riots

"coachella" by lovelytheband

"Dream" by Bishop Briggs

"Everyone Requires a Plan" by The Lumineers

"Explode" by Patrick Stump

"Flawless" by The Neighbourhood

"Green Eyes" by Coldplay

"It's a Process" by Say Anything

"Let the Flames Begin" by Paramore

"Mean" by Taylor Swift

"Nervous" by K.Flay

"Numb Without You" by The Maine

"Rainy Girl" by Andrew McMahon in the Wilderness

"Simple Song" by The Shins

"The Archer" by Taylor Swift

"The Only Exception" by Paramore

"watch" by Billie Eilish

"When It Rains" by Paramore

"when the party's over" by Billie Eilish

BB EASTON

DYING FOR RAIN

THE RAIN TRILOGY
BOOK 3

*This book is dedicated to anyone who's ever had to fight for their own happiness.
Especially me.*

May 5
Rain

IT'S AMAZING HOW YOUR whole life can change in an instant. How forces beyond your control can just reach out and rip entire chunks of your life away from you—the best chunks, the biggest chunks—without so much as a *please* or a *thank you.* And those forces always wait until your guard is down. They want to hear you exhale, to sigh in quiet contentment, before they strike.

I was in my tree house after sundown, exhaling a calming stream of smoke from one of my daddy's cigarettes, when three shotgun blasts made me an orphan.

I was creeping down the highway on the back of Wes's motorcycle, relieved that we'd survived April 23 and excited about what we might find outside of Franklin Springs, when an eighteen-wheeler exploded and almost killed my best friend, Quint.

I was wrapped in the safety of a dark, abandoned bookstore, sleeping peacefully after making love to Wes, when he ripped *himself* out of my life without so much as a goodbye.

And I'm in the safety of Wes's arms now, in the living room of my childhood home, surrounded by a newly polished hardwood floor and freshly painted walls, when I feel myself exhale again.

Watch my fear flutter to the floor like a silk robe.

Smile as hope and peace and gratitude tickle my flushed skin and whisper promises in my ear.

Wes wraps my thighs around his waist and kisses that smile away— feverishly, impatiently. As if he has more love to give me than time.

I sigh into his mouth, and three knocks on the door immediately signal my mistake. I let my guard down again, and now, the forces have come to take the only good thing I have left.

My eyes slam open, and Wes grabs my face.

"Hey, it's okay. You're gonna be okay."

"What's gonna be okay? What's happening, Wes?"

Bang, bang, bang!

"Georgia State PD. Open up!"

I shriek and cover my mouth with my hands. My stupid, sighing mouth.

"We have the premises surrounded! Open up!"

"Oh my God!" I search Wes's face for answers, search the room for a place to hide.

"They're not here for you." He shushes me, cupping my cheek in his warm, rough hand. "You did nothing wrong, okay? Just promise me you'll stay here. You're safe here."

"What's happening, Wes?" My voice goes shrill as the banging gets louder.

"It's open!" Wes yells, holding my stare as the door behind me—the brand-new country-blue door that he installed while he was away—flies open.

"That's him," a voice I've known—a voice I've *trusted*—my entire life snarls from the doorway. "That's the man who procured the antibiotics."

I spin around as my mouth falls open, shock and betrayal slicing me from back to front as I turn. "Mrs. Renshaw! What are you doing?"

I block Wes with my body as my eyes dart from Carter's mom to the massive police officer standing next to her. Rage and hurt and a desperate kind of fear surge through me, making my movements jerky and forcing words out of my mouth.

"It was me!" I scream. "Take me! I gave Quint the antibiotics! Not Wes!"

The cop flashes Mrs. Renshaw a questioning look as Wes calmly walks around my outstretched arms and kneels before me in the middle of my living room. My fingers weave through his hair, pulling it away from his face as tears blur my vision.

"No …" I whisper.

"It was me. I saved Quinton Jones's life," Wes announces without taking his eyes off me. "And even if it wasn't, you can't execute her …"

I shake my head down at him, pleading with him to do something.

And he does. He presses a single kiss to my belly and smiles up at me, a mixture of pride and heartbreak carved into his beautiful features.

"She's pregnant."

Those words bounce off my brain, heard but rejected, as the cop yanks Wes off the ground by his arm.

"You have the right to remain silent. Anything you say can and will be used against you—"

"No!" I scream, lunging for Wes. I grab his blue Hawaiian shirt with both hands as the meathead standing behind him clasps a pair of metal handcuffs around his innocent wrists.

He might as well be tightening a noose around his neck.

"Stop it! You're killing him!" I shout.

"You will be given an audience with the governor within seventy-two hours—at which point, you may defend yourself against the charges being brought against you."

I glance up at Wes's face, expecting to find panic mirroring my own, but for once, his pale mossy eyes aren't analyzing or angry or guarded or cold. They're just sad.

Sad and so, so sorry.

"Eyewitness testimony and evidence collected at the scene of the crime will be taken into consideration," the officer drones on, ignoring me as he continues his speech, but Mrs. Renshaw gives me her full attention.

"Rainbow, let go!" she hisses, taking a step toward me. "This man is a danger to everyone in the community. One day, you'll see—"

"You're killing him!" I scream again, this time directing my rage at the woman standing next to the officer. I've never wanted to hit anyone so badly in my life, but my hands won't let go of Wes.

I can't let go of Wes.

Instead, I wrap my arms around his shoulders, bury my face in his chest, and scream directly into the thick flesh and thin cotton separating me from his heart.

How many beats does it have left?

How many would it have had if he'd never met me?

Wes presses his lips to the top of my head as my lungs finally run out of air, and it breaks me all the way.

Because I know this kiss. I know all of his kisses.

Wes is trying to comfort me.

But who's going to comfort him?

"Ramirez? You need backup?" a gruff voice calls from my open doorway.

"Yeah. Looks like we got a stage five clinger."

"Ma'am," the second officer snaps, "I'm gonna need you to let go of the suspect and step aside."

I hear the order, but I don't look up or even acknowledge it. It doesn't matter anyway. I couldn't let go of Wesson Patrick Parker if I tried.

And I've been trying for weeks.

"Ma'am, this is your final warning. I will not ask you again. Let go of the suspect and put your hands on your head."

"Rainbow! Let go!" Mrs. Renshaw yells.

"Let go, baby," Wes whispers into my hair. "I love you so fucking much. Just do what they say, okay?"

But I can't. His shirt is so soft. His chest, so warm. His heart, so steady and strong where it pounds against my cheek. I clutch his shoulders tighter and stifle a sob as I press up onto my toes and kiss his worried mouth. Wes's bottom lip pulls free from his teeth just before it collides with mine. Then, he stills, holding the moment along with his breath.

He doesn't kiss me like our time is running out.

He kisses me like it's already up.

And he's right. Because before I have a chance to whisper that I love him too—before I can say goodbye to the man who taught me how to live—fifty thousand volts of electricity say it for me, seizing my muscles and bringing me to my knees.

Wes

THE FEELING OF RAIN'S body seizing against mine, the helplessness of watching her tumble to the floor at my feet—my handcuffed arms unable to catch her convulsing body—it destroys whatever's left of me.

As the officer drags me toward the front door, I feel my soul, my heart, my fucking will to live disappearing with every step I take. They don't belong to me anymore. Honestly, they never did. They belong to the little black-haired rag doll twitching on the floor back there.

By the time that asshole shoves me down the front steps, the crushing pressure in my chest is reduced to a hollow ache—just phantom pains from my amputated heart. By the time we get to his pig mobile, I hardly remember having feelings at all. And by the time he shoves me inside and slams the door, I've gone completely … fucking … numb.

I was never meant to get the girl. To have the happily ever after. That's not how my world works, and this shit right here is proof. Rain has shelter, a means of self-defense, and money to get supplies. There's nothing left for me to do. My girl—and my kid, if my suspicions are right—are going to have as good a life as anyone could hope for post–April 23.

And me?

In a few days, I'll be fucking fertilizer, and I won't have to feel this shit at all.

Rain

"SWEETHEART, I DID YOU a favor. I did all of us a favor. One day, you'll see.

"Are you *really* expecting, dear? How long has it been since you got your cycle?

"A baby! Oh my goodness. What a blessing!

"Don't you worry. Mama Renshaw's gonna help you every step of the way. And Carter—oh, he's gonna be such a good daddy.

"I'm gonna be a grandma!

"Sit up, child. I got you some water."

When I don't comply, Mrs. Renshaw cuts the happy rambling and switches into high school administrator mode. "Rainbow, *sit up,*" she hisses, snapping her fingers at me. "Don't be so dramatic. I know you think you loved that man, but in time, you'll realize that you only got attached to him because you'd just lost your folks. He was a monster, dear. You saw what he did to my sweet Carter. We're all safer with him gone."

"You're the monster." The words aren't much louder than a whisper as they leak out of my parted lips and dribble down my cheek onto the hardwood floor.

"Excuse me?"

I swallow, tasting blood and feeling pulses of pain radiating from one side of my tongue. I must have bitten it during the tasing.

"*You're* the monster," I repeat, clearing my throat.

I don't open my eyes. Don't lift my head. I'm in the same sloppy fetal position I ended up in after the volts hit me, and I don't plan on moving. Ever.

A new pain, deep and dull, throbs in my lower back, right where Wes tucked his gun into my waistband before the cops showed up.

I squeeze my eyes shut tighter and silently thank him for this last gift.

"Rainbow, I know you're upset, but when you're feeling better—"

"I will never feel better."

And as soon as you leave, I'm gonna put a bullet in my head to match the one you just gave Wes.

"I remember feeling that way too, when I was expecting Sophie. I thought I'd never feel better. But after the first trimester, you'll get your spark back."

I hear metal scraping wood just a few feet away from my head and realize that Mrs. Renshaw must be picking up the key that I dropped. The one Wes placed in my palm right after we got here. A few minutes—that's all it took for this woman to rip my future away from me. A few minutes is all it ever takes.

"Is that my front door? It is, isn't it? Goodness gracious! If that ain't a sign from God, I don't know what is. It's like he's sayin', *Welcome home, Agnes!*" Mrs. Renshaw's voice cracks, and she sniffles back a sob.

"We're gon' be all right, baby girl." Her weathered hand pats my exposed shoulder. "The Lord is my shepherd; I shall not want."

"Get out," I manage to rasp even though my lungs feel like they're going to collapse under the weight of my despair.

"You're right. I should go. You probably want some alone time. I'll be back to check on you a little later, dear. Be sure to drink your water."

Just as I hear her footsteps retreat toward the door, they stop a moment later and return to my side twice as fast as they left. "Oh, I almost forgot …"

The back of my tank top lifts, and the revolver Wes tucked into my waistband is jerked free. I hear the *click, spin, clack* of Mrs. Renshaw checking the barrel for bullets on her way out the door.

Then, I pull my knees to my chest, wrap my arms around them, and sob myself unconscious.

No dreams come to distract me from my thoughts of death. No visions of my parents or Wes arrive to soothe me. When I wake up—minutes later, hours maybe—I am empty. I am alone.

I am dead.

I just have to muster the strength to get up and make it official.

I push myself onto my hands and knees and crawl over to the stairs. The third one creaks under my weight. So does the fifth. And the sixth. This is the only home I've ever known, and it feels like it's saying goodbye with every squeaking floorboard and groaning joist.

For the first time since I heard those shotgun blasts, I'm not afraid to go into my parents' room. Nothing can hurt me anymore.

Not for long, at least.

I turn the corner into the master bedroom, but this time, I don't find the faceless body of my mother lying in a pool of blood with the shades drawn shut. I find an empty wooden bedframe, illuminated by the afternoon sun. The curtains are wide open. The mattress and bedding, long gone. All traces of what happened here … erased. It almost makes me feel bad for what I'm about to do. For leaving another bloody mess in the house that Wes spent so much time cleaning up.

Maybe I should do it in the backyard, I think.

Maybe it doesn't fucking matter anymore.

I flip the light switch in my parents' walk-in closet out of habit and am surprised when the overhead bulb actually comes on.

The second I see their clothes, the smell of them hits me like a sledgehammer.

Stale cigarettes and hazelnut coffee.

I want to wrap my arms around my mother's hanging dresses and make them hug me back. I want to sway with them and stroke their sleeves against my cheek. But what would be the point?

To make myself feel better?

Or to make myself feel worse?

Instead, I reach in between them and find a vintage briefcase I know will be there, hanging from a nail on the wall behind Mama's church clothes.

I set the brown tweed case on the floor, spin the numbers on the little dial to 503—my birthday—and pop the dull brass tabs open with a click. Inside is foam lining, molded around a small black handgun. Daddy used to let me shoot cans off a tree stump with this one, back before he turned scary. He said this one didn't have much "kick."

I hold my breath and slide the magazine out, just like he showed me. It's empty.

But not for long.

Crawling out of the closet and into the master bathroom, I sit cross-legged on the floor in front of the vanity. I open the cabinet doors and dig all the way to the back, knocking over bottles and boxes and brushes until I find it—the jewelry box where Mama hides Daddy's bullets.

Hid.

My heart pounds against my ribs as I pull the whitewashed wooden container out, both because of what it holds and because of what I find hiding behind it.

A hot-pink cardboard box.

With a picture of a manicured hand holding a pregnancy test on the front.

I set the jewelry box down beside me and reach for the pink rectangle with wide eyes and shaking fingers. The plastic sticks inside rattle when I pick it up. Opening the box, I notice that one of the tests is missing. I know Mama was pregnant for a while back when I was a kid, but she lost that baby after a bad fight with Daddy. She told me it was God's will.

I knew better.

I check the expiration date. Then, I blink and check it again.

These tests aren't twelve years old. They're current.

"Oh, Mama. What did you do?" I whisper, tears blurring the date on the side of the box.

Whatever that test told her, it went with her to the grave.

Like mother, like daughter, I think, sliding a stick out of the box.

I flip it over and read the instructions, noticing that it says this brand can detect a pregnancy seven to ten days after conception.

God. Wes might actually be right.

His words echo in my hollow soul as I wander over to the toilet.

"She's pregnant," he'd announced, cupping my belly, his eyes shining with sorrow and pride.

I couldn't process those words at the time. I was too busy watching my entire world crumble at my feet. Too busy dismissing it as just a clever tactic to keep me from taking his place. But as I wait for the results—loading bullet after bullet into the magazine of my daddy's gun, even though I only need one, just to give my shaking fingers something to do—I think about what he said again.

And realize that I never got my birth control shot in April.

I never even thought about it. The world was about to end, and my boyfriend—*ex*-boyfriend—had just left for Tennessee.

But then I met Wes.

And the world didn't end.

It was handcuffed and ripped out of my arms instead.

I slide the clip back into the handle and take a deep breath. The gun is heavier when it's fully loaded, both with the weight of the bullets and the weight of what they could do. But when I pick up the plastic stick lying on the counter, when I read those eight letters glowing on its digital screen, it feels even heavier than the gun.

PREGNANT.

I lift my head to look at my reflection in the mirror above the sink, but I don't even recognize the girl staring back. Short black hair. An inch of blonde roots. Pistol in one hand. Positive pregnancy test in the other. And a dark, desperate madness in her sunken eyes that I haven't seen since the day my daddy put a shotgun in his mouth.

I drop both the test and the gun into the sink and take a step backward with a gasp.

You're pregnant, the girl in the mirror whispers to me.
"Honey, we're home," a voice calls from downstairs.

Rain

MRS. RENSHAW'S CHEERY VOICE from downstairs spurs me into action. My jeans are too tight to stick the gun in my pocket, so I tuck it into the back of my waistband, replacing the one Mrs. Renshaw stole. I shove everything else back inside the cabinets and shut them as quietly as I can. Then, I turn off the lights and dart across the hallway to my bedroom. I find what I'm looking for on the floor by the closet, right where I left it—Carter's oversize Twenty One Pilots hoodie. I pull it on and sigh in relief when I see how well it hides the pistol.

"Rainbooow!" This time, it's Sophie's voice I hear.

Guilt seizes my chest when I think about what she might have found up here if …

I push those thoughts out of my mind and try to clear the emotion from my throat. "Hey, Soph!" I croak out, testing my fake smile. I go to tell her that I'll be down in a minute, but before the words can form in my mouth, I hear the clomping of eager footsteps flying up the stairs.

"Rainbow!"

I barely have time to spread my arms before I find myself being tackle-hugged by my favorite ten-year-old. I expect her to begin chattering away about how she got here, but instead, she buries her face in my sweatshirt and bursts into tears.

"Hey … what's going on?" I smooth my hand over her long braids and pull her tighter.

"I'm just … I'm just so happy." She sniffles, wiping her wet eyes on the soft black cotton. "I didn't think we were ever gonna get outta that place. I didn't like it there. There were no beds and we had to shower in the rain and the big kids were so mean. And then your friend beat up Carter and took you away, and I was so scared."

Sophie lifts her little face and gives me a grin so big that I notice she's missing at least two teeth. "But Mama knew what to do. She called the police, and they found you! And they put that bad man in jail!"

Her hug lit a candle of joy in my heart, but her words blew it right back out.

"When Mama came back, she said God was so proud of her that he blessed us with a new house *and* a new baby!" Her little overwhelmed eyes fill with tears again, and all I can do is hug her tighter so that I won't have to look at them anymore.

Instead, I have to look at her brother as his six-foot-three-inch frame fills my bedroom doorway. His shirt is splattered with blood. His lips and one eyebrow are split open. His left eye is swollen shut. His nose is puffy and slightly crooked, and his usual cocky swagger has been replaced by a dark thundercloud of anger.

His one open eye narrows at the sight of me. Mine widen at the sight of him.

"Is it true, Rainbow?" Sophie squeals. "Are you really gonna have a baby?"

I hold Carter's stare, feeling the same question hanging in the air between us. Then, I sigh and tell her the truth, "Yes, sweetie, I am."

Carter's gaze drops to his sister's back as he takes in those four little words.

"Are we really gonna live here? With you? Forever?"

"Of course we are, shrimp," Carter grumbles through his mangled mouth, cutting me a warning glance. "Look." His eyes dart to something over my shoulder. "Rain's already got your bed ready."

Sophie and I both turn, and I'm shocked to discover that he's right. The last time I saw it, my bed had a shotgun blast right through the middle, but now it's covered in a pristine unicorn-mermaid-cat comforter. Wes must have gone next door and swapped out my mattress and bedding for Sophie's. He mentioned that he was able to salvage some stuff from the front half of their house.

I didn't realize he'd meant a whole bed.

With every step I take toward it, I feel closer to him. Closer and yet so much further away. I lift one knee and crawl onto the soft surface, my hand sliding across the place where a giant hole used to be. I lie with my back to my uninvited guests and pull the spare pillow to my chest. It doesn't even smell like smoke.

It smells like fabric softener.

He even washed it.

Closing my eyes, I surrender to my tears. The first ones I've let fall since he was ripped from my arms.

Wes might be the one who was taken away in handcuffs, but I'm the one facing a life sentence. This house is my prison. This baby and that little girl behind me—they're my wardens. As long as they're alive, I'll be here, suffering, because I can't take the easy way out if it means causing them pain.

"Rainbow? Are you crying?"

"Nah, she's just snorin'. Growing a baby makes you real tired. Why don't you go tell Mama that your bed's here? She'll be so happy."

"Okay!"

I hear Sophie stomp back down the stairs just before the door closes with a quiet snick.

The hair on the back of my neck stands up as the floorboards creak under Carter's heavy feet. I expect to feel the bed sag under his weight, but when it doesn't, I turn and find him pacing back and forth across my matted carpet.

His eyebrows are furrowed, his swollen lips move as if he's mumbling to himself, and his long fingers are tugging on his overgrown black curls.

I've never seen him so distraught. It makes me nervous.

"How did you guys get here?" I ask, hoping to take his mind off of whatever has him acting this way.

"My mom went back to our house, got my dad's truck out of the garage, and drove to the mall to pick us up." He shrugs. "Told us she was takin' us home."

"How did your dad get to the truck with his broken leg?"

"I pushed him in that rolly chair you gave him."

"And y'all didn't see any Bonys?"

Carter turns and glares at me with his one good eye. "Can we not do this?"

"What?"

"Pretend like everything's fucking fine."

I sigh and roll onto my back, feeling my dad's gun dig into my spine. "Fine with me."

Carter doesn't say anything. He just keeps pacing, and I just keep staring at his battered face.

"I'm sorry," I finally mutter, not knowing where else to begin.

"It's not your fault," he replies without taking his eyes off the floor. "Birth control is only, like, ninety-nine percent effective."

Wait. What?

"I just … I'm not ready to be a dad."

Oh my God. That's what he's upset about? He thinks this baby is his?

The thought seems absurd, but when I think about it, it's probably only been about two months since Carter and I were together. Two months that feel like two lifetimes. That was back before his family packed up and left me in Franklin Springs without a second glance. Back when my parents were still alive.

Back when my birth control shot was still effective.

"You're not gonna be a dad." I sigh, trying not to roll my eyes.

"I'm not?" Carter stops pacing and looks over at me again.

I shake my head, bracing for the brunt of his anger when he realizes that the man who mangled his face is the same one who knocked me up. But instead, Carter's split lips spread into a wide grin as he bounds over to give me a hug.

"Holy shit, girl! You had me worried there for a sec. I'm so glad we're on the same page! Listen, I got you. I'll take you to the clinic, I'll pay for the procedure, whatever you need. Just do me a favor and tell my mom you had a miscarriage, okay?"

I'm stunned speechless as Carter squeezes me a second time.

"Hey, boy!" Mr. Renshaw's gruff voice calls from the bottom of the stairs. "Your mother says the highway's clear all the way into town now. I'm goin' on a Burger Palace run. You wanna come with?"

"Hell yeah!" Carter fixes his one open eye on me and grins.

That's when I notice that he's missing about as many teeth as his sister. Wes really did a number on him.

Makes me love him even more.

"Dude, I haven't had a King Burger in weeks! You want one? Wait. Duh. Of course you want one. Pregnant chicks are always hungry. I'll get you two!"

Carter bounds out of my room, leaving the door wide open as I curl even tighter around the pillow in my arms.

"Will you boys get a King Burger combo for me, a Big Kid box for Sophie, and—oh, what the heck? Grab us some milkshakes, too! We're celebratin'!"

"Mama, I found a DVD player! Can I watch a movie?"

"Of course, princess! You can watch whatever you want! And while we wait for the boys to get back, Mama's gonna go take a nice hot bath. Praise be to God!"

I get up and close my bedroom door, locking it as quietly as possible before sagging against it and sliding to the floor. I stare at Sophie's bed, standing in the spot where mine used to be, and realize that I don't even have a home anymore.

This is *their* house now.

I'm just the ghost that haunts it.

Wes

THE RIDE DOWNTOWN HAS taken hours so far, thanks to all the roads that still haven't been cleared. At one point, the cops pulled over and called for an industrial-sized snow plow to come and escort us the rest of the way in, which has given them even more time to talk about which steroids to use now that they're legal and what the going rate for pussy is on the open market.

I checked out of their conversation somewhere near the Mall of Georgia and have been staring out the window ever since. It's a game I used to play on the school bus to take my mind off whatever the fuck had happened at my foster home the night before or whatever the fuck was gonna happen when I got to school that morning. I watch for road signs, streetlights, telephone poles—shit like that—and give each one a different sound in my mind. Telephone poles are the bass line. *Bum, bum, bum, bum.* Nice and steady. When a Stop sign comes by, it's a hi-hat. *Ching!* Road signs might be hand claps or dog barks or fucking jingle bells—whatever. It doesn't matter. What matters is that by the time I get to whatever shithole I'm going to, I've already forgotten about the one I just came from.

But when the street signs morph into double razor-wire fencing and the telephone poles are replaced by watchtowers, the symphony in my head fades away. Now, all I can hear is the steady beat of blood rushing into my extremities. *Fulton County Jail* the words above the front entrance announce. Hell, even the building looks like it could stab you. Beige concrete with hallways jutting out in all directions like a twelve-story high asterisk. I'm sure the inside is even less inviting, but I wouldn't know.

I've never been to jail before.

Not because I didn't deserve it. Just because I never got caught.

We approach the main entrance, but instead of pulling in and getting cleared by a guard, we drive right past the front gates. The guard stand is empty, and the gates are wide open.

Then, I remember what that French bitch, the director of the World Health Alliance, said on the April 24 announcement.

"In an effort to protect the law of natural selection going forward and to ensure that our population never again faces extinction due to our irresponsible allocation of resources to the weakest, most dependent members of society, all social services and subsidies are to be discontinued. Life support measures are to be discontinued. Government-provided emergency services are to be discontinued, and all incarcerated members of society will be released."

The jails are empty.

"Where are you taking me?"

"And if you pay her in hydro … ooooh-wee! She'll do this thing with her tongue where—"

I debate raising my voice and asking again, but then I realize that it doesn't fucking matter.

Nothing matters anymore.

I turn and look back out the window. As I follow the razor wire with my eyes, a sizzle beat begins to float into my head. Like the sound of an electric chair being warmed up.

A few turns later, just as the shiny gold dome of the capitol building comes into view in the distance, we encounter something I haven't seen in weeks. Maybe months.

Traffic.

Cars are parked and double-parked along every main street and side street as far as I can see. Some aren't even facing the right direction, and some are pulled right up onto the sidewalks—probably so their drivers can solicit the services of the naked ladies Officer Friendly and Deputy Dickface were talking about. That, or they're buying drugs from the pop-up bong stands a few feet away. They definitely aren't down here to window shop. Every store I've seen since we passed the jail has either been looted or burned.

Downtown Atlanta feels like Times Square on New Year's Eve—only instead of confetti, it's raining ashes from a nearby car fire; instead of fireworks, you hear gunshots; and instead of wearing stupid plastic sunglasses and carrying inflatable noisemakers, the women aren't wearing anything, and the men are carrying machine guns.

The cops flip on their siren to try to get through, but nobody pays them any attention. Nobody, except for the working girls who turn and twiddle their fingers at their best customers.

"Damn it!" The cop driving slams his palms against the steering wheel. "We're gonna have to call Hawthorne again."

"I'm on it." The cop in the passenger seat snatches the CB radio off the dash. "Hey, Sheryl. It's Ramirez. Can you send Hawthorne to help bring us in? We're on the corner of Northside Drive and MLK."

"Again? Don't y'all know not to go that way?"

"It's blocked every damn which-a-way, Sheryl. Just send Hawthorne. I ain't walkin' this suspect ten blocks down MLK."

"Okay, fine. You don't have to be so salty about it."

"And tell him to hurry up!" Ramirez slams the CB back in its cradle.

Gunshots ring out in the distance, but like the siren, nobody on the street seems to notice.

"They really need to get us a damn helicopter. This is bullshit," Ramirez huffs, crossing his arms and shifting in his seat. His knee is bouncing so fast it's making the car shake, and I realize that he's jonesing for something.

"Hey, I'mma go get a blow job real quick. You want anything?"

"Come on, man. Hawthorne's gonna be here in less than ten minutes."

"It'll only take me five," Ramirez sneers. As soon as he pushes his door open, white noise explodes into the car—a deafening mixture of hip-hop, techno beats, gunshots, car horns, dogs howling, women screaming, and alarm systems going off. But when Ramirez slams his door shut, it goes almost completely silent again.

Must be the bulletproofing.

"Fuckin' dumbass," Officer Friendly mutters under his breath.

Opening the center console, he takes out a flask and unscrews the cap with a flick of his hairy-knuckled thumb. As he brings it to his lips, his eyes, shadowed by a Neanderthal-like brow bone, cut to mine in the rearview mirror. He takes a swig. Then, he turns to face me.

"Want some?" he asks, holding the flask out and giving it a little shake.

When I shrug, he chuckles, his meaty face contorting into something even uglier.

"Oh, right. You're a little tied up, huh?"

Suddenly, something slams into the windshield, causing Officer Asshole to drop his flask and scramble for his gun. I look up to find a guy crouching on the hood of the car, peering in at us through the eyeholes of a King Burger mask. Skeleton features have been smeared onto it with neon-orange paint, matching the bone-like stripes spray-painted on his black hooded sweatshirt.

The car begins to bounce violently as another Bony, and then another, leap onto the hood, the roof, the trunk. The zombified King Burger twists his head from side to side, like a raptor studying its prey, before he takes a gun out of his hoodie pocket and presses the barrel to the glass.

I duck just before the concussion of bullets and splintering glass rings in my ears.

Ka-boom!
Ka-boom!
Ka-boom!
Ka—
Thud.
The car stops shaking.
The bullets stop flying.
And the sounds of downtown Atlanta fill the air again as Ramirez hops back inside and slams the door.

"Goddamn, I hate those motherfuckers!"

I sit back up to find King Burger slumped against the bulletproof glass, his lifeless eyes halfway open as blood trickles down his mask, filling every crack in the shattered windshield.

"That's the third car we've fucked up this week! The chief is gonna be so pissed."

"If he'd buy that damn helicopter, this wouldn't keep happening!"

Officer Friendly turns to look out his side window. "'Bout fucking time."

I follow his gaze and notice blue flashing lights reflecting in the broken shop windows on MLK Jr. Drive as a behemoth of a SWAT tank comes barreling into view. It's two lanes wide, and it has a metal blade on the front that's at least a foot thick. People on the street scatter like rats, jumping into their parked cars and trying to get the fuck out of the way before they get smashed.

Officer Friendly flips on the PA system and grabs the microphone. "Thanks a lot, good buddy," he announces through the loudspeakers as the tank grinds past. Then, he throws the car in drive and turns left onto MLK once the intersection is clear, leaning all the way to the left to see around the shattered windshield and the dead body on the hood.

"Why don't *we* ever get to drive the Scorpion?" Ramirez whines.

"Because we weren't military, remember?"

"Hawthorne should at least let me shoot the cannon some time."

Officer Friendly drives a few blocks and turns left onto Central Avenue where a huge crowd of people is gathered in a park.

"Oh shit! We got a dead man walkin'!"

The cop car slows to a crawl, and I do the stupidest thing I could possibly do.

I turn and look out my window.

The left and right sides of the park are lined with spectators, standing behind metal barricades and kept at bay by at least a dozen riot cops holding machine guns. On the far side of the plaza, a woman in a burlap jumpsuit is standing with her back to me. A row of freshly planted saplings stretches out to her left, and Governor Fuckface and a TV crew are standing to her right.

My guts twist.

No. No, no, no, no, no.

Keep driving!

But they don't. They pull to a complete stop and watch as the woman's head suddenly snaps backward. Her body jerks, her knees buckle, and the earth swallows her whole.

Stomach acid claws its way up my throat, but I swallow it down and squeeze my eyes shut. I tell myself that it's not a bad way to go. It's instant. Clean. There are way worse ways to die. Cancer is worse. Disembowelment, terrible. I could be burned at the stake or locked in an iron maiden. I could be—

Ramirez lets out a low whistle. "There goes Nora. What a waste of a good pair of tits."

"Didn't she bite you?"

"Fuck yeah, she did. Had to get a tetanus shot and everything. But you know I like 'em feisty."

As Officer Friendly chuckles and shifts into drive, I take a deep breath and one last look at the place where Nora used to be.

And that's when I see him.

The executioner.

Black mask.

Black police uniform.

Black fucking soul.

And when his head follows our car as it pulls into the police station across the street, I know he sees me too.

Wes

"Goddamn it, Riggins! That's the third car this week!"

"It wasn't my fault, sir! We got stuck in traffic, and the Bonys swarmed us!"

"I told him not to take Northside Drive, sir."

"Shut up, Ramirez! Y'all are lucky you still have jobs, you know that?"

I drum my fingers against the molded plastic armrest of the 1970s-era chair I'm handcuffed to as Ramirez, Officer Friendly—who I guess is named Riggins—and their police chief argue about the dead Bony they rode in with. The lobby of the Fulton County Police Department feels like a DMV waiting room from 1975—other than the flat screen TV glowing on the wall. Reporter Michelle Ling is interviewing Governor Fuckface in Plaza Park right down the street. The sound is off—thank God. But even without being able to hear his pompous-ass voice, that jowly grin and puffed-out belly speak volumes. He's as proud of his "duty to protect the laws of natural selection" as Michelle Ling is nauseated by the sight of him. I can see it on her face. Either she polished off a fifth of gin before this interview or this man makes her sick to her stomach.

Maybe both.

Probably both.

Just then, an officer breezes in through a side hallway with the swagger of a seasoned drag queen. He seems vaguely familiar, but it might just be because he looks like RuPaul with a little more meat on his bones and a lot less style.

"Miss me, bitches?" He sweeps a hand across the nearly empty room and then grimaces when his eyes land on the chief. "Sorry, Your Majesty." He curtsies.

"Elliott," the police chief snaps. "Deal with *that* until Hoyt and MacArthur get back." He points directly at me and then goes back to ripping Riggins and Ramirez a pair of new assholes.

"Ugh. Processing?"

The chief cuts him a warning glance, and Elliott pouts pretty hard before coming over. But as he crosses the dingy tiled floor, his face morphs from annoyed to impressed.

"Well, helloooo, sailor. I'm loving the Hawaiian print." He swirls a long index finger at me. "Very '90s Leo."

I lift an eyebrow, waiting for him to get to the point, and he lifts one right back as if he's waiting for me to respond.

Finally, he huffs, "You don't know who I am?"

Now, both of my eyebrows are raised. I shake my head a fraction of an inch, and his face falls.

"Really? Okay, maybe this will jog your memory." He backs up about ten feet and walks toward me again, this time with a blank expression on his face and an invisible person on the crook of his arm.

Considering that I just saw a sneak preview of my own death a few minutes ago, I'm not really in the mood for fucking charades, but I decide to throw the guy a bone. Maybe because he's the only person around here who isn't acting like a 'roided-out douche bag.

"The bailiff? From the executions?" I tilt my head toward the glowing screen in the corner of the room.

"Ding-ding-ding!" He beams, clapping his hands with every *ding*. "You probably didn't recognize me because I'm sooo butch on TV." The sound of footsteps entering the lobby makes him snap his head toward the back hallway. "Aren't I, Mac?"

"Aren't you what?" the gruff, middle-aged guy walking in mutters back. He doesn't even look at us. His gaze is fixed on the cubicle he's walking over to, and his shoulders are rounded from carrying the weight of the world on them.

"Aren't I so butch on TV? Our new suspect—" Elliott turns to me and asks, "What's your name, handsome?"

"Wesson Parker," I deadpan.

"Ooh, Wesson. Like the gun? I like that. Very *Dirty Harry*."

Elliott turns back to the guy who is now sitting with his back to us at a computer screen. "Wesson here didn't even recognize me! Can you believe that?"

"Nope," he mutters. Then, he pulls the trash can out from under his desk and blows a snot rocket into it.

"That's MacArthur. He's a sourpuss, but he loves me. Don't you, Mac?"

"Hmmph," the old guy grumbles, pecking at his yellowed keyboard with two stiff index fingers.

Just then a dude about as wide as the hallway he's walking through comes lumbering into the station lobby.

"Oh, thank God! Hoyt! Hoyt, c'mere, sweetie!" Elliott waves at him like a damsel in distress.

About thirty slow-motion strides later, the slack-jawed, sleepy-eyed, shaggy-haired officer makes it over to us. He reminds me of a sheepdog, both in his appearance and general IQ, but sheepdogs probably smell better.

"Hoyt, the chief told me *to tell you* to process this fine young man as soon as you got back." Elliott tosses me a wink that goes completely unnoticed by Officer Hoyt.

He simply nods and produces a key ring from his front pocket. Unlocking the metal bracelet attached to the armrest, he gestures for me to stand and secures my wrists behind my back again. Hoyt doesn't make eye contact once. He simply takes me by the arm and shuffles me over to a cubicle next to MacArthur's.

After he takes my fingerprints, name, and basic info—with as few words uttered as possible—Officer Hoyt uses a key card to escort me through a security door and into a dimly lit hallway. He stops at a metal cabinet, digs around inside for a minute, and pulls out a cup, a toothbrush, an orange jumpsuit, and a plastic bottle marked *De-Licer*.

"Sorry, man," he mumbles, his head hanging even lower than before. "Gotta hose ya down."

"Better you than the bailiff," I deadpan.

Officer Hoyt opens the floor-to-ceiling cabinet door a little wider until it blocks the small black video camera attached to the ceiling behind it. Then, for the first time since we met, he lifts his head and looks me dead in the eye. The pity and remorse I see there hit me right in the fucking gut. He doesn't look at me like I'm a suspect or a convict or "the accused." He looks at me like I'm a man who just found out that he only has a few days left to live.

"For what it's worth," he whispers, blinking his red-rimmed eyes, "I really am sorry."

I nod and press my lips together to keep my chin from wobbling like a little bitch.

I'm gonna fucking die here, I think as he escorts me to the showers.

"Dead man walkin'."

May 6
Rain

I COULDN'T SLEEP, SO I came out to the front porch to get some fresh air and escape Jimbo's snoring. He and Mrs. Renshaw dragged their king-size mattress over from next door and flopped it across my parents' queen-size bedframe last night, and Carter tossed his mattress on the floor in our junk room. Now the whole house smells like smoke.

It smells like their house.

Because it *is* their house now.

The morning fog has settled in Old Man Crocker's field across the street. It looks like a fallen cloud being pierced by orange and pink lasers as the sun rises behind the pine trees.

And that's when I realize … I'm outside.

I haven't been able to come outside without having a panic attack in weeks, but here I am. *Not* panicking.

Probably because there's nothing left to fear.

I step off the porch and walk down the stairs where Wes and I sat just yesterday afternoon.

My feet carry me past my daddy's rusted old truck—the one that Wes siphoned all the gas out of the day we met—and they don't stop.

They take me down to the end of the driveway, where about six envelopes are scattered on the gravel. I pick them up one by one.

Franklin Springs Electric.

Franklin Springs Natural Gas.
Franklin Springs Water and Sewer.
First Bank of Georgia.
They're all addressed to Mr. and Mrs. Phillip Williams.

I run my fingertips over their names, but I feel nothing. Just the slick surface of the clear plastic film covering them. Then, I fold the stack of unpaid bills in half and tuck it into my hoodie pocket.

I pick my fallen mailbox up next. The wooden post is broken off at the ground level, so I shove what's left of it into the soft Georgia clay next to the driveway. It only sticks about two feet above the ground now, but I don't care.

I don't care about anything anymore.

"Welcome to *Fuck*lin Springs!" the sign across the street greets me as I pass, not reading my mood.

I haven't walked down the highway into town by myself in months. Not since the crime rate skyrocketed, the roads got clogged with wrecks and cars that had run out of gas, and the local cops stopped showing up for work. After that, I mostly kept to the trail that snaked through the woods. But I'm not worried about the bad guys getting me now.

In fact, I hope they do.

The birds seem to be singing louder than ever as I walk past the torched and dilapidated farmhouses that used to belong to my neighbors. Maybe it's because I haven't heard one in weeks. They're damn-near deafening now.

I have to walk in the middle of the street because all the wreckage has been shoved to the sides of the highway. Thanks to Quint. When the world was busy going insane on April 23, he grabbed his little brother and his daddy's bulldozer and figured out a way to get the hell out of town.

A lot of good that did. Quint almost died in a bulldozer explosion, and now Wes is going to be executed for saving his life. I wish we'd never followed them out of town.

The second I think it, I want to take it back. If we hadn't followed them, if we hadn't been there, Quint would have died. I picture him and Lamar, all alone with that evil bitch, Q, and her crazy gang of runaways, and I shake my head. She's gonna eat them alive.

Maybe I can convince Carter to take the truck back to the mall and get them, too.

As the glowing Burger Palace billboard rises over the trees in the distance, King Burger appears to be galloping toward me with his French fry staff held high. In the place where it used to say, *Apocasize it!* above a photo of the King Burger combo meal, it now says, *Natural selection is the king's way!* with a digital slideshow of all their combo selections below.

The sign disgusts me so much it makes my stomach turn. A wave of nausea brings me to a halt, and I barely manage to pull my hair away from my face before I buckle at the waist and puke on the side of the road. Once the last heave leaves me, I prop my forearm on the wrecked minivan next to me and drop my forehead onto it. As the hurricane in my stomach dies down, I open my eyes and glance at the woman reflected in the tinted glass.

"*You're pregnant,*" she whispers to me again.

"I know that," I snap back.

Pushing away from the burgundy van, I continue walking, but this time with a destination in mind.

The closer I get to Burger Palace, the louder the sounds of civilization become. Cars stretch down the street in the oncoming lane, waiting to pull in to the parking lot. Toddlers tantrum and mothers yell and grown men curse at each other from their driver's seats as they jockey for position and cut each other off in line.

In front of Burger Palace, walking up and down the side of the highway, are street vendors pandering to the captive audience.

"AK-47 for sale! Perfect condition! Only fired once!"

"Spare change? I gotta feed my babies, y'all! Spare change?"

"Hydro! Oxy! Adderall! Viagra! No prescription necessary!"

"You fellas like to party? Fifty bucks each. Seventy-five if it's at the same time."

I flip my hood up and stick to the opposite side of the road. Cars and trucks and four-wheelers and even a few tractors pass me as they pull out of Burger Palace, but nobody stops.

They can tell I've got nothing left to offer.

I walk past the hollowed-out shell of the old library and inhale the scent of scorched books.

I walk past *Shart*well Park, careful not to step on any used hypodermic needles.

And finally, once the sun has risen above the tree line and the sweat has begun to trickle down my back, I see it.

Fuckabee Foods.

The nausea returns full force as I look across the nearly empty parking lot and remember what happened here just a few weeks ago. The three thugs who died right outside those sliding glass doors—one from overdosing on the pills Wes had given him to pay our way inside, the other two from a spray of bullets.

Fired by me.

Even though the few businesses that haven't been looted or torched are up and running again, I knew better than to expect Huckabee Foods to be one of them. The redneck mafia of Franklin Springs would rather burn this place to the ground than relinquish control. Which is why I'm not at all surprised to see a new red-bandana-wearing, facial-tattoo-sporting, machine-gun-carrying asshole sitting in a lawn chair outside.

The sight of those guys used to make me want to turn and run in the opposite direction, but that was back when I still cared about what happened to me.

Now all I care about is getting what I need and getting the hell out of here.

I pull the gun out of the back of my jeans and approach the front door with it pointed toward the ground.

Captain No-Neck looks up from his cell phone and does a double take when he sees me.

"Daaaamn, girl. That sassy walk you got is makin' my dick hard. Come on over here and give me some sugar." He spreads his legs and rubs the crotch of his pants. "I'll make it worth ya while."

I feel my heart begin to race as I stop about fifty feet away. From here, I can see that the glass in the sliding door has been replaced with a blue tarp, and there's still a red stain on the cement in front of it.

"Here's how this is gonna work," I say, trying to keep my voice as steady as possible. "You're gonna go inside and get me all the prenatal vitamins you can find, plus some canned fruits and veggies and soup with meat in it. It's gotta have meat. When you come back out, there'll be a hundred-dollar bill tucked underneath the windshield wiper of that blue Toyota." I tip my head in the direction of the car closest to him. "You take the money and leave the groceries, and nobody gets hurt."

The guard snorts through his nose before erupting into full-blown laughter. "Homegirl, the only thing that's gonna get hurt around here is yo' pussy."

"That's what the last guy said who was sittin' in that chair."

His face hardens. "What the fuck did you say?"

"He was a big fella, too, just like you. In fact, I think that's his gun you're holdin'. I know 'cause I used it to shoot your two friends over there." My eyes cut to the red stain on the cement next to him.

His jaw snaps shut, and his eyes narrow in hatred. "You tellin' me you killed Skeeter and Lawn Boy?" His voice sounds like a dangerous combination of rage and grief, so I soften my tone.

"Only 'cause they fired first. Like I said, I don't wanna hurt anybody. But you got what I need in there, and I ain't leavin' without it."

The tattooed testosterone machine's nostrils flare as he considers my proposition. Then, he stands up and swings the Uzi toward me, biceps flexing as he squeezes the handle in anger. I close my eyes and hold my breath, but the *br-r-r-r-ap* never comes.

"Two hundred," he finally says with a frustrated growl. "For Skeeter and Lawn Boy."

I nod solemnly. "Two hundred."

When the behemoth turns and passes through the sliding tarp door, I exhale in relief and dig a wad of cash out of my back pocket with a shaking hand. It's everything I had hidden in my sock drawer. Figured I'd better keep it on me now that my house has been overrun by Renshaws.

With knocking knees, I walk over to the blue Toyota and tuck all my twenties under the passenger windshield wiper. Then, I retreat to the F-150 a few parking spaces away.

Visions of an ambush flood my mind while I wait. I picture the guard running out with five, ten, fifteen thugs on his heels, all of them blasting the parking lot with semiautomatic weapons until the dumb girl in the baggy hoodie is just another red stain on the cement.

Maybe that's the real reason I came here.

Maybe I *want* them to kill me.

But they don't. What feels like hours later, the tarp door slides open again, revealing guard number two holding four plastic grocery bags and looking none too pleased about it.

He makes murderous eye contact with me as he lumbers toward the blue sedan. Then, he drops the bags on the hood and snatches the cash out from under the wiper blade. Counting it twice, the leathery redneck spits on the ground in my direction. Then, he turns and walks back to his station.

I wait until he's back in his lawn chair and as far away from me as he's going to get before I approach the car. He watches me walk with a predatory stare but doesn't make a move as I inspect the bags. It's all here—the vitamins, the soup, the fruits and veggies. This time, I can't keep my tears at bay as an overwhelming mixture of pride and disbelief swells in my chest.

"Thank you," I say, my voice cracking as I give the ogre a small, sincere smile.

"Fuck you," he replies, dropping his eyes back down to the phone in his lap.

Wes

THREE HUNDRED FIFTY-FOUR.

No matter how many times I count the gray cinder blocks lining my six-by-six cell, it always comes out to three hundred and fifty-fucking-four.

It's so small I can't even lie down on the cot without bending my knees, which is exactly what I'm doing as I stare at the ceiling with my pillow pressed against my ears, trying to block out the sobs of the guy in the holding cell next to me.

Sad bastard kept me up all night. I'd felt bad for him at first, but now, I wish somebody would come put him out of his misery. I don't know how much more of this shit I can take.

His guttural wails finally die down—*thank God*—but before I can roll over and try to get some shut-eye, the fucker decides he wants to chat.

"Hey, neighbor? You doing okay?" He sniffles, blowing his nose on God knows what.

Ugh. Do we really have to do this?

"Yep," I deadpan.

"I'm sorryyyyy." His voice breaks on the last syllable, and the tears start up again. "I'm trying to be quiet … I really am."

Jesus fucking Christ.

"It's cool," I mutter without an ounce of sincerity. I'm not exactly long on compassion right about now.

"I'm Doug." He sniffle-snorts like a rusty trumpet.

"Wes."

"Hi, Wes. What are you in for?"

Oh my God.

I roll my eyes. This guy sounds like a pocket-protector-wearing Trekkie with a comb-over and a degree in Norse mythology. He must have heard that line in a prison movie on Netflix.

"Antibiotics." Accepting that I'm never going to sleep again, I sit up and stretch my legs out in front of me. It's weird to see them wrapped in an orange jumpsuit. I wore the same Hawaiian shirt and pair of jeans ever since the fires broke out in Charleston. All I got out of town with were the clothes on my back and my buddy's dirt bike.

Now, I don't even have those.

"Antibiotics? Wow. That's all it takes, huh?"

"Guess so. What about you?" I ask, suddenly curious about what this cubicle-dweller could have possibly done to land himself here.

"I ... I stole an incubator from the hospital for m-m-my premature son." He starts weeping again, and I immediately regret asking the fucking question. "My wife and I, we ..."

"Hey, man. You don't have to—" I interrupt, trying to spare myself a fucking sob story, but Doug just keeps on going.

"We'd been trying to have a baby for years. We did everything—spent our life savings on medical procedures—but nothing worked." He clears his throat, trying to pull his shit together, and continues, "When the nightmares began, we were almost relieved. There was no point in trying if the world was going to end, you know? But as soon as we gave up, that's when it happened. My wife finally got pregnant ... but the baby wasn't due until *June.*"

Fuck. I shake my head, staring at the floor now instead of the ceiling. I think I liked it better when he was crying.

"My wife, she ... she lost it. The nightmares, the hormones, the fact that she was growing a child she'd never get to hold—it took its toll. You know how the announcement said that the April 23 hoax was designed to increase the global stress levels until the weakest members of society self-destructed?"

"Yeah," I rasp.

"My wife was weak, Wes."

Was. Past tense.

"Doug ... fuck, man ... I'm—"

"She ... she made herself go into labor. I don't know how she did it, but on April 20, I found her in a bathtub full of blood ... holding our s-s-son."

The sobbing starts again, and I can't help but think about Rain. I think about the night I found her on the verge of death with a stomach full of pills. I think about the hours I spent with my fingers down her throat, saving her life. I think about her panic attacks and trauma triggers and the days she spent holed up in an abandoned mall because she was too scared to go outside without me. Then, I think about the baby she might be growing, and I realize that my girl and Doug's girl have a lot in fucking common.

Maybe too much.

"I'm sorry for yer loss," a third voice mumbles, pulling me away from my spiraling thoughts.

I look up to find Officer Hoyt standing outside our cells, holding a pair of ankle shackles and staring at the floor.

"Oh God. Is it time? I … I'm not ready!"

"Not yet," Officer Hoyt mutters to my neighbor. "Governor Steele has a sentencin' to do first."

Then, he flashes me a remorseful, sidelong glance.

"Mr. Parker, I'm afraid I have to escort you to the courtroom now. Please stand with your back against the bars."

Regret and panic shoot through my veins as Hoyt gestures for me to step forward.

"Stick your foot out through the bars, please."

I do as he said and feel a metal shackle clamp down around my ankle.

"Other foot now."

"Doug," I ask, suddenly needing to know how his story ends, "if you're in here, does that mean you saved your son's life?"

Hoyt finishes shackling my legs and instructs me to stick my hands out through the bars next.

"Yes." Doug sniffles as cold steel greets my wrists. "I think he's going to pull through. My sister has him now."

My cell door opens with a deafening squeak. As Hoyt leads me out by the elbow, I turn and glance at the man imprisoned beside me. He's an older guy—maybe forty? Forty-five? His hair is thinning, and his skin is so pale I wouldn't be surprised if the only light it saw was the glow of a computer screen. He's wearing a blue button-up shirt with jeans and athletic shoes that have obviously *never* been used for athletics. He lifts his head as I pass and meets my sympathetic frown with one of his own, despair oozing out of his unshaven pores.

He looks like something I've always wanted. Something I'll never get the chance to become.

He looks like a dad.

A damn good one.

Rain

TWENTY-FOUR HUNDRED.

I take the last bottle of prenatal vitamins out of the plastic Huckabee Foods bag and place it on the floor of my tree house next to the others.

Twenty-seven hundred.

I don't know how far along I am, but I'm guessing that two thousand seven hundred prenatal vitamins is more than enough to get me through.

I slump back in my beanbag chair.

If Wes had seen me, he would have been so proud.

And so pissed.

I smile, remembering how mad he got the last two times we went to *Fuckabee* Foods. He told me I was "impulsive" and had a "death wish."

Yeah, and he got shot in the shoulder because of it.

My face falls.

And I let the wound get infected.

I pull my hoodie sleeves over my hands and press my fists against my mouth.

And then he almost died in Carter's house fire because I rushed back in to get his medicine and he couldn't find me.

I close my eyes and inhale through my nose. My sweatshirt smells like the vanilla candles I used to burn in my bedroom. The ones he brought with him when he came back to get me from the mall.

It's all I have left of him now. These memories … this smell …

My stomach churns again, reminding me of one more thing he left me with. Something that, unlike a scent or a memory, will only grow bigger and stronger with time. Something that, God willing, I'll be able to keep forever and ever.

My gaze drifts over to the spot across the yard where the red dirt is piled up in two neat rows as long and wide as coffins. The spot where the people who made *me* now lie. I stare at it for what feels like hours, waiting for the panic to come—the grief I've been running away from ever since that night—but it doesn't.

All I feel right now is the still, silent, soul-crushing weight of acceptance.

I climb down the ladder and trudge across my backyard, picking my feet up high as I wade through the knee-high grass. The sun is directly overhead now, but it's shady under the oak tree where Mama and Daddy are buried. I realize once I get over to them that I don't know which is which. Wes buried them while I was passed out on the bathroom floor. The mound on the left looks a little bigger, so I decide that that one must be Daddy. I turn away from him and face the mound on the right.

"Hi, Mama."

A squirrel peeks out at me from behind a branch.

"I don't know if you know this, but … I'm gonna be a mama too."

A bird chirps in response.

"I probably won't be as good of one as you"—I ball up my sleeves in my fists—"but I'm gonna try."

The wind chimes I made in art class tinkle and twirl.

"I got vitamins today … prenatal ones. And fruits and veggies, too." I beam through my sudden tears. "Aren't you proud of me?"

A gentle breeze whips around me, ruffling my hair like one of Daddy's noogies.

Silent tears stream down my face, but I don't fall apart. I wipe my runny nose on the sleeve of my sweatshirt and tell my parents what I came over here to say, "I love you guys … I'm so sorry they did this to you."

The moment the words leave my heart, I feel a little bit lighter. Not because the weight of my grief has lessened—I don't think it ever will—but because I'm carrying it differently now. It used to feel like a ball and chain around my ankle, but now, I've picked it up and put it on like a backpack.

I feel a little bit stronger.

A little bit more capable.

And for the first time in days, I feel really, really *hungry*.

I don't want to leave them. I don't want to go back into that house with those people and all that stuff that isn't mine, but I have to start thinking about more than just myself. Everyone I've lost has a chance to live on through this baby. Their blood flows in its tiny veins. If I can bring it into the world safe and sound, I might even get to see them again.

The baby might have my mother's mischievous smile or my father's button nose. I might be able to gaze into Wes's pale green eyes again or run my fingers through his soft brown hair.

My heart skips a beat as I turn and head for the back door.

Water. I need water. And a can opener. And a spoon.

I jiggle the handle and sigh when I realize that it's locked. *Of course.* I knock on my own damn door and wait for someone to let me in.

Seconds later, I hear the click-clack of the deadbolt. The door swings open, revealing one squeaky-clean Carter Renshaw wearing nothing but a pair of loose athletic shorts, as shiny and black as his sopping wet curls and bruised eye.

"There you are." He tries to smile but then hisses as his fat lip splits open again. He dabs the cut with his finger and steps aside to let me in. "We were looking for you everywhere."

"Really?" I deadpan as I walk past him into my dining room. *Their* dining room.

The sight of Carter with his shirt off used to instantly turn me on.

Now, it just pisses me off.

"Where were you? My mom made pancakes."

My mouth waters instantly as I pass through the doorway into the kitchen. The aromas of pancakes and sausage and coffee fill the air. My eyes land on Mrs. Renshaw, drying her hands on a dishtowel as Sophie wipes down the counter.

"Well, good mornin', sunshine." She beams, turning to face me.

I'm shocked at how different she looks. She must have found a wig in the wreckage of their old house because her hair is suddenly sleek and shoulder-length, like she used to wear it, and I swear she even has on mascara. Her dress is ironed. Sophie's, too. And they're both wearing probably every piece of jewelry they own.

"Rainbow!" Sophie cheers, bouncing over to give me a hug. Her plastic bracelets rattle with every step.

I mechanically wrap my arms around the girl and glare at her mother over her head. It's the first time I've seen Mrs. Renshaw since Wes was taken yesterday, but my urge to stab a utensil in her eye is put on hold when she grins and lifts a plate in my direction. My stomach growls out loud when I see what's on it.

"How did you—"

"When life gives you a box of Hungry Jack, runnin' water, and a freezer full of thawed deer sausage, you make breakfast! And lucky for us, y'all had pancake syrup!"

Sophie releases me and skips back over to the counter to get me a fork and knife from the drawer.

"Thank you," I say to Sophie instead of her mother, accepting the cutlery as Mrs. Renshaw's sparkling eyes land on her son.

"Carter, why don't you keep Rainbow company while she eats?"

The intention I see in them makes my stomach turn and my jaw clench but not enough to keep me from devouring this food.

I walk back into the dining room with Carter on my heels and sit down without acknowledging his presence. Not that he even notices. He plops down across from me and begins rambling on about everybody he saw at Burger Palace last night.

"Yo, you remember JJ, right? From the football team? That motherfucker is *swole* now. He was standing right out front, sellin' steroids and workout videos! Can you believe that shit? And I swear to God, I saw Courtney Lampros blowin' somebody between two parked cars. I'd know that fake red hair anywhere."

Yeah, I bet you would.

I swallow my last bite without even tasting it and hear someone begin talking even louder than Carter up in the living room.

"Good morning. This is Michelle Ling, reporting live from inside the Fulton County Courthouse."

My fork clatters onto my plate as I dart up the five or six stairs to the living room, where Mr. Renshaw is sprawled out on the couch with his poorly splinted leg propped up on the coffee table, messing with the remote control. He points it at the TV, mashing buttons with his knobby thumb in vain.

"Gotdamn it! I was right in the middle of watchin' *Hillbilly Handfishin'*! Now I ain't gonna know what happens!"

"We are hours away from today's public execution—"

"Then why in the hell are you interruptin' my show *now*?" Mr. Renshaw barks, chucking the now-worthless remote onto the coffee table.

"But we are going to start bringing you even more exclusive, behind-the-scenes footage from the capitol as Governor Steele works tirelessly to enforce the new law"—her face is sallow and lifeless, and she sounds as if she's reading from a script, no doubt prepared by the governor himself—"beginning with the first-ever televised sentencing."

Michelle Ling sweeps an apathetic hand out beside her and pushes open a massive wooden door. It swings wide, revealing a courtroom as big as a grocery store and as empty as church on Monday.

There's no jury.

No plaintiffs or defendants.

No witnesses waiting to be called forward.

The pews are all vacant, except for a few uniformed officers.

And there, standing next to the raised wooden judge's podium, is a tall, slender, bald man I recognize instantly as the bailiff from the executions.

Upon seeing the camera, he adjusts his uniform, lifts both hands as if he's about to conduct a symphony, and shouts, "All rise! The honorable Governor Beauregard Steele is presiding."

The two officers in the front row stand as Governor Steele breezes in through the doorway behind the bailiff. He's wearing a black judge's robe, but he left it wide open in the front to accommodate his sizable belly, and the sleeves are about three inches too short.

"Be seated."

The chair behind the podium squeaks loudly as Governor Steele sits and taps the tiny microphone in front of him, "Ladies and gentlemen, I declauh that the Georgia State Superiuh Court is now in session. I hereby call to order the case of the People Versus …" Governor Steele shuffles a few papers around on the podium until the bailiff comes over and whispers something in his ear. "Wesson Patrick Parkuh!"

He slams his gavel down, and I feel the blow directly in my own chest.

No. No, no, no.

"Bailiff!" He swings his gavel in the direction of the man on his right with the enthusiasm of a game show host. "Bring out the accused!"

I'm no longer in my body. I'm not even in my living room. I'm in the back row of that courtroom, clutching the smooth wooden bench in front of me so hard that my knuckles turn white as the bailiff pushes through the door behind him and reenters the room, dragging Wes by the elbow.

My Wes.

The camera zooms in on his beautiful face, and thanks to the power of HDTV, I can count every black eyelash as he stares at the floor, every stubborn strand of hair that refuses to stay tucked behind his ear, and every worried crease in his lips as he chews on the corner of his mouth. He's right there. Larger than life. So close I can touch him.

So, I do.

I step toward the TV as Mrs. Renshaw and Sophie and Carter come running up the stairs. Wes's eyes stare back at me the moment my fingertips graze his cheek, but they're not happy to see me.

They're downright hateful.

"Rainbow! Get away from there!" Mrs. Renshaw snaps. "Jimbo, don't just sit there! Turn that godforsaken thing off!"

"I tried, Agnes! They're broadcastin' it on every damn channel!"

"Well, try harder!"

"Your Honor." The camera cuts away from Wes and over to the judge's stand, where one of the police officers in the front row is now addressing the governor.

I yank my hand back and stumble away from the screen.

"The accused has been charged with violating the one and only true law, the law of natural selection, by procuring and administering life-saving antibiotics to a mortally wounded citizen. The evidence will show that an open bottle of Keflex was found at the scene of the crime with the accused's fingerprints on it, and the accused was identified on sight by an eyewitness. I motion to find the accused guilty as charged."

Governor Steele leans back in his chair and folds his hands across his stomach. "Very good then. Very good. Does the, uh, defense have anything to say?" He turns a beady eye on the second officer in the front row, who stands at attention and violently shakes his head.

"Jimbo! Turn! It! Off!"

"I'm tryin', woman!"

"Very well then." Governor Steele nods at the mute officer in approval, and his chair squeaks loudly as he leans forward and breathes into the microphone. "Mistuh Parkuh …"

The bailiff drags Wes over to the judge's stand, but Wes doesn't hurry. He crosses the courtroom on long, lazy legs, taking his time as the bailiff jerks on his elbow. With his hands cuffed and ankles shackled, he still manages to make that orange jumpsuit look cool as he stands in a carefree pose before the governor. Wes, the Ice King. He only acts that way when he feels threatened. It makes me want to reach into the TV and hug him from behind. Wrap my arms around his waist and rest my cheek on his back, like I used to when we would ride through the woods on his dirt bike.

Back when we thought the world was going to end.

Right now, I wish it had.

"Mistuh Parkuh, in the face of such irrefutable evidence, I hereby find you guilty of defying the one true law, the law of natural selection. You shall be sentenced to death by public exe—"

The screen goes black as Mrs. Renshaw yanks the plug out of the wall behind the TV stand.

"There!" she huffs, smiling at her son's busted face. "Justice is served. Now, let's all get back to enjoying this beautiful—"

I lunge. One look at Mrs. Renshaw's painted red lips, spread in a wide smile, and I see red everywhere. I let out a primal, soul-deep scream as we both tumble to the floor, synthetic hair and synthetic pearls flying as I wrap my hands around the neck of the woman who single-handedly took everything from me that April 23 hadn't already claimed.

"Rainbow! What the fuck?"

"Stop it, Rainbow. You're hurting her!"

"Gotdamn it, child! Get offa her!"

Mrs. Renshaw's eyes bulge out of her face, but I only squeeze harder, unable to stop myself even if I wanted to. Her arms flail, slapping, clawing, and tugging at my arms and wrists, but I'm too far gone. All I hear is her voice over and over in my head.

"Justice is served!"

"Justice is served!"
"Justice is served!"

I jerk her neck after every declaration. Just as her arms go limp and her eyes roll back in her head, I feel a pair of hands as big as dinner plates wrap around my waist and lift me off of her lifeless body.

"What the fuck is wrong with you?" Carter shouts as he jerks my arms behind my back, tangling them in a knot so tight I feel like the slightest move might break my shoulders.

Mrs. Renshaw comes to with a gasp, blinking and panting as she rubs the red marks around her neck.

Sophie picks up her mother's lost wig and kneels by her side, gently helping her sit up so she can place the nightmarish thing back on her head.

"What in the Sam Hill has gotten into you, child?" Mr. Renshaw asks as he hobbles over to help his wife stand.

Smoothing her dress over her wide hips, Mrs. Renshaw adjusts her wig and levels me with a lethal stare. It's the same look she saved for the really bad kids back when she was an administrator at our high school.

"Carter, Sophia … tie her up."

Wes

KEEP YOUR POSTURE LOOSE. *Stop clenching your fucking jaw. Look bored. More bored.*

"Mistuh Parkuh, in the face of such irrefutable evidence, I hereby find you guilty of defying the one true law, the law of natural selection. In the great state of Georgia, those who commit crimes against naychuh shall be *returned* to naychuh; therefore, I sentence you to death by public execution. This court is adjourned!" Governor Fuckface bangs his gavel and points it at the news crew standing in the back of the courtroom. "Back to you, missy!"

I glance over my shoulder just in time to see the reporter roll her eyes in disgust before turning to face the camera.

"This is Michelle Ling, reporting live from the Fulton County Courthouse. This sentencing was brought to you by Buck's Hardware … because the *buck* stops here. We'll be broadcasting live from Plaza Park this afternoon for another Green Mile execution event. Stay safe out there, and may the fittest survive."

Her tone is about as shitty as my mood.

I appreciate that.

"All rise," Elliott says in his most authoritative voice, which is fucking ridiculous—not only because he's a shit actor, but also because we're all already standing.

Governor Steele stands and almost knocks his microphone off the podium with his belly when he turns to leave. I can't believe this piece of shit is the one who decides whether I live or die.

Decided.

Fuck me.

Once the camera crew leaves, Officer Elliott blows out a breath and folds at the waist like he just ran a marathon. "Good Lawd! If I had to suck my stomach in for one more minute, I was gonna fall out on the floor!"

Ramirez and Riggins, the two cops who brought me in yesterday, chuckle as they head past us toward the door.

"You deserve an Emmy for that performance, Elliott," Ramirez taunts.

"Pssh. Please. I deserve a Oscar!" He flips his nonexistent hair over his shoulder as the two glorified beat cops laugh their way to the exit.

Elliott's smiling eyes land on me, and suddenly, they're not so smiley anymore.

"You deserve a Oscar too," he says, his mouth forming a flat line. "You did good, handsome."

I give him the same bored expression I gave Governor Fuckface and let him lead me by the elbow out the door, down a metal staircase, and through the underground tunnel that connects the courthouse to the police station across the street.

While Elliott fills the silence with tales about all the celebrity trials he's done, I find myself analyzing the path of the pipes and air-conditioning vents overhead, the placement of the lights and security cameras, the weapons holstered on Elliott's belt.

"Most actors are short as hell in person, but Chris Tucker? Ooh…now, that's a tall drink of water! Nice, too! Have you ever seen *The Fifth Element?* When I saw that movie, I told my mama I wanted to be Ruby Rhod when I grew up!"

As we climb the stairs that lead up to the police station, I find myself analyzing Elliott as well. At first, I thought he was just filling the silence because he's a self-absorbed, narcissistic star-fucker, but when he glances at me, there's a sadness in his eyes that tells me he's not trying to impress me.

He's trying to distract me.

Because I was just sentenced to fucking death, and the only thing he can do about it is try to take my mind off of it for a few minutes.

When we get back to my cell, Elliott pats me on the back. "Okay, my man. Officer Hoyt will be back with your dinner in a few minutes. You green?"

"Super green," I mumble, walking through the open bars.

"Ha! I knew you'd seen that movie! You got Korben Dallas written alllll over you, honey!" Elliott beams as he closes the door and gestures for me to turn around and stick my hands through the bars.

On second thought, maybe this asshole wasn't trying to make me feel better, I think as I face the wall and let Elliott take off my handcuffs and shackles. *Maybe he was trying to make* himself *feel better.*

Guilt. I can work with that.

"How did your sentencing go, friend?" Doug asks from the cell next to me. His voice is raw and tired.

I groan as Elliott walks away, twisting my sore wrists in front of me. "It fuckin' went."

"I'm sorry."

"It is what it is."

There's a silence, and then Doug clears his throat. "Officer Hoyt's bringing me my last meal soon. They let me choose between the chicken Alfredo and beef Wellington."

Fuck, man.

Doug's trying to sound tough, and for some reason, that makes it even worse.

I swallow the lump forming in my throat and ask, "What'd you go with?"

"The beef," he says with a sniffle. "My wife never let me eat red meat." His voice breaks at the mention of his girl, erupting into the kind of sob that's so painful it doesn't make a sound. Only gasps and gurgles and deep, guttural moans.

I let my head fall back against the cinder-block wall and close my eyes, but I don't fucking cry.

Because unlike Doug, I'm gonna see my girl again.

I thought I could do this.

I thought I had changed.

I thought I could sacrifice myself for her and make God happy for once in my shitty waste of a life.

But fuck that.

If God wanted a martyr, he shouldn't have chosen a motherfucker who knows how to pick locks with a plastic fork.

Rain

OUR GARAGE DOESN'T HAVE windows.

My garage.

Their garage.

Their garage doesn't have windows.

It's pitch-black in here, day or night.

I don't know which one it is anymore.

The sound of cockroaches scurrying around makes me think it must be getting dark outside. They usually only come out at night.

Thank God I have my boots on.

Not that I can feel my feet anyway. I haven't been able to straighten my legs for hours. Sophie dragged a chair from the dining room out here, and Carter duct-taped me to it. He bound my ankles to the wooden legs and taped my wrists to the armrests.

Now I can't feel my hands either.

I spent the first hour or two tugging on my restraints, trying to shuffle my chair across the floor without making noise, trying to think of something in here that I could use as a tool or a weapon, but once my anger wore off, I remembered that it doesn't really matter.

What's the point of escaping when you have nowhere else to go?

This used to be my home.

Then, Wes became my home.

And now ... I'm just homeless.

I picture Wes's face, bitter but not broken, defiant but not desperate, as he stood before the governor. Since the moment they ripped him away from me, I've thought of him as dead. But he's not. I looked at him, and he looked at me. And somehow, that makes it hurt more. Knowing he's out there and I can't get to him. Touching his cheek and feeling nothing but dust and static beneath my fingers. Knowing that he's locked in a cell somewhere, while I'm locked in one of my own.

If the tables were turned, Wes would come for me. I know he would. He would storm the castle and slay the dragons and burn the entire kingdom to the ground to save me.

But no one's coming for him.

And the saddest part is that no one ever has.

The door to the kitchen swings open, and I wince when the overhead fluorescent lights come on. Squeezing my eyes shut, I try to bury my face in my shoulder to hide from the unbearable brightness.

"Dinnertime." Mrs. Renshaw's voice is raspy but strong as she drags another dining room chair across the cement floor.

I hear the click-clack of high heels and the crinkle of a paper bag, which I assume holds the French fries and greasy hamburger I'm smelling.

Once my eyes adjust to the light, I blink them a few times and find Mrs. Renshaw sitting directly across from me—legs crossed, pantyhose on, wig smoothed down, jewelry for days. She glares at me like I'm in an interrogation room, and with this lighting, I might as well be.

Mrs. Renshaw places a Styrofoam to-go cup in my right hand, which is still lashed to the armrest, and then rips the piece of duct tape covering my mouth off in one swift motion, taking the skin off of my dry, chapped lips along with it.

I open and close my mouth, working my sore jaw. Then, I lean forward and take a huge slurp from the red plastic to-go cup straw. Cool water fills my mouth, but it could be gasoline for all I care. I haven't had anything to drink all day.

"Let's get one thing straight," Mrs. Renshaw says, her penciled-on eyebrows arching to the heavens as she leans forward, wrapping her forearms around the bag in her lap. "I ain't sorry for what I done. You can be mad at me all you want, Rainbow, but I will never apologize for trying to protect my family." She drops her eyes to my belly. "One day, when you're a mama, you'll understand."

A wistful smile tugs at the corners of her glossy lips before she sits up straighter and furrows her brows at me. "I always thought of you as one of my own. I loved you like you was family. But I was wrong about you." She wags her finger at me like I'm sitting in the principal's office. "You are no child of mine. You are yo' daddy's child through and through. Evil. Violent. Disturbed. Just like your savage friend who attacked my boy."

I squeeze the to-go cup in my fist, digging my fingernails into the Styrofoam until I feel tiny streams of cool water running down the sides of my fingers and over my palm. When the water reaches my wrist, I get an idea.

"You're carryin' my grandbaby, so I can't turn you in, but … I can't let you come near me or my family again either."

Mrs. Renshaw reaches into the bag and pops a handful of French fries into her mouth, closing her eyes as she savors the food just to torture me. Luckily, it gives me an opportunity to twist my wrist back and forth to help the moisture make its way underneath the duct tape.

"So, I decided"—Mrs. Renshaw swallows her mouthful of fried potato and licks the salt from her freshly painted fingertips—"I'm gon' keep you out here till the baby's born."

"What?"

Her lined lips curl into a sneer as she takes in my horrified expression. "Don't worry; we'll find you somethin' to sleep on and a place to do your business, which, honestly, is more than you deserve."

Mrs. Renshaw digs around in the bag again. The crinkling sound masks the noise the tape makes when I give my wrist one final twist, breaking the adhesive bond. Water runs down my forearm and drips out the other side of the tape, causing a jolt of fear to surge through me. I hold my breath and shift my hips in my seat just in time to catch the stream on my thigh. It lands on my jeans almost silently, and I exhale.

Leaning forward, I pretend to take another sip from the cup, holding it in place with my chin so that I can let go of it with my hand. I manage to wriggle it free from the now-useless tape as Mrs. Renshaw swallows another mouthful of fries.

"Now …" she mumbles, rummaging in the bag and pulling out a King Burger wrapped in shiny yellow paper. She peels the wrapper back on one side and holds it toward me. "Open up and say—ahh!"

Mrs. Renshaw lets out a shriek as my to-go cup flies toward her face, spraying water in all directions like a loose fire hose. She drops the food and squeezes her eyes shut, shielding herself with her hands. It buys me just enough time to reach into the back of my jeans, grab my Daddy's Beretta, and hit her upside the head with it as hard as I possibly can.

Her eyes snap to mine but only for a split second before they glaze over and roll up under her eyelids. Mrs. Renshaw slumps sideways in her chair, knocking over the Burger Palace bag along the way. Golden fries spill onto the oil-stained floor as I clutch the gun between my thighs and struggle to unwrap my left wrist.

Mrs. Renshaw moans and makes a smacking sound with her mouth as I free my left hand and start on the tape around my ankles.

The moaning gets louder as I free my right foot, but when I go to work on the other side, a hand shoots out and grabs my wrist.

I scream and try to pull my arm away, but all that does is jerk her body closer to me. Mrs. Renshaw is still slumped over sideways, and her wig has fallen halfway off, but her eyes are open and trying to focus on me. A trickle of blood flows from her temple down to the corner of her eye, turning the white part bright red. Then, it darts from my face to the gun between my legs.

Shit!

Her grip around my wrist tightens violently as she strains with her free hand to grab the weapon. My heart pounds like a desperate fist against my ribs as I snatch the gun out of her reach. Then, it stops completely as I bring it down like a hammer on the top of her head.

Crack.

Mrs. Renshaw's body goes limp, landing in my lap before sliding down my legs to the floor.

Oh God.

I roll her off my feet so that I can free myself. The Burger Palace bag crinkles loudly underneath her, and my stomach growls. Once the duct tape is off, I hold my breath and roll her onto her side, pulling the pulverized burger out from under her lifeless body.

I know I should check for a pulse, but I … I just can't.

She's fine, I tell myself as I shove the flattened sandwich into my hoodie pocket. *She's gonna be fine.*

Running over to the wall, I reach up to hit the automatic garage door button, but the sound of Wes's voice stops my hand in midair.

"Supplies. Shelter. Self-defense."

I picture his face the way it looked on the morning of April 24, when we woke up and realized that the world hadn't ended after all. His exhausted green eyes, bloodshot and rimmed with red. His battle-worn face, covered in dirt and ash and stubble. His blue Hawaiian shirt, smeared with Quint's blood. And I hear his pep talk again, too, but this time, I listen. I really listen.

"All you gotta do is say, Fuck 'em, *and survive anyway,"* he said, wiping the tears from my filthy cheeks. *"That's it. First, you say,* Fuck 'em. *Then, you figure out what you need to survive. So … figure it out. What do you need today?"*

"Food," I whisper to myself.

"Good. Do you have any?"

I picture my tree house full of cans and vitamins and nod.

"Supplies … check. What else do you need?"

"A way to get to you," I mumble, dropping my forehead to the wall next to the garage door button.

"A vehicle. That can be your shelter, too. What else?"

"An army to help me get you out."

"That would be nice, but let's start with … " I picture Wes tapping the handle of the revolver sticking out of his shoulder holster with a smirk.

"My daddy's gun," I sigh.

"Self-defense. Supplies, shelter, and self-defense. That's all you need."

I remember the way Wes smiled at me after that little speech. His tired green eyes didn't even crease at the corners. There was a sadness in them I'd never seen before. A resignation that made me nervous.

"See?" he said, letting his fake grin fall as two miserable mossy eyes stared right through me. "You got this."

"No," I corrected him. "We got this."

I don't know if I believe those words any more than I did on April 24, but I take a deep breath and push open the kitchen door anyway.

Because Mrs. Renshaw was right.

When you're a mama, you really will do anything to protect your family.

And Wes is all the family I got.

Rain

I OPEN THE DOOR just a crack and listen for people inside. Footsteps, drawers opening, anything to help me figure out whether or not the coast is clear. The house is eerily still other than the sound of a man's muffled voice in the distance. I can't make out what he's saying, but his Southern drawl and grandstanding tone make me think it must be Mr. Renshaw … until the phrase, "violatin' the laws of Mutha Naychuh," rises above the white noise.

Governor Steele.

My heart sinks. They're probably all gathered around the TV, watching today's execution.

And tomorrow, they could be watching Wes's.

No! The thought practically pushes me through the door into the kitchen. My guilt over what I just did to Mrs. Renshaw dissipates when I see what she's done to the place.

Mama's watercolor landscapes that used to hang on the wall in the breakfast nook, the stained-glass sun catchers I made as a kid that she had propped up in the window, her collection of fridge magnets from places other people had visited—all gone. Now, it's nothing but roosters. Everywhere. A metal rooster crossing sign, stained black from the flames that destroyed her own kitchen. Ceramic rooster cookie jars with the glaze all melted off. Glass rooster salt and pepper shakers that are so cracked they couldn't hold a grain of either one. Mrs. Renshaw must have dug every damn rooster she could find out of the ashes of her kitchen and shoved them all in here.

A hate I have never felt before begins to swirl inside of me. I exhale it through my nose like dragon smoke. It seeps through my pores like steam from a hot sidewalk. It clouds my vision, turning everything I see as red as the comb on a rooster's head.

It takes all of my self-control to stay silent as I walk over to the breakfast table. I want to stomp and growl and rip that metal sign off the wall so that I can use it to smash every other rooster in this room. But I breathe through my mouth and avoid the squeakiest floorboards as I tiptoe over to Mrs. Renshaw's purse on the kitchen counter. It's a big, ugly sack of a thing with rhinestones all over it, but when I lift the flap and look inside, a crystal rooster keychain stares back at me … along with a key fob that says *GMC* on the back of it.

I close my eyes and say, *Thank you,* but I don't know who I think is listening.

Mama maybe?

It can't be God. He deserted us months ago.

Opening the drawer next to the oven as quietly as possible, I reach in and take out the can opener.

"Bailiff! Bring out the accused!"

Crap!

The execution's almost over. I have to hurry. I close the drawer and slide the can opener into Mrs. Renshaw's purse, and then I slowly lift the bag off the counter. I make sure that nothing inside jingles or rattles as I drape the strap over my neck and across my body. Then, I turn.

And find Sophia Elizabeth Renshaw staring at me from five feet away.

"How did you—"

I dart forward and wrap my hand around her mouth, peeking into the dining room and up the few stairs to the living room where her dad and brother are staring with wide eyes at the glowing screen.

POW!

They both jump in their seats as I pull my head back into the kitchen.

"Sweetie …" I scramble to come up with an explanation that will make sense to a ten-year-old, but as I stare into her deep brown eyes, wide with fear and confusion and blind trust, all I can think to say is, "I love you. So much. Don't ever forget that."

Sophie blinks twice and then nods a little into my hand.

"I have to go now. Do me a favor and don't tell the guys you saw me, okay? They'll be mad."

Sophie nods again, pulling her eyebrows together, and I drop to my knees to hug her.

"Once again, I'm Michelle Ling, reporting live from Plaza Park. Today's Green Mile execution event was brought to you by Garden Warehouse. On behalf of Governor Steele and the great state of Georgia, stay safe out there, and may the fittest survive."

"Dude," Carter groans from the living room. "They have *got* to start making those holes bigger. Did you see the way that guy smacked his head on the way down? Ugh." I hear the squeak of my couch cushions and know my time is up.

"Don't s'pose it matters now, does it?" Mr. Renshaw replies as I give Sophie one last squeeze.

I can't leave through the back door in the dining room because they'll see me, so I turn and tiptoe back over to the garage, pressing my finger to my lips as Sophie watches me go.

I slide through the door and close it behind me with the quietest click, relieved to see that Mrs. Renshaw's body is right where I left it.

But horrified to see a spot of blood forming on the concrete next to her head.

My stomach lurches violently, but there's nothing in it to throw up.

I realize that if I hit the garage door button, Jimbo and Carter will hear that rusty old motor and come running, and I need more time if I'm gonna grab my supplies out of the tree house.

That only leaves me with one choice.

I have to open it myself.

Pressing my vanilla-scented hoodie sleeve to my mouth and nose, I tiptoe over to the chair where I spent most of the day restrained in the dark and climb up onto it.

Don't look down. Don't look down. Don't look down, I think as I teeter over Mrs. Renshaw's lifeless body and reach for the emergency release cord hanging from the metal track above my head. I tug on it, like Wes did on April 23 when we had no power and needed to get Mama's motorcycle out of the garage, but it's stuck. So, using both hands, I yank on the cord as hard as I can.

The release mechanism pops open, knocking me off-balance and causing my feet—and the chair—to come out from under me. I swing from the cord wildly, legs flailing and teeth gritted as I wait for the crash, but it never comes. Just a soft *thud*. I realize before I even drop to my feet what must have broken my chair's fall.

Agnes Renshaw.

I don't even look as I dart past her and hoist the heavy garage door up by hand. Then, once I duck underneath and slide it back down, I tear around the side of the house and through the backyard. The sun is setting behind the trees, but there's enough light left that anybody who happens to be looking out a window right now would see me dashing up my tree house ladder. All I can do is hurry and pray that they don't.

I chuck all of the cans and vitamin bottles back into the Huckabee's Foods bags and give my parents one last glance as I sprint through the knee-high grass toward the front yard. The wind chimes on the back porch tell me goodbye as I round the side of the house. I pass my daddy's rusted old truck and Mama's motorcycle—that hopefully no one here knows how to drive—and set my sights on the silver GMC at the top of the driveway.

With my heart in my throat, I reach out and grab the driver's side door handle, seconds away from being home free, but instead of feeling the door unlatch and swing open, I feel resistance followed by sheer terror when the headlights begin to blink, and the horn begins to blare.

Shit, shit, shit!

I scramble to shift all the bags I'm carrying to one hand as I dig in Mrs. Renshaw's purse for the car key with my other. I glance at the window next to the front door where I can see Carter and Jimbo on the other side, sitting on the couch, facing the TV. Both of their heads turn in my direction, and Carter shoots to his feet.

Come on!

My thumb grazes the jagged comb on the crystal rooster's head as the front door swings wide open. Carter's furious gaze lands on me as I yank the keychain out and frantically begin mashing buttons. I tug on the door handle and push and push and push every rubbery square as Carter leaps down my front porch stairs and runs at full speed up my driveway. The door finally flies open, and I dive inside, slamming it shut just as Carter's fingers wrap around the edge of it. He screams as I pull harder and harder, trying to get the door to latch. The moment it does, I hit the lock button and jam the key into the ignition.

"You bitch!" Carter screams, cradling his smashed fingers while he kicks the side of the truck, but I don't look at him.

I shift into reverse and peel out of there, feeling a bump under my tire just before Carter screams again.

I risk one last glance at the house as I shift into drive. Mrs. Renshaw is in the garage, facedown under a wooden chair. Carter is hopping on one foot in the driveway, screaming every swear word he knows at the top of his lungs. Mr. Renshaw is standing on the front porch, using the railing as a crutch while he shakes his head in disappointment. And above the garage, where the blinds on my bedroom window are spread apart, I'm sure two big brown eyes are watching me go.

I tear my gaze away from that house of horrors and focus solely on the double yellow line stretching out before me.

"I ain't sorry for what I done."

Well, Agnes, that makes two of us.

Rain

FRANKLIN HIGHWAY CUTS THROUGH the hundred-foot-tall Georgia pines like it's always been there. The smooth curves and rolling hills help calm me down, much like the glowing blue lights on the instrument panel of Mr. Renshaw's fancy new truck. There's one red light that catches my attention, and as soon as my brain is able to process information again, I slam on the brakes and come to a screeching stop right in the middle of the highway.

"Oh my God," I mutter, lowering the parking brake that I've driven over five miles without realizing was still on.

My hands shake as I wrap them around the steering wheel again, and I wonder if it's from adrenaline or hunger. Probably both. I pull the flattened burger out of my hoodie pocket and peel back the crumpled yellow paper. It looks like roadkill, but my mouth waters at the sight of it anyway.

I devour it as I drive downhill through the darkening woods, careful to avoid all the twisted metal and broken glass that Quint's bulldozer didn't clear.

Quint.

I wonder how he and Lamar are doing.

Stuck at the mall with that psychopath, Q.

I bet she's gonna make 'em scout for her now that Wes is gone.

Oh God. They won't last five minutes outside of the mall. The Bonys are gonna eat them alive.

The truck's headlights illuminate a charred, blackened bulldozer up ahead, right in front of the mangled, overturned eighteen-wheeler that exploded when Quint and Lamar tried to push it out of the way. Visions of yellow sparks and orange flames flicker before me in my mind. The sound of flying debris landing all around us fills the quiet cab. My heart begins to race as I remember finding Quint and Lamar, unresponsive in the wreckage, blanketed with broken glass. And when I pull off onto the Pritchard Park Mall exit ramp, I know what I have to do even before I drive over the flattened chain-link fence surrounding the mall.

The whole reason Wes was sentenced to death is because he helped me save Quint's life.

If I leave him here, if Q makes him start scouting, all of that will be for nothing.

I turn my headlights off as I drive across the empty parking lot, pulling up to the curb directly in front of the main entrance. If I didn't know better, I'd think this place was just as abandoned as it had been when they boarded it up ten years ago. But I do know better. There's a whole community of armed runaways living inside, a whole farm's worth of food growing on the roof, and a whole pecking order of power that starts with Q and ends with whoever is at the bottom dying at the hands of Bonys while trying to fulfill her list of demands.

I shut off the ignition, pocket the key, and pull the gun out of my waistband. Taking a deep breath, I look around to make sure there isn't a murderous, spray-painted motorcycle gang coming my way. Then, I hop out of the truck, lock the doors behind me, and dash inside.

The building is dark and dank and smells like mildew. The sound of frogs croaking and crickets chirping echoes in the atrium up ahead, and the filthy, cracked floor tiles clatter under my boots. I can't believe I considered this place home just a few days ago. I was so blinded by my fear of the outside world that I couldn't see it for what it was.

A disgusting, disintegrating hellhole.

I creep down the darkened hallway and pull the gun out from my waistband, wishing it were a flashlight instead. I peek my head into the tuxedo rental shop where Quint and Lamar have been living ever since the accident, but no one's home.

They're probably in the food court, finishing dinner.

I consider waiting for them here to avoid a conflict with Q, but that thought lasts half a second before my feet turn and carry me straight toward the cafeteria.

Wes could be executed as soon as tomorrow. Time is a luxury I don't have.

The sounds of laughing, shouting, accordion-playing, and obnoxious singing get louder and louder as I make my way through the atrium, past the crumbling fountain—with its murky water and random swamp plants—and around the broken escalators. I remember when the idea of seeing Q used to scare me to the point that I wouldn't leave the tuxedo shop, but that feels like a lifetime ago. Back when my only goal was to avoid my own pain.

Well, there's no avoiding it now. It's here. It's in my face and in my house and on my TV and buried in my backyard.

Q can't hurt me worse than this.

Just before I walk through the food court doors, I shove the gun back into my waistband and cover it with Carter's hoodie. I don't want to cause trouble. I just want to get my friends and get the hell out of Pritchard Park. Forever.

The burn barrel in the center of the cavernous room is still smoking from tonight's dinner, but nobody is manning it. Everyone is at their designated spots—Q and the runaways are at the back table, living it up like they're at the Mad Hatter's tea party, and the Jones brothers are sitting by themselves at a table off to the right, picking at their almost empty plates in silence. It's weird to see the Renshaws' table empty, but I refuse to think about them right now.

Or ever again.

I glance at Q as I tiptoe across the room. Her head is thrown back in laughter. A cloud of pot smoke swirls above her head. She doesn't see me … yet.

But Brangelina does. Brad and Not Brad elbow each other and jerk their prominent chins at me as I tear my eyes away and focus on what I came here to get.

Quint's face lights up as I approach their table. Where there was once a shard of glass four inches long sticking out of the side of his neck, he now sports a single bandage. The beige color stands out against his dark skin.

Lamar turns his head but doesn't give me the same warm welcome as his brother. He glares at me like I'm just one more mother figure who abandoned them, his fifteen-year-old authority problem stronger than ever.

"What are you doing here?" Quint asks, wincing as he tries to turn his neck to look in Q's direction.

"I'll tell you in the truck," I whisper, crouching down next to their table. "C'mon. Let's go before the queen decides to—"

"Ho. Lee. Shit," a raspy voice announces from the back of the room. "Look what the fuck the cat dragged in, y'all."

I sigh and stand up. Turning to face Q, I hold my head up but keep my posture loose, like Wes did as he faced the judge today.

Q stands and steps onto her chair before walking across the table and leaping down to the floor with the smug swagger of an untouchable kingpin. Her baggy black men's T-shirt and dress pants, cut off at the knee, hang from her curves like high fashion as she tosses her faded green dreadlocks over her shoulder and levels me with an amused stare.

"I knew as soon as I saw Surfer Boy on TV today that yo' ass would come crawlin' back to Mama Q, and here you is. Couldn't even make it a day on ya own, huh, princess?" Q stalks toward me like a jungle cat, but I hold my ground.

"I'm not here to stay. I just came back to get my friends."

"You mean, you came back to snatch my scouts." Her tone turns venomous as she moves in closer.

"Q, please," I plead. "Just let them go. Wes scouted more than enough supplies to cover all four of our shares while he was here."

"Well, he ain't here no more, now is he?"

"No!" I shout, feeling my face get hot. "He's not! And if you don't let us go, you're gonna get to watch him die on live TV in two days!" I shove my finger in the direction of the fast-food menu screens lining the left side of the food court.

Q's dark eyebrows shoot up as she reaches out and grabs my face with her right hand. Her chunky silver rings collide with the fading bruise on my cheekbone, and her long, sharp fingernails dig into my flushed skin.

"Bitch," she hisses, baring her teeth, "you done fucked up fo' da last time. You think you can come up in *my* castle and talk shit to *the queen*?" Sinking her talons even deeper into my flesh, Q drags me by the face toward the food court entrance. "Errybody say, *Bye, bitch.*"

"Bye, bitch!" a chorus erupts behind us, followed by laughing and clanking and banging around.

I squeal into her palm, but she only tightens her grip on my face. My skin splits in all five places where her nails stab into it. I wrap my hands around her wrist—not to pull her hand away, but to pull it closer. Q cackles as she walks backward in front of me, dragging me down the hall, completely at her mercy. I consider pulling my gun out, but if Q saw me reach for my waistband, she'd probably grab my gun and stick it down my throat before I could even get a hand on it.

I grunt in frustration and dig my own nails into her wrist.

"Ow!" She jerks my face violently, opening the wounds even more. "Calm the fuck down, ho!"

"Let me go!" I scream, but it comes out as three muffled syllables against her palm.

Suddenly, Q shoves me away from her, and I land with a surprisingly soft thud. I open my eyes and find myself in a small room, sprawled out on a mattress on the floor. Q reaches behind a counter, and with a quiet *click*, a few strands of battery-powered Christmas lights come on. They snake back and forth across the ceiling, illuminating the small space just enough to indicate that it must have been a tiny boutique once, maybe even a candle store or a tobacco shop. Now, it just houses a wooden counter where the register once was, a mattress on the floor covered in black bedding, and an entire wall of shelves that now hold all of Q's personal belongings.

Out of every store in the entire mall, I never would have pictured her choosing such a cozy, modest spot to claim as her bedroom.

I scramble to my feet and reach for my gun, but Q beats me to it, pulling hers out even faster.

"Goddamn, you suck at this. Put it in the *front* of yo' pants or somethin'. I coulda shot yo' ass fifteen times by now."

"Why haven't you?" I snap.

"'Cause it's mo' fun to fuck wit' you than it would be to mop you up." She shoves her gun back into the pocket of her baggy shorts and smirks. "Put that thing down, bitch. You ain't gonna shoot nobody."

I sigh and wrestle the gun into the front of my jeans, the waistband already starting to feel a little bit tighter than usual.

Q walks behind the checkout counter and opens a cabinet underneath. "You really gon' try to bust Surfer Boy outta jail?"

"Um ... yeah. I guess." I shrug, losing confidence by the second.

"Good. Here." A pink bundle flies across the room, hitting me square in the chest.

I groan as I catch it, smelling a hint of cigarette smoke and hazelnut coffee wafting off the shiny fabric.

"Is this ... my duffel bag?" I hold it out and look it over in the dim light. I haven't seen it since Carter dumped it out in front of Q yesterday—*God, was that only yesterday?*—when he tried to bust Wes for hoarding supplies. It feels like everything must still be in here.

"Take ya shit, and go get my boy. Hawaii Five-Oh's too damn pretty to get turned into muhfuckin' plant food." Q shakes her head with sincerity. "Best scout I eva had."

I don't even know what to say. I thought she was going to kill me—or at least beat the crap out of me—and here she is ... helping me?

"What about Quint and Lamar?"

"Who, them?" Q flicks her chin at something over my shoulder.

I turn my head to find the Jones brothers standing on the other side of the hall, huddled together but still watching my back.

"I ain't got no use for those pussies. I *hope* you fuckin' take 'em."

"But you said—"

"Listen, bitch. I said what I said 'cause you was disrespectin' me in front of my crew. I snatched ya face 'cause you was disrespectin' me in front of my crew. But the truth is, the faster y'all get the fuck up out my castle, the betta. I got enough mouths to feed."

"Thank you, Q. Really. I don't—"

"Eh, eh, eh, eh," she cuts me off with an aggravated wave of her hand. "Get the fuck outta here. Go on now, 'fore I change my mind and shoot yo' ass."

I nod at the dreadlocked lioness and turn around to claim my last remaining friends.

Quint's and Lamar's eyes go wide as I walk out of the queen's lair with blood dripping down my face and a pink duffel bag in my arms.

"Y'all wanna take a ride downtown?" I ask with an exhausted smile.

"Fuck yeah!" Lamar punches the air in front of him.

"You sure about this?" Quint asks, his eyebrows pulling together as we turn and walk toward the main entrance.

"Quint," I warn. "Without Wes, you'd be—"

"I know; I know. I'm in. I just wanna make sure you thought about—oh shit. Look!" Quint raises a finger, and I follow his stare down the hall to the main entrance doors.

Right outside, perfectly visible through all the panes of missing glass, a swarm of Bonys has descended upon the Renshaws' truck like it's a two-ton piñata. Hoots and hollers and glass breaking and metal smashing echo down the corridor as they take their crowbars and spray-paint cans and steel-toed boots to the massive GMC.

"No!" I scream, shoving my duffel bag into Lamar's arms as I take off running down the hallway.

"Rain! Stop!"

But I can't. This is the moment when Wes would chastise me for being "impulsive." Yell at me for "not listening." Tell me I have "a death wish." But Wes isn't here. And the only hope I have of getting to him before he's *not here* for good is that damn truck.

Crash!

A man in a leather jacket and a motorcycle helmet with nails drilled through it from the inside out smashes the driver's side window as his buddy in a zombified clown mask spray-paints the words *DEATH TO SHEEP* in two-foot-tall letters on the side of the dented white truck. A third guy wearing a *Scream* mask climbs up onto the hood and holds a crowbar over his head in a stabbing motion aimed at the windshield. All three of them have on black jackets with neon-orange skeleton bones spray-painted on them.

"Stop!" I scream, pushing through the exit door and waving my hands in the air. "Stop! Stop! Stop!"

My hands drop to my sides in relief when they actually do stop, but then my heart climbs into my throat as I look for an escape route when all three of their heads turn toward me like snakes spotting a mouse.

"Please," I say, holding my hands up. "There's a purse on the passenger seat. Take it. Take whatever you want, just … please leave the truck."

Pinhead and the undead clown glance at each other with a chuckle, which turns into full-blown maniacal laughter as they turn and walk toward me in unison.

"Take whatever we want, huh?" the guy with the nails sticking out of his helmet asks with a snaggletooth sneer.

The rotting clown makes a slurping sound as he flicks his tongue in and out of the rubbery mouth hole on his mask.

I don't even realize I've been walking backward until my heel hits one of the metal doors behind me.

"Whoa!" the guy in the *Scream* mask exclaims from somewhere near the truck.

His friends turn, and I watch as he pulls my dad's Smith & Wesson revolver out of Agnes's purse. She must have stashed it in there after she swiped it from me yesterday.

"Holy shit, bro!" Pinhead exclaims. "That looks like the gun from *Dirty Harry*!"

"Who the fuck carries a .44 Magnum?" The creepy clown chuckles. "Fuckin' thing weighs, like, six pounds and only shoots six bullets!"

The guy holding the revolver lifts his mask to reveal the rounded baby face of a kid no older than Lamar. But these guys don't treat him like a kid. They step aside so that he can approach me, eyes narrowed, gears turning.

"I know a dude who carries a gun just like this," he says, lifting the revolver in his hand. "You know him?"

I don't have to ask who he's talking about. There's a sadness in his tone, a fondness, a sense of loss that I recognize.

"Yeah." I nod, this single ounce of compassion making my chest ache and my eyes sting.

"I saw him on TV today," the kid says, softening his tone.

"Oh shit! The nerd?" Pinhead asks.

"No, dumbass," the boy snaps back. "The dude from the sentencing. He was the one who used to come into the CVS all the time and pay me in hydro."

"Ohhhh, that guy. Yeah, he cool."

"That's ..." I clear my throat, hoping they won't hear my voice shaking. "That's why I need the truck. I'm gonna go to the capitol, and ... I don't know ... try to ..." I can't even say it out loud. It sounds so stupid. It is stupid.

But it wouldn't be if I had help.

"Hey ... you guys could come too." I try to smile, but it feels like a grimace. "Since you knew him. *Know* him, I mean. You could help me—"

The zombified clown snorts into his rubber mask as his helmeted buddy erupts into hysterics.

"Do we look like muhfuckin' customer service to you?" The clown chuckles.

"Yeah," Pinhead blurts out through his hyena-like laughter, clicking his heels together and giving me a salute. "Do we look like fuckin' Captain America and shit?"

As his friends keel over, laughing, the kid shakes his head and levels me with a sympathetic stare. "Listen, I'm sorry your man caught a case, but we ain't exactly in the helpin' business."

"We in the *stayin' the fuck alive* bidness, and bidness is gooood." The clown flicks his tongue at me again.

"Tell you what … I keep the bag, you keep the truck, and if anybody fucks with you"—the kid sets the purse and the gun on the hood of the GMC and picks up a can of orange spray paint one of them had tossed aside—"just tell 'em you're reppin' Pritchard Park."

I stand, petrified by a potent mixture of fear and shock and gratitude, as this Bony kid spray-paints stripes across my chest and down my arms to match his.

Dropping the can to the ground, the boy grabs Mrs. Renshaw's purse and climbs onto a motorcycle parked in front of the truck. He slides his *Scream* mask back into place and motions with his head for the two guys who had to be twice his age to follow.

"Dude"—the clown elbows Pinhead, and they walk over to their bikes— "did you see somebody spray-painted the highway sign to say Bitch-Ass Park?"

"Fuck yeah! I did that shit, man."

As the Bonys cackle and pull out of the parking lot on squealing tires, I stand like a newly decorated Christmas tree and wait for Quint and Lamar to come out from their hiding places.

When the door beside me finally squeaks open, Lamar is the one who speaks first, "I just want you to know, we totally had your back, Rainy Lady."

"A hundred percent," Quint chimes in.

"Just shut up and get in the truck," I snap.

"Yes, ma'am."

Wes

THE GREEN MILE. THAT'S what Officer MacArthur called it when he came to get Doug for his execution a few hours ago. After he sobbed all over his shitty fucking beef Wellington.

"Time to walk the Green Mile, buddy."

Who says that? Heartless motherfucker. That must be why they sent him instead of Hoyt or Elliott. Those two still have some shred of humanity left. But Mac? He's older. Harder. His tightly cropped gray hair tells me he's probably ex-military, and the trench-deep lines around his eyes and mouth tell me that he's definitely seen some shit. That asshole looks like he eats nails for breakfast and tacks for snacks.

Speaking of nails, I've spent the last hour feeling around under my cot and the sink-slash-toilet unit in my cell, trying to find one.

As it turns out, I do not know how to pick a lock with a plastic fork.

I mean, I do—I had to do it all the time in foster home number ten. Or was it eleven? My foster mom wanted to keep her whole government check for herself, so she used to keep a lock on the fridge and the pantry to keep me from eating the good shit. All she left out was a loaf of generic white bread and a jar of government peanut butter.

So, I got real good at picking locks.

Before she kicked me out, of course.

As soon as Officer MacArthur left with Doug—poor fucking bastard— I knew I had a solid hour to get to work before everybody came back from the execution. They won't let you keep forks, for obvious reasons, but I managed to break one of the tines off without getting caught. That's all I needed to pick Ms. Irene's pantry lock, but the motherfucker on my holding cell is a beast. There's not a *single* mechanism you have to push inside—there are, like, five, and the fifth one is so far back I can't even reach it.

But maybe if I had a nail and figured out a way to bend the tip of it …

"What are you mopin' around fo'? I'm the one who had to walk his ass over to the hole!" Officer Elliott whines from somewhere down the hall.

I stand and quietly step toward the bars.

The mumbling I hear in response must be from Hoyt. He never talks much louder than a whisper. I can't make out a word he's saying.

"Mm-mm-mm. Pissed himself right there on live TV. What a gotdamn shitshow. I need a drink."

I hear the unmistakable rumble of a file cabinet drawer opening, followed by clinking glasses and a painful hiss that, after working in a dive bar for the last few months, I know was probably caused by a throatful of cheap whiskey.

"I think you need another one, big fella."

Clink.

Hiss.

"You know, when I got into this job, all I had to do was wear a uniform, walk some big, sexy men back and forth, listen to all that juicy drama in the courtroom, and collect my paycheck at the end of the month. I did *not* sign up for this shit."

Click.

Hiss.

Mumble. Mumble. Mumble.

"Right? Good benefits. Good retirement plan. Now, they got us killin' muhfuckas on the daily."

Mumble. Mumble.

"I know, hoss. They good folks. This shit ain't right."

Mumble. Mumble.

"You know what you need to do? You need to start workin' on yo' side hustle. Like me. I'mma get me some headshots done, get me a manager, a agent. What you gon' do?"

As Hoyt murmurs, I hear the file cabinet drawer close, and their voices grow louder as they move into the hallway. Elliott goes one way, and Hoyt heads toward me. I can tell it's him by the slow, heavy shuffling of his feet across the dirty floor. I lean against the bars and wait for him to pass.

When he does, he doesn't even look at me.

"Officer Hoyt?" I ask, using my least shitty tone.

Hoyt stops walking but keeps his eyes on the floor.

"I heard you guys talkin'. I just … I just want you to know that I don't blame you for … you know. Doing what you gotta do. You and Elliott, y'all are good dudes."

Hoyt doesn't say a word. He simply nods at the floor and keeps walking.

"Hey, Hoyt? Sorry, *Officer* Hoyt? Can I ask you a question?"

Hoyt stops again.

"You know how you let Doug choose his last meal? That was real nice, man. Meant a lot to him."

The big guy's chin drops almost to his chest, and I know I got him. It's shitty of me to prey on someone's kindness, but you know what else is shitty?

Being shot in the face on live TV.

"You know, I used to work in a bar, and we had last call. Everybody got one last drink before the bar closed for the night. It was good times, man. Some of the best times of my life. Anyway, I was wondering if, since I only got a day and half left, maybe I could get a drink. Like last call, you know? Somethin' strong, to take the edge off."

Hoyt shakes his head and staggers a little on his feet. He must have had more of that whiskey than I realized.

"Can't let ya have nuthin' glass in yer cell."

"Here. You can use this." I grab the plastic cup, with my toothbrush and comb inside, off the sink and shove it in between the bars, knocking the toothbrush to the body fluid–covered floor in the process.

"Shit."

I crouch down and pick up the toothbrush as Hoyt shuffles over.

"I'll get ya a new one," he mumbles, taking the cup from my outstretched hand as he glances up at the ceiling at the end of the hall.

A security camera. Of course.

"Thanks, man." I stand up, palming the toothbrush so that it's out of sight and hopefully out of mind. "You know, for what it's worth, Doug really did like you."

Hoyt finally looks at me, trying and failing to make eye contact as his glassy eyes swim in his bloated, ruddy face. He smells like a potent mixture of brown liquor and body odor, and I genuinely feel bad for the guy.

Just not as bad as I feel for myself.

He returns a few minutes later with a new cup and toothbrush.

"Got you a clean set," he mumbles, glancing at the camera and then back at his feet. "Wash up. It's gon' be lights out soon."

From the weight of the cup, I know as soon as he hands it to me that it's full of bottom-shelf whiskey, but that's not really what I was after.

What I wanted was an ally.

The spare toothbrush was just a bonus.

Rain

"IN ONE MILE, TURN right onto West Paces Ferry Road."

Evidently, Jimbo got all the bells and whistles when he bought this truck. It even has GPS built right into the dashboard. And thank God because even though I found my phone in the duffel bag Q gave me, it's dead as a doornail, and there was no way I'd have been able to find my way to downtown Atlanta with the back roads being as clogged up as they are.

"So … are you gonna tell us what's goin' on or what?" Quint asks, eyeing me suspiciously from the passenger seat.

"I already told you. We're going to get Wes."

"Not about that. I'm talkin' 'bout how your man beat the shit outta Carter yesterday; then Jimbo almost shot his ass and chased y'all outta the mall; then Agnes called the cops, and they took her to find you guys; then she came back *in this truck* to pick up Carter, Sophie, and Jimbo; and now, *you're* drivin' it even though they hate your ass right now."

"Oh. That." My mouth goes dry, and my palms begin to sweat as I think about the events that led up to me stealing this truck. I picture Agnes, facedown and bleeding in the garage. I picture sweet Sophie and Jimbo finding her there. Then, I picture Carter, sprinting up the driveway toward me, his mangled face twisted in rage.

I focus on the road in front of my headlights and try my best to breathe as I blink the unwanted images away. "The Renshaws stole my house, so I stole their truck."

I hope that's enough of an explanation for them, but of course, it's not.

"Stole your house? How the hell do you steal a house?" Lamar yells over the sound of the wind whipping through the busted-out windows from his spot on the tiny, fold-down backseat.

"They literally just moved in and took it over. I was too shocked and upset to fight back right away, but after I saw Wes's sentencing, I just … I don't know … I snapped. Agnes had Carter tie me up in the garage and said she was gonna keep me out there 'til the baby was born, but I escaped and stole their truck."

Quint's and Lamar's questions come rapid-fire after that.

"They tied you up?"

"The garage? Hell nah!"

"She was gonna keep you out there 'til *what* baby was born? The second coming of Christ?"

"Wait."

"Hold up."

"Are you …"

"No."

"You're *pregnant?*"

"Do you know who the daddy is?"

I glare at Lamar, who asked that last question.

"What?" He holds his hands up. "No shade. I probably got a coupl'a baby mamas out there I don't know about."

"Boy!" Quint reaches into the backseat and smacks Lamar upside the head. "You can't get a girl pregnant just by starin' at her, and that's about as far as you ever got."

"Pssh! You don't know my life. I got hos in different area codes."

"You been ridin' your bike to all those area codes? 'Cause you know you ain't got no license."

"It's Wes's," I snap, cutting them both off.

"Ohhhh shit." Quint's expression goes flat as he turns to face me again.

"Yeah."

"Sorry, Rain." Lamar drops his voice and gives me an awkward pat on the shoulder.

"Don't be sorry," I say, swerving to avoid a mangled muffler in the road. "Just help me get him out."

"Yes, ma'am." I see Lamar give me a little salute in the rearview mirror.

Quint nods in agreement.

Thankfully, the GPS lady chooses that exact moment to change the subject. "Turn right onto West Paces Ferry Road."

"Somebody should really make a post–April 23 GPS system," Lamar jokes. Then, he switches to his best robotic lady voice. "Turn right at the burning school bus."

Quint chuckles. "Or how 'bout, *Ignore that Stop sign unless you would like to be robbed at gunpoint.*"

I can't help but smile. Even Quint's GPS voice sounds Southern.

"I don't think we have to worry about getting robbed in a giant truck that says *DEATH TO SHEEP* on the side of it," I say, rolling my eyes.

"You know it probably just has dicks on the other side." Lamar laughs. "You can't give a dude a can of spray paint and *not* end up with a buncha dicks."

"Oh shit." Quint laughs, rummaging in the glove box until he finds a flashlight. Then, he leans out the broken passenger window and shines it on the side of the truck. "Gotdamn it! There's one right here on my door! Why does it hafta be on my side?"

We all laugh, which feels strange and wrong, considering the circumstances, before Quint pulls his head back into the truck.

"Jesus. Who the hell do you s'pose lives there?"

I follow his gaze out the window and find a house—no, a mansion—set back from the road behind a perfectly manicured lawn and a brightly lit fountain. The brick monstrosity is illuminated from all sides, making the white plantation-style columns—and the police cars lining the circular driveway—glow in the dark.

"That's the governor's mansion," Lamar says. "They didn't make y'all go there on a field trip?"

Quint and I shake our heads.

"Pssh. Y'all lucky. They made us go in sixth grade. Pissed me off so bad. How you gonna drag a buncha country kids all the way into the city just to show us a buncha shit we ain't never gonna have?"

"Yeah, especially when our tax money paid for all that shit," Quint adds, still staring out the window.

The property seems to go on forever.

"I didn't even learn nuthin'. 'Cept that Governor Steele has, like, thirty rooms in his house, a heated pool, a helicopter pad, some kinda marble floors that came from Italy or France or some-fuckin'-place. Oh, and at Christmastime every year, somebody makes a giant gotdamn four-foot-wide gingerbread house that looks just like the mansion, and then they just throw the whole thing away in January. Homeless people down the street would eat tha hell outta that thing!"

"And they say sharing what we got with sick people and old people is why we were facin' extinction. If you ask me, it was from assholes like this taking all the damn *resources* for themselves." Quint clicks off his flashlight and tosses it back into the glove box. "I saw on TV that one percent of the world's population owns ninety-nine percent of the wealth. If anything goes against nature, it's that shit."

"You're right." I nod, trying to keep my eyes on the road instead of the mansion my mama and daddy helped pay for with their hard-earned money. "I remember watchin' an episode of *Hoarders* once where they said that no other species on Earth hoards like humans do. I mean, animals will store food for winter or whatever, but they never take more than they actually need. Not like us."

By the time we get to the end of the property and pass the fully illuminated tennis court, I'm convinced that Governor Beauregard Steele's house is more than *anybody* actually needs.

"Turn left onto Northside Drive," the GPS lady says.

"How much longer?" Lamar whines from the backseat.

I glance at the glowing screen in the dashboard. "That's weird."

"What?"

"It says we're only nine miles away, but …"

"Ten hours?" Lamar yells, his face between Quint and me as he reads the dash for himself.

I assume it's a mistake until I come around a curve and have to jerk the wheel to avoid hitting a stopped car. The truck bounces as I careen over the curb and onto the grass, slamming on the brakes and coming to a stop inches away from a telephone pole.

Lamar flies into the dashboard and lands in Quint's lap. "What the hell, Rain?"

"Look!" I point through my broken window at the sea of parked cars stretching all the way down Northside Drive. At first, I assume there's just a bad wreck up ahead that never got cleared, but then I hear the sound of bass in the distance.

And screaming.

And gunshots.

The streetlights are still working, but that's more than I can say for the businesses lining the road. Smashed windows, busted neon signs … the bank has an actual car sticking out the side of it.

"We still have nine miles to go?" Quint asks.

"Uh-huh."

"There is heavier than expected traffic up ahead," the GPS lady announces.

"Yeah, no shit," Lamar grunts as he peels himself off the dash.

"I have an idea." I flip on the high beams and decide to try to drive down the side of the road. There are a few cars and mangled, twisted bumpers blocking the sidewalk, but I think I have just enough space to maneuver around them in the truck.

"Rain, are you sure we should go this way?" Quint asks.

The *br-r-r-r-ap* of a machine gun in the distance answers him with a resounding *no*.

"This is how the GPS said to go," I snap. "You got any better ideas?"

Quint shuts his mouth, and we creep alongside the road in silence, the sound of thumping hip-hop and excitement and fear and desperation growing louder with every passing second.

"Where is everybody?" Lamar asks, securely buckled in the backseat this time.

"I think we're about to find out."

We creep over the top of a hill, and the scene laid out before us looks like an anthill after it's been stepped on. There are people everywhere—fighting in the street, having sex in the street, standing on cars while watching other people fight and have sex in the street, shooting up in doorways, firing guns into the air, and walking around with homemade signs advertising whatever weapons, drugs, sex acts, or snacks they're selling.

I see two guys holding leashes and fistfuls of dollar bills while their pit bulls maul each other.

I see a guy pushing a grocery cart full of colorful bongs.

I see a man holding a machine gun, guarding a naked woman dancing on the corner in clear six-inch heels.

Then, I see a body lying facedown on the sidewalk in my headlights, and I have to slam on the brakes.

"Dude, are you crazy? You can't stop here," Lamar whines.

"I can't run her over either!"

"That bitch is already dead!"

"What if she isn't?"

"Maybe somebody should go check," Quint offers.

"One, two, three—"

"Not it!" We all shout in unison.

"Ahh! That was you, big bro! Go do it!"

"Whatever! We all said it at the same time!"

"Nuh-uh. You said it late."

"Ugh!" I groan. "*I'll* do it, okay?" I go to pull the gun out of my waistband when the sound of motorcycle engines perks my ears.

I lift my head and stare through the windshield as a group of neon-orange skeletons on motorcycles rushes down the street toward us like an approaching tidal wave. They crisscross between the parked cars, bashing them with baseball bats and shooting out their windshields with wolf-like howls.

Br-r-r-r-r-ap!

One of them mows down a group of semiconscious junkies leaning against a dumpster with a machine gun that's been mounted to the front of his motorcycle. Their bodies jerk and fall to the ground as screams fill the air. The folks on the street scatter like rats, diving for the alleys and huddling in vacant doorways.

"What the hell are y'all waitin' for? Let's go!" Lamar yells, pushing on the back of his brother's seat.

I reach out to grab my door handle when I notice the neon-orange bones painted on my sleeve.

"No," I mumble, letting go of the door.

"Rain!"

"Just … just shut up, okay?" I wave Quint off while keeping my eyes locked on the leader of the pack. I couldn't look away if I wanted to.

"Fuck this!" Quint goes to open his door, but my hand shoots out and grabs a fistful of his T-shirt.

"The Bony kid said to tell 'em we're from Pritchard Park, remember? Maybe they can help us!"

Quint stares at me like I just sprouted a third eye. "Are you fuckin' crazy?"

"You're crazy if you think they aren't gonna shoot you the second you jump outta this truck!" I yell over the sound of approaching motorcycles and gunfire and howling.

It's so loud now I know they're on top of us … even before Quint's terrified eyes look past me and out the broken window.

"License and registration, ma'am," a sinister voice bellows in my ear.

With a deep breath, I turn and smile, which I realize a moment too late is the exact opposite of the hardened gangster vibe I was supposed to be going for. It's also the exact opposite of what I want to do when I take in the blood-spattered King Burger mask staring back at me. The eyes and nose have been painted black, and his grinning mouth has extra-white teeth painted on either side of it to resemble the lip-less smile of a skull. But instead of *Día de Muertos* designs painted on the cheeks and forehead, it's pot leaves and dollar signs. Not that I can see much of the forehead. The top half of the Bony's mask is shaded by the brim of an old velvet top hat, and his neon-orange bones have been spray-painted directly onto a fur coat that looks like it was made from the hides of a thousand calico cats. I can't really see his eyes, but I can *feel* them looking us over.

"Um …" I swallow. "We represent Pritchard Park?"

"Oh, do you now?"

The Bony's pack begins to surround the truck. I wince as the one on the dirt bike drives right over the woman on the sidewalk to position himself next to Quint's door.

"Mmhmm." My voice trembles as I force myself to stare into the black voids where his eyes should be.

"A'ight." He nods. His voice is calm—loud due to the engine noise but calm. Then, just as I begin to relax, he throws me a curveball.

"You say you a Bony bitch? Then, tell me … who's ya prez?"

My prez? Like, my president?

I assume he doesn't mean the president of the United States. It must be a biker-gang thing. Like who's my leader.

Crap.

My mind hurtles back in time to our run-in with the Pritchard Park Bonys. None of them mentioned any names, let alone the name of their leader. Come to think of it, I haven't seen any Bonys anywhere who seemed like leadership material.

Except for this guy.

"You?" I say, going out on a limb.

"You damn right!"

The masked man tips his head back and laughs. The sound allows me to breathe again. And sounds strangely familiar.

"What brings y'all to A-town?"

"I … uh …"

I glance at Quint, who looks like he's about to piss himself, but thankfully, Lamar pipes up from the backseat, trying to sound more hood than country, "Her baby daddy caught a case, yo. So, we goin' to the capitol to bust his ass out!"

"Ohhhh shiiiiiit!" The leader of the Bonys covers his toothy rubber mouth with a fist. Then, he offers it to Lamar for a bump. "Yo, Fat Sacks!" he yells to the Bony in front of the truck, wearing a black ski mask and a neck full of heavy gold chains. "These muhfuckas is gonna storm tha castle!"

The other Bony says something, but evidently, I'm not the only one who can't hear it because the prez shouts at him to repeat it. The gold-chain guy pulls up his ski mask and shouts louder, and everyone in the car gasps audibly.

"Holy shit!" Quint whisper-shouts.

"Is that Big Boi?" Lamar asks.

"From OutKast?" I squint, trying to get a better look at him before he pulls his ski mask back down. "No way."

Lamar, Quint, and I all turn to stare at The Prez in unison. I want to ask him if he's André 3000 so bad, but I also want to live, so I keep my mouth shut and pray that Lamar does the same for once in his life.

"It's y'alls' lucky day," The Prez announces, slapping the roof of the truck and making us jump. "My VP and his boys here are gonna give you cats a lift. It'd take y'all ten hours to get through this shit in that redneck mobile."

"Oh my God! That's what the GPS lady said!" Lamar whispers as Quint and I open our doors.

May 7
Wes

THREE HUNDRED FIFTY-FOUR cinder blocks, and not a damn one of them is even a little bit fucking loose.

I know because I stayed up all goddamn night, checking every single one.

The air vent is too small for a toddler to crawl through.

The floor is solid cement.

There are no fucking windows.

No fucking outlets.

And because the lock is unpickable without a bent nail, they put everything in here together with screws.

Out of options and ideas, I've been lying on my cot for the last few hours with my hands under my pillow, whittling the end of my bonus toothbrush into a spike, using the side of a screw. I don't want to have to hurt these guys. I actually kind of like them—well, except for Mac. But if it comes down to them or me …

"Mornin', sunshine. How you doin'?" Elliott calls from the hallway before appearing with a plastic tray. His smile fades as soon as he sees me. "Sorry. I guess that's a silly question, ain't it?"

I sit up, leaving the evidence of my shiv-making operation under my pillow, and scrub a hand down my face. "I was hoping I'd get some sleep with Doug bein' gone, but"—I shrug—"not so much."

Elliott shakes his head. "That was the cryin'-est damn man we eva had in here." He lifts a hand to the ceiling. "God rest his soul."

While Elliott reaches for his key, the rusty-ass gears in my brain slowly begin to turn again. "Since nobody took his spot, I guess this is a slow week for arrests, huh?"

"Why? You lookin' for a cellmate?" Elliott wiggles his eyebrows at me while he unlocks my door.

I know he's cracking jokes to keep things light, but heavy is the name of the game right now.

"Nah. I was just thinking, it's probably nice for you guys to have a day with no executions. No burlap jumpsuits. Nobody crying or pissing themselves. No last meals or last words. That's gotta be hard, day after day."

Elliott narrows his eyes at me as he sets my tray on my sink. "You tryin'a guilt-trip me, handsome? 'Cause I ain't fallin' for it."

"No. I just know you guys didn't exactly sign up for this," I say, repeating his drunken words from last night. "But hey, at least you won't have to do it much longer. Now that they're televising the sentencings, I'm sure you'll get some acting work soon."

Elliott steps back out of my cell and closes the door with a loud clang. He can't look at me until he wipes the flattered smirk off his face.

What a shit actor.

"When you said, 'All rise,' in the courtroom yesterday … I got chills, man. Didn't even sound like you."

Elliott purses his lips to keep from smiling as he rests a hand on the billy club hanging from his utility belt. "I'm just tryin'a shine. That's all."

"Well, good fuckin' job." I stand up and grab the tray off the sink by the door.

"Pssh." Elliott drops his eyes and waves me off, but he doesn't leave.

We're only about three feet apart now, separated by a few dozen metal bars.

"For real," I say, going in for the kill. "You know, I have some friends in the TV industry. Maybe they'll notice you tomorrow. I'm sure they'll be watching my … you know."

Elliott's face falls.

"I would offer to put in a good word for you, but I'm sure you're not allowed to let me talk to anyone. Or maybe you can. I mean … it's not like there are any laws anymore."

"Nice try, handsome, but no laws means that the chief can skin me alive and wear me like a Gucci fedora if he wants to, so ixnay on the calling your friends-ay."

I shrug. It's not like I have anyone to call anyway. I just want him to think I have something he wants.

"Why you tryin'a help me anyway? You know I can't let you go."

"I don't know, man. I've got, like, eighteen hours to live. It couldn't hurt to do somethin' nice for somebody before ..."

"Before you meet your maker."

I clench my jaw and nod.

"Well, for what it's worth"—Elliott glances up at the camera at the end of the hall and turns his back to it, finishing his thought under his breath while he locks my cell—"anybody who walks the Green Mile already got themselves a one-way ticket into the pearly gates, as far as I'm concerned."

Elliott pockets his key and steps away from the bars. Using his normal volume and level of sarcasm, he says, "Eat up, buttercup. I'll be back for that tray in half an hour."

"Thanks, man," I say in a tone as low and sincere as the one he used ten seconds ago.

Then, as soon as he's gone, I shovel the gruel he brought me into my mouth in about three angry bites. I can't tell if it's oatmeal or grits or regurgitated fucking Cream of Wheat, and I don't really give a shit. I have eighteen hours to con, fight, or fucking dig my way out of here.

I'm gonna need all the energy I can get.

Rain

I DON'T KNOW HOW many times in the last few weeks that I've woken up and had no idea where I was. I've woken up in my tree house, in a tree house inside of an abandoned bookstore, on the floor in my bathroom, on the floor of an abandoned mall, in Carter's bed, and even tied up in my own garage. It usually only takes me a second or two to remember where I am and how I got there, but as I stare into the absolute darkness on this particular morning, I got nothing.

Not until I try to stretch.

My hands and feet don't get more than a foot away from my body before they're stopped by immovable walls. My eyes go wide as I reach out in front of me and hit a ceiling that's just as close. My heart begins to race, and my lungs stop working altogether as I pat and slap and thrash against the box I'm locked inside of.

I kick the roof of my prison, hearing a metallic *bang* with every blow.

Then, I hear a similar banging coming from the other side.

"Help!" I scream, kicking harder. "I'm trapped! Help!"

"Pull the handle, dumbass!" a familiar voice calls back through the steel.

Handle?

Handle!

I reach up and feel around until I find a cord with a plastic grip attached. Then, I pull it as hard as I can. The trunk lid pops open, and morning sunlight blinds me as the events of last night come back in a rush—getting a ride from the Bonys to the capitol, getting swarmed by junkies and dealers and prostitutes as soon as they left, deciding to hide in the trunk of a wrecked Dodge Charger so that I could actually get some sleep.

Guess it worked.

As I sit up and stretch my arms over my head, I groan in appreciation. My muscles feel the kind of sore that only comes from a really good night's sleep.

The gold dome of the capitol building looms over Lamar's head as a steady stream of homeless, strung-out Atlantans shuffle past us on the sidewalk. Quint fits right in as he walks over from the busted blue Toyota he spent the night in. He's been wearing the same clothes since April 23, his once-tightly-cropped hair is overgrown and matted, and for the first time in his life, he has a beard.

"Gotdamn, woman." Lamar chuckles. "It's, like, ten in the mornin'. I was about to bust in there to make sure you wasn't dead."

"Not dead yet." I yawn. "How'd you guys sleep?"

"Like shit," Quint and Lamar complain in unison.

Quint rolls his neck, careful not to stretch the side with the bandage too far, as Lamar sits down on the bumper next to me.

"Next time we decide to sleep in abandoned cars," he huffs, "I'm findin' me a Caddy or a Lincoln or somethin' with some legroom."

"Boy, you're the same height as Rain," Quint teases.

I grab my duffel bag out of the trunk and slam it shut.

"Not for long! I got them growin' pains. I'mma be taller than Carter pretty soon!"

My stomach sours at the mention of his name. I drop the bag on the trunk lid and pull out a couple of cans of soup, each one less appetizing than the one before it, but Lamar snatches the chicken and dumplings like it's made of solid gold.

"Dibs on the dumplin's!"

When the Bonys offered to give us a ride down here last night, I managed to shove all the groceries I got from Huckabee Foods into my duffel bag before climbing onto the back of a perfect stranger's dirt bike. I should have been terrified as we zigzagged through the crowded streets of Atlanta, but it just reminded me of the days I spent hugging Wes on the back of his dirt bike as we tore up the woods in Franklin Springs, looking for a bomb shelter.

Before I knew it, they were dropping us off right in front of the capitol building with nothing more than a, "Fuck 'em up, y'all," and a pat on the back.

And here we are. We've got supplies, shelter, and a means of self-defense.

If only we had a damn can opener. The one I got from home was still in Agnes's purse when it got stolen.

After scouring the abandoned cars nearby for tools and coming up empty, we end up trading a can of Mexican chicken and rice soup to an exceptionally crazy-looking homeless guy in exchange for the use of his sword.

Yeah, I said sword.

Over breakfast, the Jones brothers and I decide to start our search for Wes at the capitol building. Not for any real reason other than the fact that we are sitting right in front of it. As we walk up to the front steps, past marble life-size statues of men on horseback and toward actual, real-life men holding machine guns, I begin to get cold feet.

I stop in the middle of the cobblestone walkway and turn to face the guys.

"Uh … Rain? You okay?"

"What are we doing?" I whisper, trying to catch my breath. "The place is surrounded by cops. We can't just walk through the front door."

"First of all, we haven't done anything wrong, and second of all—"

"Look!" Lamar finishes for him, pointing at something behind me.

I lift my head and follow his gaze to a small sign posted beside the front steps.

THE GEORGIA STATE CAPITOL IS OPEN TO THE PUBLIC FOR SELF-GUIDED TOURS FROM 8 A.M. TO 5 P.M., MONDAY THROUGH FRIDAY, AND IS CLOSED ON WEEKENDS AND HOLIDAYS.

I turn back to face Quint. "I don't even know what day it is. Do you know what day it is?"

"Let's go find out." He smiles. "The worst they can do is tell us no."

"Actually, the worst they can do is shoot us in the dick," Lamar corrects.

"Boy, shut up."

I swallow my panic, along with a mouthful of saliva, and follow them up the imposing staircase to the even more imposing guards waiting for us at the top.

"Mornin', sir," Quint says to the cop blocking our entrance at the top of the stairs, cranking his Southern accent all the way up to eleven. "We've been watchin' the executions on TV and came all the way from Franklin Springs to see one in person. I noticed on your sign down there that y'all allow folks to tour the capitol. Is that right?"

The cop shares a glance with his buddy and then nods once.

"Well, ain't that a treat!" Quint slaps his knee.

"Leave all weapons and personal belongings with the officer inside before going through the metal detector. Enjoy your visit," he deadpans, eyeing my Bony sweatshirt. Then, he opens one of the heavy front doors and holds it for us.

The moment we walk over the threshold, it's like stepping through a portal into the late 1800s. The foyer is three stories high with a sweeping marble staircase right in the center. The floors are marble. The columns are marble. The statues and busts of old white men are marble. But the doors lining every wall on all three floors? Those are dark and wooden and at least eight feet tall each.

"Ma'am." A woman's voice snaps me out of my daze. "You need to check all bags, weapons, and outside food with me, please."

I stare at the female officer in disbelief. It's been so long since I've been somewhere with rules or uniforms—or employees for that matter. It's actually kind of … nice.

I tuck my gun into my duffel bag and hand it to the cop. She gives me a ticket in return and motions toward the metal detector.

We walk through and get the okay from the male officer on the other side, and as we wander aimlessly into the foyer, tears begin to blur my vision.

For the first time in months, I feel safe.

Protected.

Secure.

There are rules here.

People follow them.

No weapons allowed.

No outside food or drinks.

There are business hours.

And little yellow claim tickets.

This place has been spared from the anarchy raging outside.

And I hate how much I like it.

How good it makes me feel.

Especially when there is a twenty-five-foot-long banner hanging from the third-story railing with Governor Steele's face on it staring down at me. The quote, *There is only one true law—the law of nature,* is printed above his jowly scowl. It reminds me of the banners from the nightmares—the ones with the four horsemen of the apocalypse and the date April 23. Only this banner is even more terrifying.

Because this monster is real.

Then, I notice along the bottom of the banner, in a tidy little row, are the logos for half a dozen local businesses—Buck's Hardware. Huckabee Foods. Pizza Emporium. Lou's Liquor Superstore.

It makes me sick.

"What now, Rainy Lady?" Lamar asks.

I scan every floor, but all I see is wooden door after wooden door, the names stamped in bronze next to each one announcing which distinguished member of Congress works inside.

Or *worked* inside, I guess.

No laws probably means no congressmen. No senators. No secretaries answering phone calls.

No wonder they allow the public inside—this place is nothing more than a museum now.

"Nobody's here," I mumble as the dead eyes of every life-size portrait stare straight through me.

Nobody ... including Wes.

"'Scuse me," Quint says, turning toward the officer stationed at the metal detector. "Can you point us in the direction of where the, uh, *accused* are bein' held?"

"They are in a secure, off-site location, sir."

"Off-site? Like, in another buildin'?"

"I am not at liberty to say, sir."

"Well, shoot. We was hopin' to see one up close and personal."

"Then, I suggest you come back for the Green Mile execution event tomorrow afternoon. There are spectator stands on either side of Plaza Park, but if you get a seat on the right side, the accused will walk right past you."

"Ooh, we'll do that. Thank you kindly, sir." Quint tips his invisible hat while I rush over to the desk with my yellow ticket outstretched.

I can't get out of here fast enough. Not only because the sight of Governor Steele's gaping pores makes me want to puke, but also because of what the guard just said.

Tomorrow.

We only have until tomorrow.

"Off-site," Quint repeats as we walk across the capitol building lawn, stately oaks and ancient magnolia trees shading us from the May sun.

"Oh God. Do you think they're keeping him at the jail? I assumed they were keeping the accused somewhere else because they released everybody from jail, but maybe he's there."

"Where even is the jail?" Quint asks.

"I don't ..." The words disappear on my tongue as I look across the street at a row of baby oak trees, as tidy and perfectly spaced as the list of sponsors on Governor Steele's banner.

Plaza Park looks so much smaller in real life. It's just a patch of grass in the middle of the city. Metal risers line the left and right sides, a group of police officers in riot gear laughs and drinks coffee near their patrol cars on the far side of the park, and right here in front, not much taller than the people they're now feeding on, is a row of freshly planted saplings.

I don't want to, but I find myself walking across the street, moving between the abandoned cars toward the spot where Wes's grave will be dug.

The grass is perfect—just like him. Another beautiful thing that will be destroyed here tomorrow. I kneel and run my fingers over the short green blades. I want to lie on top of them until the gravediggers come. Stop them with my body. I want to stage a protest, start a fire. But I don't know how.

I'm not that girl. I'm the one who smiles and does as she's told. I'm the one who gets good grades and doesn't start trouble. I'm the one who blends in with the bad guys instead of rising up against them.

At least, that's who I used to be. I don't even know what I am anymore. Besides desperate.

"No!" a woman shouts, which isn't anything out of the ordinary around here, except for the fact that she sounds really, really close.

"I told you, I don't have anything!"

I sit up on my knees and swing my head in all directions. Quint must be alarmed, too, because he's standing behind me with my duffel bag slung across his chest, frantically digging inside.

"Stop!" she screams. "Get off of me!" It sounds like it's coming from the direction of a black BMW with the windows broken out.

I hear a slap, followed by another scream, and before I can think better of it, I'm on my feet, darting over to Quint. I reach into the bag and find the gun tucked inside a folded pair of jeans, right where I stashed it. Quint gestures for me to give it to him, but I can't.

Because at that moment, I hear the woman growl a single word, "No."

It's long and bitter and broken and angry, but under that frustrated rage, I hear her powerlessness.

And I feel it as if it came from between my own gritted teeth.

Flipping the safety off, I sprint toward the muffled sounds of struggle—shoes scraping against asphalt, body parts thudding against the back of the car, grunting, whimpering. The noises are horrible, but they're nothing compared to the scene I find when I come around the side of the BMW. Bare skin and bare breasts and fresh blood and flailing limbs. A hand wrapped around a throat. A hand wrapped around a gun. Panties around ankles and pants around thighs. Fingernails clawing. Lips turning blue.

I want to shoot. For the first time in my life, I *want* to shoot someone. But I can't. He's too close to her.

I growl the same powerless, "No," that she did, point my gun at the sky, and fire a frustrated bullet into the air.

The greasy-haired man looks up—yellow eyes wide in surprise and yellow teeth gnashing in anger—but before he can swing his pistol in my direction, Lamar jumps out from the other side of the car, holding a whiskey bottle like a club. He bashes the sleazeball over the head so hard the bottle shatters, raining glass and the lifeless body of a possibly dead rapist down on the victim.

Quint grabs the guy's gun out of his hand as Lamar rolls his body off the traumatized woman beneath him. She's so exposed. Her skirt is bunched around her waist. Her blouse and bra are shoved up over her petite breasts. Just witnessing the emotion on her face feels like a violation, like even her soul has been bared without her consent.

"Can y'all get him out of here?" I ask, reaching for her hands to help her up.

Quint and Lamar nod and drag the scumbag away while I pull his victim to a sitting position as gently as I can. The woman cries and gasps for breath, her ruffled black hair stuck to her tears and fluttering in front of her mouth as I pull off my hoodie and drape it over her mostly naked body. She clutches it to her chest with one hand and pushes the wet strands away from her face with the other.

And now it's my turn to gasp.

The battered, bluish face in front of me belongs to Michelle Ling, the TV reporter who's been covering the executions since day one.

I kneel down beside her and place a hand on her arm. "Are you okay?"

Her chin crumples as she shakes her head. "No," she wails again, only this time, it's not angry or frustrated. There's a defeated finality to it that makes me think she's not okay for more reasons than one.

"Hey, he's gone now. Do you want to go into the capitol building? It feels safe in there."

She shakes her head again.

"Sweetie …" I don't know why I'm calling her sweetie. She's probably ten years older than me. "Do you have an office around here or a news van?"

She nods.

"Okay. Let's get you covered up, and we'll go there."

I help her adjust her clothes and pull my spray-painted hoodie on over her head. She manages to stand and pull her panties back up, wobbling on an expensive pair of red slingback heels.

They match the lipstick smeared across her face.

"Here we go," I say, wrapping an arm around her waist.

I notice Quint and Lamar standing by a dumpster about half a block away and give them a thumbs-up. I hope they threw that monster inside.

"Where to?"

Michelle points down the street, and we begin to walk.

"What were you doin' out here by yourself, honey?"

"Scouting locations." She sniffles. "I'm a reporter."

"I know who you are." I force a small smile.

Michelle hangs her head in a way that tells me she's more embarrassed about me knowing who she is than me seeing her almost naked. "There's no execution today because the governor took off to go golfing, and the station is breathing down my neck about it. They want me to get some kind of behind-the-scenes footage to show during that time slot."

She covers her face and starts to cry again. "I hate this job! I hate it!" she screams. "I hate these people!"

"Can you quit?" I ask, not knowing what else to say.

Michelle shakes her head. "I need the money." She swipes her long, thin fingers under her eyes and sniffles. "My husband died two months ago. In a car accident. I didn't find him until three days after he went missing because none of the ambulances or cops were working at that point."

"Oh my God. I'm so sorry."

"Don't be." Michelle wraps an arm around my shoulders and keeps walking. She's still shaking from the attack. "When I found him, there was a half-naked woman in the car with him, and our bank account was empty."

I shake my head. "That's so awful, Michelle. And you know what's worse? I think everybody who lived through April 23 has a story like that."

"What's yours?" she asks. Her voice sounds like an echo, like the words were formed in some hard, empty, faraway place.

I take a deep breath and try to compress my grief into as few syllables as possible. "A few days before April 23, my dad tried to kill my mom and me in our sleep with a shotgun before he turned it on himself. But I wasn't in bed like he thought."

"That is awful," Michelle mutters. No *I'm sorry*. No pity or sympathy. Just the factual observation of a jaded journalist.

It's kind of nice.

"My dad was always anxious and depressed," I continue, "a nonproductive, like the World Health Alliance lady said, but the nightmares finally made him snap. Just like they wanted them to."

Michelle shakes her head. "They're murderers. All of them. The World Health Alliance, our government leaders—they killed twenty-seven percent of the population with a few clicks of a mouse, *admitted to it*, and we're just supposed to say *thank you*?" She sounds so cold, so bitter, but her skinny arm is still wrapped around my shoulders like she needs me to keep her going. "We should be executing *them*."

The E-word makes my breath catch and my steps falter.

Michelle looks me up and down like I'm the one who needs help. "You okay?"

Leaning into her side, I nod, but then I shake my head as I inhale warm traces of vanilla on the hoodie she's wearing.

"My fiancé is supposed to be"—I have to swallow back a sob before I can say the word—"executed tomorrow."

"Oh my God. Wesson Parker? I covered his sentencing yesterday."

Michelle leads me around a corner where a sudden rotten stench slaps me in the face and makes my stomach turn on contact. Without warning, I lean over and puke on the sidewalk, right next to a dead Bony wearing a King Burger mask covered in flies.

"And I'm pregnant," I cry, wiping my mouth with the back of my hand as we stumble away from the bloated corpse. "I don't even know what I'm doing here. I don't even know where he is."

"I do," Michelle says, stopping about fifty feet short of the Channel 11 news van. Lifting a shaking finger with a jagged, broken nail clinging to the end, she points in the direction of a modern-looking building across the street.

Fulton County Police Department, the sign announces.

"He's in there."

My shoulders slump, and my heart breaks all over again as I take in the fortress in front of me.

"I'm guessing they don't have visiting hours," I mumble in complete and utter defeat.

Michelle reaches into the neck of my sweatshirt and pulls out a laminated card on the end of a lanyard. "They do if you've got one of these."

Rain

BUZZ.

The exterior door unlocks after Michelle flashes her media pass at the bulletproof window. She pushes her way through with the grace of a seasoned professional despite the fact that she's wearing my spray-painted hoodie, ripped jeans, and filthy hiking boots.

The cops inside reach for their guns as soon as they see those neon-orange bones but immediately relax when the cameraman and I walk in. Or should I say, hobble in. Michelle's feet are a full size smaller than mine, so these slingback pumps are killing me.

"Good afternoon, Officers," she announces as we walk into the center of the police department lobby.

I've never been in a police station before. I expected it to feel more like a jail and less like the Department of Motor Vehicles. There is a counter where you talk to someone through a window, a few cubicles with yellowing desktop computers that look like you might have to crank 'em to start 'em up, and a sea of mismatched plastic chairs bolted to the floor.

"Officer Elliott, Officer Hoyt, this is my cameraman, Flip, and our new reporter"—Michelle looks at me with a blank expression on her face, and I freeze, realizing that I never told her my name—"Stella McCartney," she declares without missing a beat.

It's the same name that I saw printed on the label inside her skirt.

I manage to squeak out a tiny, "Hello," without letting my voice shake too much.

"Gentlemen, as you know, there will be no sentencing or execution today, so the governor has demanded that I get some behind-the-scenes coverage to show during that time slot to ensure that the one true law stays top-of-mind for the citizens of Georgia. However, as you can see"—she gestures to her outfit—"I've been involved in an … *incident.* So, Stella here is stepping in as my replacement."

The two officers—one thin, bald, and dark; the other round, shaggy, and pasty—glance at each other skeptically. They're so quiet I can hear my own heartbeat in my ears, fast and hard, before the lanky one's face splits into a grin.

"I knew it!" he yells, clapping his hands together. "I knew as soon as y'all walked in here that you were gonna interview me. Finally!" He raises his palms to the sky. "I told myself—I said, 'Marcel, you just keep doin' what you doin', baby. They gon' notice. And when they do … oooooh … you goin' to Hollywood!'" He turns to face his partner and slaps him on the arm with the back of his hand. "What did I say? What did I say?"

"Officer Elliott." Michelle clears her throat. "I'm afraid the governor has instructed us to interview the *accused,* not the staff."

The police officer's face goes somber, and that's when I recognize him. He's the bailiff from TV.

"It would be fantastic if we could have the use of a private room with good lighting, perhaps an interrogation room or—"

"Absolutely not," a gruff voice interrupts as a man appears from the back hallway. He's older, weathered, and sporting a military haircut.

"With all due respect, Officer MacArthur, we didn't bring a lighting crew, and—"

"You will interview the inmate through the bars, and if the *governor* has a problem with the lighting situation, he can take it up with me."

"Yes, sir." Michelle nods before casting me a quick, apologetic look over her shoulder.

My heart sinks.

My palms begin to sweat.

Wes is here.

And I'm going to see him.

Through the bars.

"Very well …" She turns to glance at Flip and me before addressing the officers again, "Shall we get started?"

Here we go.

After a quick pat-down and a trip through the metal detector, we follow all three officers through a security door and down a series of poorly lit hallways. I try to imagine how Wes must have felt while walking down these exact same passageways.

Was he scared? Was he sad? Does he miss me? Have they been mean to him?

The *click-clack* of my heels and *jingle-jangle* of the officers' tool belts echo off the tiled floor as we walk in silence. Each officer is standing next to one of us, and each one has a hand resting on his holstered weapon. We're completely unarmed—Michelle made sure of that, knowing that we'd be searched and sent through a metal detector—so even though we're succeeding in getting closer to Wes, my hopes of breaking him out feel further and further away with every step.

Officer Elliott stops in front of an open doorway, bringing our little caravan to a halt. "Can y'all at least get a clip of me introducing the accused before you interview him?" he begs, blocking our path. "Pleeeeease?"

Michelle and Flip exchange a look.

"Uh, sure." She shrugs.

Officer Elliott's face morphs from hopeful to elated as he disappears through the doorway. "Hey, handsome! Get up! A reporter lady's here to interview you on TV, and *I* get to introduce you! And for God's sake, comb your hair or somethin'! You look a mess!"

My heart leaps into my throat when I realize who he's talking to. Who's on the other side of that doorway.

Oh my God.

It's him.

It's actually him.

He's here.

And I'm here.

How did I even get here?

It doesn't matter. I'm gonna see Wes.

And it's gonna be on TV.

Oh no.

I have to interview him.

I don't know what to say!

I don't even remember my name! McCartney? Something McCartney!

"Okay, Officer Elliott," Michelle calls out after getting the thumbs-up from her cameraman, "we're ready to roll."

Elliott appears in the doorway with the exuberance of a spokesmodel. He accepts the microphone Flip hands him and takes a deep breath, dropping into the serious bailiff character he plays on TV.

Michelle turns to me. "You ready, Stella?" she asks under her breath.

Stella! That's it!

I nod and smile through my nerves.

"Okay then. In three … two …" Flip points at Officer Elliott.

"Good afternoon, good people of Georgia. My name"—Elliott turns slightly, giving the camera his best three-quarter profile—"is Officer Marcel Elliott. I'm coming to you from a secure, undisclosed location along with reporter Stella McCartney to bring you an exclusive, behind-the-scenes interview with one of our very own *accused*. You might remember him from yesterday's sentencing. He's a heartthrob with a heart of gold. Ladies and gentlemen, I give you ... Wesson ... Patrick ... Parker!"

Elliott steps to the side and sweeps his hand in the direction of the doorway as Michelle gives me a gentle shove from behind. I stumble three steps forward, almost rolling an ankle in her red stilettos, and look up to find one pale green eye staring at me from beneath a worried, dark brow.

And time.

Stands.

Still.

He's here.

And I'm here.

And everyone else fades away. Because a lock of shiny brown hair has fallen in front of Wes's right eye, and all I can think about is reaching through the bars and tucking it behind his ear.

Michelle clears her throat as Elliott shoves the microphone into my hand. I glance behind me at the blinking red light on top of the camera. Then, with my heart thundering in my chest and my legs as wobbly as a newborn foal's, I take another step closer to the man in the cage.

I watch his posture relax, his attitude go cool. He has no pockets to shove his hands into, so he drapes one over the crosspiece between the bars, resting his weight on his forearm.

His body is playing for the camera, for the cops, and the audience, but his face is all mine. The way he bites the inside of his bottom lip. The way the black of his pupils swallows the green. The way his Adam's apple bobs in his throat as he tries to force down his emotions.

I try to swallow mine too.

"Ms. McCartney?" Elliott prods.

Wes raises an eyebrow at me and shifts his gaze to the camera over my shoulder.

"Oh, right," I mumble to myself, looking at the microphone like it's an alien tool that I have to figure out how to operate. I tap the soft black dome with my finger before I lift it to my mouth. I tell myself to face the camera and say something, but I can't bear to pull my eyes away from the man standing in front of me.

So, I don't.

"Mr. Parker—" I clear my throat, hoping no one notices that I sound like I'm about to cry.

"Please, call me Wes."

He smiles, just for me, and the warmth I feel brings tears to my eyes.

I blink them away and try again.

"Wes"—I swallow—"how are you? I mean, in here. How are you holding up in here?"

God, I'm bombing this!

"How am I?" Wes's eyes widen in surprise. "I'm …" He shakes his head, looking for the words before a tiny smirk tugs at the corner of his mouth. "I'm better than I was a few minutes ago."

Warmth floods my cheeks as I try to come up with an actual question.

"Well … that's good. Mr. Parker—"

"Wes."

"Wes." I blush. "I saw your sentencing on TV yesterday. It was the first one ever televised. Personally, I was shocked by the lack of evidence and eyewitness testimony presented by the state as well as the lack of deliberation before you were found guilty. Do you believe you were given a fair trial?"

I exhale, relieved that I managed to ask a professional-sounding question without bursting into tears.

Wes snorts. "A fair trial? No. I was given a speaking part in *The Governor Steele Show.*"

"Had you been given a fair trial, do you think you still would have been found guilty?"

Please say no. Please say no.

"The only thing I'm guilty of is trying to help somebody I love," Wes responds, the word *love* wrapping around me like a ghost blanket.

He reaches through the bars and takes the microphone from my hand, letting his fingers graze mine in the process. The callused tips leave a trail of fire in their wake, and the moment they're gone, I have to twist the sides of my skirt in my fists to keep from reaching for him so that I can feel it again.

Wes faces the camera and gives the people of Georgia his best smolder. "I want everyone out there to picture the person they care about most. Your mother. Your child." Wes looks at me. "Your best friend. Your wife. Now, picture them injured or sick. Would you give them medicine if you thought it would save their life? Bandage their wounds? Because if so, it's just a matter of time before you're standing where I am."

I catch the sight of Michelle out of the corner of my eye, making the sign for *cut* with her hand across her throat. I guess Wes's little speech might have gone a bit too far. I reach up to take the microphone back, but he holds on to it, forcing me to stand there with my hand wrapped around his. Electricity courses through my veins as he tilts it toward my mouth so that I can speak, but I can't.

I'm touching Wes.

He's here.

He's alive.

And the only question I have left for him is one I can't ask out loud.

How do I get you out of here?

Wes

SHE'S HERE.

She's actually fucking here.

I touch her again just to make sure. I can't stop touching her.

She's so fucking beautiful—camera-ready with that slicked-back hair and red lipstick. Her big blue eyes are framed by a million jet-black lashes, but the tears welling up inside them are already starting to make her mascara run.

I want to reach up and run a thumb over her cheek, but the blinking red light on the camera five feet away keeps me from doing it. I don't know how Rain got in here or what kind of trouble she'll be facing if I blow her cover, so as much as it fucking kills me, I let go of the mic.

I let go of *her.*

"Mr. … I mean, Wes." Rain drops her eyes as a blush creeps up her neck.

I count her breaths—one, two, three—before she lifts her eyes to me again. When she does, a black tear slides down the side of her face that the camera can't see.

"You don't seem scared," she says with a worried wrinkle in her forehead.

"I'm not," I answer honestly.

"Why? Have you just … *accepted* what's gonna happen to you?" Her perfect reporter diction falters as her voice rises in frustration.

"No."

Rain straightens her spine for the camera and regains control of her Southern accent. "Then, can you tell us what's going through your mind right now?"

Her eyes plead with me to give her hope. To promise her that I have a plan. But all I have is the knowledge that I've survived every shitty fucking thing this life has thrown at me so far, and somehow, that feels like enough.

It has to be.

"Right now?" I say, staring into her eyes as if my gaze alone could dry her tears. "Right now, I'm only thinking about *right now*. About how a beautiful woman can walk into your life when you least expect it. About how quickly things can change." Rain drops her eyes again, and I can't help but smile. "And I'm also thinking of about a million and one ways I can try to escape."

Elliott snatches the microphone away from Rain with an awkward laugh and faces the camera, forcing his way in between us.

"Ha! My man Parker's got jokes, y'all! Tune in tomorrow at six to see him, and yours truly, walk the Green Mile! Stay safe out there, and may the fittest survive!"

Elliott holds his serious TV news anchor face until Flip indicates that the recording is over. Then, he lights up like a Christmas tree. "Am I a natural or what? Listen"—he steps forward and places his hands on Flip and Michelle's shoulders, turning them toward the hallway—"if y'all ever need another guest reporter, I'd be more than happy to ..." His voice trails off as he walks them down the hall.

It's suddenly just me.

And Rain.

And about two-dozen steel bars in between us.

"There's a camera," I spit out before she has a chance to do or say anything incriminating.

"Don't you worry about that," Elliott's voice sings from the doorway, making Rain jump.

"Boy, when you said you had friends in the TV industry, I didn't know you meant you had *friends in the TV industry*. Haaaay!" He snaps his fingers.

"Did y'all see me? I killed that shit! I ... murdered ... that ... shit!" Elliott claps his hands to punctuate every word. "Ooooh lawd, that felt good. Did it look good? Don't answer that. I know it looked good! Ha-*ha*!"

Rain gives me a nervous glance.

"You came through, handsome. I don't know how, but you said you was gonna help me out, and you did that shit. I'mma have me my own show in no time!"

Then, like a switch being flipped, he goes into cop mode as he turns to face Rain.

"But it's real obvious that your little friend, *Ms. McCartney,* here ain't who she says she is."

My jaw clenches shut.

No, you motherfucker. Leave her alone.

"Y'all couldn't keep ya damn hands off each other during that whole interview."

At the mention of hands, mine ball into fists.

I will fucking kill you.

"Stand-in reporter? *Please.* This bitch has about as much charisma as a mug shot. The second she walked in, I knew you two was fuckin'."

Elliott reaches into his pocket, and I try to gauge whether or not he's close enough for me to choke him through the bars.

"So I'mma do you a solid, lover boy." Elliott pulls his hand out of his pocket, producing a set of keys, and sticks one in the lock on my cell.

Then, with a wink, he yanks open the squeaky door and gives Rain a shove. Her heels click against the concrete floor as she stumbles forward, landing directly against my chest.

"Consider this your last meal." He smirks. "You got twenty minutes."

Slam!

My heart thuds in time with his footsteps as they echo down the hallway, and Rain's heart beats even faster where it's pressed against my chest.

She's here.

Holy shit.

She's right fucking here.

I wrap my arms around her trembling body and squeeze so hard I'm afraid I might crush her. Even when she's in heels, her head fits under my chin. I don't move. I don't breathe. I close my eyes and pretend that time has stopped, just for us. That tomorrow isn't coming. That we're fleshy statues now, and we can stay like this forever.

But we can't because Rain's trembles are now full-body shudders as the sob she's been trying to hold in leaks out all over my orange jumpsuit.

"Wes," she cries, burying her face in my neck. "I'm so sorry! I shouldn't have let them take you! I should have—"

"Shh." I smooth a hand over her hair and feel her breath, hot and desperate, on my skin.

Rain lifts her tear-streaked face. Her pouty red lips tremble as they pull into a frown, but before she can let out another sob, I seal her mouth with mine. She tastes sad and girlie—all salty tears and cherry lip gloss—but she kisses me back with the determination of a woman. Her tongue slides and swirls around mine. Her tits, practically bursting out of that too-tight blouse, press against my chest. And her hands dive into my hair, holding me like a balloon in danger of floating away. Then, her kisses begin to roam.

"I love you so much," she murmurs, kissing my cheek.

"Oh my God, I missed you." Her kisses trace the line of my jaw.

"This is all my fault." She breathes against my neck. "I'm gonna get you out. I promise. I'll … I'll figure something out."

"Hey." I capture her face in my hands and tilt it back so that I can stare directly into her wide, panicking eyes when I tell her, "I'll get myself out. Do you hear me? You shouldn't be here."

Rain's eyelids close as she exhales a quiet, shuddering sob. "This is the only place I want to be."

Without looking up, Rain grips my zipper and slides it down my chest. I grit my teeth as she reaches in and wraps her arms around my exposed torso, pressing her wet cheek against my bare skin. My eyes sting. My lungs scream for air. Nothing fucking hurts as much as this woman's touch. It filets me like a dull knife. At first, it hurt because I realized that no one had ever cared for me like that before. Then, it killed me because I knew once she left, no one ever would again. But now? Now, her love cuts me down where I stand because I can no longer deny how much I want it.

I don't want to die for her or let her go or try to convince myself that she belongs with someone else. I never did. The soul-crushing truth is that I want her more than I've ever wanted anything. I want her by my side and in my bed and in my life forever. I still don't believe that God will let me have her, but until he pries her out of my cold, dead hands, I'm going to keep fighting.

Rain pushes the orange fabric over my shoulders, and I shrug it off like a skin I've outgrown. Her fingernails graze my sides as she kisses my tattoos, lingering over the wilted pink lily on my ribs. My fist grips her hair as her fingertips trace the edge of my government-issued boxers. Rain slides them down slowly as she sinks to her knees. I can feel my heartbeat in my cock as it falls forward, seeking her warmth. As badly as I want to yank her back up and fuck her properly, the image of her red lips wrapped around my dick is one I simply can't go to my grave without seeing.

Rain's black lashes fan out across her flushed cheeks as she licks me from base to tip, swirling her tongue around my swollen, throbbing head. My chest aches as she takes me into her mouth, as I watch her crimson lips slide over my cock and her cheeks hollow as she sucks me off, but when she opens her big blue eyes and looks up at me, the sensation is more intense than I ever fucking imagined.

This is her love for me. This is her selflessness. This is her risking her life to get to me, just to spend what little time we have left trying to make me feel good.

"Come here," I whisper, cupping her face and wiping the mascara from under her eyes with my thumbs.

Rain doesn't break eye contact as she slides her lips down my length one last time, and I'm overwhelmed with the need to feel her everywhere. I pull her to her feet and make quick work of the buttons on her blouse as I nip and suck at the overheated skin beneath her ear.

"We don't have much time left, and I want to spend it inside you," I growl, feeling a ripple of goose bumps pebble under my lips.

Yanking her tight skirt up over her full hips, I palm her perfect, round ass as I kiss my way down to her bra. Sucking one straining nipple through the black lacy fabric, I slide my hand between her legs and tease her slit over her panties. They're already soaked through. My mouth waters. I know we don't have much time left, but I need to lick her. I need to taste her.

If this is my last meal, I'm gonna fucking savor it.

Dropping to my knees, I trace the edge of Rain's silky panties with my finger before sliding them to one side. I don't take my time, and I don't ease her in. I run my tongue along her soft, slippery flesh and stifle a moan as the flavor coats my tongue.

Fucking perfect.

Rain hisses and grabs my hair as I suck and lick and devour her pussy, alternating between pulling me closer and trying to push me away.

"Wes," she whispers, her voice needy and breathless. "Please. I need you."

Those words are my undoing. I press her back against the one cinder-block wall that's hidden from the hallway, pull her knee over my hip, and fill her so deep and so hard that she has to bite my lip to keep from moaning.

"Fuck," I snarl, filling her again.

She feels so fucking good, so warm and soft and right and *mine*, that for a minute, I wonder if I'm already dead.

Not even heaven could feel as good as this.

"I love you," Rain whispers against my mouth.

The sadness in her shaky voice hits me like a fist to the heart.

I wrap my hand around her jaw and force her to look at me as I thrust into her again. "I love you more."

It's not a fucking question.

"If I can't get you out of here …" Her words trail off with a gasp.

"That's not your job. Do you hear me? You just stay safe."

Rain closes her eyes, and I feel her chin buckle under my palm. "I can't lose you, Wes."

"Hey, look at me."

Rain opens her tortured eyes and slays me with a single sentence. "*We* can't lose you."

We.

I gaze down the length of her beautiful torso, over her swollen, flushed-pink tits, and down to her still-flat belly. I realize I'm no longer fucking her.

I'm marveling at her.

"I took a test." She swallows. "You were right."

"Fuck. Rain …" I cup her face in my hand and kiss her again, not out of lust or loss or the elapsing of time, but out of pure, soul-crushing love.

When I fill her again, it's because that's the only way I can get closer to her. And when I feel her contract around me, when her breaths turn to whimpers and she whispers that she loves me again, I pour myself into her on a muffled cry.

I thought I wanted to be a good dad, like Doug.

But fuck that.

Good dads die for their families.

I'm gonna live for mine.

Rain

I STAND IN THE center of Wes's cell with my arms wrapped around his waist and my cheek pressed against his chest, waiting, counting his heartbeats until the next horrible thing happens.

Eighteen ... nineteen ... twenty ...

"Remember what I said," Wes whispers into my hair.

I nod, feeling my own heart beating about twice as fast as his. I tighten my fist around my balled-up panties. Any second now, that door is going to open, and Wes is going to attack Officer Elliott. As soon as Wes has his arms pinned behind his back, my job is to strangle Officer Elliott until he passes out. Wes said it might be too hard for me to do with my bare hands, so I should wrap my panties around his neck and tighten them instead.

I can't believe we're about to do this.

The calming thump of Wes's heartbeat is suddenly drowned out by the panic-inducing clomp of hard-sole shoes coming down the hall.

I squeeze my eyes shut and cling to him tighter.

"Okay, lovebirds," Elliott sings from the hallway behind me as his footsteps come to a stop. "Time's up."

I feel Wes bristle in my arms, so I look over my shoulder at the man on the other side of the bars. Officer Elliott has a huge grin on his face ... and a small handgun in his fist.

"Ms. McCartney, you come on over here, hon." He gestures to the door with the barrel of the gun. "Handsome, you go stand in the corner with ya hands up."

And just like that, our escape plan is ruined. Wes can't jump Elliott if he's got a gun pointed at him at point-blank range.

And we all know it.

"Fuck," Wes hisses, squeezing me tighter.

"Shh … it's okay," I whisper, tilting my head back to look at him. His nostrils flare with every breath. "I'll see you tomorrow, okay?"

I don't even know why I said that. Maybe because it's the closest thing to goodbye I can bring myself to say, or maybe it's because it's true. One way or another, I'm gonna see him tomorrow. Either in my arms after I rescue him or in Plaza Park when I lose him forever.

"Tomorrow? Oh my goodness, are you goin' to the Green Mile event?" Officer Elliott asks enthusiastically. "Ooh! Maybe you could talk to Michelle Ling for me! See if I can introduce *the governor* this time!"

"Yeah, okay," I mumble, not taking my eyes off Wes's beautiful, tortured face. "Tomorrow," I promise again, pushing up onto my toes to kiss his tightly drawn lips.

"Tomorrow," Wes growls before his mouth crashes into mine, finally letting every ounce of the panicked desperation he's been feeling make itself known.

My back arches as I try to absorb the brunt of his brutal kiss, the feral force of his love, the overwhelming power of his will to survive. I feel Wes becoming a caged animal in my arms, and my heart breaks, both for him and for anyone in this building who makes the mistake of coming too close to him.

Clang! Clang! Clang!

Officer Elliott taps his gun against the bars. "You got three seconds to get in the corner with your hands up before I shoot, boy. Don't make me hafta drag yo' dead ass down the Green Mile tomorrow!"

I break our kiss and wriggle out of Wes's death grip, walking him backward into the corner of his cell.

"I love you," I whisper, holding him at arm's length.

A lock of hair falls over one pale green eye as he stares down at me. Unbridled rage swims in the other. "Tomorrow," he grinds out through clenched teeth.

I force a smile through my tears and nod. "Tomorrow."

Tearing myself away from him and tearing my own heart out in the process, I turn and take three steps over to the bars.

Officer Elliott unlocks the door and yanks me out without once taking his eyes off of Wes. As soon as the door slams shut, he turns to me and beams. "So, here's my vision. Instead of Michelle doing her usual boring-as-hell intro, what if the camera follows *me*, leading the accused all the way down the Green Mile? Make folks feel like they're really there!"

As he walks me away, with a grin on his face and a gun pressed between my shoulder blades, I glance over my shoulder.

I used to love nothing more than watching Wes watch me. His rapt attention. His intense gaze. With a single look, he could make me feel seen. Studied. Special.

But watching him watch me go is an entirely different experience. I don't feel special.

I feel split apart.

Officer Elliott rambles the entire way back to the lobby about all his TV show ideas, but I'm not listening. I'm too busy trying to remember how to breathe. Just before he buzzes us into the lobby, he holsters his gun and starts laughing like we're old friends.

"Y'all come on back anytime, Ms. McCartney," he says, giving me a little shove.

Officer Hoyt looks up from the front desk but drops his gaze the moment our eyes meet.

"Thank you, Officer Elliott," I mumble without turning around. And I'm surprised to realize that I mean it.

I really hope Wes doesn't kill you.

"Thank *you*, honey child. And be sure to tell ya boy Flip to get my good side tomorrow!"

"Which side is your good side?" Officer Hoyt asks as I click-clack over to the main entrance, trying to hold my head up and my sobs in.

"Both sides, silly!" Officer Elliott howls with laughter as the door buzzes open.

I walk outside and squint into the daylight.

The world before me looks just as abused and miserable and desperate and filthy as I feel.

But the sun is still shining.

Wes is still alive.

And the Channel 11 news van is still waiting for me out front.

And for that, I'm grateful.

As I drag my grieving bones across the street to the Channel 11 news van, the passenger door opens, and Michelle climbs out.

"You okay?" she asks, her battered face mirroring my battered spirit.

I nod. Then shrug. Then shake my head as she comes over to give me a hug.

"If it makes you feel any better, I think this footage is gonna have everybody in Georgia on Team Wes as soon as it airs. He's a hottie, huh?" Michelle forces a smile as she tugs me closer to the van.

Opening the side doors, she gestures for me to climb inside. Flip is in the driver's seat while Quint and Lamar are sitting in two small fold-out chairs. The three of them are chowing down on soup straight out of the can.

A skinny counter wraps around the back and driver's side of the van, and above it are rows of monitors, lights, switches, and buttons.

Lamar greets me with a grin. "Hey, Rainy Lady!"

"How'd it go?" Quint asks, setting his can on the counter.

I sit in the middle of the floor and try to pry off one of Michelle's cruel shoes. It's so tight on my foot that I end up yanking it off with both hands and throwing it across the van. "Ugh!"

"So … not good?" Lamar summarizes.

I screw my eyes shut and shove my hands into my hair, tugging as hard as I can to distract myself from the pain. A squeal emanates from somewhere deep inside of me, high and pained and pressured, like a teakettle about to blow.

"What the hell happened?" Michelle asks, climbing in behind me and shutting the doors. "You were in there for, like, half an hour!"

"I had him!" I shout, hot, angry tears leaking through my closed eyelids. "I had him, and I fucking lost him!" I take a few deep breaths and try to calm down. Try to force my brain to think.

Think, Rain. Keep it together.

"He's right there!" I growl, shoving my hand in the direction of the police station. "He's right here, and I can't get him out!"

"What happened in there?" Michelle repeats her question as she climbs back into the passenger seat.

I suck in another deep breath and cover my mouth with my hands. "They have guns. That's what happened."

"We have guns," Quint offers.

"We have two guns." I snort.

Flip lifts his pant leg, revealing a small silver pistol in an ankle holster.

"Okay, three guns. Even if we managed to take out the cops in the lobby without getting shot, there are probably more officers inside. All they'd have to do is seal the doors, and then we'd be sitting ducks."

Michelle shakes her head. "This whole Green Mile operation is run by, what … the governor, a handful of police officers at the station, maybe a dozen riot cops, and a couple of security guards at the capitol? What is that, like, twenty people?"

"If we could just get the Bonys on our side, we'd have enough people to fight back or even the runaways from the mall." Lamar raises his voice in excitement. "Q is fuckin' crazy. I bet she'd kill a cop."

I sigh. "I tried to get her to come, but you know her. Q only does what's good for Q."

"You know who would probably love to help? All those prisoners they just released," Quint suggests. "Nobody hates cops more than criminals, right?"

"There's enough guns in this country to arm every man, woman, and child," Flip mumbles around a mouthful of loaded potato soup. "All you need is, like, a hundred of 'em."

My shoulders slump. "How do we even find that many people? Look around. Everybody's just tryin'a survive. They're not gonna put their necks on the line for people they don't know."

"Damn." Michelle's mouth draws into a frown as she reaches for a bottle of vodka next to a monitor. "I wish we could broadcast a message for you, but they'd kill us as soon as they saw it."

I stare into the black monitor next to her as she takes a long pull from the bottle, seeing only my reflection staring back at me.

Broadcast.

Message.

As soon as they saw it.

"What if they don't see it?" I blurt out, my eyes darting back to Michelle's. "What if we fight fire with fire?"

"What are you talkin' about?" Flip asks as Michelle chokes on her last swallow of vodka.

"I'm talking about subliminal messaging! That's how they programmed us to think the world was gonna end, right? How they drove a quarter of us insane enough to kill ourselves or get ourselves killed. What if we do the exact same thing *against* them? We could plant a subliminal message in the interview footage that makes people want to fight back!"

Michelle shakes her head. "Stella …"

"My name is Rain."

"Rain … we only have a few hours to get back to the newsroom and upload that interview. Where are we gonna find that kind of content? Or software even?" Michelle turns to Flip. "Can our programs even splice images in at intervals that small?"

Flip shrugs as Quint gestures to the computer screens. "Can't you just find the images online?"

Michelle's mouth falls open. "Have you guys not been online since April 23?"

We shake our heads in unison.

Michelle huffs in exasperation. "It's unusable! With no laws, it's been completely overrun by hackers. If you go online through anything other than a secure government server, you'll have your identity stolen, your bank account emptied, and you'll be locked out of your device in seconds."

I groan and fall back in my chair, rubbing my eyes with both hands. "So, where do we find a secure server?"

"Well, they have one at the TV station, but I am *not* working on this there." Michelle takes another gulp from her bottle before passing it to Flip.

He accepts it with a polite nod and turns to face me. "Pretty much any government buildin' should have a secure server. You just gotta be able to get inside and plug in."

My eyes drift over to the heavily tinted windows on the side of the van. Just beyond them, rising like both a beacon of hope and symbol of death, is the glowing gold dome of the capitol building.

"Michelle"—I swallow—"you still got that media pass?"

Wes

ONCE, WHEN I WAS, like, eight, I went on a school field trip to the zoo. My mom was too fucked up on whatever her drug of choice was at the time to sign the permission slip, but my teacher must have forged that shit because, when the day came, they let me get on the bus right along with everybody else.

I'd never been to the zoo before. Hell, I'd never been on a field trip before. I was so fucking excited, but once we got there, all I felt was sad. These big, magical beasts—creatures I'd only ever seen on TV—were locked up in cages like criminals. They hardly moved. They ignored us completely. Even the lions, the kings of the fucking jungle, were just lying on rocks, waiting to die. Every motherfucker there had accepted their fate.

Except the fucking tiger.

The tiger was the only animal there who was in solitary confinement. And he was the only animal there who was pacing. Not lazy, *I'm just gonna stretch my legs* pacing, but fucking-head-down, eyes-on-the-prize, *I'm gonna find a way out of this motherfucker* pacing. He would do a lap around the perimeter of his cage, pushing on the Plexiglas walls with his body. Then, he would do figure eights around all the trees, which had been cut short to keep him from climbing out.

There was something different about him. Something that made him refuse to accept his circumstances, like the others. And now, I know what it was.

Somewhere out there, that motherfucker had a mate.

I could live in here quite fucking comfortably if Rain were locked up too. We could fuck and talk and feed each other and make fun of Elliott all goddamn day. But without her, I feel like that fucking tiger. I want to climb the walls. I want to scrape the mortar out from in between the cinder blocks with my bare hands. I want to rip the face off the next piece of shit who rattles my bars.

But unlike that tiger, I *am* gonna get the fuck out of here.

Because unlike that tiger, I'm not gonna let them know I'm restless.

If he had acted as lazy as the lions, those zookeepers might have gotten lazy too. Maybe let his trees grow a little too long. Maybe used a little less caution when they opened the door to feed him. An opportunity would have presented itself.

Which is exactly why I'm lying on my cot, staring at the ceiling, trying to act bored, when all I want to do is punch holes in the walls and wear a figure eight into the floor with my pacing.

Clomp. Clomp. Clomp.

Hard-sole shoes approach, but they're not the spirited footsteps of Officer Elliott. Nor are they the slow shuffles of Officer Hoyt. No, these punishing footsteps belong to someone angrier. Someone who must be picturing the faces of his mortal enemies on every unpolished floor tile. Someone with a gray buzz cut and a burgeoning beer gut.

Officer MacArthur appears outside my door with a scowl on his leathery face and the scent of cheap whiskey emanating from his pores.

"Parker," he snaps, addressing me like I'm one of his soldiers.

But I don't fucking salute.

"That's me," I deadpan, tucking my hands behind my head.

"I'm here to take you to the showers. The governor insists on the accused looking decent for the Green Mile."

"Did you pull the short straw or somethin'?" I ask. "Why isn't Elliott or Hoyt takin' me?"

"That's Officer Elliott and Officer Hoyt to you, son," he growls. "And I'll be taking you because the accused tend to get a little aggressive at this point in their sentence."

"Ah," I say, sitting up with a stretch. "So you're the muscle, huh?"

"Step over to the door and place your hands through the bars."

I do as he said, my movements as slow and despondent as a caged lion's.

He clamps a pair of handcuffs around my wrists as tight as they'll go before saying, "Now, stick your feet out, one at a time."

I do that, too, watching for signs of intimidation or fear. He's not shaking, not nervous. But he's shackling me just as tightly as he cuffed me, which tells me I haven't fully convinced him of my apathy.

I wait for him to unlock my door and marvel at how clear-eyed he seems for somebody who smells like the bottom of a bottle of Jim Beam.

"You former military?" I ask as he guides me by the bicep into the hall.

He grumbles in response but eventually spits out, "Army. Special Forces."

"No shit? That's pretty badass, man. Were you, like, a paratrooper or something?"

"Sniper," he mutters under his breath.

Sniper. My fists flex, and blood surges to my extremities. *There's only one thing they need a sniper for around here.*

We walk past an open office door, and the image of my own face stops me in my tracks. There's a monitor above the desk broadcasting the interview Rain did earlier. I watch myself lean against the bars, orange polyester from the neck down, poorly masked shock and awe from the neck up. The back of Rain's head and a sliver of the side of her face are visible on the screen. I want to reach out and run my fingers through her slicked-back black hair as she stutters and stumbles over her first question to me.

"Mr. Parker—"

"Please, call me Wes."

"Wes … how are you? I mean, in here. How are you holding up in here?"

My throat tightens at the sound of her shaky voice. On camera, she looks fucking amazing, but from where I was standing, she was all teary eyes and trembling hands.

And red fucking lips.

"How am I? I'm … I'm better than I was a few minutes ago."

Mac coughs out a laugh and claps me on the shoulder. "Pretty smooth, boy. That replacement they got for Michelle Ling was a stone-cold fox, wasn't she?" He tugs me by the arm down the hall, coughing and chuckling and coughing some more.

I grind my teeth and try to concentrate on keeping my breathing even. I want to put my fist through the guy's face, but I can't let him see me sweat.

I try to figure out an angle as we turn down the next hallway and stop in front of the cabinet where they keep the soap and towels. I can't play on his guilty conscience like Hoyt because this dude is literally a trained killer. I can't play to his vanity like Elliott because … fucking look at him. But maybe, since he's a military guy, I can appeal to his sense of justice. Make him see that what they're doing here is wrong.

That what *he's* doing is wrong.

"Michelle Ling looked pretty roughed up, huh? I wonder what happened to her."

"Probably got jumped by a meth-head or a Bony." Mac shrugs, pulling a towel out of the cabinet and draping it over his arm.

"That has to be hard for a guy like you … seeing all that crime happening right outside your door and not being able to do anything about it."

Mac grabs a nondescript white bottle, which I assume has some kind of shampoo in it, and closes the cabinet. "It's not a crime if it's legal," he mutters, but there's no conviction in his voice. It sounds rehearsed, like it's just something he tells himself so he can sleep at night.

Mac pulls open the shower room door without looking at me, and I walk in without being asked.

After setting the towel on a hook next to one of the open shower stalls, Mac puts the shampoo bottle on a shelf inside and turns on the faucet. The pipes are rusty and exposed, and they rattle and hiss louder than an oncoming earthquake.

Good.

"Just because it's legal doesn't make it *right*," I say as Mac bends down to take off my shackles. "Attacking an innocent woman? Robbery? Rape? Isn't that why you got into this job in the first place? To protect the good guys and punish the bad guys?"

"I don't make the rules," Mac snaps, obviously annoyed with my line of questioning. "I just enforce 'em."

The shackles clatter to the ground as Mac stands, pressing a hand to the small of his back as his knees and random other joints snap, crackle, and pop.

"That's apparent." I snort, holding my wrists out for him to uncuff next. "The bad guys are literally getting away with murder while you're busy shooting good guys in the head on live TV."

Mac's eyes slam up to mine the moment the second cuff falls free.

"Yeah, I know you're the executioner. I figured it out as soon as you said you were a sniper. But it's cool, man. You're just doing what you gotta do, right?" I unzip my jumpsuit, pausing when I get to the sharpened toothbrush stashed in the waistband of my boxers. "And so am I."

Grabbing the shiv, I catch Mac completely off guard as I plunge it into the side of his neck, using my left arm to block him from going for his gun. He yells in pain, but the thumps and rattles and hissing and splashing from the shower muffle his cry.

Mac goes for his gun with his left hand as I struggle with his right, but the awkward cross-body reach doesn't allow him to flip the snap to unlock the weapon from his holster. Doing some kind of spin move, he twists out of my hold, but I grab his billy club and duck the second he gets a hand on his gun. When Mac spins around to shoot, I bash him in the kneecap with it, sending him to the floor. I grab the hand holding the gun on his way down and try to pry his fingers off by pulling his trigger finger back as far as it will go. He yells in pain and punches me in the side of the head with his free hand. Repeatedly. I feel his arthritic knuckles crunch against my skull. I shift my weight and curl around the hand holding the gun so that he can only punch me in the back now. Then, I bite his thumb *and* pull backward on his finger as hard as I fucking can until the gun falls free. We both scramble for it, sending it sliding across the tile floor.

"Shit," I hiss right before Mac rears back and clocks me right in the jaw.

I see spots as I reach into the shower for the dropped billy club and crack him over the head with it. Instead of knocking him out, Mac's eyes glaze over with rage, and he attacks me with everything he's got.

Fists rain down on me as I back up into the scalding hot spray of the shower. I try to block his swings with one hand while using the other one to swing and stab at him with the club. I can't connect with anything other than his sides and shoulders, so I change tactics and shove the club up under his chin, pushing until he can't breathe and is forced to let go of me. The second he does, we both scramble for the gun again, and again it turns into a bloodbath. My ribs crack under his fists. His nose breaks against my palm. My elbow drops into his gut. His knee comes up to meet mine. What I have on Mac by way of youth and agility, he more than makes up for with skill. We are nothing but sopping wet fists and teeth and adrenaline and fear. But I have something Mac doesn't have.

A damn good reason to live.

My lungs burn and my eyes burn and my entire fucking body feels like it's been pulverized by a meat grinder as we wrestle under the searing hot water, but it's not quite as bad as I let on. See, I might not be able to use Mac's guilt or his vanity or even his sense of justice to get what I want, but he's got something even easier to exploit.

Pride.

Good thing I got that shit beat out of me by the eighth grade.

Leaving myself open to a few blows that feel like sledgehammers, I let Mac think he has the upper hand. I can almost see his ego swell as he lands a solid right cross to the cheekbone of the punk twenty-two-year-old who dared to take on the legendary Officer MacArthur. And I can almost hear it shatter into a million pieces when he rears back to clock me again and feels a solid steel cuff click into place around his wrist.

Scurrying backward out of the shower on my elbows, I watch as Mac's eyes go wide in horror. He sits up on his haunches and thrashes in place as he realizes that I've handcuffed him to the shower pipe.

I reach the gun across the room just as he reaches for his taser, but when he holds it up, it's dripping wet and completely worthless.

The look on his face as he drops the taser and raises his hands in the air is something I'll never forget as long as I live. I've seen it on TV a few times now but never in person. Never staring down the barrel of my own gun.

It's the look of a man who knows he's about to die.

His nose is gushing blood, which the shower dilutes into a pink stream that courses over his swollen mouth and down his neck. His chest is heaving even harder than mine, but his hands aren't shaking nearly as bad.

"You fought well, son." He spits through the bloody water.

"So did you, old man." I close one eye and aim for his forehead. "Between the eyes, right? That's your style?"

He nods without remorse. "Instant kill."

His words send a shiver down my wet, bruised spine as I tighten my finger around the trigger.

But I'm not like Mac.

I'm not a cold-blooded killer.

Which is exactly why the fuck I need him.

Rain

"YOU GOT IT UPLOADED and everything?" I whisper as Flip closes his laptop.

"Uploaded. Broadcasted. It's done." He looks over at me, the blue digital glow from the servers illuminating his tired face.

"Oh my God." I cover my mouth with my hoodie sleeves.

"And you got all the images in there without them being too obvious?" Michelle asks, rubbing her exposed arms to stay warm. They must keep the air-conditioning on full blast in here to cool off all the equipment.

"Yes, ma'am." Flip stands up and stretches. "Folks are gonna have some real wild dreams tonight."

I launch myself at him and wrap my arms around his middle. "Thank you. Thank you so much. You have no idea ..." I ramble as Flip awkwardly pats me on the back.

"I hope it works, hon. Now, if you don't mind, I'd like to get the hell outta here before nightfall."

Michelle stands up and smooths her hands over her black pencil skirt, which I can see now is actually a little loose on her. She's probably lost weight since she bought it from all the stress.

I let go of Flip and attack her with my gratitude next.

Hugging me right back, Michelle says, "You gonna be okay tonight? If you need a place to stay ..."

"I'll be all right. I wanna stay nearby in case something happens."

What I mean is, *I'm going to spend the night locked in the trunk of a car outside the police station, praying that my boyfriend escapes before they execute him.*

I look over at the Jones brothers, who are sitting against a shelving unit full of servers on the other side of the room. Their eyes are closed, and their heads are propped against one another's.

"Y'all go ahead," I say, nodding toward my sleeping friends. "I seriously can't thank you enough."

"You sure?" Michelle asks, holding me at arm's length.

I nod. "I'm sure. I'll see you tomorrow." Those words remind me of the last person I said that to just a few hours ago. The place where my heart used to be aches in response.

"Yes, you will." She smiles, but it looks all wrong on her.

As Michelle and Flip tiptoe out of the capitol's server room, I walk over to Quint and gently shake his shoulder.

"Wake up, guys. It's done. Time to go."

"Hmm?" Quint smacks his lips without opening his eyes.

"We gotta go. We've been in here for, like, two hours. The guards are probably already lookin' for us."

Lamar sits up with a yawn. "Did you do it?"

"I think so. Come on!"

The boys grumble but slowly pull themselves to their feet.

I grab my duffel bag off the floor and toss it over my shoulder before pressing my ear to the door. When I don't hear anything, I open it just a crack.

"You get what you need, Ms. Ling?" The voice of the male security guard echoes through the rotunda.

"Yes, thank you. There was no way we could have made it to the station to upload our footage in time with the roads being the way they are," Michelle replies with her patented, matter-of-fact reporter voice.

"Happy to help."

"That was a great interview, by the way," the female guard adds.

"Thank you. My stand-in, Ms. McCartney, will be along shortly. She just had to … use the restroom."

"I think we're good," I whisper to Quint and Lamar as I open the second-story door and tiptoe out into the wide hallway.

There's significantly less light coming in from the windows in the main entryway than when we got here, increasing my sense of urgency.

I've seen this place at night. If we want to live to see morning, we need to find a place to hide before dark.

We should be talking, I think as we near the end of the hall. *We're being too quiet. They're gonna know something's up.*

I turn to say something to Quint, *anything,* but the words shrivel up and die in my mouth when I notice that his brother is no longer following us.

I swing my head in all directions and find him just before he disappears through a door.

A massive wooden door with the words *Office of the Governor* painted on the frosted-glass window in white and gold letters.

"Lamar!" I whisper.

"Shit!" Quint hisses.

We follow him as quietly as possible but freeze when voices ring out from the atrium behind us.

"Governor! We didn't expect you back until tomorrow morning. How was your outing?"

"Pretty damn good, Officuh. Pretty damn good. I suspect those old bastards let me win, but a win's a win in my book."

"Spoken like a true politician," a third voice that I don't recognize jokes, causing everyone to laugh.

Quint and I glance at each other in horror and dash inside the governor's office to grab Lamar. The lights are on inside, illuminating what looks like a time capsule from the 1900s. The front room must be a lobby. It's filled with heavy wooden furniture upholstered in navy blues and deep reds, regal-looking carpet, brass light fixtures, and oil paintings of ducks and dogs and old white men.

Through the open door across from the entrance is Governor Steele's office. His land yacht of a wooden desk is parked in the back, in front of a navy-blue curtain with the golden seal of Georgia in the center. But I'm more interested in the person standing in front of his desk, relieving himself all over Governor Steele's rug.

"Lamar! What the hell you doin'?" Quint snaps as I shield my eyes. "We gotta go! Now!"

"I just needed to stop by the little boy's room on the way," Lamar says with a chuckle.

"Well, put your pecker away, and let's go! Are you fuckin' crazy?"

I hear the zip of Lamar's fly and lower my hand.

"Calm down. I was just leavin' a little surprise for this asshole to find when he gets back from his—"

Lamar's eyes go wide as we hear the creak of the main door. He bolts, diving behind the governor's desk, as Quint and I duck behind a pair of leather wing chairs.

"Tell the SWAT team I'm gonna hafta move the execution to tomorrow mornin'. I've got a meetin' with Tim Hollis in the aftuhnoon to discuss some *sponsuhship* opportunities," a familiar old-South accent announces as he walks into the lobby.

"The CEO of Burger Palace?" the other male voice I heard in the atrium asks.

"The one and only. Good man. Shit golfuh." The governor chuckles as they walk through the door into the main office. "I convinced that son-of-a-bitch to pay five billion dolluhs to be the official sponsuh of the Green Mile execution event!"

"No fucking way."

"Yes, suh! That's why I need that hundred-year-old bottle of scotch. You and I gon' celebrate tonight! We're gonna rename Plaza Park *Burger Palace Park* and use drones to film the executions from all angles. We'll have aerial shots of the bodies fallin' in the holes. It's gonna be glorious."

My stomach turns, and my palms get so sweaty one of them slides off the leather chair, causing me to almost lose my balance. Quint glares at me in warning.

"You'll get national coverage for sure," the other man says.

I can see him now as they walk right through the wet spot that Lamar left on the rug. He's dressed in all black, like a bodyguard.

The governor clicks his tongue and shoots a finger gun at the man. "Bingo. The only thing left to figyuh out is whether it'll be bettuh to paint King Burger on the lawn or use a projector to make him all animated-like."

"I think the real question is, where are you gonna hang all your deer heads once you move into the White House?"

Governor Steele chuckles as he comes around the side of the desk. "Once *we* move into the White House. I'm gonna make you head of the Secret Service, my friend."

I reach out and grab Quint's arm, the ghost of my heart slamming against my ribs as the governor opens his top drawer and takes out a bottle of liquor. Shutting it, he looks down at his overstuffed chair with a frown.

"Now, why in the hell is my chair pulled out?"

"Hey, Beau?" his security guy asks, pulling a gun from his side holster. "You didn't leave your lights on last night when you left, did you?"

I clutch Quint's arm tighter as the governor's bodyguard pushes him out of the way and points the barrel of his gun at the cavernous opening under his desk.

Please don't let them find him, I pray. *Please, God. He's just a kid. Please, please, please don't let them—*

Suddenly, I feel a kiss on my cheek, so quick I think I might have imagined it, before the arm that I was clutching slips out of my grasp. I look up from my crouched position and reach for Quint, but my fingers grasp nothing but the last breath he exhaled before he disappeared around the front of his chair.

No! Quint!

"Death to sheep!" he cries, running for the door.

And then there's a bang so loud I almost scream.

And a thump.

And a deep, guttural groan.

I clutch the chair for support and hold in my cries as Quint slaps at the floor, trying to drag himself into the lobby.

"What in the hell?" the governor shouts, clutching his chest.

"Goddamn it, Beau! I told you we gotta stop allowing tours!"

I bite my lip as their footsteps approach and screw my burning eyes shut as the men stand beside my oldest friend.

BLAM!

Then … nothing.

"Nice job, Jenkins. You really were Special Forces, huh?"

"Green Berets, sir."

Governor Steele slaps him on the back. "Come on. Now, I really need a drink. I'll have Edna and the cleaning crew take care of that."

The two men leave as I cling to the chair like it's a loved one, silently crying into the Italian leather, my fingers wedged between the brass rivets.

But it doesn't hold me back.

My face contorts against the wet hide as pain slices me from ear to ear, stretching my mouth in a wordless scream.

Loss.

Loss.

Loss.

Loss.

Every week, every day, another one. No matter what I do, no matter how hard I try to save them, I can't.

Powerless.

Weak.

Worthless.

Stupid.

And now, Wes is going to be executed tomorrow for saving the life of someone who died anyway.

Pointless.

Meaningless.

Hopeless.

Death.

Slowly, the sound of agony, high-pitched and constant, breaks through the fog of silence in the room. It feels like mine. Sharp. Brittle. Unending. Unrelenting.

But it's coming from under the desk.

I want to go to him. Hold him like a mother. Shush him and tell him it's going to be all right.

But I can't.

Because it's not.

And it never will be again.

"Get up," I bark, standing from my hiding spot.

Quint's body is laid out in the middle of the doorway between the lobby and the office, a maroon blanket covering his back and seeping into the carpet all around him.

Lamar sniffles, but then he begins sobbing even louder.

He always does this. He gets in trouble, and then Quint takes the punishment. How many times did Quint get a whooping from their drunk old man for something that Lamar had done, and how many more times did Lamar get in trouble, knowing Quint would show up just in time to take the fall?

Selfish.

Spoiled.

Ungrateful.

Brat.

Stomping over the desk, I pull the chair out even further, prepared to scream at Lamar—to unleash the pain and rage and helplessness and injustice bottled up inside of me—but the boy I find huddled under there, hugging his knees and weeping into his elbows, looks so much like his brother at that age that I slump to the floor and crawl inside with him.

Wrapping my arms around Lamar's shuddering body, I realize how small he still is. How young.

"Shh," I whisper, rocking him back and forth. "Shh …"

"I killed him," Lamar whispers back. "I killed him, Rain."

"No," I choke out, his short, unkempt dreadlocks soaking up my tears. "*They* killed him, baby. They kill everybody. It doesn't matter what you do." My voice disappears on a sob as I realize that I was right all along.

None of this matters.

And we're all gonna die.

Rain

LAMAR AND I STRUGGLE to carry Quint's body out the heavy wooden door and into the darkened hall as the security guards from the entrance make it to the top of the stairs. I fully expect them to shoot us, and I don't even care. I'm not leaving Quint here.

"What the hell happened up here?" the male officer asks.

Lamar has his back to them. He's carrying Quint's legs, and I have him under the armpits. He's so heavy. I lift a knee to help support his weight and feel my jeans soak through with blood as soon as it touches his back. Setting his butt down on the floor, I sit with his upper body in my lap and cry.

"Good Lord, Ms. McCartney. When Mr. Jenkins said he shot an intruder, I didn't realize it was your partner."

"It was my fault," Lamar says, sitting across from me, hugging Quint's shins to his chest. "I shouldn't have gone in there." His face collapses into a broken, silent sob.

"Well ..."

The two officers look at each other, perplexed.

"You want us to help you carry him out?" the male officer asks.

I nod. The two cops rush over and each take a shoulder. They lift him off of me, and I miss the weight of him as soon as they do. Taking a leg from Lamar, we share a brief, miserable moment before we carry our brother and best friend down the marble steps, right under the watchful, beady eye of Governor Steele and his collection of sponsors.

When we reach the bottom of the stairs, the female officer hands Quint off to her partner and runs over to the welcome desk to grab my duffel bag.

I don't know why, but their kindness makes it hurt even more.

She opens the door for us and walks us down the front steps and into the twilight.

"Where should we take him?" the male officer grunts, shifting Quint's weight in his arms.

I shake my head. "I don't know."

The sound of anarchy fills the air—motorcycle engines revving, screams, howls, laughter, gunshots.

"How about over there?" his partner suggests, pointing to a dogwood tree in full bloom. "Just until you figure something out."

I nod and shuffle over to the tree in a daze. We lay Quint down beneath it on a bed of pine needles and dogwood petals, and the lady cop places a hand on my shoulder.

"I'm so sorry, Ms. McCartney."

"For what it's worth," her partner adds, his voice gruff and sincere, "that was a damn good interview."

"Thank you." I don't know if I spoke the words or simply thought them, but the officers walk away.

Now, it's just me.

And Lamar.

And a sleeping Quint.

At least, that's what it looks like.

That's what I want to tell myself.

I don't know why, but I reach over and gently peel the Caucasian-colored bandage off his neck.

Then, I snort out something that might almost be a laugh if it wasn't so goddamn painful and ironic.

"His wound is healed."

Lamar sits with his legs crossed and his face buried in his hands. "It was all for nuthin'," he mumbles. "Us livin' in that mall, you takin' care of him, Wes getting' arrested … it was all to save Quint, and now …" He shakes his head as his shoulders begin to rise and fall.

"Maybe this was supposed to happen," I say, rubbing his back like my mom used to rub mine when I was upset. "Maybe it was his destiny."

I don't believe a word I'm saying. And neither does Lamar.

"I don't believe in destiny," he says. "Look around. It's all just fuckin' chaos. It's just bad shit happening to good people. That's all life is. I fuckin' hate it!" he yells on a broken sob.

"Me too."

"I want my mom."

"Me too," I whisper around the swollen lump in my throat.

I wrap my arm around him and pull him close. Quint and Lamar's mama abandoned them when they were little. Rumor has it that their daddy beat her so bad that, one night, she just upped and left. Never heard from her again. But I wouldn't be surprised if that's just a story their daddy made up, and she's really buried out back behind their house somewhere.

Just like my mama.

"I wanna go home."

"Me too, buddy."

But my home isn't in Franklin Springs anymore. It's locked in a cage three blocks away. Wes is my home now, and by this time tomorrow, he'll be gone, too.

Because being good is a terminal disease around here.

Which probably means that I'm next.

I've been a good girl my whole entire life. Straight As and church on Sundays. Smile for the camera. Say *please* and *thank you*. Cheer at your boyfriend's games. Suck his dick when he wants it. Always wear makeup, but not too much makeup. Look pretty, but not too pretty. Tiptoe around your daddy. You know he has issues. Don't drink. Don't smoke. Don't curse. Respect your elders. Do as they say.

That's what my mama taught me. She was as good as they come.

And she was the first one to go.

"Death to sheep," the Bonys say.

How right they are.

As I rub Lamar's back, the neon-orange stripes on my sleeve almost seem to glow in the dark. I follow them up to my shoulder and across my chest.

I might be a sheep, I think. *But this sheep is wearing wolf's clothing.*

"Come on," I say, giving Lamar a squeeze. "Help me pick him up."

"What?" He sniffles, looking up at me with heartbroken brown eyes. "Why? Where are we going?"

"We're going to do something bad."

24

May 8
Wes

I TAKE A DEEP *breath, savoring the scent of burning leaves in the cool fall air until my lungs feel like they're burning too.*

The woods are a blazing blur of red and orange as my dirt bike flies over miles and miles of trail. It seems to go on forever, and that's perfectly fucking fine with me. There's no sense of urgency anymore, no doomsday clock, no guillotine hanging over my head. It's just me and my girl and the woods I've called home since I was young enough to have one.

We bounce over a tree root in our path, and Rain giggles in my ear, squeezing me tighter. I used to love the way her tits felt while smashed against me whenever she rode on the back of my bike, but I think I love the way her round belly feels even more.

I suck in another breath and marvel at this fucked up new feeling.

It's not just happiness. I was happy sleeping in a puddle on the floor of an abandoned mall with Rain by my side. No, this is something else.

This is everything else.

All of it. All the things I ever wanted but wasn't stupid enough to hope for. Safety. Security. Love. Life. Fun. Freedom.

A future.

I close my eyes and inhale another lazy lungful of fresh air, but when I open them, I have to slam on the brakes. Rain squeals and clings to me for dear life as I skid sideways and stop inches away from a fifty-foot-long banner as it unfurls from an oak branch and blocks our path.

Like so many banners I've seen before, I expect one of the four horsemen of the apocalypse to be staring down at me—a cloaked demon riding on the back of a smoke-breathing black stallion, ready to chop my head off or light me on fire—but what I find there instead is even more terrifying.

The putrid, pasty scowl of Governor Fuckface. His jowly mouth opens, baring razor-sharp teeth that slam down again and again, missing us by millimeters.

I grab Rain and stumble away from the banner just as my bike disappears into the void of his cavernous mouth. From this distance, I can see the whole image now. It's in similar shades of black and red and gray, like the April 23 banners we all saw in our nightmares, but instead of April 23 at the top, this one simply has a bull's-eye.

Right in the middle of Fuckface's forehead.

His bloodshot eyes dart left and right as his teeth continue to gnash at nothing, but just when I begin to feel like he's no longer a threat, the trees shed their vibrant leaves in a single, sudden explosion. Rust-colored confetti rains from the sky as every tree in the forest begins to age in reverse. They shrink and shrivel up, twisting and contorting until they're nothing but saplings again.

Then, they reach for us.

"Mwa-ha-ha-ha-ha!" The banner man cackles as spindly branches grab for us like claws.

The sky goes dark, and the wind howls through the barren woods as I grab Rain's hand and turn to run back the way we came.

"Wes!" she screams just before her hand is ripped away from mine.

"Rain!" I turn to find her six feet above the ground, suspended in the branches of a sapling.

She's floating in some sort of pink primordial ooze, and the tree appears to be fucking feeding on her, growing bigger and stronger than all the others.

"We must return to the one true law!" Fuckface howls. "The law … of naychuh!"

My vision blurs. My fists ball at my sides. And when he opens his mouth to cackle again, I take off in a sprint. I'm going to rip him down and rip him apart and fucking feed him to himself until he chokes on his own evil hypocrisy, but before I get there, I notice his eyes go wide in fear as they focus on something behind me. I slow to a jog and turn around as people from all walks of life begin to march into the forest. The collective crunch, crunch, crunch *of the leaves under their feet is deafening as they surround us, each one with a fist in the air.*

"Seize them!" Fuckface shouts.

The trees come alive, snatching children from their mother's arms, ripping families apart as they scream and reach for one another. Pink plasma surrounds their tangled, trapped loved ones as the trees feed on their screaming bodies.

*But the people in the woods are undaunted. They continue to march forward, in unison—*crunch, crunch, crunch—*as the bull's-eye in the center of Fuckface's forehead begins to glow like a flashing neon sign.*

I glance at Rain, her face distorted through the ooze, and she begins pointing frantically at something below me.

When I look down, I'm holding her dad's .44 Magnum.

I kiss the barrel and say a silent, Thank you. *Then, I close one eye and aim for the target.*

When I squeeze the trigger, I expect that fucker to disappear, go up in smoke, burn to the ground, something, but instead, he simply laughs at me.

"Mwa-ha-ha-ha-ha!"

I raise my gun and fire three more rounds into that shithead's forehead, but still … nothing.

Then—crunch, crunch, crunch—*the sea of men, women, and children behind me step up to join me on the front line. They stand shoulder to shoulder with me, lowering their fists as they draw their weapons—shotguns, rifles, flame-throwers, hand grenades—an arsenal as diverse as they are.*

This time, when I raise my gun, they all take aim with me.

This time, when I squeeze my trigger, the entire traumatized, hungry, tired, homeless, grieving, fucked up population fires their weapons alongside me. And this time, when my bullet hits the bull's-eye, it's joined by a thousand others.

The target jerks and flashes and rings like a carnival bell before it explodes in a giant ball of fire. I have to shield myself from the heat as Governor Fuckface lets out a pained, defeated cry.

Gasps and cheers and laughter spread through the crowd, so I lower my arm and watch as the banner burns away. The breeze blows its sparkling ashes around us like swirling silver glitter as the saplings twist and grow and sprout new green leaves.

I run to Rain's tree and catch her in my arms as she leaps from the growing branches. The smile on her face is brighter than fucking sunshine as I spin her around, watching everyone in the woods do the same.

This time, when I inhale, the air doesn't smell like burning leaves.

This time, it smells like burning governor.

I exhale with a content sigh as the sound of knuckles on a steel bar wakes me from my dream.

What the fuck was that? I wonder as I scrub a hand down my face.

I haven't had a dream like that since the government was pumping them into my head, pre–April 23. Of course, those always ended with four demonic horsemen destroying everyone and everything in their path in an apocalyptic blaze of glory, not with the citizens banding together to defeat the enemy. Big fucking improvement.

I open my eyes to find Hoyt standing at my door. He's staring at the floor even harder than usual, his mouth forming a perfect frown. It's not until

I see what he's holding that the bliss from my dream wears off and the nightmare that is my fucking reality comes crashing down around me.

It's a bundle of brown.

Fucking.

Burlap.

"The governor moved the Green Mile up to this mornin'." Hoyt clears his throat. " 'Fraid I'm gonna hafta ask you to put these on."

The sadness in his voice makes me have to clear my own fucking throat.

Jesus, Hoyt.

I stand up and approach the bars.

"How long have I got?" I ask, pulling the jumpsuit from Hoyt's reluctant arms.

"Don't know." He sighs and shakes his head, his chin practically resting on his chest.

I notice that he's still holding something—a white plastic cup filled with caramel-colored liquid.

"A little hair of the dog?" I ask, trying to lighten the mood.

Hoyt's eyes jump to mine in a panic. "I … uh … no. I just … thought you might want a fresh cup … you know … to brush your teeth."

He brought me whiskey. Sweet fucking bastard.

"Officer Hoyt, I could kiss you."

I grab the cup from my sink and exchange it for the one in his meaty hands. "Thanks, man."

Hoyt nods at the ground before shuffling away.

I swirl the alcohol around in the cup, taking a deep whiff until his footsteps fade in the distance.

Then, I pour it down the drain and brush my teeth.

I have a date with the fucking devil today.

I'll drink when it's over.

Rain

AFTER LYING WIDE AWAKE next to Lamar's skinny, snoring body all night, I decide I've had enough. If I don't stretch my legs soon, I'm gonna scream, and I don't want to wake Lamar up. I'm sure wherever his mind is right now, it's a hell of a lot better than what's waiting for him here.

Reaching up, I feel around with my hand until it hits a dangling handle. Then, I yank as hard as I can. The lid pops open with a quiet click, and sunlight floods the spacious trunk. We went with a Cadillac this time—at Lamar's request. A metallic purple one sitting on blocks.

I sit up and stretch before climbing out of the trunk, but when I do, a wave of nausea almost brings me back down to the fetal position. The blood on my jeans must have dried and stuck to my skin overnight. Every movement severs the crusty bond a little more—like a bandage being pulled off—and I smell like a corpse.

Once my feet are planted firmly on asphalt again, I suck in a few breaths of fresh air. Then, I turn and unzip the duffel bag as quietly as possible, pulling out a bottle of water Michelle gave me yesterday and a prenatal vitamin.

I just hope I can keep it down.

As I unscrew the cap, Lamar throws an elbow over his face and groans.

"Morning," I mumble, tossing the giant, chalky pill into my mouth. I swallow with a shudder.

"Why's everybody so loud?" he whines, making me realize that it *is* pretty loud out here.

I turn in the direction of soon-to-be Burger Palace Park, and my jaw almost hits the Cadillac's chromed-out bumper. Dozens—no, *hundreds* of people have gathered around our handiwork.

Last night, Lamar and I laid Quint's body in the middle of Plaza Park, his arms and legs spread out like a human X. Then, we went and found the dead Bony I'd seen on the side of the road yesterday. I took his King Burger mask to put over Quint's face, and Lamar took a can of orange spray paint he'd found in the guy's hoodie pocket. Once the bloodstained mask was in place, I painted the words *HERE'S YOUR SPONSOR* in a circle around Quint's body.

"Lamar." I shake his shoulder. "Lamar, look!"

He grumbles and sits up, dreadlocks smashed against the side of his head as he turns and squints in the direction of our human protest sign … and the crowd gathering around it.

"Oh shit …" he says, almost to himself. "It worked."

Turning to me, Lamar's brown eyes go wide. "The sublimi-whatever thing! It worked! People are coming! Holy shit, Rain! What pictures did y'all use?"

"Just some photos I found on Google. People marching with their fists in the air. People rioting in the streets. Oh, and a picture of Governor Steele's banner from the capitol building with a bull's-eye Photoshopped right onto his forehead." I smirk.

Lamar snorts and shakes his head. "You 'member, before all this shit started, you had blonde hair and wore cowboy boots and dresses. Now, look at you." He gestures from my head to my waist. "Black hair. Boned out. Savage as fuck. You're like … Post-Apocalypse Barbie now."

"I feel more like Morning Sickness Barbie," I say with a forced smile. But it fades the moment I let my gaze drift over to the growing crowd circling the body of my dead best friend.

I wrap an arm around Lamar's shoulders and exhale.

"What do we do now that they're here?" he asks.

"I don't know," I say with an honest shrug. "Go start a riot, I guess."

Lamar nods. "For Quint."

"And Wes."

"And your folks." He gives me a sympathetic look.

"And Franklin Springs."

"And all the people pushin' up oak trees down there."

Sliding my free hand into the front pocket of my hoodie, I splay my trembling fingers across the biggest reason of all.

And for you, little one.

My matted hair suddenly blows into my face as a van flies past us on the road, weaving around all the abandoned cars like an Olympic downhill skier. Then, it slams on its brakes with an ear-splitting screech. A second later, the

Channel 11 news van backs up next to us. Michelle rolls her tinted window down, revealing a fresh-faced reporter with a sparkle in her eye, an entire tube of concealer covering her bruises, and a breaking story to chase.

"Do you see that crowd?" she shouts. "It worked! Come on! Let's get over there!"

I grab the duffel bag as Lamar climbs out of the trunk. Michelle hops out and opens the giant side door on the van for us.

"Where's Quint?" she asks as we pile inside.

Lamar drops his eyes, and I raise a single finger in the direction of the park.

"Oh, he's already over there?"

"You could say that," I mutter.

Ever the good journalist, Michelle's eyes narrow to slits as they shift back and forth between Lamar and me. It doesn't take her more than a second to deduce from our tear-streaked faces and blood-soaked clothes what happened.

"Oh my God. No."

I nod.

"Quint is …"

I nod.

"Are you serious?"

I nod.

Lamar stares out the window, practically catatonic, as I fill her and Flip in on what happened.

Michelle reaches for the bottle of vodka in her cupholder and takes a long swig as I tell her the story, her red lipstick staying perfectly intact.

"And the governor said they're moving the execution up to this morning?"

After everything I just told her, that's what she's focused on?

"Yeah, but I don't know when."

"Oh my God." Michelle takes another swig. "We have to start broadcasting now. Here, put this on."

She tosses a bundle of soft red material at me. I catch it in my lap as the scent of lavender fabric softener fills the air.

"I grabbed you a wrap dress from my closet since it's kind of one-size-fits-all. It was the best I could do on such short notice." She gives me an apologetic look. "At least it's red—the color of revolution."

"Revolution?"

"You got 'em here. Now, you gotta tell 'em what to do."

All of our heads turn toward the crowd flooding into Plaza Park as we drive past. I can hear their shouts from inside the van as the riot cops with Plexiglas shields try to push people off the field.

My palms begin to sweat as I turn my back to everyone in the van and strip my hoodie off over my head, followed by my once-white tank top. I then pull off my hiking boots and peel my blood-encrusted jeans off my legs. The skin underneath is stained maroon, and fresh tears fill my eyes as images from last night flash before them. Quint's body in my lap. The kindness of the security guards who helped us—I don't even know their names. Holding Lamar as he cried himself to sleep. I consider taking the bottle of water and rinsing my legs clean, but it doesn't matter.

I'll probably be covered in my own blood by the end of the day anyway.

Or Wes's.

With a heavy sigh, I slip on the wrap dress and tie it around my waist. The fabric is soft and clean and somehow comforting.

"Here." Michelle hands me a tube of lipstick and a comb from her purse. "You don't want people to just hear you. You want them to *listen* to you. A bold lip draws their eyes to your mouth."

I remember another woman I saw on TV with a bold red mouth.

"My name is Dr. Marguerite Chapelle. I am the director of the World Health Alliance. If you are seeing this broadcast, congratulations. You are now part of a stronger, healthier, more self-sufficient human race."

I shudder.

We sure as hell listened to her, didn't we?

"What do I even say to them?" I wonder out loud, using the reflective surface of the lipstick cap as a mirror to help me apply it.

Michelle thinks for a minute, vodka sloshing out of her bottle as Flip pulls up onto the curb next to Plaza Park. "I read a study a few years ago about social media that said that people are addicted to outrage. It said that news stories about major events got way fewer likes and shares and comments than posts from people reacting to those events with outrage. We're drawn to that kind of fiery passion. It makes us feel alive, powerful … connected. No successful movement was ever started without outrage, so I say, you get up there and get pissed off."

"I'm not trying to start a movement. I just want these people to help me save Wes."

"What do you think *they* want?" she asks, opening the passenger door to the sounds of chaos and anger. To a sea of people with locked elbows and fists in the air.

I sigh as I yank the comb through my tangled hair. "A revolution."

"You built this bomb, girl. Time to go set it off." Flip winks at me in the rearview mirror before opening his door and climbing out too.

I turn to Lamar. "How do I look?"

He furrows his eyebrows at me, the right one still scarred from the bulldozer accident. "Like a reporter."

"You don't like it?"

"I liked Post-Apocalyptic Barbie better." Lamar shrugs. "Maybe take the hoodie … just in case."

I give him a sad smile as I reach for my sweatshirt. Anything to make him happy. "You doin' okay?" I ask, tying the sleeves around my waist.

He shakes his head and drops his eyes. His chin begins to wobble, but he grits his teeth and squashes it.

"Me too, buddy." I pat his knee. "Me too."

"Guys …" Flip calls out, slapping the side of the van to get our attention. "Looks like we might be too late."

Lamar and I scramble outside and notice that everyone's heads are craned back and tilted to the right as a helicopter descends onto a small, oval-shaped patch of grass next to the capitol building.

Michelle turns to me with an apologetic look on her face. "Shit! I have to get into position. He's gonna go inside the capitol for a minute and then make a big entrance by coming down the capitol steps. I usually meet him at the end of the main walkway and introduce him. Then, we walk over to the park together."

"Introduce him!" I shout, my eyes going wide. "How much time do we have?"

"Before he comes out? Maybe twenty minutes? Thirty, tops."

"Perfect! I'll be right back!" I tighten the sleeves around my waist and take off running.

"Rain! Where are you going?"

"Call me Stella!" I yell over my shoulder.

"*Did I ever tell you you're my heeee-rooooo?*" Elliott sings to me as we jog down the block, take a right, pass the now-maskless dead Bony, take a left, and sprint past the crowd in Plaza Park.

"Ooh! Look at that! My fans await!" Elliott cups his hand and waves at them like the Queen of England as I pull him to a stop next to the news van.

"Michelle," I huff, trying to catch my breath. "Officer Elliott here would like to introduce the governor on today's broadcast."

Michelle narrows her eyes in confusion. Then, she pops them open again once she connects the dots. "Of course! We'd love for you to do the honors, Officer Elliott. Thank you for coming on such short notice. The governor surprised us by moving the execution up, unannounced."

"Tell me about it, honey. We're runnin' around like chickens with our heads cut off over at the station. Got my boy Wes all suited up and ready to go though. He's gon' break some hearts, that one." Elliott shakes his head, and I can tell that one of the hearts is going to be his.

I know the feeling.

"We don't have much time, so I'll cut right to the chase. In a few minutes, the governor is going to walk down those steps, and we need you to—"

"Don't worry 'bout me, honey. I got this!" Officer Elliott interrupts, flicking his fingers at Flip. "Gimme a mic! Where do I stand? How's my hair?" He runs a hand over his perfectly bald head and cackles.

Flip grabs his camera bag out of the van and leads Officer Elliott toward the capitol building as he continues to ramble. Then, glancing behind him at Michelle, he jerks his head in the direction of Plaza Park.

Go. Now, he mouths.

Michelle doesn't hesitate. She leans into the van and grabs a large, padded black bag. Unzipping it, she says, "Lamar … I'm gonna need you to be my cameraman for the day." Turning around, Michelle presents him with a full-size TV camera.

"Oh my God. Can you even hold that thing up?" I ask.

"Pssh." He dismisses me as he accepts the equipment with straining, spindly arms.

"I'll start the broadcast," she says, positioning the camera on his shoulder. "All you have to do is hold it, like this."

"So, is Flip just not gonna turn his camera on or somethin'?" Lamar asks, shifting his weight to support the load.

"That's right. He'll use it to record; it just won't be live. Yours will be."

Turning toward me, Michelle contorts her crimson lips into something I assume is supposed to look reassuring, but her wild eyes are just as manic as the cheering, shouting, fist-pumping crowd swelling behind her. She wants this just as bad as they do. Everyone here has lost someone or something because of Operation April 23, including Michelle. That's why the dream spoke to them, motivated them to pick up their weapons and fight their way down here. The question is, are they here to start a revolution?

Or do they just want their pound of flesh?

"Let's go!" Michelle grins.

She leads the way, squeezing in between Bonys and housewives and pimps and homeless teenagers. "Excuse me!" she yells. "Michelle Ling! Channel 11 Action News!"

But nobody can hear her, and we're starting to get separated.

Somebody grabs my wrist just as she and Lamar disappear through a group of old rednecks carrying hunting rifles. I try to yank my arm away, but the grip is surprisingly strong for a hand so small. I follow the skeletal arm it's attached to up to the face of a woman who's probably in her early forties but looks about fifteen years older. Everything about her is thin—her body, her skin, the limp blonde hair hanging around her sad, wrinkled face.

"Ms. McCartney?" she asks, a pair of familiar green eyes lighting up in recognition. "Oh my God, it *is* you!" She wraps her other hand around my forearm. "You saw my boy yesterday!"

Turning her head, she yells to a rough-looking crew of tattooed men and women behind her, "Y'all! It's the reporter who interviewed my Wesson!"

Her what?

"Ms. McCartney, I'm Wesson Parker's mama, Rhonda. I saw him on the TV yesterday, and I ..."

Her face crumples in on itself, and tears spill down her cheeks as my mind struggles to process the words she just said.

Wes's mama.

I never really thought of her as a real person before. More like a ghost. A part of Wes's past that he didn't like to talk about. All I know is that she was a drug addict who neglected her children to the point that Wes's baby sister died of starvation, and she's been in prison ever since.

But here she is, in the flesh. Wes got her eyes, her perfect nose. She must have been so beautiful once.

"You can't let them kill my baby!" Her voice goes shrill as she clings to me for strength. "Please, Ms. McCartney! Please! You gotta help him! That's my boy! My baby boy!"

Tears fill my own eyes as I watch the grandmother of my child beg for the life of her own son. Not only because I share her pain, but also because there's someone else on this planet who loves him. He deserves all the love in the world.

"I'm trying to," I say, not loud enough for anyone to hear over the crowd noise.

"I'm going to!" I shout, shifting my gaze from her to her terrifying group of friends.

They look like they all just got out of prison, which ... I realize ... they did.

"I'm going to rally everybody to help me, but I need to get to the middle of the crowd first."

Rhonda's eyes—Wes's eyes—fill with hope. "Really?" She jerks my arm. "Really? Did y'all hear that?" she shouts over her shoulder. "Let's get her to the clearing!"

Two big, burly men with facial tattoos and necks wider than my thighs step forward and, without so much as a hello, lift me onto their shoulders.

"Ahh!" I cling to their shaved heads as they push their way through the crowd like human bulldozers, the rest of the released prisoners pushing through behind them.

"Hey!"

"Watch out!"

"Ow!"

"Fuck you!"

Fistfights and shouting matches break out in the wake of my ex-con caravan as the clearing in the center of the crowd gets closer and closer.

The tops of Michelle's and Lamar's heads come into view, and I exhale. They made it. Lamar's camera lens turns to face me, and the red light is already blinking as the bodybuilders barrel their way into the circular opening that has formed around Quint's body.

Michelle is standing on one side of my blood-soaked friend while Lamar stands on the other, trying to keep a brave face.

Poor baby.

Michelle snaps her fingers at Lamar, instructing him to turn the camera toward her.

"This is Michelle Ling, reporting live from Plaza Park minutes before the Green Mile execution event is scheduled to begin. As you can see"—she does a spinning motion with her finger, instructing Lamar to turn the camera in a circle to get footage of the entire crowd—"quite a crowd has gathered here today to express their outrage over what many are calling 'senseless, government-sanctioned murders' and 'public executions for profit.'"

Michelle gestures toward me, and Lamar takes the cue, unsteadily swinging the giant camera in my direction.

"I have our newest reporter, Ms. McCartney, here with the inside scoop on the allegations against Governor Steele and his controversial Green Mile event. Ms. McCartney, can you please tell us why today's execution was rescheduled for this morning?"

I hear her question, but I don't look into the camera, and I don't climb down from my human throne. I don't care about the people sitting at home. They can't help me. The people I need to talk to are right here. Right now.

Sticking the microphone between my teeth, I cling to the stubbled heads of my helpers and slowly push myself to stand on their shoulders. They grab my ankles with their viselike hands, holding me perfectly still as I straighten my spine and look out over the park. Thousands of people have filled the space now, the tops of the saplings barely visible above their heads at the edge of the park. Riot cops line the perimeter, but they're outnumbered a hundred to one. Anger and adrenaline rise off the crowd in waves as thick as steam. It's a deadly powder keg of chaos.

And I'm holding a microphone shaped like a match.

While the crowd quiets to a hush, I scan the sea of faces for one to focus on. I think it will help me feel less nervous if I have one specific person to talk to. But I don't find just one person. I find all the people.

Q and the runaways are front and center, horsing around like little kids. Brad has Not Brad on his shoulders, chicken-fighting Q, whose thighs are wrapped around Tiny Tim's head. Loudmouth and the other runaways I never got a chance to meet are standing in front of them, cheering and trying to help Q win.

A sea of Bonys takes up the left half of the crowd. I pick out The Prez in his fur coat immediately as well as the kids from Pritchard Park who spray-painted our truck—I'd know that helmet with the nails sticking out of it anywhere.

But the person I decide to focus on, the one who makes me think that everything might actually be all right, belongs to an older man with a face like Santa Claus and a body like a grizzly bear. A man I've known my whole life. A man who was more of a father to me than my own sometimes. A man who has a broken leg that I should yell at him for standing on right now.

Mr. Renshaw.

When I lock eyes with him, I don't see anger there. I see forgiveness. Remorse. Understanding. It is not the face of a man whose wife just died. It's the face of a man whose wife did something regrettable, and he's come to make amends for it. Agnes must be okay. And when Jimbo presses his lips together and gives me a single nod, I know we're going to be okay, too.

If we survive what I'm about to do.

Clutching the microphone with two shaky hands, I inhale the crowd's desperation and exhale the terrifying truth. "Today's execution was rescheduled for this morning because Governor Steele has a meeting this afternoon."

The crowd grumbles at the mention of our shared enemy.

"At that meeting, the CEO of Burger Palace is going to pay him five billion dollars to be the official sponsor of the Green Mile execution event."

The grumbles turn to growls.

"They're going to rename this place Burger Palace Park and project King Burger's picture right onto the field. I know this because I heard the governor say it with my own two ears, and so did my friend here … right before he was shot in the back by Governor Steele's bodyguard."

Lamar pans the camera down to his brother's body on the ground and almost drops it as his eyes squeeze shut in pain.

You gotta get through this, buddy. Stay with me.

"How do y'all feel about Governor Steele making five billion dollars for killing our friends and family members—good people—on live TV?"

Fists and shouts fill the air.

"Greed. That's why our species was facing extinction. Not because we were wasting our resources on 'nonproductive citizens,' but because our resources were being hoarded by them!" I shove my finger in the direction of the capitol building, feeling the hands around my lower legs tighten to keep me from falling.

"One percent of our population owns ninety-nine percent of the wealth on this planet! Think about that. That's not nature's way! No other species hoards resources like that. They take what they need, and they leave what they don't. That's the true law that was being violated. This isn't about survival of the fittest; it's about survival of the richest!"

Mr. Renshaw nods his head in agreement, and a surge of pride fills the empty hole in my chest, turning the dark, decaying tissue into something pink and pulsing again.

"Have you seen the governor's mansion?" I ask, shouting as loud as I can.

The people yell and raise their fists in response.

"Your taxes paid for that! Have you seen his fancy new helicopter?" I gesture toward the landing pad behind me.

Their shouts and fists rise up again.

"Well, you bought it for him! Have you seen the CEO of Burger Palace's private island?"

"No!"

"You paid for that, too, when they started charging forty dollars for a King Burger Combo! They're killing us for profit, y'all. And that's what's about to happen right here, right now, to Wesson Parker if we don't rise up and say *enough*!"

The crowd shouts the word, "Enough!" in unison, throwing their fists in the air.

The force of their conviction almost knocks me over. It hits me in the chest like a wrecking ball, overwhelming me with support. I felt like I was fighting this battle on my own for so long, clinging to this person I love tooth and nail while the entire world tried to take him from me. But I'm not alone anymore.

And neither are they.

"The folks who have been murdered here by Governor Steele and his executioner are good people. They're your family, your doctors, your friends, your loved ones. They are people who were willing to die to save someone else."

To save me.

"They are not the enemy. Doing everything we can to help each other survive isn't what made us weak; it's what made us *human*. The real enemy is the one percent of our population who took ninety-nine percent of our resources! The one percent who almost made us go extinct because of their greed. The one percent who killed a quarter of us off through mind control to make up for the lack they'd created and then told us it was our fault for turning our backs on natural selection!"

I lean over and give the microphone to Wes's mom, who's watching me with glistening eyes. *Hold this, please,* I mouth to her.

I untie the sleeves wrapped around my waist and pull the hoodie on over my head, careful not to let my gun fall out of the front pocket. As soon as those orange bones are visible, the left half of the crowd—the side with jackets matching mine—goes wild. I take the microphone back from Rhonda with a hopeful look.

Standing back up, I shove my fist into the air, and when the entire crowd does the same, it feels like the ocean itself is rising up to meet me. Except for Q, who's smirking with her arms folded across her chest.

"They say they want the strongest to survive? Well, I say, there's strength in numbers! Let's show them—"

"Shoot her!" a booming Southern voice shouts from somewhere behind me.

My head swivels in that direction, and I find Governor Steele marching across the capitol lawn, pointing at me in anger, with Officer Elliott and Flip hot on his trail. Three riot cops rush across the street to drag Governor Steele away but not before he produces a gun from somewhere inside his three-piece suit and aims it directly at me.

The brute squad drops me immediately, catching me in their heavily tattooed arms as two bullets whiz through the air over my head.

The microphone slips through my fingers.

And the powder keg explodes.

Rain

THE SECOND THOSE SHOTS are fired, a hundred more follow as the crowd erupts into a pushing, shoving, screaming, stampeding, mindless thing. Michelle, Lamar, and I are swallowed by the mob in an instant. People trample over Quint's body as they push in all directions to get away from the madness. I watch as his mask goes flat under a cowboy boot, and I have to choke down my own vomit.

But there's no time to process. I'm going to end up just like him if I don't stay upright. With every jarring shove, every push and pull, I feel myself getting smaller. It's like that time my parents took me to the beach, and I got sucked away from the shore by the undertow. I remember feeling so weak, my little muscles no match for the all-powerful ocean. The only difference is that if I get pulled under here, I won't drown. I'll have my internal organs liquefied under the stomping, panicking feet of Bonys and rednecks and newly released prisoners.

Shots ring out every few seconds, followed by more screaming, and I don't know if the riot cops are firing at us or if we're firing at the riot cops.

The giant ex-cons who were holding me up are able to force their way through the chaos, but when the crowd closes in behind them, it swallows me whole and forces me under, like a crashing wave.

Fight! I scream at myself. *Stay on your feet!*

Another *ka-pow* reverberates through the air as a man no more than five feet away from me topples into the crowd like a cut tree. I can't get out of the way, and he lands on me, coughing up blood as we both go down.

I scream as I hit the grass under two hundred pounds of bleeding human. "Help! Helllllllp!"

I struggle to roll the dying man off of me as motorcycle boots and cowboy boots and combat boots and hunting boots stomp on my feet and trip over my legs and kick me in the side and crush my arms. Fear and pain hijack my brain as the assault continues. Instead of rolling him off, I pull the dying man back on top of me, using him as a human shield to protect my belly as I try to remember to breathe. Panic grips my throat and squeezes, stealing my voice as it whispers into my ears.

Weak.

Stupid.

Powerless.

Girl.

But then I hear another voice in my ear, one that sounds less like me and more like a female rapper who smokes two packs a day. Faded green dreadlocks tumble into my face as the voice chuckles.

"Bitch, how you gonna start a riot and then lie down and take a nap? That's some gangsta shit right there."

Two hands grab me under the armpits and hoist, lifting me out from under the now-dead body just before another surge of people tramples him as well.

I turn and find the feral, feline eyes of Q staring back at me, a smirk on her full lips and a spatter of blood on her right cheek.

"You came," I mutter in disbelief.

"Pssh. Not from that speech, I didn't." She grins. "Come on. Let's go get ya man."

Before I can ask her how in the hell she thinks we're going to get out of here, Q climbs the bodies around her like a jungle gym.

"Ow!"

"Fuck!"

"What the hell?"

"Come on, you little pussy!" she yells down at me, crawling on top of the angry mob like it's her own personal magic carpet.

I do the same, but much more apologetically, and follow her every move as she crawls on her hands and feet over the undulating sea of bodies. But with the way the crowd is pushing back and forth, we take two steps forward and find ourselves three feet farther away.

"Ugh! Don't these muhfuckas know who you is?"

Q squats on the shoulders of a bearded, plaid-covered redneck and places her fingers in her mouth. The whistle that follows is deafening and brings everyone immediately around us to a halt.

"Y'all need to get dis bitch to the front 'fore I start shootin' muhfuckas just to make a path!"

Everyone's stare shifts from Q to me, and suddenly, a sidewalk of hands, palms up, appears before me.

Q's mouth twists into a self-satisfied sneer as she gestures for me to go ahead.

I give her a grateful nod and begin placing my wobbly knees and shaking hands on their open palms.

"Nah, bitch. Not like dat. Like dis." Q gives me a shove, and I scream and grasp at nothing as I topple over sideways.

But I don't hit the ground. The crowd catches me and carries me like a conveyor belt toward the front of Plaza Park. I blink and try to catch my breath as I wave at Q, who gives me a smug smile before slapping the crap out of the guy she's crouching on for trying to pull her off.

From up here, I can see that droves of angry people are flooding in from the streets—probably thanks to our live broadcast—but the new rioters are only making it harder for the ones trying to flee to get out. Because the longer sides of the park are walled off by risers—which the riot cops are now standing on, firing at anybody who tries to climb up to their level—the only way in and out of the park are the two shorter sides. Folks are either fighting to get out, fighting to get in, or fighting just for the hell of it, but when I see the news van pull away from the curb, I know who's not fighting.

Michelle and Lamar.

I catch a glimpse of Lamar's messy dreadlocks in the passenger side window as the van takes off down the street. I want to feel relieved that they got out, but instead I feel the sudden pull of gravity as a bullet whizzes past me and into the crowd holding me up. I start to fall as everyone around me screams scatters, but I manage to hold onto somebody's shirt to keep my upper body from hitting the ground. When I finally get my feet under me, I notice that the man I was clinging to is standing perfectly still, staring at the ground through a bullet hole in the middle of his hand.

Then, I hear a scream.

It might be mine. I don't even know anymore.

I keep my head down and keep pushing forward. Too low, and I'll get trampled. Too high, and I might get shot. I trip and stumble over other people who have fallen, their bodies reminding me why I have to succeed today.

No more deaths in vain. No more blood spilled on this ground.

Especially not Wes's.

Someone nearby raises her fist in the air and shouts, "Here's your sponsor!" The words I spray-painted around Quint's body.

Emotion squeezes my chest as the people around her do the same.

Chants of, "Here's your sponsor!" spread like a ripple through the crowd, fists pumping and feet stomping.

It gives me an opportunity to get a little lower and weave my way under their raised fists.

Then, a fresh round of panic breaks out. I didn't hear any shots fired, so I'm not sure what the threat is until I see a shiny metal canister spewing smoke careen through the air over my head.

"Tear gaaaasssss!" someone cries, and the pushing starts again.

I'm crushed by bodies moving in all directions as thick smoke pours in, filling what little open space there is left. Just before it gets to me, I pull the neck hole of my hoodie up to my forehead. Then, I yank the hood down past my chin. I can't see anything through the layers of thick black fabric, but I can feel, and I can climb.

Keeping my breaths as shallow as possible, I try to pretend like I'm Q. I climb the jerking, screaming bodies around me until I'm grabbing hair instead of clothing. Then, I move forward. My eyes and nose and throat begin to burn as I blindly crawl over the coughing, crying heads of strangers.

I called them here, I think as stinging tears soak into the black cotton covering my face. *I did this to them.*

Someone in the crowd behind me fires aimlessly into the air, screaming about his eyes, just as something sharp pokes me in the cheek. I reach out and feel leaves. A branch.

A tree!

I yank the hood off my face and peek out of the neck of my sweatshirt just as the person below me succeeds in bucking me off. I tumble to the ground and land on my feet, but the mob pushes me forward, slamming me into the trunk of a recently planted oak tree.

The first of Governor Steele's victims is decaying under this dirt, but I don't have time to think about that.

I have to figure out how the hell to save the next one.

I want to fight my way down the line of saplings until I make it to Wes's hole, but before I can take the first step, another wave of chaos breaks out. I cling to the tree as wailing police sirens get louder and louder and louder, followed by screaming and pushing and shoving worse than anything I've experienced up to this point. Reaching as high as I can, I grab the spindly branches and pull myself into the tree, praying that it will hold my body weight so that I can escape the crowd threatening to rip me to shreds below.

As soon as I climb above them, I see what all the panic is about. A massive tank, as wide as the entire street with a cannon the size of a telephone pole on the front, is charging straight toward the crowd, followed by two police cars and a SWAT SUV. People are climbing all over one another, trying to get out of the way as the tank lurches up over the curb and into the park. I can't see if anyone gets run over, but a chunk of them seems to disappear in front of the tank as it turns and forces itself in between the hole that was dug for Wes's grave and the rest of the mob.

Blue lights spill over everything as the police cars and SWAT utility vehicle pull in behind the tank and form a tight, square barricade around the hole. I notice that the riot cops have moved from their stations on the risers and are now marching up to the cop cars with their shields raised. One by one, they climb on top of the vehicles, facing outward in a ring of human turrets.

No!

My heart thunders in my chest, my hands shake, and my guts twist into violent knots as the driver's side door to one of the police cars opens. Officer Elliott steps out, and with a solemn look on his face, he opens the back door to the cruiser. Governor Steele hoists himself out on the third try, and the car lifts a full six inches higher off the ground before Flip climbs out behind him.

Flip turns on his camera, which I assume is live now that Michelle is nowhere to be seen, and instructs the governor to stand in the center of their barricade with the SWAT vehicle behind him. I expect Officer Elliott to do another introduction, but Governor Steele doesn't give him the chance.

He simply opens his mushy, shapeless mouth and bellows loud enough for me to hear over the madness, "Bailiff, bring out the accused!"

No! No, no, no, no! Somebody, do something! Elliott, please!

But Officer Elliott simply nods his head once, turns, and walks over to the other cruiser. Opening the back door, he reaches in and pulls Wes—*my Wes*—out by the elbow.

His hands are bound behind his back, and he's wearing a burlap jumpsuit.

Not orange. Burlap.

The sight of him dressed like that rips a scream from my body. Somewhere in the crowd, another woman howls in the same heartbroken pitch, and I know his mama sees him, too.

"Elliott, do something!" I shout. "Somebody! Help him!"

But everyone is screaming. The riot cops are shooting people who try to climb onto the vehicles or who shoot at them first. Tear gas canisters are being tossed out like candy. The crowd is surging against the vehicles, making them rock back and forth. No one can possibly hear me.

But still, I scream.

I look to the driver's seat of the patrol car Wes got out of and find Officer Hoyt gripping the steering wheel and staring straight ahead, his eyes at half-mast.

"Hoyt!"

Governor Steele says something I can't hear and motions to the tank. A man steps out of it and walks across the clearing, but it's not until he stands directly in front of Wes and turns to face him that I can tell who it is.

The executioner.

He's wearing an all-black police uniform, and he has on a loose black mask that covers his entire head with two small eyeholes cut out. His hand is on a pistol holstered on his tool belt, and his focus is lasered in on Wes.

My Wes.

"Flip! Flip, do something!"

The cameraman takes his spot off to the side, next to Governor Steele. Everything is moving so fast. The crowd continues to slam against the vehicles in waves, making all but the tank rock back and forth, but with the riot cops standing on top, firing at anyone who climbs too high or shoots at them, nobody is able to do anything to stop them.

My hand dives into the front pocket of my hoodie, and I'm shocked to find my gun still tucked inside.

The moment my finger wraps around the trigger, I'm back outside Huckabee Foods, staring at a beautiful boy in a blue Hawaiian shirt, who is smiling at me with perfect white teeth. His light eyes sparkle under a canopy of black lashes, and I'm lost in them until his face contorts in pain. Blood explodes from his shoulder, and I don't hesitate. I don't think. I grab the machine gun off the dead guard beside me, turn, and pull the trigger, spraying two men and a sliding glass door with enough bullets to take out an entire army of meth-head gangbangers.

I've done this before, I tell myself.

I can do it again.

But I don't have a machine gun this time. And I can't be impulsive.

As the executioner raises his weapon, I realize that I can only get one shot off before the riot cops see me and take me out.

This is it.

I pull the gun out of my pocket.

Time slows down.

And I'm forced to make the hardest decision of my life in an instant.

Assassinate the governor and end the Green Mile once and for all but risk Wes still being executed in the process?

Or kill the executioner and give Wes a chance to escape in the confusion?

His legs aren't shackled. He could slip between the vehicles and disappear into the crowd.

But how many more "accused" would die in his place? How much longer would the governor's reign of terror last?

Do I sacrifice one life to save the others?

Or sacrifice the others to save *the one*?

My one.

My Wes.

My decision is made.

Ten Minutes Earlier
Wes

WHEN HOYT TOLD ME that "Ms. McCartney" came to get Elliott to introduce the governor, I knew she had some shit up her sleeve. When he wordlessly put me in the back of a police cruiser instead of walking me through the tunnel, I knew it must be bad. But when he pulled up behind another cruiser, a SWAT vehicle, and Mac's fucking tank just to escort me into Plaza Park, that's when I knew.

That dream was no fucking fluke.

That dream was planted by a certain little black-haired rag doll with a death wish.

As soon as the park comes into view, my mouth falls open in a silent curse. I've never seen so many people shoved into one square block before. The entire crowd is fighting and flailing and pounding their fists in the air as tear gas canisters sail overhead, and gunshots loud enough to hear inside Hoyt's bulletproof cruiser ring out.

What the fuck have you done, baby?

I shake my head as adrenaline floods into my extremities, and panic seizes my lungs. My eyes scan the mob, frantically searching for a familiar heart-shaped face, but everything is just a blur of fists and weapons and smoke and mouths twisted in pain and anger.

I told you I'd get out of this. What the fuck have you done?

Hoyt glances at me in the rearview mirror. All the shaggy, unwashed hair in the world couldn't hide the pity and remorse written all over his doughy face. I don't have to pretend to be fucking terrified when I look back at him. I am.

Just not for me.

The tank barrels into the crowd, and the screams of the people in its path bounce off the windshield.

"Goddamn." I cringe and cling to the seat with cuffed hands as people flood into the risers to get out of the way.

Hoyt and the other two vehicles pull into the park behind the tank, and the four of them form a perfect little square.

I don't have to be able to see the ground to know what they're protecting. *My fucking grave.*

Hoyt throws the car in park and sits with his thick hands wrapped around the steering wheel. He doesn't move. He doesn't speak. And gauging from the amount of swallowing and throat-clearing he's doing, he's not real happy about what's about to happen.

Or at least, what he *thinks* is about to happen.

Poor bastard. I want to let him in on my plan just to put him out of his misery, but I can't fucking trust him to play along. He's a worse actor than Elliott. Look at him. He can't even pretend to be professional.

My attention is pulled away from Hoyt when I notice riot cops in gas masks, carrying full-body bulletproof shields, marching over to the car. The first three climb directly on top of our cruiser, standing on the hood, the trunk, and the roof.

The fuck?

One by one, cops fill in from the sides of the park until all four vehicles have at least three riot cops standing on top of each.

Governor Fuckface is now standing between the tank and the gaping hole in the ground as Flip lifts a TV camera onto his shoulder and points at him.

As his pasty, bloated face opens and closes, my hands begin to shake.

No! I yell at myself, balling them into fists. *Stop it! You don't fucking end here. You survive, and so does Rain. That's what you do. That's how this shit works.*

But as the crowd surrounds the vehicles and begins rocking them back and forth, including the one I'm presently freaking out in, I realize that I'm not so fucking sure anymore.

Yeah, I have a plan. But I didn't exactly factor in an angry mob or tanks or riot cops or my girl getting trampled to death while I sit here and do nothing either.

I swallow back a surge of bile as Elliott marches over to my door and yanks it open.

Here we go. God, you better fucking have my back.

I step out into a three-hundred-and-sixty-degree assault on my senses. The crowd noise is deafening, the air is thick and humid and tainted with tear gas, and the mid-morning sun is blinding as it bounces off the cruisers and shines directly into my face.

But even through all of the sensations I'm being blasted with, one ear-splitting scream rises over the rest.

She's out there.

She's fucking out there.

Goddamn it.

I don't need this. I need to focus, but now, all I can think about is kicking Elliott right in the fucking face and diving into that crowd, so I can find my girl and drag her ass to safety.

Elliott steers me by the elbow to stand in front of a five-foot-by-five-foot hole in the ground—*oh, look at that; they widened it just for me*—and gives me a little pat on the shoulder before letting me go.

I have to physically shake my head to clear my thoughts of Rain.

Focus, fucker!

I blink and stare straight ahead, finding the cameraman and the devil himself standing across from me with their backs to the SUV.

Governor Fuckface sneers, and I spit at his feet.

"Mistuh Parkuh," he begins, condescension oozing through every missing consonant, "you were arrested on May 5 for allegedly procuring and administering life-saving drugs to a young man with a fatally infected wound. On May 6, you were found guilty of this crime, and as such, you have been sentenced to death."

Someone gets out of the tank behind me. A cop wearing a black executioner's mask trudges past, coming to stand directly across from me. Fuckface is still talking, but I'm searching the man in black for some assurance that this is gonna go down the way I planned.

"I would offuh you a few last words, but as you can see, the little interview you gave yesterday has the *constituency* all riled up. So, I'm afraid those are gonna be the last words you eva get to speak in *my* state, boy. Executionuh"—he steps aside and gestures toward the man in black—"fire at will."

Come on. Come on …

My entire body sways with every forceful pump of blood through my veins as the cop unsnaps his holster and draws his weapon. It's a small handgun, probably a .22—something large enough to kill me without blowing the back of my head off in the process.

How considerate.

I swallow and hold my breath as the executioner lifts the gun and steadies it with the palm of his left hand under the clip. And that's when I notice that every knuckle on both of his hands are as scabbed and mangled as mine.

Mac.

I exhale and close my eyes.

And for a fraction of a second, I'm at peace.

With the blinding sun and flashing blue lights and screaming mob and sinister scowl of pure fucking evil finally blocked out, it's just me and the life I've placed in the bloody hands of a complete stranger.

Until I hear *her.*

Over the roar of the crowd, over the cruisers being rocked back and forth, over the shouted warnings from the riot cops, I hear *her.*

"Somebody, do something!"

She's close. Too fucking close.

My eyelids slam open, and my head swivels automatically in the direction of her voice. Rain is the first thing I see, tangled in the branches of a baby oak tree, just like the dream I had last night. Only she's not being devoured. Quite the opposite. She has her gun raised, and she's aiming it directly at Mac.

Fuck!

Without thinking, I drop to the ground and sweep my leg out, knocking Mac clean off his feet as three gunshots ring out in rapid succession. The first one Mac fired into the air just before he hit the dirt. The second one shattered the passenger window of the SWAT vehicle he was standing in front of, splintering the glass—where his head would have been—like a spiderweb. And the third one came from somewhere to the left of me.

I turn in that direction and find Hoyt standing beside his cruiser, holding a smoking gun over the roof of his car. His face is slack-jawed and wide-eyed, just like the girl in the tree fifty feet behind him. Rain lowers her gun in stunned shock and raises one shaking finger to point at something on the other side of me.

Before I can even turn in that direction, I feel a rush of putrid air ruffle my hair as something hits the ground beside me like a three-hundred-pound sack of rotten potatoes. I swing my head around to find Governor Fuckface lying on the ground, bleeding out from the neck as he coughs and gurgles. His mouth opens and closes like a fish out of water as he holds one of his three chins with one hand and reaches out to me with the other.

"Ew!" Officer Elliott squeals as he walks over and lifts one perfectly polished hard-sole shoe, firmly placing it over the governor's ribs. "Hoyt, did you have to shoot him in the neck? That's so nasty!" With a disgusted grimace and a shove, Elliott rolls Beauregard Steele's gasping body into the hole that was dug for me.

Or was it?

I did notice that it was a little bit wider than usual.

Another man in all-black civilian clothes, like a bodyguard, steps out of the tank and tells the riot cops to stand down. As soon as they holster their weapons, the crowd erupts in cheers. I walk on my knees over to Mac. I can't help him up because my hands are still fucking cuffed behind my back, but he groans and sits up on his own, pulling his mask off in the process.

"You okay, old man?"

He nods and glares at Hoyt, who's now getting a shoulder massage from Elliott.

"You're jealous that he got the kill and not you, aren't you?" I tease.

Mac's jaw grinds, and his eyes narrow as they cut back to me. "Who knew those two clowns would have their own fucking plan?"

I chuckle. "Evidently, my girl had one, too. She damn near blew your head off, man."

"You mean, *that* girl?"

I follow Mac's smirk over my shoulder and find the riot cops helping Rain climb onto the hood of Hoyt's cruiser. She's wearing that fucking red lipstick again, and she has a red skirt or dress or some shit on under her spray-painted, blood-splattered hoodie.

I pull my lip between my teeth and stare as she hops down, the wind ruffling her hair and blowing her skirt up before she lands with a graceful thud just a few feet away from me.

She's here.

She's right fucking here.

I barely register the click of my handcuffs before I'm on my knees with my face buried in my girl's belly and my arms wrapped around her thighs.

"Don't look at me like that, little missy," Mac's deep voice grumbles behind me. "I wasn't gonna kill him."

I laugh. I fucking laugh until I damn near cry as Rain's fingers comb through my hair and her body sinks into my lap and her swollen, red eyes stare through mine.

"Did you get tear-gassed?" I ask, swiping my thumbs over her wet cheeks.

"No, I'm just really happy," she sobs, her red lips splitting into a smile that I've wanted to put on her face since the moment I fucking met her.

I let myself watch her smile for a whole second, maybe two, just long enough for me to take a picture of it with my mind. Then, I kiss that fucking grin right off her face.

Somewhere in the back of my mind, a voice tells me that I need to be careful. Stay vigilant. That my story doesn't end like this. That I don't get to be happy. That my world doesn't work that way.

But I tell that voice to shut the fuck up.

It's a new world now.

And in this world, we can be whatever the fuck we want to be.

Even happy.

EPILOGUE

One Year Later
Rain

I SLIDE THE CAR *seat into the red vinyl booth and sit down next to it while Wes goes up to the front to order. Lily smiles back at me as I rock her gently, cooing and kicking her feet under her blanket. She's so incredibly beautiful. Soft brown hair like her daddy— only hers is fuzzier and sticks straight up. She has giant blue eyes, like mine, but hers sparkle with the kind of pure, innocent joy that only someone who didn't live through April 23 can know.*

By the time Lily arrived, the world was safe again. Orderly. Militant. After Governor Steele was assassinated, we went from zero laws to martial law in the span of about a week. It turns out that all over the country, members of the military were gearing up for a government takeover. Officer MacArthur and Governor Steele's bodyguard, Jenkins, were in the Green Berets together and had already been in talks with Army officials about organizing a coup in Georgia when Wes suggested that they do it at his execution.

It's kind of hilarious that Officer Hoyt beat them to it.

Georgia was the first state to fall, but after that, the other forty-nine toppled like dominoes. Within a few days, the military completely seized power. Existing laws were reinstated, mandatory curfews were enforced, and the released prisoners were put to work— rebuilding businesses, clearing the roads, cleaning up the graffiti, and burying the dead. It's still weird to see tanks driving down the street every night at 8 p.m. and generals giving press conferences instead of men in ten-thousand-dollar suits, but if it means my daughter and I can go to the grocery store without getting raped, robbed, killed, or kidnapped, I'll take it.

Once the state governments started being overthrown, the president read the writing on the wall and just … disappeared. Rumor has it that he flew off to Tim Hollis's private island along with a bunch of the other "one-percenters" and is living quite comfortably in the tropics.

Burger Palace didn't survive though. After Lamar's footage of what happened at Plaza Park made the national news, boycotts and vandalism spread across the country. Here's your sponsor, Fuck your sponsor, Not my sponsor, *or some other variation was spray-painted over every image of King Burger from California to Connecticut.*

After the Burger Palace in Franklin Springs shut down, Mr. and Mrs. Renshaw bought it for cents on the dollar and turned it into a mom-and-pop barbeque joint. They'd actually liked cooking for all the runaways at the mall and decided to try their hand at the service industry. It's the only restaurant in town, so even though it's not the best-tasting barbeque you've ever had—and every once in a while, you might find some buckshot in your brisket—they do a ton of business.

I'm happy for them. I might not ever be on speaking terms with Agnes again, and I still low-key hate her guts, but ... I guess we came to some kind of a truce. When Wes kicked them out of my house after the riot, Jimbo forced Agnes to apologize for having Wes arrested and for tying me up, and I apologized for knocking her out and stealing their truck. But I did not *apologize for running over Carter's foot. He deserved that shit.*

Carter ended up getting a job as a police officer, and get this, his first assignment as a rookie is to patrol the area around the Pritchard Park Mall and make sure there's no resurgence of Bony activity. He's a real mall cop now! Q would die! Actually, I'm sure she already knows. Her mattress is probably a regular stop on his route. Gross. They deserve each other.

My phone dings from somewhere inside my diaper bag.

"Hold on, little lady," I say, pinching my munchkin's toes. "I just gotta ... err ..." *I dig around in the bottomless bag as Lily watches me in amusement. "Got it!"*

I yank my phone out and illuminate the screen, giggling at Michelle's all-caps text.

THREE MONTHS OF MATERNITY LEAVE IS BULLSHIT. IS IT NEXT WEEK YET?

I smirk and drop the phone back in my bag. I always thought I would go to school to become a nurse like my mama, but I think I've seen enough bloodshed for one lifetime. After the Green Mile riot, Michelle insisted that I keep working as her co-reporter and personal assistant. I couldn't tell her no after everything she'd done for me, but I also realized that I didn't want to. Nobody had ever listened to me until Michelle handed me a tube of red lipstick and a microphone. She showed me that I don't have to roll over and let bad things happen to me anymore. To the people I love. I can fight for them with nothing more than a camera and a press pass.

Only now, I do it under my new name, Rain Parker, instead of Stella McCartney.

My mama's wedding rings gleam on my left hand as I walk my short nails up baby Lily's chubby thigh. I blow a raspberry on her squishy cheek and feel my insides turn to mush when she lets out a tiny, breathy giggle.

I had no idea that Wes had saved Mama's rings for me until he surprised me on Mother's Day, a few days after the assassination. He took me to the Fulton County Courthouse, and in the exact same spot where Governor Steele had sentenced him to death, Officer Marcel Elliott pronounced us husband and wife. When I asked Wes why he wanted to do it there, he said it felt like "a nice fuck you."

And it did. It felt perfect actually. Lamar walked me down the aisle. Officer Hoyt and Officer MacArthur were our maid of honor and best man. Michelle and Flip were in the audience, taking pictures and videos, and Wes even invited his mama, who cried like a baby the whole time.

After Lily was born, Wes had a tattoo artist transform the wilted pink flower on his ribs into a vibrant orange tiger lily. He said he didn't want to be marked by what had happened to his sister anymore. He wanted to move on. And a big part of that was letting his mama back into his life. Rhonda has stepped up and become the mother he and I both needed. She's clean and sober, she has a job and an apartment, and she comes over for dinner every Sunday. We don't let her babysit though. Wes's trust only goes so far. Besides, we have Lamar for that. At least, until he goes off to college.

I turn my head and smile as Wes saunters over. He's wearing his blue Hawaiian shirt—my favorite—and carrying a tray full of the world's most mediocre barbeque. We don't normally eat at the Renshaws' place—things are still pretty tense between us—but today is special. This is the anniversary of the day we met, right here in this very restaurant—or as Wes likes to call it, the day he kidnapped me at gunpoint from Burger Palace. But he knows he saved me that day. I was as lost as a person could possibly be. My house was a crime scene. My parents, the victims. My friends were gone. My boyfriend had abandoned me. I was being jumped by half the town while high as a kite on my daddy's pain pills. And the world was supposed to end in a matter of days. All I wanted to do was stay numb and die.

All Wes wanted was someone to help him survive.

But somehow, together, we figured out how to live.

Wes's full lips curl into a smug grin the second he catches me staring, and my heart does a little backflip. I can't believe I get to keep him. I can't believe we actually got our happily ever af—

Without warning, the lights go out, and the doors on either side of the restaurant burst wide open. Police sirens blare, and blue lights splash across the darkened walls as hundreds of shoving, screaming bodies run full speed into the restaurant. The customers all around us stand up on their chairs and benches, and they're all wearing riot cop gear—gas masks and shields and billy clubs and guns. When I look back at Wes, he's gone, swallowed by the chanting, fist-thrusting mob.

Chairs and punches are thrown at cops. Tear gas and bullets fly into the crowd. Noxious smoke fills the room as Lily begins to cough and cry behind me.

I pull her blanket over her face and stand up on my seat, hugging the car seat to my chest as I try to find Wes in the crowd. I scream his name, but I can't see or hear anything through my own stinging, watering eyes and the painful wails of my baby girl. I get closer to the edge of the crowd, searching through the blinding, burning smoke when someone reaches out and grabs me, pulling me in.

The crush of fighting, clawing, panicking bodies is so forceful that I can't breathe. I can't even move, except when they shove me in one direction or another. Someone climbs onto my back, trying to get above the crowd, and my knees buckle under the weight. I curl my body around Lily's car seat, trying to protect her as feet and fists and billy clubs rain down on my head and back.

"Help!" I scream as loud as I can. "Help! I have a baby!"

Then, two hands reach out from the smoky darkness and grip me by the shoulders.

"Baby," Wes whispers, gently shaking me. "You fell asleep nursing again."

I open my eyes with a gasp to find a shirtless green-eyed man smiling down at me and a sleeping infant in my arms.

"Oh my God," I cry, clutching Lily to my chest. "Oh, thank God." My heart is pounding as my brain sluggishly tries to grasp the fact that we're not going to be trampled to death.

"Another nightmare?" Wes asks, his dark eyebrows pulling together as he crouches down next to me.

I'm sitting in a rocking chair in my old bedroom—Lily's room now—in the dark. My white nursing gown seems to glow in the moonlight, and my breast is still exposed from her midnight feeding.

I nod and reach a hand out to cup Wes's concerned face. I thought the nightmares would go away after April 23, but they're just different now. Instead of demonic horsemen, it's real monsters. Ones we've already defeated whose ghosts now haunt us while we sleep.

But that's okay. As long as I get to wake up in this beautiful dream, I don't mind a few nightmares now and then.

"You okay?"

I smile and nod again. "Better than I was a few minutes ago," I whisper, echoing the flirty response he gave me from inside his jail cell.

Wes smiles and kisses me on the forehead. "Here, I'll put her down."

He scoops the sleeping bundle out of my arms, and I watch, awestruck, as he lazily carries her across the room. She's barely the size of one of his biceps, but he's so gentle and loving with her. He kisses her fuzzy head before laying her down in the middle of her crib, his back muscles rippling as he leans over. Wes is wearing nothing but a pair of gray sweatpants, and when he turns to face me, his lips curl into a sinister smirk. I follow his gaze down to my chest and laugh silently as I go to pull my nursing gown back up.

"Don't you dare," Wes growls, stalking toward me.

He started a construction company, rebuilding houses that had been damaged during Operation April 23, and one of the perks of the job is this body. Good Lord. He was cut before, but now he belongs on the cover of a romance novel.

A really gritty one where the hero has tattoos and drives a motorcycle and cusses a lot.

Wes reaches his hands out, and I take them, letting him pull me to my feet. Then, I let out a surprised yelp as he grabs my fuller than usual ass and lifts me off the ground. My legs wrap around his waist, and my arms wrap around his shoulders as he chuckles softly, smiling against my parted lips.

"How long until she wakes up?" he whispers, carrying me out of the nursery.

I cringe as we walk past Lamar's room, thankful that his door is shut and lights are off.

"Two or three hours, depending on how long I was asleep."

"Challenge accepted." He smirks, kicking the master bedroom door shut behind him.

When we moved back in, we got all new furniture, painted the walls a dark gray, and I even had a pastor from my old church come and say a blessing, just in case. We made it our own, and I love it. It's not *home*—Wes is my home—but it's not scary anymore either. It's just a house—wood and nails and screws and paint ... and bedroom doors that lock.

Holding me up with one arm, Wes turns the silvery latch on the doorknob. The *click* sends an excited shiver down my spine. I tighten my thighs around his waist and let my longer hair fall around us as I tilt my head down to kiss his parted lips. Wes captures my mouth with an appreciative moan. Squeezing my ass with one hand, he reaches up and hooks a finger into the top edge of my nursing gown, yanking the stretchy, gauzy white fabric down until my other breast is exposed as well.

"That's better," he murmurs into my mouth as his rough palm caresses my tender, swollen flesh.

I arch my back as his thumb swirls around my oversensitized nipple, breaking our kiss and allowing Wes to suck and nip his way along my jaw and neck.

I can feel him pressed against me through his sweatpants, so reaching between us, I slide my fingers into his waistband and shimmy it down over his swollen length. Hot, velvety flesh fills my hand, and I lick my lips as I pump him slowly.

"Fuck," Wes growls, his teeth scraping my collarbone as he grabs my ass with both hands again. "I want you just like this."

I squeal as he pushes away from the door, tightening my grip around his broad shoulders as he crosses the room and sits on the edge of the bed. I land on his lap with my knees spread on either side of him and moan when he bends me backward and pulls one straining pink nipple into his mouth. His heavy cock presses against my slippery center, and my hips grind against it instinctively, needing more.

Wes's tongue swirls and flicks and sucks until my breasts begin to tingle and burn.

"Wes!" I hiss, trying to pull away, but he only chuckles and continues his assault. Milk drips from my other nipple and down my breast as I grab his head and try to pull him off me. "Wes, you're gonna get milk in your—"

Holding my stare with blazing emerald eyes, Wes slowly drags the flat of his tongue over my nipple, collecting every drop of milk that falls.

Swallowing, he brings his lips back to my mouth. "I told you …" he rasps, lifting my ass until the head of his cock drags through my folds and presses against my entrance. "I want you just … like … this."

I sink down onto him as he claims my mouth, swirling and exploring with his expert tongue as he guides my body up and down his length. I run my fingers through his hair and cup his chiseled face in my hands as I kiss the mouth that he worships me with.

I don't deserve him. I don't deserve a love like this. It overwhelms me, filling me up until I spill over, milk dripping from my breasts and tears cascading down my cheeks as I come again and again into the night.

But my husband doesn't care. He licks up every drop that I spill and fills me up again.

That's the thing about life after April 23. When you fall in love at the end of the world, you live every day like it's your last.

At least, until the baby wakes up.

I hope you enjoyed The Rain Trilogy! If you did, I think you'll love SKIN. *It's a gritty, taboo, forbidden love story full of '90s nostalgia, dark humor, and heart-wrenching teenage angst. Plus, the entire 44 Chapters About 4 Men series is being adapted into a steamy dramedy for Netflix called* Sex/Life! *Read on for a sneak peek!*

mybook.to/bbeastonskin

SKIN
Chapter One

Positive, positive, positive.

It was my first day of tenth grade, and I was *not* going to be nervous. I was going to think deliriously happy, positive thoughts. I was going to skip down the familiar halls of Peach State High School with a bounce in my steel-toed step and a self-confident smirk on my face because *this* was going to be the year that Lance Hightower finally proclaimed his undying love for me. It just *had* to be.

I wasn't going to beat myself up about the fact that I had been trying and failing to make out with that boy since middle school, *nor* was I going to focus on the fact that I still had zero breasts at the age of fifteen. No, I was going to fantasize about all the wildly spontaneous, highly public ways Lance might choose to propose. After all, I'd just learned—thanks to my dad's unhealthy obsession with watching CNN—that it was totally legal for teenagers to get married in Georgia as long as they had written permission from one of their parents. That wouldn't be a problem for me, seeing as how I'd perfected my mom's signature by the age of twelve.

I was also feeling pretty damn good because I knew I'd picked out the *perfect* back-to-school outfit. My trademark black combat boots and wingtip eyeliner were firmly in place; I was rocking some kick-ass black spiderweb fishnets under my favorite pair of too-short-for-school cutoff jeans; my gray midriff T-shirt boasted the logo of an indie band I was absolutely *certain* no one had heard of; and my arms were practically pinned to my sides with the weight of a thousand metal, beaded, and leather bracelets. Also, I'd started smoking over the summer (for real this time), and my shorter, edgier, more angled haircut got tons of compliments, even from Lance (which was the whole point).

Of course, all my positivity went to shit as soon as I made it to the church parking lot for a smoke between classes.

It was no secret at Peach State High School that if you wanted to do something bad, all you had to do was walk out past the rust buckets in the student parking lot, step over a guardrail, and clear the tree line. That was it. On the other side, you would find yourself in a magical wooded wonderland called *the church parking lot*, a place where kids could escape the oppression of our overcrowded, underfunded public learning institution to laugh, smoke, and be merry (if only for seven minutes at a time). The church was a long, abandoned one-room chapel that was in the process of being reclaimed by the forest, and its parking lot was nothing more than a patch of gravel, but to a band of misfit teenagers, it was heaven.

Or so I'd heard. I'd never actually ventured out to the church parking lot during school hours before, but this was my year. I just knew that on the other side of those woods, I'd find *my people*. Artsy, quirky, free spirits who shared my appreciation for alternative rock, avant-garde art, and experimental photography. The group that would embrace me with open arms, invite me to sit with them at lunch, and host raging keggers like the ones I saw on TV.

Instead, what I found was the most intimidating group of human beings I'd ever seen in one place. *Fuck me.* Those kids were cool with a capital *C* and twenty-seven *O*s. They had *multicolored* hair. They had *piercings*. They had expertly painted red lips that I could never pull off with my redheaded complexion. And the accessories—more chokers and studded belts than you could shake a flannel shirt at. One girl was even wearing denim overalls with the legs cut off and one shoulder strap undone. I wasn't punk rock; I was Punky fucking Brewster.

At least my combat boots were vintage and my eyeliner was flawless. That I knew for sure. I'd been perfecting that goddamn cat eye since the age of ten. As long as I kept my grades up, my hippie parents never really gave a shit how much makeup I wore, or what I dressed like, or how many F-bombs I dropped at the dinner table. (And by dinner table, I mean, my TV tray in the living room.) So I stood on the periphery and tried not to stare, clinging to both my Camel Light and the hope that someone would at least admire my eyeliner art.

I watched the guys all squeezing and kneading and nuzzling their girlfriends, and I watched their girlfriends' giant boobs bounce with every giggle.

I bet they have sex, I thought. *Every one of them.*

My face and neck suddenly felt itchy and hot.

Annnnd, now I'm blushing. Fantastic.

I dropped my head and stared down at my boots, which I could see with no problem at all, thanks to my complete and total lack of breasts.

Why can't the heroin-chic look still be in? Maybe it'll make a comeback. Please let it make a comeback.

Everyone out there looked like Drew Barrymore, and I looked like somebody drew a smiley face and freckles on one of Drew Barrymore's pinkie fingers.

My BFF, Juliet Iha, was supposed to be meeting me out there, but after a few minutes, it became pretty clear that she'd flaked out on me yet again.

She's probably out here somewhere, fogging up Tony's car windows.

Juliet was dating a grown-ass man who'd dropped out of high school at least a decade prior and never seemed to have anywhere pressing to be. Without fail, that creepy fucker always seemed to be lurking around wherever we were, leaning up against his busted-ass, old Corvette like an actor cast to play the part of Potential Child Molester in a PSA from 1985. Tony definitely gave me the "no feeling," but Juliet really liked him, and he was old enough to buy us cigarettes, so I kept my mouth shut.

Just as I was about to stamp out my Camel Light and drag my sad ass back inside, I felt two solid arms wrap around my body from behind. One snaked around my rib cage, and the other hoisted me up from behind my knees. Before I could scream, *Rape!* I was flipped completely upside down and plopped, ass up, on the shoulder of a giant. It wasn't until he swatted my backside and laughed in that glorious, soft tone that made my body go all warm and bubbly that I realized I'd been captured by my immortal beloved, Lance Hightower.

Lance Motherfucking Hightower. God, he was perfection. Lance was in my grade, but he was easily half a foot taller than most of the upperclassmen and already filled out like a man. Dude had a permanent five o'clock shadow at the age of fifteen. Despite having the dark, chiseled features of a Disney prince, Lance was a punk rock icon. Every day, he sported the same effortlessly badass look: faded black Converse, faded black jeans, and a faded black hoodie covered in patches advertising obscure European underground punk bands and anarchist political statements that he painted on with Wite-Out during class. That hoodie was so well known, it probably had its own fanzine.

Topping off all that faded black packaging was an equally faded, slightly grown-out green Mohawk. It probably would have added another three inches to Lance's already six-foot-three-inch frame if he ever bothered to style it, and the color totally brought out the green flecks in his coppery-hazel eyes.

Oh, Lance. I had been obsessing over him since the sixth grade. I admired him from afar until last year when we fatefully wound up sharing a pottery wheel in art class. The flirting that ensued was incendiary. Atomic. The only problem was that I was technically "dating" his best friend, Colton, at the time, so things never really got off the ground.

Then, a goddamn miracle happened. Colton upped and moved to Las Vegas to live with his dad right in the middle of the spring semester. I pretended to be sad for a few hours, out of respect. Then, I immediately resumed my campaign to become the mother of Lance's children. The only problem was that Lance and I didn't have any classes together, so all of my flirting had to be done in seven-minute increments between periods. But in tenth grade, what I was sure would be the best year ever, Lance and I had been assigned to the same motherfucking lunch period. I was going to be sporting his last name by May. I just knew it.

"Lance! What are you doing?" I giggled. "Put me down! I can't breathe with your shoulder in my stomach!"

Lance chuckled. "That's so sweet. You take my breath away too, girl."

God, his voice. Like fucking angel bells. For such a big dude with such an in-your-face look, Lance's voice was surprisingly soft and flirty. It was a total mindfuck the first few times I'd heard that sweet sound come out of that ruggedly handsome face. And the pick-up lines. I swear to Jesus he had a new one every time I saw him. I fucking loved Lance Hightower.

I giggled harder, which made my stomach hurt even worse, and swatted at his perfect, patch-covered ass. "Put me down, asshole!"

Before he could comply, we heard a sickening smack from across the parking lot, followed by a deep voice shouting, "Say it again, motherfucker!"

Lance held on tight to the backs of my thighs and swung around to face the commotion, making me even dizzier as I grabbed his waist and peeked around his side to see what was going on.

Although I couldn't make out exactly what was happening due to the blood rushing into my eyeballs, I recognized the assailant immediately. I'd never met him, but I'd heard stories. Everybody had. He was "the skinhead," the only one at our entire four-thousand-student suburban high school.

I'd noticed him in ninth grade because he was literally the only person I'd ever seen wear suspenders (skinny ones, called braces) to school. In a world full of studded belts and chain wallets, that motherfucker wore suspenders—the epitome of dorkiness—and made them look as scary as the stripes on a venomous snake.

A snake who was standing about thirty feet away, looming over a little skater boy who was clutching his rapidly swelling jaw and trying not to cry.

When the kid didn't say whatever it was the skinhead wanted to hear, he buried his fist deep in Skater Boy's stomach, causing him to lurch forward and release a noise so guttural, I assumed something important must have ruptured.

With his left hand, the skinhead yanked the guy's head back by his chin-length brown hair and screamed into his terrified face, "Say that shit again!"

I felt like I might throw up. My heart was racing, and my head was pounding from being upside down, but all I could register was a sickening sense of helplessness and humiliation for that poor kid. I'd been raised in a house with pacifist parents and no siblings. I'd never seen anyone get hit before—at least, not in real life—and I felt that punch as if it had been dealt directly to me.

In a way, it had. That punch shook me to my core. It showed me that senseless violence and cruelty really did exist, and they came wearing boots and braces.

When Skater Boy remained silent, the skinhead responded by shoving his head so hard that he flew sideways and landed, hands- and face-first, in the gravel. His body slid a few feet before finally coming to a stop. The kid scrambled to pull himself into a ball and made little screeching sounds as if struggling to suppress a scream.

Instead of attacking again, his assailant began to circle him slowly, like a hawk. I held my breath and gripped Lance's waist tighter, ignoring the throbbing in my eyeballs, and watched upside down as he assessed his victim. I was horrified by how calm he was. He wasn't angry or upset, just … calculating. Cold and calculating.

The skinhead approached the kid, who was now trembling and sobbing quietly, and slowly rolled him onto his side with one very heavy-looking combat boot. Still curled up tightly, Skater Boy choked out what sounded like a muffled, garbled apology. Unimpressed, his attacker bent down toward the kid's face and placed a meaty hand firmly on the side of his head. I didn't know what he was doing at first, but when the brown-haired kid started screaming in pain, I realized that the skinhead was pressing his face into the gravel.

"What was that?" he asked calmly, tilting his head to one side as if genuinely interested, the veins in his muscular arm beginning to bulge as he applied more pressure.

"I'm sorry! I'm sorry! I didn't mean it! Please stop! Please!" The scream at the end of his apology got increasingly louder as that heartless, hairless demon crushed his face further into the jagged rocks.

The skinhead released Skater Boy's head and stood up. I exhaled and felt my body relax into Lance's shoulder and then watched in disbelief as he kicked the kid directly in the lower back one, two, three times. By the time my eyes registered the strikes and my ears registered the resulting scream, it was over, but my spirit was forever changed.

It said, *These people fuck and they fight and you'd better get used to it, little girl.*

Lance set me down, slowly, and I wrapped myself around him like a tree trunk for stability.

I stared, partially hidden behind Lance's sturdy frame, as the skinhead idly spit on the ground next to his victim, lit a cigarette, and walked with long, confident strides … directly toward me. The gravel crunched under the weight of his steel-toed boots, which emerged from the bottom of a tightly rolled pair of blue jeans. Bright red laces wound themselves up the front of his boots, and bright red braces slashed across his muscular chest—a chest which was wrapped in a tight black T-shirt emblazoned with the word *Lonsdale.*

Steeling myself behind Lance's comforting presence, I mustered the courage to peek up at the skinhead's face. It was like looking at a ghost. He resembled a person, but there was no color to help differentiate his features.

His skin was white. His hair and eyelashes were virtually transparent, and his eyes … his eyes were a ghostly, icy gray-blue. Like a zombie's. And when they landed on mine, my hair stood up on end so violently, it felt like a million tiny needles were stabbing me at once.

Those zombie eyes flicked from mine to Lance's with a look of irritation as he approached. I could feel a buzzing electric current of malice radiating off of him well before he reached us, and I winced as he passed, as if bracing myself for his wrath. When nothing happened, I carefully opened my eyes, relieved by the change in the atmosphere. The static charge was gone. *He* was gone. But he left a broken boy, a still-burning Marlboro Red, and my scattered wits on the ground in his wake.

As traumatizing as my first smoke break had been, that wasn't the reason I was having trouble concentrating in my honors economics class. It was because as soon as the bell rang, I knew I was going to have lunch with Lance Motherfucking Hightower—and my best friends, Juliet and August—but mostly *Lance Motherfucking Hightower*.

I saw the teacher's mouth moving, but all I could hear were my own racing thoughts. *I'm totally going to sit next to him. But what if I get there first? Will he sit next to me? Maybe I should hide and wait for Lance to sit down and then run over and sit next to him before anyone else has a chance. Yes. Totally. Then, I'll find an excuse to touch him. And I'll laugh at all his jokes. Not that it'll be hard. He's so funny. And beautiful. And tall. And edgy. And fucking dreamy.*

When the bell finally rang, I jumped up as if my ass were on fire and sprinted to the bathroom to touch up my makeup. Then, I hightailed it to the cafeteria to scope out the cool-kid table. Every punk, goth, druggie, drama nerd, vegan, hippie, skater, and metal head at our high school wanted a spot at that table, and even though he was only in tenth grade, Lance was the reigning king of them all. Getting a spot next to him was going to be tricky.

When I ran up, I realized that not only had Lance already taken his seat—right in the middle of the fifteen-foot-long table—but goddamn Colton Hart was also sitting right next to him.

Shit.

Shit, fuck, damn.

When the hell did he get back?

Colton was going to be a major fucking obstacle in my quest to become Mrs. Hightower. He was the world's biggest cockblocker—that was actually how I'd wound up dating him in the first place. He'd just kept inserting himself between Lance and me until I gave in and let him kiss me. Which he did. A lot. Don't get me wrong; making out with Colton Hart was a spectacular way to spend an afternoon. He was super fucking cute. And cocky. And sarcastic. And *bad*. But he just wasn't Lance.

But technically, he *was* still my boyfriend.

Oh my God. What if he thinks we're still a couple? No. There's no way. He never even called me after he left. He probably screwed all kinds of future strippers while he was living with his dad and brother in Las Vegas, and now, I'm small potatoes. I'm just the girl he left back in Georgia who wouldn't let him touch her boobs. It's totally fine. No. Big. Deal.

As I walked up, I couldn't help but admit to myself that he did look damn good. Better than I'd remembered. He was like a wicked Peter Pan. Spiky brown hair with blond tips, pointy ears, perfect male model smile. When he'd left, he'd had a definite punk rock style, like a mini Lance, but I guessed his skateboarding older brother had worn off on him while he was in Vegas. Colton had traded in his boots for a pair of shell-toed Adidas, his bondage pants for a pair of black cargo shorts, and his studded belt for a chain wallet.

There was a spot open next to both of them, but I made sure to sit next to Lance just to establish whose girl I was. Or at least, whose girl I wanted to be.

As soon as I walked up and set down my backpack, Colton cried, "Kitten! Get your ass over here!"

I glanced down at Lance, who made no attempt to rescue me, and sighed. Getting up and walking around him, I embraced Colton, who had stood up and was waiting for me with open arms.

Feigning excitement, I said, "Hey, Colton! Oh my God! When did you get back?" as he squeezed the shit out of me.

"Last week," he said, rocking me from side to side. "My moms got lonely. What can I say? Living without me is hard." He pulled away and gave me a wink. "Isn't it?"

I rolled my eyes in response, but I couldn't help my traitorous smile. He really was cute. And he smelled squeaky clean. Like a girl. Colton had a thing for products—hair products, skin products. He was vain as hell and proud of it.

After giving me the once-over, Colton whistled. "Look at you. You're making me wonder why I left in the first place." I blushed and looked at the ground. "You wanna ride the bus home with me this afternoon? Just like old times? My mom just stocked the fridge with PBR ..."

Yes. No. Kinda?

Before I could say something stupid, Juliet swooped in and rescued me. "She's riding home with me, Colton. BB is *my* bitch now."

Juliet set her tray down across from my backpack and glared at Colton. She never liked him. For starters, I'd kind of forgotten she existed after he and I started dating. I just started riding the bus home with him every day instead of her—a dick move, I knew, but I was fourteen, and he was my first real boyfriend. I was pretty sure "first real boyfriend" would be accepted as just cause for a temporary insanity plea in a court of law. But Juliet also hated him because I'd kind of blabbed to her about how hard he'd been pressuring me to do *stuff* with him. I would have given in, too, if he hadn't told me he was moving. I was *not* giving it up to somebody who was just going to leave in a few weeks. Besides, I was saving myself for Lance Hightower.

Colton glared back at her for a minute. Then, he smiled and asked, "Can I watch?"

We all laughed, even Lance, who was watching the show with piqued interest. When I sat back down next to him (and away from the pheromone cloud that was Colton Hart), I let out a shaky breath and stared straight ahead at Juliet, thanking her silently. Lance, who had resumed his conversation with Colton, reached under the table and gave my thigh a reassuring squeeze. He left his hand there, and I prayed to every deity I'd ever learned the names of that he would slide it up a little farther. He didn't, but he did absentmindedly lace his fingers through the holes in my fishnets as he spoke, causing me to stop breathing long enough to almost actually fucking die.

My mind was sufficiently scrambled when August, whom I hadn't even noticed, spoke to me from the spot next to Juliet.

I had been friends with August Embry since first grade, when we wound up in the same first grade class. Back then, he was a shy, pudgy little thing with no friends, and I was a bossy, talkative little thing with no friends, so we'd just clicked. I loved him like a brother.

August was still a shy, round little thing. He hid his warm chocolate-brown eyes behind a curtain of dyed black hair, and every night, he painted his fingernails black to match. Of course, every day, he would pick them clean again—leaving little black flecks behind, like a trail of breadcrumbs everywhere he went. August was the sweetest, most sensitive person I'd ever met.

I could tell from his body language that August wasn't exactly happy to see Colton either. He and Lance had become kind of close since Colton left. They both liked the same terrible music and competed over who had the best, rarest punk records in their collections, so Lance getting his best friend back didn't bode well for August.

"Hey, A!" I cheered, trying way too hard to sound like a girl who *didn't* have a boy's fingers stroking her inner thigh at that exact moment. "I didn't know you had this lunch period too! Are you growing your hair out? I love it!"

August just smiled and looked down at the food on his tray, which he suddenly decided needed rearranging.

I turned to ask Juliet if I could ride home with her and Tony, but she was gone. Her stuff was still on the table though, and I thought I could hear the sound of her voice. As much as it killed me, I moved Lance's hand so that I could peek under the table. There she was, sitting cross-legged on the floor, talking on her cell phone, which was strictly forbidden at school. There was only one person she could possibly be talking to.

"Juliet," I whispered.

She looked up, annoyed. "What?"

"Ask Tony if he minds giving me a ride this afternoon."

She winked at me and whispered into her brick-sized Nokia, "Hey. BB's gonna ride home with us this afternoon, okay?" She gave me a thumbs-up after hearing his response.

Cool.

Just then, I felt Lance's hand press down on the back of my head and saw his crotch rise up to meet the side of my face. I screamed and tried to sit up, causing my head to smash Lance's hand into the underside of the table. Laughter erupted from the cafeteria as I emerged, red-faced, looking like a girl who'd just eaten a punk rocker's cock for lunch.

I glared at Lance, trying my best to look angry, but his eyes were shut, and he was laughing so hard, he wasn't even making noise. Just the sight of that giant, Mohawked motherfucker smiling ear to ear had me reduced to a puddle of swoon juice in an instant. I burst out laughing right along with him and anxiously glanced over at Colton.

He was laughing, too, but his smile didn't quite reach his eyes. Guess he didn't appreciate the entire lunchroom thinking *his* girlfriend was giving his best friend a BJ under the table.

In that moment, I knew that Colton wasn't going to be a problem. Lance had just established, with dramatic flair and in front of everyone, that I was his girl.

All the hope and hormones had my insides on the verge of spontaneous combustion, so I barely noticed the loud *slam* that came from somewhere behind me. I hardly felt the resulting shudder that rippled down the length of the lunch table. And I didn't turn to look for the source until the faces of all my friends fell and glanced anxiously over my shoulder. Swiveling around on my stool, I followed everyone's gaze to an empty seat at the end of the table.

Um, anyway. Where was I? Oh, right. Planning my spring wedding …

That afternoon, I fought against the current of teenagers fleeing the building, dragging my swollen backpack behind me by one strap, in search of my new locker. According to my homeroom teacher, my old one had to be torn out over the summer to make room for the new science lab. She had given me a little slip of paper with my new locker number and combination on it, saying only that it was "somewhere over on C Hall." I couldn't wait to find that shit so that I could finally offload a few of the ten-pound textbooks I'd been given that day.

Clutching the piece of paper with my new digits on it, I scanned dozens of identical metal doors until I found the one I'd been assigned. It was almost at the end of the hallway, of course, near the exit doors that led out to the student parking lot. I felt relief wash over me immediately.

My first day of tenth grade was a wrap, and overall, it had been a smashing success. I'd smoked with the coolest of the cool kids; wound up with the same lunch period as Lance, Juliet, and August; got a bunch of compliments on my fishnets and new haircut; and now, I had a new locker on the same hall as all the seniors. Okay, so maybe it took me a few attempts to get my code to work, but once that shit was open, it was glorious.

As I bent over to take the last load of books out of my straining backpack, I stopped short, paralyzed by the sight of two black steel-toed boots with blood-red laces planted just inches away from my face ... and pointing directly at me.

Fuck.

Fuck, fuck, fuck.

Not him. Anyone but him.

I took my time gathering my stuff, hoping that ignoring him would make him magically disappear. When I finally stood up, arms full of books, I mustered all the courage I had and looked him in the eye.

Zombie eyes. God, his irises were such a pale, pale gray-blue that his pupils looked like two endless black holes in contrast. Two black holes that were sucking me in.

Speak dumbass!

"Um, hey," I said in a voice that didn't sound like it belonged to me.

He didn't reply. He simply cocked his head to the side and studied me with those cold, dead eyes. It was the same way he'd looked at the kid in the parking lot, right before he smashed his face into the ground.

Swallowing hard, I forced myself to break the silence.

"I'm sorry, do you need something?" I squeaked out, trying to sound cute and tiny. I blinked and opened my eyes a little wider, feeling like a woodland creature in danger of being squished by a massive black boot.

"Your shit is in front of my locker," he said. His voice was deep and clear and humorless.

"Oh my God! I'm so sorry!" Tripping over myself, I slid my lightened backpack behind me with my foot.

The skinhead immediately grasped the metal latch on the locker beside mine and gave the lower left corner of the door a swift kick, causing the fucker to pop right open, no code necessary. I shuddered involuntarily as my mind conjured images of that same boot landing square in the back of a scared little skater boy just a few hours earlier.

Afraid that he could smell my fear, I quickly hid my face behind the metal door of my own locker, busying myself by arranging my books and notebooks by size, color, the Dewey fucking decimal system, *anything*. Then, something occurred to me. Before I knew it, my stupid mouth was moving.

"Shouldn't you be suspended?"

I felt my face blush crimson as the blond with the buzzcut slammed his locker shut and asked, point blank, "Why?"

Was he teasing me? We both knew what the fuck he had done.

"That, that fight. Today. In the church parking lot," I said into my locker.

Thinking about that … *attack* had my blood pumping into my extremities and my mind screaming for me to run. I turned and went back to my organizing, hoping to conceal the terror and embarrassment that I was sure my big, dumb doe eyes were doing a shit job of concealing. My face always snitched on me, broadcasting my every thought. My every feeling.

My thin metal makeshift shield vibrated as he spoke, "I didn't get suspended for the same reason you're not sitting in detention right now for smoking. That shit happened off-campus."

"Is he okay?"

God! My fucking mouth! Filter, BB. Filter!

"Who? That little pussy wipe from the parking lot? He'll be pissing blood for a week, but he'll live."

Slowly, the door I had been cowering behind began to close. Moving out of the way so that the metal wouldn't graze my face, I reluctantly turned toward the boy with the cadaverous eyes, who was deliberately pushing my locker shut. Once the door was firmly closed and I had nowhere left to hide, Zombie Eyes leaned toward me and reached around my body with his left hand. I squeezed my eyelids shut and braced myself for something violent and potentially bloody to happen.

With his voice lowered so that only I could hear, he said, "If you hit a fucker in the kidney hard enough … right here"—I suddenly felt a thick finger jam directly into one side of my lower back—"he'll piss blood."

My eyes shot open, and I immediately wished that they hadn't. That gray-blue gaze was way too close, too intense. His finger lingered way too long, and there was a crackle in the air that had my senses on high alert.

Danger! Danger! Skinhead Boy is fucking touching you! He could kill you with that finger, BB! Kill you and eat your brains!

But those zombie eyes wouldn't let me move. Up close, they were so clear. Like two crystal balls that I wished would give me a glimpse into this twisted creature's soul. In my curious state of hypnosis, again, words tumbled unbidden from my mouth.

"Why'd you hit him?"

After a pause long enough to let me hope that maybe I hadn't actually asked my question out loud, he answered, "Because he called your little boyfriend a faggot."

About three million follow-up questions slammed into my throat at once:

A) Why would a Neo-Nazi looking motherfucker beat someone up that he doesn't even know for calling some other dude he doesn't know a faggot?

B) Shouldn't he have given the kid a high five instead?

C) Why would he call Lance my boyfriend? Lance is NOT my boyfriend. I mean, I want him to be my boyfriend. Jesus, I want to ride him like a pony everywhere I go and have all of his babies, but he's not my boyfriend.

D) Why would anyone think Lance was gay in the first place? He's sooo dreamy.

But the only thing I could squeak out was, "You were defending Lance?"

I never knew an eye roll could be so terrifying. *Shit.* I'd done it. I'd finally pissed him off with all my stupid fucking questions. Why did I always have to talk to the scary ones?

My mom still loved to tell people about the time I'd picked up my Happy Meal and sat down with a group of leather-clad bikers at McDonald's when I was three just so that I could ask the gnarliest-looking one why he had a ponytail. According to her, my exact words were, "Only girls are 'apposed to have ponytails."

My curiosity was going to get me straight murdered one day.

The skinhead, who now looked positively murderous himself, removed his hand from my back and placed it on my locker, just above my head. Cocking his head to the side again, he watched me, as if mulling over the best way to skin me alive, and of course, I just stood there, blinking up at him like a fucking dumbass.

Basic bodily functions like speaking, breathing, and running were completely out of my grasp. It was as if I'd been cornered by a coiled rattlesnake. A rattlesnake that just so happened to smell like dryer sheets, cigarettes, and a sweet hint of cologne.

"No," he said. "I was defending *you.*"

Too much. It was too intense. I broke eye contact and took a step backward, landing on the backpack I had forgotten was behind me and almost losing my balance. Turning around to pick it up, I took a deep breath and tried to regroup before facing him again. When I did, his ghostly eyes were crinkled at the corners, and his mouth was tipped up just slightly on one side. *Fucker.* He was actually enjoying watching me squirm.

Smirk still in place, he said, "When I was outside, I heard that little shit telling his buddy about the hard-on he had for 'the little redhead in the fishnets.' Couldn't argue with him there, Punk. I think you gave every guy in that parking lot a semi."

My face was suddenly on fire. *Oh God. I'm blushing! Is this really happening?*

He continued, but his smirk had been replaced by something that made my blood run cold. "When he saw that giant motherfucker's hands on you, he turned into a pissy little bitch." He spat the last word out through gritted teeth. "Told his buddy you must love taking it up the ass to be wasting your time with that queer."

Gulp. Breathe. What?

"S-so, so you punched him?"

The zombie-eyed skinhead leaned down toward my ear and didn't stop until I could feel his hot, venomous breath on my neck. "I. Beat. His. Fucking. Ass."

My limbs were moving on their own accord. Legs stumbling backward. Hands fumbling with backpack straps. "Um, thanks?" I mumbled, eyes darting everywhere but his. "I, uh, have to go … I'm gonna miss my … thanks again …"

"Knight," he announced as I turned and sprinted for the double doors. "Thanks, *Knight.*"

Fuck me.

Read the rest of BB and Knight's story at: https://mybook.to/bbeastonskin

PLAYLIST

THIS PLAYLIST IS A collection of songs that I either mentioned in *Dying for Rain* or that I felt illustrated a feeling or a scene from the book. I am grateful to each and every one of the brilliant artists listed below. Their creativity fuels mine.

You can stream the playlist for free on Spotify: https://spoti.fi/380bOey

"Army of Me" by Björk

"Artist and Repertoire" by Envy on the Coast

"Bandito" by Twenty One Pilots

"Black Out Days" by Phantogram

"Champion" by Bishop Briggs

"Champion" by Fall Out Boy

"False God" by Taylor Swift

"Graveyard" by Halsey

"Hallelujah" by Paramore

"I Will Follow You into the Dark" by Death Cab for Cutie

"Jumpsuit" by Twenty One Pilots

"My Cell" by The Lumineers

"Neon Gravestones" by Twenty One Pilots

"Nightmare" by Halsey

"ocean eyes" by Billie Eilish

"Oh No!!!" by grandson

"Prison Sex" by TOOL

"Slip on the Moon" by DREAMCAR

"Start a Riot" by Duckwrth, Shaboozey

"Team" by Lorde

"The Ruler and the Killer" by Kid Cudi

"Weaker Girl" by BANKS

"you should see me in a crown" by Billie Eilish

BOOKS BY BB EASTON

STANDALONE ROMANTIC COMEDIES

44 CHAPTERS ABOUT 4 MEN
This steamy memoir inspired the Netflix Original Series SEX/LIFE.

GROUP THERAPY
A fun, forbidden psychologist/celebrity client romance.

THE 44 CHAPTERS SPIN-OFF SERIES
Darkly funny. Deeply emotional. Shockingly sexy.

SKIN

SPEED

STAR

SUIT

THE RAIN TRILOGY
Intense, immersive, end-of-the-world romance.

PRAYING FOR RAIN

FIGHTING FOR RAIN

DYING FOR RAIN

DEVIL OF DUBLIN
A dark mafia romance steeped in Irish folklore.

DEVIL OF DUBLIN

THE DEVIL HIMSELF

For updates on new releases, sales, and giveaways, sign up at https:// www.artbyeaston.com/subscribe

ACKNOWLEDGMENTS

If you're reading this, that means you made it all the way to the end of The Rain Trilogy: The Complete Collection! Thank you so, so much for taking this journey with me. I've never written fiction before. My five previous books are all based on my real life, so this was a challenge of epic proportions. But if you've read *SUIT*, you know that I love nothing more than a good challenge. I learned so much during this process—mostly that writing fiction is hard as hell, but also that I have the best readers in the entire world. You guys show up. Whether I'm writing a sexy, comedic memoir; an angsty, semi-autobiographical New Adult series; or a gritty, dystopian romantic suspense trilogy, you guys are here for it. I love you for that.

I also love **Ken Easton**. I joke that I don't carry a purse; I carry a man. I bring Ken with me everywhere I go. He is the holder of my lipstick, the keeper of my schedule, the doer of my taxes, the mower of my lawn, and the hand on my elbow, preventing me from walking into traffic when I'm too busy talking to you all on social media to pay attention to my surroundings. He keeps me alive and fed and laughing and out of prison so that I can do what I love, and for that, we should *all* say, *Thank you.*

I'm also indebted to **my mom**, **Ken's mom**, and **Ken's sister** for watching my kids at the drop of a hat so that I can meet a deadline or catch a plane. It takes a village, y'all. Thank God I have a good one.

It also takes a village to edit these damn books. A huge, huge thank-you to my content editors, **Karla Nellenbach** and **Traci Finlay**; my copy editors, **Jovana Shirley** and **Ellie McLove**; my beta readers, **Sammie Lynn**, **Sara Snow**, and **Tracey Frazier**; and my proofreaders, **April C.**, **Michelle Beiger DePrima**, and **Rhonda Lind** for always, always squeezing me in when I need you, at least pretending to be excited about my books, and polishing them up quickly and thoroughly every single time. You guys are the first people I let read my work, and your sensitivity and enthusiasm are what give me the confidence to hit publish. I hope you know how much I appreciate you.

And as if editing them isn't hard enough, then I have to turn around and sell the damn things. Thank God I have the magical unicorns of **Bookcase Literary Agency—Flavia Viotti, Meire Dias**, and **Maria Napolitano—** and the rock stars of **Social Butterfly PR—Jenn Watson, Sarah Ferguson,** and **Brooke Nowiski—**on my team. Anytime I have good news to share, a book to publish, or a karaoke bar calling my name, you guys are always there with a thoroughly researched plan, a handful of Advil, and your Uber app on standby. Thank you for spreading the word about these stories and for getting them into as many new hands as possible. You are the wind beneath my wings.

And speaking of spreading the word, I couldn't do it without **all of my author friends—**especially you, **Colleen**, only because I haven't mentioned your name in this book yet. Thank you for selflessly sharing your platforms, your resources, your time, and your expertise to help me succeed. I've said it before, and I'll say it again. I don't have competitors; I have coworkers. I love you guys.

To **Larry Robins** and **J. Miles Dale**, thank you for believing in me. You took a quirky debut Frankenbook that was too sexy to be a comedic memoir and too autobiographical to be a romance novel and somehow turned it into a Netflix series. I don't know what the hell I did to deserve you, but I am eternally grateful to you both. I can't wait to squeeze you on the red carpet!

And as always, to the **readers, bloggers, and bookstagrammers of** #TeamBB, you guys are my ride-or-dies. Thank you for the gorgeous teasers, the comments and shares, the reviews that never fail to make me cry, the thoughtful gifts, and the relentless, rabid support you've showered me with over the years. You overwhelm me with your love, and I hope when you come see me at an event or interact with me online that you feel it returned tenfold. Also, all of your affection totally makes up for the fact that Ken is an emotional cyborg, so he thanks you, too. I yell at him a lot less now that I have you.

ABOUT THE AUTHOR

BB Easton is the Wall Street Journal bestselling author of 44 CHAPTERS ABOUT 4 MEN, the hilarious, steamy, tell-all memoir that inspired the Netflix Original Series, SEX/LIFE. Within the first month, SEX/LIFE was viewed by 67 million households worldwide, making it the 3rd Most-Watched Netflix Original Series of all time.

BB was a stressed-out school psychologist and mother of two when the inspiration to write 44 CHAPTERS ABOUT 4 MEN struck. Through that process, she rediscovered her passion for writing, became dangerously sleep-deprived, and finally mustered enough courage to quit her job and become a full-time author.

BB went on to publish four more wickedly funny, shockingly steamy, and heartwarmingly autobiographical books in the 44 CHAPTERS world: SKIN, SPEED, STAR, and SUIT. Since then, she's been hard at work writing fictional stories that appeal to her love for us-against-the-world romance, including a dystopian trilogy (PRAYING FOR RAIN), a psychologist-client rom-com (GROUP THERAPY), and a dark mafia romance series (DEVIL OF DUBLIN).

You can find BB procrastinating in all of the following places:

Website: www.authorbbeaston.com

Instagram: www.instagram.com/author.bb.easton

TikTok: https://vm.tiktok.com/ZMeEKRLyS/

Facebook: www.facebook.com/bbeaston

\#TeamBB Facebook Group: www.facebook.com/groups/BBEaston

Twitter: www.twitter.com/bb_easton

Pinterest: www.pinterest.com/artbyeaston

Goodreads: https://goo.gl/4hiwiR

BookBub: https://www.bookbub.com/authors/bb-easton

Spotify: https://open.spotify.com/user/bbeaston

Selling signed books, mugs, and apparel on Etsy: www.etsy.com/shop/artbyeaston

And giving away free e-books from her bestselling author friends every month in her newsletter: www.artbyeaston.com/subscribe

www.ingramcontent.com/pod-product-compliance
Lightning Source LLC
Chambersburg PA
CBHW020717310726
48979CB00004B/962